LINDA HOWARD

ANN MAJOR
SUSAN MALLERY

WHAT
THE
HEART
CAN'T
HIDE

Silhouette Books

Published by Silhouette Books

America's Publisher of Contemporary Romance

SILHOUETTE BOOKS

WHAT THE HEART CAN'T HIDE

Copyright © 2002 by Harlequin Books S.A.

ISBN 0-373-48494-1

The publisher acknowledges the copyright holders
of the individual works as follows:

ALL THAT GLITTERS
Copyright © 1982 by Linda Howard

THE GOODBYE CHILD
Copyright © 1991 by Ann Major

THE BEST BRIDE
Copyright © 1995 by Susan W. Macias

This edition published by arrangement with Harlequin Books S.A.

® and TM are trademarks of Harlequin Books S.A., used under license.
Trademarks indicated with ® are registered in the United States Patent
and Trademark Office, the Canadian Trade Marks Office and in other
countries.

Visit Silhouette at www.eHarlequin.com

Printed in U.S.A.

PRAISE FOR THESE
award-winning authors:

New York Times **bestselling author**
Linda Howard

"Howard's writing is compelling."
—*Publishers Weekly*

"You can't read just one Linda Howard!"
—*New York Times* bestselling author
Catherine Coulter

New York Times **bestselling author**
Ann Major

"Want it all? Read Ann Major."
—*New York Times* bestselling author Nora Roberts

"Compelling characters, intense,
fast-moving plots and snappy dialogue
have made Ann Major's name synonymous
with the best in contemporary romantic fiction."
—*Rendezvous*

Award-winning author
Susan Mallery

"A gifted storyteller, Ms. Mallery fills the pages
with multi-faceted characters, solid plotting
and passion that is both tender and sizzling."
—*Romantic Times Magazine*

"If you haven't read Susan Mallery, you must!"
—*New York Times* bestselling author
Suzanne Forster

Linda Howard says that whether she's reading them or writing them, books have long played a profound role in her life. She cut her teeth on Margaret Mitchell, and from then on continued to read widely and eagerly. In recent years her interest has settled on romance fiction, because she's "easily bored by murder, mayhem and politics." After twenty-one years of penning stories for her own enjoyment, Ms. Howard finally worked up the courage to submit a novel for publication—and met with success! Happily, the Alabama author has been steadily publishing ever since, and has made multiple appearances on the *New York Times* bestseller list.

Ann Major lives in Texas with her husband of many years, and is the mother of three college-age children. She has a master's degree from Texas A&M at Kingsville, Texas, and has taught English in high school and college. She is a founding board member of the RWA and a frequent speaker at writers' groups. Ann loves to write; she considers her ability to do so a gift. Her hobbies include hiking in the mountains, playing tennis, sailing, reading, playing the piano, but most of all enjoying her family. She can be reached at www.eHarlequin.com or http://annmajor.com.

Susan Mallery is the *USA Today* bestselling author of over forty books for Harlequin Books & Silhouette Books, as well as mainstream and historical romances. Frequently appearing on bestseller lists, she makes her home in the Pacific Northwest with her handsome prince of a husband and her two adorable-but-not-bright cats. She can be reached through www.eHarlequin.com or www.susanmallery.com.

CONTENTS

ALL THAT GLITTERS
Linda Howard

Chapter 1

Charles said bluntly, without warning, "Constantinos arrived in London this morning."

Jessica looked up, her mind blank for a moment, then she realized what he had said and she smiled ruefully. "Well, you did warn me, Charles. It seems you were right." Not that she had ever doubted him, for Charles's instincts in business were uncanny. He had told her that if she voted her stock in ConTech against the Constantinos vote, she would bring down on her head the wrath of the single largest stockholder and chairman of the board, Nikolas Constantinos, and it appeared that once again Charles had been exactly right. The vote on the Dryden issue had been yesterday. Despite Charles's warnings, she had voted against the takeover and her vote had carried the majority. Less than twenty-four hours later, Constantinos had arrived in London.

Jessica had never met him, but she had heard enough horror tales about him to count herself lucky in that respect. According to gossip, he was utterly ruthless in his business dealings; of course, it stood to reason that he would not have achieved his present position of power by being meek and mild. He was a billionaire, powerful even by Greek standards; she was only a stockholder, and she thought humorously that it was a case of overkill for him to bring out his heavy artillery on her, but it looked as though no problem was too small for his personal attention.

Charles had pointed out that she could have voted for the takeover and saved herself a lot of trouble, but one of the things that Robert had taught her in the three years of their marriage was to stand up for herself, to trust her instincts and never to sell herself short. Jessica had felt that the move against Dryden was underhanded and she voted against it. If Constantinos was unable to accept that she had the right to vote her stock as she wanted, then he would just have to learn to deal with it. Regardless of how much power he wielded, she was determined not to back down from her stand, and Charles had found that she could be very stubborn when she set her mind to something.

"You must be very careful around him," Charles instructed her now, breaking into her thoughts. "Jessica, my dear, I don't believe you realize just how much pressure the man can bring to bear on you. He can hurt you in ways you've never imagined. Your friends can lose their jobs; mortgages can be called in on their homes; banks will cease doing business with you. It can even extend to such small things as repairs to your auto being delayed or seats on flights suddenly becoming unavailable. Do you begin to see, my dear?"

Disbelievingly, Jessica stared at him. "My word, Charles, are you serious? It seems so ludicrous!"

"I regret that I am very serious. Constantinos wants things done his way, and he has the money and the power to ensure that they are. Don't underestimate him, Jessica."

"But that's barbaric!"

"And so is Constantinos, to a degree," said Charles flatly. "If he gives you the option of selling your stock to him, Jessica, then I strongly urge you to do so. It will be much safer for you."

"But Robert—"

"Yes, I know," he interrupted, though his voice took on a softer tone. "You feel that Robert entrusted that stock to you, and that he would have voted against the Dryden takeover, too.

Robert was a very dear and special man, but he's dead now and he can't protect you. You have to think of yourself, and you haven't the weapons to fight Constantinos. He can demolish you.''

"But I don't want to fight him," she protested. "I only want to carry on as I always have. It seems so silly for him to be upset over my vote—why should he take it so personally?''

"He doesn't take it personally," explained Charles. "He doesn't have to. But you've gone against him and you'll be brought into line, regardless of what he has to do to accomplish it. And don't think that you can appeal to his better nature—"

"I know," she broke in, her soft mouth curving into a smile. "He doesn't have one!''

"Exactly," said Charles. "Nor can he be feeling very charitable toward you; your record in voting against him, my dear, is very nearly perfect.''

"Oh, dear," she said wryly. "I hadn't realized. But at least I'm consistent!''

Charles laughed unwillingly, but his cool eyes gleamed with admiration. Jessica always seemed in control of herself, capable of putting things into their proper perspective and reducing crises to mere annoyances, though he feared that this time she was in over her head. He didn't want her hurt; he never again wanted to see the look in her eyes that had been there after Robert's death, the despair, the pain that was too deep for comforting. She had recovered, she was a strong woman and a fighter, but he always tried to protect her from any further hurt. She had borne enough in her young life.

The phone rang and Jessica got up to answer it, her movements, as always, lithe and as graceful as a cat's. She tucked the receiver against her shoulder. "Stanton residence.''

"Mrs. Stanton, please," said a cool, impersonal male voice, and her sharp ear caught the hint of an accent. Constantinos already?

"This is Mrs. Stanton," she replied.

"Mrs. Stanton, this is Mr. Constantinos's secretary. He would like to see you this afternoon—shall we say three-thirty?"

"Three-thirty?" she echoed, glancing at her wristwatch. It was almost two o'clock now.

"Thank you, Mrs. Stanton," said the voice in satisfaction. "I will tell Mr. Constantinos to expect you. Good day."

The click of the receiver made her take the phone from her ear and stare at it in disbelief. "Well, that was cheeky," she mused, hanging up the instrument. It was possible that he had taken her echo of the time as an affirmation, but her instincts told her otherwise. No, it was simply that she was not expected to make any protest, and it wouldn't have mattered if she had.

"Who was that, my dear?" asked Charles absently, gathering up the papers he had brought for her signature.

"Mr. Constantinos's secretary. I've been summoned into the royal presence—at three-thirty this afternoon."

Charles's elegant eyebrows rose. "Then I suggest you hurry."

"I've a dental appointment at four-fifteen," she fretted.

"Cancel it."

She gave him a cool look and he laughed. "I apologize, my dear, and withdraw the suggestion. But be careful, and try to remember that it would be better to sell the stock than to try to fight Constantinos. I have to go now, but I'll ring you later."

"Yes, 'bye," she said, seeing him out. After he had gone, she dashed upstairs and took a shower, then found herself dawdling as she selected her dress. She was unsure what to wear and stood examining the contents of her wardrobe for long moments; then, in swift impatience with herself, she took down a cool beige jersey dress and stepped into it. It was classically simple and she wore it with four-inch heels to give her enough height to make her look more than a child.

She wasn't very tall, and because she was so fragile in build she tended to look about sixteen years old if she didn't use a host of little tricks to add maturity to her appearance. She wore simple clothing, pure in cut, and high heels whenever possible. Her long, thick, tawny hair she wore twisted into a knot at the back of her neck, a very severe hairstyle that revealed every proud, perfect line of her classically boned face and made her youth less obvious. Too much makeup would have made her look like a child playing grown-up, so she wore only subtle shades of eye shadow, naturally tinted lipsticks, and a touch of peach blusher. When she looked into the mirror, it was to check that her hair was subdued and her expression cool and reserved; she never saw the allure of long, heavily lashed green eyes or the provocative curve of her soft mouth. The world of flirtations and sexual affairs was so far removed from her consciousness that she had no concept of herself as a desirable woman. She had been a child when Robert had taken her under his protective wing—a sullen, self-conscious, suspicious child—and he had changed her into a responsible adult, but he had never attempted to teach her anything about the physical side of marriage and she was as untouched today at the age of twenty-three as she had been when she was born.

When she was ready, she checked the clock again and found that she had three-quarters of an hour to reach the ConTech building, but in the London traffic she would need every minute of that time. She snatched up her bag and ran downstairs to check on her dog, Samantha, who was very pregnant. Samantha lay in her bed, contentedly asleep even though her sides were grotesquely swollen by the puppies she carried. Jessica made certain there was water in her dish, then let herself out and crossed to her car, a sleek dark green sports model. She loved its smooth power and now she needed every ounce of it as she put it through its paces.

The traffic signals were with her and she stepped out of the lift on the appropriate floor of the ConTech building at precisely three-twenty-nine. A receptionist directed her to the royal chambers and she opened the heavy oak door at the appointed time.

A large room stretched before her, quietly furnished with chocolate-brown carpeting and chairs upholstered in brown and gold. Set to one side of massive double doors was a large desk, and seated at that desk was a slim, dark man who rose to his feet as she entered.

Cool dark eyes looked her up and down as she crossed the room to him, and she began to feel as if she had violated some law. "Good afternoon," she said, keeping all hint of temper out of her voice. "I am Mrs. Stanton."

The dark eyes swept over her again in a manner that was almost contemptuous. "Ah, yes. Please be seated, Mrs. Stanton. I regret that Mr. Constantinos has been delayed, but he will be free to see you shortly."

Jessica inclined her head and selected one of the comfortable chairs, sitting down and crossing her graceful legs. She made certain that her face remained expressionless, but inside she was contemplating scratching the young man's eyes out. His manner set her teeth on edge; he had a condescending air about him, a certain nastiness that made her long to shake the smug look off his face.

Ten minutes later she wondered if she was expected to cool her heels here indefinitely until Constantinos deigned to see her. Glancing at her watch, she decided to give it another five minutes, then she would have to leave if she was to be on time for her dental appointment.

The buzzer on the desk sounded loudly in the silence and she looked up as the secretary snatched up one of the three telephones on his desk. "Yes, sir," he said crisply, and replaced the receiver. He removed a file from one of the metal cabinets beside him and carried it into the inner sanctum, returning almost immediately and closing the double doors behind him. From all indications, it would be some time yet before Constantinos was free, and the five minutes she had allowed were gone. She uncrossed her legs and rose to her feet.

Coolly uplifted eyebrows asked her intentions.

"I have another appointment to keep," she said smoothly, refusing to apologize for her departure. "Perhaps Mr. Constantinos will call me when he has more time."

Outraged astonishment was plain on the man's face as she

took up her bag and prepared to leave. "But you can't go—" he began.

"On the contrary," she interrupted him, opening the door. "Good day."

Anger made her click her heels sharply as she walked to her car, but she took several deep breaths before she started the engine. No sense in letting the man's attitude upset her, perhaps enough to cause an accident, she told herself. She would shrug it off, as she had learned to do when she had been battered with criticism following her marriage to Robert. She had learned how to endure, to survive, and she was not going to let Robert down now.

After her dental appointment, which was only her annual checkup and took very little time, Jessica drove to the small dress shop just off Piccadilly that her neighbor Sallie Reese owned and operated, and helped Sallie close up. She also looked through the racks of clothing and chose two of the new line of evening gowns that Sallie had just stocked; perhaps because she had never had anything pretty when she was growing up, Jessica loved pretty clothes and had no resistance to buying them, though she was frugal with herself in other matters. She didn't wear jewelry and she didn't pamper herself in any way, but clothing—well, that was another story. Robert had always been amused by her little-girl glee in a new dress, a pair of jeans, shoes; it really didn't matter what it was so long as it was new and she liked it.

Remembering that made her smile a little sadly as she paid Sallie for the gowns; though she would never stop missing Robert, she was glad that she had brought some laughter and sunshine into the last years of his life.

"Whew, it has been a busy day," sighed Sallie as she totaled up the day's revenue. "But sales were good; it wasn't just a case of a lot of people window-shopping. Joel will be ecstatic; I promised him that he could buy that fancy stereo he's had his heart set on if we had a good week."

Jessica chuckled. Joel was a stereo addict, and he had been

moaning for two months now about a marvelous set that he had seen and just had to have or his life would be blighted forever. Sallie took all of his dire predictions in stride, but it had been only a matter of time before she agreed to buy the new stereo. Jessica was glad that now her friends could afford a few luxuries without totally wrecking their budget. The dress shop had turned their fortunes around, because Joel's income as an accountant was just not enough nowadays to support a young family.

When Robert had died, Jessica had found herself unable to live in the luxurious penthouse without him and she had left it, instead buying an old Victorian house that had been converted into a duplex and moving into the empty side herself. Joel and Sallie and their twin five-year-old hellions, who went by the names of Patricia and Penelope, lived in the other side of the old house and the two young women had gradually become good friends. Jessica learned how Sallie had to scrimp and budget and make all of their clothing herself, and it was Sallie's needlework that had given Jessica the idea.

The Reeses had not had the capital to open a shop, but Jessica had, and when she found the small, cozy shop off Piccadilly, she leaped on it. Within a month it was remodeled, stocked, and in business with the name of SALLIE'S RAGS on the sign outside. Patty and Penny were in kindergarten and Sallie was happily installed in her shop, making some of the clothing herself and gradually expanding until now the shop employed two salesgirls full time, besides Sallie herself, and another woman who helped Sallie with the sewing. Before the first year was out, Sallie had repaid Jessica and was flushed with pride at how well it had turned out.

Sallie was now rounding quite nicely with a third little Reese, but she and Joel no longer worried about expenses and she was ecstatic about her pregnancy. She was fairly blooming with good health and high spirits, and even now, when she was tired, her cheeks had a pink color to them and her eyes sparkled.

After they had closed up, Jessica drove Sallie by to pick up Patty and Penny, who stayed late on Friday nights with their baby-sitter, as that was the night Sallie closed out the week. The twins were in school for the best part of the day, and when summer holidays came, Sallie intended to stay home from the shop with them, as her pregnancy would be advanced by then. When Jessica pulled up outside the baby-sitter's home, both of the little girls ran to the car shrieking "Hello, Auntie Jessie! Have you any candy for us?" That was a standard Friday-night treat and Jessica had not forgotten. As the girls mobbed her, Sallie went laughing to pay the sitter and thank her, and by the time she came back with her hands full of the girls' books and sweaters, Jessica had them both settled down in the car.

Sallie invited Jessica to eat dinner with them, but she declined because she did not like to intrude too much on the family. Not only was she rather reserved herself, but she sensed that Sallie wanted to be with Joel to celebrate the good news of the week's business in the shop. It was still new enough to them that it was a thrill, and she didn't want to restrain them with her presence.

The phone started ringing just as she opened the door, but Jessica paused for a moment to check on Samantha before she answered it. The dog was still in her basket, looking particularly peaceful, and she wagged her tail in greeting but did not get up. "No pups yet?" asked Jessica as she reached for the phone. "At this rate, old girl, they'll be grown before they get here." Then she lifted the phone on the kitchen extension. "Mrs. Stanton speaking."

"Mrs. Stanton, this is Nikolas Constantinos," said a deep voice, so deep that the bass notes almost growled at her, and to her surprise the accent was more American than Greek. She clutched the receiver as a spurt of warmth went through her. How silly, she chided herself, to melt at the sound of a faint American accent just because she was American herself! She loved England, she was content with her life here, but nevertheless, that brisk sound made her smile.

"Yes, Mr. Constantinos?" she made herself say, then wondered if she sounded rude. But she would be lying if she said something trite like "How nice it is to hear from you" when it wasn't nice at all; in fact, it would probably be very nasty indeed.

"I would like to arrange a meeting with you tomorrow, Mrs. Stanton," he said. "What time would be convenient for you?"

Surprised, she reflected that Constantinos himself did not seem to be as arrogant as his secretary; at least he had *asked* what time would be convenient, rather than *telling* her what time to present herself. Aloud she said, "On Saturday, Mr. Constantinos?"

"I realize it is the weekend, Mrs. Stanton," the deep voice replied, a hint of irritation evident in his tone. "However, I have work to do regardless of the day of the week."

Now that sounded more like what she had expected. Smiling slightly, she said, "Then any time is convenient for me, Mr. Constantinos; I haven't any commitments for tomorrow."

"Very well, let's say tomorrow afternoon, two o'clock." He paused, then said, "And, Mrs. Stanton, I don't like playing games. Why did you make an appointment with me this afternoon if you did not intend to keep it?"

Stung, she retorted coldly, "I didn't make the appointment. Your secretary phoned me and told me what time to be there, then hung up before I could agree or disagree. It rushed me, but I made the effort and waited for as long as I could, but I had another appointment to keep. I apologize if my effort was not good enough!" Her tone of voice stated plainly that she didn't care what his opinion was, and she didn't stop to think if that was wise or not. She was incensed that that cockroach of a secretary had *dared* to imply that she was at fault.

"I see," he said after a moment. "Now it is my turn to apologize to you, Mrs. Stanton, and *my* apology is sincere. That will not happen again. Until tomorrow, then." The phone clicked as he hung up.

Jessica slammed the phone down violently and stood for a minute tapping her foot in controlled temper, then her face cleared and she laughed aloud. He had certainly put her in her place! She began almost to look forward to this meeting with the notorious Nikolas Constantinos.

When Jessica dressed for the meeting the next day, she began early and allowed herself plenty of time to change her mind about what she would wear. She tried on several things and finally chose a severely tailored dull-gold suit that made her look mature and serious, and this she teamed with a cream-colored silk shirt. The muted gold picked up the gold in her tawny hair and lightly tanned skin, and she didn't realize the picture she made or she would have changed immediately. As it was, she looked like a golden statue come to life, with gleaming green jewels for eyes.

She was geared up for this meeting; when she walked into the outer office at two o'clock, her heart was pounding in anticipation, her eyes were sparkling, and her cheeks were flushed. At her entrance the secretary jumped to his feet with an alacrity that told her some stinging comments had been made concerning his conduct. Though his eyes were distinctly hostile, he escorted her into the inner office immediately.

"Mrs. Stanton, sir," he said, and left the office, closing the doors behind him.

Jessica moved across the office with her proud, graceful stride, and the man behind the desk rose slowly to his feet as she approached. He was tall, much taller than the average Greek, and his shoulders strained against the expensive cloth of his dark gray suit. He stood very still, watching her as she walked toward him, and his eyes narrowed to slits. She reached the desk and held out her hand; slowly her fingers were taken, but instead of the handshake she had invited, her hand was lifted and the black head bent over it. Warm lips were pressed briefly to her fingers, then her hand was released and the black head lifted.

Almost bemused, Jessica stared into eyes as black as night beneath brows that slashed across his face in a straight line. An arrogant blade of nose, brutally hard cheekbones, a firm lip line, a squared and stubborn chin, completed the face that was ancient in its structure. Centuries of Greek heritage were evident in that face, the face of a Spartan warrior. Charles had been right; this man was utterly ruthless, but Jessica did not feel threatened. She felt exhilarated, as if she was in the room with a tiger that she could control if she was very careful. Her heartbeat increased and her eyes grew brighter, and to disguise her involuntary response, she smiled and murmured, "Are you trying to charm me into voting my shares the way you want before you resort to annihilation?"

Amazingly, a smile appeared in response. "With a woman, I always try charm first," he said in the deep tones that seemed even deeper than they had last night over the phone.

"Really?" she asked in mock wonder. "Does it usually work?"

"Usually," he admitted, still smiling. "Why is it that I have the feeling, Mrs. Stanton, that you'll be an exception?"

"Perhaps because you're an unusually astute man, Mr. Constantinos," she countered.

He laughed aloud at that and indicated a chair set before his desk. "Please sit down, Mrs. Stanton. If we are to argue, let us at least be comfortable while we do it."

Jessica sat down and said impulsively, "Your accent is American, isn't it? It makes me feel so much at home!"

"I learned to speak English on a Texas oil field," he said. "I'm afraid that even Oxford couldn't erase the hint of Texas from my speech, though I believe it was thought by my instructors that my accent is Greek! Are you from Texas, Mrs. Stanton?"

"No, but a Texas drawl is recognizable to any American! How long were you in Texas?"

"For three years. How long have you been in England, Mrs. Stanton?"

"Since shortly before I married, a little over five years."

"Then you were little more than a child when you married," he said, an odd frown crossing his brow. "I'd assumed that you would be older, at least thirty, but I can see that's impossible."

Lifting her dainty chin, Jessica said, "No, I was a precocious eighteen when I married.'' She began to tense, sensing an attack of the type that she had endured so many times in the past five years.

"As I said, little more than a child. Though I suppose there are countless wives and mothers aged eighteen, it seems so much younger when the husband you chose was old enough to be your grandfather.''

Jessica drew back and said coldly, ''I see no reason to discuss my marriage. I believe our business concerns stocks.''

He smiled again, but this time the smile was that of a predator, with nothing humorous in it. ''You're certainly correct about that,'' he allowed. ''However, that issue should be solved rather easily. When you sold your body and your youth to an old man of seventy-six, you established the fact that monetary gain ranks very high on your list of priorities. The only thing left to discuss is: how much?''

Chapter 2

Years of experience had taught Jessica how to hide her pain behind a proud, aloof mask, and she used that mask now, revealing nothing of her thoughts and feelings as she faced him. "I'm sorry, Mr. Constantinos, but you seem to have misjudged the situation," she said distantly. "I didn't come here to accept a bribe."

"Nor am I offering you a bribe, Mrs. Stanton," he said, his eyes gleaming. "I'm offering to buy your stock."

"The shares aren't for sale."

"Of course they are," he refuted her silkily. "I'm willing to pay more than market value in order to get those stocks out of your hands. Because you are a woman, I've given you certain allowances, but there is a limit to my good nature, Mrs. Stanton, and I'd advise you not to try to push the price any higher. You could find yourself completely out in the cold."

Jessica stood and put her hands behind her back so he couldn't see how her nails were digging into her palms. "I'm not interested at any price, Mr. Constantinos; I don't even want to hear your offer. The shares aren't for sale, now or at any other time, and especially not to you. Good day, Mr. Constantinos."

But this man was no tame secretary and he did not intend to let her leave until he had finished with his business. He moved with a lithe stride to stop her and she found her path blocked by a very solid set of shoulders. "Ah, no, Mrs. Stanton," he murmured softly. "I can't let you leave now, with nothing settled between us. I've left my island and flown all the way to England for the express purpose of meeting you and putting an end to your asinine notions, which are wreaking havoc with this company. Did you think that I'd be put off by your high-and-mighty airs?"

"I don't know about my high-and-mighty airs, but your king-of-the-mountain complex is getting on my nerves," Jessica attacked, her voice sarcastic. "I own those shares, and I vote them as I think I should. The Dryden takeover was underhanded and stank to the heavens, and I voted against it. I would do it again if the issue arose. But a lot of other people voted against it as well, yet I notice that it's *my* stock you want to buy. Or am I only the first of the group to be brought into line?"

"Sit down, Mrs. Stanton," he said grimly, "and I will attempt to explain to you the basics of finance and expansion."

"I don't wish to sit down—"

"I said *sit!*" he rasped, and abruptly his voice was harsh with menace. Automatically Jessica sat down, then despised herself for not facing him and refusing to be intimidated.

"I am *not* one of your flunkies," she flared, but did not get up. She had the nasty feeling that he would push her down if she tried to leave.

"I am aware of that, Mrs. Stanton; believe me, if you were one of my employees, you would have learned long ago how to behave yourself," he retorted with heavy irony.

"I consider myself quite well-behaved!"

He smiled grimly. "Well-behaved? Or merely cunning and manipulative? I don't imagine it was very difficult to seduce an old man and get him to marry you, and you were smart enough to select a man who would die shortly. That set you up very nicely, didn't it?"

Jessica almost cried aloud with the shock of his words; only her years of training in self-control kept her still and silent, but she looked away from him. She could not let him see her eyes or he would realize how deeply vulnerable she was.

He smiled at her silence. "Did you think that I didn't know your history, Mrs. Stanton? I assure you, I know quite a lot about you. Your marriage to Robert Stanton was quite a scandal to everyone who knew and admired the man. But until I saw you, I never quite understood just how you managed to trap him into marriage. It's all very clear now; any man, even an old one, would jump at the chance to have your lovely body in his bed, at his convenience."

Jessica quivered at the insult and he noticed the movement that rippled over her skin. "Is the memory less than pleasing?" he inquired softly. "Did you find the payment more than you'd expected?"

She struggled for the composure to lift her head, and after a moment she found it. "I'm sure my private life is no concern of yours," she heard herself say coolly, and felt a brief flare of pride that she had managed that so well.

His black eyes narrowed as he looked down at her and he opened his mouth to say more, but the phone rang and he swore under his breath in Greek, then stepped away from her to lift the phone to his ear. He said something in harsh, rapid Greek, then paused. His eyes slid to Jessica.

"I have an urgent call from France, Mrs. Stanton. I'll only be a moment."

He punched a button on the phone and spoke a greeting, his language changing effortlessly to fluent French. Jessica watched him for a moment, still dazed with her inner pain, then she realized that he was occupied and she seized her chance. Without a word, she got to her feet and walked out.

She managed to control herself until she was home again, but once she was safely enclosed by her own walls, she sat down on the sofa and began to sob softly. Was it never to end, the nasty comments and unanimous condemnations of her marriage to Robert? Why was it automatically assumed that she was little more than a prostitute? For five years she had borne the pain and never let it be known how it knifed into her insides, but now she felt as though she had no defenses left. Dear God, if only Robert hadn't died!

Even after two years she could not get used to not sharing amusing thoughts with him, to not having his dry, sophisticated wisdom bolstering her. He had never doubted her love, no matter what had been said about their December-May marriage, and she had always felt the warmth of his support. Yes, he had given her financial security, and he had taught her how to care for the money he willed to her. But he had given her so much more than that! The material things he had bestowed on her were small in comparison to his other gifts: love, security, self-respect, self-confidence. He had encouraged her development as a woman of high intelligence; he had taught her of his world of stocks and bonds, to trust her own instinct when she was in doubt. Dear, wise Robert! Yet, for his marriage to her he had been laughed at and mocked, and she had been scorned. When a gentleman of seventy-six marries a gorgeous young girl of eighteen, gossips can credit it to only two things: greed on her part, and an effort to revive faded appetites on his.

It hadn't been that way at all. Robert was the only man she had ever loved, and she had loved him deeply, but their relationship had been more that of father to daughter, or grandfather to granddaughter, than of husband to wife. Before their marriage Robert had even speculated on the advantages of adopting her, but in the end he'd decided that there would be fewer legal difficulties if he married her. He wanted her to have the security she'd always lacked, having grown up in an orphanage and been forced into hiding herself behind a prickly wall of sullen passivity. Robert was determined that never again would she have to fight for food or privacy or clothing; she would have the best, and the best way to secure that way of life for her was to take her as his wife.

The scandal their marriage had caused had rocked London society; vicious items concerning her had appeared in the gossip columns, and Jessica had been shocked and horrified to read several accounts of men who had been "past lovers of the enterprising Mrs. S." Her reaction had been much the same as Robert's: to hold her head even higher and ignore the mudslingers. She and Robert knew the truth of the marriage, and Robert was the only person on earth whom she loved, the only person who had ever cared for her. Their gentle love endured, and she had remained a virgin throughout their marriage, not that Robert had ever given any indication that he wished the situation to be different. She was his only family, the daughter of his heart if not his flesh, and he schooled her and guided her and went about settling his financial affairs so they could never be wrested out of her control. And he trusted her implicitly.

They had been, simply, two people who were alone in the world and had found each other. She was an orphan who had grown up with a shortage of any type of love; he was an old man whose first wife had died years before and who now found himself without family in his last years. He took in the wary young girl and gave her every comfort, every security, even marrying her in an effort to make certain she never wanted for anything again. Jessica, in turn, felt a flood of love for the gentle, elderly man who gave her so much and asked for so little in return. And he had loved her for bringing her youth and beauty and bright laughter into the fading years of his life, and had guided her maturity and her quick mind with all the loving indulgence of a father.

While Robert had been alive, their scarcity of friends had not really bothered her, though she had suffered under the cuts she had received. There were a few real friends, like Charles, and they had been sufficient. But now Robert was gone and she lived alone, and the poisonous barbs she still received festered in her mind, making her ache and lie awake at night. Most women refused to speak to her and men acted as if she was fair game, and the fact that she kept quietly to herself was evidently not enough to change anyone's opinion of her. Thinking about it now, she acknowledged that, outside of Charles and Sallie, she had no friends. Even Sallie's Joel was a bit stiff with her, and she knew that he disapproved.

It wasn't until the shadows of early evening had darkened the room that she roused from her dejected seat on the sofa and went slowly upstairs to stand under the shower. She felt deadened, and she stayed under the needlelike spray for a long time, until the hot water began to go, then she got out, dried off, and dressed in a pair of faded old jeans and a shirt. Listlessly she brushed her hair out and left it loose on her shoulders, as it usually was when she was at home. Only when she was going out did she feel the need for the more severe hairstyle, to give her an older look, and she would not be going anywhere tonight. Like an animal, she wanted only to find a dark corner and lick her wounds.

When she went into the kitchen, she found Samantha moving about restlessly in her basket; as Jessica watched, frowning, the dog gave a sharp little whine of pain and lay down. Jessica went over and stroked the silky black head. "So, it looks like tonight is the night, my girl! Not before time, either. And if I remember correctly, it was on a Saturday that you ran away from me and got yourself in this fix, so I suppose it's poetic justice."

Samantha didn't care about philosophy, though she licked the gentle hand that stroked her. Then she laid her head down and began that sharp whining again.

Jessica stayed in the kitchen with the dog, and as time wore on and no puppies were born, she began to get worried, for Samantha appeared to be in distress. Was something wrong? Jessica had no idea what kind of four-legged Romeo Samantha had met; was it possible that she had mated with a larger breed and now the puppies were too big to be born? Certainly the little black dog was very swollen.

She rang over to Sallie's side of the house, but the phone rang endlessly and she hung up. Her neighbors were out. After chewing her lip indecisively for a moment, Jessica took the phone directory and began looking for the vet's number. She didn't know if Samantha could be moved while she was in labor, but perhaps the vet made house calls. She found the number and reached for the phone, which rang just as she touched it. She gave a startled cry and leaped back, then she grabbed up the receiver. "Mrs. Stanton."

"This is Nikolas Constantinos."

Of course it was, she thought distractedly. Who else had such a deep voice? "What do you want?" she demanded.

"We have unfinished business—" he began.

"It will just have to stay unfinished," she broke in. "My dog is having puppies and I can't talk to you. Good-bye, Mr. Constantinos." She hung up and waited a second, then lifted the receiver again. She heard a dial tone as she checked the vet's number again, then began dialing.

Half an hour later she was weeping in frustration. She could not get her vet, or any other, on the phone, probably because it was Saturday night, and she was sure that Samantha was going to die. The dog was yelping in agony now, squirming and shuddering with the force of her contractions. Jessica felt appallingly helpless, and grief welled up in her so that the tears streamed down her cheeks.

When the doorbell rang, she scrambled to answer it, glad to have some company, even if the caller knew nothing about dogs. Perhaps it was Charles, who was always so calm, though he would be as useless as she. She jerked the door open and Nikolas Constantinos stepped in as if he owned the house, closing the door behind him. Then he swung on her and she had a glimpse of a grim, angry face before his expression changed abruptly. He took in her jean-clad figure, her mane of hair and tear-streaked face, and he looked incredulous, as if he didn't believe it was really her. "What's wrong?" he asked as he produced a handkerchief and offered it to her.

Without thinking, Jessica took it and scrubbed at her cheeks. "It—it's my dog," she said thinly, and gulped back fresh tears. "I don't think she can have her puppies, and I can't get a vet on the phone...."

He frowned. "Your dog is really having puppies?"

For answer, she burst into a fresh flow of tears, hiding her face in the handkerchief. Her shoulders shook with the force of her sobs, and after a moment she felt an arm slide about her waist.

"Don't cry," Constantinos murmured. "Where is she? Perhaps I can help."

Of course, why not? She should have thought of that herself; everyone knew billionaires were trained in animal husbandry, she told herself hysterically as she led the way into the kitchen.

But despite the incongruity of it, Nikolas Constantinos took off his jacket and slung it over the back of a chair, removed the gold studs from his cuffs and slid them into his pants pocket, then rolled up the sleeves of his white silk shirt. He squatted on his heels beside Samantha's bed and Jessica knelt next to him, because Samantha was inclined to be snappy with strangers even when she was in the best of moods. But Samantha did not offer to snap at him, only watched him with pleading, liquid eyes as he ran his hands gently over her swollen body and examined her. When he had finished, he stroked Samantha's head gently and murmured some Greek words to her that had a soft sound to them, then he turned his head to smile reassuringly at Jessica. "Everything seems to be normal. We should see a pup any minute now."

"Really?" Jessica demanded, her excitement spiraling as her fears eased. "Samantha is all right?"

"Yes, you've worried yourself to tears for nothing. Hasn't she had a litter before?"

Ruefully Jessica shook her head, explaining, "I've always kept her in before. But this time she managed to slip away from me and, well, you know how it goes."

"M'mmm, yes, I know how it goes," he mocked gently. His black eyes ran over her slim build and made her aware that he had a second meaning for his statement. He was a man and he looked on her as a woman, with a woman's uses, and instinctively she withdrew from his masculine appraisal. But despite that, despite everything he had said to her that afternoon, she felt better now that he was here. Whatever else he was, the man was capable.

Samantha gave a short, sharp yelp and Jessica turned anxiously to her dog. Nikolas put his arm about Jessica's shoulders and pulled her against his side so that she felt seared by the warmth of his body. "See, it's beginning," he murmured. "There's the first pup."

Jessica knelt there enthralled, her eyes as wide and wondrous as a child's, while Samantha produced five slick, squirming little creatures, which she nudged one by one against the warmth of her belly. When it became obvious that Samantha had finished at five, when all of the squeaking little things were snuggled against the furry black belly and the dog was lying there in tired contentment, Nikolas got to his feet and drew Jessica to hers, holding her for a moment until the feeling had returned to her numb legs.

"Is this the first birth you've witnessed?" he asked, tilting her chin up with his thumb and smiling down into her dazed eyes.

"Yes...wasn't it marvelous?" she breathed.

"Marvelous," he agreed. The smile faded from his lips and he studied the face that was turned up to him. When he spoke, his voice was low and even. "Now everything is fine; your tears have dried, and you are a lucky young woman. I came over here determined to shake some manners into you. I advise you not to hang up on me again, Jessica. My temper is"—here he gave a shrug of his wide shoulders, as if in acceptance of something he could not change—"not calm."

Half-consciously she registered the fact that he had used her given name, and that his tongue had seemed to linger over the syllables, then she impulsively placed her hand on his arm. "I'm sorry," she apologized warmly. "I wouldn't have done it if I hadn't been so worried about Samantha. I was trying to call the vet."

"I realize that now. But at the time I thought you were merely getting rid of me, and very rudely, too. I wasn't in a good mood anyway after you had walked out on me this afternoon. But when I saw you…'' His eyes narrowed as he looked her up and down again. ''You made me forget my anger.''

She stared at him blankly for a moment before she realized that she hadn't any makeup on, her hair was tumbled about her shoulders, and worse than that, she was barefoot! The wonder was that he had even recognized her! He had been geared up to smash a sophisticated woman of the world, and instead he had found a weeping, tousled girl who did not quite reach his shoulder. A blush warmed her cheeks.

Nervously she pushed a strand of hair away from her face. ''I—ummm—I must look a mess,'' she stammered, and he reached out and touched the streaked gold of her hair, making her forget in midsentence what she had been saying.

''No, you don't look a mess,'' he assured her absently, watching the hair slide along his dark fingers. ''You look disturbingly young, but lovely for all your wet lashes and swollen lids.'' His black eyes flickered back to hers. ''Have you had your dinner yet, Jessica?''

''Dinner?'' she asked vaguely, before she mentally kicked herself for not being faster than that and assuring him that she had indeed already had her meal.

''Yes, dinner,'' he mocked. ''I can see that you haven't. Slip into a dress and I'll take you out for dinner. We still have business to discuss and I think it would be wiser if the discussion did not take place in the privacy of your home.''

She wasn't certain just what he meant by that, but she knew better than to ask for an explanation. Reluctantly she agreed. ''It will take me about ten minutes,'' she said. ''Would you like a drink while I'm dressing?''

''No, I'll wait until you can join me,'' he said.

Jessica ran upstairs and washed her face in cold water, which made her feel immensely better. As she applied her makeup, she noticed that her mouth was curved into a little smile and that it wouldn't go away. When she had completed her makeup, she took a look at herself and was disturbed by the picture she presented. Because of her bout of weeping, her lids were swollen, but with eye shadow and mascara applied, they looked merely sleepy and the irises gleamed darkly, wetly green, long Egyptian eyes that had the look of passions satisfied. Her cheeks bloomed with color, natural color, because her heart was racing in her breast, and she could feel the pulse throbbing in her lips, which were still smiling.

Because it was evening, she twisted her hair into a swirl atop her head and secured it with a gold butterfly clasp. She would wear a long dress, and she knew exactly which one she wanted. Her hands were shaking slightly as she drew it out of the closet, a halter-necked silk of the purest white, almost glittering in its paleness. She stepped into it and pulled the bodice up, then fastened the straps behind her neck. The dress molded itself to her breasts like another skin, then the lined silk fell in graceful folds to her feet—actually, beyond her feet, until she stepped into her shoes. Then the length was perfect. She slung a gold gauze wrap over her arm and she was ready, except for stuffing a comb and lipstick into a tiny evening bag—and remembering at the last minute to include her house key. She had to descend the stairs in a more dignified manner than she had gone up them, for the delicate straps of her shoes were not made for running, and she was only halfway down when Nikolas appeared from the living room and came to stand at the foot of the stairs, waiting for her. His gleaming eyes took in every inch of her in the shimmering white silk and she shivered under the expression she could see in them. He looked...hungry. Or...what?

When she reached the bottom step, she stopped and looked at him, eye to eye, but still she could not decide just what it was that glittered in those black depths. He put his hand on her arm and drew her down the last step, then without a word took the gold wrap and placed it about her bare shoulders. She quivered involuntarily under his touch, and his gaze leaped up to hers; this time it was all she could do to meet it evenly, for she was disturbed by her response to the lightest touch of his fingers.

"You are...more than beautiful," he said quietly.

What did that mean? She licked her lips uncertainly and his hands tightened on her shoulders; a quick glance upward revealed that his gaze had fastened on her tongue. Her heart leaped wildly in response to the look she saw, but he dropped his hands from her and stepped back.

"If we don't go now, we won't go at all," he said, and she knew exactly what that meant. He wanted her. Either that, or he was putting on a very good act, and the more she thought about it, the more such an act seemed likely. Hadn't he admitted that he always tried his charm on a woman in order to get his own way?

He certainly must want those shares, she mused, feeling more comfortable now that she had decided that he was only putting on the amorous act in order to get around her on the shares. Constantinos in a truly amorous mood must be devastating to a woman's senses, she thought, but her own leaping senses had calmed with the realization of what he was up to and she was once more able to think clearly. She supposed she would have to sell the shares; Charles had advised it, and she knew now that she would certainly not be able to continuously defy this man. She would tell him over dinner that she was willing to sell the shares to him.

He had turned out all of the lights except for a dim one in the kitchen for Samantha, and now he checked to make certain the door was locked behind them. "Haven't you any help living in with you?" he asked, frowning, his hand sliding under her elbow as they walked to his car.

"No," she replied, amusement evident in her voice. "I'm not very messy and I don't eat very much, so I don't need any help."

"But that means you're alone at night."

"I'm not frightened, not with Samantha. She sets up a howl at a strange footstep, and besides, Sallie and Joel Reese are in the other side, so I'm not really alone."

He opened the door of the powerful sports car he was driving and helped her into the seat, then went around to his side. She buckled her safety belt, looking with interest at the various dials and gauges. This thing looked like the cockpit of an airplane, and the car was at odds with what she had expected of him. Where was the huge black limousine with the uniformed chauffeur? As he slid into his seat and buckled up, she said, "Do you always drive yourself?"

"No, but there are times when a chauffeur's presence isn't desirable," he said, smiling a little. The powerful engine roared into life and he put the car into gear, moving forward with a smooth rush of power that pushed her back into her seat.

"Did you sell the country estate?" he asked from out of nowhere, making her wonder just how much he did know about her. More than just that vicious gossip, evidently; but he had known Robert before their marriage, so it was only natural that he should know about Robert's country home.

"Robert sold that a year before he died," she said steadily. "And after he died, I let the penthouse go; it was far too big and costly for just me. My half-house is just large enough."

"I would have thought a smaller apartment would have been better."

"I really don't like apartments, and then, there was Samantha. She needs room to run, and the neighborhood is friendly, with a lot of children."

"Not very glamorous," he commented dryly, and her ire rose a bit before she stifled it with a surge of humor.

"Not unless you think lines of drying laundry are glamorous," she agreed, laughing a little. "But it's quiet, and it suits me."

"In that dress, you look as if you should be surrounded by diamonds and mink, not lines of laundry."

"Well, what about you?" she asked cheerfully. "You in your silk shirt and expensive suit, squatting down to help a dog have puppies?"

He flashed her a look that glinted in the green lights from the dash. "On the island, life is much simpler than in London and Paris. I grew up there, running wild like a young goat."

She had a picture of him as a thin young boy, his black eyes flashing as he ran barefoot over the rough hills of his island. Had the years and the money and the layers of sophistication stifled the wildness of his early years? Then, even as she formed the thought in her mind, she knew that he was still wild and untamed, despite the silk shirts he wore.

Conversation died after that, each of them concerned with their own thoughts, and it wasn't until he pulled up before a discreetly lit restaurant and a doorman came to open the doors for them that Jessica realized where he had brought her. Her fingers tightened into fists at the curl of apprehension that twisted in her stomach, but she made her hands relax. He couldn't have known that she always avoided places like this—or could he? No, it was impossible. No one knew of her pain; she had always kept her aloof air firmly in place.

Taking a deep breath, she allowed herself to be helped out of the car, then it was being driven away and Nikolas had his hand on her elbow, escorting her to the door. She would not let it bother her, she told herself fiercely. She would talk with him and eat her meal and it would be finished. She did not have to pay any attention to anyone else they might meet.

After a few dinners out after their marriage, Robert had realized that it was intensely painful to his young bride to be so publicly shunned by people who knew him, and they had ceased eating out at the exclusive restaurants he had always patronized. It had been at this particular restaurant that a group of people had literally turned their backs on her, and Robert had gently led her away from their half-eaten dinner before she lost all control and sobbed like a child in front of everyone. But that had been five years ago, and though she had never lost her horror at the thought of eating in such a place—and this place in particular—she held her head proudly and walked without hesitation through the doors being held open by the uniformed doorman.

The maître d' took one glance at Nikolas and all but bowed. "Mr. Constantinos, we are honored!"

"Good evening, Swaine; we'd like a quiet table, please. Away from the crowd."

As they followed the maître d', winding their way between the tables, Jessica recovered herself enough to flash an amused glance up at the tall man beside her. "An isolated table?" she queried, her lips twitching in a suppressed smile. "So no one will notice the mayhem?"

The black head inclined toward her and she saw his flashing grin. "I think we can keep it more civilized than that."

The table that Swaine selected for them was as isolated as was possible on a busy Saturday night. It was partially enclosed by a bank of plants that made Jessica think of a jungle, and she half-listened for the scream of birds before she chided herself for her foolishness.

While Nikolas chose a wine, she glanced about at the other tables, half afraid that she would see a familiar face; she had noticed the little silence that had preceded them as they made their way to their table, and the hiss of rapid conversation that broke out again in their wake. Had Nikolas noticed? Perhaps she was overly sensitive, perhaps the reaction was for Nikolas rather than herself. As a billionaire, he was certainly more noticeable than most people!

"Don't you like the table?" Nikolas's voice broke in on her thoughts and she jerked her eyes back to him, to find that he wore an irritated expression on his hard, dark face as he stared at her.

"No, the table's fine," she said hastily.

"Then why are you frowning?" he demanded.

"Black memories," she said. "It's nothing, Mr. Constantinos. I just had an…unpleasant experience in here once."

He watched her for a moment, then said calmly, "We can leave if it bothers you."

"It bothers me," she admitted, "but I won't leave. I think it's past time I got over my silly phobias, and what better time than now, when I have you to battle with and take my mind off old troubles?"

"That's twice you have alluded to an argument between us," he commented. He leaned closer to her, his hard brown hand reaching out to touch the low flower arrangement between them. "There won't be any arguments tonight. You're far too lovely for me to want to spend our time together throwing angry words about. If you start to argue, I'll simply lean over and kiss you until you're quiet. I've warned you now, so if you decide to spit defiance at me like a ruffled kitten, I can only conclude that you want to be kissed. What do you think about that, hmmm?"

She stared at him, trying to control her lips, but they parted anyway in a delicious smile and finally she laughed, a peal of laughter that brought heads swinging in their direction. She leaned over the table, too, and said confidentially, "I think, Mr. Constantinos, that I'll be as sweet and charming as it's possible for me to be!"

His hand left the flowers and darted out to capture her wrist, his thumb rubbing lightly over the delicate blue veins on the inside of her arm. "Being sweet and charming will also get you kissed," he teased huskily. "I think that I'll be the winner regardless! And I promise you that I'll kiss you hard if you call me mister again. Try to say Nikolas; I think you'll find it isn't that difficult. Or call me Niko, as my friends do."

"If you wish," she said, smiling at him. Now was the time to tell him about the shares, before he became too serious about his charming act. "But I want to tell you that I've decided to sell the shares to you, after all, so you don't have to be nice to me if you don't want to. I won't change my mind even if you're nasty."

"Forget the shares," he murmured. "Let's not talk about them tonight."

"But that's why you asked me to dinner," she protested.

"Yes, it was, though I haven't a doubt I could have come up with another good excuse if that one had failed." He grinned wickedly. "The little waif with the tear-streaked face was very fetching, especially as I knew a cool, maddeningly sophisticated woman was lurking behind the tears."

She shook her head. "I don't think you understand, Mr.

Con—er—Nikolas. The shares are yours. There's no need to keep this up.''

His lids drooped over the dark brilliance of his eyes for a moment and his hand tightened on her wrist. "Very well, let's discuss the damned shares and be finished with it, as you won't leave the subject alone. Why did you change your mind?"

"My financial advisor, Charles Welby, had already told me to sell rather than try to fight you. I was prepared to sell them, but your manner made me angry and I refused out of sheer contrariness, but as usual, Charles is right. I can't fight you; I don't want to become embroiled in boardroom politics. And there's no need for that outrageous price you mentioned, market value will do nicely.''

He straightened, dropping her wrist, and he said sharply, "I have already given you an offer; I won't go back on my word."

"You'll have to, if you want the shares, because I'll accept market value only." She faced him calmly despite the flare of temper she saw in his face.

He uttered something short and harsh in Greek. "I fail to see how you can refuse such a sum. It's a stupid move."

"And I fail to see how you'll remain a billionaire if you persist in making such stupid business deals!" she shot back.

For a moment his eyes were like daggers, then laughter burst from his throat and he threw back his head in sheer enjoyment.

Oblivious of the many interested eyes on them, he leaned forward once more to take her hand. "You are a gorgeous snow queen," he said huskily. "It was worth losing the Dryden issue to meet you. I don't think I will be returning to Greece as soon as I had planned."

Jessica's eyes widened as she stared at him. It seemed he was serious; he was actually attracted to her! Alarm tingled through her, warming her body as she met the predatory gaze of those midnight eyes.

Chapter 3

The arrival of the wine brought her a welcome relief from his penetrating gaze, but the relief was only momentary. As soon as they were alone again, he drawled, "Does it bother you that I'm attracted to you? I would have thought you would find it commonplace to attract a man's desire."

Jessica tried to retrieve her hand, but his fingers closed firmly over hers and refused to let her go. Green sparks began to shoot from her eyes as she looked up at him. "I don't think you are attracted," she said sharply. "I think you're still trying to put me in my place because I won't bow down and kiss your feet. I've *told* you that the shares are yours, now please let go of my hand."

"You're wrong," he said, his hand tightening over hers until the grip was painful and she winced. "From the moment you walked into my office this afternoon, every nerve in my body has been screaming. I want you, Jessica, and signing those shares over to me won't get me out of your life."

"Then what will?" she demanded, tight-lipped. "What is your price for leaving me alone?"

A look of almost savage anger crossed his face; then he smiled, and the smile chilled her blood. The midnight eyes raked over her face and breasts. "Price?" he murmured. "You know what the price would be, to leave you alone...eventually. I want to sate myself with you, burn you so deeply with my touch that you will never be free, so that whenever another man touches you, you will think of me and wish me in his place.''

The thought—the image it provoked—was shattering. Her eyes widened and she stared at him in horror. ''No,'' she said thickly. ''Oh, no! Never!''

''Don't be so certain,'' he mocked. ''Do you think I couldn't overcome any resistance you might make? And I'm not talking about forcing you, Jessica; I'm talking about desire. I could make you want me; I could make you so hungry for my love-making that you'd beg me to take you.''

''No!'' Blindly she shook her head, terrified that he might really force himself on her. She wouldn't permit that, never; she had endured hell on earth because everyone saw her as a gold-digging little tart, but she would never let herself be reduced to the level of a kept woman, a mistress, all of the ugly things they had called her. ''Don't you understand?'' she whispered rag-gedly. ''I don't want to get involved with you—with any man—on any level.''

''That's very interesting,'' he said, his eyes narrowing on her face. ''I can understand that you'd find your marriage duties to an old man to be revolting, but surely all of your lovers can't have been so bad. And don't try to pretend that you went into that marriage as pure as the driven snow, because I won't believe you. An innocent wouldn't sell herself to an old man, and be-sides, too many men claim to have...known you.''

Jessica swallowed hard on the nausea that welled up in her and her head jerked up. White-faced, green eyes blazing, she spat at him, ''On the contrary, Robert was an angel! It was the other men who left a bad taste in my mouth—and I think, Mr. Constantinos, that in spite of your money, you give me the worst taste of all.''

Instantly she was aware that she had gone too far. His face went rigid and she had only a second of warning before the hand that held her fingers tightened and pulled, drawing her out of her chair until she was leaning over the table. He rose and met her halfway, and her startled exclamation was cut off by the pressure of his mouth, hot and hard and probing, and she had no defense against the intrusion of his tongue.

Dimly she could hear the swelling murmurs behind her, feel a flash of light against her lids, but the kiss went on and on and she was helpless to pull away. Panic welled in her, smothering her, and a whimper of distress sounded in her throat. Only then did he raise his punishing mouth, but he still held her over the table like that, his eyes on her white face and trembling lips, then he very gently reseated her and resumed his own seat. "Don't provoke me again," he said through his teeth. "I warned you, Jessica, and that kiss was a light one compared to the next one you will get."

Jessica didn't dare look up at him; she simply sat there and stared at her wine, her entire body shaking. She wanted to slap him, but more than that she wanted to run away and hide. That flash of light that she had noticed had been the flash of a camera, she knew, and she cringed inside to think of the field day the scandal sheets would have with that photo. Nausea roiled in her stomach and she fought fiercely against it, snatching up her wineglass with a shaking hand and sipping the cool, dry wine until she had herself under control again.

A rather uncomfortable-looking waiter appeared with the menus and Jessica used every ounce of concentration that she possessed in choosing her meal. She had thought of allowing Constantinos to order for her; in fact, he seemed to expect her to do so, but it had become very important that she cling to that small bit of independence. She had to cling to something when she could feel the eyes boring into her from all corners of the room, and when across from her sat a man who made man-eating tigers seem tame.

"It's useless to sulk," he said now, breaking in on her thoughts with his smooth, deep voice. "I won't allow that, Jessica, and it was only a kiss, after all. The first of many. Would you like to go sailing with me tomorrow? The weathermen are predicting a warm, sunny day and you can get to know me as we laze about all day in the sun.''

''No,'' she said starkly. ''I don't ever want to see you again.''

He laughed outright, throwing back his gleaming dark head, his white teeth flashing in the dimness like a wild animal's. ''You're like an angry child,'' he murmured. ''Why don't you scream that you hate me, and stamp your feet in a temper so I may have the pleasure of taming you? I'd enjoy tussling with you, rolling about until you tired yourself out and lay quietly beneath me.''

''I don't hate you,'' she told him, regaining some of her composure despite his disturbing words. She even managed to look at him quite coolly. ''I won't waste the energy to hate you, because you're just passing through. After the shares have been signed over, I'll never see you again, and I can't see myself shedding any tears over your absence, either.''

''I can't let you continue to delude yourself,'' he mocked. ''I'm not merely passing through; I've changed my plans—to include you. I'll be in London for quite some time, for as long as it takes. Don't fight me, my dear; it's only a waste of time that's better spent in other ways.''

''Your ego must be enormous,'' she observed, sipping at her wine. ''You seem unable to believe that I simply don't fancy you. Very well, if that's what it takes to rid myself of you, when you take me home we'll go upstairs and you may satisfy your odd little urges. It won't take much effort, and it'll be worth it to see the back of you.'' Even as the words left her mouth, Jessica almost jumped in amazement at herself. Dear heaven, how did she manage to sound so cool and disinterested, and say such dreadful things? What on earth would she do if he took her up on it? She had no intention of going to bed with him if she had to scream her silly head off and make a scandal that would force both of them out of the country.

His face had turned to stone as she talked and his eyes had narrowed until they were mere slits. She had the urge to throw up her arms to protect her face, even though he didn't move a muscle. At last he spoke, grinding the words out between his teeth. "You cold little bitch, you'll pay for that. Before I'm finished with you, you'll regret opening your mouth; you'll apologize for every word. Go upstairs with you? I doubt I'll wait that long!"

She had to get out, she had to get away from him. Without thinking, she clutched her bag and said, "I have to go to the ladies—"

"No," he said. "You aren't going anywhere. You're going to sit there until we've eaten, then I'll drive you home."

Jessica sat very still, glaring at him, but her hostility didn't seem to bother him. When their meal was served, he began to eat as if everything was perfectly calm and normal. She chewed on a few bites, but the tender lamb and stewed carrots turned into a lump in her throat that she couldn't swallow. She gulped at her wine, and there was a flash of a camera again. Quickly she set down her glass and paled, turning her head away.

He missed nothing, even when it seemed that he wasn't paying attention. "Don't let it upset you," he advised coolly. "The cameras are everywhere. They mean nothing; it's merely something to fill the space in their empty little tabloids."

She didn't reply, but she remembered the earlier flash, when he had been kissing her so brutally. She felt ill at the thought of that photo being splashed all over the gossip pages.

"You don't seem to mind being the target of gossip," she forced herself to say, and though her voice was a bit strained, she managed the words without gulping or bursting into tears.

He shrugged. "It's harmless enough. If anyone is really interested in who I had dinner with, or who stopped by our table for a moment's conversation, then I really have no objection. When I want to be private, I don't go to a public place."

She wondered if he had ever been the subject of such vicious gossip as she had endured, but though the papers were always making some mention of him closing a deal or flying here and there for conferences, sometimes with a vague mention of his latest "lovely," she could recall nothing about his private life. He had said that he lived on an island....

"What's the name of the island where you live?" she asked, for that was a subject as safe as any, and she dearly needed something that would allow her time to calm herself.

A wicked black brow quirked upward. "I live on the island of Zenas, which means Zeus's gift, or, more loosely translated, the gift of the gods. I'm using the Greek name for the god, of course; the Roman version is Jupiter."

"Yes," she said. "Have you lived there for long?"

The brow went higher. "I was born there. I own it."

"Oh." Of course he did; why should he live on someone else's island? And she had forgotten, but now she remembered, what he had said about growing up wild on the island. "Is it a very large island? Does anyone else live there, or is it just you alone on your retreat?"

He grinned. "The island is roughly ten miles long, and as much as five miles wide at one place. There is a small fishing village, and the people graze their goats in the hills. My mother lives in our villa year round now; she no longer likes to travel, and of course, there's the normal staff in the villa. I suppose there are some two hundred people on the island, and an assortment of goats, chickens, dogs, a few cows."

It sounded enchanting, and she forgot her troubles for a moment as she dreamed about such a quiet, simple life. Her eyes glowed as she said, "How can you bear to leave it?"

He shrugged. "I have many interests that require my time and attention, and though I'll always look on the island as my home, I'm not quite a hermit. The modern world has its attractions, too." He raised his wineglass to her and she understood that a large amount of the world's attraction was in its women. Of course, on a small Greek island the young women would be strictly supervised until they wed, and a healthy man would want to relieve his more basic urges.

His gesture with the wineglass brought her attention back to her own wineglass, and she saw that it was nearly empty. "May I have more wine?"

"No," he refused smoothly. "You've already had two glasses, and you've merely pushed your food around on your plate instead of eating it. You'll be drunk if you continue. Eat your dinner, or isn't it the way you like it? Shall I have it returned to the kitchen?"

"No, the food is excellent, thank you." What else could she say? It was only the truth.

"Then why aren't you eating?"

Jessica regarded him seriously, then decided that he was a big boy and he should certainly be able to handle the truth. "I'm not exactly enjoying myself," she told him. "You've rather upset my stomach."

His mouth twitched in grim amusement. "You haven't upset mine, but you have without doubt upset my system in every other way! Since meeting you, I totally absolve Robert Stanton of foolishness, except perhaps in whatever overly optimistic expectations he may have had. You're an enchanting woman, even when you're insulting me."

She had never mentioned her relationship with Robert to anyone, but now she had the urge to cry out that she had loved him, that everyone was wrong in what they said of her. Only the years of practice in holding herself aloof kept her lips sealed on the wild cry of hurt, but she did allow herself to comment, "Robert was the least foolish man I have ever met. He knew exactly what he was about at all times."

Nikolas narrowed his eyes. "Are you saying that he knew you married him only for his money?"

"I'm saying nothing of the kind," she retorted sharply. "I won't discuss my marriage with you; it's none of your business. If you're finished with your meal, I'd like to go home now."

"*I've* finished," he said, looking pointedly at her plate. "However, you've hardly even begun to eat. You need food to absorb some of the wine you've had, and we won't leave here until you eat."

"I would bolt it down without chewing if that would free me from your company," she muttered as she lifted her fork and speared a morsel of meat.

' He waited until she had the meat in her mouth and was chewing before he said, "But it won't. If I remember correctly, you have invited me upstairs when I take you home. To satisfy my 'odd little urges,' I think was how you phrased it. I accept your invitation."

Jessica swallowed and attacked another piece of meat. "You must have misunderstood," she said coldly. "I wouldn't let you inside my house, let alone my bedroom."

"My apartment will do just as well," he replied, his eyes gleaming. "Or the ground, if you prove difficult about the matter."

"Now see here," she snapped, putting her fork down with a clatter. "This has gone far enough. I want you to understand this clearly: I'm *not* available! Not to you, not to any man, and if you touch me, I'll scream until everyone in London hears me."

"If you can," he murmured. "Don't you imagine that I'm capable of stifling any screams, Jessica?"

"Oh?" she demanded with uplifted brows. "Are you a rapist? Because it would be rape, have no doubt about it. I'm not playing at being difficult; I'm entirely serious. I don't want you."

"You will," he said confidently, and she wanted to scream now, in frustration. Could he truly be so dense, his ego so invulnerable, that he simply couldn't believe that she didn't want to go to bed with him? Well, if he didn't believe that she'd scream, he'd certainly be surprised if he tried anything with her!

In one swift motion she stood up, determined not to sit there another moment. "Thank you for the meal," she said. "I believe it would be best if I took a taxi home, and I'll have Charles contact you Monday about the settlement of the shares."

He stood also, calmly laying his napkin aside. "I'm taking you home," he said, "if I have to drag you to my car. Now, do you want to make your exit in a dignified manner, or slung over my shoulder? Before you decide, let me assure you that no one will come to your aid. Money does have its uses, you know.''

"Yes, I know,'' she agreed frigidly. "It allows some people to act like bullies without fear of retribution. Very well, shall we leave?''

He smiled in grim triumph and placed a bill on the table, and even in her anger she was startled at the amount he had laid down. She looked up in time to see him nod to the maître d', and by the time they had made their way across the room her wrap was waiting. Nikolas took the wrap and gently placed it about her shoulders, his hands lingering there for a moment as his fingers moved over her flesh. A blinding flash of light told her that this, too, had been photographed, and involuntarily Jessica shrank closer to him in an effort to hide. His hands tightened on her shoulders and he frowned as he looked down at her suddenly pale face. He looked around until he located the photographer, and though he said nothing, Jessica heard a muttered apology somewhere behind them. Then Nikolas had his arm firmly around her waist and he led her outside, where his car was just being driven up.

When the doorman and the young man who had brought the car had been settled with and Nikolas had seen that she was securely buckled into her seat, he said, "Why do you flinch whenever a flash goes off?''

"I dislike publicity,'' she muttered.

"It scarcely matters whether you like it or not,'' he said quietly. "Your actions have made certain that you will have it, regardless, and you certainly should be used to it by now. Your marriage made quite a lot of grist for the mill.''

"I'm aware of that,'' she said. "I've been called a bitch to my face and a lot worse to my back, but that doesn't mean that I've ever become accustomed to it. I was eighteen years old, *Mr. Constantinos*''—she stressed the word—"and I was crucified by the press. I've never forgotten.''

"Did you think no one would notice when you married a rich,

elderly man of Robert Stanton's reputation?'' he almost snarled. ''For God's sake, Jessica, you all but begged to be crucified!''

''So I discovered,'' she said, her voice catching. ''Robert and I ceased going out in public when it became obvious that I would never be accepted as his wife, though he didn't care on his own account. He said that he would find out who his true friends were, and there were a few. He seemed to cherish those few, and never said anything that indicated he wanted his life to be any different, at least in my hearing. Robert was endlessly kind,'' she finished quietly, for she found that even the memories of Robert helped to calm her. He had seen life so clearly, without illusions and with a great deal of humor. What would he think about this predatory man who sat beside her now?

He drove in silence and she leaned her head back and closed her eyes, tired and rather drained. All in all, it had been a long day, and the worst part was still to come, unless he decided to act decently and leave her alone. But somehow she doubted that Nikolas Constantinos ever acted in any way except to please himself, so she had best brace herself for war.

When he pulled up in the drive on her side of the house, she noticed thankfully that Sallie and Joel were home and were still awake, though her watch told her that it was ten-thirty. He cut off the engine and put the keys in his pocket, then got out and came around to open her door. He leaned in and helped her to gather her long skirt, then all but lifted her out of the car. ''I'm not an invalid,'' she said tartly as his arm slid about her waist and pulled her against his side.

''That's why I'm holding you,'' he explained, his low laughter brushing her hair. ''To prevent you from running.''

Fuming helplessly, Jessica watched as he took the key from her bag and opened the door, ushering her inside with that iron arm at her back. She ignored him and marched into the kitchen to check on Samantha. She knelt and scratched the dog behind the ears, receiving a loving lick on the hand in return. A puppy squeaked at being disturbed and it too received a lick of the warm tongue, then Jessica was startled as two hard hands closed over her shoulders and pulled her to her feet.

She had had enough; she was tired of him and his arrogance. She exploded with rage, hitting at his face and twisting her body in his grasp as he tried to hold her against him. "No, damn you!" she cried. "I told you I won't!"

Samantha rose to her feet and gave a growl at seeing her mistress treated so roughly, but the puppies began to cry in alarm as she left them and she turned back to look at her offspring. By that time Nikolas had swept Jessica off her feet and into his arms and was back through the kitchen door with her, shouldering it shut behind him. He wasn't even breathing hard as he captured her flailing arms, and that made her even angrier. She arched her back and kicked in an effort to wiggle out of his arms; she hit out at that broad chest, and when that failed to stop him, she opened her mouth to scream. Swiftly he forced her head against his shoulder and her scream was largely muffled by his body. Blinded and breathless with fury, she gave a strangled cry as he suddenly dropped her.

Soft cushions broke her fall, then her body was instantly covered by his hard weight as he dropped down on her and pinned her. "Damn you, be still," he hissed, stretching a long arm up over her head. For a sickening moment she thought he would slap her, and she caught her breath, but no blow fell. Instead, he switched on the lamp at the end of the sofa and a soft light bathed the room. She hadn't realized where they were until he turned on the lamp and now she looked about her at the comfortable, sane setting of her living room. She turned her head to look up with bewilderment into the furious dark face above her.

"What's the matter with you?" he barked.

She blinked. Hadn't he been attacking her? He had certainly been manhandling her! Even now his heavy legs pressed down on hers and she knew that her skirt was twisted above her knees. She moved restlessly under him and he let his weight down more heavily on her in warning. "Well?" he growled.

"But...I thought...weren't you attacking me?" she asked, her brow puckering. "I thought you were, and so did Samantha."

"If I *had* been attacking you, the situation was reversed before I got very far," he snapped. "Damn you, Jessica, you don't know how tempting you are—and how infuriating—" He broke off, his black eyes moving to her lips. She squirmed and turned her head away, a breathless little "No" coming from her, but he captured her head with a hand on each side of her face and turned her mouth back to him. He was only a breath away and she tried to protest again, then it was too late. His hard mouth closed over her soft one, forcing her lips open, and his warm, wine-fragrant breath filled her mouth. His tongue followed, exploring and caressing her inner mouth, flicking at her own tongue, sending her senses reeling.

She was frightened by the pressure of his big, hard body over hers and for a moment her slim hands pushed uselessly at his heavy shoulders. But his mouth was warm and he wasn't hurting her now, and she had never before been kissed like this. For a moment—only one moment, she promised herself—she allowed herself to curve in his arms, to respond to him and kiss him back. Her hands slid over his broad shoulders to clasp about his neck, her tongue responded shyly to his; then she no longer had the option of returning his caresses or not. He shuddered and his arms tightened painfully about her and his mouth went wild, ravaging, sucking her breath hungrily from her body. He muttered something, thickly, and it took her dazed mind a minute to realize he had spoken in French and to translate the words. When she did, her face flamed and she tried to push him away, but still she was helpless against him.

He slid one hand under her neck and deftly unhooked the halter strap of her bodice. As his mouth left hers and trailed a fiery path down her neck, she managed a choked "No," to which he paid no attention at all. His lips moved the loosened straps of her bodice down as he planted fierce kisses along her shoulder and collarbone, licking the tender spot in the hollow of her shoulder until she almost forgot her rising fear and quivered with pleasure, clutching his ribs with helpless hands. He became impatient with the straps, still in the way of his wandering mouth, and jerked roughly at them, intent on baring her to the waist, and panic erupted in Jessica with the force of a volcano.

With a strangled cry she twisted frantically in his arms, holding her bodice up with one arm while, with the other, she tried to force his head away from her. He snarled in frustration and jerked her arm above her head, reaching for the material of her dress with his other hand. Her heartbeat came to a standstill and with superhuman effort she pulled her hand free, beating at his back. "No!" she cried out, nearly hysterical. "No, Nikolas, don't; I beg you!"

He stilled her words with the forceful pressure of his mouth, and she realized in a jolt of pure terror that she couldn't control him; he was bent on taking her. A sob erupted from her throat and she released her bodice to beat at him with both hands, crying wildly and choking out the muffled words, "No! No...." He raised his lips from hers and she moaned, "Please! Nikolas! Ah, don't!"

The savage movements of his hands stopped and he lay still, his breath heaving raggedly in his chest. She shook with sobs, her small face drenched with tears. He groaned deep in his throat and slid off the sofa, to kneel beside it and rest his black head on the cushion beside her. Silence fell on the room again and she tried to choke back her tears. Hesitantly she put her hands on his head, sliding her fingers through his thick hair, not understanding her need to comfort him but unable to resist the impulse. He quivered under the touch of her hands and she smelled the fresh sweat on his body, the maleness of his skin, and she realized how aroused he had been. But he had stopped; he hadn't forced her, after all, and she could feel all of her hostility draining away. For all her inexperience she knew enough about men to know that it had been quite a wrench for him to become so aroused and then stop, and she was deeply grateful to him.

At length he raised his head, and she gasped at the strained, grim expression on his face. "Straighten your dress," he said thickly, "or it may be too late yet."

Hastily she hooked her straps back into place and pushed the skirt down over her legs. She would have liked to sit up, but with him so close it would have been awkward, so she remained lying against the cushions until he moved. He ran his hand wearily through his hair. "Perhaps it's just as well," he said a moment later, getting to his feet. "We made no preparations, and I know I couldn't have— Was that what frightened you, Jessica? The thought of the risk we'd have been taking with an unwanted pregnancy?"

Her voice was husky when she spoke. "No, it…it wasn't that. You just…frightened me." She sat up and wiped at her wet cheeks with the palms of her hands. He looked at her and grimly produced the handkerchief that she had used earlier, to dry her eyes when he had first arrived—was it only a few hours ago? She accepted the square of linen and dried her face, then gave it back to him.

He gave a short, harsh laugh. "So I frightened you? I wanted to do a lot of things to you, but frightening you wasn't one of them. You're a dangerous woman, my dear, deadly in your charm. You leave a man aching and empty after you've pulled away." He inhaled deeply and began to button his shirt, and only then did she notice that somehow his jacket had been discarded and his shirt unbuttoned and pulled loose from his pants. She had no memory of opening his shirt, but only she could have done it, for his hands had been too busy on her to have accomplished it.

His face still wore that taut, strained look and she said in a rush, "I'm sorry, Nikolas."

"So am I, my dear." His dark gaze flickered to her and a tight little smile touched his mouth. "But you're calling me Nikolas now, so something has been accomplished." He tucked his shirt inside his pants and dropped down on the sofa beside her. "I want to see you again, and soon," he said, taking her hand. "Will you come sailing with me tomorrow? I promise that

I won't rush you; I won't frighten you as I did tonight. I'll give you time to get to know me, to realize that you'll be perfectly safe with me. Whoever frightened you of men should be shot, but it won't be like that with me. You'll see,'' he said encouragingly.

Safe? Would she ever be safe with this man? She strongly doubted it, but he had been nicer than she would have expected and she didn't want to make him angry, so she tempered her words. ''I don't think so, Nikolas. Not tomorrow. It's too soon.''

His mouth pressed into an ominous line, then he sighed and got to his feet. ''I'll call you tomorrow, and don't try anything foolish like trying to hide from me. I'd only find you, and you might not like the consequences. I won't be put off like that again. Do you understand?''

''I understand that you're threatening me!'' she said spiritedly.

He grinned suddenly. ''You're safe so long as you don't push me, Jessica. I want you, but I can wait.''

Jessica tossed her head. ''It could be a long wait,'' she felt compelled to warn.

''Or it could be a short one,'' he warned in his turn. ''As I said, I'll call you tomorrow. Think about the sailing; you'd like it.''

''I've never been sailing; I don't know the first thing about it. I could be seasick.''

''It'll be fun teaching you what you don't know,'' he said, and he meant more than sailing. He leaned over and pressed a warm kiss to her mouth, then drew away before she could either respond or resist. ''I'll let myself out. Good night, Jessica.''

''Good night, Nikolas.'' It felt odd to be saying good night to him as if those moments of passion and terror had never happened. She watched as he picked up his jacket from the floor and walked out, his tall, lean body moving with the wild grace of a tiger. When he was gone, the house felt empty and too quiet, and she had a sinking feeling that Nikolas Constantinos was going to turn her life upside down.

Chapter 4

Despite feeling edgy when she went to bed, Jessica slept deeply and woke in a cheerful frame of mind. She had been silly to let that man work her into a state of nerves, but she would try to avoid him in the future. Charles could handle all the details of selling the stock.

Humming to herself, she fed Samantha and praised the puppies to their proud mother, then made toast for herself. She had not acquired the English habit of tea, so instead she drank coffee; she was lingering over the second cup when Sallie rapped on the window of the back door. Jessica got up to unlock the door and let her in, and she noticed the worried frown that marred Sallie's usually smiling face. Sallie held a folded section of newspaper.

"Is anything wrong?" asked Jessica. "But before you tell me, would you like a cup of coffee?"

Sallie made a face. "Coffee, my girl? You're not civilized yet! No, Jess, I think you should see this. It's a nasty piece, and just when all of that business was beginning to die down. I wouldn't have brought it over, Joel thought I shouldn't, but— well, you'll be hit with it when you go out, and I thought it would be better for you to see it privately."

Jessica held out her hand wordlessly for the paper, but she

already knew what it was. Sallie had folded it to the gossip and society pages, and there were two photographs there. One, of course, was of Nikolas kissing her. She noticed dispassionately that it was a good picture, Nikolas so dark and strong, she much slighter in build, their mouths clinging together over the table. The other photo was the one taken when they had been leaving and Nikolas had had his hands on her shoulders, looking down at her with an expression that made her shiver. Raw hunger was evident in his face in that photo, and remembering what had happened when he brought her home made her wonder anew that he had stopped when she became frightened.

But Sallie was pointing to the column under the photos and Jessica sat down at the table to read it. It was a witty, sophisticated column, tart in places, but at one point the columnist became purringly vicious. Nausea welled in her as she skimmed over the lines of print:

> London's notorious Black Widow was observed spinning her web over another helpless and adoring victim last night; the elusive Greek billionaire Nikolas Constantinos appeared to be completely captivated by the Widow's charm. Can it be that she had exhausted the funds left to her by her late husband, the esteemed Robert Stanton? Certainly Nikolas is able to maintain her in her accustomed style, yet from all reports this man may not be as easy to capture as she found her first husband. One wonders just who will be the victor in the end. The Widow seems to stop at nothing— but neither does her chosen prey. We will observe with interest.

Jessica dropped the paper onto the table and sat staring blindly across the room. She shouldn't let it bother her; she had been expecting this to happen. And certainly she should be accustomed to it, after five years, but it seemed that rather than becoming hardened, she was more sensitive now than she had been years ago. Then she had had Robert to buffer her, to ease the pain and make her laugh, but now she had no one. Any pain she suffered was suffered alone. The Black Widow—that phrase had been coined immediately after Robert's death, and it had stuck. Before that they had at least referred to her by name. The cutting little bits had always been nasty but stopped short of libel, not that she would ever have pursued the matter. The publicity involved in a suit would have been even nastier, and she would rather live a quiet life, with her few friends and small pleasures. She would even have returned to the States if it hadn't been for Robert's business interests, but she wanted to see to them and use the knowledge Robert had given her. Robert would have wanted that, too, she knew.

Sallie was watching her anxiously, so Jessica pulled a deep, shuddering breath into her lungs and forced herself to speak. "Well, that was certainly a vicious bit, wasn't it? I had almost forgotten how really rotten it can be.... But I won't make the mistake of going out again. It isn't worth it."

"But you can't hide away all your life," protested Sallie. "You're so young; it isn't fair to treat you like—like a leper!"

A leper—what an appalling thought! Yet Sallie wasn't so wrong, even though Jessica had yet to be stoned out of town. She was still welcome in very few homes.

Sallie cast about for a different subject, for although Jessica was trying to act casual about the whole matter, her face had gone pale and she looked stricken. Sallie jabbed the photo in the newspaper and said, "What about this dish, Jess? He's a gorgeous man! When did you meet him?"

"What?" Jessica looked down and two spots of color came back to her cheeks as she gazed at the photo of Nikolas kissing her. "Oh...actually, I only met him yesterday."

"Wow! He certainly is a fast worker! He looks the strong, masterful type, and his reputation is mind-boggling. What's he like?"

"Strong, masterful, and mind-boggling," Jessica sighed. "Just like you said. I hope I don't have to meet with him again."

"You've mush in your head!" exclaimed Sallie indignantly. "Honestly, Jess, you are unbelievable. Most women would give their right arm to go out with a man like that, rich *and* handsome, and you aren't interested.''

"But then, I'm wary of rich men," Jessica replied softly. "You've seen an example of what would be said, and I don't think I could go through that again."

"Oh! I'm sorry, love," said Sallie. "I didn't think. But—just think! Nikolas Constantinos!"

Jessica didn't want to think of Nikolas; she wanted to forget the entire night. Looking at her friend's pale, closed face, Sallie patted her shoulder and slipped away. Jessica sat for a time at the table, her mind blank, but when she stood up to place her cup and saucer in the sink, it suddenly became more than she could handle and the tears fell freely.

When the bout of weeping ended, she was exhausted from the force of it and she wandered into the living room to lie down on the sofa, but that reminded her of Nikolas lying there with her, and instead she collapsed into a chair, pulling her feet up into the seat and wrapping her robe about her legs. She felt dead, empty inside, and when the phone rang, she stared at it dumbly for a long moment before she lifted the receiver. "Hello," she said dully.

"Jessica. Have you—"

She took the receiver away from her ear when she heard the deep voice, and listlessly let it drop back onto the cradle. No, she couldn't talk to him now; she hurt too deeply.

When the doorbell pealed some time later, she continued to sit quietly, determined not to answer it, but after a moment she heard Charles's voice call out her name and she got to her feet.

"Good morning," she greeted him while he eyed her sharply. She looked beaten.

"I read the paper," he said gently. "Go upstairs and wash your face and put on some clothes, then you can tell me about it. I intended to call you yesterday, but I had to go out of town, not that I could have done anything. Go on, my dear, upstairs with you."

Jessica did as she was told, applying cold water to her face and smoothing the tangles from her hair, then changing out of her nightgown and robe into a pretty white sundress with tiny blue flowers on it. Despite her numbness, she was glad that Charles was there. With his cool lawyer's brain he could pick at her responses until they were all neatly arranged where she could understand them, and he would analyze her feelings. Charles could analyze a rock.

"Yes, much better," he approved when she entered the living room. "Well, it is rather obvious that my fears for you were misplaced; Constantinos was obviously quite taken with you. Did he mention the Dryden issue?"

"He did," said Jessica, and even managed a smile for him. "I'm selling the stock to him, but don't imagine everything was sweetness and light. We get along like the proverbial cats and dogs. His comments on my marriage make that gossip column seem mild in comparison, and I have walked out on him and hung up on him once each—no, I've done it twice; he called this morning and I didn't want to talk to him. It would be best if I don't see him again, if you could handle all of the details of the stock transaction."

"Of course I will," replied Charles promptly. "But I feel certain you're underestimating your man. From that photo in the newspaper, he's attracted to more than your ConTech stock."

"Yes," admitted Jessica, "but there's no use. I couldn't live with that type of publicity again, and he attracts reporters and photographers by the dozens."

"That's true, but if he doesn't want something to be published, it isn't published. His power is enormous."

"Are you trying to argue his side, Charles?" Jessica asked in amazement. "Surely you understand that his attraction is only temporary, that he's only interested in an affair?"

Charles shrugged. "So are most men," he said dryly. "In the beginning."

"Yes, well, I'm *not* interested. By the way, the shares are going for market value. He offered much more than that, but I refused it."

"I see Robert's standards there," he said.

"I'll sell the stock to him, but *I* won't be bought."

"I never thought you would. I wished myself a fly on the wall during your meeting; it must've been diverting," he said, and smiled at her, his cool, aristocratic face revealing the dry humor behind his elegant, controlled manner.

"Very, but it stopped short of murder." Suddenly she remembered and she smiled naturally for the first time since reading that horrid gossip column. "Charles, Samantha had her puppies last night, five of them!"

"She took time enough," he observed. "What will you do with five yelping puppies about the house?"

"Give them away when they're old enough. There are plenty of children in the neighborhood; it shouldn't be that difficult."

"You think so? When have you last tried to give away a litter of unknown origin? How many females are there?"

"How should I know?" she demanded, and laughed. "They don't come with pink and blue bows around their necks, you know."

Charles grinned in return and followed her into the kitchen, where she proudly displayed the pups, all piled together in a little heap. Samantha watched Charles closely, ready to nip if he came too near her babies, but he was well aware of Samantha's tendencies and kept a safe distance from her. Charles was too fastidious to be an animal lover and the dog sensed this.

"I see you've no tea made," he commented, looking at the coffeepot. "Put the water on, my dear, and tell me more about your meeting with Constantinos. Did it actually become hot, or were you teasing?"

Sighing, Jessica ran water from the tap into a kettle and put it on the stove. "The meeting was definitely unfriendly, even hostile. Don't let the photo of that kiss fool you, Charles; he only did that as a punishment and to make me shut up. I can't—" She started to say that she couldn't decide if she trusted him or not, but the ring of the doorbell interrupted her and she stopped in her tracks, a chill running up her spine. "Oh, glory," she gulped. "That's him now; I know it is! I hung up on him, and he'll be in a raging temper."

"I'll be brave and answer the door for you while you make the tea," offered Charles, searching for an excuse to get to Constantinos before he could upset her even more. That shattered look was fading from her eyes, but she was still hurt and vulnerable and she wasn't up to fending off someone like Constantinos. Jessica realized why Charles offered to get the door; he was the most tactful man in the world, she thought as she set out the cups and saucers for tea. And one of the kindest, always trying to shield her from any unpleasantness.

She stopped in her tracks, considering that. Why hadn't Charles offered to meet with Constantinos and work out the deal on the shares rather than letting her go herself? The more she thought about it, the more out of character it seemed. A wild suspicion flared and she dismissed it instantly, but it crept back. Had Charles deliberately thrown her into Nikolas's path? Was he actually *matchmaking?* Horrors! What had he been thinking of? Didn't he know that Nikolas Constantinos, while very likely to ask her to be his mistress, would never even consider marriage? And Charles certainly knew her well enough to know that she would never consider anything but!

Marriage? With Nikolas? She began to shake so violently that she had to put the tray down. What was wrong with her? She had only met the man yesterday, yet here she was thinking that she would never settle for less than being his wife! It was only that he was physically attractive to her, she told herself desperately. But Jessica was nothing if not honest with herself and she knew immediately that she was hiding from the truth. It wasn't only a physical attraction that she felt for Nikolas. She had seen a great many men who were handsome and physically appealing to her, but none that she had wanted as she had wanted Nikolas last night. Nor would she have been so receptive to Nikolas's caresses if her mind and emotions hadn't responded to him, too. He was brutal and ruthless and maddeningly arrogant, but she sensed in him a masculine appreciation for her femininity that tore down her barriers of hostility. Nikolas wanted her. That was fairly obvious, and she could have resisted that, had she not been aware that he delighted in her sharp mind and equally sharp tongue.

All in all, she was dangerously attracted to him, even vulnerable to falling in love with him, and that realization was a blow that surpassed the unpleasant shock of that vicious gossip column. White-faced, trembling, she stared at the kettle of boiling water, wondering what she was going to do. How could she avoid him? He was not a man to accept no for an answer, nor was she certain that she could say no to him, anyway. Yet to be in his company was to invite even greater pain, for he would not offer marriage and she would not be satisfied with less.

Eventually the shrill whistle of the kettle drew her mind back to the present and she hurriedly turned the heat off and poured the water over the tea. She had no idea if Nikolas would drink tea and decided that he wouldn't, so she poured coffee for him and also for herself; then, without allowing herself time to think about it, she picked up the tray and carried it through to the living room before she could lose all her courage.

Nikolas was lounging on the sofa like a big cat, while Charles had taken a chair; they both got to their feet as she entered, and Nikolas stepped forward to take the heavy tray from her hands and place it on the low table. She shot him a wary glance from under her lashes, but he didn't look angry. He was watching her intently, his gaze so penetrating that she shivered. He immediately noted her reaction and a sardonic half-smile curved his mouth. He put his hand on her arm and gently forced her to a seat on the sofa, then took his place beside her.

"Charles and I have been discussing the situation," he said easily, and she started, shooting a desperate look at Charles. But Charles merely smiled and she could read nothing from his expression.

"What situation?" she asked, reaching for some hidden well of calmness.

"The position our relationship will put you in with the press," he explained smoothly as she handed Charles's tea across to him. By some miracle she kept from dropping the cup and saucer, though she felt her entire body jerk. When Charles had rescued his drink, she turned a pale face up to Nikolas.

"What are you saying?" she whispered.

"I think you know, my dear; you're far from stupid. I'll take certain steps that will make it plain to all observers that I don't feel I need the press to protect me from you, and that any long noses poked into my private life will rouse me to…irritation. You won't have to worry any longer about being the subject of a nasty Sunday-morning column; in fact, after I finish convincing the press to do as I want, all sympathy will probably swing to you."

"That's quite unnecessary," she said, lowering her lashes as she offered a cup of coffee to him. She felt confused; it had not occurred to her that Nikolas might use his influence to protect her, and rather than feeling grateful, she withdrew into a cool reserve. She didn't want to be indebted to Nikolas and drawn further into his sphere of influence. The paper had gotten it all wrong; he was the spider, not she! If she allowed it, he would weave silken threads all about her until she was helpless against him.

"I'll be the judge of that," Nikolas snapped. "If you'd told me last night why you were so upset about that damned photographer, I could have prevented both the column and the photos from being printed. Instead, you let your pride stand in the way, and look what you've endured, all for nothing. Now I know the extent of the situation and I'll act as I think best."

Charles said mildly, "Be reasonable, Jessica. There's no need for you to endure spiteful gossip. You've suffered it for five years; it's time that state of affairs was ended."

"Yes, but…" She halted, for she had been about to say, But not by *him,* and she wasn't certain enough of Nikolas's temper to risk it. She took a deep breath and began again. "What I meant was, I don't see the need for any intervention, because there won't be another opportunity for this to happen. I'd have to be a fool to allow myself to get into that situation after what happened last night. I'll simply live here as quietly as possible; there's no need for me to frequent places where I'd be recognized.''

''I won't allow that,'' Nikolas put in grimly. ''From now on, you'll be by my side when I entertain or when I go out. People will meet you, get to know you. That's the only sure way of forever stifling the gossip, to let these people become acquainted with you and find out that they like you. You *are* a likable little wench, despite your damnable temper.''

''Thank you!'' she returned smartly, and Charles grinned.

''I could kick myself for missing your first meeting,'' he put in, and Nikolas gave him a wolfish grin.

''The first wasn't as interesting as the second,'' he informed Charles dryly. ''And the third meeting isn't beginning all that well, either. It'll probably take me all day to convince her not to be obstinate over the matter.''

''Yes, I can see that.'' Charles winked and replaced his empty cup on the tray. ''I'll leave you to it, then; I've some work to do.''

''Call me tomorrow and we'll settle about the shares,'' said Nikolas, getting to his feet and holding out his hand.

Jessica's warning sirens went off. ''The shares are already settled,'' she said in fierce determination. ''Market value only! I told you, Nikolas, I won't sign the papers if you try to buy me off with a ridiculously high price!''

''I shall probably break your neck before the day is out,'' returned Nikolas genially, but his eyes were hard. Charles laughed aloud, something very rare for him, and Jessica glared at him as he and Nikolas walked to the door. They exchanged a few low words and her suspicions flared higher. Then Nikolas let him out and returned to stand before her with his hands on his hips, staring down at her with an implacable expression on his hard face.

''I meant what I said,'' she flared, scrambling to her feet to stand before him and braving the volcanic heat of his eyes.

"So did I," he murmured, raising his hand and absently stroking her bare shoulder with one finger, his touch as light and
delicate as that of a butterfly. Her breath caught and she stood
very still until the caress of that one finger drove her beyond
control and she began to tremble. The finger moved from her
shoulder to her throat, then up to press under her chin and raise
her face to his. "Have you decided if you want to go out on the
boat with me?" he asked as his eyes slipped to her mouth.

"I—yes. I mean, yes, I've decided, and no, I don't want to
go," she explained in confusion, and the corners of his mouth
lifted in a wry smile.

"Then I suggest we go for a drive, something to keep me
occupied. If we stay here all day, Jessica, you know what will
happen, but the decision is yours."

"I haven't invited you to stay at all, much less all day!" she
informed him indignantly, pulling away from him.

His arm dropped to his side and he watched sharply as the
color rose in her cheeks. "You're afraid of me," he observed
in mild surprise. Despite her brave, defiant front, there had been
a flash of real fear in her eyes, and he frowned. "What is it
about me that frightens you, Jessica? Are you afraid of me sexually? Have your experiences with men been so bad that you
fear my lovemaking?"

She stared numbly at him, unable to formulate an answer. Yes,
she was afraid of him, as she had never before feared any other
human being. He was so lawless—no, not that. He made his
own laws, his influence was enormous; he was practically un-
touchable by any known power. She already knew that her emotions were vulnerable to him and that she had no weapons
against him at all.

But he was waiting for an answer, his strong features hardening as she moved involuntarily backward. She gulped and
whispered wildly, "You—you wouldn't understand, Nikolas. I
think that a woman would be in very good hands with you, so
to speak, wouldn't she?"

"I like to think so," he drawled. "But if it isn't that, Jessica, what is it about me that makes you as wary as a frightened doe? I promise I won't slaughter you.''

"Won't you?"

The whispered, shaking words had scarcely left her mouth before he moved, closing the distance between them with two lithe strides and capturing her as she gave an alarmed cry and tried to dart away. His left arm slid about her waist and pulled her strongly against him, while his right hand caught a fistful of her tawny hair and pulled firmly on it until her face was tilted up to his.

"Now," he growled, "tell me why you're afraid."

"You're hurting me!" she cried, anger chasing away some of her instinctive fear. She kicked at his shins and he gave a muffled curse, releasing her hair and scooping her up in his arms instead. Holding her captive, he sat down on the sofa and pinned her squirming body on his lap. The struggle was woefully unequal and in only a moment she was exhausted and subdued, lying quietly against the arm that was so hard and unyielding behind her back.

He chuckled. "Whatever you're afraid of, you're definitely not afraid to fight me. Now, little wildcat, tell me what bothers you."

She was tired, too tired to fight him right now, and she was beginning to understand that it was useless to fight him, in any event. He was determined to have everything his way. Sighing, she turned her face into his shoulder and inhaled the warm, earthy male scent of him, slightly sweaty from their struggle. What could she tell him? That she feared him physically because she had known no man, that it was a virgin's instinctive fear? He would never believe that; he would rather believe the tales that many men had made love to her. And she couldn't tell him that she feared him emotionally, that she was far too vulnerable to his power, or he would use that knowledge against her.

Then an idea struck her. He had given it to her himself. Why not let him believe that she had been so mistreated that she feared all men now? He had seemed receptive to that idea....

"I don't want to talk about it," she muttered, keeping her face turned into his shoulder.

His arms tightened about her. "You have to talk about it," he said forcefully, putting his mouth against her temple. "You have to get it out in the open, where you can understand it."

"I—I don't think I can," she said breathlessly, for his arms were preventing proper breathing. "Give me time, Nikolas."

"If I must," he said into her hair. "I won't hurt you, Jessica; I want you to know that. I can be very considerate when I get what I want."

Yes, he probably could, but he was thinking only of an affair while she was already beginning to realize that her heart was terrifyingly open, his for the taking—except that he didn't want it. He wanted only her body, not the tender emotions she could give him.

His hands were moving restlessly, one stroking over her back and bare shoulders, the other caressing her thigh and hip. He wanted to make love, *now,* she could feel the desire trembling in his body. She groaned and said, "No, Nikolas, please. I can't—"

"I could teach you," he muttered. "You don't know what you're doing to me; a man isn't a piece of rock!"

But he was, pure granite. Her slim body arched in his arms as she tried to slip away from him. "No, Nikolas! No!"

He opened his arms as if he was freeing a bird and she slid from his lap to the floor, sitting on it like a child, her head resting on the sofa. He sighed heavily. "Don't wait too long," he advised, his deep voice hoarse. "Run upstairs and do whatever you have to do before we go for a drive. I have to get out of here or there won't be any waiting."

He didn't have to tell her a second time. On trembling legs she ran upstairs, where she combed her hair and put on makeup, then changed her shoes for modest heels. Her heart was pounding wildly as she returned downstairs to him. She hardly knew him, yet he was gaining a power over her that was frightening. And she was helpless to prevent it.

When she approached him, he stood and pulled her close with a masterful arm, and his hard warm mouth took hers lazily. When he released her, he was smiling, and she supposed he had reason to smile, for her response had been as fervent as it was involuntary.

"You'll be a blazing social success," he predicted as he led her to the door. "Every man will be at your feet if you continue to look so fetching and to blush so delightfully. I don't know how you can manage a blush, but the how really doesn't matter when the result is so lovely."

"I can't control my color," she said, miffed that he should think her capable of faking a blush. "Would you rather your kisses had no effect on me?"

He looked down at her and gave her a melting smile. "On the contrary, my pet. But if it's excitement that brings the flush to your cheeks, I shall know when you are becoming aroused and will immediately whisk you away to a private place. You must tell me all of your little signals."

She managed a careless shrug. "Before you whisk me away to be ravished, I suggest that you first make certain I'm not in the midst of a fight. Anger brings on the same reaction, I'm told. And I don't imagine that even your backing will smooth away all the rocks!"

"I want to know about any rocks that stub your toe," he said, and his voice grew hard. "I insist on it, Jessica. I won't have a repeat of the sort of trash I read this morning, not if I have to muzzle every gossip columnist in London!"

To her horror, it did not sound like an empty threat.

Chapter 5

When the doorbell rang, Jessica went very still. Nikolas put his hand on her waist and squeezed gently, then that hand urged her inexorably toward the door. Involuntarily she resisted the pressure and he looked down at her, his hard mouth curving into a dry smile. "Don't be such a little coward," he mocked. "I won't let the beasts eat you, so why not relax and enjoy it?"

Speechless, she shook her head. In the few days that she had known Nikolas Constantinos he had taken her life and turned it upside down, totally altered it. This morning he had given his secretary a list of people to call and invite to his penthouse that night, and naturally everyone had accepted. Who turned down Constantinos? At four o'clock that afternoon Nikolas had called Jessica and told her to dress for the evening, he would pick her up in two hours. She had assumed that they would be dining out again, and though she hadn't looked forward to it, she had realized the futility of resisting Nikolas. It wasn't until he had her at his penthouse that he had told her of his plans.

She was angry and resentful that he had done all of this without consulting her, and she had scarcely spoken to him since her arrival, which seemed to bother him not at all. But underneath her anger she was anxious and miserable. Though well aware that, with Nikolas backing her, no one would dare be openly cold or hostile, she was sensitive enough that it didn't really matter if their dislike was hidden or out in the open. She knew it was there, and she suffered. It didn't help that Nikolas's secretary, Andros, was there, his contempt carefully hidden from Nikolas but sneeringly revealed to her whenever Nikolas wasn't looking. It had developed that Andros was a second cousin to Nikolas, so perhaps he felt he was secure in his position.

"You're too pale," observed Nikolas critically, pausing with his hand on the handle to open the door. He bent and kissed her, hard, deliberately letting her feel his tongue, then straightened away from her and opened the door before she could react in any way other than the delicate flush that rose to her cheeks.

She wanted to kick him, and she promised herself that she would have his hide for his arrogant action, but for now she steeled herself to greet the small clusters of people who were arriving. Stealing a glance at Nikolas, she saw that his hard masculine lips wore a light coat of her lipstick and she blushed anew, especially when several of the sharp-eyed women noted it also, then darted their glances to her own lipstick as if matching the shades. Then he stretched out one strong hand and pulled her closer to his side, introducing her as his "dear friend and business partner, Jessica Stanton." The dear friend description brought knowing expressions to many faces, and Jessica thought furiously that he might as well have said *"chère amie,"* for that was how everyone was taking it. Of course, that was Nikolas's intention, but she did not plan to fall meekly in with his desires. When the second half of his introduction sank in, everyone immediately became very polite where for a moment she had sensed a direct snub. *Chère amie* was one thing, but business partner was another. He had made it obvious, with only a few well-chosen words, that he would take any insult to Jessica as an insult to himself.

To her surprise and discomfiture, Nikolas introduced one tall, smartly dressed blonde as a columnist, and by the pressure of his fingers she knew that this was the gossip columnist who had written that vicious little bit about her for the Sunday paper. She greeted Amanda Waring with a calm manner that revealed nothing, though it took all of her self-control to manage it. Miss Waring glared at her for a fraction of a second before assuming a false smile and mouthing all of the conventional things.

Her attention was jerked back to Nikolas by the spectacle of a stunning redhead sliding a silken arm about his muscular neck and stretching up against him to kiss him slowly on the mouth. It wasn't a long kiss, nor a deep one, but nevertheless it fairly shouted of intimacy. Jessica went rigid as an unexpected and unwelcome flame of jealousy seared her. How dare that woman touch him! She quivered and barely restrained herself from jerking the woman away from him, but if Nikolas himself hadn't released the woman's arm from his neck and stepped back from her, she might still have created a scene. The glance Nikolas gave her was as apologetic as one could expect from him, but the effect was ruined by the gleam of amusement in the midnight depths of his eyes.

Deliberately Nikolas drew his handkerchief out of his pocket and wiped the redhead's coral-beige lipstick from his mouth, something he hadn't done when he had kissed Jessica. Then he took Jessica's hand and said, "Darling, I'd like you to meet an old friend, Diana Murray. Diana, Jessica Stanton."

Lovely dark blue eyes turned on Jessica, but the expression in them was savage. Then the soft lips parted in a smile. "Ah, yes, I do believe I've heard of you," Diana purred.

Beside her, Jessica felt Nikolas turn as still as a waiting panther. She tightened her fingers on his hand and responded evenly, "Have you? How interesting," and turned to be introduced to Diana's escort, who had been watching with a guarded expression on his face, as if he didn't want to become involved.

Despite Nikolas's bombshell, or perhaps because of it, the room was fairly humming with conversation. Andros was moving from group to group, quietly taking over some of the duties of the host, thereby freeing Nikolas for the most part. For a while Nikolas steered Jessica about from one small knot of people to another, talking easily, bringing her into the conversations and making it obvious by his possessive hand on her arm or the small of her back that she was his, and had his support. Then, callously, she felt, he left her on her own and went off to talk business.

For a moment she was panic-stricken and she looked about, hunting for a corner seat. Then she met Andros's cold, smiling look and knew that he expected her to make a fool of herself. She took a firm grip on her wavering nerves and forced herself to approach a small group of women who were laughing and discussing a current comedy play. It wasn't until she had joined the group that she saw it contained Amanda Waring. Immediately a little silence fell over the women as they looked at her, assessing her position and wondering just how far good manners went.

She lifted her chin and said in a calm voice, "Isn't the lead role played by that actress Penelope something-or-other who was such a smash in America last year?"

"Penelope Durwin," supplied a plumpish, middle-aged woman after a moment. "Yes, she was nominated for their best-actress award, but she seems to like live theater better than films."

"Aren't you an American?" asked Amanda Waring in a velvet little voice, watching Jessica with her icy eyes.

"I was born in America, yes," said Jessica. Was this to become an interview?

"Do you have any plans to return to America to live?"

Jessica stifled a sigh. "Not at this time; I like England and I'm content here."

Conversation ceased for a stiff moment, then Amanda broke the silence again. "Have you known Mr. Constantinos long?" Whatever Amanda's personal feelings, she was first and foremost a columnist, and Jessica was good copy. More—Jessica was fantastic copy! Aside from her own notorious reputation, she was apparently the current mistress of one of the world's most powerful men, an elusive and sexy Greek billionaire. Every word that Jessica said was newsworthy.

"No, not for long," Jessica said neutrally, and then a different voice broke into the circle.

"With a man like Nikolas, it doesn't take long, does it, Mrs. Stanton?" purred a soft, openly hostile voice. Jessica quivered when she heard it and turned to look at Diana, meeting the woman's impossibly lovely blue eyes.

For a long moment Jessica looked at her quietly and the silence became so thick that it was almost suffocating as they all waited to see if a scene would develop. Jessica couldn't even summon up anger to help her; if anything, she pitied this gorgeous creature who watched her with such bright malice. Diana so obviously adored Nikolas, and Jessica knew how helpless a woman was against his charm, and his power. When the silence was almost unbearable, she replied gently, "As you say," and turned back to Amanda Waring. "We met for the first time this past Saturday," she said, giving the woman more information than she had originally intended, but she would be foolish to let the woman's antagonism live when she could so easily put it down.

Her ploy worked. Miss Waring's eyes lit, and hesitantly the other women rejoined the conversation, asking Jessica if she had any plans to visit Mr. Constantinos on his island. They had heard it was fabulous; was he leaving England soon; was she going with him? In the midst of answering their questions Jessica saw Diana leave the group, and she gave an inward sigh of relief, for she had felt that the woman was determined to provoke a scene.

After that, the evening was easier. The women seemed to unbend a little as they discovered that she was a rather quiet, perfectly well-behaved young woman who did not act in the least as if she coveted their husbands. Besides, with Nikolas Constantinos to control her, they certainly felt safe. Though he kept himself to the knot of men discussing business, every so often his black eyes would slide to Jessica's slim figure, as if checking on her. Certainly his alert gaze convinced any unattached male that it would be wise not to approach her.

Only once, when Jessica slipped away for a moment to check her hair and makeup, did she feel uneasy. She saw Diana talking very earnestly to Andros, and even as she watched, Andros flicked her a cool, contemptuous look that chilled her. She hurried away to Nikolas's bedroom and stood for a moment trying to calm her accelerated heartbeat, telling herself that she shouldn't be alarmed by a look. Heavens, she should be accustomed to such looks!

A knock on the door made her shake off her misgivings and she turned to open the door. Amanda Waring stood there. "May I disturb you?" she asked coolly.

"Yes, of course; I was just checking my hair," said Jessica, standing back for the woman to enter. She noticed Amanda looking around sharply at the furnishings, as if expecting black satin sheets and mirrors on the ceilings. In fact, Nikolas was rather spartan in his tastes and the large bedroom seemed almost bare of furniture. Of course, the huge bed dominated the room.

"I wanted to speak with you, Mrs. Stanton," began Amanda. "I wanted to assure you that nothing you said will be repeated in my column; Mr. Constantinos has made it clear that my job hangs in the balance, and I'm not a fool. I stand warned."

Jessica gasped and swung away from the mirror where she had been smoothing her hair. Horrified, she stared at Amanda, then recovered herself enough to say frostily, "He did *what?*"

Amanda's thin mouth twisted. "I'm sure you know," she said bitterly. "My editor told me this morning that if another word about the Black Widow appeared in my column, it would not only mean my job, I would be blacklisted. It took only a phone call from Mr. Constantinos to the publisher of the newspaper to accomplish that. Congratulations, you've won."

Jessica's lips tightened and she lifted her chin proudly. "I must apologize for Nikolas, Miss Waring," she said in calm, even tones, determined not to let this woman guess her inner turmoil. "I assure you that I didn't ask him to make the gesture. He has no use for subtlety, has he?"

In spite of the coldness in the woman's eyes, her lips quirked a bit in humor. "No, he hasn't," she agreed.

"I'm sorry he's been so nasty. I realize you have a job to do, and of course I'm fair game," Jessica continued. "I'll have to talk with him—"

The door opened and Nikolas walked in, staring coldly at Amanda Waring. "Miss Waring," he said forbiddingly.

Immediately Jessica knew that he had seen the columnist enter the room after her and had come to her rescue. Before he could say anything that would alienate the woman even more, she went to him and said coolly, "Nikolas, have you really threatened to have Miss Waring dismissed if she prints anything about me?"

He looked down at her and his lips twisted wryly. "I did," he admitted, and his glance slashed to Amanda. "I won't have her hurt again," he said evenly, but his tone was deadly.

"I'm perfectly capable of taking care of myself, thank you, Nikolas," Jessica said tartly.

"Of course you are," he said indulgently, as if she was a child.

Furious, Jessica reached out for his hand and dug her nails into it. "Nikolas—*no.* I won't stand by and watch you throw your weight around for my benefit. I'm not a child or an idiot; I'm an adult, and I won't be treated as if I don't have any sense!"

Little gold flames lit the blackness of his eyes as he looked down at her, and he covered her hand with his free one, preventing her nails from digging into him any longer. It could have looked to be a loving gesture, but his fingers were hard and forceful and held hers still. "Very well, darling," he murmured, carrying her hand to his mouth. After pressing a light kiss on her fingers, he raised his arrogant black head and looked at Amanda.

"Miss Waring, I won't mind if your column mentions that the lovely Jessica Stanton acted as my hostess, but I won't tolerate any more references to the Black Widow, or to Mrs. Stanton's financial status. For your information, we have just completed a business deal that was very favorable to Mrs. Stanton, and she has not, is not, and never will be in need of funds from anyone else.''

Amanda Waring was not a woman to be easily intimidated. She lifted her chin and said, ''May I quote you on that?''

Suddenly Nikolas grinned. ''Within reason,'' he said, and she smiled back at him.

''Thank you, Mr. Constantinos...Mrs. Stanton,'' she added after a moment, glancing at Jessica.

Amanda left the room and Nikolas looked down at Jessica with those little gold lights still dancing in his eyes. ''You're a little cat,'' he drawled lazily. ''Don't you know that now you'll have to pay?''

Not at all frightened, Jessica said coolly, ''You deserved it, for acting like a bully.''

''And you deserve everything you get, for being such a provocative little tease,'' he said, and effortlessly pulled her into his arms. She tried to draw away and found herself helpless against his iron strength.

''Let me go,'' she said breathlessly, trying to twist away from him.

''Why?'' he muttered, bending his head to press his burning lips into the hollow of her shoulder. ''You're in my bedroom, and it would take only a slight tug to have this gown around your ankles. Jessica, you must have known that this gown would heat the blood of a plaster saint, and I've never claimed to be that.''

She would have been amused at his statement if the touch of his mouth on her skin hadn't sent ripples of pleasure dancing through her veins. She was glad that he liked her gown. It *was* provocative; she knew it and had worn it deliberately, in the manner of a moth flirting with the flame that will singe its wings. It was a lovely gown, made of chiffon in alternating panels of sea green and emerald, swirling about her slim body like waves, and the bodice was strapless, held up only by the delicate shirring above her breasts. Nikolas was right, one tug would have the thing off, but then, she hadn't planned on being alone with him in his bedroom. She saw his head bend down again and she turned her mouth away just in time. "Nikolas, stop it! You have guests; you can't just disappear into the bedroom and stay there!"

"Yes, I can," he said, capturing her chin with one strong hand and turning her mouth up to his. Before she could reply again he had opened his mouth over hers, his warm breath filling her. His tongue probed, teasing her into response, and after a moment she forgot her protests, going up on tiptoe to strain against his hard body and offer him completely the sweetness of her mouth. Without hesitation he took it, his kisses becoming wilder and deeper as he hungrily tasted her. He groaned into her mouth and his hand began to slide up her ribs. It wasn't until his strong fingers cupped one soft breast that she realized his intentions and once again cold fear put out the fires of her own desire. She shuddered and began trying to twist out of his embrace; his arm tightened painfully about her and he arched her slim body against him, his mouth ravaging.

Jessica stiffened and cried out hoarsely, "No, please!"

He swore in Greek and pulled her back into his arms as she tried to get away from him, but instead of forcing his caresses on her, he merely held her tightly to him for a moment and she felt the thunderous pounding of his heart against her. "I won't force you," he finally said as he pressed kisses onto her temple. "You've had some bad experiences, and I can understand your fear. But I want you to understand, Jessica, that when you come to me, I won't leave you unsatisfied. You can trust me, darling."

Weakly she shook her head. "No, you don't understand," she muttered. "Nikolas, I—" She started to tell him that she had never made love, that it was fear of the unknown that made her shrink from him, but he laid a finger against her lips.

"I don't want to know," he growled. "I don't want to hear of another man's hands on you. I thought I could bear it, but I can't. I'm too jealous; I never want to hear you talk about an-other man."

Jessica shook her head. "Oh, Nikolas, don't be so foolish! Let me tell you——"

"No," he snapped, gripping her shoulders and shaking her violently.

Growing angry, Jessica jerked away from him and threw her head back. "All right," she rejoined tartly. "If you want to be such an ostrich, by all means go bury your head. It doesn't matter to me what you do!"

He glared at her for a moment, then his tense broad shoulders relaxed and his lips twitched with barely suppressed laughter. "It matters," he informed her mockingly. "You just haven't admitted it to yourself yet. I can see that I'll have to destroy your stubbornness as I'll destroy your fear, and in the same way. A few nights of lovemaking will turn you into a sweet, docile little kitten instead of a spitting wildcat."

Jessica stepped around him to the door, her tawny head high. As she opened the door, she turned and said coolly, "You're not only a fool, Nikolas, you're an arrogant fool."

His soft laughter followed her as she returned to the gathering, and she caught the knowing glances of several people. Diana looked furious, then turned her back in a huff. Sighing, Jessica wondered if Nikolas included Diana in many of his entertainments. She hoped not, but had the feeling that her hopes would be disappointed.

From that evening on, Nikolas completely took over her life. Almost every evening he took her to some small party or meeting, or out to dine in the poshest, most exclusive restaurants. She hardly had any free time to spend with Sallie, but that practical young woman was delighted that her friend was going out more and that no other vicious items about her had appeared in the press. Amanda Waring often mentioned Jessica's name in tandem with Nikolas's, and even hinted that the prolonged presence of the Greek in London was due entirely to the charms of Mrs. Stanton, but she made no mention of the Black Widow or of Jessica's reputation.

Even Charles was delighted that Nikolas had taken over, Jessica often thought broodingly. She felt as if a trusted friend had deserted her, thrown her into the lion's den. Didn't Charles really understand what Nikolas wanted of her? Surely he did; men were men, after all. Yet more and more it seemed that Charles deferred to Nikolas in decisions concerning her assets, and even though she knew that Nikolas was nothing short of a financial genius, she still resented his intrusion into her life.

She was bitterly disappointed but not really surprised when, shortly after Nikolas's takeover of her affairs, Charles gave her some papers to sign and told her they concerned minor matters only. She had trusted him implicitly before, but now some instinct made her read carefully through the papers while Charles fidgeted. Most of the papers did concern matters of little importance, but included in the middle of the stack was the document selling her shares in ConTech to Nikolas for a ridiculously high price and not the market price she'd insisted on. Calmly she pulled the paper out and put it aside. "I won't sign this," she told Charles quietly.

He didn't have to ask what it was. He gave her a wry smile. "I was hoping you wouldn't notice," he admitted. "Jessica, don't try to fight him. He wants you to have the money; take it."

"I won't be bought," she told him, raising her head to give him a level look. "And that's what he's trying to do, buy me. Surely you have no illusions about his intent?"

Charles studied the tips of his impeccable shoes. "I have no illusions at all," he murmured. "That may or may not be a sad thing. Unvarnished reality has little to recommend it. However, being the realist I am, I know that you haven't a prayer of besting Constantinos in this. Sign the papers, my dear, and don't wake sleeping tigers."

"He's not sleeping," she mocked. "He's only lying in wait." Then she shook her head decidedly. "No, I won't sign the papers. I'd rather not sell the stock at all than let him think he's got me all bought and paid for—or I'll sell to a third party. At market price those shares will be snapped up in a minute."

"And so will you," Charles warned. "He doesn't want those stocks in anyone else's hands."

"Then he'll have to pay me market price." She smiled, her green eyes taking on a glint of satisfaction. Just once, she thought, she had the upper hand on Nikolas. Why hadn't she thought of threatening to sell the shares to a third party before now?

Charles left with the paper unsigned and Jessica knew that he would inform Nikolas immediately. She had an engagement with Nikolas that night to attend a dinner with several of his business associates, and she toyed with the idea of simply leaving town and standing him up rather than argue with him, but that would be childish and would only postpone the inevitable. She reluctantly showered and dressed, choosing with care a gown that didn't reveal too much of her; she knew that she could trust Nikolas's thin veneer of civilization only so far. Yet the modest gown was provocative in its own way, the stark severity of the black cloth against her pale gold skin a perfect contrast. Staring at her reflection in the mirror, she thought with wry bitterness of the Black Widow tag and wondered if anyone else would think of it.

As she had half-expected, Nikolas was a full half-hour early, perhaps hoping to catch her still dressing and vulnerable to him. When she opened the door to him, he stepped inside and looked down at her with such grimness in his black eyes that she was startled, even though she'd been expecting him to be angry.

The door was hardly closed behind him when he took her wrist and pulled her against him, dwarfing her with his size and strength. "Why?" he gritted softly, his head bent down so close to hers that his breath was warm on her face.

Jessica knew better than to struggle against him; that would only fan his anger. Instead, she made herself lie pliantly against him and answered him evenly, "I told you what I'd accept, and I haven't changed my mind. I have my pride, Nikolas, and I won't be bought."

The black eyes snapped angrily at her. "I'm not trying to buy you," he snarled, his hands moving to her slim back in a caressing movement that was the direct opposite of the anger she sensed in him. Then his arms wrapped about her, welding her to his hard frame, and he dipped his head even closer to press swift, light kisses on her upturned mouth. "I only want to protect you, to make you so secure that you'll never again have to sell your body, even in marriage."

Instantly she went rigid in his arms and she flashed him a glance that scorched. "Beware of Greeks bearing gifts," she retorted hotly. "What you mean is, you want to ensure that you're the only buyer!"

His arms tightened until she gasped for breath and pushed against his shoulders in protest. "I've never had to buy a woman!" he ground out between clenched teeth. "And I'm not buying you! When we make love, it won't be because money has passed between us but because you want me as much as I want you."

Desperately she turned her head away from his approaching mouth and gasped out, "You're hurting me!" Instantly his arms loosened their hold and she gulped in air, her head dropping to rest on his chest. Was there nothing she could say that would make him understand her point of view?

After a moment he put her away from him and drew a folded paper from the inner pocket of his jacket. Spreading it open, he placed it on the hall table and produced a pen, which he held out to her. "Sign it," he ordered softly.

Jessica put her hands behind her back in the age-old gesture of refusal. "Market value only," she insisted, her eyes holding his calmly. She played her last ace. "If you don't want them, I'm certain there are other buyers who would be glad to get those shares at market value."

He straightened. "I'm sure there are," he agreed, still in that soft, calm voice. "And I'm also certain that if you sell that stock to anyone but me, you'll regret it later. Why are you being so stubborn about money? The amount of money you sell the stock for will in no way influence the outcome of our relationship. That's already been decided.''

''Oh, has it?'' she cried, clenching her small fists in fury at his arrogance. ''Why don't you just go away and leave me alone? I don't want anything from you, not your money, nor your protection, and certainly not *you!*''

''Don't lie to yourself,'' he said roughly, striding forward to lace his arms about her and hold her to him. She flung her head back to deny that she was lying; that was the only chance he needed. He bent his black head, and his mouth closed over hers. His kiss wasn't rough but moved seductively over her lips, inviting her response and devastating her, sucking away her breath and leaving her weak in his arms. Her eyes closed, her lips opened helplessly to his mastering tongue, and she let him kiss her as deeply as he wished until she lay limply against him. His tenderness was even more dangerous than his temper, because her response to him was growing more passionate as she became accustomed to him and she sensed her own capitulation approaching. He was no novice when it came to women, and he knew as well as she did that the need he stirred in her was growing stronger.

''Don't lie to me, either,'' he muttered against her mouth. ''You want me, and we both know it. I'll make you admit it.'' His mouth came down again to fit completely against her lips, and he took full possession of them, molding them as he wanted. He began to touch her breasts, deliberately asserting his mastery over her, trailing his fingertips lightly over the upper curves and leaving a growing heat behind. Jessica made a whimpering sound of protest, muffled by his mouth; she gasped under his onslaught, searching desperately for air, and he gave her his heated breath. Now his hand slid boldly inside her gown and cupped the round curves in his palm. At his intimate caress, Jessica felt herself drowning in the sensual need he aroused, and she gave in with a moan, twining her arms around his neck.

Swiftly he bent and slid his arm under her knees, lifting her and carrying her to the lounge, where he placed her on the sofa and eased down beside her, never ceasing the drugging kisses which kept her under his sensual command. She moved restlessly, her hands in his hair, trying to get closer to him, aching with a need and emptiness which she didn't understand but couldn't ignore.

Triumph glittered in his eyes as he moved to cover her with his body, and Jessica opened her eyes briefly to read the look on his face, but she saw him through a haze of desire, her senses clouded. Nothing mattered right now, if only he would keep on kissing her....

His fingers had explored her satiny breasts, had teased the soft peaks into firm, throbbing proof of the effect he was having on her. Sliding his body down along hers, he investigated those tempting morsels with his lips and tongue, searing her with the heat of his mouth. Her hands left his head and moved to his shoulders, her fingers digging into the muscles which flexed with his every movement. Golden fire was spreading throughout her body, melting her, dissolving her, and she let herself sink into her own destruction. She wanted to know more, she wanted to have more of him, and she thought she would die from the pleasure he was giving her.

He left her breasts to move upward and kiss her mouth again, and now he let her feel the pressure of his entire body, the force of his arousal.

"Let me stay with you tonight," he breathed into her ear. "You want me, you *need* me, as much as I want and need you. Don't be afraid, darling; there's no need to be afraid. I'll take good care of you. Let me stay," he said again, though despite the soft words it wasn't a plea, but a command.

Jessica shuddered and squeezed her eyes tightly shut, her blood boiling through her veins in frustration. Yes, she wanted him—she admitted it—but he had some terrible ideas about her, and she found it hard to forgive him for that. As soon as he spoke, she began to recover her senses and remember why she didn't want to let him make love to her, and she turned her face away from his kisses.

If she let him make love to her, he would know as soon as he possessed her that he was wrong in his accusations; but she also knew in her bones that to go to him under those circumstances would lower her to exactly what he thought her to be now, and her standards were too high to allow that. He offered nothing but physical gratification and material gain, while she offered a heart that had been battered and was now overly sensitive to each blow. He didn't want her love, yet she knew that she loved him, against all logic and her sense of self-preservation.

He shook her gently, forcing her eyes open, and he repeated huskily, "Will you let me stay, darling? Will you let me show you how sweet it will be between us?"

"No," she forced herself to reply, her voice hoarse with the effort she was making. How would he react to a denial at this stage? He had a violent temper; would he be furious? She stared up into his black gaze, and her fear was plain for him to read, though he couldn't guess the cause. "No, Nikolas. Not...not yet. I'm not ready yet. Please."

He drew a deep breath, mastering his frustration, and she collapsed in intense relief as she realized that he wasn't angry. Roughly he drew her head against his shoulder and stroked her hair, and she breathed in the hot male scent of his skin and let him comfort her. "You don't have to be afraid," he insisted in a low tone. "Believe me. Trust me. It has to be soon; I can't wait much longer. I won't hurt you. Just let me show you what it means to be my woman."

But she already knew, she thought in despair. His confident masculinity lured her despite her better sense. His lovemaking would be sweet and fiery, burning away her control, her defenses, leaving her totally helpless in the face of his marauding mastery. And when he was finished, when his attention was attracted by another challenge, she would be in ashes. But how long could she hold him off, when every day increased her need of him?

Chapter 6

Her heels clicking as she strode into the ConTech building, Jessica strove to control her temper until she was alone with Nikolas, but the determined clatter of her heels gave her away and she tried to lighten her step. Her soft lips tightened ominously. Just wait until she saw him!

"Good afternoon, Mrs. Stanton," said the receptionist with a friendly smile, and Jessica automatically returned the greeting. In a few short weeks, Nikolas had turned her world around; people smiled and greeted her now, and everyone connected with ConTech treated her with the utmost courtesy. But recognizing his enormous influence didn't make her feel more charitable toward him; she wanted to throttle him instead!

As she left the elevator, a familiar figure exited Nikolas's office, and Jessica lifted her chin as she neared Diana Murray. Diana paused, waiting for Jessica to approach her, and good manners forced Jessica to greet her.

"My, isn't Nikolas busy this afternoon?" purred Diana, her beautiful eyes watching Jessica sharply for any signs of jealousy.

"I don't know; is he?" countered Jessica coolly. "It doesn't matter; he'll see me anyway."

"I'm sure he will. But give him a minute," Diana advised in a sweet voice which made Jessica long to slap her. She preferred unvarnished hostility to Diana's saccharine poison. Diana smiled and added, "Let him have time to smooth himself down. You know how he is." Then she walked away, her hips swaying with just the right touch of exaggeration. Men probably found Diana irresistible, Jessica thought savagely, and she promised herself that if Nikolas Constantinos didn't walk carefully, he was going to find a storm breaking over his arrogant head.

She thrust open the door, and Andros looked up from his never-deserted post. As always when he saw her, his eyes conveyed cold dislike. "Mrs. Stanton. I don't believe Mr. Constantinos is expecting you."

"No, he isn't," agreed Jessica. "Tell him I'm here, please."

Reluctantly Andros did her bidding, and almost as soon as he had replaced the receiver, Nikolas opened the doors and smiled at her. "Hello, darling. You're a pleasant surprise; I didn't expect to see you until later. Have you decided to sign the papers?"

This reference to his purchase of her shares only served to fan higher the flame of her anger, but she controlled herself until she had entered his office and he had closed the doors firmly behind them. Out of the corner of her eye, she saw him approaching, obviously intent on taking her in his arms, and she briskly removed herself from his reach.

"No, I haven't decided to sign anything," she said crisply. "I came here to get an explanation for this." She reached into her purse and withdrew a slim packet of papers attached with a paper clip to a creased envelope. She thrust them at him and he took them, a frown wrinkling his forehead.

"What are these?" he asked, studying the darkened green of her eyes and gauging her temper.

"You tell me," she snapped. "I believe you're the responsible party."

He removed the paper clip and rapidly scanned the papers, flipping them one by one. It took only a minute; then he replaced the paper clip. "Is anything wrong? Everything looks in order."

"I'm certain everything is in perfect legal order," she said impatiently. "That isn't the problem, and you know it."

"Then exactly what is the problem?" he inquired, his lashes drooping to cover the expression in his eyes, but she knew that he was watching her and saw every nuance of her expression before she, too, shuttered her face.

He hooked one leg over the corner of the desk and sat down, his body relaxed. "I don't see why you're upset," he said smoothly. "Suppose you tell me exactly what you don't like about the agreement. It hasn't been signed yet; we can always make changes. I hadn't meant for you to receive your copy by mail," he added thoughtfully. "I can only suppose that my attorney tried to anticipate my wishes, and he'll certainly hear from me on that."

"I don't care about your attorney, and it doesn't make any difference how I received this piece of trash, because I won't sign it!" she shouted at him, her cheeks scarlet with anger. "You're the most arrogant man I've ever met, and I hate you!"

The amusement that had been lurking in his eyes vanished abruptly, and when she spun on her heel and started for the door, too incensed even to yell at him, he lunged from his position on the desk to intercept her before she'd taken three steps. As his hand closed on her arm, she lashed out at him with her free hand. He threw his arm up to ward off the blow, then deftly twisted and caught that arm, too, and drew her against him.

"Let me go!" she spat, too infuriated to care if Andros heard her. She twisted and struggled, heaving herself against the iron band of his arms in an effort to break free; she was given stamina by her anger, but at last even that was exhausted. When she shuddered and dropped her head against his shoulder, he lifted her easily and stepped around the desk, where he sat down in his chair and cradled her on his lap.

Jessica felt faint, drained by her rage and the struggle with him, and she lay limply against him. His heart was beating strongly, steadily, under her cheek, and she noticed that he wasn't even breathing rapidly. He'd simply subdued her and let her tire herself out. He stretched to reach the telephone and dialed a single number, then spoke quietly. "Hold all calls, Andros. I don't want to be disturbed for any reason." Then he dropped the receiver back onto the cradle and wrapped both arms about her, hugging her securely to him.

"Darling," he whispered into her hair. "There's no need to be so upset. It's only a simple document—"

"There's nothing simple about it!" she interrupted violently. "You're trying to treat me like a high-priced whore, but I won't let you! If that's the way you think of me, then I don't want to see you again."

"I don't think of you as a whore." He soothed her. "You're not thinking clearly; all you're thinking now is that I've offered you payment for going to bed with me, and that isn't what I intended."

"Oh, no, of course it wasn't," she mocked in a bitter tone. She struggled to sit up and get away from the intimate heat of his body, but his enfolding arms tightened and she couldn't move. Tears sparkled in her eyes as she gave up and relaxed against him in defeat.

"No, it wasn't," he insisted. "I merely want to take care of you—thus the bank account and the house. I know you own the house where you live now, but admit it, the neighborhood isn't the best."

"No, it isn't, but I'm perfectly happy there! I've never asked for anything from you, and I'm not asking now. I don't want your money, and you've insulted me by asking me to sign a document swearing that I'll never make any demands against your estate for 'services rendered.'"

"I'd be extremely foolish if I didn't take steps to secure the estate," he pointed out. "I don't think you'd sue me for support, darling, but I have other people to consider and a responsibility to uphold. A great many people depend on me for their livelihood—my family as well as my employees—and I can't in good conscience do anything that might jeopardize their well-being in the future."

"Do all of your mistresses have to sign away any claims on you?'' she demanded, angrily brushing away the single tear which dropped from her lashes. "Is this in the nature of a form letter, everything filled in except for the name and date? How many other women live in apartments or houses you've so kindly provided?''

"None!'' he snapped. "I don't think I'm asking too much. Did you truly think I'd establish you as my mistress and leave myself vulnerable to any number of other claims? Is that why you're so angry, because I've made certain you can't get any money from me except what I freely give to you?''

He'd made the mistake of releasing her arm, and she swung wildly at him, her palm striking his face with enough force to make her hand tingle. She began to cry, tears flooding down her face while she gulped and tried to control them, and in an effort to get away from him she started fighting again. The results were the same as before: he simply held her and prevented her from landing any more blows, until she was breathless and worn out. Pain and anger mingled with her sense of helplessness at being held like that, her raw frustration at being unable to make him see how utterly wrong he was about her, and she gave up even trying to control her tears. With a wrenching sob she turned her face into his shoulder and gave in to her emotional storm.

"Jessica!'' he ground out from between clenched teeth, but she barely heard him and paid no attention. A small part of her knew that he had to be furious that she'd slapped him—Nikolas wasn't a man to let anyone, man or woman, strike him and get away with it—but at the moment she just didn't care. Her delicate frame heaved with the convulsive force of her weeping. It would never end, the gossip and innuendo concerning her marriage; even though Nikolas wouldn't allow anyone else to talk about her, he still believed all of those lies himself. What he didn't seem to realize was that she could endure everyone else's insults, but she couldn't endure his, because she loved him.

"Jessica.'' His voice was lower now, softer, and the biting power of his fingers eased on her arms. She felt his hands touching her back, stroking soothingly up and down, and he cuddled her closer to his body.

With tender cajoling he persuaded her to lift her face, and he wiped her eyes and nose with his handkerchief as if she were a child. She stared at him, her eyes still luminous with tears, and even through her tears she could see the red mark on his cheek where she'd hit him. With trembling figures she touched the spot. "I—I'm sorry," she said, offering her apology in a tear-thick voice.

Without a word he turned his head and kissed her fingers, then bent his head and lifted her in the same motion, and before she could catch her breath he was kissing her, his mouth hot and wild and as hungry as an untamed animal's, tasting and biting and probing. His hand searched her breasts and moved down-ward to glide over her hips and thighs, on down to her knees, moving impatiently under the fabric of her dress. With a shock she realized that he was out of control, driven beyond the control of will by his own anger and the struggle with her, the softness of her body twisting and straining against him. He wasn't even giving her a chance to respond to him, and fear made her heart-beat speed up as she realized that this time she might not be able to stop him.

"Nikolas, no. Not here. No! Stop it, darling," she whispered fiercely, tenderly. She didn't try to fight him, sensing that at this stage it would only excite him more. He was hurting her; his hands were all over her, touching her where no man had ever touched before, pulling at her clothing. She reached up and placed her hands on both sides of his face and repeated his name softly, urgently, over and over until, abruptly, he was looking at her and she saw that she'd gained his attention.

A spasm crossed his face, and he ground his teeth, swearing beneath his breath. He slowly helped her to her feet, pushing her from his lap, and then got to his feet as if in pain. He stood looking at her for a moment as she swayed against the desk for support; then he cursed again and walked a few feet away, standing with his back to her while he wearily massaged the back of his neck.

She stared at his broad, muscular back in silence, too drained to say anything to him, not knowing if it was safe to do so. What should she do now? She wanted to leave, but her legs were trembling so violently that she doubted her ability to walk unaided. And her clothing was disheveled, twisted, and partially unbuttoned. With slow, clumsy fingers she restored her appearance, then eyed him uncertainly. His stance was that of a man fighting himself, and she didn't want to do anything that might annoy him. But the silence was so thick between them that she was uneasy, and at last she forced her unsteady legs to move, intending to retrieve her purse from where she'd dropped it and leave before the situation worsened.

"You aren't going anywhere," he said in a low voice, and she halted in her tracks.

He turned to face her then, his dark face set in weary lines. "I'm sorry," he said with a sigh. "Did I hurt you?"

His apology was the opposite of the reaction she had expected, and for a moment she couldn't think of a response. Then she dumbly shook her head, and he seemed to relax. He moved close to her and slid his arm around her waist, urging her close to him with gentle insistence. Jessica offered no resistance and pressed her head into the sheltering hollow of his shoulder.

"I don't know what to say," he muttered. "I want you to trust me, but instead I've frightened you."

"Don't say anything," she answered, having finally mastered her voice. "There's no need to go over it all again. I won't sign the paper, and that's that."

"It wasn't meant as an insult, but as a legal necessity."

"But I'm not your mistress," she pointed out. "So there's no need for the document."

"Not yet," he agreed. "As I said, my attorney anticipated my wishes. He was in error." His tone of voice boded ill for the poor attorney, but Jessica was grateful to the unknown man. At least now she knew exactly what Nikolas thought of her, and she preferred the painful truth to living in a dream.

"Perhaps it would be better if we didn't see each other anymore," she began, but his arm tightened around her and a scowl blackened his brow.

"Don't be ridiculous," he snapped. "I won't let you go now, so don't waste your breath suggesting it. I promise to control myself in the future, and we'll forget about this for the time being."

Lifting her head from his shoulder, Jessica gave him a bitter look. Did he truly think she could forget that he thought her the sort of woman who was available for a price? That knowledge was a knife thrust into her chest, but equally painful was the certainty that she didn't want him to vanish from her life. Whatever he had come to mean to her, the thought of never seeing him again made her feel desolate. She was risking her emotional well-being, flirting with disaster, but she could no more walk away from him now than she could stop herself from breathing.

Several weeks passed in a more restrained manner, as if he'd placed himself on his best behavior, and she managed to push away the hurt. He insisted that she accompany him whenever he went out socially, and she was his hostess whenever he entertained.

The strain on her was telling. At yet another party, she felt smothered and escaped into the coolness of the dark garden, where she sucked in deep lungfuls of fresh, sweet air; she had been unable to breathe in the smoke-laden atmosphere inside. In the weeks since she had met Nikolas, she had learned to be relaxed at social gatherings, but she still felt the need to be by herself occasionally, and those quiet times had been rare. Nikolas had the power of a volcano, spewing out orders and moving everyone along in the lava flow of his authority. She wasn't certain just where he was at the moment, but she took advantage of his lapse of attention to seek the quietness of the garden.

Just before leaving for the dinner party tonight, they'd had a flaming argument over her continued refusal to sell the stock to him, their first argument since the awful scene in his office. He wouldn't back down an inch; he was furious with her for defying him, and he had even accused her of trying to trick him into increasing his offer. Sick to death of his lack of understanding and tired of the running battle, Jessica had grabbed the paper and signed it, then thrown it to the floor in a fit of temper. "Well, there it is!" she had snapped furiously. It wasn't until he'd leaned down and picked up the paper to fold it and replace it in his pocket that she'd seen the speculative gleam in his eyes and realized that she'd made a mistake. Signing now, after he had accused her of holding out for a higher price and assured her that she wouldn't get it, had convinced him that she'd been doing exactly that all along, biding her time and hoping for a higher price. But it was too late now to do anything about it, and she had grimly conquered the tears that sprang to her eyes as the pain of his suspicions hurt her.

Strolling along the night-dewed path of white gravel, she wondered sadly if the sense of ease which had come into their relationship lately had been destroyed. He had ceased pressuring her to let him make love to her, had in fact become increasingly tender with her, as if he was at last beginning to care. The thought made her breathless, for it was like a dream come true. In a thousand ways, he spoiled her and curbed his impatient nature for her, and she no longer tried to fight her love for him. She didn't even want to any longer, so thoroughly had he taken her under his influence.

But all of that might be gone now. She should never have signed that agreement! She'd given in to his bullying tactics in a fit of temper, and all she had done was to reinforce his picture of her as a mercenary temptress. What ground she'd gained in his affections had been lost in that one moment.

Moving slowly along, her head down while she dreamed wistfully of marrying Nikolas and having his children—something not likely to happen now—it was some moments before she heard the murmur of voices. She was almost upon the couple before she realized it. She halted, but it seemed that they hadn't noticed her. They were only a dim shape in the darkness, the pale blur of the woman's gown blending into the darkness of the man's dinner jacket as they embraced.

Trying to move quietly, Jessica stepped back with the intention of withdrawing without attracting attention to herself, but then the woman gave a sharp sigh and moaned, "Nikolas! Ah, my love..."

Jessica's legs went numb and refused to move as strength drained away from her. Nikolas? *Her* Nikolas? She was too dazed to feel any pain; she didn't really believe it. At last she managed to turn and look again at the entwined couple. Diana. Most assuredly Diana. She had recognized that voice. And— Nikolas? The bent black head, the powerful shoulders, *could* be Nikolas, but she couldn't be certain. Then his head lifted and he muttered in English, "What's wrong, Diana? Has no one been taking care of you, as lovely as you are?"

"No, no one," she whispered. "I've waited for you."

"Were you so certain I would return?" he asked, amusement coming into his voice as he raised his head higher to look into the gorgeous upturned face.

Jessica turned away, not wanting to see him kiss the other woman again. The pain had started when she saw for certain that Nikolas was the man holding Diana so passionately, but she determinedly forced it down. If she let go, she would weep and make a fool of herself, so she tilted her chin arrogantly and ignored the vise that squeezed her chest, the knife that stabbed her insides. Behind her, she heard him call her name, but she moved swiftly across the patio and into the protection of the house and the throng of people. People smiled at her now, and spoke, and she put a faint smile on her stiff lips and made her way very calmly to the informal bar.

Everyone was getting their own drinks, so she poured herself a liberal portion of tart white wine and sipped it as she moved steadily about the room, smiling, but not allowing herself to be drawn into conversation. She could not talk to anyone just now; she would just walk about and sip her wine and concentrate on mastering the savage thrust of pain inside her. She wasn't certain how she would leave the party, whether she was strong enough to leave with Nikolas or if it would be best to call a taxi, but she would worry about that later. Later, after she had swallowed enough wine to dull her senses.

Out of the corner of her eye she saw Nikolas moving toward her with grim determination, and she swung to the left and spoke to the couple she nearly collided with, marveling that her voice could be so natural. Then, before she could move away, a strong hand closed on her elbow and Nikolas said easily, "Jessica, darling, I've been chasing you around the room trying to get your attention. Hello, Glenna, Clark...how are the children?"

With a charming smile he had Glenna laughing at him and telling him about her two young sons, whom it seemed Nikolas knew personally. All the time they talked, Nikolas kept a tight grip on Jessica's arm, and when she made a move to break away from him, his fingers tightened until she nearly gasped with pain. Then he was leading her away from Glenna and Clark and his fingers loosened, but not enough to allow her to escape.

"You're hurting my arm," Jessica said coldly as they wove through milling groups of laughing, chattering people.

"Shut up," he ground out between his teeth. "At least until we're alone. I think the study is empty; we'll go there."

As he literally pulled her with him, Jessica had a glimpse of Diana's face before they left the room behind, and the expression of pure triumph on the woman's face chilled her.

Pride stiffened her back, and when Nikolas closed the door of the study behind them and locked it, she turned to face him and lifted her chin to give him a haughty stare. "Well?" she demanded. "What do you want, now that you've dragged me in here?"

He stood watching her, his black eyes grim and his mouth set in a thin line that at any other time would have made her apprehensive but now left her curiously unmoved. He had thrust his hands into his pants pockets as if he didn't trust himself to control his temper, but now he took them out and his eyes gleamed. "It always amazes me how you can look like a queen, just by lifting that little chin."

Her face showed no reaction. "Is that all you brought me in here to say?" she demanded coolly.

"You know damned well it isn't." For a moment he had the grace to look uncomfortable, and a dull flush stained the brutal cheekbones. "Jessica, what you saw...it wasn't serious."

"That really doesn't matter to me," she thrust scornfully, "because our relationship isn't serious, either. You don't have to explain yourself to me, Nikolas; I have no hold on you. Conduct your little affairs as you please; I don't care."

His entire body jerked under the force of her words and the flush died away to a white, strained look. His eyes grew murderous and an instant before he moved she realized that she had gone too far, pushed him beyond control. She had time only to suck in her breath to cry out in alarm before he was across the room with a lithe, savage movement, his hands on her shoulders. He shook her violently, so violently that her hair tumbled down about her shoulders and tears were jerked from her eyes before his mouth closed on hers and his savage kiss took her breath away. When she thought that she would faint under his onslaught, he lifted her slumping body in his arms and carried her to the soft, worn sofa where their host had obviously spent many comfortable hours. Fiercely he placed her on it and covered her body with his, holding her down with his heavy shoulders and muscular thighs. "Damn you!" he whispered raggedly, jerking her head back with cruel fingers tangled in her hair. "You have me tied in knots; I can't even sleep without dreaming about you, and you say you don't care what I do? I'll make you care, I'll break down that wall of yours—"

He kissed her brutally, his lips bruising hers and forcing a moan of protest from her throat, but he paid no attention to her distress. With his free hand he slid down the zipper of her dress and pulled the cloth from her shoulders, and only then did his mouth leave hers to press his sensual attack on the soft mounds of her breasts.

Jessica moaned in fright when her mouth was free, but as his hot lips moved hungrily down her body, a wanton need surged through her. She fought it fiercely, determined not to surrender to him after what had passed between them tonight, knowing that he thought her little better than a whore. And then he had gone straight into Diana's arms! The memory of the smugly victorious smile the woman had given her sent tears streaming down her face as she struggled against his overpowering strength. He ignored her efforts to free herself and moved to press completely over her, his hands curving her against his powerful, surging contours. He was feverish with desire and she was helpless against him; he would have taken her, but when he raised his head from her throbbing breasts, he saw her tear-drenched face and stopped cold.

"Jessica," he said huskily. "Don't cry. I won't hurt you."

Didn't he understand? He had already hurt her; he'd torn her heart out. She turned her head away from him with a jerky movement and bit her bruised lip, unable to say anything.

He eased his weight from her and pulled his handkerchief from his pocket to wipe her face. "It's just as well," he said grimly. "I don't want to make love to you for the first time on a sofa in someone else's house. I want you in a bed, *ma chère,* with hours in which I can show you how it should be between a man and a woman."

"Any woman," she said bitterly, remembering Diana.

"No!" he refuted fiercely. "Don't think of her, she means less than nothing to me. I was foolish—I'm sorry, darling. I wanted to ease myself with her, to relieve the tension that you arouse and won't satisfy, and instead I found that she leaves me cold."

"Really?" Jessica taunted, glaring at him. "You didn't look so cold to me."

He tossed the tear-wet handkerchief aside and captured her chin with one hand. "You think not? Did I act as if I was carried away by passion?" he demanded, forcing her to look at him. "Did I kiss her as I kiss you? Did I say sweet things to her?"

"Yes! You called her— No," she interrupted herself, becoming confused. "You said she was lovely, but you didn't—"

"I didn't call her darling, as I call you, did I? One kiss, Jessica! One kiss and I knew that she couldn't even begin to damp down the fires you've lit. Won't you forgive me for one kiss?"

"Would you forgive me?" she snapped, trying to turn her head away, but he held her firmly. Against her will she was softening, letting him talk her out of her resolve. The heavy weight of his limbs against her was comforting as he wrapped her in the security of his strength, and she began to feel that she could forgive any transgression so long as she could still touch him.

"I would have snatched you away from any man foolish enough to touch you," he promised her grimly, "and broken his jaw. I don't think I could control myself if I saw someone kissing you, Jessica. But I'd never walk away from you; I'd take you with me."

She shuddered and closed her eyes, recalling those awful moments when she had watched their embrace. "Neither can I control *my*self, Nikolas," she admitted hoarsely. "I can't bear to watch you make love to another woman. It tears me apart."

"Jessica!"

It was the first admission she had made that she cared for him, even a little. Despite their closeness over the past weeks, she had still resisted him in that, had refused to tell him that she cared. Now she could no longer hide it.

"Jessica! Look at me. *Look at me!*" Fiercely he shook her and her eyes flew open to stare into his blazing, triumphant eyes. "Tell me," he insisted, bending closer to her, his mouth poised above hers. His hand went to her heart, felt the telltale pounding, and lingered to tenderly stroke the soft womanly curves he found.

"Tell me," he whispered, and brushed his lips against hers.

Her arms went about his shoulders, clinging tightly to his strength as her own was washed away in the floodtide of her emotion. "I love you," she moaned huskily. "I've tried not to— you're so…arrogant. But I can't help it."

He crushed her to him so tightly that she cried out, and he loosened his hold immediately. "Mine," he muttered, pressing hot kisses over her face. "You're mine, and I'll never let you go. I adore you, darling. For weeks I've been half-mad with frustration, wanting you but afraid of frightening you off. You'll have no more mercy from me, you'll be my woman now!" And he laughed exultantly before he sat up and helped her to pull her gown back up. He zipped it for her, then his hard hands closed about her waist.

"Let's leave now," he said, his voice rough. "I want you so badly!"

Jessica shivered at the raw demand in his voice, elated but also frightened. The time had come when he would no longer allow her to draw away from him, and though she could feel her heart blooming at his admission of love, she was still wary of this man and the control he had over her.

Nikolas sensed her hesitation and pulled her close to him with a possessive arm. "Don't be frightened," he murmured against her hair. "Forget whatever has happened to you; I'll never do anything to hurt you. You said that you aren't frightened of me, but you are, I can tell. That's why I've suffered through these weeks of hell, waiting for you to lose your fear. Trust me now, darling. I'll take every care with you."

She buried her face against his shoulder. Now was the time to tell him that she had never made love before, but when she gathered her courage enough to raise her head and open her mouth, he forestalled her by laying his fingers gently across her bruised lips. "No, don't say anything," he whispered. "Just come with me, let me take care of you."

Her hair was a tumbled mass about her shoulders and she lifted her hands to try to twist it up again. "Don't bother," Nikolas said, catching her hand. "You look adorable, if anyone should see you, but we'll leave by the back way. Wait here while I make our excuses to our host; I'll only be a moment."

Left by herself, Jessica sat down and tried to gather her dazed and scattered thoughts. Nikolas loved her, he had admitted it. Love was the same as "adore," wasn't it? Certainly she loved him, but she was also confused and uncertain. She had always thought that a mutual declaration of love led to sweet plans for the future, but instead Nikolas seemed to plan only on taking her to bed. She tried to tell herself that he was an extremely physical man, and that afterward he would want to talk about wedding plans. It was just that she had always dreamed, in her heart, of going to her husband in white, and of deserving the symbol of purity. For a moment she toyed with the idea of telling Nikolas she didn't want to leave, but then she shook her head. Perhaps she had to prove her love for Nikolas by trusting him as he had requested and giving him the full measure of her love.

Then it was too late to worry, because Nikolas came back, and she drowned in the possessive glow of his dark eyes. Her nervousness was swamped by her automatic response to his nearness and she leaned pliantly against him as he led her out of the house by the back way and to his car parked down the narrow, quiet street.

London was a golden city by night, gleaming like a crown on the banks of the Thames, and it had never seemed more golden to her than it did tonight, sitting quietly beside Nikolas as he drove through the city. She looked at the familiar landmarks as if she had never seen them before, caught by the unutterable loveliness of the world she shared with Nikolas.

He didn't drive her home, as she had expected, but instead they went to his penthouse. That alarmed her, though she wasn't sure why, and she hung back, but he pulled her into the elevator and held her close, muttering hot words of love to her. When the elevator doors slid open, he took her hand and led her down the quiet, dim hallway to his door. Unlocking it, he let her inside and followed, locking the door behind him with a final-sounding click. She had gone a few steps forward and now stood very still in the darkness, and with a flick of his finger he switched on two lamps. Then he went over to his telephone console to make sure his automatic answering service was on.

"No interruptions tonight," he said, turning to her now. His eyelids drooped sensuously over his gleaming eyes as he came to her and drew her against his hard body. "Do you want anything to drink?" he asked, his lips moving against her temples.

She closed her eyes in ecstasy, breathing in the heady male scent of him, basking in his warmth. "No, nothing," she replied huskily.

"Nor do I," he said. "I don't want alcohol dulling my senses tonight; I want to enjoy every moment. You've obsessed me from the first moment I saw you, so forgive me if I seem to..." He paused, trying to find the word, and she smiled tenderly.

"If you seem to gloat?" she murmured.

"Gloat is too strong a word, but I do admit to a sense of triumph." He grinned.

She watched with a pounding heart as he shed his dinner jacket and draped it over a chair. His tie followed, and his satin waistcoat, then he came to her and she shrank back at the look on his face. So would the Spartan warriors of long ago have looked, proud and savage and lawless. He frightened her, and she wanted to run, but then he had her in his arms and his mouth covered hers and all thoughts fled as her senses were filled with him.

He lifted her and carried her along the corridor to his bedroom, shouldering the door closed behind them, then crossing to the huge bed and standing her before it.

Sanity fought with desire and she choked, "No, Nikolas, wait! I have to tell you—"

"But I can't wait," he interrupted huskily, his breathing ragged. "I have to have you, darling. Trust me, let me wipe out the touch of the others who have hurt you."

His mouth shut off anything else she might have said. He was far more gentle than she would ever have expected, his hands moving over her with exquisite tenderness, molding her to him as his lips drank greedily of hers. She gasped at the surge of pleasure that warmed her, and she curled her slender arms about his neck, arching herself against his powerful form and hearing his deep groan reverberating in her ears like music. With shaking hands he unzipped her gown and slid it down her hips to lie in a silky pool about her feet. He caught his breath at the slim, graceful delicacy of her body, then he snatched her close to him again and his mouth lost its gentleness as he kissed her hungrily. He muttered love words in French and Greek as his strong, lean fingers removed her underwear and dropped it carelessly to the floor, and she thrilled at the hoarse desire so evident in his voice. It was right, it had to be right, he loved her and she loved him....

Feverishly she unbuttoned his silk shirt, her lips pressing hot little kisses to his flesh as she revealed it. She had never caressed him so freely before, but she did so now, discovering with delight the curling hair that roughened his chest and ran in a narrow line down his abdomen. Her fingers flexed mindlessly in that hair, pulling slightly, then her hands dropped to his belt and fumbled awkwardly with the fastening.

"Ah...darling," he cried, his fingers closing almost painfully on hers. Then he brushed her hands aside and helped her, for she was trembling so badly that she couldn't manage to undo the belt.

Rapidly he stripped, and she caught her breath at the sight of his strong, incredibly beautiful body. "I love you," she moaned, going into his arms. "Oh, Nikolas, my love!"

He shuddered and lifted her, placing her on the bed and following her down, his mouth and hands all over her, rousing her to wilder, sweeter heights, then slowing and letting her drift back to awareness before he intensified his efforts again and took her to the brink of madness before drawing away. He was seducing her carefully, making certain of her pleasure, though he was going wild with his own pleasure as he stroked her lovely curves and soft hollows.

At last, aching with the need for his complete possession, Jessica moved her body urgently against him. She didn't know how to demand what she needed; she could only moan and clutch at him with frantic fingers. Her head moved mindlessly from side to side, rolling on the tawny pillow of her hair. "Nikolas—ah, beloved," she moaned, scarcely knowing what she said as the words tripped over themselves coming from her tongue. She wanted only his touch, the taste of his mouth on hers. "I never knew—oh, darling, please! Being your wife will be heaven." Her hands moved over his muscled ribs, pulling at him, and she called out to him with surrender plain in her voice. "Nikolas...Nikolas!"

But he had gone stiff, pulling away from her, and he rose up on his elbow to look at her. After a moment she realized that she had been deserted and she turned her head to look at him questioningly. "Nikolas?" she murmured.

The silence lengthened and thickened, then he made an abrupt, savage movement with his hand. "I've never mentioned marriage to you, Jessica. Don't delude yourself; I'm not that big a fool."

Jessica felt the blood draining from her face and she was glad of the darkness, of the dim lights that left only black and white images and hid the colors away. Nausea roiled in her stomach as she stared up at him. No, he wasn't a fool, but *she* was. Fiercely she fought back the sickness that threatened to overwhelm her, and when she spoke, her tone was even, almost cool.

"That's odd. I thought marriage was a natural result of love. But then, you've never actually said that you love me, have you, Nikolas?"

His mouth twisted and he got out of bed, walking to the window to stand looking out, his splendid body revealed to her in its nudity. He wasn't concerned with his lack of dress, standing there as casually as if he wore a suit and tie. "I've never lied to you, Jessica," he said brutally. "I want you as I've never wanted another woman, but you're not the type of woman I would ever take as my wife."

Jessica ground her teeth together to keep from crying out in pain. Jerkily she sat up against the pillows and drew the covers up over her nakedness, for she couldn't be as casual about it as he could. "Oh?" she inquired, only a slight strain revealed in her voice, for, after all, hadn't she had years of experience in hiding her feelings? "What type of woman am I?"

He shrugged his broad shoulders. "My dear, that's rather obvious. Just because Robert Stanton married you doesn't make it any less an act of prostitution, but at least he married you. What about all the others? They didn't bother. You've had some unpleasant experiences that have turned you against men, and I was prepared to treat you with a great deal of consideration, but I've never considered making you my wife. I wouldn't insult my mother by taking a woman like you home to be introduced to her."

Pride had always been a strong part of Jessica's character and it came to her rescue now. Lifting her chin, she said, "What sort of woman would you take home to Mama? A nun?"

"Don't get vicious with me," he snarled softly in warning. "I can deal with you in a way that will make your previous experiences seem like heaven. But to answer your question, the woman I marry will be a virgin, as pure as the day she was born, a woman of both character *and* morals. I admit that you have the character, my dear; it's the morals that you lack."

"Where will you find this paragon?" she mocked, not at all afraid of him now. He had already hurt her as badly as she could ever be hurt; what else could he do?

He said abruptly, "I have already found her; I intend to marry the daughter of an old family friend. Elena is only nineteen, and she's been schooled in a convent. I wanted to wait until she's older before we became betrothed; she deserves a carefree youth."

"Do you love her, Nikolas?" The question was torn from her, for here, after all, was an even deeper pain, to think that he loved another woman. By contrast to this unknown, unseen Elena, Diana seemed a pitiful rival.

"I'm fond of her," he said. "Love will come later, as she matures. She'll be a loving, obedient wife, a wife I can be proud of, a good mother to my children."

"And you can take her home to Mama," Jessica mocked in pain.

He swung away from the window. "Don't mock my mother," he hissed between his teeth. "She's a wonderful, valiant woman; she knew your late husband—are you surprised? When she heard of his disastrous marriage, she was shocked and dismayed, as most people were. Her friends here in London who wrote to her about you didn't ease her worries for an old friend. Should I insult her now by showing up with you in tow and saying, 'Mother, do you remember the gold-digger who took Robert Stanton for all he was worth and ruined the last years of his life? I've just married her.' Were you really such a fool as to think that, Jessica?"

Jessica flung aside the covers and stood up, her bearing erect and proud, her head high. "You're right about one thing," she said in a clipped voice. "I'm not the woman for you."

He watched silently as she went over to her gown and picked it up from the floor, slipping quickly into it. As she slid her feet into her shoes, she said, "Good-bye, Nikolas. It's been an interesting experience."

"Don't be so hasty, my dear," he jeered cruelly. "Before you walk out that door, you should consider that you could gain even more by being my mistress than you did by marrying Robert Stanton. I'm prepared to pay well."

Bitter pride kept her from reacting to that jibe. "Thanks, but no, thanks," she said carelessly, opening the door. "I'll wait for a better offer from another man. Don't bother seeing me out, Nikolas. You aren't dressed for it."

He actually laughed, throwing back his arrogant head. "Call me if you change your mind," he said by way of good-bye, and she walked out without looking back.

She called Charles early the next morning and told him that she would be out of town for several weeks. She hadn't cried, her eyes had remained dry and burning, but she knew that she couldn't remain in London. She would return only when Nikolas had left, flown back to his island. "I'm going to the cottage," she told Charles. "And don't tell Nikolas where I am, though I doubt that he'll bother to ask. If you let me down in this, Charles, I swear I won't ever speak to you again."

"Had a spat, did you?" he asked, amusement evident in his voice.

"No, it was really a rather quiet parting of the ways. He called me a whore and said I wasn't good enough to marry, and I walked out," she explained coolly.

"My God!" Charles said something under his breath, then said urgently, "Are you all right, Jessica? Are you certain you should go haring off to Cornwall by yourself? Give yourself time to calm down."

"I'm very calm," she said, and she was. "I need a holiday and I'm taking it. You know where I am if anything urgent comes up, but other than that, I don't expect to see you for several weeks."

"Very well. Jessica, dear, are you certain?"

"Of course. I'm perfectly all right. Don't worry, Charles. I'm taking Samantha and the pups with me; they'll enjoy romping around Cornwall."

After hanging up, she made certain everything in the house was turned off, picked up her purse and walked out, carefully locking the door behind her. Her luggage was already in the car, as were Samantha and her wiggling, energetic family, traveling in a large box.

The rest in Cornwall would do her good, help her to forget Nikolas Constantinos. She had had a close call and she was grateful that she had escaped with her self-respect intact. At least she had prevented him from realizing how shattered she was.

Turning it over and over in her mind as she made the long drive to Cornwall, she wondered if she hadn't known all along just what Nikolas thought of her. Why else had she mentioned marriage at such a moment, when he was on the brink of making love to her? Hadn't she subconsciously realized that he would not let her think he intended marriage in order to seduce her?

She was glad that she hadn't told him that she was a virgin;

he would have laughed in her face. She could have proved it to him, he would no doubt have demanded proof, but she was too proud. Why should she prove anything to him? She had loved Robert and he had loved her, and she would not apologize for their marriage. Somehow she would forget Nikolas Constantinos, wipe him out of her thoughts. She would not let his memory destroy her life!

Chapter 7

For six weeks Jessica pored over the newspapers, searching for any notice, however small, to indicate that Nikolas had returned to Greece. He was mentioned several times, but it was always to say that he was flying here or there for a conference, and a day or so later she would read that he had returned to London. Why was he staying in England? He had never before remained for so long, always returning to his island at the first opportunity. She had no contact with Charles, so she couldn't ask him for any information, not that she would have anyway. She didn't want to know about Nikolas, she told herself fiercely time and again, but that didn't ease the ache in her heart that kept her lying awake night after night and turned food to ashes in her mouth.

She lost weight, her already slim figure becoming fragile. Instead of recovering, she was in danger of going into a Victorian decline, she told herself mockingly, but no amount of willpower could make her swallow more than a bite or two of food at any meal.

Long walks with Samantha and the gamboling puppies for company tired her out but did not reduce her to the state of exhaustion that she needed in order to sleep. After a while she began to feel haunted. Everything reminded her of Nikolas, though nothing was the same as it had been in London. She heard his voice, she remembered his devouring kisses, his fierce possessiveness. Perhaps he hadn't loved her, but he had certainly wanted her; he had been quite blatant about his desire.

Had he expected her to return to him? Was that why he was still in London? The thought was heady, but she knew that nothing had changed. He would take her on his terms, or not at all.

Still she lingered at the cottage, walking every day down to the beach, where the vacationers romped and children went into ecstatic fits over the five fat, prancing puppies. They had been weaned now, and mindful of their increasing size she gave them away one by one to the adoring children. Then there was only Samantha left with her, and the days trickled slowly past.

Then, one morning, she looked at herself in the mirror as she was braiding her hair, really looked at herself, and was stunned at what she saw. Had she really allowed Nikolas Constantinos to turn her into this pale, fragile creature with huge, dark-circled eyes? What was wrong with her? She loved him, yes; in spite of everything he had said to her, she still loved him, but she wasn't so weak in spirit that she would let him destroy her!

She began to realize that it solved nothing to hide away here in Cornwall. She wasn't getting over him; if anything, she was being eaten alive by the need to see him, to touch him.

Suddenly her chin lifted as an idea came to her. She still loved him, she could not rid herself of that, but it was no longer the pure, innocent love that she had offered him the first time. Bitter fires had scorched her heart. For the burned remains of that sweetness, physical love might be enough. Perhaps in his arms she might find that all of her love had been burned out and she would be free. And if not—if she found that in spite of everything she continued to love him—in the years to come, when he was married to his pure, chaste little Elena, she would have the memories and knowledge of his passion, passion such as Elena would never know.

Then she realized that when she became his mistress he would know that no other man had ever touched her. What would he think? Would he apologize, beg her forgiveness? The thought left her curiously unmoved, except for the bitterly humorous thought that the only way she could prove her virtue to him was by losing it. The situation was ironic, and she wondered if Nikolas would appreciate the humor of it when he knew.

Without consciously admitting it, her mind was made up. She would accept Nikolas on his terms, give up her respectability and chastity for the physical gratification that he could give her. But she would not let him support her; she would keep her independence and her pride, and when he married his pure little Greek girl, she would walk away and never see him again. She would be his mistress, but she would not be a party to adultery.

So she packed her clothing and closed up the cottage, put Samantha in the car and began the long drive back to London. The first thing she did was call Charles and tell him that she had returned, assuring him that she was fine. He had to go out of town that afternoon or he would have come over, and she was glad that their meeting was postponed. If Charles saw her now, so thin and wan, he would know that something was dreadfully wrong.

That same problem worried her the next morning as she dressed. She couldn't get up the courage to call Nikolas; he might tell her that he was no longer interested, and she felt that she had to see him again even if he turned her down to her face. She would go to his office, be very calm and nonchalant about it—but could she carry it off when she looked so very fragile?

She used her makeup carefully, applying slightly more blusher than she normally used and taking extra care with her eyes. Her hair would have to be left down to hide the thin lines of her neck and soften the fleshless contours of her cheekbones. When she dressed, she chose a floaty dress in a soft peach color, and was satisfied when she looked in the mirror. Nothing could quite disguise how delicate she had become, but she looked far from haggard.

As she drove to ConTech, she remembered the first time she had made this drive to meet Nikolas. She had been rushed, irritable, and not at all pleased. Now she was going to offer him what she had never thought to offer any man, the use and enjoyment of her body without benefit of marriage, and the only comfort she could find was that her body was all he would have. She had offered him her heart once, and he had scorned it. Never again would she give him the chance to hurt her like that.

Everyone recognized her now as she went up in the elevator, for she had often met Nikolas for lunch. Surprised murmurs of "Good morning, Mrs. Stanton" followed her, and she wondered for the first time if Nikolas was pursuing someone else now, but it really made no difference if he was. He could only turn her down if he was no longer interested, and any other rival would eventually have to give way to the precious, innocent Elena.

The receptionist looked up as she entered, and smiled warmly. "Mrs. Stanton! How nice it is to see you again!"

The greeting seemed genuinely friendly, and Jessica smiled in return. "Hello, Irena. Is Nikolas in today?"

"Why, yes, he is, though I believe he's planning a trip this afternoon."

"Thank you. I'll go in, if I may. Andros is here?"

"On guard as usual," Irena said, and wrinkled her nose in a private little communication that actually made Jessica laugh aloud. Evidently Andros had not endeared himself to the rest of the staff.

Calmly she walked into the office, and immediately Andros rose from his seat. "Mrs. Stanton!" he exclaimed.

"Hello, Andros," she returned as he eyed her with frank dislike. "I'd like to see Nikolas, please."

"I'm sorry," he refused in coolly neutral tones, though his eyes sparkled with delight at being able to turn her down. "Mr. Constantinos has someone with him right now and will be unable to talk to you for some time."

"And he's leaving on a business trip this afternoon," said Jessica dryly.

"Yes, he is," Andros said, his lips quirking in triumph.

Jessica looked at him for a moment, anger building in her.

She was sick and tired of being treated like dirt, and from this moment on she planned to fight back. "Very well," she said. "Give him a message for me, please, Andros. Tell him that I'm willing to agree to his terms, if he's still interested, and he can get in touch with me. That's all."

She turned on her heel and heard Andros strangle in alarm. "Mrs. Stanton!" he protested. "I can't—"

"You will have to," she cut in as she opened the door, and had a glimpse of the consternation in his black eyes as she left the office. He had damned himself either way now, for if he passed on the message Nikolas would know that Andros had refused her entrance, and he would not dare withhold the message, for if Nikolas ever found out—and Andros knew that Jessica would make certain he did—there would be hell to pay. Jessica smiled to herself as she walked back to the elevator. Andros had had that coming for a long time.

The elevator took its time arriving, but she wasn't impatient. The way she figured it, Nikolas would hear from Andros in about ten minutes, and he would try to reach her on the phone when he had decided that she had enough time to get home. If she was late getting back, that was all to the good. Let Nikolas wait for a while.

Several other people were in the elevator when it finally did arrive, and it was necessary to stop at every floor before she finally reached the entrance level. She crossed to the glass doors, but as she reached out to push them open, a dark-clothed arm reached past her and opened it for her. She raised her head to thank the man for his courtesy, but the words stuck in her throat as she stared up into the leaping black eyes of Nikolas.

"You've terrified Andros out of ten years of his life," he said easily, taking her arm and ushering her through the door.

"Good. He deserved it," she replied, then eyed him curiously. He was carrying his briefcase, as if he had left for the day. "But how did you get down so fast?"

"The stairs," he admitted, and grinned down at her. "I wasn't taking a chance of letting you get away from me today and not being able to find you before I have to leave this afternoon. That's probably the only reason Andros found the courage to give me your message so promptly; he knew I'd break his neck if he waited until later. You *were* serious, Jessica?''

"Perfectly," she assured him.

He still held her arm, his fingers warm and caressing, but his grip was unbreakable nonetheless. A limousine had drawn up to the curb and he led her to it. The driver jumped out and opened the back door and Nikolas helped her into the spacious back seat, then got in beside her. He gave the driver her address and then closed the sliding window between them.

"My car is here," she told him.

"It'll be perfectly safe until we return," he said, carrying her fingers to his lips for a light kiss. "Or did you think I could calmly leave on a dull business trip after receiving a message like that? No, darling, it's impossible. I'm taking you with me." And he gave her a look of such burning, primitive hunger that she shivered in automatic reaction to his sexuality.

"But I can't just leave," she objected. "Samantha—"

"Don't be silly," he interrupted softly. "Do you think I can't arrange to have a small dog looked after, or that I'd allow such a small thing to stand in my way? Samantha can be taken to an excellent kennel. I'll handle all the details; all you have to do is pack."

"Where are we going?" she asked, turning her head to look at the passing city streets. Evidently his desire had not waned, for there was no hesitation in his manner.

"To Paris, just for a couple of days. A perfect city to begin a relationship," he commented. "Unfortunately I'll be busy during the day with meetings, but the nights will be ours completely. Or perhaps I'll simply cancel the meetings and keep you in bed the entire time."

"Not good business practice," she said lightly. "I won't nag at you if you have to go off to your meetings."

"That's not very good for my ego," he teased, rubbing her wrist with his strong fingers. "I'd like to think that you burn for my touch as I do for yours. I'd nearly reached the limit of my patience, darling; another week and I'd have gone to Cornwall after you."

Startled, she looked at him. "You knew where I was?"

"Of course. Did you think I'd let you simply walk out on me? If you hadn't come back to me, I was going to force the issue, make you mine even if you bit and clawed, but I don't think you'd have resisted for long, h'mmm?"

It was humiliating to think that she hadn't been out of his reach even in Cornwall; he had known where she was and been content to let her brood. She turned her head again to stare blindly out the window, vainly trying to find comfort in the fact that he was, after all, still attracted to her. He might not love her, not as she understood love, but she did have some power over him.

He lifted her hand again and gently placed his lips on her soft palm. "Don't pout, darling," he said softly. "I knew that you'd come back to me when you decided to be realistic. I can be a very generous man; you'll want for nothing. You'll be treated like a queen, I promise you."

Deliberately Jessica pulled her hand away. "There are several things I want to discuss with you, Nikolas," she said in a remote tone. "There are conditions I want met; otherwise, I'm not interested in any sort of a relationship with you."

"Of course," he agreed dryly, his strong mouth curving into a cynical smile. "How much, my dear? And do you want it in cash, stocks or jewels?"

Ignoring him, she said, "First, I want to keep my own house. I don't want to live with you. You can visit me, or I'll visit you if you prefer that, but I want a life apart from yours."

"That's not necessary," he snapped, his straight brows pulling together over suddenly thunderous eyes.

"It's very necessary," she insisted evenly. "I don't delude myself that any relationship with you will be permanent, and I don't want to find myself forced to live in a hotel because I've given up my own home. And as I said, I'm not interested in living with you.''

"Don't be so certain of that," he mocked. "Very well, I agree to that condition. You're always free to move in with me when you change your mind."

"Thank you. Second, Nikolas"—here she turned to him and fixed him with an even stare, her green eyes clear and determined, her soft voice nevertheless threaded with steel so that he knew she meant every word—"I will never, under any circumstances, accept any money or expensive gifts from you. As you told Amanda Waring, I don't need your money. I'll be your lover, but I'll never be your kept woman. And finally, on the day you become engaged to your Elena, I'll walk away from you and never see you again. If you're an unfaithful husband, it won't be with me."

A dark blush of anger had swept over his features as she spoke, then he became motionless. "Do you think my marriage would change the way you feel about me?" he demanded harshly. "You might feel now that you could walk away from me, but once you've known my touch, once we've lain together, do you truly think that you could forget me?"

"I didn't say I would forget you," she said, her throat becoming thick with anguish. "I said I'd never see you again, and I mean it. I believe very strongly in the marriage vows; I never looked at another man when I was married to Robert."

He shoved a hand roughly through his hair, disturbing the tidy wave and making it fall down over his forehead. "And if I don't agree to these last two conditions?" he wanted to know. He was obviously angry, his jaw tight, his lips compressed to a grim line, but he was controlling it. His eyes were narrowed to piercing slits as he watched her.

"Then I won't go with you," she replied softly. "I want your word that you'll abide by those conditions, Nikolas."

"I can make you go with me," he threatened almost soundlessly, his lips scarcely moving. "With one word from me, you can be taken away from England without anyone knowing where you are or how you left. You can be secluded, forced to live as I say you will live.''

''Don't threaten me, Nikolas,'' she said, refusing to be frightened. ''Yes, I know you can do all of those things, but you'll be defeating your own purpose if you ever resort to such tactics, for I won't be bullied. You *do* want a willing woman in your arms, don't you?''

''You damned little witch,'' he breathed, pulling her to him across the seat with an iron grip on her wrist. ''Very well, I agree to your conditions—if you think you have the willpower to enforce them. You can probably refuse any gifts from me without being bothered by it, but when it comes to leaving me— we'll see. You're in my blood, and I'm in yours, and my marriage to Elena won't diminish the need I have to sate myself with your soft body, my dear. Nor do I think you could leave me as easily as you've planned, for haven't you come back to me now? Haven't you just offered yourself to me?''

''Only my body,'' she made clear. ''*You* set those terms, Nikolas. You get only my body. The rest of me stays free.''

''You've already admitted that you love me,'' he said roughly. ''Or was that just a ploy to try to trap me into marriage?''

Despite the pain in her wrist where he held her so tightly, she managed a nonchalant shrug. ''What do you know of love, Nikolas? Why talk about it? I'm willing to sleep with you; what more do you want?''

Abruptly he tossed her wrist back into her lap. ''Don't make me lose my temper,'' he warned. ''I might hurt you, Jessica. I'm aching with the need to possess you, and my patience is thin. Until tonight, my dear, walk softly.''

From the look on his face, it was a warning to be taken seriously. She sat quietly beside him until the chauffeur stopped the limousine outside her house, then she allowed him to help her out. He leaned down and gave instructions to the chauffeur to pick up his luggage and return, then he and Jessica went up the walk. He took the key from her and unlocked the door, then opened it for her. "Can you be ready in an hour?" he asked, glancing at his watch. "Our flight leaves at noon."

"Yes, of course, but don't I need a booking?"

"You're taking Andros's seat," he replied. "Andros will be taking a later flight."

"Oh, dear, now he certainly will be cross with me," she mocked as she crossed to the stairway.

"He'll have to control his irritation," said Nikolas. "Go on; I'll arrange for Samantha and the pups."

"Just Samantha," she corrected. "I gave the pups away while we were in Cornwall."

"That should certainly make things easier," he said, grinning.

Jessica went up to her room and pulled her suitcases out again. All of this packing was becoming monotonous. Carefully she folded clothing and essentials into her leather cases, matching her outfits with shoes and accessories. Nikolas sauntered in when she was only half-finished and stretched out on the bed as if he had every right to be there, surveying her through half-closed eyes.

"You've lost weight," he said quietly. "I don't like it. What have you been doing to yourself?"

"I've been on a diet," she replied flippantly.

"Diet, hell!" He came off the bed and caught her arm, his other hand cupping her chin and turning her face up to his. Black eyes went sharply over her features, noting the shadows under her eyes, the defenseless quiver of her soft mouth. His hand quested boldly down her body, cupping her breasts and stroking her belly and hips. "You little fool!" he breathed sharply. "You're nothing but a shadow. You've nearly made yourself ill! Why haven't you been eating?"

"I wasn't hungry," she explained. "It's nothing to act up about."

"No? You're on the verge of collapse, Jessica." He put his arms about her and pulled her tightly to him, lowering his head to kiss her temples. "But I'll take care of you now and make certain that you eat enough. You'll need your strength, darling, for I'm a man with strong needs. If I were a gentleman, I would allow you a few days to regain your strength, but I'm afraid that I'm too selfish and too hungry for you to allow you that.''

"I wouldn't want you to," she whispered against his chest, her arms moving slowly about him, feeling with growing desire his strong, hard body pressing to her. She had missed him so badly! "I need you, too, Nikolas!"

"I would take you now," he murmured, "but the car will be back soon and I really need more time than that to satisfy these weeks of frustration. But tonight—just wait until tonight!"

For a long moment she simply rested her head on his broad chest; she was tired and depressed, and glad to have his strength to rest upon. Though she had made her decision, it was against her basic nature to go against the morals of a lifetime, and sadly she realized that her love for Nikolas had not diminished despite her bitter pride. She would have to come to terms with that, just as she had accepted that, while he wanted her physically, he did not love her and probably never would. Nikolas had planned his life and he was not a man to allow anyone to upset his plans.

Only a few hours later, Jessica sat alone in the luxurious suite that Nikolas had reserved, staring about as if dazed. After their flight had landed at Orly, Nikolas had bundled her through customs at top speed and into a taxi; after a mad ride through the Paris traffic, he had deposited her in this hotel and left immediately for his meeting. She felt abandoned and desolate, and her nerves were beginning to quiver as feeling returned to them. For weeks she had been numbed, not feeling anything except the agony of rejection, but now, as she looked about her, she began to wonder just what she was doing here.

Vaguely she studied her surroundings, noting how exactly the pale green carpet picked out the green threads in the blue-green brocade of the sofa she sat upon and the heavy swag of the curtains. A lovely suite...even the flowers were color-coordinated. A perfect setting for a seduction, when the lights were low and Nikolas turned his smoldering dark eyes on her.

Her mind shied away from the image of Nikolas, not wanting

to think of the coming hours. She had agreed to be his lover, but now that the time was here, she felt rebellious. She thought of what he would say if she refused to go through with it and decided that he would be furious. She pushed the idea away, but as the minutes ticked away, the thought returned again and again, stronger each time, until at last she got up and paced the room in agitation as pain crawled along her nerves.

Had the pain of rejection unhinged her mind? Whatever had she been thinking of? She wouldn't be Nikolas Constantinos's mistress; she wouldn't be any man's mistress! Hadn't Robert instilled more self-respect into her than that? Nikolas didn't love her; he would never love her. His sole motivation was lust, and giving her virginity to him to prove her innocence would be her loss and mean nothing to him. Virginity wouldn't make him love her.

She remembered the tales from her teenage years, tales of girls whose boyfriends pressured them to "prove their love." Then, in a few weeks, the boyfriends were running after some other girl. She had been too withdrawn herself to get into such a situation; she had never really even dated, but she had thought at the time that the girls were such fools. Anyone could see that the boys were just after sex, any way they could get it. Wasn't it the same situation now? Oh, Nikolas was a far cry from a fumbling teenage boy, but all he wanted was sex. He might pretty it up with words like "want" and "need," and call her darling now and then and tell her that he adored her, but basically it was the same urge.

It was simply that she was a challenge to him, that was why he was so determined to make love to her. He couldn't accept defeat; he was far too fiery and arrogant. Everything about her challenged him, her coolness, her resistance to his lovemaking.

She had been standing at the window, looking out at the twinkling Parisian lights as they blinked on in the darkness, for some time when Nikolas returned. She didn't turn as he entered the room and he said softly, "Jessica? What's wrong, darling?"

"Nothing," she said flatly. "I'm just looking."

She heard the muffled thud as he dropped his briefcase and then he came to stand behind her, his warm hands sliding over her arms and crossing in front of her, pulling her back against his body. His head bent and his lips burned on the side of her neck. For a moment she went limp as a spark of desire arced across her nerve endings, then she twisted away from him in a rush of panic.

He frowned at her and took a step toward her; as he did, she retreated, holding her hands out to ward him off.

"Jessica?" he questioned, baffled.

"Don't come near me!"

"What do you mean?" he demanded, his brows snapping together. "What kind of game are you playing now?"

"I—I've changed my mind," she blurted. "I can't do it, Nikolas. I'm sorry, but I just can't go through with it."

"Oh, no, you don't!" he exploded, closing the distance between them with two long strides and catching her arm as she tried to whirl away from him. "Oh, no, you don't," he breathed savagely, jerking her to him. "No more waiting, no more putting me off. Now, Jessica. *Now.*"

She read his intent in his glittering black eyes as he bent down to lift her in his arms. Terror bloomed in her mind and she twisted madly in an effort to evade his lips, trying to throw herself out of his grasp. Tears poured out of her eyes and she began sobbing wildly, begging him not to touch her. Hysteria began to build in her as she realized she could not escape his brutal hold and her breath strangled in her chest.

Suddenly he seemed to realize that she was terrified; startled, he put her on her feet and stared down into her twisted, bloodless face.

Chapter 8

"All right," he said in a strained voice, backing away from her, his hands held up as if to show he was unarmed. "I won't touch you, I promise. See? I'll even sit down." He suited his actions to his words and stared at her, his black eyes somber. "But God in heaven, Jessica, *why?*"

She stood there on trembling legs, trying to control her sobs and find her voice to explain, but no words would come and she only returned his gaze dumbly. With a groan he brought his hands up and rubbed his eyes as if he was tired, and he probably was. When he dropped his hands loosely onto his knees, his expression was grim and determined. "You win," he said tonelessly. "I don't know what your hang-up about sex is, but I accept that you're too frightened to come to me without some assurance about the future. Damn it, if marriage is what it takes to get you, then you'll have your marriage. We can be married on the island next week."

Shock made her grope weakly for the nearest chair, and when she was safely sitting down, she said in a quavering voice, "No, you don't understand—"

"I understand that you have your price," he muttered angrily. "And I've been pushed as far as I can be pushed, Jessica, so don't start an argument now. You *will* sleep with a husband, won't you? Or do you have another nasty little surprise saved up for me after you have the ring on your finger?''

Anger saved her—clean, strength-giving anger spurting into her veins. It stiffened her spine and dried her tears. He was too arrogant and bullheaded to listen to her, and she was tempted for a minute to throw his offer back in his face, but her heart stopped her. Maybe he was proposing for all the wrong reasons, but it was still a proposal of marriage. And however angry he was now, at both her and himself, he would calm down and she would be able to tell him the truth. He would have to listen; she would make him. He was frustrated now and in no mood to be reasoned with; the best thing to do was not make him angry.

"Yes," she said almost inaudibly, lowering her head. "I'll sleep with you when we're married, no matter how frightened I get."

He heaved a sigh and leaned forward to rest his elbows on his knees in a posture of utter weariness. "Only that saved you tonight," he admitted curtly. "You really were frightened, you weren't faking it. You've really been treated roughly down the line, haven't you, Jessica? But I don't want to hear about it, I can't take it now."

"All right," she whispered.

"And stop looking like a whipped kitten!" he shouted, getting to his feet and pacing angrily to the window. He shoved his hands deeply into his pockets and stood staring out at the brightly lit streets. "I'll telephone Maman tomorrow," he said, reining in his temper. "And I'll try to get out of my meeting fairly early so we can shop for your wedding gown. Since we'll have to get married on the island, all of the trimmings will be expected," he explained bitterly.

"Why does it have to be on the island?" she questioned hesitantly.

"Because I grew up there," he growled. "The island belongs to me, and I belong to the island. The villagers would never forgive me if I got married anywhere but there, with all the traditional celebrations. The women will want to fuss over my bride; the men will want to congratulate me and give me advice on handling a wife.''

''And your mother?''

He turned to face her and his eyes were hard. ''She'll be hurt, but she won't question me. And let me warn you now, Jessica, that if you ever do anything to hurt or insult my mother, I'll make you wish you'd never been born. Whatever you've been through before will seem like heaven compared to the hell I'll put you through.''

She gasped at the hatred in his eyes. Desperately she tried to defend herself and she cried out, ''You know I'm not like that! Don't try to make me a villain because things haven't gone as you'd have liked them! I didn't want it to be this way between us.''

''I can see that,'' he said grimly. ''You'd have preferred it if I'd been as gullible as Robert Stanton, seeing only your angelic face and willing to give you anything you wanted. But I know you for what you are, and you won't take me to the cleaners like you did that old man. You had a choice, Jessica. As my mistress, you'd have been spoiled rotten and treated like a queen. As my wife, you'll have my name and very little else, but you made your choice and you'll live with it. Just don't expect any more generous settlements like I gave you for those stocks, and above all, remember that I'm Greek, and after the wedding you'll belong to me body and soul. Think about that, darling.'' He gave the endearment a sarcastic bite and she winced away from the savagery of his tone.

''You're wrong,'' she said in a trembling voice. ''I'm not like that, Nikolas; you know I'm not. Why are you saying such awful things? Please, let me tell you how it was—''

''I'm not interested in how it was,'' he shouted suddenly, his face filled with the rage he could no longer control. ''Don't you know when to shut up? Don't push me!''

Shaking, she turned away from him and crossed to the bedroom. No, she couldn't do it. No matter how much she loved him, it was plain that he'd never love her, and if she made the mistake of marrying him, he would make her life a misery. He'd never forgive her for bringing him to the point where he'd agreed to marriage. He was proud and angry, and as he had said, he was Greek. A Greek never forgot a grievance; a Greek went after vengeance.

It would be better to make a clean break, never to see him again. It would be impossible to forget him, of course, but she knew that any sort of marriage between them was impossible. She had lived with scorn and suspicion from strangers, but she couldn't take it from her husband. It was time she left England completely, returned to the States, where she could live in quiet seclusion.

"Put that suitcase back," he said in a deadly voice from the doorway as she lifted her case from the closet.

Paling, she cast him a startled glance. "It's the only way," she pleaded. "Surely you see that marriage between us wouldn't work. Let me go, Nikolas, before we tear each other to pieces."

His mouth twisted cynically. "Backing out, now that you know you won't be able to twist me around your little finger? It won't work, Jessica. We'll be married next week—unless you want to pay the price for walking out of this hotel without me?"

She knew what he meant and her chin went up. Without a word, she shoved her suitcase back onto the shelf and closed the door.

"I thought so," he murmured. "Don't get any more ideas about running out on me, or you'll regret it. Now come back in here and sit down. I'll order dinner sent up and we'll work out the details of our arrangement."

He was so cold-blooded about it that the last thing she wanted to do was talk to him, but she went ahead of him and took a seat on the sofa, not looking at him.

He ordered dinner without asking her preference, then he called Andros, who was on the floor below them, and told him to come to the suite in an hour, he wanted him to take some notes. Then he replaced the receiver and came to take a seat on the sofa beside her. Uneasily Jessica edged away from him and he gave a short bark of laughter.

"That's odd behavior for a prospective bride," he mocked. "So standoffish. I won't let you get away with that, you know. I'm paying for the right to touch you when I please and however I please, and I don't want any more playacting."

"I'm not playacting," she denied shakily. "You know I'm not."

He eyed her thoughtfully. "No, I suppose you're not. You're afraid of me, aren't you? But you'll do what I want, if I marry you first. Too bad that kills any sense of mercy I might have possessed."

There was no convincing him. Jessica fell silent and tried to draw together the shreds of her dignity and composure. He was furious, and her attempts to establish her innocence were only making him that much angrier, so she decided to go along with him. If nothing else, she could salvage her pride.

"Nothing else to say?" he jeered.

She managed a cool shrug. "Why waste my time? You'll do what you want anyway, so I might as well go along for the ride."

"Does that mean you've agreed to marry me?" The tone was mocking, but she sensed the seriousness underlying the mockery and she realized that he wasn't certain that she'd stay.

"Yes, I'll marry you," she replied. "On the same conditions that I agreed to be your mistress."

"You backed out of that," he pointed out unkindly.

"I won't back out of this."

"You won't get a chance to. The same conditions, eh? I seem to remember that you didn't want to live with me; needless to say, that condition doesn't stand."

"The part about the money does," she said, turning her green eyes on him, opaque and mysterious with the intensity of her thoughts. "I don't want your money. Anything that I want, I'll pay for myself."

"That's interesting, even if it isn't convincing," he drawled, putting one strong brown hand on her throat and lightly stroking her skin. "If you're not marrying me for my money, why are you marrying me? For myself?"

"That's right," she admitted, meeting his gaze squarely.

"Good, because that's all you're getting," he muttered, leaning toward her as if drawn irresistibly by her mouth.

His lips fastened angrily on hers; his hands were hard and punishing and he pulled her close to him, but she didn't struggle. She rested pliantly against him and let him ravage her mouth until the anger began to fade and the hungry desire in him became stronger. Then she kissed him back, tentatively, and the pressure of his hard mouth lessened.

The long kiss provided an outlet for his black anger and she could sense him growing calmer even as his passion flared. He was prepared to wait now; he knew that she would be his within a week. He drew back and stared down into her pale face with its soft, trembling lips, then he kissed her again, hard.

The arrival of their dinner interrupted them and he released her to get to his feet and open the door. He seemed in a calmer frame of mind now, and as they ate, he even made small talk, telling her about his meeting and the problems that had been discussed. She relaxed, sensing that the worst of his temper had passed.

Andros arrived right on cue just as they were finishing the meal, and his dark eyes flashed at her in silent hostility before he gave his attention to Nikolas.

"Jessica and I are going to be married," Nikolas announced casually. "Next week, on the island. Tuesday. Make all the arrangements and notify the press that an engagement has been announced, but give them no details about when the wedding will take place. I'll call Maman myself, early tomorrow morning."

Andros's astonishment was plain, and though he didn't look at Jessica again, she sensed his dismay. No doubt his nose was more than a little out of joint to learn that the woman he actively disliked was going to marry his employer!

"We'll also have a prenuptial agreement drawn up," Nikolas continued. "Take all of this down, Andros, and have it on Leo's desk tomorrow morning. Tell him I want it back the day after tomorrow at the latest. It will be signed before we go to the island."

Andros sat down and opened his pad, his pen at the ready. Nikolas gave Jessica a considering stare before he started speaking again.

"Jessica renounces in advance all monetary claims against my estate," he drawled, sitting down and stretching his long legs out before him. "Should we be divorced, she will be entitled to no alimony and no property except such gifts as I have made to her, which will be her personal property."

Andros flashed Jessica a startled look, as if expecting her to disagree, but she sat quietly, watching Nikolas's dark, brooding face. She felt calm now, though she knew that her entire future was at stake. Nikolas had agreed to marriage when she had thought that he never would, so it was a start.

"While we're married," Nikolas continued, leaning his black head back against the sofa, "Jessica will conduct herself with strict propriety. She's not to leave the island without my personal escort, or with my permission and a substitute escort that I've chosen. She will also turn over the handling of all her income from her first husband to me." Now he, too, looked at Jessica, but still she made no protest. Her business affairs would be in marvelously competent hands with Nikolas, and she had no fears of him cheating her.

Then a thought occurred to her, and before she could halt herself, she said evenly, "I suppose that's one way of getting back the money you paid for my stocks."

Nikolas's jaw went rigid and she wished that she'd held her tongue rather than make him even angrier. She wasn't even protesting letting him have control of the money; she hadn't wanted it anyway. He wanted to have her completely under his power and she was willing to go along with him. It was a chance she was taking, but she had to hope that when he found out how wrong he was, he would soften his stand.

After a tense moment Nikolas delivered his final condition. "Last of all, I shall have final authority over any children that we should have. In case of divorce, I'll retain custody, though of course Jessica will be permitted visitation rights if she wants to come to the island. Under no circumstances will she be permitted to take the child or children away from the island or to see them without my permission."

Pain twisted her heart at that last and she hastily turned her head away so they couldn't see the welling of tears in her eyes. He seemed so hard! Perhaps she was being a fool; perhaps he'd never come to love her. Only the thought that he would know beyond a doubt that she came to him an innocent gave her the courage to agree to his conditions. He would at least realize that she wasn't going to corrupt their children.

If only there would be children! Nikolas seemed to take it for granted that their marriage wouldn't last, but already she knew that for her it was forever. No matter what he did, she would always be married to him in her heart. She wanted to have his children, several children, miniature replicas of him with black hair and black, flashing eyes.

"No comments, Jessica?" Nikolas asked softly, the jeering tone plain in his voice.

Jerking her thoughts back from a delightful vision of herself holding a tiny black-eyed baby in her arms, she stared at him for a moment as if she didn't recognize him, then she gathered herself and replied almost inaudibly, "No. I agree to everything you want, Nikolas."

"That's all," he said to Andros, and when they were alone again, he snapped, "You won't even make a token protest to keep any children, will you? Or are you hoping that I'll pay you to stay away from them? If so, disillusion yourself. You won't get a penny from me under any circumstances!"

"I agreed to your conditions," she cried shakily, her control broken by a heavy pain in her chest. "What more do you want?

I've learned that I can't fight you, so I won't waste my breath. As for any children we might have, I want children—I want *your* children—and the only way I'll ever leave them will be if you physically throw me off the island. And don't insult me by insinuating that I won't be a good mother."

He stared down at her, a muscle in his jaw jerking out of control. "You say you can't fight me," he muttered hoarsely, "but you still deny me."

"No, no," she moaned, despairing of ever making him understand. "I'm not refusing you. Can't you see, Nikolas? I'm asking more from you than you're offering, and I'm not talking about money. I'm talking about yourself. So far you've offered me only the same part of yourself that you gave Diana, and I want more than that."

"And what about you?" he growled, getting to his feet and pacing restlessly about the room. "You won't even give me that much; you hold yourself away and demand that I give in to you in every respect."

"You don't have to marry me," she pointed out sharply, abruptly weary of their bickering. "You can let me walk out that door, and I promise you that you'll never see me again, if that's what you want."

His mouth twisted savagely. "You know I can't do that. No, you've got me so twisted inside that I've got to have you; I'll never be worth a damn if I can't satisfy this ache. It's not a wedding, Jessica, it's an exorcism."

His words still rang in her ears the next day as she paced the suite, waiting for him to return from his meeting. Andros was there; he had been there all morning, watching her, not talking, and his silent vigilance rasped painfully on her nerves. It had been a hellish night, sleeping alone in the big bed that Nikolas had intended to share with her, listening to him turn restlessly on the sofa. She had offered to take the sofa and let him have the bed, but he had glared at her so fiercely that she hadn't insisted. They had both slept very little.

Earlier, he had phoned his mother and Jessica had shut herself in the bathroom, determined not to listen to the conversation. When she came out of the bathroom, Nikolas had gone and Andros was there.

Just when she thought she couldn't stand the silence any longer, Andros spoke, and she nearly jumped out of her skin. "Why did you agree to all of Niko's conditions, Mrs. Stanton?"

She looked at him wildly. "Why?" she demanded. "Do you think he was in any mood to be reasonable? He was like a keg of dynamite waiting for some fool to set him off."

"You're not afraid of him, though," Andros observed. "At least, you're not afraid of his temper. Most people are, but you've always dared him to do his worst. I've been turning it over and over in my head, and I can think of only one reason why you'd let him make those insulting conditions."

"Oh? What have you decided?" she asked, pushing her heavy hair away from her eyes. She had been too upset that morning to put it up and now it tumbled untidily over her shoulders.

"I think you love him," Andros said quietly. "I think you're willing to marry him under any conditions because you love him."

She gulped at hearing it put into words. Andros was watching her with a different light in his dark eyes, a certain acceptance and the beginnings of understanding. "Of course I love him," she admitted in a tight whisper. "The only problem is making him believe it."

Suddenly Andros smiled. "You don't have a problem, Mrs. Stanton. Niko is besotted with you. When he calms down, he'll realize, as I did, that under the conditions he set, the only reason you had for marrying him is love. It's only because he's so angry now that it hasn't already occurred to him."

Andros didn't know the whole of it, but still his words gave her hope. He said that Nikolas was besotted with her. That was a little hard to believe; Nikolas was always so much in control, but it was true that he was willing to marry her if he couldn't have her any other way.

Nikolas arrived then, preventing her from talking with Andros any longer, but she felt better. The two men conferred over a sheaf of papers that Nikolas took out of his briefcase, then Andros took the papers to return to his room and Nikolas turned to Jessica.

"Are you ready?" he asked remotely.

"Ready?" She didn't understand.

He sighed impatiently. "I told you that we'd shop for your wedding dress. And you'll have to have rings, Jessica, they'll be expected."

"I'll have to put up my hair," she said, turning to the bedroom, and he followed her.

"Just brush it and leave it down," he ordered. "I like it better down."

Wordlessly she obeyed him and took out her lipstick. "Wait," he said, catching her wrist and pulling her around to him. She knew what he wanted and her heart lightened as she leaned against him and lifted her mouth for his kiss. His lips pressed on hers and his hot breath filled her mouth, making her dizzy. He wanted more; he wasn't content with kisses, but with a quiver of his body he pulled away from her and once again the look in his eyes bordered on the murderous.

"Now you can put on your lipstick," he muttered, and slammed out of the bedroom.

With a shaking hand she applied the lipstick. His temper hadn't improved, and she was afraid that to deny him even her kisses would make him that much worse. No, nothing would satisfy Nikolas but her full surrender, and she wished fervently that the next week would fly past.

But how could an entire week fly by when even the afternoon dragged? She could feel the tension building up in her as they sat at the quiet, exclusive jewelers and examined the trays of rings that he set out. Nikolas was no help at all; he merely sat back and told her to pick out what she liked, he didn't care. Nothing he could have said would have been better calculated to demolish any joy Jessica might have felt in the proceedings. On the other hand, the jeweler was so nice and tried to be so helpful that she hated to disappoint him with her disinterest, so she forced herself to carefully examine each and every ring that he thought she might like. But try as she might, she couldn't choose one. The brightly winking diamonds might have been glass for all she cared; she wanted only to find a quiet corner and weep her eyes out. At last, with tension cracking in her voice, she said, "No—no! I don't like any of them!" and made as if to get to her feet.

Nikolas stopped her with an iron grip on her wrist and he forced her back into her chair. "Don't get upset, darling," he said in a gentler tone than he had used all day. "Calm down; you mustn't weep or it will upset Monsieur. Shall I pick one out for you?"

"Yes, please," she said in a stifled voice, turning her face away so he couldn't see her eyes brimming with the tears he had said she mustn't shed.

"I don't care for the diamonds either, Monsieur," Nikolas was saying. "Her coloring needs something warmer...yes, emeralds to match her eyes, in a gold setting."

"Of course—I have just the thing!" Monsieur said excitedly, taking the trays of diamonds away.

"Jessica?"

"What?" she asked, still not turning around to face him.

She should have known that he'd never allow her to keep her head turned away from him. One long forefinger stroked along her jaw, then gently forced her face to turn to him. Black eyes took in her pallor, her tense expression, noted the wetness that threatened to overflow from her eyes.

Without a word, he took out his handkerchief and wiped her eyes as if she was a child. "You know I can't bear for you to cry," he whispered. "If I promise not to be such a beast, will you smile for me?"

It wasn't in her to deny him anything when he was being so sweet, even if he had been as cold as ice only a moment before. Her lips parted in a gentle smile and Nikolas touched her mouth with his finger, tracing her lip line. "That's better," he mur-

mured. "You understand why I won't kiss you here, but I want
to, very much."

She kissed his fingers in answer, then he saw the jeweler returning and he straightened up, taking his hand away, but his
brief attentions had put color in her cheeks and she was smiling
hazily.

"Ah, this is more like it," Nikolas said, pouncing on a ring
as soon as the jeweler set the tray down before them. He took
Jessica's slender hand and slid the ring onto it; it was too big,
but she caught her breath at the sight of it.

"What a lovely color," she breathed on a sigh.

"Yes, this is what I want," Nikolas decided. The square-cut
emerald was not so big that it looked awkward on her graceful
hand, and the rich, dark green looked better on her than a thousand diamonds would have. Her golden skin and tawny hair were
a perfect setting for her mysterious Egyptian green eyes, and the
emerald ring was only an echo of her own coloring. Brilliant
diamonds surrounded the emerald, but they were small enough
that they didn't detract from the deep color of the gem. He removed it gently from her finger and gave it to the jeweler, who
carefully put it aside and measured Jessica's finger. "And a wedding ring," Nikolas added.

"Two," inserted Jessica bravely, meeting his eyes. After a
moment he gave in, nodding his permission.

"I don't like wearing rings," he said as they left the jewelers,
his arm hard about her waist.

"We're going to be married, Nikolas," she said, turning to
face him and putting both hands on his chest. "Shouldn't we
try as hard as we can to make a success of our marriage? Or are
you going into it with divorce already on your mind?" Her voice
quivered at that thought, but she met his dark gaze squarely.

"I don't have anything on my mind except having you," he
said bluntly. "Rings aren't important to me. If you want me to
wear a wedding ring, then I'll wear one. A ring won't stop me
if I want to be free of you."

She nearly choked on the pain that welled up in her chest and

she turned abruptly away, fighting for composure. By the time
he caught up with her she had managed to pull her cool mask
in place again and she revealed nothing of her inner hurt.

When they were in the taxi, she heard him give the address
of a well-known couturier and she said quietly, "I don't know
what you have in mind, Nikolas, but there isn't time to have a
gown made. A ready-to-wear gown will be fine with me."

He didn't even glance at her, and after his gentleness in the
jewelry shop, the chill was that much colder. "You're forgetting
who I am," he snapped. "If I want a gown ready for you by
tomorrow afternoon, the gown will be ready."

There was nothing to say to that, because it was true, but she
thought of the people who would be sitting up all night to do
the delicate stitchery that had to be done by hand and she knew
that it wasn't worth it. But Nikolas had a set to his jaw that
dissuaded her from arguing with him, and she sat back in miserable silence.

So far as Jessica knew, Nikolas was not inclined to personally
select clothing for his women, but he was recognized the instant
he stepped into the cool foyer of the salon. Immediately a tall,
slender woman with severely styled ash-blond hair was gliding
across the dove-gray carpet toward them, welcoming them to the
salon, and if Monsieur Constantinos wished to see anything in
particular...

Nikolas was all charm, raising the woman's fingers to his lips,
his wolfish black eyes bringing a wave of color to her cheeks
that owed nothing to artificiality. Nikolas introduced Jessica,
then said smoothly, "We're to be married next week in Greece.
I managed to convince her only yesterday, and I want to have
the wedding immediately, before she can change her mind. But
this leaves very little time for the gown, you understand, as we
are leaving for Greece the day after tomorrow."

The woman snapped to attention and assured him that a gown
could indeed be ready, if they would like to see some models....

A parade of models appeared, some wearing white, but the
majority in pastel colors, delicately flattering colors that were

nevertheless not virginal white. Nikolas looked them all over carefully and finally chose a gown with classically simple lines and requested it in a shade of pale peach. Jessica suddenly frowned. This was her wedding gown, and she was entitled to wear the traditional white.

"I don't like peach," she said firmly. "In white, please, Madame."

Nikolas glared at her and the woman looked startled, but Jessica stood her ground. It was to be white or nothing. At last Nikolas gave in, for he didn't want to make a scene in front of extremely interested witnesses, and Jessica was taken into the dressing room to be measured.

"You made a fool of yourself, insisting on white," Nikolas said curtly on the way back to the hotel. "Your name is recognized even in France, Jessica."

"It's my wedding, too," she said stubbornly.

"You've already been married, my sweet; it should be old hat to you by now."

Her lower lip trembled at that cut and she quickly firmed it. "Robert and I were married in a civil ceremony, not a religious one. I'm entitled to a white gown, Nikolas!"

If he caught her meaning, he ignored it. Or perhaps he simply didn't believe it. He said grimly, "After your history, you should count yourself lucky I'm marrying you at all. I have to be the world's biggest fool, but I'll worry about that afterward. One thing is for certain, as my wife you'll be the most well-behaved woman in Europe."

She turned her head in frustration, staring out the window at the chic Parisian shoppers, the elegant cafés. She had seen nothing of Paris except fleeting glimpses through the window of the taxi and the gay, mocking lights of the night winking up into her hotel window.

It was too late to back out now, but she was aware of the awful, creeping knowledge that she had made a mistake in agreeing to the marriage. Nikolas was not a man to forgive easily, and not even the knowledge that she was not promiscuous would make him forget that, to his way of seeing it, she had sold herself to him for a price—marriage.

Chapter 9

"There!" Andros shouted to Jessica above the roar of the helicopter blades. "That is Zenas."

She leaned forward to watch eagerly as the small dot in the blue of the Aegean began to grow bigger, then it was rushing toward them and they were no longer over the sea but over the stark, barren hills with the shadow of the helicopter flitting along below them like a giant mosquito. Jessica glanced at Nikolas, who was at the controls, but he didn't acknowledge her presence by so much as the flicker of an eyelash. She wanted him to smile at her, to point out the landmarks on his island, but it was only Andros who touched her arm and directed her attention to the house they were approaching.

It was a vast, sprawling house, built on the cliffside with a flagstone terrace enclosing three sides of the house. The roof was of red tile; the house itself was white and cool amid the shade of orange and lemon trees. Looking down, she could see small figures leaving the house and walking up to the helipad, which was built off to the right of the house on the crest of a small hill. A paved drive connected the house to the helipad, but Andros had told her that there was only one vehicle on the island, an old army jeep owned by the mayor of the village.

Nikolas set the helicopter down so lightly that she didn't even feel a bump, then he killed the engine and pulled off his headset. He turned a grim, unsmiling face to Jessica. "Come," he said in French. "I will introduce you to Maman—and remember, Jessica, you're not to upset her."

He slid open the door and got out, ducking his head against the wind whipped up by the still-whirling rotors. Jessica drew a deep breath to steady her pounding heart and Andros said quietly, "Not to worry. My aunt is a gentle woman; Nikolas is not at all like her. He is the image of his father, and like his father before him he is protective of my aunt."

She gave him a grateful smile, then Nikolas beckoned impatiently and she clambered out of the helicopter, holding desperately to the hand Nikolas had extended to help her. He frowned a little at the coldness of her fingers, then he drew her forward to the group that had gathered at the edge of the helipad.

A small woman with the erect bearing of a queen stepped forward. She was still beautiful despite her white hair, which she wore in an elegant Gibson Girl style, and her soft, clear blue eyes were as direct as a child's. She gave Jessica a piercing look straight into her eyes, then she looked swiftly at her son.

Nikolas bent down and pressed a loving kiss on the delicately pink cheek, then another on her lips. "Maman, I've missed you," he said, hugging her to him.

"And I've missed you," she replied in a sweet voice. "I'm so glad you're back."

With his arm still about his mother, Nikolas beckoned to Jessica, and the look he gave her as she stepped closer warned her to behave. "Maman, I'd like you to meet my fiancée, Jessica Stanton. Jessica, my mother, Madelon Constantinos."

"I'm happy to meet you at last," Jessica murmured, meeting that clear gaze as bravely as possible, and she discovered to her astonishment that she and Madame Constantinos were nearly the same size. The older woman looked so fragile that Jessica had felt like an Amazon, but now she found their eyes on the same level and it was a distinct shock.

"And I'm happy to meet you," Madame Constantinos said,

moving out of Nikolas's embrace to put her own arms around Jessica and kiss her on the cheek. "I was certainly surprised to receive Niko's phone call announcing his intentions! It was… unexpected."

"Yes, it was a sudden decision," Jessica agreed, but her heart sank at the coolness of the old woman's tone. It was obvious that she was less than happy over her son's choice of a bride. Nevertheless, Jessica managed a tremulous smile, and Madame Constantinos's manners were too good to permit her to exhibit her displeasure any more openly. She had spoken in English, very good English with a slight drawl that she could only have picked up from Nikolas, but as she turned to introduce Jessica to the other people she switched to French and Greek. Jessica didn't understand any Greek, but all of the people spoke some French.

There was Petra, a tall, heavyset woman with black hair and eyes and the classic Greek nose, and laughter shining in her face. She was the housekeeper and her employer's personal companion, for they had been together since Madame Constantinos had come to the island. There was a natural grace and pride about the big woman that made her beautiful despite her almost manly proportions, and a motherly light gleamed in her eyes at the barely concealed fear and nervousness on Jessica's face.

The other woman was short and plump, her round face as gentle as any Jessica could remember. She was Sophia, the cook, and she patted Jessica's arm with open affection, ready to accept immediately any woman that Kyrios Nikolas brought home to be his bride.

Sophia's husband, Jason Kavakis, was a short, slender man with solemn dark eyes, and he was the groundskeeper. He and Sophia lived in their own cottage in the village, but Petra was a widow and she had her own room in the villa. These three were the only staff at the villa, though the women from the village were all helping with the preparations for the wedding.

The open, unrestrained welcome that she received from the staff helped Jessica to relax and she smiled more naturally as

Madame Constantinos linked arms with Nikolas and began organizing the transfer of their luggage to the villa. "Andros, please help Jason carry the bags down." Then she removed her arm and gave Nikolas a little push. "And you, too! Why should you not help? I will take Mrs. Stanton to her room; she is probably half-dead with fatigue. You've never learned to take a trip in easy stages."

"Yes, Maman," he called to her retreating back, but his dark eyes looked a warning at Jessica.

Despite the coolness of her welcome from Madame Constantinos, Jessica felt better. The old lady was not an autocratic matriarch, and Jessica sensed that beneath her restraint she was a pert, gentle old woman who treated her son as if he was simply her son, rather than a billionaire. And Nikolas himself had immediately softened, becoming the Niko who had grown up here and who had known these people since babyhood. She couldn't imagine him intimidating Petra, who had probably diapered him and watched his first toddling steps, hard as it was for Jessica to picture Nikolas as an infant or a toddler. Surely he had always been tall and strong, with that fierce light in his dark eyes.

The villa was cool, with the thickness of its white walls keeping out most of the brutal Greek sun, but the quiet hum of central air-conditioning told her that Nikolas made certain his home was always at a comfortable temperature.

She had already realized that Nikolas's tastes were Greek, and the villa bore that out. The furnishings were sparse, with vast amounts of open floor space, but everything was of the highest quality and built to last for years. The colors were of the earth, soft brick tones for the tiles of the floor, over which were scattered priceless Persian rugs, muted greens and natural linen for the furniture upholstery. Small statues in different shades of marble were set in niches, and here and there were vases of incredible delicacy, sitting comfortably in the same room with pottery that had surely been produced by the villagers.

"Your bedroom," said Madame Constantinos, opening the door of a square white room with graceful arched windows and furnishings done in shades of rose and gold. "It has its own bath attached," she continued, crossing the room to open a door and indicate a tiled bath. "Ah, Niko, you must show Jessica about the villa while Petra unpacks for her," she said without pause when Nikolas appeared with Jessica's luggage and set it in the middle of the floor.

Nikolas smiled, his eyes twinkling. "Jessica would probably like a bath instead; I know I would! Well, darling?" he asked, turning to Jessica with the smile still lingering in his eyes. "You have your choice, shall it be a guided tour or a bath?"

"Both," she said promptly. "Bath first, though."

He nodded and left the room with a careless "I'll be along in half an hour, then," thrown over his shoulder. Madame Constantinos took her leave soon after, leaving Jessica standing in the middle of the floor looking about the charming room and feeling deserted. She pulled off her travel-worn clothing and took a leisurely bath, returning to the room to find that Petra had efficiently unpacked for her in the meantime. She dressed in a cool sun dress and waited for Nikolas, but the time passed and after a while she realized that he didn't mean to return for her. He had simply offered to give her a tour to please his mother; he had no intention of spending that much time in her company. She sat quietly on the bed and wondered if she had a prayer of ever winning his love.

It was much later, after a light dinner of fish and *soupa avgolemono,* which was a lemon-flavored chicken soup Jessica found delicious, that Nikolas approached her as she stood on the terrace watching the waves roll onto the beach so far below. She would have liked to avoid him, but that would have looked odd, so she remained at the wall of the terrace. His hard fingers clasped her shoulders and drew her back against him; his head bent down to hers and it must have looked as though he was whispering sweet nothings in her ear, but what he said was, "Have you said anything to Maman to upset her?"

"Of course not," she whispered vehemently, giving in to the force of those fingers and leaning against his chest. "I haven't

seen her at all from the time she took me to my room until
dinner. She doesn't like me, of course. Isn't that what you
wanted?''

"No," he said, his mouth curving bitterly. "I didn't want you
here at all, Jessica."

Her chin rose proudly. "Then send me away," she dared him.

"You know I can't do that, either," he snapped. "I'm living
in torment, and I'll either crawl out of it or I'll pull you down
with me." Then he released her and walked away, and she was
left with the bitter knowledge of his hatred.

The day of her wedding dawned clear and bright with the
remarkable clarity that only Greece had. She stood in the window and looked out at the barren hills, every detail as sharp and
clear as if she had only to reach out her hand to touch them.
The crystalline sunlight made her feel that if she could only open
her eyes wide enough she would be able to see forever. She felt
at home here, on this rocky island with its bare hills and the
silent company of thousands of years of history, the warm and
unquestioning welcome of the dark-eyed people who embraced
her as one of their own. And today she would marry the man
who owned all this.

Though Nikolas's hostility was still a barrier between them,
she felt more optimistic today, for today the terrible waiting was
over. The traditional ceremony and the exuberant celebrations
that followed would soften him; he would have to listen to her
tonight, when they were alone in his bedroom, and he would
know the final truth when she gave him the unrivaled gift of her
chastity. Smiling, she turned away from the window to begin
the pleasant ritual of bathing and dressing her hair.

In the few days that she had been on the island she had already
become steeped in the traditions of the people. She had imagined
that they would be married in the small white church with its
arched windows and domed roof, the sunlight pouring through
the stained glass, but Petra had set her right about that. The
religious ceremony was seldom performed in the church, but
rather in the house of the groom's godfather, or *koumbaros,* who

also provided the wedding entertainment. Nikolas's godfather was Angelos Palamas, a rotund man of immense, gentle dignity, his hair and eyebrows white above eyes as black as coal. An improvised altar had been set in the middle of the largest room of Kyrios Palamas's house, and she and Nikolas would stand before the altar with the priest, Father Ambrose. She and Nikolas would wear wreaths of orange blossoms on their heads, the wreaths blessed by the priest and linked by a ribbon, as their lives would be blessed and linked.

With measured, dreamy movements, she braided her hair in a fat single braid and coiled it on her head in the hairstyle that signified maidenhood. In a little while Madame Constantinos and Petra would come in to help her dress, and she went to the closet and took down the zippered white plastic bag that held her wedding gown. She hadn't looked at it before, exercising a childish delight in saving the best for last, and now her hands were tender as she laid the bag on the bed and unzipped it, being careful not to catch any of the material in the zipper.

But when she drew the delicate, lovely dress out, her heart and breathing stopped, and she dropped it as if it had turned into a serpent, turning blindly away with hot tears pouring down her cheeks. He had done it! He had countermanded her instructions while she was in the dressing room being measured, and instead of the white dress she had dreamed of, the creation that lay crumpled on the bed was a pale peach in color. She knew that the salon hadn't made a mistake; she had been too positive in her request for white for that. No, it was Nikolas's doing, and she felt as if he had torn out her heart.

Wildly she wanted to destroy the dress, and she would have if she had had anything else suitable, but she hadn't. Neither could she bring herself to pick it up; she sat in the window with the scalding tears blinding her and sticking in her throat, and that was how Petra found her.

Strong, gentle arms went about her and she was drawn against the woman's bosom and rocked tenderly. ''Ah, it is always so,''

Petra crooned in her deep voice. "You weep, when you should laugh."

"No," Jessica managed in a strangled voice, pointing in the direction of the bed. "It's my gown."

"The wedding gown? It is torn, soiled?" Petra went over to the bed and picked up the gown, inspecting it.

"It was supposed to be *white*," Jessica whispered, turning her small, drowned face back to the window.

"Ah!" Petra exclaimed, and left the room. She returned in only a moment with Madame Constantinos, who went at once to Jessica and put her arm about her shoulders in the first warm gesture she'd made.

"I know you're upset, my dear, but it's still a lovely gown and you shouldn't let a mistake ruin your wedding day. You'll be beautiful in it—"

"Nikolas changed the color," Jessica explained tautly, having conquered the rush of tears. "I insisted on white—I was trying to make him understand, but he wouldn't listen. He let me think the dress would be white, but while I was in the dressing room, he changed the color."

Madame Constantinos caught her breath. "You insisted— what are you saying?"

Wearily Jessica rubbed her forehead, seeing that now she would have to explain. Perhaps it was just as well for Madame Constantinos to know the whole story. She searched for a way to begin and finally blurted out, "I want you to know, Madame—none of the things you've heard about me are true."

Slowly Madame Constantinos nodded, her blue eyes sad. "I think I had already realized that," she said softly. "A woman who had traveled as many roads and known as many lovers as have been attributed to you would have had some of that knowledge in her face, and your face is innocent of any such knowledge. I had forgotten how gossip can spread like a cancer and feed on itself, but you have reminded me and I promise I won't forget again."

Encouraged, Jessica said hesitantly, "Nikolas told me that you were a friend of Robert's."

"Yes," Madame Constantinos acknowledged. "I had known Robert Stanton for most of my life; he was a dear friend of my father's, and beloved of the entire family. I should have remembered that he saw things far more clearly than the rest of us. I've thought many harsh things about you in the past, my dear, and I'm deeply ashamed of myself. Please, can you possibly forgive me?"

"Of, of course," Jessica cried, jumping to her feet to hug the older woman and wipe at the tears that welled anew. "But I want to tell you how it was, how I came to marry Robert. After all, you have a right to know, since I'm going to marry your son."

"If you'd like to tell me, please do so, but don't feel that you owe an explanation to me," Madame Constantinos replied. "If Niko is satisfied, then so am I."

Jessica's face fell. "But he isn't satisfied," she said bitterly. "He believes all of the tales he's heard, and he hates me almost as much as he wants me."

"Impossible," the older woman gasped. "Niko couldn't be that much of a fool; it's so plain that you're not a scheming adventuress!"

"Oh, he believes it, all right! It's partly my fault," she admitted miserably. "At first, when I wanted to hold him off, I let him think that I—I was frightened because I'd been mistreated. I've tried since then to explain to him, but he simply won't listen; he refuses to talk about my 'past affairs' and he's furious because I won't go to bed with him—" She stopped, aghast at what she had blurted out to his mother, but Madame Constantinos gave her a startled look, then burst into a peal of laughter.

"Yes, I can imagine that would make him wild, because he has his father's temperament." She chuckled. "So, you must convince my blind, stubborn son that your experience is wholly fictional. Do you have any idea how you might accomplish such a thing?"

"He'll know," Jessica said quietly. "Tonight. When he realizes that I have a right to a white wedding dress."

Madame Constantinos gasped as at last she realized the significance of the dress. "My dear! But Robert—no, of course not. Robert was not a man to wed a young girl for physical gratification. Yes, I think I must hear how this came about, after all!"

Quietly Jessica told her of how she had been young and alone and Robert had wanted to protect her, and of the vicious gossip she had endured. She left out nothing, not even how Nikolas had come to propose to her, and Madame Constantinos was deeply troubled when the tale ended.

"There are times," she said slowly, "when I would like to smash a vase over Niko's head, even if he is my son!" She looked at the wedding gown. "Have you nothing else to wear? Nothing white?"

Jessica shook her head. "No, nothing. I'll have to wear it."

Petra brought crushed ice and folded it in hand towels to make compresses for her eyes, and after half an hour all traces of her tears had gone, but she was unnaturally pale. She moved slowly, all vitality gone from her, all sparkle killed. Gently Madame Constantinos and Petra dressed her in the peach gown and set the matching veil on her head, then they led her from the room.

Nikolas wasn't there; he was already at the home of his godfather, but the villa was filled with relatives, aunts and uncles and cousins who smiled and chattered and patted her as she passed. None of her friends were there, she realized with a start, but then, there were only two: Charles and Sallie. That made her feel more alone, chilled as if she would never again be warm.

Andros was to escort her down the path that led to the village, and he waited for her now, tall and dark in a tuxedo, and momentarily looking so much like Nikolas that she gasped. Andros smiled and gave her his arm; his manner had warmed over the past few days and now he was frankly solicitous as he discovered how she trembled, how cold her hands were.

Nikolas's female relatives rushed outside to form an aisle from the top of the hill down to the village, standing on both sides of the path. As she and Andros reached them, they began to toss orange blossoms down on the path before her, and the village women were there in traditional dress, tossing small, fragrant white and pink blossoms. They began to sing, and she walked on flowers down the path to join the man she would marry, but still she felt frozen inside.

At the door of Kyrios Palamas's house Andros gave her over to the arm of Nikolas's godfather, who led her to the altar, where Nikolas and Father Ambrose waited. The altar, the entire room, danced with candles, and the sweet smell of incense made her feel as if she was having a dream. Father Ambrose blessed the wreaths of orange blossoms that were set on their heads as they knelt before the altar, and from that moment on it was all a blur. She had been coached on what to say and she must have made the proper responses; when Nikolas made his vows, his deep, dark voice reverberated inside her head and she looked around a little wildly. Then it was over, and Father Ambrose joined hands with them and they walked around the altar three times while little Kostis, one of Nikolas's innumerable cousins, walked before them waving a censer, so they progressed through clouds of incense.

Almost immediately the crowded room burst into celebration, everyone laughing and kissing each other, while cries of "The glass! The glass!" went up. The newly married couple was laughingly shoved to the hearth, where a wineglass was turned upside down. Jessica remembered what she should do but her reactions were dulled by her misery and Nikolas easily beat her, his foot smashing the wineglass while the villagers cheered that Kyrios Constantinos would be the master in his house. As if it could ever be any other way, Jessica thought numbly, turning away from the devilish gleam in Nikolas's black eyes.

But he caught her back to him, his hands hard on her waist and his eyes glittering as he forced her head up. "Now you're legally mine," he muttered as he bent his head and captured her lips.

She didn't fight him, but the response that he had always

known was lacking. He raised his head, frowning when he saw
the tears that clung to her lashes. "Jessica?" he asked questioningly, taking her hand, his frown deepening when he felt its
iciness, though the day was hot and sunny.

Somehow, though afterward she wondered at her stamina, she
made it through the long day of feasting and dancing. She had
help in Madame Constantinos and Petra and Sophia, who gently
made it clear that the new Kyria was weak with nerves and not
able to dance. Nikolas threw himself into the celebration with
an enthusiasm that surprised her until she remembered that he
was Greek to the bone, but even with all the laughing and dancing and the glasses of ouzo he consumed, he returned often to
his bride and tried to entice her appetite with some delicacy he
had brought. Jessica tried to respond, tried to act normally, but
the truth was that she couldn't make herself look at her husband.
No matter how she argued with herself, she couldn't escape the
fact that she was a woman, and her woman's heart was easily
bruised. Nikolas had destroyed all of her joy in her wedding day
with the peach gown and she didn't think she would ever be
able to forgive him.

It was late; the stars were already out and the candles were
the only illumination in the house when Nikolas approached her
and gently swung her up into his arms. No one said anything;
no jokes were made as the broad-shouldered man left the house
of his godfather and carried his bride up the hill to his own villa,
and after he had disappeared from view, the celebration began
again, for this was no ordinary wedding. No, the Kyrios had
finally taken a bride, and now they could look forward to an
heir.

As Nikolas carried her up the path with no visible effort, Jessica tried to gather her scattered wits and push her unhappiness
aside, but still the cold misery lay like a lump in her chest. She
clung to him with her arms around his neck and wished that it
was miles and miles to the villa and perhaps then she would be
more in control of herself by the time they arrived. The cool
night air soothed her face and she could hear the rhythmic thun-

der of the waves as they pounded against the rocks, and those seemed more real to her than the flesh-and-blood man who carried her in his arms.

Then they were at the villa and he carried her around the side of the terrace until he reached the double sliding glass doors of his bedroom. They opened silently at his touch and he stepped inside, letting her slide gently to the floor.

"Your clothes have been brought in here," he told her softly, kissing the hair at her temple. "I know you're frightened, darling; you've been acting strange all day. Just relax; I'll fix myself a drink while you're changing into your nightgown. Not that you'll need a nightgown, but you do need some time to calm down," he said, grinning, and suddenly she wondered just how many glasses of ouzo he'd had.

He left her and she stared wildly around the room. She couldn't do it; she couldn't share that big bed with him when she felt as she did. She wanted to scream and cry and scratch his eyes out, and in a sudden burst of tears and sheer temper she tore the peach gown off and looked around for scissors to destroy it. There were no scissors to be found in the bedroom, however, so she tore at the seams until they ripped apart, then she threw the gown on the floor and kicked it.

She drew a deep, shuddering breath into her lungs and wiped the furious tears off her cheeks. The gesture had been childish, she knew, but she felt better for it. She hated that gown, and she hated Nikolas for ruining her wedding day!

He would be returning soon, and she didn't want to face him while wearing nothing but her underwear, but neither did she have any intention of putting on a seductive nightgown for his benefit. She threw open the closet door and grabbed the one pair of slacks she had with her and a pullover top. Hastily she snatched the top over her head just as the door opened.

Thick silence reigned as Nikolas took in the tableau of her standing there clutching a pair of slacks and staring at him with anger and fear plain in her wide eyes. His black gaze wandered to the tattered wedding gown on the floor, then back to her.

"Settle down," he said softly, almost in a whisper. "I'm not going to hurt you, darling, I promise—"

"You can keep your promises," she cried hoarsely, dropping the slacks to the floor and pressing her hands to her cheeks as the tears began to slide from her eyes. "I hate you, do you hear? You—you *ruined* my wedding day! I wanted a white gown, Nikolas, and you had them use that horrible peach! I'll never forgive you for that! I was so happy this morning, then I opened the bag and saw that ugly peach thing and I—I— Oh, damn you, I've cried enough over you; I'll never let you make me cry again, do you hear? I hate you!"

Swiftly he crossed the room to her and put his hands on her shoulders, holding her in a grip that didn't hurt but nevertheless held her firmly. "Was it so important to you?" he murmured. "Is that why you haven't looked at me all day, all over a silly gown?"

"You don't understand," she insisted through her tears. "I wanted a white one, and I wanted to keep it and give it to our daughter for *her* wedding—" Her voice broke and she began to sob, trying to turn her head away from him.

With a muttered curse he pulled her to him and held her tightly in his arms, his dark head bent to rest atop her tawny one. "I'm sorry," he whispered into her hair. "I didn't understand. Don't cry, darling; please don't cry."

His apology, so unexpected, had the effect of startling her out of her tears, and with a caught breath she raised her tear-wet eyes to stare at him. For a moment, their eyes held; then his midnight gaze slipped to her mouth, and as quickly as that he was kissing her, pulling her even closer to his powerful frame as if he could make her a part of himself, his mouth hungrier and more devouring than it had ever been before. She tasted the ouzo he had been drinking, and it made her drunk, too, so that she had to cling to him even to stand upright.

Impatiently he scooped her up in his arms and carried her to the bed, and for a moment she stiffened in alarm as she remembered that she still hadn't told him the truth. "Nikolas...wait!" she cried breathlessly.

"I've been waiting," he said thickly, his restless mouth raining kisses across her face, her throat. "I've waited for you until I thought I would go mad. Don't push me away tonight, darling—not tonight."

Before she could say anything else, his mouth closed over hers again. In the sweet intoxication sweeping over her at the touch of his lips, she momentarily forgot her fears, and then it was too late. He was beyond listening to her, beyond the reach of any plea as he responded only to the force of his passion.

Still she tried to reach him. "No, wait!" she said, but he ignored her as he pulled her top over her head, momentarily smothering her in the folds of material before he freed her from it and tossed the garment aside. His eyes were glittering feverishly as he stripped her underwear away, and her pleas for patience stuck in her throat as he dropped his robe and covered her with his powerful body. Panic bloomed in her, and she tried to control it, forcing herself to think of other things until she regained some small measure of self-control, but it was useless. A thin sob tore out of her throat as Nikolas drew her down into the fathomless well of his desire, and blindly she clung to him as the only tower of strength in a wildly shaking world.

Chapter 10

Jessica lay in the darkness listening to Nikolas's even breathing as he slept, and her flesh shrank when he moved in his sleep and his hand touched her breast. Slowly, terrified of waking him, she inched away from his hand and off the bed. She couldn't just lie there beside him when every nerve in her body screamed for release; she'd go for a walk, try to calm herself down and sort out her tangled emotions.

Silently she pulled on the discarded slacks and top and let herself out through the sliding doors onto the terrace. Her bare feet made no sound as she walked slowly around the terrace, staring at the faint glow of the breakers as they crashed onto the rocks. The beach drew her; she could walk down there without taking the risk of waking anyone, though she doubted that anyone would still be up now. It had to be nearing dawn; or perhaps it wasn't, but it seemed as though she had spent hours in that bedroom with Nikolas.

Depression weighed on her shoulders like a rock. How silly and stupid she had been to think she would be able to control Nikolas even for a moment. If he had loved her, it might have been possible, but the raw truth of the matter was that Nikolas felt nothing for her except lust, and now she had to live with that knowledge.

She walked slowly along the rim of the cliff, hunting for the narrow, rocky path that led down to the beach, and when she found it, she began a careful descent, well aware of the treacherously loose rocks along the path. She gained the beach and found that only a thin strip of sand was above the tide and that the incoming waves washed about her ankles as she walked. The tide must be coming in, she thought absently; she'd have to keep watch on it and climb up before the water got too deep.

For just a moment she had managed to push away thoughts of Nikolas, but now they returned, swooping down on her tired mind like birds of prey. She had wagered her happiness in the battle with him and she had lost. She had given her innocence to a man who didn't love her, all for nothing. Nothing! In the dark, savage hours of the night it had been forced into her consciousness that she had gained nothing, and he had gained everything. He had wanted only the release he could find with her flesh, not her virginity or her love. She felt used, degraded, and the bitterest knowledge of all was that she had to see it through. He'd never allow her to leave him. She had learned to her cost that mercy was not a part of Nikolas's character.

She almost choked on her misery. It hadn't been at all as she had imagined. Perhaps if Nikolas had been tender, adoring, easy with her, she wouldn't feel so shocked and shattered now. Or perhaps if he hadn't been so frustrated, if he hadn't drunk so much ouzo, he would have been more patient, better able to cope with her fright. If, if! She tried to excuse him by telling herself that he had been pushed past control; she told herself over and over that it was her own fault; she should have made him listen before. But after a day of unbroken pain and unhappiness, it was too much for her to handle just now.

A wave suddenly splashed above her knees and with a start she looked about. The tide was still coming in, and the path was a long way down the beach. Deciding that it would be easier to climb over the rocks than to resist the tide, she clambered up on the jagged rocks that lined the beach and began picking her way over them. She had to watch every step, for the moonlight was treacherous, making her misjudge distances. Several times she wrenched her ankles, despite taking all the care in the world, but she persisted and at last, when she looked up, she saw that she was only a few feet from the path.

In relief she straightened and stepped onto a flat rock; but the rock was loose and she dislodged it, sending it skittering down, to splash into the water. For a moment she teetered, trying to regain her balance, but another rock slipped under her foot and with a cry she fell sideways. Her head banged against a rock and instant nausea boiled in her stomach; only instinct kept her clawing at the rocks, trying to catch herself before she fell the entire distance. Her hands tore other rocks loose and she fell painfully, the loose rocks bouncing down onto her and knocking others loose in their turn. She had started a small avalanche and they piled up against her.

When the hail of rocks had stopped, she raised her head and gasped painfully for breath, not certain what had happened. Her head throbbed alarmingly, and when she put her hand up, she felt the rapidly swelling knot under her hair. At least she wasn't bleeding, as far as she could tell, and she hadn't fallen into the water. She sat for a moment trying to still the alarming sway of her vision and the nausea that threatened. The nausea won, and she retched helplessly, but afterward she didn't feel any better. Slowly she realized that she must have hit her head harder than she had first thought, and her exploring fingers told her that the swelling now extended over almost the entire side of her head. She began to shiver uncontrollably.

She wasn't going to get any better sitting here; she needed to get to the villa and wake someone to call a doctor. She tried to stand and groaned aloud at the pain in her head. Her legs were like dead weights; they didn't want to move. She tried again to stand, and it wasn't until another rock was dislodged by her struggles that she saw the rocks lying across her legs.

Well, no wonder she couldn't stand, she told herself fuzzily, pushing at the rocks. She could move some of them, despite the dizziness that made her want to lay her head down and rest, and she pushed those into the sea where it boiled only a few feet below her.

But some of the rocks were too heavy, and her lower legs were securely pinned. She had made a mess of her midnight walk, just as she had made a mess of her marriage; it seemed she couldn't do anything right! Helplessly she began to laugh, but that hurt her head and she stopped.

She tried shouting, knowing that no one would hear her above the booming of the tide, especially as far away as she was from the villa, and shouting hurt her head even worse than laughing had. She fell silent and tilted her head back to stare at the two moons that swung crazily in the sky. Two moons. Two of everything.

A wave hit her in the face and it cleared her senses for a moment. The tide was still coming in. How high did the tide get here? She couldn't remember noticing. Was it nearly high tide now? Would the water soon start dropping? Smiling wearily, she leaned over and rested her throbbing head on her curled-up arm.

A long time later she was roused by the sound of someone shouting her name. Oddly, she couldn't raise her head, but she opened her eyes and stared through the dim gray light of dawn, trying to see who had called her. She was cold, so cold, and it hurt to keep her eyes open. With a sigh, she closed them again. The shout came again, and now the voice was strangled. Perhaps someone was hurt and needed help. Gathering her strength, she tried to sit up, and the explosion of pain in her head sent her reeling into a tunnel of darkness.

Nightmares tormented her. A black-eyed devil kept bending over her, hurting her, and she screamed and tried to push him away from her, but he kept coming back when she least expected it. She wanted Nikolas, he would keep the devil from hurting her, but then she would remember that Nikolas didn't love her and she knew she had to fight alone. And there was the pain in her head, her legs, that stabbed at her whenever she tried to push the devil away. Sometimes she cried weakly to herself, wondering when it would end and someone would help her.

Gradually she realized that she was in a hospital. She knew the smells, the sounds, the starchy white uniforms that moved around. What had happened? Oh, yes, she had fallen on the rocks. But even when she knew where she was, she still cried out in fear when that big, black-eyed man leaned over her. Part of her knew now that he wasn't a devil; he must be a doctor, but there was something about him…he reminded her of someone….

Then at last she opened her eyes and her vision was clear. She lay very still in the high hospital bed, mentally taking stock of herself and discovering what parts worked, what parts didn't work. Her arms and hands generally obeyed commands, though a needle was taped to the inside of her left arm and a clear plastic line attached it to an upside-down bottle that hung over her head. She frowned at the apparatus until that became clear in her mind and she knew it for what it was. Her legs worked also, though every movement was painful and she was stiff and sore in every muscle.

Her head. She had banged her head. Slowly she raised her right arm and touched the side of her head. It was still swollen and tender, but her hair was still there, so she knew that the injury hadn't been serious enough to warrant surgery. All in all, she was extremely lucky, because she hadn't drowned, either.

She turned her head and discovered immediately that it wasn't a smart move; she closed her eyes against the bursting pain, and when it had subsided to a tolerable ache, she opened her eyes again, but this time she didn't move her head. Instead, she looked about the hospital room carefully, moving nothing but her eyes. It was a pleasant room, with curtains at the windows, and the curtains were drawn back to let in the golden crystal of the sunshine. Comfortable-looking chairs were set about the room, one right beside her bed and several others against the far wall. An icon was set in the corner, a gentle little statue of the Virgin Mary in colors of blue and gold, and even from across the room Jessica could make out the gentle, glowing patience on her face. She sighed softly, comforted by the delicate Little Mother.

A sweet fragrance filled the room, noticeable even above the hospital smells of medicine and disinfectant. Great vases of flowers were set about the room, not roses as she would have expected, but pure white French lillies, and she smiled as she looked at them. She liked lillies; they were such tall, graceful flowers.

The door opened slowly, almost hesitantly, and from the corner of her eye Jessica recognized the white of Madame Constantinos's hair. She wasn't foolish enough to turn her head again but she said, "Maman," and was surprised at the weakness of her own voice.

"Jessica, love, you're awake again," Madame Constantinos said joyously, coming into the room and closing the door behind her. "I should tell the doctor, I know, but first I want to kiss you, if I may. We've all been so worried."

"I fell on the rocks," Jessica said by way of explanation.

"Yes, we know," Madame Constantinos said, brushing Jessica's cheek with her soft lips. "That was three days ago. To complicate the concussion you had, you developed an inflammation in your lungs from the soaking you received, all on top of shock. Niko has been frantic; we haven't been able to make him leave the hospital even to sleep."

Nikolas. She didn't want to think about Nikolas. She thrust all thoughts of him out of her tired mind. "I'm still so tired," she murmured, her eyelashes fluttering closed again.

"Yes, of course," Madame Constantinos said gently, patting her hand. "I must tell the nurses now that you're awake; the doctor will want to see you."

She left the room and Jessica dozed, to be awakened some unknown time later by cool fingers closing around her wrist. She opened her eyes to drowsily study the dark, slightly built doctor who was taking her pulse. "Hello," she said when he let her wrist down onto the bed.

"Hello, yourself," he said in perfect English, smiling. "I am

your doctor, Alexander Theotokas. Just relax and let me look
into your eyes for a moment, h'mmm?''

He shone his little pencil flashlight into her eyes and seemed
satisfied with what he found. Then he listened intently to her
heart and lungs, and at last put away his chart to smile at her.

''So, you've decided at last to wake up. You sustained a rather
severe concussion, but you were in shock, so we postponed surgery until you had stabilized, and then you confounded us by
getting better on your own,'' he teased.

''I'm glad,'' she said, managing a weak smile. ''I don't fancy
myself bald-headed.''

''Yes, that would have been a pity,'' he said, touching a thick
tawny strand. ''Until you consider how adorable you would have
been with short baby curls all over your head! Nevertheless,
you've been steadily improving. Your lungs are almost clear
now and the swelling is nearly gone from your ankles. Both legs
were badly bruised, but no bones were broken, though both ankles are sprained.''

''The wonder is that I didn't drown,'' she told him. ''The tide
was coming in.''

''You were soaking wet anyway; the water reached at least to
your legs,'' he told her. ''But you've improved remarkably; I
think that perhaps in another week or ten days you may go
home.''

''So long?'' she questioned sleepily.

''You must wait until your head is much better,'' he said,
gently insistent. ''Now, you have a visitor outside who is pacing
a trench in the corridor. I will light a candle tonight in thanks
that you have recovered consciousness, for Niko has been a wild
man and I was at my wits' end trying to control him. Perhaps
after he has talked to you he will get some sleep, eh, and eat a
decent meal?''

''Nikolas?'' she asked, her brow puckering with anxiety. She
didn't feel up to seeing Nikolas now; she was so confused. So
many things had gone wrong between them....

· ''No!'' she gasped, reaching out to clutch the doctor's sleeve with weakly desperate fingers. "Not yet—I can't see him yet. Tell him I've gone back to sleep—"

"Calm down, calm down," Dr. Theotokas murmured, looking at her sharply. "If you don't want to see him, you don't have to. It's simply that he has been so worried, I thought perhaps you might tell him at least to go to a hotel and get a good night's sleep. He has been here for three days, and he's scarcely closed his eyes."

Madame Constantinos had said much the same thing, so it must be true. Taking a deep breath, she steadied her wildly tingling nerves and breathed out an assenting murmur.

The doctor and his retinue of nurses left the room, and immediately the door was pushed open again as Nikolas shouldered his way past the last nurse to leave. After one shocked glance, Jessica looked away. He needed to shave and his eyes were hollow and red with exhaustion. He was pale, his expression strained. "Jessica," he said hoarsely.

She swallowed convulsively. After that one swift glance, she knew that the devil who had tormented her in her nightmares was Nikolas; the devil had had those same dark, leanly powerful features. She remembered him bending over her that night, her wedding night, and she shuddered.

"You—you look terrible," she managed to whisper. "You need to sleep. Maman and the doctor said you haven't slept—"

"Look at me," he said, and his voice sounded as though he was tearing it out of his throat.

She couldn't. She didn't want to see him; his face was the face of the devil in her nightmares, and she still lingered halfway between reality and that dream world.

"Jessica, my God, look at me!"

"I can't," she choked. "Go away, Nikolas. Get some sleep; I'll be all right. I just—I just can't talk to you yet."

She sensed him standing there by her side, willing her to look at him, but she closed her eyes again on an acid burning of tears, and with a smothered exclamation he left the room.

It was two days before he visited her again and she was grate-

ful for the respite. Madame Constantinos had carefully explained
that Nikolas was asleep, and Jessica believed it. He had looked
totally exhausted. According to his mother, he slept for thirty-
six hours, and when she reported with satisfaction in her voice
that Niko had finally woken up, Jessica began to brace herself.
She knew that he would be back, and she knew that this time
she wouldn't be able to put him off. He had given in to her the
last time only because she was still so groggy and he had been
tired; she wouldn't have that protection now. But at least now
she could think clearly, though she still had no idea what she
would do. She only knew her emotions; she only knew that she
bitterly resented him for ruining her wedding day, childish
though she knew she was being about that. She was also angry,
with him and with herself, because of the fiasco of their wedding
night. Anger, humiliation, resentment and outraged pride all
warred within her, and she didn't know if she could ever forgive
him.

She had improved enough that she had been allowed out of
bed, even though she went no farther than the nearest chair. Her
head still ached sickeningly if she tried to move rapidly, and in
any case her painful ankles did not yet permit much walking.
She found the chair to be marvelously comfortable after lying
down for so long, and she talked the nurses into leaving her
there until she tired; she was still sitting up when Nikolas came.

The afternoon sun streamed in through the windows and
caught his face, illuminating starkly the strong bone structure,
the grim expression. He looked at her silently for a long moment,
and just as silently she stared back, unable to think of anything
to say. Then he turned and hung the DO NOT DISTURB sign
on the door, or at least she thought that was what it said, as she
couldn't read Greek.

He closed the door securely behind him and came around the
foot of the bed to stand before her chair, looking down at her.
"I won't let you run me out this time," he said grimly.

"No," she agreed, looking at her entwined fingers.

"We have a lot to talk about."

"I don't see why," she said flatly. "There's nothing to say. What happened, happened. Talking about it won't change anything."

His skin tightened over his cheekbones and suddenly he squatted down before her so he could look into her face. His chiseled lips were pulled into a thin line and his black eyes burned over her face. She almost flinched from him; fury and desire warred in his eyes, and she feared both. But she controlled herself and gave him back look for look.

"I want to know about your marriage," he demanded curtly. "I want to know how you came to me still a virgin, and damn it, Jessica, I want to know why in hell you didn't tell me!"

"I tried," she replied just as curtly. "Though I don't know why. I don't have to explain anything to you," she continued, unable to give in to his anger. She had endured too much from Nikolas; she couldn't take any more.

A vein throbbed dangerously in his temple. "I have to know," he muttered in a low tone, his voice becoming strained. "God in heaven, Jessica—please!"

She trembled to hear that word from him, to hear Nikolas Constantinos saying please to anyone. He, too, was under a great deal of tension; it was revealed in the rigid set of his shoulders, the uncompromising lines of his mouth and jaw. She let out her breath on a shuddering sigh.

"I married Robert because I loved him," she finally muttered, her fingers picking unconsciously at the robe she wore. "I still do. He was the kindest man I've ever known. And he loved me!" she asserted with a trace of wildness, lifting up her tangled tawny head to glare at him. "No matter how much filth you and people like you throw at me, you can't change the fact that we loved each other. Maybe—maybe it was a different kind of love, because we didn't sleep together, didn't try to have sex, but I would have given my life for that man, and he knew it."

His hand lifted, and even though she shrank back in the chair, he put his hand on her throat, caressing her soft skin and letting his fingers slide warmly to her shoulder, then downward to cup a breast where it thrust against her robe. Despite the tingle of alarm that ran along her skin, she didn't object to his touch, because she had learned to her cost that he could be dangerous when he was thwarted. Instead, she watched the raw hunger that leaped into his eyes.

His gaze lifted from where his thumb teased and aroused her flesh to probe her face. "And this, Jessica?" he asked hoarsely. "Did he ever do this to you? Was he incapable? Did he try to make love to you and fail?"

"No! No to all of it!" Her voice wobbled out of control and she took a deep breath, fighting for poise, but it was hard to act calm when the mere touch of his thumb on her breast was searing her flesh. "He never tried. He said once that love was much sweeter when it wasn't confused by basic urges."

"He was old," Nikolas muttered, suddenly losing patience with the robe and tugging it open, exposing the silky nightgown underneath. His fingers slid inside the low neckline to cup and stroke the naked curves under the silk, making her shudder with mingled response and rejection. "Too old," he continued, staring at her bosom. "He'd forgotten the fires that can burn away a man's sanity. Look at my hand, Jessica. Look at it on your body. It drove me mad to think of an old man's spotted, shriveled hand touching you like this. It was even worse than thinking of you with other men."

Involuntarily she looked down and a wild quiver ran through her at the contrast of his strong, dark fingers on her apricot-tinted flesh. "Don't talk about him like that," she defended shakily. "I loved him! And one day you, too, will be old, Nikolas."

"Yes, but it will still be *my* hand doing the touching." He looked up again and now two spots of color were spreading across his cheekbones as he became more aroused. "It wouldn't have made any difference how old he was," he admitted raggedly. "I couldn't bear the thought of any other man touching you, and when you wouldn't let me make love to you, I thought I'd go mad with frustration."

She couldn't think of anything to say and she drew back so that his hand was dislodged from her breast. Temper flared in his eyes and she realized that Nikolas would never be able to accept her will over his, even in the matter of her own body. The thought killed the tiny heat of response in her and she threw out coolly, "None of that matters now; it's over with. I think it would be best if I returned to London—"

"No!" he snapped savagely, rising to his feet and pacing about the small room with the restless stride of a panther. "I won't let you run away from me again. You ran away the other night and look what happened to you. Why, Jessica?" he asked, his voice suddenly husky. "Were you so frightened of me that you couldn't stay in my bed? I know that I— My God, why didn't you tell me? Why didn't you make me listen? By the time I realized, it was impossible for me to stop. It won't be like that again, sweet, I promise. I felt so guilty; then, when I saw you lying across those rocks, I thought that you'd—" He stopped, his face grim, and suddenly Jessica remembered the voice she thought had been pure imagination, calling out her name. So it had been Nikolas who had found her.

But his words froze her emotions in her breast. He felt *guilty*. She could think of a lot of reasons he could have given her for wanting her to stay, but few of them would have so insulted her sense of pride. She'd *swim* back to England before she'd stay with him merely to let him assuage his sense of guilt! She wanted to rage at him in her hurt and humiliation, but instead she pulled a mantle of deceptive calm about her and strove instinctively for her mask of cool disdain, so carefully cultivated over the years. "Why should I have told you?" she asked in a remote little voice, ignoring the fact that she had tried to do that very thing for weeks. "Would you have believed me?"

He made a slashing movement with his hand, as if that wasn't important. "You could have had a doctor examine you, given me proof," he growled. "You could have let me find out for myself, but in a manner much less brutal than what you endured. If you'd told me, if you hadn't fought…"

For a moment she merely stared at him, astonished at his unbelievable arrogance. Regardless of his billions and his surface sophistication, underneath he was Greek to the core of him and a woman's pride counted for nothing.

"Why should I prove anything to you?" she jeered out of the depths of her misery. "Were you a virgin? Who set you up to judge my character?"

Dark anger washed into his face and he took one long stride toward her, reaching out as if he longed to shake her, but then he remembered her injuries and he let his arms fall. She glared at him stonily as he drew a deep breath, obviously trying to control his temper. "You brought it on yourself," he finally snapped, "if that is your attitude."

"Is it my fault you're a bully and a tyrant?" she challenged, hearing her voice rise with temper. "I tried to tell you from the day we met that you were wrong about me, but you categorically refused to listen, so don't try to throw it all back on me! I should never have come back from Cornwall."

He stood looking down at her, his hard face unreadable, then his mouth twisted bitterly. "I'd have come after you," he said.

She pushed away the disturbing words and sought for control over her temper. When she could speak without any heat, she said distantly, "It's all over, anyway; it's no use crying about what might have been. I suggest a quiet, quick divorce—"

"No!" he gritted murderously. "You're my wife, and you'll stay my wife. I'm a possessive man, and I don't let my possessions go. You're mine, Jessica, in fact as well as in name, and you'll stay on the island even if I have to make you a prisoner."

"What a charming picture!" she cried in sudden desperation. "Let me go, Nikolas. I won't stay with you."

"You'll have to," he told her, his black eyes gleaming. "The island is mine, and no one leaves without my permission. The people are loyal to me; they won't help you to escape no matter how you charm them."

Impotently she glared at him. "I'll make you a laughing-stock," she warned.

"Try it, my dear, and you'll find out the extent of a Greek husband's authority over his wife," he warned. "I won't look such a laughingstock when you're sitting on pillows."

"You'd better not lay a hand on me!" she said furiously. "You may be Greek, but I'm not, and I won't be punished by you."

"I doubt if it will be necessary," he said, drawling now, and she knew that he was once more in command of the situation and aware of what he was going to do. "You'll be more cautious now about pushing me, won't you, love?"

"Get out!" she shouted, rising to her feet in a temper that made her forget her tender head, and she was forcefully reminded of her injuries as nauseating pain crashed into her skull and she wobbled on her unsteady feet. Instantly he was beside her, lifting her in his arms and placing her on the bed, easing her down onto the pillows. Through a haze of pain she said again, "Go away!"

"I'll go, until you've calmed down," he told her, leaning over her like the devil in her dreams. "But I'll be back, and I'll take you back to the island with me. Like it or not, you're my wife now and you'll stay my wife." On those final words he left her, and she stared through a mist of tears at the ceiling, wondering how she could endure such open warfare in the place of marriage.

Chapter 11

But it wasn't open warfare. Nikolas wouldn't allow that, and she was helpless to fight him. The only weapon she had was her coldness, and she used that relentlessly, not giving an inch to him when he came to visit her. He ignored her lack of response and talked to her pleasantly, telling her of the day-to-day happenings on the island and the people who asked about her. Everyone sent their love and wanted to know when she would be out of the hospital, and she found it extraordinarily difficult to keep from responding to that. In the few short days she had been on the island she had been made so welcome that she missed the people there, especially Petra and Sophia.

It was on the morning that she was released from the hospital that Nikolas shredded her self-possession, and he did it so easily that afterward she realized he had only been waiting until she was stronger to take action. When he sauntered into her room and found her already dressed and ready to leave, he kissed her casually before she could draw back, then released her before she could react to that, either.

"I'm glad you're ready," he commented, picking up the small suitcase containing the few clothes he had brought for her stay in the hospital. "Maman and Petra gave me strict orders to bring you back as soon as possible, and Sophia has cooked a special dinner for you. Would you like to have *soupa avgolemono,* eh? You liked that, didn't you?''

"Why don't you save yourself the trouble of taking me back and just put me on a plane for London?'' she asked coolly.

"And what if you did go to London?'' he returned, looking down at her with exasperation in his eyes. "You'd be alone, the butt of more cruelty than you can imagine, especially if you're pregnant.''

Stunned, she looked up at him and he said mockingly, "Unless *you* took precautions? No? I didn't think so, and I confess that the thought never entered my mind.''

Impotently she glared at him. She wanted to hit him, and at the same time she melted oddly inside at the thought of having his baby. Damn him, in spite of everything, she knew with a bitter sense of resignation that she still loved him. It wasn't something she would recover from, yet she wanted to hurt him because he had hurt her. She was shocked at the violence of her feelings and she tore her gaze away from him, looking down at her hands.

It took every ounce of her willpower to keep the tears from falling and she said defeatedly, "All right. I'll stay until I know if I'm going to have a baby or not.''

"That could take a while,'' he told her, smiling smugly. "After your fall, your entire system could be out of balance. And I intend to do everything I can to make you pregnant if that's what it takes to keep you on the island.''

"Oh!'' she cried, drawing away from him, shattered at the thought. Her panic was plain in her eyes as she stared at him. "Nikolas, no. I can't take that again.''

"It won't be like that again,'' he assured her, reaching out to catch her arm.

"I won't let you touch me!''

"That's another right husbands have over wives.'' He grinned, pulling her to him. "Make up your mind to it now, pet; I'm going to be exercising my marital rights. That's why I married you.''

She was so upset that she went without protest to the taxi he had waiting, and she didn't talk to him at all on the drive through Athens to the airport. At any other time she would have been enchanted with the city, but now she was frightened by his words and her head had begun to ache.

Nikolas's own helicopter was at the airport, fueled up and ready for flight, and through a haze of pain Jessica realized that he must have brought her to the hospital in the helicopter. She had no memory of anything after the last time she fainted on the rocks, and suddenly she wanted to know what had happened.

"Nikolas, you found me, didn't you? When I fell?"

"Yes," he said, frowning. He slanted a look down at her and his gaze halted, surveying her pale, strained face.

"What happened then? After you found me, I mean."

He took her arm and led her across the tarmac to the helicopter, walking slowly and letting her lean on him. "At first I thought you were dead," he said remotely, but the harsh breath he drew told her that the memory wasn't something he could handle easily, even now. "When I got down to you, I found that you were still alive and I dug you out from under those rocks, then carried you back up to the villa. Sophia was already up; she was beginning to cook when she saw me coming up the path with you, and she ran to help me."

They had reached the helicopter and he opened the door, then lifted her onto the seat and closed the door securely. He walked around and slid his long frame onto the seat in front of the controls and reached for the headset. He looked at it in his hand, frowning absently. "You were soaked, and shivering," he continued. "While Andros contacted the hospital and made arrangements for transportation from the airport to the hospital, Maman and I stripped you and wrapped you in blankets, then we flew here. You were in deep shock and surgery was postponed, though the doctors were concerned, but Alex told me that you almost certainly wouldn't survive major surgery at that time; your condition had to stabilize before he could even consider it."

"Then I got better," she finished for him, smiling wanly.

He didn't smile in return. "Your responses were better," he muttered. "But you developed a fever, and your lungs were inflamed. Sometimes you were unconscious; sometimes you were delirious and screamed whenever I or any of the doctors came near you." He turned his head to look at her, his eyes flat and bitter. "At least it wasn't just me; you screamed at every man."

She couldn't tell him that it had been him she had feared, and after a moment of silence he put the headset on and reached for the radio controls. Jessica leaned her head back and closed her eyes, willing the throb in her temples to go away, but when the rotors began turning, it increased the pain and she winced. A hand on her knee brought her eye-lids fluttering open and at Nikolas's concerned, questioning gaze she put her hands over her ears to let him know what was wrong. He nodded and patted her leg sympathetically, which made her want to cry. She closed her eyes again, shutting out the vision of him.

Unbelievably, she slept on the flight back to the island. Perhaps there was something in the medication she was still taking that made her drowsy, but Nikolas had to wake her when the flight was over and she sat up in confusion to see what seemed like the entire population of the island turned out for her arrival. Everyone was smiling and waving and she waved back, touched to tears by the warmth she felt from the islanders. Nikolas jumped from the helicopter, yelling something that made everyone laugh, then he reached her side as she released her seat belt and he slid the door open.

With an ease that both frightened and elated her, he reached in and lifted her against his chest. "I can walk," she protested.

"Not down the hill," he said. "You're still too wobbly. Put your arms around me, love; let everyone see what they want to see."

It was true that when she slid her arms around his muscular neck it seemed to please everyone, and several jocular-sounding remarks were made to him, to which he responded with grins and several remarks of his own. Jessica promised herself that she would learn Greek without delay; she wanted to know what he was saying about her.

He carried her down to the villa and straight to his bedroom, for she couldn't think of it as theirs. As he placed her on the bed, she looked around wildly, and before she could choke the words back, she cried out, "I can't sleep here, Nikolas!"

With a sigh he sat down on the edge of the bed. "I'm sorry you feel that way, darling, because you'll have to sleep here. Rather, you'll have to sleep with me, and that's what has you worried, isn't it?"

"Can you blame me?" she questioned fiercely.

"Yes, I can," he returned calmly, his black eyes implacable. "You're an intelligent, adult woman, and you should be capable of realizing that future lovemaking between us will be nothing like our wedding night. I was half-drunk, frustrated, and I lost control. You were frightened and angry and you fought me. The result was predictable and you got hurt. It won't be like that again, Jessica. The next time I take you, you'll enjoy it as much as I will."

"Can't you understand that I don't want you?" she flashed, unreasonably angry that he should so calmly plan on making love to her when she had said he couldn't. "Really, Nikolas, your conceit must be colossal if you imagine that I'd want to sleep with you after that night."

Temper flared in his eyes. "You can thank God that I know you so well, Jessica, or I'd make you regret those words!" he snapped. "But I *do* know you, and I know that when you're hurt and frightened you strike back like a spitting, clawing kitten, and you have years of practice in putting on that cold mask of yours. Oh, no, darling, you don't fool me. No matter how your pride tells you to resist me, I remember a night in London when you came to me and whispered that you loved me. You were sweet and shy that night; you weren't acting. Do you remember it, too?"

Jessica's eyes closed in horror. That night! How could she

forget? And how like Nikolas to remember the secret she had said aloud, thinking that he'd return the sweet words and admit to loving her. But he hadn't, not then and not since. Words of passion had come from his lips, but never words of love. Shaking, she cried out, "Remember? How can I forget? Like a fool I let you get too close to me, and the words were barely out of my mouth when you slapped me in the face with your true opinion of me. At least you opened my eyes, jerked me out of my silly dream. Love isn't immortal, Nikolas. It can die."

"Your's didn't die," he murmured confidently, a smile curving his hard, chiseled lips. "You married me, and you wanted your white gown for the wedding. You wore your hair in the style of a virgin; yes, I noticed. Everything you did shouted that you were marrying me forever, and that's how it will be. I've hurt you, darling, and I've made you unhappy, but I'll make it up to you. By the time our first baby is born, you'll have forgotten that I ever made you shed a tear."

That remark almost made her leap off the bed, and to prove him wrong she promptly burst into tears, which played havoc with her headache. With a comforting murmur Nikolas took her in his arms and lay down on the bed with her to hold her close and whisper soothingly to her, and perversely his nearness did calm her. At last she hiccupped into silence and nestled closer against him, her face buried in his shirt. Out of that doubtful sanctuary she said hesitantly, "Nikolas?"

"Yes, darling?" he muttered, his deep voice rumbling under her ear.

"Will—will you give me a little time, please?" she asked, raising her tear-stained face to him.

"I'll only give you time to recover completely," he replied, brushing her hair back from her temples with gentle fingers. "Beyond that, I won't wait. I can't. I still want you like mad, Mrs. Constantinos. Our wedding night was a mere appetizer."

She quivered in his arms at the sudden vision she had of being devoured by him, as if he were a hungry animal. She felt torn by indecision, loving him but unable to give in to him, to trust him or know what he was about. "Please don't rush me," she whispered. "I'll try; I really will. But I—I don't know if I'll ever be able to forgive you."

One corner of his mouth jerked before he firmed his lips together and said, "Forgive me or not, you're still mine, and I'll never let you go. I'll repeat it as many times as I have to to make you believe me."

"We've made a mess of it, Niko," she whispered painfully, tears filling her eyes again as she used the shortened, affectionate version of his name for the first time.

"Yes, I know," he muttered, his eyes going bleak. "We'll just have to try to salvage something and make our marriage work."

After he had gone, Jessica lay on the bed trying to quiet her confused emotions; she felt so many things at once that she was helpless to sort them out. With part of herself she wanted to melt into his arms and give in to the love which she still felt for him in spite of everything that had happened; the other part of her was bitterly angry and resentful and wanted to get as far away from him as possible. For years, she had suppressed pain and loneliness, but Nikolas had ripped away the barrier of her self-control and she could no longer push away or ignore the aches. Her long-controlled emotions were boiling out of her in a bitter release, and she resented the way he had torn away her defenses.

What a mockery of a marriage, she thought tiredly. A woman shouldn't require defenses against her husband; a marriage should be based on mutual trust and respect, and even now Nikolas felt neither of those things for her. She had thought that when he realized how wrong his assumptions concerning her had been, his entire attitude would change, but she'd been wrong. Perhaps he no longer resented her so bitterly, but he still would not allow her any authority concerning her own life. He wanted to control her, make her every movement subject to his whim, and Jessica didn't think she could tolerate a life like that.

After a time she dozed, and woke to the long shadows of late afternoon. Her headache had eased; in fact, it was gone, and she felt better than she had since the accident. Getting out of bed, she walked carefully to the bathroom, fearing an onset of her headache, but it didn't return and gratefully she stripped off her wrinkled clothing and ran water in the huge, red-tiled sunken tub. Petra had supplied the bathroom with an assortment of toiletries that surely Nikolas had never used, unless he had a hidden passion for perfumed bubble bath, and she poured the liquid liberally into the tub until it had mountains of foam in it.

After pinning her hair up, she stepped into the tub and sank down until the bubbles tickled her chin. She reached for the soap, then gave a frightened squeal as the door opened without warning. Nikolas stepped through, a worried frown creasing his brow, but the frown turned into a grin as he surveyed her where she lay, all but submerged in the bubbles. "Sorry, didn't mean to startle you," he said.

"I'm taking a bath," she said indignantly, and his grin spread wider.

"So I see," he agreed, dropping his tall frame onto the floor by the tub and sprawling out to lean on his elbow. "I'll keep you company, since this is the first time I've been privileged to witness your bath and wild horses couldn't drag me away."

"Nikolas!" she wailed, her cheeks flushing red.

"Now, calm down," he soothed, reaching out to run a finger over her nose. "I promised you that I wouldn't make a pass at you, and I won't, but I didn't promise that I wouldn't get to know my wife and let her become accustomed to me."

He was lying. Suddenly she knew that he was lying and she jerked away from his hand, tears springing to her eyes. "Get away from me!" she cried hoarsely. "I don't believe you, Nikolas! I can't stand it. Please, please go away!" If he stayed, he would take her to bed and make love to her, regardless of his promise. He had only told her that to catch her off guard, and she couldn't submit to him again. Shuddering sobs began to quake through her body, and with a muffled curse he got to his feet, his face darkening with fury.

"All right," he said through gritted teeth. "I'll leave you

alone. God, how I'll leave you alone! A man can take only so
much, Jessica, and I've had it! Keep your empty bed; I'll sleep
elsewhere.'' He stormed out of the bathroom, slamming the door
behind him with a force that jarred it on its hinges, and a second
later she heard the bedroom door slam, too.

She winced and drew a shuddering breath, trying to control
herself again. Oh, it was useless; this marriage would never
work. Somehow she'd have to convince Nikolas to set her free,
and after tonight that shouldn't be too difficult.

Nikolas, however, proved himself unyielding in his refusal to
let her leave the island. She was aware that he looked at the
situation as a battle he had every intention of winning, despite
her constant maneuvering to keep a comfortable distance between them. She also saw that his anger at her in the bathroom
had been largely staged, for what reason she didn't know. He
was irritated that she didn't fall into his arms whenever he
touched her, the way she had prior to their marriage, but he had
no intention of denying himself the pleasures of her body if he
could find the slightest weakness in her resistance. He was simply waiting, watching her carefully, ready to pounce.

The strain of keeping up a front of calmness and serenity
before everyone else was telling on her, but she didn't want to
distress Nikolas's mother, or even Petra or Sophia. Everyone had
been so kind to her—after her release from the hospital she had
been coddled shamelessly by the entire household—that the last
thing she wanted was to worry them with a warlike atmosphere.
By silent, mutual consent, she and Nikolas let it be assumed that
he slept in another room because her head still ached and his
restlessness interfered with her sleep. As she was still plagued
by headaches if she tried to exert herself in any way, the explanation was accepted without question.

Without making a big production out of it, she pretended that
she was not recovering as rapidly as she really was, using her
physical condition as a weapon against Nikolas. She rested frequently and would sometimes slip away without comment to lie
down with a cold, damp cloth over her eyes and forehead. Some-

one would usually check on her before too long, and in that manner she made certain the entire household was aware of her delicacy. She hated to trick them like that, but she had to protect herself, and she was aware that she would have to take whatever chance presented itself if she was to escape from the island. If everyone thought her weaker than she actually was, she had a better chance of succeeding.

The opportunity presented itself the next week when Nikolas informed them at the dinner table that he and Andros were flying to Athens the following morning; they would spend the night and return to the island the next day. Jessica was careful not to look up, certain that her expression would give her away. This was it! All she had to do was to hide on board the helicopter, and once they had landed in Athens and Nikolas and Andros had left to attend their meeting, she could slip out of the craft, walk into the terminal building, and purchase a ticket for a flight out of Athens.

She spent the evening making her plans; she retired early and packed the essentials she would take with her in the smallest suitcase she had, then replaced the case in the closet. She checked her purse to make certain that the money she had brought was still in her wallet; it was, as Nikolas no doubt felt certain that no one on the island was susceptible to a bribe, and in that he was probably correct. But she hadn't even thought of that, and now she was glad that she hadn't, as he would probably have taken the money away from her if she had tried something like that.

She counted the money carefully; when she had left England to travel to Paris with Nikolas, she had provided herself with enough cash to buy anything she might want, or to cover any emergency she was likely to encounter. Every penny was still there. She wasn't certain that it was enough to purchase a ticket to London, but she could certainly get out of Greece. Even if she could only get as far as Paris, she could telephone Charles and have him wire extra funds to her. Nikolas had control of her business concerns, but she hadn't emptied her bank account, and those funds were still available to her.

Later, when everyone had retired, she would take the suitcase and hide it in the helicopter. From her previous trips in it, she knew that there was a small space behind the rear seats, and she thought that there was enough room for both herself and the suitcase. To be certain, she would take a dark blanket and huddle under it on the floor if she couldn't get behind the seats. Remembering the construction of the helicopter, she thought it would be possible for someone to hide in that manner. The helicopter was built to carry six passengers, and the seats were broad and comfortable. Nikolas would pilot the craft himself, and Andros would be in the seat next to him; there would be no reason for them to look behind the rear seats.

As a plan, it had a lot of drawbacks, relying too heavily on chance and happenstance, but it was the only plan she had and probably the only chance she would have, as well, so she had to take the risk. It wasn't in her mind to disappear forever, but only until she'd had the chance to become certain within herself how she felt about Nikolas, and whether or not she wanted to continue with their marriage. All she asked was a little time and a little distance, but Nikolas wouldn't willingly give her what she needed. Jessica felt that she had been pushed and pulled more than she could stand. From the moment she had met Nikolas, he had maneuvered and manipulated her until she felt more like a doll than a woman, and it had become essential to her that she regain control of her own life.

Once, naïvely, she had thought that love could solve any problem, but that was another dream that had been shattered. Love didn't solve anything; it merely complicated matters. Loving Nikolas had brought her a great deal of pain and very little in the way of happiness. Some women could have been content with the physical gratification that he offered and accepted that he didn't love them in return, but Jessica wasn't certain that she possessed the sort of strength that required. That was what she had to discover about herself: whether she loved Nikolas enough to live with him regardless of the circumstances, whether she could make herself accept the fact that she had his desire but not his love. A lot of marriages were based on less than love, but she had to be certain before she let herself be maneuvered once again into a corner with nowhere to turn.

She knew her husband; his plan was to get her pregnant, thereby tying her irrevocably to the island and to him. She also knew that she had very little time left before he began putting his plan into action. He'd left her alone thus far, but she was nearly fully recovered now, and she sensed with sharpened instincts that he was now entirely unconvinced by her charade and would come to her bed at any time. She knew that she had to escape now if she was to have that time by herself to decide on a calm, reasonable level whether she could continue living with him.

After putting her purse away, she prepared for bed and turned out the lights, not wanting to do anything suspicious. She lay quietly in bed, her body relaxed but her mind alert to every sound in the villa.

The bedroom door opened, and a tall, broad-shouldered form threw a long shadow over her. "Are you awake?" Nikolas asked quietly.

For answer, Jessica reached out and switched on the lamp. "Is something wrong?" She struggled up to prop herself on her elbow, her eyes wide and wary as she watched him enter the room and close the door behind him.

"I need a few things from the closet," he informed her, and her heart stopped as she watched, paralyzed, while he crossed to the closet and slid the doors open. What if he should take the suitcase that contained the clothing she had packed? Why hadn't she insisted that he take his things out of the closet? But that would have looked odd to his mother, and in all honesty he hadn't taken advantage of the situation. What clothing he needed, he took from the closet sometime during the day, and never at times when he might find her undressed.

He took down one of his own suitcases made of dark brown

leather, and she drew a shuddering breath of relief. He looked at her sharply. "Are you feeling all right? You look ill."

"Just the usual headache." She forced herself to answer calmly, and before she could stop herself she blurted out, "Do you want me to pack for you?"

A grin slashed the darkness of his face. "Do you think I'll make an unholy mess of folding my shirts? I manage well enough, but thank you for the offer. When I return," he added thoughtfully, "I think I'll take you back to Dr. Theotokas for another examination."

She didn't want that, but as she planned to be gone before then she made no protest. "Because of the headaches? Didn't he say that it would take time for them to go away?"

He took a shirt from the clothes hanger and folded the garment neatly before placing it in the opened suitcase. "Yes, but I think you should be making a better recovery than you are. I want to make certain there aren't any other complications."

Like a pregnancy? The thought sprang without warning into her mind, and she began to tremble. It was possible, of course, but surely too early to tell. She didn't have any idea herself as yet. But wouldn't it be ironic if she managed to escape Nikolas's clutches and found that she was already pregnant? She wasn't certain what she would do if those circumstances arose, so she pushed the thought from her mind.

Conversation lapsed, and she propped herself higher on the pillow and watched as he completed his packing. When he closed the case and set it aside, he came to sit beside her on the bed. Uneasy at his nearness, she didn't say anything, her eyes unwavering as she watched him. A crooked little smile twitched at his lips. "I'll be leaving at dawn," he murmured, "so I won't wake you up. Will you give me a good-bye kiss tonight?"

She wanted to refuse, yet part of her yielded, held her motionless as he bent down and lightly pressed his mouth to hers. It wasn't a demanding kiss, and he straightened away from her almost immediately. "Good night, darling," he said softly, and putting his hands on her ribcage he eased her down beneath the light covers and began to tuck them in around her. She raised her eyes to meet his and gave him a small, timid smile, but it was enough to still his hands in their occupation.

He caught his breath, and his dark eyes began to gleam as the muted glow of the lamp caught their expression. "Good night," he said again, and leaned over her.

This time his mouth lingered, moving over her lips and molding them to meet the pressure of his. The pressure wasn't intense, but still the contact remained, warm and enticing, his breath sweet and heady with the wine they had had with dinner. Unconsciously she put her hand on his arm and stroked her fingers upward to clasp his shoulder, then on to curve about his neck. He deepened the kiss, his tongue meeting hers and exploring, making exciting forays against the sensitive places he found, and Jessica felt herself drifting into the red haze of sensual pleasure, not yet alarmed by his touch.

With a slow movement he folded the covers down far enough to let the soft curves of her breasts become visible to his avid gaze. He lifted his head from hers and watched as his long fingers slid beneath the thin silk of her nightgown and curved over the rich flesh, then moved up again to catch the strap and draw it down her arm. Jessica made a small gesture of fear, but he was being so slow and gentle that she didn't struggle; instead her lips sought his flesh eagerly, tasting the slightly salty taste of the skin along his cheekbone, the curve of his jaw. He turned his head and their mouths met again, and her eyelashes fluttered closed. The leisurely movement of his hand urged the pink silk slowly lower, baring the upper curve of one breast. Then the delicate rosy nipple was free and his hand left the strap to capture her exposed beauty.

"Now I'll kiss you good night," he whispered and he shifted so that his mouth slid down the arched curve of her throat. He paused, and his tongue explored the sensitive hollow between her neck and shoulder blade, making her shiver with a delight which was rapidly growing beyond her control. She didn't care. If he had only been this slow and tender on their wedding night, perhaps none of their problems would still exist. She lay quietly under his wandering touch, enjoying the delicate sensations and the spreading heat in her body.

Then his lips continued their journey and moved down the satin slope to close hotly over the throbbing bud. She moaned aloud and arched her back, her hand clenched in the rich thickness of his hair as she held his head to her. The gently pulling motions of his mouth set sharp twinges of pure physical desire shooting along her nerve endings. Her trembling intensified, and she started to reach for him; then he released her flesh and lifted his head, drawing back from her.

He was smiling, but the smile was sharp with triumph. "Good night, darling," he murmured, drawing the strap onto her shoulder again. "I'll see you in two days." Then he was gone, taking the suitcase and closing the door silently behind him, and Jessica lay on the bed, biting her lips to keep from screaming in both fury and frustration. He'd done that deliberately, seducing her with his gentleness until she forgot her fear, then not taking her to fulfillment. Were his actions motivated by revenge for the way she'd refused his advances before, or was it all a calculated maneuver to bring her to heel? She rather thought it was the latter, but she was more determined than ever not to give in to him. She would *not* be his sexual slave!

The thought of her escape gave her grim pleasure. He was so certain of his victory; let him wonder what had gone wrong when he found that his wife had fled rather than sleep with him. Nikolas was far too selfish and self-confident; it would do him a world of good to have someone stand up to him every so often.

She set the alarm on the clock for 2:00 a.m., then settled down in the bed, hoping she could sleep. She did, eventually, but had had only a few hours of rest when the alarm went off. She silenced it quickly and got out of bed, then used the flashlight that was always in the drawer of the table by the bed to find her jeans, shirt, and a pair of crepe-soled shoes. She inched the closet door open and removed the small suitcase, then went over to the sliding glass doors that led to the terrace. She released the lock with only a faint click, her hands steady as she slid the door open just enough to allow her to slip through the opening. Hastily she switched off the flashlight, hoping no one was up at this hour to see the betraying light.

There was no moon, but the faint starlight was enough to guide her as she avoided the furniture set about the terrace and made her way silently around to the front of the house. She left the terrace and followed the flagstone path which led up the hill to the helicopter pad. She had gone only a short distance when her legs began to ache and tremble with fatigue, an unwelcome reminder that she truly wasn't completely recovered. Her heart was hammering in her chest when she finally reached the helicopter, and she paused for a moment, breathing rapidly.

The door of the aircraft opened easily, and she crawled inside, banging her hip painfully with the suitcase and muttering an imprecation at the unwieldy luggage. She switched the flashlight on again to pick her way between the seats to the rear. The space behind the rear seats was a mere two feet deep, and she found immediately, by trying to curl up inside it, that it could not accommodate both herself and the suitcase. She placed the suitcase on the floor between the last two sets of seats, but decided that it could be seen too easily in that location.

She studied the interior of the helicopter for a minute, then folded herself once again into the hiding place and stood the suitcase between herself and the back of the seat; the seat was tilted forward a little, but not enough to be noticeable, she hoped. The position was cramped, and she wouldn't be able to move at all until they had landed in Athens and Nikolas and Andros had left, but it was the best she could manage. She left the suitcase in position and crawled out, her legs and arms already stiff from the short time she had been crouching there. She had intended to bring a blanket but had forgotten it, and now she promised herself that when she hid herself prior to takeoff she would have a blanket to cushion the hardness of the cold metal.

Elated, she carefully crept down the hill and into her bedroom and closed the sliding door behind her. She could have waited in the helicopter, but she had a cautious hunch that Nikolas might look in on her before he left, and she intended to be snug in her bed; underneath the nightgown, though, she would still have on her clothes.

Then she saw that she would have to remove her shirt if she didn't want it to be visible above the nightgown, and she wouldn't have a chance to put it on again. She would have very little time in which to reach the helicopter ahead of the two men, and she didn't want to waste any of it in dressing. She would keep the shirt on, and pull the covers up under her chin.

She kicked her shoes off and stood them beside the bed on the side away from the door, then lay down to rest. She wasn't even tempted to nap; her blood was racing through her veins in excitement, and she waited impatiently for the faint sounds in the silent house that would indicate that someone was moving around.

The sky was just beginning to lighten when she caught the sound of water running and knew that she hadn't long to wait now. She turned on her side to face the door and pulled the covers up snugly under her chin. Forcing herself to breathe deeply and steadily, she waited.

She didn't hear his footsteps; he moved as silently as a big cat, and the first indication she had of his presence was when the door opened almost without a sound and a thin sliver of light fell across the bed. Jessica concentrated on her breathing and peeped through her lashes at him as he stood in the doorway watching her. The seconds ticked away and panic began to coil in her stomach; why was he waiting? Did he sense that something was out of the ordinary?

Then he closed the door with a slow movement, and she drew a deep, shuddering breath of relief. She threw back the covers and slid her feet into the waiting shoes, then snatched up the dark brown blanket that she had gotten out earlier but forgotten to take with her, and let herself out the sliding doors.

Her heart was in her throat, interfering with her breathing as she ran as silently as she could around the house and up the hill.

How long did she have? Seconds? If they left the house before she was inside the helicopter, they would see her. Had Nikolas been dressed? She couldn't remember. Panting, she gained the crest of the hill and threw herself at the helicopter, wrenching at the door. It had opened so easily before, but now it was stubborn, and she fumbled at it for several agonizing seconds before the handle turned and the door opened. She scrambled in and closed the door, throwing a hasty look at the house to see if they were coming. No one was in sight yet, and she slumped in the front seat, limp with relief. She hadn't known that escaping would be so nerve-racking, she thought tiredly. Her entire body ached from the unaccustomed exertion, and her head had begun to throb.

Her movements were slower as she crawled to the back of the helicopter and tilted the seat forward to allow her into her hiding place. She spread the blanket and curled up in the small space, her head pillowed on her arm. She was so tired that, despite the uncomfortable position, she felt herself begin to drift into sleep, and it wasn't until Nikolas and Andros boarded the helicopter that she jerked herself back to awareness. They had noticed nothing unusual, it seemed, but she held her breath.

They exchanged a few words in Greek, and she gnawed her lip in frustration that she couldn't understand them. Madame Constantinos and Petra had taught her a few words, but she hadn't made much progress.

Then she heard the whine of the rotor as it began turning, and she knew that her plan had worked.

The vibration of the metal made her feel as if her skin were crawling, and already she had a cramp in her left calf. She cautiously moved her arm to rub the painful cramp, glad that the beating roar of the blades drowned out all sound. The noise reached a peculiar whine, and they lifted off, the aircraft tilting forward as Nikolas turned it away from the house and toward the sea that lay between the island and Athens.

Jessica had no idea how long the flight lasted, for her head was aching so badly that she closed her eyes and tried to lose herself in sleep. She didn't quite succeed, but she must have dozed because it was the cessation of noise as the blades slowed that alerted her to the fact that they had landed. Nikolas and Andros were talking, and after a moment they both left the helicopter. Jessica lay there listening to the dying whir of the blades. She was afraid to get out immediately in case they were still in the area, so she counted slowly to one thousand before she left her hiding place.

She was so stiff that she had to sit in a seat and rub her protesting legs before they would obey her, and her feet tingled as the circulation was restored. Retrieving the suitcase from behind the seat, she peered out, but could see no one who resembled her husband; so she took a deep breath, opened the door, and climbed out of the helicopter.

It surprised her that no one paid any attention to her as she walked casually across the tarmac and entered the terminal building. She knew from her own experiences that comings and goings at air terminals were carefully watched, and the very fact that no one stopped her to ask her business made her uneasy. It was still early, and though there were a good many people in the building it lacked the crush of the later hours; the women's rest room was almost empty, and none of the women there noticed her as she slipped into one of the stalls and locked the door, then opened her suitcase and took out her purse and the dress she was going to wear. Marveling at the modern fabrics which didn't wrinkle, she stripped off her jeans and shirt and folded them into the open case, then struggled into panty hose and pulled the dress over her head. The smooth, silky fabric felt good against her skin, and she settled the ice blue garment into place, then contorted her arms behind her back to do up the zipper. Comfortable, classic pumps completed the outfit. She placed her other shoes in the suitcase, then fastened it and picked it up in one hand, together with her purse, and left the cubicle.

She did a quick job on her hair, twisting it up and securing it loosely with a few pins, and added glossy coral color to her mouth. Her eyes stared back at her from the mirror, wide and filled with alarm, and she wished that she had sunglasses to hide behind.

Leaving the security of the rest room, she approached the ticket counter and asked the cost of a tourist class ticket to London. Luckily the fare was well within her means, and she purchased a ticket for the next available flight, but there she was stalled. The next flight wasn't until after lunch, and Jessica quailed at the thought of waiting that long. She would be missed on the island long before that; probably even now it had been noticed that she wasn't to be found. Would they search the island first, or notify Nikolas that his wife had disappeared? If only she'd thought to leave a note telling them that she'd gone with Nikolas! That way, no one would have known that she was missing, until Nikolas returned without her.

Her stomach protested its emptiness; so she went to the restaurant and ordered a light breakfast, then sat at the small table trying to force the food down her tight throat. The thought of something going wrong at this late stage was horrifying.

Leaving most of her meal on the plate, she purchased a fashion magazine and tried to ignore her anxiety as she flipped through the glossy pages, noting the newest styles. A glance at her watch increased her anxiety; surely Nikolas had been notified by now. What would he do? He had endless resources; he could tighten security to make certain that she didn't leave the country. She had to be on that jet before he discovered that she had left the island.

The clock ticked slowly, laboriously on. She forced herself to sit quietly, not wanting to draw attention to herself by pacing or in any way betraying her nervousness. The terminal was crowded now as tourists poured into Athens, and she tried to concentrate on the stream of people. How much longer? It was almost noon now. An hour and a half and she would be on her way, provided that there were no delays in takeoff.

When she felt someone at her elbow, she didn't respond immediately, hoping that it was a stranger, but the utter stillness told her that this was a forlorn hope. Fatalistically, Jessica turned her head and gazed calmly into the stony black eyes of her husband.

Though his face was expressionless, she could feel the force of his anger, and she knew that he was livid. Never before had she seen him this angry, and it took more courage than she had known she possessed to stand before him and give him back look for look, but she did it, lifting her chin defiantly. A savage glitter lit his eyes for a brief second, then he disciplined himself and leaned down to pick up her suitcase. "Come with me," he uttered between clenched teeth, and his long fingers wrapped around her arm to ensure that she did as he had ordered.

Chapter 12

He took her out to the parking area, where a dark blue limousine waited; to her embarrassment, Andros sat in the back. He moved to the opposite end of the seat, and Nikolas helped Jessica in, then climbed in beside her. He spoke sharply to the driver, and the vehicle was set in motion.

It was an utterly silent drive. Nikolas was grim, unspeaking, and she had no intention of unleashing his temper if she could avoid it. In a way, she decided that she was grateful for Andros's presence, as it forced her husband to restrain himself. She couldn't even think about later, when they would be alone.

The limousine stopped at the front entrance of a hotel so modern it would have fit in in the middle of Los Angeles more than in a city which had existed for thousands of years. Dragged along like a child in tow, she was forced to match Nikolas's long strides as they entered the hotel and took the elevator up to the penthouse. He probably owned the hotel, she thought wryly.

She was braced for the worst, and it was an anticlimax when he opened the door and ushered her inside the luxurious apartment, said tersely to Andros, "Don't let her out of your sight," and then left without even glancing at her.

When the door had closed behind him, Andros whistled

soundlessly between his teeth. He looked at Jessica ruefully. "I've never seen him so angry before," he told her.

"I know," she said, letting out her breath in a long sigh. "I'm sorry you had to be involved."

He shrugged. "He won't be angry with me unless I let you escape from me, and I don't intend to do that. I'm attached to my neck, and prefer to remain so. How did you leave the island?"

"I hid on the helicopter," she explained, sitting down in one of the extremely comfortable chairs and running her fingers over the royal blue upholstery. "I had it all planned, and it worked like a charm—except that the flight to London wasn't until after lunch."

He shook his head. "It wouldn't have made any difference. Don't you know that Niko would have traced you long before your flight landed, and you would have been met as you left the plane? Met and detained?"

She hadn't thought of that, and she sighed. If only she had left that note! "I wasn't leaving him for good," she explained, her voice troubled. "But I need some time by myself to think…" She halted, unwilling to discuss her marriage with Andros. He was much friendlier than he had been before he discovered that she loved Nikolas, but some basic reserve made it difficult for her to be so open.

Andros sat down across from her, his lean, dark face anxious. "Jessica, please remember that Niko isn't a man of compromises; yet he has constantly compromised his own rules since he met you. I don't know what has gone wrong between you. I thought that after the wedding things would be better. Would it make you feel more confident to know that Nikolas must care for you, or he wouldn't act as he does?"

No, that didn't help. Sometimes she thought that Nikolas was capable of feeling nothing but lust for her, and guilt that their wedding night had been such a fiasco for her. Their relationship was so tangled that she wondered if anything could save it now.

"Where did he go?" she asked, her spirit draining from her

as she remembered how he had refused to look at her. She had insulted him, deceived him, and he wouldn't easily forgive her.

"Back to the meeting he was attending," answered Andros. "It was urgent, or he wouldn't have returned."

Another black mark against her. He had left an important meeting to collect her, and he would be furious that others knew his wife was attempting to leave him.

"No one else knew," said Andros, guessing her thoughts. "He told me only when we were on the way to the airport."

Thank heaven for small favors, she thought, though she doubted that it would make much difference to Nikolas's temper.

There was nothing to do but wait for him to return; though there were books aplenty in the apartment, she couldn't settle down to read. Andros ordered lunch for both of them, and again she had to force herself to eat. After that, time dragged. She put records on the stereo and tried to relax, a useless effort; instead she paced the room, rubbing her arms as if she were chilled.

The magnificent sun was setting when the door finally opened and Nikolas entered, his dark face still a mask which revealed nothing. He didn't say a word to Jessica but conversed with Andros in rapid Greek. Finally Andros nodded and left the apartment, and she was alone with Nikolas.

Her stomach tightened in anticipation, but still he didn't look at her. Pulling his tie loose from his neck, he muttered, "Order dinner while I shower. And don't even try to leave; the staff will stop you before you reach the street."

She believed him and bit her lip in consternation as he disappeared into one of the rooms that opened off the lounge area. She hadn't explored the apartment, having been too nervous to have any interest in her surroundings, so she had no idea of what the different rooms were. Obediently she lifted the telephone and ordered dinner from someone who spoke excellent English, subconsciously choosing those foods that she had noticed Nikolas particularly liked. Was it a feminine instinct, to soothe away male ire by an offering of food? she wondered. When she realized what she had done, she smiled wryly at herself, feeling a strange kinship with cavewomen from thousands and thousands of years ago.

The food arrived as Nikolas reentered the lounge, his black hair still damp from his shower. He was simply dressed in black pants and a white silk shirt which clung to his body in patches where his skin was wet, leaving his dark skin visible beneath the thin fabric. She watched his face, trying to gauge the extent of his anger, but it was like trying to read a blank wall.

"Sit down," he said remotely. "You've had a busy day; you need to replenish your strength."

The lamb chops and artichoke hearts were the best she had ever tasted, and she was able to eat with an improved appetite despite his hostile presence across from her. She was nearly finished before he spoke again, and she realized that he had waited until then to keep from upsetting her and ruining her appetite.

"I called Maman," he said, "and told her that you were with me. She was frantic, of course; they all were. You'll apologize for your thoughtlessness when we return home, though I managed to gloss over it by telling Maman that you had smuggled yourself to Athens in order to be with me. She was glad that you felt well enough to pursue me so romantically," he finished sarcastically, and Jessica flushed.

"I didn't think of leaving a note until it was too late," she confessed.

He shrugged. "No matter. You'll be forgiven."

She placed her fork carefully beside the plate and gathered her courage. "I wasn't leaving you," she offered in explanation. "At least—"

"It damned well looked as though you were!" he snapped.

"Not permanently," she persisted.

"You're right about that. I would have had you back within two days at the most." He appeared to be on the verge of saying something else, but he bit back the words and said instead, "If you've finished, it would probably be wise if you took your bath now. I'll probably break your neck if I have to listen to your excuses right now!''

For a moment, Jessica sat there defiantly; then she pressed her lips together and did as he had directed. He was in no mood to be reasonable right now, and if she listened to very much more of his sarcasm she was likely to lose her own temper, and she didn't want that to happen. Scenes between herself and Nikolas could quickly become violent and always ended in the same manner, with him making love to her.

She locked herself in the giant bathroom and took a shower, not being in the mood for a long, relaxing bath in the tub. As she toweled herself dry, she noticed a dark blue robe hanging on a hook on the door, and as she hadn't brought a nightgown with her she borrowed the robe and tied it about her. It was enormous, and she had to roll the sleeves up before her hands peeped out. She had to lift the hem in order to walk, and she held the gathered material in her hand as she left the bathroom.

''Very fetching,'' Nikolas drawled from his reclining position on the bed.

Jessica stopped cold, glaring at him. He had turned off all the lights except for the bedside lamp, and the covers on the bed were turned back. He had also undressed.

She didn't pretend to misunderstand his intentions. Nervously she pushed her hair back from her face. ''I don't want to sleep with you.''

''That's good, because I have no intention of sleeping.''

Her face flamed with temper. ''Don't play word games with me! You know very well what I mean.''

His black eyes were narrowed as he surveyed her from her bare feet to her disheveled hair. ''Yes, I know very well that you have an aversion to sharing a bed with me, but I'm your husband, and I'm tired of my empty bed. It's obvious that if you're well enough to smuggle yourself to Athens, you're well enough to fulfill your wifely obligations.''

''You're strong enough that I can't fight you off,'' she said fiercely. ''But you know that I'm not willing. Why can't you listen to me? Why do you refuse to let me decide for myself how I feel?''

He merely shook his head. ''Don't try to throw up a smoke screen of words; it won't work. Take off the robe and come here.''

Defiantly she crossed her arms and glared at him. ''I wasn't leaving you!'' she insisted. ''I just wanted some time by myself to—to think and get myself on an even keel again, and I knew you'd never loosen the chains and let me go if I asked you.''

''I'm sorry you feel that way about our marriage,'' he replied in a silky voice, his expression dangerous. ''Jessica, darling, are you going to come here, or am I going to have to fetch you?''

''I expect you'll have to fetch me,'' she stated, not giving in an inch. She tensed all over at the thought of a repeat of his earlier lovemaking, and her face must have revealed the fear she felt because some of the sternness left his expression.

''You don't have to be afraid,'' he said, uncoiling his length from the bed with a wild grace. Her breath caught in her throat at the untamed beauty of his naked male body, but at the same time she stepped back in alarm.

''No. I don't want to,'' she said childishly, putting up a hand to ward him off. He merely caught it and used it to pull her close to him, the male scent of him enveloping her and making her feel surrounded by him.

''Don't fight me,'' he whispered, opening the robe with his free hand and pushing it away from her shoulders to let it drop about her feet in a blue pool. ''I promise you won't be hurt, darling. It's time you learned about being my wife, and it's a lesson you'll enjoy.''

Jessica shivered, rigid with anxiety, and goose bumps roughened her skin as he leaned down to press his hot mouth into the tender hollow of her shoulder. She remembered the night before, when he had roused her gently into desire, then left her unfulfilled, a calculated move that had left her feeling both insulted and frustrated. His physical desires were hot and demanding, but his brain always remained alert and cool, unaffected by the wildly shifting emotions that kept her so unsettled. Was this merely another calculated maneuver as he tried to break her spirit, tame her into accepting his authority?

She wrenched away from him, shaking her head in denial. "No," she said again, though she had no hope that he would accept her refusal.

He moved swiftly, lifting her into his arms and carrying her the few steps to the bed. He placed her on the cool sheet and followed her down, his arms and legs securing hers and holding her motionless. "Just relax," he crooned, trailing soft kisses over her shoulder and neck, then up to her trembling lips. "I'll take care of you, darling; there's nothing to be afraid of this time."

Violently Jessica turned her head away from him, and he pressed his lips instead to the line of her jaw, the sensitive shell of her ear. She made a strangled sound of protest, and he murmured soothingly to her, continuing the light kisses as he trailed his fingers over her body, learning the soft slopes and curves and reassuring her that this time he wasn't going to be impatient with her.

She tried to hold herself away from the seductive quality of those light, elusive touches on her skin, but she wasn't cold by nature, and eventually her sense of awareness began to dim and grow hazy. Imperceptibly she began to relax in his arms, and her skin warmed, taking on the flushed glow of a woman who was awakening to desire. Still he lingered over her, stroking and petting her almost as if she were a cat, and finally she let her breath out in a tremulous sigh and turned her head to seek his mouth with hers.

His kiss was slow and deep, passionate without being demanding, and he continued until at last her control broke and she moved eagerly against him, her arms winding around his neck. Excitement coursed through her veins and she felt on fire, her skin burning, and only the touch of his hands and body gave her any relief.

Finally she could stand it no longer and clutched at him with desperate hands, and he moved over her and possessed her soft body with the urgent masculinity of his. Jessica caught her breath on a sob and arched herself beneath him, glorying in the sensation of oneness with him, intent on nothing but the growing, pulsing need of her body that he gently satisfied.

But he wasn't that easily satisfied; she had wounded his arrogant Greek pride in trying to leave him, and he spent the long hours of the night making her admit time and again that he was her physical master. He wasn't brutal; at no time did he lose control. But he aroused her with his insistent, prolonged caresses and forced her to plead with him for release. At the time, she was so submerged in sensuality that nothing mattered to her except being in his arms and accepting his lovemaking. It wasn't until she woke the next morning and looked over at her sleeping husband that a chill ran over her, and she wondered at his motivation.

Had the night been only a demonstration of his mastery of her? Not once, even in the depths of his own passion, had he uttered a word of love. She began to feel that his lovemaking had been as calculated as before, designed only to make her accept his domination; there was also his stated intention of making her pregnant.

She turned her head restlessly on the pillow, aware of a cold knot of misery in her stomach. She didn't want to believe any of that; she wanted him to love her as she loved him; yet what else could she think? Tears slipped down her cheeks as she stared at the ceiling. Charles had warned her from the beginning not to challenge Nikolas Constantinos. His instinct was to conquer; it was part of his nature, and yet she had thrown her own will into opposition to his at every turn. Was it any wonder that he was so determined to subdue her?

Since she had met him, she had been on an emotional seesaw, but suddenly the never-ending strain had become too much. She was crying, soundlessly, endlessly, and she couldn't stop, the pillow beneath her head becoming wet with the slow rain of her tears.

"Jessica?" she heard Nikolas ask sleepily, lifting himself onto his elbow beside her. She turned her head and looked at him, her lips trembling, her eyes desolate. A concerned frown puckered his brow as he touched his fingers to her wet cheek. "What's wrong?"

She couldn't answer; she didn't know what was wrong. All she knew was that she was so miserable she wanted to die, and she wept softly.

Some time later, a stern Dr. Theotokas gave her an injection and patted her arm. "It's only a mild sedative; you won't even go to sleep," he assured her. "Though it's my opinion that rest and time are all that are required to make you well again. A severe concussion isn't something one recovers from in a matter of days. You've overexerted yourself, both physically and emotionally, and now you're paying the price."

"I know," she managed to say, giving him a weak smile. Her tears had slowed, and already the sedative was making itself felt in the form of a creeping relaxation. Was her weeping a form of hysteria? Probably so, and the doctor wasn't a fool. She was nude in her husband's bed; he'd have had to be blind not to know how they had spent the night—therefore the discreet warning about overexerting herself.

Nikolas was talking to Dr. Theotokas in Greek, his voice hard, rough, and the doctor was being very positive in his replies. Then the doctor was gone, and Nikolas sat down on the bed beside her, putting one arm on the other side of her and propping himself up on it. "Are you feeling better?" he asked gently, his dark eyes examining her closely.

"Yes. I'm sorry," she sighed.

"Shhh," he murmured. "It's I who should be apologizing. Alexander has just cursed me for being seven kinds of fool and not taking better care of you. I won't tell you what he said, but Alexander knows how to make a point," he finished wryly.

"And…now?" she asked.

"Now we return to the island, and you're to spend your time doing nothing more tiring than lying on the beach." His gaze met hers squarely. "I've been forbidden to share your bed until you've completely recovered, but we both know the concussion isn't the only problem. You win, Jessica. I won't bother you again until it's what you want, too. I give you my word on that."

Seven weeks later, Jessica stood on the terrace and stared absently at the gleaming white yacht anchored out in the bay; unconsciously her hand went to her stomach, her fingers drifting over the flatness. His promise had been scrupulously kept, but it had been given too late. It would still be some time yet before her condition began to show, but already she had seen the little smiles that Petra and Sophia exchanged whenever she was unable to eat any breakfast yet raided the kitchen later with a ravenous appetite. In a thousand ways, she had betrayed herself to the women, from her increased sleepiness to the way she had learned to move slowly to prevent the dizziness which swept over her if she stood abruptly.

A baby! She wavered between a glowing contentment that she was actually carrying Nikolas's child, and a deep depression that the relationship between them hadn't improved at all since they had returned to the island. He was still restrained, cool. She knew that it distressed Madame Constantinos, but she couldn't bring herself to make up to Nikolas, and he wasn't doing any making up, either. He'd made it plain that she would have to take the next step, and she had backed off. If anything, she was more confused than before, with the knowledge of her pregnancy weighing on her. The yo-yo effect the pregnancy had on her emotions kept her unsettled, unable to decide on any course of action. But right now, she was just recovering from a bout of nausea and feeling resentful that Nikolas should have made her pregnant so easily, and she glared at the yacht below.

Andros had brought the yacht in yesterday. Nikolas had worked like a demon these past weeks, both to catch up on his work and to divert himself, but he had decided that a cruise would be a welcome change, and he had sent Andros to the marina where the yacht was berthed to bring it to the island. Nikolas had planned to leave in two days, with Jessica and his mother along, and Jessica was beginning to suspect that he meant to settle things between them whether she liked it or not once he had her on the yacht. He had given his word that he wouldn't bother her, but he had probably never thought that the situation would last this long.

She resentfully turned away from the sight of the graceful ship and met Sophia's smiling dark eyes as she held out a glass of cool fruit juice. Jessica took the glass without protest, though she wondered how Sophia always knew just when her stomach was upset. A tray with dry toast and weak tea was also brought to her every morning now, and she knew that the coddling would intensify as her pregnancy advanced. The women hadn't said anything yet, knowing that she hadn't informed Nikolas of his impending fatherhood, but she would have to tell him soon.

"I'm going for a walk," she told Sophia, giving the empty glass back to her, and their ability to communicate had improved to the extent that Sophia understood her the first time and beamed at her.

Walking slowly, careful to avoid the sun whenever she could, Jessica picked her way cautiously down the steep path that led to the beach. She was joined by a leaping, prancing Samantha. Nikolas had even had the small dog brought over, and Samantha was having the time of her life, romping with unlimited freedom. The village children spoiled her terribly, but she had attached herself to Nikolas, and now Jessica made a face at her. "Traitor!" she told the dog, but Samantha barked so happily that she had to smile.

She found a piece of driftwood and amused herself by throwing it for Samantha to retrieve, but halted the game when the dog showed signs of tiring. She suspected that Samantha had managed to get in the family way again; Nikolas had reported, laughingly, that he'd seen her being very friendly with a native dog. She sat down on the sand and stroked the dog's silky head. "Both of us, my girl," she said ruefully, and Samantha whined in pleasure.

At length, she began retracing her steps up the path, concentrating on her footing to make certain she didn't fall. She was taken totally by surprise when a gruff voice behind her barked playfully, "What are you doing?" She shrieked in alarm, whirling about, and the sudden movement was too much. She had a glimpse of Nikolas's dark, laughing face before it swam sickeningly away from her, and she flung out both hands in an effort to catch herself as she pitched forward. She didn't know if she hit the ground or not.

When she woke, she was in her bedroom, lying on the bed. Nikolas was sitting on the edge of the mattress, washing her face with a cold wet cloth, his dark face set in stern lines.

"I—I'm sorry," she apologized weakly. "I can't think why I fainted."

He gave her a brooding glance. "Can't you?" he asked. "Maman has a very good idea, as do Petra and Sophia. Why haven't you told me, Jessica? Everyone else knows."

"Told you what?" She delayed, pouting sulkily, trying to put off the moment when she actually had to tell him.

His jaw tightened. "Don't play games with me," he said harshly, leaning over her with determination. "Are you having my baby?"

In spite of everything, a certain sweetness pierced her. There were only the two of them in the room, and this moment would never happen again. A slow smile, mysterious in its contentment, curved her lips as she reached for his hand. With a timeless gesture she placed his palm over her still-flat abdomen, as if he could feel his tiny child growing there. "Yes," she admitted in perfect serenity, lifting her glowing eyes to him. "We've made a baby, Nikolas."

His entire body quivered, and his black eyes softened incredibly, then he stretched out on the bed beside her and gathered her into his arms. His hand stroked her tawny mane of hair, the strong fingers trembling. "A baby," he murmured. "You impossible woman, why haven't you told me before? Didn't you know how happy you would make me? Why, Jessica?"

The heady sensation of his warm body lying against her so

dazed her mind that she forgot to think of anything else. She had to gather her thoughts before she could answer. "I thought you'd gloat," she said huskily, running the tip of her tongue over her dry lips. "I knew you'd never let me go if you knew about the baby...."

His gaze went to her mouth as if drawn by a magnet. "Do you still want to go?" he muttered. "You can't, you know; you're right in thinking that I'll never let you go. Never." His tone thickened as he said, "Give me a kiss, darling. It's been so long, and I need your touch."

It had been a long time. Nikolas had been strict about not touching her, perhaps doubting his control if he allowed himself to kiss and caress her. And once Jessica had recovered from her shock, she had missed his touch and his hungry kisses. Trembling slightly at the memory, she turned to him and lifted her face.

His mouth touched hers lightly, sweetly; this was not the type of kiss she had received from Nikolas before. She melted under the petal-soft contact, nestling closer to him and lifting her hand to his neck. Automatically her lips opened and her tongue darted out to touch his lips and move within to seek the caress of his own tongue. Nikolas groaned aloud and abruptly the kiss changed; his mouth became ravenous as the pressure increased. Instantly heat rose in Jessica's middle, the same mindless desire he had roused in her before pride and anger had forced them apart. She ached for him; she felt as if she would die without his touch. Her body arched to him, seeking relief that only he could give.

With a deep moan, Nikolas lost control. Every muscle in his big body was shaking as he opened her dress and removed it. The wild light in his eyes told her that he might hurt her if she resisted, reminding her for a stricken moment of their wedding night, but then that frightening vision faded and she moved against him. Her own shaking fingers unbuttoned his shirt, her lips searching across his hairy chest and making his breath catch.

By the time she reached for his belt, his hand was there to help her and impatiently he shed his pants and moved over her.

His mouth was drink to a woman dying of thirst; his hands created ecstasy wherever they touched. Jessica gave herself to him simply, sweetly, pliant to his every whim, and he rewarded her tenfold with his care of her, his hungry enjoyment of her. She loved this man, loved him with all her heart, and suddenly that was all that mattered.

When she floated back to earth, she was lying in his arms, her head pillowed on his shoulder while he lazily stroked her body as one would a cat. Smiling, Jessica lifted her head to look at him and found that he was smiling, too, a triumphant, contented smile. His black eyes were sleepy with satiation as he met her gaze. "I had no idea pregnant women were so erotic," he drawled, and a fiery blush burned her face.

"Don't you dare tease me now!" she protested, not wanting anything to spoil the golden glow that still enveloped her.

"But I'm not teasing. You were desirable before, God knows, but now that I know you have my child inside you, I don't want to turn you loose for even a moment." His deep voice went even deeper, became thick. "I don't think I can stay away from you, Jess."

Silently she played with the curls of hair on his chest. This afternoon had changed everything, not least of all her own attitude toward him. She loved him, and she was helpless before that fact. She had to put away her resentment and concentrate on that love, or she wouldn't have a life worth living, because she was bound mind and body to this man. Perhaps he didn't love her, but he was certainly not indifferent toward her. She would give him her love, wrap him about so tightly with the tender bonds of her heart that someday he would come to love her, too. And she had a powerful weapon in the child she carried; Nikolas would adore the baby.

A gnawing worry had been lifted from her mind. Since their return to the island, she had been terrified that he would make love to her, haunted by her contradictory but still bitter memories of their wedding night and the one other night she had spent with him. This afternoon, in the golden sunlight, he had proved to her that lovemaking could be sweet, too, and he had satisfied her with all the skill of an experienced lover. She knew now that with time those bitter memories would fade, lost in the newer memories of nights in his arms.

"No more empty nights," he growled, echoing her thoughts. He leaned over her, and his dark face was hard, almost brutal with a resurgence of his desire; unfortunately she was still thinking of their wedding night, and she gasped in alarm when she saw his face looking so much as he had looked then. Before she could stop herself, her hands were pushing at his shoulders, and she had cried out, "Don't touch me!"

He jerked back as if he had been slapped, his face going pale.

"Don't worry about that," he said tightly, swinging off the bed and grabbing up his pants. "I've done everything I can think of to make it up to you, and you've thrown it all back in my face. I have no more arguments, Jessica, no more persuasions. I'm tired, damn it, tired of—" He broke off and jerked his pants on, and Jessica came out of her frozen horror at what she had done.

"Nikolas, wait—it isn't—"

"I don't give a damn what it isn't!" he ripped out savagely, his jaw set like granite. "I won't bother you again." He slammed out of the bedroom without looking at her again and Jessica lay on the bed, stunned by the violence of his reaction and by the raw emotion that had been in his voice. She had hurt him, something she hadn't thought possible. Nikolas had always seemed so tough, so impervious to anything she said or did, except to be angry when she defied him. But he had his pride, too; perhaps he had finally tired of a woman who resisted him at every turn. The thought made her shrink inside, thinking of being without his absorbing interest in everything she did, his open appreciation of her body.

She left the bed, too, and pulled on her robe. Restlessly, miserably, she paced the room. How *could* she have done that to him? Just when she had admitted that she needed him, she had let her silly fears drive him away and she was totally lost without him. What would she do without his arrogant strength to bolster her when she was depressed or upset? From the day they had met he had supported her, protected her.

Her head had begun to throb and she rubbed her temples abstractedly. At last she gathered up her courage and pulled on her clothing with trembling hands. She had to find Nikolas and make him listen, explain why she had pushed him away.

When she entered the living room, Madame Constantinos was there and she looked up from her book as Jessica entered. "Are you all right, my dear?" she asked in her soft French, her sweet face worried.

"Yes," Jessica muttered. "I— Do you know where Nikolas is, Maman?"

"Yes, he and Andros have locked themselves in the study with strict orders not to be disturbed. Andros is flying to New York tomorrow and they are finalizing a merger."

Andros was handling that? Jessica passed a shaking hand over her eyes. Nikolas should have been handling that merger, she knew, but he was delegating the responsibility to Andros so he could take time to be with her on the yacht. How could she have been so blind?

"Is anything wrong?" Madame Constantinos asked worriedly.

"Yes—no. Yes, there is. We've had a quarrel," Jessica confessed. "I need to see him. He misunderstood something that I said."

"M'mmmm, I see," said his mother. She looked at Jessica with those clear blue eyes. "You told him of the child, then?"

Evidently her condition was well-known to all the women of the household, she reflected. She sat down and sighed wearily. "Yes. But that isn't why he's angry."

"No, of course not. Nikolas would never be angry at the thought of becoming a father," mused Madame Constantinos, smiling a little. "He is undoubtedly as proud as a peacock."

Yes," Jessica admitted huskily, remembering the look on his face when she had told him of the baby.

Madame Constantinos was looking out the glass doors of the terrace, smiling a little. "So Niko is angry and upset, is he? Let him alone for tonight, my dear. He probably wouldn't listen to you anyway, right now, so let him stew in his own misery for a little while. That is a small-enough punishment for the misery he has caused you. You've never said why you were on the beach so early in the morning, my dear, and I haven't liked to ask, but I do have a fairly accurate picture of what happened that night. Yes, let Niko worry for tonight."

Tears welled in Jessica's eyes. "It wasn't all his fault, Maman," she defended Nikolas. She felt as if she would die. She loved him, and she had driven him away.

"Don't fret," Madame Constantinos advised serenely. "You cannot think clearly now. Tomorrow everything will be better, you'll see."

Yes, thought Jessica, gulping back her tears. Tomorrow she would try to make up to Nikolas for her past coldness, and she didn't dare think what she would do if he turned away from her.

Chapter 13

By the time morning came, Jessica was pale with her own unhappy thoughts. She wanted only to heal the breach between her and Nikolas, and she was unsure how to go about it or if he even wanted to mend things between them. She was in agony from the need to see him and explain, to touch him; more than anything she needed to feel his arms about her and hear his deep voice muttering love words to her. She loved him! Perhaps there was no rhyme or reason to it, but what did that matter? She'd known from the first that he was the only man who could conquer the defenses she'd built about herself and she was tired of denying her love.

She dressed hurriedly, without regard for how she looked, and merely brushed her hair, then left it hanging down her back. As she rushed into the living room she saw Madame Constantinos sitting on the terrace and she went through the glass door to greet her. "Where is Niko, Maman?" she asked in a trembling voice.

"He's on board the yacht," the older woman answered. "Sit down, child; have your breakfast with me. Sophia will bring something light. Have you been ill this morning?"

Surprisingly she hadn't. That was the only good thing about

this morning that she could see. "But I must see Nikolas as soon as possible," she insisted.

"All in good time. You cannot talk to him now, so you might as well have your breakfast. You must take care of the baby, dear."

Reluctantly Jessica sat down, and in just a moment Sophia appeared with a tray. Smiling, she set out a light breakfast for Jessica. In the halting Greek that Jessica had acquired in the weeks she'd been on the island she thanked Sophia and was rewarded by a motherly pat of approval.

Gulping, Jessica chewed at a roll, trying to force it past the lump in her throat. Far below them she could see the white gleam of the yacht; Nikolas was there, but he might as well be a thousand miles away. There was no way she could get out to him unless one of the fishermen would take her, and for that she would have to walk to the village. It wasn't such a long walk, and before, she would have done it without a second thought, but her pregnancy had badly undermined her stamina and she was hesitant about making it that far in the fierce heat. As Madame Constantinos had said, she had to take care of the precious life inside her. Nikolas would hate her if she did anything that could harm his child.

After she'd eaten enough to satisfy both her mother-in-law and Sophia, and had pushed the tray away, Madame Constantinos said quietly, "Tell me, dear, do you love Niko?"

How could she ask? wondered Jessica miserably. It must be evident in every word she'd said since Nikolas had stormed out of her bedroom the day before. But Madame Constantinos's soft blue eyes were on her and she admitted in a strained whisper, "Yes! But I've ruined it—he'll never forgive me for what I said to him! If he loved me, it might be different—"

"How do you know that he doesn't love you?" demanded the older woman.

"Because all he's been concerned with since we met was going to bed," Jessica confessed in deep depression. "He says he wants me—but he's never said that he loves me."

"Ah, I see," said Madame Constantinos, nodding her white head knowingly. "Because he's never told you the sky is blue, you know that it can't possibly be that color! Jessica, my dear, open your eyes! Do you truly think Niko is so weak in character that he would be a slave to his lust? He wants you, yes—physical desire is a part of love."

Jessica didn't dare hope that it could be true that Nikolas loved her; on too many occasions he had totally ignored her feelings and she said as much to Madame Constantinos.

"I never said he is an amiable man," the other woman retorted. "I'm speaking from personal experience. Niko is the image of his father; they could be one and the same man. It wasn't always comfortable, being Damon's wife. I had to do everything his way or he would fly into a rage, and Niko is the same. He is so strong that sometimes he fails to understand that most people do not have that same strength, that he needs to soften his approach."

"But your husband loved you," Jessica pointed out softly, her eyes trained on the remote gleam of the yacht on the crystalline sea.

"So he did. But we had been married for six years before he told me so, and then only because I was suffering from the loss of our second child, a still-birth. When I asked him how long he had loved me, he looked at me in amazement and said, 'From the first. How can a woman be so blind? Never doubt that I love you, even when the words aren't said.' And so it is with Niko." Quietly, her clear blue eyes on Jessica, Madame Constantinos said again, "Yes, Niko loves you."

Jessica went even paler, shaken at the wild surge of hope that shot through her. Did he love her? Could he *still* love her, after yesterday?

"He loves you," reassured his mother. "I know my son, as I knew my husband. Niko lost his head over you; I have seen him look at you with such yearning in his eyes that it took my breath away, for he is a strong man and he doesn't love lightly."

"But—but the things he's said," protested Jessica shakily, still not daring to let herself hope.

"Yes, I know. He's a proud man, and he was angry with himself that he couldn't control his need for you. It is partly my fault, this trouble between you and Niko. He loves me, and I was upset when I thought my dear friend Robert had married a gold-digger. Niko wanted to protect me, but he couldn't make himself leave you alone. And you, Jessica, were too proud to tell him the truth."

"I know," said Jessica softly, and tears welled in her eyes. "And I treated him so badly yesterday! I've ruined it, Maman; he'll never forgive me now." The tears dripped from her lashes as she remembered the look that had been in Nikolas's eyes as he'd left her bedroom. She wanted to die. She felt as if she'd smashed paradise with her own hands.

"Don't fret. If you can forgive him for his pride, my dear, he'll forgive you for yours."

Jessica gasped at the thrust, then admitted to herself the truth of it. She had used her pride to hold Nikolas away, and now she was paying for it.

Madame Constantinos placed her hand on Jessica's arm. "Niko is leaving the yacht now," she said gently. "Why don't you go to meet him?"

"I—yes," gulped Jessica, getting to her feet.

"Be careful," called Madame Constantinos after her. "Remember my grandchild!"

Her eyes on the small rowboat steadily narrowing the gap between it and the beach, Jessica made her way down the path that led to the water. She went down it with a hammering heart, wondering if Madame Constantinos was right that Nikolas truly loved her. Thinking back, it seemed to her that he did—or had. If only she hadn't ruined it!

Nikolas had beached the rowboat and was securing it against the tide when she walked across the sand up to him. He wore only a pair of blue cut-off jeans and his nearly nude, muscular body rippled with lithe grace as he moved. She caught her breath in sheer admiration and stopped in her tracks.

Nikolas straightened and saw her. His black eyes were impossible to read as he stood there looking at her, and she drew in a quivering breath. He wouldn't make the first move, she knew; she'd have to do it. Taking her courage in both hands, she said quietly, "Nikolas, I love you. Can you possibly forgive me?"

Something flickered in the black depths of his eyes, then was gone. "Of course," he said simply, and walked toward her.

When he was so close that she could smell the clean sweat of his body, he stopped and asked, "Why?"

"Your mother opened my eyes," she said, swallowing with some difficulty. Her heart was lodged in her throat and was pounding so hard she could barely speak. He wasn't going to make it easy for her, she could see. "She made me realize that I've been allowing my pride to ruin my life. I—I love you, and even if you don't love me, I want to spend the rest of my life with you. I hope you love me; Maman thinks you do, but even if you c-can't love me, it doesn't matter."

He shoved his fingers through his black hair, his face suddenly grim and impatient. "Are you blind?" he demanded roughly. "All of Europe knew I took one look at you and went mad. Do you think I'm such a slave to lust that I'd have pursued you so single-mindedly if I'd only wanted you for sex?"

Her heart leaped wildly as he spoke words that were so similar to those his mother had used. So Madame Constantinos did know her son! And as she'd said, Niko was much like his father. She reached out shaking hands and her fingers clutched at the warm skin that covered his ribs. "I love you," she whispered shakily. "How can you ever forgive me for being so blind and stupid?"

A quiver ran through his entire body, and with a deep groan, he snatched her to him, burying his face in her tangled hair. "There's no question of forgiving you," he muttered fiercely. "If you can forgive me, if you can still love me after the way

I've hounded you so mercilessly, how can I hold a grudge against you? Besides, my life won't be worth living if I let you go. I love you.'' Then he lifted his head and repeated, ''I love you.''

Her entire body began to quiver as she heard his deep voice at last saying those words, and once he had admitted it, he kept on saying it, over and over, while she clung to him with desperate strength, her face buried in the warm, curly hair that covered his chest. He cupped her chin in his palm and turned her face up to his and she was engulfed in his hungry, possessive kiss. Wild little tingles began to shoot along her nerves and she stood on tiptoe to press herself against him, her arms sliding up to twine about his neck. His firm, warm skin beneath her fingers made her feel drunk and now she no longer wanted to resist him; she responded to him without reserve. At last she could indulge her own need to touch him; to stroke his darkly tanned skin and bite sensuously at his lips. A deep groan came from his chest as she did exactly that, and the next moment he had scooped her up in his arms and was striding across the sand.

''Where are you taking me?'' she whispered, trailing her lips across his shoulder, and he answered her in a strained voice.

''Over here, to where the rocks hide us from view.'' And in a moment they were surrounded by the rocks and he carefully placed her on the sun-warmed sand. Despite the urgency she sensed in him, he was gentle as he made love to her, holding himself back, as if he feared hurting her. His skilled, patient attention carried her to rapture, and when she floated back to earth, she knew that their lovemaking had been clean and healing, wiping out all of the pain and anger of the past months. It had sealed the pact of their confessed love, made them truly man and wife. Clasped tightly in his arms, her face buried against his heaving chest, she whispered, ''All of this time wasted! If only I'd told you—''

''Shhh,'' he interrupted, stroking her hair. ''No self-recriminations, darling, because I'm not free from guilt either, and I'm not good at admitting when I'm wrong.'' His strong mouth curved into a wry smile and he moved his hand to her back, the stroking motion continuing as if she was a cat. "I understand now why you were so wary of me, but at the time every rejection was like a slap in the face," he continued softly. "I wanted to leave you alone; you'll never know how much I wanted to be able to walk away and forget about you, and it made me furious that I couldn't. I'm not used to anyone having that kind of power over me," he confessed in self-mockery. "I couldn't admit that I'd finally been defeated; I did everything I could to get the upper hand again, to try to manage my emotions, but nothing worked, not even Diana."

Jessica gasped at his audacity in even mentioning that name to her and she raised her head from his chest to glare at him jealously. "Yes, what about Diana?" she asked sharply.

"Ouch," he winced, flicking the tip of her nose with a long brown finger. "I've opened my bloody mouth when I should've kept it shut, haven't I?" But his black eyes sparkled and she knew that he was enjoying her jealousy.

To get back at him, she refused to be put off. "Yes, you did," she agreed. "Tell me about Diana. That night you said you'd only kissed her once, is that true?"

"Within reason," he hedged.

Furious, she clenched her fist and struck him in the stomach with all her strength, which wasn't enough to really hurt him but which made him grunt. "Hey!" he protested, grabbing her fist and holding it. But he was laughing, a carefree laugh that she'd never heard from him before. He looked exultant, he looked happy, and that made her even more jealous. "Niko," she bit out, "tell me!"

"All right," he said, his laughter fading to a faint smile. His black eyes watched her sharply as he admitted, "I meant to take her. She was willing, and she was balm to a battered ego. Diana and I had a brief affair some months before I met you, and she made it clear that she wanted to resume our relationship. You had me so confused, so frustrated, that I couldn't think of anything but trying to break the hold you had on me. You wouldn't let me have you, but I kept coming back for more of that delicate cold shoulder and I was furious with myself. You acted as if you couldn't stand my touch, while Diana made it obvious that she wanted me. And I wanted a responsive woman in my arms, but when I began kissing her, it just wasn't right. She wasn't you, and I didn't want her. I wanted only you, even if I couldn't admit to myself just then that I loved you.''

His explanation hardly mollified her, but as he still held her fist and her other arm was effectively pinned to her side by his encircling arm, she couldn't take out her anger on him physically. She still glared at him as she ordered, ''You're not to kiss another woman again, do you hear? I won't stand for it!''

''I promise,'' he murmured. ''I'm all yours, darling; I have been from the moment you walked across my office toward me, if you'd only wanted me. But I admit that I like that green fire in your eyes; you're beautiful when you're jealous.''

His words were accompanied by a wickedly charming grin that accomplished its purpose, for she melted at the look of loving ownership he gave her. ''I suppose it tickles your ego that I'm jealous?'' she asked, letting herself relax against him.

''Of course. I went through torture, I've been so jealous of you; it's only fair that you be a little jealous, too.''

He followed his admission with a searching kiss that had her flowing against him; it was as if her desire for him, so long denied, had burst out of control and she couldn't hold back her pleasure. Like an animal he sensed that and took advantage of it, deepening his kiss, stroking her body with sure, knowing hands. ''You're beautiful,'' he whispered raggedly. ''I've dreamed so many times of having you like this; I don't want to let you go for even a minute.''

''But we have to,'' Jessica replied dreamily, her green eyes sleepy with love and need. ''Maman will be waiting for us.''

''Then I suppose we'd better return,'' Nikolas growled, sitting up and raising her with an arm behind her back. ''I wouldn't like for her to send someone looking for us. And you *are* sleepy, aren't you?''

"Sleepy?" she asked, startled.

"You won't be able to stay awake, will you?" he continued, his black eyes sparkling. "You'll have to take a nap."

"Oh!" she exclaimed, her eyes widening as understanding dawned. "I believe you're right; I'm so sleepy I won't be able to stay awake until lunch."

He laughed and helped her dress, and hand in hand they walked up the path. Holding his strong hand tightly, Jessica felt the golden glow of love inside her expand until it included the whole world. For the first time in her life everything was as it should be; she loved Nikolas and he loved her, and already she carried his child. She would tell him the full story of her marriage, explain why she had hidden behind the lies others had told, even from him, but it would make no difference to their love, she knew. In deep contentment she asked, "When did you admit to yourself that you love me?"

"When you were in Cornwall," he admitted gruffly, his fingers tightening. He stopped and turned to face her and his dark face had a grim expression as he remembered. "It was two days before Charles deigned to tell me where you'd gone, and I was on the verge of insanity before he decided I'd been punished enough. I'd spent two days trying to get you on the phone, waiting hours outside your house for you to come home. I kept thinking of the things I'd said to you, remembering the look in your eyes as you left, and I was in a cold sweat thinking I'd lost you. That was when I knew I loved you, because the thought of not seeing you again was agony."

She looked at him in surprise. If he'd loved her that early, why had he insisted on those insulting conditions in the prenuptial agreement? She asked him as much, her voice troubled, and in response to the echo of pain he saw in her eyes, he pulled her into his arms and laid his cheek on her head.

"I was in pain, and I lashed out," he muttered. "I'm sorry, darling, I'll have that damned thing torn up. But I kept thinking that you were holding out for a ring so you could get your hands on my money, and it drove me wild because I loved you so much I had to have you, even thinking all you wanted was money.''

"I've never wanted your money. I'm even glad you took control of my money, because I was furious with you for bullying me into taking such a large sum for the shares of ConTech when I didn't want it.''

"I know that now, but at the time I thought that that was *exactly* what you wanted. My eyes were opened on our wedding night, and when I woke up and you were gone—'' He broke off the sentence and closed his eyes, his expression tormented.

"Don't think of that,'' she said gently. "I love you.''

His eyes opened and he looked at her, the clear depths of her eyes shining with the love she felt. "Even when I'm mad with jealousy and frustration, I still have a spark of sanity left,'' he said, his mouth curving in amusement. "I still had the sense to make you my wife.'' He leaned down and swept her up in his arms. "Maman is waiting for us. Let's give her the good news, then take that nap. I'll take you home, love''—and he started up the path to their home, his stride long and effortless as he carried her. Jessica curled her arms about his neck and rested against him, knowing she was safe in the strength of his love.

THE GOODBYE CHILD
Ann Major

This book is dedicated to Tara Gavin, my editor.
This story owes its very existence
to her gentle guiding hand.

Prologue

It was raining, and the wind had dropped to nothing. Evangeline Martin looked up impatiently at her lifeless sail and then at the thick fog bank up ahead. White plumes were rolling over the wide Mississippi and silently blanketing everything.

Suddenly she was afraid.

She should never have taken the boat out on a day like this. No matter how awful she'd felt about what *Grand-mère* had done.

"Mon dieu," she sighed, utterly miserable, fighting tears that always came so embarrassingly easily.

She was heartbroken.

She was furious.

Less than an hour ago, her grandmother had offered her irrefutable proof that Eva's fiancé, her adoring Armand, was not twenty-two as he had claimed. Nor was he a medical student at Tulane. No, he was twenty-seven years old, and he had a pregnant girlfriend in Baton Rouge. Another scoundrel of the first order—this one with a prison record—who had been after Eva for her money.

She could sure pick them. Or rather she couldn't. That was the problem.

"You're too softhearted, *chère*. Too sweet and trusting," her grandmother had said, attempting to console her. "You always let men who need you pick you."

But *Grand-mère* was wrong. Eva had chosen him because he'd seemed so proper, and she'd felt so sure her wealthy, conventional family would approve of him. She was the baby of the family, and even though she was in college, they still treated her like one. She wanted to do something right for once, but this was the third time she'd chosen the wrong man. The third time her family had hired a private investigator. Eva was disgusted with herself for always failing them.

She sipped the last of her diet cola and tossed the empty can into the cockpit. She heard a splash and quickly glanced into the cockpit. The can floated beside her life preserver in a pool of water. The plug was gone! The cockpit was rapidly filling. Even as she fought panic and tears, she told herself not to worry. The boat had flotation.

The boom swung lazily across to the other side of the boat and she ducked. Then the sail flapped and was still. The icy rain fell more thickly. The boat was dead in the shallows under the lee of the levee. At this rate she would never get home.

Eva shivered. She'd forgotten the pants to her foul-weather gear, and her legs were drenched. She pulled up her yellow, waterproof hood to cover her hair, and considered her dilemma. She felt safer near the shore, but if she didn't steer the boat into deeper water where the current was stronger, where the trees and levee didn't block what little air there was, she'd never get home.

She warily nudged the tiller. She had sailed upwind against the current; she would drift sluggishly toward the bayou and home.

A green-and-white buoy that marked the edge of the shallows slowly slid by. She was in deep water now, the most dangerous part of the river because of the river traffic. She heard the eerie sound of a foghorn somewhere downriver.

Her tiny boat glided by the von Schönburg oil docks and refinery. A huge barge was tied up there. On the other side of the river, hidden behind the levee, was an alley of live oaks leading to Sweet Seclusion, the tumbledown, white-columned plantation house that belonged to Raoul Girouard.

All her life her family had warned her against the Girouards, especially Raoul. They said the Girouards had never been a proper southern family. They had a long history of spawning pirates and river gamblers. But Raoul was the worst of them all. He was such a scoundrel that he was even an outcast among his own family—his father having thrown him out years ago for trying to seduce his young stepmother.

According to rumor, Raoul had only grown wilder after that. He'd become a gambler, a womanizer, a mercenary who would sell his own soul for money. He'd been expelled from every college he'd ever attended. He'd been a merchant marine and a soldier of fortune. He'd lived in Africa like an Arab, taken a trek across the Sahara on a camel and written a book about it. When he'd finally settled down, had he chosen the proper sort of career? No, he'd gone to work for an impoverished prince, Otto von Schönburg, and infuriated all the gossipmongers of the neighborhood, who staunchly believed all scoundrels should suffer, by making both himself and his royal boss filthy rich in the spot-oil business. A gambler's business, *Grand-mère* said. She said as well that no matter how high Raoul lived, his bad character would bring him down in the end. Eva had listened to these stories spellbound, never admitting even secretly to herself how blissfully, sinfully fascinating Raoul Girouard sounded.

Eva's boat drifted into the fog bank, and she couldn't see either shore. She heard another call from a foghorn, closer this time.

Out of nowhere came the violent wash of giant props. The water around her was ominously still. She twisted her neck to see, but the mist was too thick. The roar grew louder and louder.

She screamed and pushed the tiller away, but the little boat did not respond.

Then suddenly she saw a sleek white wall of aluminum and steel slicing directly toward her through the gray water like an airborne torpedo.

She stood up and screamed, but the big yacht bore down on her.

Only in that last desperate second did the captain swerve, missing her smaller hull by mere inches, but his powerboat's wake caught her boat broadside. Waves sloshed over the freeboard and deluged the half-filled cockpit. The boom swung across and slammed into the back of her head so hard she nearly lost consciousness. The hull jostled up and down, the tiller came loose in her hands and she lost her balance and slid helplessly across the slick fiberglass deck into the river.

She hit the cold water face first. She struggled to stay afloat, but her foul-weather jacket and the currents were sucking her under. A second wave from the powerboat swamped her.

She clawed the water like a wildcat, but she was weak and dazed from the blow to her head, and gagged on mouthfuls of water.

Above, the fog layer was thinning, and she could see blue sky. The powerboat was circling and coming back, its big engines cut to a purr. A tall dark man was diving in.

Her last thought was that he was too far away. He would never reach her in time. Still, she swam toward him desperately, struggling to stay afloat and to keep her head above the icy water, but the current was pulling her under. Darkness pulsed around her. She stretched her hand toward him and kicked wildly. Her fingertips touched his briefly and then fluttered helplessly away as the current pulled her deeper and deeper down into an endless liquid darkness.

"You might as well quit trying, Raoul. She's not going to make it," a young voice croaked uncertainly.

Yes, I am! Oh, yes I am—!

Eva's lips trembled with the effort to shout at the two men hovering over her, but she was too weak even to whisper. Her throat and nasal passages burned. Her stomach heaved. Her whole body ached with exhaustion and cold.

She was in too much pain to be dead!

She was suffocating, dying for a breath of air. Air was so close. So painfully close.

Her eyes were shut, and her eyelids were so heavy it seemed that leaden weights lay on top of them. But she was aware of the warmth of the sun on her skin, of the strong comfort of someone's hard arms holding her, of a firm mouth forcing itself against hers, of hot breaths being rhythmically forced down her bruised windpipe again and again.

"Breathe, damn you. Breathe," a man ordered in a rough, imperious growl that made her want to yell at him. He was so unkind, and he was hurting her—never before in her short pampered life had anyone talked to her like that. But such effort was impossible. He wound his long fingers in her thick hair, jerking her head up once more. She felt his lips on hers again. His mouth was open; so was hers. His fingers ground into her upper arms like iron bands, and she felt him push three relentless drafts of warm oxygen down her throat.

Air! At last! She was desperate for it. She gulped it in and then gagged on the vile water coming up from the opposite direction.

She struggled frantically to open her eyes. She was gasping, spitting up water, drowning all over again, and breathing in great gulps of air despite the pain in her throat and her waterlogged chest. Every nasal passage in her head felt enflamed.

His arms still around her, he helped her lean back against plump cushions.

"Pierre, get more blankets. Bring brandy."

This man with the rough hands and voice didn't ask; he commanded. And she'd never put up with that from anyone.

"Where am I?" she whispered, her voice a thin, trailing sound.

Talking was difficult. Her throat still felt paralyzed. Every muscle was cramping from the cold.

Her rescuer didn't bother to answer. "You little idiot, what the hell were you doing in the middle of the river in a sinking boat where you could have been killed? Don't you know that a barge could have crushed you? Barges can't stop on a dime the way I had to.''

She was so tired, too tired to fight him. ''I'm not as stupid as you seem to think!''

''That's not even debatable.''

''You're impossibly rude.''

''Because you're impossibly stupid!''

She snapped her eyes open and her mouth, too, intending to issue a passionate rebuke. He was a blur, but what she saw of him took her breath away. He was the most beautiful human being she'd ever seen. A Greek god, with jet-black hair, chiseled features sculpted of bronze, and a body of muscle and sinew as perfect as his face. He had a beautiful mouth. It was wide and sensual, and somehow very kissable.

She had a weakness for beauty. And apparently for kissable mouths.

She rubbed her eyes, and he was still there, her vision of him clearer. He had magnificent black eyes, and they were ablaze with fury.

''The wind died,'' she managed. ''I couldn't sail. If you know anything about sailboats…''

His hard gaze bore into her. ''I know a great deal about sailboats, and yours was being sailed by an idiot.''

She glanced nervously away. She was on board his yacht, alone with this virile, hostile stranger. ''I—I was trying to drift downstream. To get home.''

''Where's home? Who are you, anyway?''

''Eva…Martin.''

He cut her off. ''So you're the scatterbrained baby of the, er, illustrious Senator Wade Martin's family.''

''Scatterbrained! I'll have you know—''

His derisive gaze began to make a slow, assessing sweep of her, traveling down her throat, over the lush curves of her breasts. She was unaware that her wet white shorts were almost transparent. But his burning eyes made her aware of some new danger.

"I'm not scatterbrained! And I'm not a baby! I'm twenty!"
She heard herself, appalled. Just saying her age made her seem
so much younger.

"All of twenty?" His knowing smile was cynical. "I'm Raoul
Girouard. I'm afraid your family doesn't like me much."

"I'm beginning to see why." She was never, never this rude
to anyone.

"Really?"

"My grandmother's told me all about you."

A shadow passed across his handsome face, but he said
smoothly, "Then she probably told you I eat little girls like you
for breakfast." His voice was soft and low, but it vibrated
through every feminine cell in her body.

She regarded him with dark suspicion, her brow so puckered
with worry that some of his anger seemed to leave him. The
kissable mouth actually smiled.

"Then for midnight snacks?" He laughed softly and, like his
voice, his laughter was a dangerously pleasant sound.

Her lips quivered as she tried to suppress a smile of her own.
If he was a scoundrel, at least he didn't pretend he wasn't.

"And so I do," he murmured with a sardonic grin. "But
you're perfectly safe. I'm not hungry at the moment. I had a late
lunch, and it's still the middle of the afternoon."

His breath stirred the damp hair near her ear as he spoke, and
her pulse accelerated in alarm. Some part of her knew that she
could never feel perfectly safe around a man like him.

Fortunately Pierre returned with the blankets and brandy.
Raoul took the blankets and almost fiercely pressed them around
her, molding them to the shapely contours of her body. When
he was done, Raoul commanded Pierre to steer the yacht toward
Martin House. Pierre vanished again, and Eva was left alone
with Raoul.

Raoul held the glass of brandy to her lips. "Here, this will
make you feel better."

"I never drink brandy."

"Drink it."

She scowled at him, but he just scowled back. She took a sip, and the stuff burned all the way down her throat, choking her. Almost immediately she went into a paroxysm of coughing.

He slipped an arm beneath her head and patted her back gently and set the glass down.

"D-did anyone ever tell you that you're incredibly bossy?" she sputtered.

He merely smiled and kept patting her back until she stopped coughing. "I'm used to getting my way."

"So am I."

She saw her boat drifting upside down toward the shallows, and she began to shiver. It suddenly occurred to her how close she'd come to death. His arms were still around her, and when he would have pulled away, she clung to him, feeling ridiculous for her fears. Just the thought of that dark water sucking her under made her terrified all over again. She didn't know if she could ever go near the water again.

At last he let her go. Embarrassed, she pushed her wet hair from her eyes. "I must look a mess."

Raoul's glinting eyes swept her from head to toe.

"But a pretty mess." His voice was huskily pitched. "I see why they keep you under lock and key."

Just the way he spoke made her feel beautiful.

"You probably say things like that to every woman."

"Maybe I never meant them so much before."

"They say you have a way with women."

"They say...." Again a shadow came across his face, and his eyes grew grave.

He touched her chin, lifted it. Yes, she could see some sadness in his eyes—some secret pain. She met the intensity of his gaze and wondered what he was thinking.

"Was it so awful?" he murmured.

"I don't think I'll ever get over it," she admitted. "The water, the darkness of it...I never knew before how much I wanted to live."

"Thank God I stopped the boat in time," he whispered.

Then he did a strange thing. He took Eva's slender hands in his and buried his face in them. She felt the warmth of his bronzed skin, the rough texture of his close-shaven cheek. She grew aware of his heavily muscled body thrillingly close to hers. He was trembling, and she realized that this strong hard man had been just as frightened as she had been.

"I was driving like I've lived—too damned fast." He paused. "Your grandmother's right about me, you know. I'm the kind of man a girl like you should avoid."

"I don't always do what *Grand-mère* says."

He studied the tilted stubborn chin, the flame color of her hair. "So I see."

"She told me to stay out of the river."

"You should have listened."

"If I had, I would never have met you." Eva's breath caught in her throat. She had never been so bold. "I—I shouldn't have said that."

"I'm glad you did."

"I never chase men."

"Chasing the opposite sex can be a delightful pastime."

"You are terrible."

"I believe in enjoying life."

"And conceited."

"Impossibly."

"You have a bad temper."

"Horrendous." He smiled sheepishly.

"And the most scandalous reputation."

"Even worse than my temper."

"At least you're honest about it."

"A man who accepts himself is a free man."

Again she sensed a darkness in him that made her wonder. "Is he?" Eva touched his damp hair, ruffled her fingers through it and then drew her hand back in shock.

"Little girls shouldn't play with fire unless they want to get burned," he said gently, but the shadow was there in his eyes.

"This morning I thought I was in love with someone else. Only now... I—I don't know what I want...anymore."

"But I do."

Suddenly she felt his hands on her shoulders. As his head lowered toward hers, she closed her eyes, her stomach felt topsy-turvy with excitement. She was as fatally attracted as a moth to flame.

"You're sweet," he whispered. "Too sweet for a scoundrel like me." Slowly he drew her into his arms and kissed her softly on the mouth. At the touch of his lips, her own quivered. Delicious little shivers traced over her body. Never had Armand, never had anyone, aroused her emotions with a single kiss as he did.

He released her almost immediately, and she sighed in forlorn disappointment.

"I'm too old and experienced for you," he murmured hoarsely in warning.

"How old?"

"Thirty-five. An antique."

"It's lucky that I come from a long line of antique dealers."

She buried her face in the hollow of his neck and, with a glow of satisfaction, she heard the harsh rasp of his indrawn breath.

"Very lucky," he groaned, pulling away, his dark eyes devouring her.

Something elemental seemed to hover in the air, charging it with tension.

"Your family doesn't like me." His swarthy face was a hard mahogany mask as he issued the warning one final time.

"Maybe if you went into a respectable career—like law or medicine..."

"So law is respectable?" He laughed harshly. "*Chère,* you are very young."

"At least my family already knows all about you and won't have to hire a private investigator."

"What?"

"Nothing."

"Do you always live so dangerously?" he murmured. His lean muscled frame stretched out beside her with graceful ease. The sun broke through the fog. Its flooding brilliance caught the side of his face and made the gray at his temple stand out against his black hair.

"Never—until today."

Carelessly he took her hand in his. Just his nearness and his most casual touch caused an emotional upheaval in her.

He was the forbidden. A known scoundrel.

She should get up and run.

But as his hand slid caressingly along the length of her arm, she stayed right where she was.

He made her feel alive in every cell in her body. She sensed a beauty in him that was more than physical.

If he was a scoundrel, she would simply have to redeem him.

Chapter 1

He had hung up the phone, but he could not forget the call.

So—Otto had found him out, in the nick of time to stave off the ruin of his vast von Schönburg empire. Otto would stop at nothing now that he had learned his enemy's true identity.

The man at the desk had learned that bitter truth the hard way. Beneath his silk dress shirt, there were tangled coils of flesh that ran the length of his back, scars from his stay in a terrorist prison camp. Because of a bullet wound to his left thigh, he would walk with a limp for the rest of his life. But the worst scars were carved like fissures into his soul. Betrayal, prison, the desert—*Africa*. All these tortures he had endured because of one man, Prince Otto von Schönburg.

Now Otto was playing a new deadly game—with the woman Nicholas had once loved.

Nicholas had always known he would have to deal with her someday.

But not like this.

Evangeline was in dreadful danger.

Because of him. Because of that single governing emotion that had driven him since Africa—his fierce desire for revenge against von Schönburg for almost destroying him, for blackening his name; revenge, too, for those men who'd fought under him and died.

Nicholas didn't want his carefully laid plans to get even with von Schönburg blown away because of Eva. He didn't want to be involved with her at all.

He curled his fist into an iron-tight knot of flesh and bone.

But he was.

Just as he knew all of Otto's weaknesses, Otto knew his.

And Evangeline Martin had been one of them from the first moment he'd pulled her from the Mississippi River and breathed life back into her.

Not that Nicholas loved her. Not anymore. She belonged to another time, another world. He had been another man, and she had been part of his foolish dream. The emotion that now filled his heart ran deep, but it was of a darker strain.

He lighted a cigarette and carefully shook out the match. It was Friday before a beautiful European summer weekend. Everyone else had gone home. Even Zak. The trading room on the fifth floor of Z.A.K. World Oil was ominously quiet. The telephones no longer buzzed constantly; the remote-control video screens were blank. During the day the room was a war zone as his agents scrambled for cargoes and markets. Z.A.K. was a key trader in the international spot-oil market.

The man who had called himself Nicholas Jones for the past eight years was seated alone in the dark staring unseeingly out the windows at the quiet Rotterdam neighborhood of centuries-old brick town houses beneath his glass office building. Every muscle in Nicholas's lean six-foot frame ached with exhaustion. He was forty-five. His once-black hair was winged with silver. Deep worry lines grooved his handsome dark face. His expression was harsh and set. His black eyes that had once flashed with youthful dreams were world-weary and cynical, as though cruel experiences in his life had obliterated all softness in him.

He should have known cornering von Schönburg had been too easy.

"Raoul," Otto had whispered in his guttural German accent

into the telephone. That dreadful voice. Nicholas had known it instantly. "So you really are alive."

"No thanks to you."

"You're the owner of Z.A.K., the genius pulling the strings of his puppets from backstage. You've done well, my friend." The German voice lowered to a gravelly purr. "Thanks to me. Or rather at my expense. But no more. And to think—once you worked for me instead of against me."

"No more. I put the noose around your neck. I have only to pull it tight to strangle you."

"You still don't get it. I have Evangeline."

Evangeline. He hadn't seen her for eight years, yet at the mere sound of her name Nicholas had gripped the armrests of his chair with clenched fingers. A silence had filled the office—the still, alert silence of terror.

"The noose is around *your* neck, my friend."

"Otto, you listen to me—"

"No, you listen to me, Girouard. You're good at what you do, but you lack the killer instinct. I don't. Last night I held her in my arms. We made love until dawn. The silly little fool thinks I want to marry her. She wants marriage and children. She still wants her family's approval, and who could not but approve the most eligible bachelor in Europe?" Otto laughed. "I was always so careful about my image when you were not so careful about yours. But imagine, me choosing her, an American and a little nobody—even if her father was a senator—when I could have any of a dozen princesses. But she is a very beautiful woman. A delicate, fragile woman. You and I always did have common tastes."

"We have nothing in common, you bastard" came Nicholas's raw, angry drawl.

"Do as I say, or she dies."

"What do you want?"

As if he couldn't guess. Because of Nicholas, Otto was involved in a complex tangle of disastrous deals in the spot-oil market. Otto wasn't getting his money because Pelican Oil had filed for bankruptcy. Other companies weren't getting their money, either, and they were refusing to pay. The feds had just seized six ships. Otto had been a key buyer in each of the multiple chains of buyer-seller deals having to do with the distressed cargoes. Six distressed cargoes meant demurrage charges of more than three thousand dollars a day. Nearly ninety-three million dollars was at stake to be exact. And Otto owed immense interest payments next week on his vast real estate holdings.

"Get on that telex of yours first thing Monday morning, my friend, and get Velmar Oil to pay on those letters of credit."

"I own only a small interest in Velmar. Pelican was the weak link in all those chains. Why should Velmar pay money Pelican owes?"

"It's because of you that Pelican is in trouble. Pay them what you owe them."

"Pelican sold me East bloc oil and didn't deliver."

"Use your influence. Z.A.K. could issue Velmar a letter of indemnity."

So there it was.

"A letter of indemnity when Z.A.K. wasn't even involved?" Nicholas's low rasp rose to a roar. "Do you think I'm mad? You're asking me to ruin my own company, to jeopardize all my own deals, to betray all my contacts, my suppliers, everyone I do business with—I'd be washed up in Europe for good—all this to save you!"

"To save Evangeline."

"She means nothing to me." Nicholas's voice softened, but even that low tone held a steel edge. "We were always wrong for each other."

"You mean a great deal to her."

"You're a liar."

"Maybe. Maybe not. You knew about Pelican. You stayed out of the deals, hoping to lure me into them by tempting me to recapture markets you took from me. It took me a long time to figure you had to be behind Z.A.K. and Velmar, too. There was only one man who could play this game better than me."

"If you thought I was so good, you shouldn't have sold me out in Africa."

"I was in a tight spot. I made a deal. You were expensive. I had to cut...costs."

"Cut the throats of my men, you mean."

"Enough said. I can't wait to settle this through the courts."

"Where can I reach you if I need...more time?"

"Portofino. *La Dolce Vita*. While you scramble, I shall be enjoying champagne, and sunsets, and...your woman."

Nicholas felt the blood rise up his neck. His face flushed as he thought of the two of them together—Eva, always trusting the wrong man, unsuspecting of any danger, completely at Otto's mercy. Otto would tell her all the bodyguards were for her protection. It would never occur to her they would be her assassins.

La Dolce Vita was Otto's yacht. Two hundred and twenty feet of sleek white aluminum—it had been custom made in an Italian shipyard by one of the world's leading designers. It was a floating palace with multiple layers of afterdecks, a pool, a helipad. Its security was impregnable.

"Either pay yourself or get Velmar to pay. If you don't, then Eva dies. London is a very dangerous city. There are cars, motorcycles, bombs. My friend, she's still in love with you."

"The hell you say."

"But that won't stop me from sleeping with her."

The line went dead.

Nicholas held the phone for a long time. Otto was asking him to commit financial suicide to save a woman he hadn't seen in eight years.

What did one woman matter? One life? Nicholas had learned a long time ago just how cheap a life could be. A hundred men had died because Raoul had trusted Otto. Later Raoul had seen more men die as easily as flies, in prison and in the desert.

He leaned back in his chair and ran both his hands through his thick black hair. His tie was loose and the top button of his shirt was undone.

He was determined not to think of her.

Not yet.

Raoul Girouard. His real name. Odd how alien it sounded. It brought back the past as nothing else could. So many years ago he'd gone by that name...yet it seemed a stranger's now. Just as his own past almost seemed a stranger's life instead of his own.

Had he really ever been von Schönburg's man? He had worked for him, yes. Right after the oil embargo when OPEC ripped up all its old contracts and proved they weren't worth the paper they were written on. Spot-oil traders had begun to provide cargoes of oil to countries that couldn't get them through conventional markets. Otto had been just another impoverished aristocrat who'd gotten into the spot-oil business and done reasonably well. Then he'd hired Raoul, and Raoul's brilliance had made him into a billionaire. Otto had invested in everything— from African oil fields to stocks, bonds and art.

Back in those golden years when crude-oil prices soared from less than four dollars a barrel to nearly forty dollars a barrel, a trader could make a million dollars on one deal alone. Raoul had been incredibly successful.

But the good times hadn't lasted. The North Sea had come on-line; U.S. regulation had been stamped out. Things had happened so fast that the oil industry had never been the same since. Now the expense of stockpiling oil inventories had led refiners to rely on the spot market as much as possible.

But the game was different now. Smaller. Tougher. More dangerous. It took more skill to play than it had before.

At the height of his successful partnership with Otto, Raoul had met Eva and fallen in love.

She had seemed a dream. She and her family had represented the kind of loving, stable world to which Raoul had always secretly wanted to belong. His own mother had died when he'd been an infant, and his father had shown him the door when he was barely seventeen. After that loveless start, Raoul had been an angry young man. The anger and the hardship of starting on his own too young had made him do reckless things he later regretted. He'd been toughened, changed forever. Then he'd met Eva, and her softness had almost made him believe he could erase his whole life and start afresh with her. But she had never trusted in him, in the man he was. Right from the start, she'd wanted to change him, to smooth away all his rough edges, and he'd let her try. Until he discovered that no matter what he did, he would never be good enough for either her or the Martins.

He'd been so desperately in love with her, for her sake, he'd even applied to law school. Without a care how she hurt him, she'd broken off their engagement—to spare her grandmother the pain of having Raoul Girouard for a grandson-in-law.

His male pride obliterated because the woman he loved thought so little of him, Raoul had been only too willing to leap at the first chance to get away from her. And that had been Africa.

Because Raoul knew Africa and Arabic, Otto had asked him to go to Rana, a tiny, war-torn North African nation to assess the danger to the newly acquired von Schönburg oil interests there. A nearby terrorist nation had been fighting to seize control of them. Raoul had jumped at the chance, even though at the last minute Eva had begged him to stay.

Once in Africa, Raoul had analyzed the situation and told Otto he would eventually lose his investment, but Rana could probably put up a fight for a year. Otto had used this information to make a profitable, self-serving deal with the terrorist aggressor nation. Not only had he sold his oil interests, but he'd sold the vital intelligence Raoul had given him as well, information that would shorten the costly war from a year to days. The terrorists had moved in fast, trapping Raoul and his men in Rana. Most of them died defending von Schönburg's interests.

Otto, always so careful about his own image, had spoken to newsmen around the world and twisted the truth, telling them Raoul had sold him and all his men out in Africa. These lies had been printed in all the right papers. Otto had emerged blameless and a much wealthier man.

But Otto had made one mistake. He hadn't made sure of his kill.

Not that he hadn't tried.

A man by the name of Nicholas Jones had been shot on that last brutal day. Badly wounded in the left thigh, Raoul had lain beside Jones's body. When Raoul saw the terrorists checking the papers of all the foreigners' bodies, some instinct had warned him to exchange identification papers with the dead Jones.

When the terrorists had found Raoul Girouard's papers on Jones's body, they'd stopped asking questions. Raoul's own face had been bloodied beyond recognition. The terrorists had hauled him back across their border to prison, but not before he'd witnessed Otto's bodyguard and hit man, Paolo, sinking a bayonet into Jones's body.

Raoul hadn't died from his wounds, nor from the starvation diet of the prison camp. Nor from the labor, the heat or the beatings with rubber hoses. He'd met Zak, a black who was half English, half Egyptian. After thirteen months they'd escaped. They both spoke Arabic and knew camels. They'd groped their way across the Sahara from well to well.

Before he'd gone to Africa, Raoul had authorized a Swiss bank to pay the note on Sweet Seclusion, his home on the bayou. When he didn't return in two years, the bank quit paying. It had hurt to learn that Otto had bought Sweet Seclusion on the auction block. But what had hurt even more was the discovery that Eva had helped Otto restore it.

With his name blackened by a scandal so terrible neither Eva nor her family could ever accept him, Raoul had not returned to Louisiana. He'd withdrawn his money from his Swiss account, kept his assumed name and set himself up in business, with Zak as the front man for Z.A.K. World Oil. In the years that followed, deal by deal, Nicholas had worked behind the scenes of his own company to destroy the von Schönburg fortune that he had helped build. Again and again he'd made better deals in the spot-oil market, always working to steal Otto's markets, to get close to Otto's contacts, to hurt Otto at the only enterprise that really mattered to the man—making money. Recently there had been articles in the London papers that the foundations of the von Schönburg empire were crumbling.

Companies like Z.A.K. didn't produce or refine oil; they were middlemen, buying and selling cargoes of crude that might not be delivered for months, oil that hadn't even been pumped out of the ground. The right call meant big profits; the wrong calls meant equally huge losses.

Nicholas had guessed right so often that there were those who believed he was infallible.

Maybe he'd been too damned good.

Maybe von Schönburg was right. Maybe all he'd done was place the noose around his own neck. If he did what Otto wanted, Z.A.K., and everybody who worked for Z.A.K., were finished.

Was one woman worth so much?

Otto had said he lacked the killer instinct.

But the man Otto had sent to Africa and betrayed was dead.

Nicholas Jones was a different breed entirely.

What was Eva like now? The woman Nicholas read about in the papers attended the smartest London charity balls, lunched at Harry's Bar, spent late nights at Annabel's, and took ski trips to Saint Moritz. She had an expensive antique shop to finance. Otto was royalty. Did Evangeline want success and status and respect more than anything? The girl he'd known had wanted love.

Otto and Evangeline. Thank God it was impossible for him to picture them together.

The only way Nicholas could ever remember Eva was as she'd looked that day he'd last seen her, that soft rainy afternoon when she'd driven to New Orleans and thrown herself into his arms at the airport and he'd pushed her away. He'd been too furious and disillusioned to listen to her.

She'd been twenty-two with long red hair, great, dark, tear-filled eyes and a sleek slim body. When he'd pushed her away, he'd felt as if he'd torn away a part of his body and cast it off.

The pain of it had been so fierce, he'd almost relented. Almost.
Instead he turned and walked up the ramp to his waiting plane.
She'd called after him, but he'd walked on. Whatever her faults,
that girl who'd loved too easily and cried too easily, who had
never learned she couldn't please everybody had been nothing
like the glitzy, social climber he now read about in the London
papers.

One thing about her was unchanged—she still had a penchant
for picking the wrong men.

Eva had been in London a long time. Nicholas read the London papers, so he'd kept up with her struggle to rise in the art
and antique world. He'd even learned of her financial problems.
They didn't surprise him—she was too softhearted and disorganized to run an efficient shop.

Otto was an antique collector. Otto and Eva had a thing for
antiques. Now it seemed Otto and Eva had a thing for each other.

Otto was a collector—not only of beautiful objects—but of
people who fascinated him or who might prove useful as well.
It was all too obvious that Otto had kept Eva on the string all
these years just in case he ever needed her.

Nicholas's gaze wandered downward to a tree-lined canal
where reddish-gold sunlight sparkled and children played in a
park. He took a deep, bitter breath.

Eight years was a long time to remember a woman. To remember her arrogant, prestigious family he'd longed to be a part
of. To remember a woman who couldn't accept him for the man
he was, who couldn't really trust him, who valued her family
more than the man she professed to love.

Still, it was odd that the thought of Eva being in danger—and
all because of him—made every nerve ending in his body tense
with alarm.

Hours later, after Nicholas got back to his flat, he went upstairs to his bedroom. His thoughts kept returning to his telephone conversation with Otto.

My friend, she's still in love with you.

Then why the hell was she engaged to Otto?

Why the hell was she still single at all?

Nicholas yanked open a drawer and pulled out a ring with a black onyx stone and a broken golden chain that sparkled against his brown palm. He had given it to Eva and, when he went to Africa, she'd given it back to him as a symbol of good luck.

It was time he got rid of the thing. He pulled out a black velvet box, black paper and gold ribbon. Then he picked up the phone and dialed.

A woman answered in German; her voice was light, eager. Too eager. Anya was Otto's beautiful, rebellious daughter. Like Otto, Raoul collected people who might prove useful.

"I can't see you tonight, Anya," he said. "Not for a week or two."

"But..."

"I will see you in Portofino at the party you're giving your father."

"What? What of Papa?"

"Pretend we're meeting for the first time."

She laughed huskily. "The danger will make everything more exciting."

He hung up the phone.

Of one thing Nicholas was sure: Otto wasn't bluffing. Nicholas had till Monday to deliver.

Nicholas had to get Eva before then.

Or Otto would kill her.

Chapter 2

As always, Eva's shop on fashionable Pimlico Road was in chaos.

Eva had had another of her sleepless nights. She'd awakened, startled from one of her much-dreaded dreams about Raoul. More than anything she longed to forget him, to hate him, to fall in love and marry someone else. But she who had once fallen in love so easily had never been able to love again.

Not after him.

He had ruined her.

He still haunted her.

Not that she would have admitted it to anyone.

Her family had been full of I-told-you-so's. They couldn't understand why she hadn't married. And she couldn't tell them.

After her dream, she had walked her floors till dawn, and the next morning she was tired and on edge. So tired she would have loved to scream or do something else that was equally unladylike.

At the moment her cat was the center of her shop's crisis.

The afternoon was dark and rainy, the streets jammed with traffic. Eva hated rain.

Inside the shop the phone was ringing. Eva hoped it was Mr. Jeffries calling, the fat little man with the wire spectacles and

bald head who owned the magnificent, twelfth-century, illuminated manuscript Eva was trying to buy for Otto. Her shop,
Connoisseurs, would be in the black if she could negotiate this
sale. She hoped Mr. Jeffries had a better price than his outrageous sum of nine million pounds.

On another line, Prince Otto von Schönburg was on hold.
Nigel, the shop's manager, had gone to an auction on Bond
Street. There were stacks of unpaid bills on Eva's desk. The
constant pressure of keeping Connoisseurs afloat was too much
for Eva on any morning, but today it was worse than usual.

Why didn't Zola answer the phone? Lady Vivien Balfoure
was waiting in Nigel's velvet-walled, beige office for Eva to
return so they could haggle over the price of a certain urn made
of the finest Sèvres porcelain, an urn that Vivien had coveted
for months but Lord Balfoure refused to buy for her.

The front doorbell tinkled. High heels tripped across marble
floors and hesitated before some tempting art object. Doubtless,
another customer who needed instant service. And the phone
kept ringing.

While all this was going on, Evangeline was trapped in the
warehouse behind Connoisseurs. There were so many important
things clamoring for attention. But first she had to rescue Victor
from the jammed drawer of an eighteenth-century armoire made
of glowing mahogany and padauk, before she bundled it off to
her restorers. He had scratched her twice when she'd stuck her
bandaged hand inside and grabbed the only thing she could
reach—his fluffy black tail.

What a morning! It had begun at one a.m. with her nightmare
about Raoul. Then on her way to the shop a motorcycle had
almost run her down in the rain. As a result she had stumbled
over a water hydrant and sprained her wrist. Otto kept bom-
barding her with telephone calls. He refused to discuss the manuscript. Instead he was carrying on about the motorcyclist, saying that he and his family had received death threats because of
an arms conference he was to attend. He was demanding that

she drop everything and come to Portofino so he could protect her. Tonight!

And now Victor.

Eva leaned down and peered into the drawer. She pulled at it, but it wouldn't budge.

Yellow cat's eyes stared at her from the dark.

"Victor, please...*chère.* Kitty, kitty. The movers are here," Evangeline pleaded in Cajun French, his native tongue, and most decidedly his favorite language.

Victor yawned and showed a mouthful of needle-sharp teeth. Like all males, he loved being difficult. His yellow eyes became disdainful slits. His ears flattened. His black tail flicked back and forth as if to say he hadn't the slightest intention of coming out unless he heard something really fascinating like the can opener. The phone kept ringing.

"Zola! Haven't you found Victor's sardines yet?"

Two burly men with a dolly and furniture quilts shifted their weight impatiently in the shadowy warehouse. Finally one of them spoke in a surly undertone. "Look, luv, how wuz I ter know 'e was in there when I shut the drawer? But sardines or no sardines, we ain't got all day. Not to wait for no bloomin' cat."

The bad grammar grated, but the casual endearment was unendurable.

"Love!" Every nerve in Eva's body bristled. Very slowly Eva pushed her tortoiseshell glasses up the bridge of her nose. She arose and studied the gum-chewing, tangle-haired hulk lounging against a crate of Venetian crystal. Red letters blazed Party Animal from his black T-shirt.

"You're new, aren't you?" she demanded briskly.

For the first time he looked at her.

Her severe, double-breasted black jacket with white pinstripes, matching pleated trousers and black spike heels accentuated her pencil-slim figure. Her red hair was pulled back. There were touches of gold at her throat and ears. Every detail of her costume, even her overlarge glasses, was deliberately calculated to make her seem more suave and professional than she secretly doubted she could ever be.

But the big boy bought her look of competence. "Give me a break, lady," he muttered, shuffling uneasily.

"Who interviewed you for this job?"

"A...a...Miss Zola."

"I suppose she told you nothing about what to wear to work?"

"Nothing."

"First, I am not your 'love.' I am Miss Martin, your boss. Second and third, no message T-shirts and no gum in Connoisseurs."

The boy gulped his gum. He hung his head.

One party animal tamed. Eva smiled softly, triumphantly.

The phone rang again. Outside it was pouring. Victor still held command of his drawer. Lady Balfoure was still waiting. The sale of the manuscript and the future solvency of Connoisseurs was still very much up in the air, but Eva felt better because she had won this minor battle.

Suddenly Zola flew into the warehouse and waved a can of sardines that flashed in the dim light like a victory signal. "I found them."

"If you'd just put things where they belong in the first place—" Eva began.

"If you'd just leave Victor at home where he belongs—"

They both stopped, each realizing it was useless to try to reform the other.

Zola was black, beautiful and original. She'd come from Louisiana with Eva. She adored antiques. Tall and thin, Zola had prominent cheekbones, huge eyes and a shower of ebony ringlets. She always wore miniskirts and painted her nails to match. She was the last sort of person one would have expected to find in a shop like Connoisseurs. She kept the accounts in a jumble. She forgot to place orders and relay telephone messages. But she loved the customers, and they adored her.

"Now where's Victor—that rascal?" Zola murmured.

"In there." Eva pointed to the armoire.

"I can handle it from here if you want to get the phone, Eva."

"If…"

Zola pushed a pair of lime-green bracelets that looked like huge frosted doughnuts up her golden arms. She opened the can and held it against the drawer. The movers were as entranced by the curve of golden thigh as was Victor by the delectable vapors of sardines. "Here, kitty kitty," she whispered in a tone that all three males found utterly seductive.

Eva saw his black paw poke out of the drawer just as she raced out of the warehouse for the phone. Otto's line was blinking. She grabbed it.

"*Liebchen,* for a moment I was afraid—" He sounded tense.

Eva rubbed her bandaged wrist. "You're not still carrying on about that idiot on the scooter?"

"I won't be able to rest until you're safe with me—tonight."

"You're just using that to order me to come. I told you I never go to birthday parties," Eva insisted firmly.

"Not even mine?"

"I explained months ago. And you know how I hate boats."

"*La Dolce Vita* isn't a boat. She's a palace."

For fifty-eight years Otto had been used to getting his way. Eva held the phone away from her ear for a minute and took a deep breath and counted to five.

She put the phone back to her ear. "I've been single too long to put up with this sort of nonsense from any man—even a prince."

He laughed. "This prince has asked for your hand in marriage."

"Things were perfect before you became obsessed with marriage."

"They will be so again, once you marry me. I want to announce our engagement at my party."

"I—I'm not sure I should marry anyone." She decided to make a joke of her doubts. "Why should I subject myself to the whims and tyrannies of a husband—even a royal one?'' She was only half teasing.

''Because you are an idealist when it comes to people and money, and I am not. Because I have money, and you need it. Because I am the only man you've dated that your family has ever approved of. Because you want children. Because you are a woman, the kind of woman who can never be complete without a man. Because you get lonely living alone, *liebchen*. I see it sometimes in your eyes. Because, you see, you need me, and I want you.''

He had struck a nerve—several nerves.

She was tired, so tired of struggling all by herself, so tired of trying to prove herself, and failing. So tired of trying to forget Raoul. All she had ever wanted was to marry and be happy.

''If you come, we can discuss the manuscript,'' Otto purred.

Nine million pounds. Did he think he was buying a manuscript or her?

Nigel had warned her. ''Prince Otto buys his wives just as he buys his masterpieces.'' And after all, there had been three others.

Otto used her silence to change tactics abruptly.

''*Liebchen…*'' There was a new element in Otto's voice. ''Something else rather unpleasant has occurred. I've had news of…Raoul.''

Otto hated Raoul and almost never mentioned him.

She felt a tingle of unwanted excitement as well as a tingle of some new and very surprising emotion—danger. ''What?''

''There's a man who says he was with Raoul in Africa when he died.''

''Who?''

''You will have to come to Portofino to meet him. I can tell you nothing but his name, Nicholas Jones.''

''The name means nothing.''

''He says he has a message to deliver.''

''I'm not interested in Raoul,'' she murmured, struggling to keep her voice flat and emotionless.

But in the antique, gilt-edged mirror across the room she saw that her face was as still as death, as gray as ash. Only the frantic pulse in her throat told her she was very much alive.

"The sun is shining in Portofino," Otto whispered.

Her pulse became quick erratic thuds.

"I am offering you a paradise of sun, sea and cobblestones. A mysterious stranger who knows something of my former, treacherous protégé and your 'friend.' What kind of woman would prefer staying in London and working?

Outside the window there was nothing but gray wet.

"It's supposed to rain in London—all weekend," Otto persisted.

Rain always reminded Eva of Louisiana. Of Raoul. Of the girl she'd been so long ago. Of the months of horror and scandal after his death, when all the vicious stories about him had been printed and the local gossips had linked her name to his. Rain reminded her of everything she had run away from Louisiana to forget.

Her pulse drummed like the rain against the window. The dark day coupled with her sleepless night and her approaching birthday must have made her more susceptible to the slightest mention of Raoul. Mr. Jones could say nothing that she did not already know. Raoul was dead, and both she and Otto wanted to forget him.

Still, she'd been working too hard at Connoisseurs. She needed a break.

Doorbells jingled and Nigel bustled into the shop, his weary arms brimming with auction-house catalogues. If she managed to negotiate the sale of the manuscript, no one at Connoisseurs would have to work as hard as each did now just to meet the overhead. Zola could have more time off for her baby.

Sun, sea and cobblestones. Eva imagined the white afterdecks of *La Dolce Vita,* the sparkling sunlight on the Ligurian sea, the warmth of the sun on her own skin. There would be elegantly served lunches on the afterdeck following a leisurely period for gossip and aperitifs. The weekend would be a blur of delectable foods, matching wines and champagne. She hated water sports, but she could watch the other guests sail, ski or swim.

And she would meet Nicholas Jones. Perhaps he could tell her something that would make her stop her inexplicable dreams of Raoul.

When Eva made up her mind, she made it up quickly. "So, it's really sunny?"

"My jet is standing by at Heathrow to pick you up, *Liebchen*."

"You were very sure of yourself."

There was a silence, and then Otto spoke, his guttural purr triumphant. "Because—you see—you are not so different from other women."

She felt like screaming at him, but he had already hung up.

She slowly set down the phone.

Sun, sea and cobblestones. And Otto's mysterious stranger, Nicholas Jones.

Everyone thought she should marry Otto. Even Nigel.

And she wanted to.

But it would be so much better if she could put the past and Raoul Girouard behind her before she did.

Hadn't she come to London to prove that she could make a life for herself and forget him?

Life was almost perfect when she managed to.

And now this.

She flipped her calendar, intending to see what was scheduled for the next week.

But the page fell open on her birthday, which was the same as Otto's although no one knew, not even Otto, because birthdays, especially her own, were occasions she no longer celebrated. An eternity ago Raoul had sent her a letter and promised to return on her birthday. He had sounded almost like he was ready to make up their quarrel. Instead, on that day, she had learned of his betrayal and death.

She would be thirty. Had Raoul lived, he would be forty-five. She had never imagined she would really ever be this age without a husband and children of her own. Her sister, Noelle, had twin girls. Otto would marry Eva, give her children. The biological clock was ticking.

Beneath the date for her birthday Eva had scribbled a single word.

"Portofino."

Suddenly it seemed that her entire life was hanging in the balance.

Chapter 3

Nicholas Jones didn't like the heavy damp wind sweeping across the balcony. Nor did he like the purple clouds towering on the southern horizon. A nasty storm was brewing in the Mediterranean, a freak, unseasonable storm that none of the weather forecasters had predicted.

He wasn't sure how to fit a storm in with his plans for tonight.

He put the thought of the storm out of his mind, and focused on the problem at hand. Nicholas felt like a common thief as he crouched in the shadows of the little balcony outside Otto's stateroom, the luxury cabin Otto had given Evangeline.

Otto had armed men everywhere. If they caught him aboard, they'd kill him.

This was hellish nonsense. It seemed like a scene from one of Nicholas's blackest nightmares.

He was insane.

But from the moment he'd spoken to Zola, he'd known he had no choice.

"A motorcycle nearly ran her down. Prince Otto says she's a target because of her close connection to him. He's involved in some sort of international arms conference. She went to Portofino so he could protect her."

Damn the clever bastard....

So here Nicholas was in Portofino, an unlikely hero in an unlikely melodrama, trying to pick what was surely the most stubborn lock in Europe. He could have been enjoying himself on board his own boat, *Rogue Wave*.

Instead his bad left leg was cramping. It was a struggle not to gag on the acrid smoke that blew up from the afterdeck. Beneath him two of Otto's men were smoking cheap Italian cigarettes and regaling one another with the filthiest jokes Nicholas had ever heard.

Carefully Nicholas placed a black-and-gold box beside the door so that both his hands would be free. Then he inserted the tiny knifelike tool back into the lock and began to jiggle it. He had to work fast before Otto came upstairs.

Nothing happened.

Noxious smoke enveloped him before the wind blew it away. Perspiration beaded his brow. Twin howls of laughter erupted over a particularly lewd item. Nicholas was too old for this game; he didn't know any of the rules or the tricks.

But he had to see Evangeline alone to try to talk her into going into hiding. He couldn't risk a public meeting.

Since she believed Raoul was dead, there was no telling what she would do when she first saw him again. Nor did he have the slightest idea what he was going to say to her, let alone how he could possibly convince her that her life was in grave danger—from Otto, her fiancé—and that he, Nicholas, had come to protect her.

Nicholas remembered her softness, her beauty, her trusting innocence. Her hair had been silken flame; her brown eyes as luminous and quiet as a fawn's. Just the memory brought a sense of hollow pain to his chest. There had been a time when he could have talked her into anything.

No. She wasn't that woman. Maybe she never had been. Now she thought she belonged to Otto.

Nicholas kept working silently, grimly, quickly, but without success. The metal blade kept clicking impotently. Anya's party would begin in less than an hour.

The blade jammed.

Damn. He didn't have the touch.

He managed to pry it loose. For hours, it seemed, the inane jokes went on beneath him as his blade strained inside the stubborn lock, as he agonized over how he was going to approach Evangeline, as the precious seconds ticked away one by one.

Then, just as he was about to give up, something in that hellish metal trap gave.

In his excitement, he dropped his tool. It clattered against the glass door as it fell. *Thowop!* It hit painted white aluminum.

Damn.

With a groan he knelt to pick it up. There was a sudden hush beneath him; the relaxed banter and jokes stopped. There was a new urgency in the Italian voices.

"*Dio!* What was that?"

Nicholas's hand froze in midair as he reached for the black-and-gold box.

"The balcony."

The men were shouting the alarm just as Nicholas opened the door and stepped silently into a gleaming cocoon of pink Carrara marble. His bad leg was throbbing, and his limp was more pronounced. The fragrance of a thousand roses filled the air. After the smoke, he felt slightly nauseated.

He saw gold vases filled with pink roses. A Titian hung on one wall; a magnificent Gobelin tapestry was on the other. Mirrored doors ran the length of the cabin. The nearest door was opened. He saw dresses hanging inside it. The last two doors were also slightly ajar. Filmy traceries of perfumed steam seeped out of them. A bathroom. The floors were covered with thick Persian carpets.

Nicholas felt repelled by Otto's extravagance. Otto hadn't changed. He had always used his money to overpower, to impress, to enslave and corrupt—to buy even those things in life that no man should ever have to buy.

In the center of the vast stateroom was a bed covered with a pink silk spread. Otto's bed. Hers, too. Nicholas flinched at the thought and then pushed it from his mind, concentrating instead on the black silk evening gown that lay there. The dress was lined with red taffeta. A heavy collar of diamonds and bloodred rubies had been tossed down beside it. Nicholas picked up the necklace and fingered it grimly. It was the kind of thing Anya wore. He pitched it back onto the bed.

It was clear as day that Eva was already Otto's mistress, that she was only too happy to be the newest piece of merchandise on Otto's auction block.

What was her price? A necklace of diamonds and rubies? No. More. Much more. On the bed beside the necklace were catalogues of priceless illuminated manuscripts, and then Nicholas remembered she had a shop to finance. Otto's money could give her success, her family's respect, status in society, all the things a man like himself could never provide.

Sour grapes, old man? Nicholas laughed mirthlessly at himself. Who was he to judge her after the things he'd done? Besides, it wasn't as if he wanted her for himself.

Where the hell was she?

Restlessly he moved farther into the bedroom. On a wing-backed chair he saw bits of fragile black lace. She had always been messy. He picked one up, examining what he discovered was a filmy brassiere. For a second longer he let it dangle against his brown arm while he imagined the creamy smooth swell of her breasts filling it. Feeling aroused somehow, he flung the intimate gossamer thing down again.

Damn Otto for forcing him into such a degrading position. He had no wish to spy, no wish to sneak around a woman's bedroom and invade her privacy, especially not Evangeline's. Still, the picture of white skin and dark nipples pushing beneath black lace lingered like an erotic dream in the back of his mind.

Nicholas heard the splash of water, the husky murmur of a familiar French love song. The very song he had once so lovingly taught her. He looked up and was electrified when he focused on that cloud of steam sifting from that last half-opened door. A bar of pink-gold light fell across the rugs.

Dear God! Just his rotten luck! She was bathing!

He should go and come back another time.

But he couldn't. There was no other time.

He moved closer to those half-opened doors, closer until he could see the flutter on cranberry tiles of her pink silk robe that lay discarded beside the marble tub. Closer until he could see her arm rise languidly from the soapy bubbles, until he could see the tantalizing curve of her naked back coated with sparkling bubbles, until he could see the damp tangle of red hair spilling in wild disarray from the confines of the towel down her long graceful neck. A pair of tortoiseshell glasses lay on the edge of the tub. She turned slightly, and the profile of a breast rose above a mountain of bubbles. She ran a thick Turkish washrag over it.

His heart began to pound violently. He told himself to move away. Instead his muscles turned to stone, and he stood there rigidly, staring at her with the awe of a raw schoolboy seeing his first woman. Her skin was golden and wet from her bath. Her voice was soft and husky as she sang that half-remembered love song, every faltering note cutting like the sharpest blade straight through to his heart. Once, long ago, on a drowsy summer afternoon, when she'd hardly been more than a girl, he had taught her that song of lost love. And afterward he had promised he would never leave her.

But he had.

She was French. And sensuous. She had loved him.

No, dear God. She had lied! How she had lied. She had wanted to remake him into some ideal man she could love. After his lonely childhood and lonely life, he had been so starved for love and for family himself, he had concocted a fantasy about her and hers. The Martins were proud. For a hundred years they'd occupied positions of power and privilege while his own family had bred gamblers and rogues. Raoul had secretly admired the Martins and longed to be one of them, and that had made their dislike hurt all the more.

The sweat on his brow was thick again. He felt a vague nostalgia, a terrible loneliness. And remorse. Why the hell should he feel remorse when she had been the one to show him she could never really love him.

She was nothing to him now! Nothing, but he couldn't just stand back and let her die—not even to save his own skin. Not even to destroy Otto.

She lifted her left hand lazily from the tub and blew the bubbles from her fingers. An immense diamond glittered in the soft pink light. She stopped singing and moved her hand so that she could admire the white stone as it flashed.

There was a new coldness in the pit of his stomach.

So, she had told Otto yes. Because of the money, the status and the fame, he supposed. Like everyone else neither she nor the Martins could see past the image Otto so carefully projected. Her shop was in trouble.

How in the hell was Nicholas going to convince Eva to jeopardize Connoisseurs and go into hiding with him? To convince her that Otto was a villain?

Someone began to pound on the pink door. Nicholas started, jumping clumsily back toward the balcony. So clumsily that his arm bumped against the wing-backed chair. The black box with the gold ribbons went flying toward the bathroom, landing right in front of the bathroom door. Nicholas swallowed hard. There was no way he could get it. No way she could come out and miss it.

Of all the abominable luck.

More pounding. *"Signorina!* It's Paolo!"

Otto's personal bodyguard. Nicholas held a special grudge against him. Half Italian, half Arab, Paolo was the loathsome bastard who'd done Otto's dirty work in Africa.

"Signorina!"

"I'm taking a bath."

"I have to check the stateroom. The guards, they hear somebody on your balcony!"

She turned off the faucet. Her voice was impatient. "All right. In a minute."

Nicholas could hear her stepping out of the tub. He heard

water gurgling down the drain. There was no time to do anything except react on instinct. He dived toward the open closet door, squirming behind a dozen hanging dresses. Just as he was about to pull the door closed, he stepped on something soft that yowled and sprang at him viciously. A set of thorny claws raked his bad leg. Needle-sharp teeth bit into his ankle.

A cat! He would have gladly paid the price of a thousand barrels of Nigerian crude to grab the squawling thing by the scruff of its neck and give it a fierce shaking. At the very least he wanted to yowl as indignantly as the cat had. He bit his lip instead.

"Victor, darling. Are you into trouble?"

Nicholas smothered his cry with the back of his hand, pushed the door open a crack and gave the monster a gentle kick. He saw a blur of black fur leap wildly toward the sliver of light. Thank God! He had the closet to himself.

The devil sat down in front of the closet to lick his tail.

"Victor...you look upset." Eva's voice was soft and husky and warm as she came toward the closet.

Through the crack Nicholas could see her. She looked alluringly soft in her pink silk robe, the roundness of her breasts too apparent against the thin material. Her glasses had fallen down to the tip of her nose. Her hair was a shower of coppery fire. She bent, and the robe gaped open, revealing too much slender leg. Her beautiful smile was radiant and adoring as she scooped the black devil into her arms. "Look what I found, sweetie."

Sweetie...Nicholas almost strangled.

She held the black-and-gold box up for the cat to inspect as if he had the wit to do so. Black paws began poking playfully at the gold ribbon as she carried him toward the door that Paolo was pounding on.

Put something else on, Nicholas wanted to yell, something that isn't so transparent and doesn't cling like a second skin.

She opened the door and smiled charmingly at the tanned brute with the moody sensual face.

The man was as dangerous as a cobra. Nicholas sucked in his

breath with hatred. Skintight suede molded Paolo's lean body. He had the look of a killer—with those opaque, soulless eyes and the hard thin lips that rarely smiled. Why couldn't she see it?

She had never been clever about men.

Nicholas remembered the opaque eyes, the way the thin lips had curved again and again when he'd plunged his bayonet into Jones's inert body before kicking him into the ravine. Paolo was the hit man Otto had sent to Africa.

The enticing charm of Eva's smile toward this monster roused a dangerous, murderous fury in Nicholas.

"*Signorina*, I need to look—"

His eyes slid over her lush body with a predatory interest.

Damn the man. Nicholas could have gladly choked him to death with his bare hands.

Paolo broke off, swaggered restlessly to the balcony and looked out, his every movement slow, suggestive, dangerous, as if he were casing the room. He lifted curtains, looked under the bed, and she watched him, unafraid.

As always she was incapable of seeing through a man like Paolo.

"There's no one here, Paolo, I can promise you. And the prince is waiting. I need to get dressed."

That was the understatement of the year.

Paolo's eyes went over her. He combed his fingers through his black hair, shrugged, and decided she was right.

When he had gone, Nicholas sagged against the wall in relief. Until he realized he was going to sneeze.

Cats! He was allergic to them!

Gently Eva set Victor and the mysterious gold-and-black box down on the bed. Then she switched on the radio. For a second it blared, so she didn't hear the two very loud sneezes in her closet. Then she turned the radio down, twisting knobs until she found a lovely Chopin nocturne.

She had to hurry; Otto was waiting. She'd stayed too long in her bath because she dreaded facing all of Anya's glamorous guests. She loosened the sash of her robe.

Victor was on the bed with the mysterious black box, and he was snatching and pulling, making a hopeless snarl of the gold ribbons. She studied the box. Curious, she picked it up and held it against her ear, shaking it lightly.

Someone had been here. Why hadn't she mentioned the box to Paolo?

She shook the box again.

Because whoever had come in hadn't bothered the diamond collar or her. Because she could never have gotten rid of Paolo if she had, and his strange eyes made her feel creepy. He didn't bathe often enough, and when he came too close she could smell sweat and leather and stale wine.

As she undid the gold ribbons, she draped the long lengths across Victor who rolled over, winding himself playfully in the glittering streamers.

Holding the box in her bandaged hand, she tore into the black paper, tossing the bits to Victor.

Inside was a gold velvet box.

A tiny vellum envelope fell out. Her name was a swirl of bold black letters. Even her middle name that no one knew. For a long moment she stared at it. Long ago that single letter from Raoul had come to her from Africa addressed in the same manner. The handwriting was identical.

A shiver traced down her spine.

Then she tore it open.

Inside was a single card and more of the same bold black scrawl. She read aloud the terse message in French.

"Once I promised to return to you on your birthday, *chère*."

It was unsigned.

Her lips quivered. *Chère*. Only one man had ever called her that. Only one man had ever made her such a promise.

Raoul.

But he was dead.

Who else? Who even knew that today was her birthday?

Her family—but they were in Louisiana, and they would never be so cruel.

Numbly her fingers lifted the lid of the box. Shimmering against black satin was a golden ring with an onyx stone set in its center.

Mon Dieu.

She was breathless, shocked.

The ring was the one that Raoul had given to her when they'd been so in love. When he'd left for Africa, she'd given it back to him—along with a gold chain so he could wear the ring around his neck.

Her heart stopped and then began to flutter chaotically. Raoul's thick gold chain was looped through the ring, but one link was broken as if the chain had been ripped violently from his neck.

She thought of Raoul lying helpless, dying. The vision came to her of some brutal hand reaching down toward that limp brown neck for the chain. She wanted to remember all the hatred she'd felt for Raoul. But all she could remember was the grief.

Through a mist of emotion Eva stared at the glittering bits of gold. The ring couldn't be hers! She didn't want it to be!

The ornate stateroom with its pink marble and Persian carpets and fine oil paintings blurred. Victor and his tangle of gold ribbons were forgotten. The sickening sweetness of the roses made her feel nauseated.

In a trance Eva lifted the ring from black velvet. She turned it over. With her fingertip she traced the familiar initials, Raoul's and hers, entertwined—E.M. and R.G.

She gave a broken cry.

Then she screamed.

Once.

Before she fainted.

For a second there was no sound other than a wildly romantic crescendo of piano notes. Chopin's *Minute Waltz.*

Then Paolo began banging against the door.

Her scream pierced through every cell in Nicholas's body. He had remained in the closet, trying to frame the exact words he would say to make her understand.

At her scream his heart seemed to explode in his chest.

He told himself to stay where he was until he got a grip on himself. He told himself that he hated her, that whatever pain she felt meant nothing.

But as she fell, he sprang from the closet, forgetting the danger to himself. Eva was lying on the floor—soft breasts, slender waist, long shapely legs—a provocative curl of voluptuous woman. The pink silk wrapper concealed very little. Her glasses had fallen to the carpet. She was lovely, fragile. And so small and feminine.

If she had been beautiful eight years ago, she was even more beautiful now. Her features were gentle and sweet. She had the high cheekbones of a Cherokee princess. Her hair was scintillatingly thick, golden red. Her slim figure was fuller and more opulently lush.

He had no real taste for the kind of women he saw now— scrawny women, cold women, women who could never touch his heart as once Eva had.

Eva was as still as death; her golden skin as white as snow. Her ring was clutched in her fingers.

With exquisite care Nicholas lifted her into his arms, cradled her tightly against him and smoothed the tangled curls back from her forehead. She was warm and damp from her bath, deliciously perfumed. She had the same sensuous, exciting body he remembered.

He ignored the familiar stirring in his loins and carried her to the bed and laid her down, smoothing her hair out on the pillow. Her eyes fluttered open, and she stared up at him. Nicholas thought he saw a glimmer of recognition, but she lowered her thick black lashes before he could be sure. Her whispery voice was so soft he could barely hear her. "You're a dream. A dream... I hate you, but why can't I forget you?"

Dear God. So, she was haunted by painful dreams, too.

She closed her eyes completely.

To shut him out.

He shook her, but she did not open them again.

"This is no dream, Eva. No dream. I've come back. To protect you. You mustn't be afraid. Not of me, *chère,* no."

"No, I don't want you to be real."

He couldn't blame her as he glanced around the lavish room. She wanted Otto and all that Otto could give her. But she didn't know what Otto was. Very carefully Nicholas lifted her into his arms. Somehow he had to get her out of here. But as he headed toward the door, he heard the thunder of footsteps outside in the hall.

Then the pink door was starting to splinter beneath Paolo's black-booted heel.

Nicholas was trapped.

"Signorina?"

Otto was shouting, too. "Here's the key you fool. Then in a softer voice that would sound evil only to Nicholas, he heard Otto say, *"Liebchen?"*

Nicholas barely had time to ease her ring onto her finger, to lay her gently back down onto the bed, and cover her completely from neck to ankle with pink silk. He grabbed the velvet box and its wrappings—not so easily done because he had to yank the golden ribbon away from the growling cat-devil—and then slipped outside onto the balcony.

They were gone now—Otto, Paolo, the doctor—having made a lengthy fuss over Eva.

She had lain in her bed like one in a trance, her red hair spread in a tangle of fire against her white pillow, a dazed expression on her face, not answering their questions.

They had pressed.

She had told them nothing.

Which was damned odd, but Nicholas was thankful nevertheless, even though he was furious at himself for bungling everything.

The doctor concluded that she was suffering from nerves, that she was overly excited about the suddenness of the engagement and the party. No one thought to search the stateroom or the balcony again.

There were guards everywhere. All Nicholas could do was wait until they left for the party. Even after she was alone in the room again, Nicholas was afraid to show himself. How could he convince her she had to go into hiding with him? How could they escape the heavily guarded yacht together? What if she screamed again and brought them all back to the stateroom? Nicholas was under no illusions about what would be his fate. No, somehow at the party he would have to find a way to approach Eva when she was not so carefully guarded. With the comings and goings of the guests, it would be easier to escape.

The curtains weren't quite shut. There was a crack. From time to time Eva would walk in front of it, and Nicholas could watch her twisting the black-and-gold ring on her bandaged hand. She looked pale, confused, distraught.

Once as she studied the ring, he'd watched her silent face. He saw her lips tremble and a tear well out of one corner of her eye and spill down her flushed cheek before she raised her hand to brush it away.

What was she thinking, feeling? She had said she hated him. What would she do when they met?

Slowly, as he watched the most tantalizing dress-tease he'd ever seen, he realized all that he had lost. He saw her naked, golden-limbed and lovely. He saw her in black lace and sheer black hose. He watched her pin up her hair. He remembered how she'd been—innocent at first and then wild in his bed. And in spite of all that had gone wrong, he wanted her.

He clenched his shaking hands into fists. In his mind's eye, visions of blood and death in the desert, all the dreadful memories of Otto's treachery rose up to haunt him.

She was sleeping with his worst enemy. Nicholas cared nothing for her. She was nothing but a pawn in a dangerous game he was playing with a dangerous man.

Nicholas had Otto where he wanted him. Only this woman stood in the way.

Nicholas was trapped on the balcony while she dressed. He should have looked away. He should have shut his eyes.

But he didn't. Instead he watched her dress, and the sight of her lighted a spark of desire that burned him to the core. He felt a madness to touch her, to know the warmth of her, to know her softness, to caress her until she burned with a madness equal to his own. Once he had been another man who had dreamed of having a real life, and she was the woman he had longed to share it with.

Just once he wanted to have her again, after the long barren years. And this treacherous need filled him with hatred because she had given herself to Otto.

Nicholas felt his stubborn, intractable will sliding away—the powerful force that had kept his mask in place all these years—and he was suddenly afraid. This woman was dangerous to him. She made him forget who he was, how he'd taught himself to live. Just the sight of her brought back the dreams.

If he wasn't careful, Otto would win after all.

Nicholas was afraid of her, afraid of even talking to her.

But he had no choice.

If he didn't get her away from Otto, she would die.

Chapter 4

Eva could not stop thinking of Raoul any more than she could forget the onyx ring on her finger. Had he come to her room? Her vision now seemed heart-stoppingly real.

But he was dead!

The horizon burst into white flame and her confused thoughts returned to the present. The heavy, rain-scented wind ruffled the harbor. The immense cigarette tender bobbed up and down in the dark waves at the stern of *La Dolca Vita.*

She hated boats and anything to do with boats—deep water, rain, electrical storms. The mere thought of jumping down into that wildly gyrating death trap filled her with dread. She had never forgotten the horror of nearly drowning.

Eva's sparkly black high-heeled shoe flailed for the last rung of the ladder. The sea breeze was whipping her gown, exposing too much leg to Paolo down below. The water splashed against the hulls; she felt salt spray against her ankle.

She gasped. If she misjudged, she would fall into the water, and her heavy gown would pull her under.

"Careful, *Liebchen!*" Otto commanded in a cool autocratic tone from above.

White-faced, she clung to the teak ladder. At last her toe found the bottom rung. Paolo's strong arms came around her waist, and he lifted her down into the tender. Otto jumped deftly after her. She grabbed the rail, and Paolo let her go and cast off.

It would soon be dusk. On the front edge of the black storm, Portofino was still jewel pink and gold—a paradise of sun and sea—all sparkle and shimmer beneath a hazy violet sky. On one hilltop Anya's villa was brilliantly lighted. Although Eva was disturbed by what had happened in Otto's cabin and frightened of the wind and water, she told herself she'd soon be up there, safe and sound on dry land.

Otto smiled reassuringly, but his smile lacked warmth. There was some new tension in him. He cupped her chin. It was all she could do to endure his cold, possessive fingers.

Otto had thick white hair, bushy black brows and fox-sharp blue eyes. Eva didn't like the way his bright, feral eyes seemed to read her every doubt.

He was shorter than she. Plump and tanned, he carried his extra thirty pounds well. He had a large head, powerful torso and an equally powerful will. He exuded power. He was the kind of man few people crossed. She remembered how furious he'd been when she'd told him a little while ago that she didn't want him to announce their engagement tonight after all.

Otto carefully honed his public image. The newspapers said he was the most eligible bachelor in Europe. Architectural magazines ran stories on his castles. Art magazines published articles about his collection. Her parents had been thrilled for her last night when she'd become engaged to him. They would be equally disappointed in her when they learned what she'd just done.

With a frown, Otto lifted Eva's left hand and studied the diamond he'd given her. He had promised her he would not make the announcement—but very reluctantly.

"You're still angry."

His face was dark and sullen. "Do you blame me? I'm used to getting any woman I want."

"I'm just not sure," she whispered. "Please..."

The powerful engine of the tender roared to life and she tried to pull her hand from his, but he wouldn't let her.

"You're still pale," Otto murmured, his penetrating blue eyes searching her face. "What upset you?"

"Nerves. I told you I'm afraid of boats."

His expression changed. He saw too much.

She turned away, her gaze fixing on a sleek black yacht moored only a few feet away. It hadn't been there earlier.

"The engagement," she began, "the party, deciding to come here at the last moment. Everything seems so hurried."

"You screamed. Why?"

She could not say: *I saw him.*

"An anxiety attack. I'm not used to parties like this, mingling with royalty."

She was looking at the black sloop. There was something mysterious about her. Eva read the bold curls of gold script on her stern. *Rogue Wave.* The yacht's lines were so graceful that she made Otto's many-decked, floating giantess with her air conditioners and stabilizers and helipad seem elaborate and top-heavy.

"Did your scream have anything to do with your wanting to postpone the announcement?"

"Don't be ridiculous," she said, not meeting his eyes.

"Nicholas Jones never showed up." There was a grim note in Otto's voice.

"Oh. I was so looking forward to meeting him."

"You will have to enjoy me instead." The grim note took on a bitter edge.

She was aware of a stealthy movement at a darkened window just above the waterline. There were no lights below on *Rogue Wave,* but Eva was almost sure that someone was watching them from the dark.

Shakily Eva twisted the slender gold-and-onyx ring on her right hand. Someone had come into her room and had returned the ring that she had given Raoul. She had fainted then, only to imagine him in her room.

What was going on? Who was Nicholas Jones? Had he left the ring? Had he really known Raoul? But Otto had told her Nicholas Jones hadn't come.

All she knew was that this afternoon when she'd found the ring she had realized she wasn't sure she could marry Otto. But she had to tread carefully. Connoisseurs was too dependent on Otto and his friends. Otto was egotistical. If she humiliated him, he would ruin her.

Otto brought her hand to his cool lips. Then he seized the controls of the boat and he became more arrogant than ever. He leaned back and steered with a single finger. The boat jetted recklessly across the harbor, careening past moored yachts and showering them with its rooster tail of white spray, sending a dangerous wake in all directions. Eva gripped the railings in true terror. The powerful rush of damp sea wind tore her hair loose from its pins, whipping it against her cheeks. By the time they roared up to Anya's private dock, one glance in a chrome mirror told her that she looked as wild as if she'd just stuck two fingers in an electric light socket.

Otto turned toward her, thrilled. "Well, *Liebchen,* what do you think of her?"

She was still terrified from the ride across dark water and now furious, too. "What do you think of my hair?"

He plucked a pin out of the red frizz and handed it to her. "I love it. You look wild—half-tamed."

Half a dozen of Otto's liveried men helped her ashore, onto the dock that led to the platform for the funicular that would carry them up the cliff to Anya's villa.

"Perfect for a part in a Tarzan film," she retorted.

"Perfect to be my future gypsy princess," he murmured. "You are the first woman who has ever denied me her bed this long."

That again. "We are not married."

"That is so rarely an obstacle." There was a predatory gleam in his eyes. "Besides, everyone believes we are lovers."

"I—I don't care." But she grew very still.

He touched the diamond necklace, lifting a single bloodred
ruby. His plump fingertip was cold against her throat.

"When a man marries at fifty-eight..."

She licked her suddenly parched lips. "For the fourth time..."

"Such a man knows exactly what he wants."

"You sound like you're buying a Renoir."

"You are worth far more than a Renoir." He smiled but his
voice was cold.

There was an answering coldness in her own heart. What was
the matter with her? Why couldn't she just do the sensible thing
and marry this man her family approved of? Why did it feel so
wrong?

He took her hand firmly and led her toward the funicular. He
stepped into the cramped metal cage himself. Eva glanced upward at the steep tumble of jagged rocks.

"There are no roads to the villas," Otto explained. "Mule
trains still carry most heavy items to the villas. I was very lucky
to convince the local committee to allow me to build this funicular."

The cliff seemed sheer and almost vertical in places. Usually
she wasn't afraid of heights, but a strong wind was blowing.

Paolo was shutting the gate on them, sending them up alone.

"No." Otto commanded. "I want you to stay with Eva—
everywhere, every moment—tonight."

A look passed between the two men, some silent order, given
and received. Otto pushed open the gate. Paolo squeezed his
great body in with them. Otto punched a red button, and the
funicular shot jerkily upward on a series of grumbling metallic
groans.

The ascent was steep and terrifying, so steep that Eva didn't
dare look down. By the time they reached the villa, the sky was
almost totally black except for a few diamond-bright stars and
flashes of lightning.

Otto left her with Paolo, and Eva found a bathroom and re-
pinned her hair. When she came out she wandered among
Anya's guests out onto the palm-shaded terraces that clung to

the vertical cliffs. White lights had been hung in the trees, and the swimming pool that had been chiseled into the rocky cliff was a dazzling aquamarine color. Flowers were everywhere.

There were dozens of beautiful women in designer gowns and jewels. The finest French champagne flowed as freely as the sparkling waves lapping against Anya's dock below. The softly scented breezes smelled of salt air and summer blossoms—geranium, gardenia and oleander. The moonlit evening was idyllic, and yet Eva couldn't relax.

There was a ring on her finger that she couldn't explain. The man she had given it to was dead. She could not stop asking herself who had returned it to her and why? The mere thought of it was enough to send a strange tremor through her.

Portofino had not changed in fifty years. Ever since she'd arrived, she had felt as if she'd lifted the curtain of time and walked back into the past.

Near the pool behind her a pair of lovers were embracing secretively.

"Nothing ever changes here except the shift of the sun in the sky."

Eva recognized the voice of Il Padrino, the local godfather. He was speaking to a dark-eyed starlet. "We read, we relax, we talk, we make love...." The girl giggled invitingly.

Eva drifted away, but his words lingered in her mind, arousing that aching, unwanted emptiness that usually haunted her only in dreams. Raoul seemed eerily near. She went into the house and admired Anya's magnificent antiques as well as the paintings on the walls, which were masterpieces. She was fascinated by two paintings. The first was of the phoenix, that great mythical bird fabled to live five hundred years, plunging itself into a wall of flame that would be its funeral pyre. The second painting was of the same subject, but in it the phoenix was rising from its own ashes. She looked up and saw that Paolo was watching her.

Bodyguards—their necessity seemed sinister somehow. She

shivered. The rich were as trapped by their wealth as were the poor by their poverty.

She moved toward Otto and his guests. As always he was using every minute to promote his businesses.

Once he had told her, "Like you, *Liebchen*, I'm a shopkeeper at heart."

"You keep a big shop."

He had laughed.

The glitterati of a dozen countries were there tonight. All were vying for attention, competing to see and be seen by the right people. There was a vicious social hierarchy even among these kings and queens of society, and she felt out of it all. But such freedom would not be hers much longer—not if she married Otto.

Hours passed. Eva moved through the throngs of guests on Otto's arm, very aware that she and his necklace of diamonds and bloodred rubies were on display just like his fabulous paintings. The guests believed what Otto wanted them to believe— that he and she were lovers.

For so many years she had worked hard for this moment.

She was the envy of everyone.

Never had she felt more utterly alone.

If she married Otto, she would have approval, success, children. But what of love?

Otto's guests expressed their interest in Connoisseurs. She found herself trying to act like Otto—using this social occasion to promote her business, but what she secretly wanted was to feel cherished and to feel wild about the man who would be her husband. She told herself that Otto was older; he'd known too much hardness in his life to ever wear his heart on his sleeve.

Suddenly she and Otto were standing beside a gold-and-marble table piled with a mountain of gifts. He was telling everyone stories of his childhood, how he'd grown up in Paris, a refugee of the Nazis.

"I learned early that life was precarious, my friends. You must seize what you want—whether it is an empire, a moment or a woman.'' The thin aristocratic lips parted in one of his sly-fox smiles. He lifted Eva's left hand so that everyone could see the diamond he had given her.

There were gasps. Then applause.

He had not actually announced their marriage. And yet he had.

Eva felt betrayed. She tried to smile but she could not be that false. She felt like her face was cracking. Her entire body was trembling. The ornate room with its velvet sofas, tall mirrors and elaborate oil paintings seemed to spin in a sickening whirl.

She felt Otto's cold lips against her cheek. "You are pale, *Liebchen*," he whispered, pretending concern.

Pale with suppressed rage. She could see the looks of envy on many of the women's faces. Again she tried to smile, but she was too angry. *Later,* she told herself. *Later. You will deal with him later, firmly but with care.*

Otto reached for the nearest gift, the largest one of all. It was wrapped in black paper and tied with golden streamers.

Black and gold.

The same paper and ribbon as the gift she'd found in her stateroom.

She glanced down at the ring on her right hand. In an instant her fury toward Otto was forgotten. All the remaining color drained from her face. Her knees felt like rubber. Uncertainly she turned to Otto, touched his arm and held on to him for support. He smiled at her, pleased.

Otto ripped into the paper and pulled out a tiny vellum enveloped and handed it to her. Otto's nine aristocratic names were mocking swirls of bold black.

Eva felt the blood rush back into her face.

On the card inside was a single word. Revenge. It was signed Nicholas Jones.

Otto caught sight of the message and then this fierce gaze flashed around the room. He spoke to her hurriedly, but she didn't hear him. The roar in her ears was too deafening.

Nicholas Jones—he was here! He was the one who had come into her room earlier.

The crowd grew quiet as everyone waited for Otto to open the gift.

She looked up desperately. "I thought you said he wasn't coming," she whispered.

She was shocked at the change in Otto. He seemed smaller somehow, as if he had shrunk a whole size. His face was very white. His thin lips were pressed together to conceal their trembling.

Across the room a tall man moved deliberately, drawing her attention away from Otto. He was tall and dark and dressed in black. He stood in the shadows beneath the golden paintings of the phoenixes.

She froze.

This time she knew.

His back was to her, but something about him was achingly familiar. She studied the way his tuxedo fit him so perfectly, emphasizing his broad muscular shoulders yet not exaggerating them, tapering at his lean waist. He was talking to Anya. He made a gesture with his hand that was peculiarly French—*Cajun French*—and yet peculiarly his alone.

Eva felt the shock of recognition go through her whole body.

The man turned slowly. There was an iridescent ribbon of golden light in his ebony hair. He lighted a cigarette and carefully shook out the match. That gesture, too, was peculiarly his.

Behind him the golden feathers of the phoenix seemed on fire.

Raoul.

Mon Dieu.

He was alive.

The vision in her stateroom had been all too real. The treacherous, lying devil who'd murdered a hundred men in cold blood for money was very much alive and prospering by the look of him.

Some part of her had always known he'd survived.

And yet this man with the black hair and the deep dark eyes and the devastatingly beautiful masculine face wasn't *her* Raoul at all. He was of some newer, crueler vintage. There were deep lines around his mouth that added a harshness and a terrible coldness to his features.

This man was ruthless. She knew that he had come into her stateroom and left a gift, his deliberate intention—to tear her heart to pieces. He was a stranger, either reborn or disguised as the man she had once loved, a stranger who mesmerized her with a vital, furious, animal magnetism that Raoul had never possessed. She had loved Raoul; this man aroused some darker, deeper emotion.

She had never quite believed Otto. Never until now. She had always believed that if only Raoul had come home, they could have proved him innocent of Otto's accusations.

Nicholas Jones appeared capable of anything.

She wanted to run, but she couldn't move a muscle.

Otto hadn't seen him yet, but his hands were shaking as he opened a case of the finest imported French champagne. He lifted a bottle and held it up for the crowd to admire. He tried to smile, but his face was a mask.

Everybody clapped and smiled. Everybody except Otto and Eva and the dark uninvited guest across the room.

For the first time the man looked directly at Eva. His cynical gaze met hers, touched hers with its mocking fire, and she felt an incredible shock go through her again. He felt it, too. Then his tanned face hardened, his black eyes narrowed, first with disbelief and then with a fresh blaze of anger and contempt. He lifted his champagne glass toward Otto and her in a mock salute before he turned back to Anya.

His face purpling, Otto jammed the bottle into its cardboard cradle and thrust the magnificent gift aside. He had spotted the swarthy uninvited guest beside his daughter. Instantly he called Paolo to his side and spoke to him in low, rapid whispers. Seconds later Paolo moved through the crowd toward Anya, but when he reached her, Raoul had vanished.

Somehow Eva and Otto got through the next hour. Otto opened his gifts while she read the cards for him in a voice that shook almost as much as his hands did. From time to time her gaze flickered about the room, searching for but not finding Raoul. After all the presents had been opened, guests began to come up to Otto and congratulate him.

Eva waited until Otto was surrounded. Then she slipped out of the house and raced down the stone steps and footpaths, past the huge rock walls embroidered with geraniums and cascading clumps of bougainvillea, past the aquamarine pool, and lost herself in the hanging gardens that clung to the cliffs in tiers of imported palms, eucalyptus, mimosas, flowing fountains, artificial waterfalls, and pines. When she reached the far corner of the garden, she came to a high glass wall that served as a windscreen and a boundary wall as well. A narrow lap pool reflected the dark shapes of the trees and the starry sky. Anya's brilliantly lighted terra-cotta mansion was almost invisible, so steep were the cliffs and dense pines, but Eva could hear the music drifting down from the house.

Where was Raoul? Why had he come back tonight?

Beneath she could see the harbor, the sparkling water and the lightning in the distance; she could smell the salt tang of the sea as well as the fragrance of nectar from the summer flowers.

More than anything she wanted to be alone.

She heard a stealthy footstep on stone. Someone had followed her from the house, someone who was hidden by the trees.

"Who..." Her voice was light and breathless.

There was no answer. Frightened, she took a faltering step back. Then another. Again she called out, but again silence was her only answer. As the heel of her shoe caught the edge of a brick, too late, she remembered the pool.

She fell backward, floundering wildly to save herself. A million reflected stars rippled across the inky liquid surface. She cried out in frustration, sputtering, as the water slopped into her sparkly shoes, then up to her waist and over her head. When she managed to stand up, her hair and her gown were a dripping mess.

"Oh!" She was pushing the oozing mass of her collapsed hairdo out of her eyes when a tall figure moved in the shadows.

"Very nice," a deep sarcastic voice drawled from the trees. A match flared. "A hell of a lot nicer than the first time we met, when I had to jump in, too."

He stepped nearer the pool. In the tiny curl of golden flame she recognized the raven hair, his harsh profile, his unsmiling, yet ever-so beautiful mouth.

"You!" she spat.

Nicholas Jones lighted his cigarette and shook out the match. In his flawlessly cut tuxedo, he was as elegant as she was not. His broad-shouldered physique was more heavily sculpted with muscle than she remembered. From her embarrassing position in that shallow pool, he seemed a gigantic being looming out of the darkness. He moved toward her with a slight limp until he stood directly above the pool, staring down at her. His face gave nothing away. The hard features seemed cast in bronze.

She swallowed.

It wasn't his vile misdeeds that she remembered. No, it was all the youthful pain of loving him and losing him that came back to her, the years of loneliness, as well as the bitter disillusionment of knowing he could never be the man she'd wanted him to be.

He had meant so much to her. She had meant so little to him. Most of all she hated him for that.

Only his eyes moved. They were insolent and black as they roamed the length of her, passing over her eyes and her red hair, to linger at her swelling breasts, clearly revealed by the ruined silk.

"Well, don't just stand there!" she hissed. "Do something!"

"The mistake I made was pulling you out of the river in the first place." At her quick frown, he grimaced. She could see his white teeth in the faint light, and there was mockery in his eyes.

She could have gladly choked him. "Please," she whispered with pretended meekness.

He leaned down and took her wet hands in his warm dry ones. Even this most casual touching was different with him than with any other man. She let her body go limp as he started to pick her up, so he had to put all his strength into the effort. Then just as he was lifting her out, she suddenly hunched, put both feet against the side of the pool and kicked.

With delight she heard his startled male yelp as he fell, then his furious splashes behind her as she heaved herself out of the pool.

A hand closed around her ankle like a vise and he dragged her roughly across the bricks into the water...into his arms.

"Not so fast, *chère*," he whispered.

"You're hurting me," she screamed, trying to protect her injured wrist.

"That was a nasty little trick," he muttered, pulling her more tightly against himself.

"And exactly what you deserved."

The damp straps of her gown fell over her shoulders, and the bodice slipped revealingly. Her wet breasts were mashed into his chest. His hard thighs trapped her legs as she thrashed to free herself. Her every movement only made her more aware of him as a man. There was something erotic about the cool water and his hot skin. Something erotic about wet clinging clothes.

"Maybe you are exactly what I deserve...." He held her tightly. He ran a caressing hand beneath her delicate chin.

"Let me go!"

His hands and eyes inspected her closely. There was something predatory in his every gesture. His masculine scent touched her nostrils. Her body had begun to tremble beneath the pressure of his hands. Her breathing became harsh and rapid.

His voice came low, like an animal growl. "You shouldn't have pulled me in if you didn't want my company."

"Why did you come back—tonight?"

"You wouldn't believe me if I told you." His fingertip started to push one of her fallen straps back up.

"Try me."

A charged silence fell between them.

She felt his finger on the naked skin of her shoulder and jerked away as if from flame. He was watching her, his dark eyes taunting as if he were as conscious as she that all that separated their bodies was two layers of thin wet fabric.

"To save you, you little fool. Otto von Schönburg is the worst scoundrel you've ever picked."

"I would be a fool if I believed you. You never cared about saving anyone but yourself," she jeered.

"Someone must have taught you that. The day we met I saved your life, remember?" His words were no more than a warm whisper. "Otto, I'll bet."

"He told me what you did—in Africa."

There was a sudden bleak wasteland of pain in Nicholas's eyes. She saw it and didn't understand it. But she felt compassion for him, which was absurd.

"I'll just bet he did. And you always were ready to believe the worst about me. You were determined to remake me into some wimpy paragon your grandmother could approve of, and when you couldn't..." He forced himself to stop. "What else did Otto teach you?" He ground out the words with rough malice. And then, before she could stop him, he caught her shoulders and pulled her closer. "What else?" he whispered. "That question has driven me mad."

With the back of his hand he traced the softness of her cheek, the length of her nose, the voluptuous fullness of her lips, reading her every feature with the exquisite gentleness of a blind man starved for the sight of the woman he loved. "You're still a very beautiful woman. Did Otto enhance your skill in bed? Not that you weren't good..." His fingertip moved insolently down her throat, and she began to quiver from the mesmerizing warmth of his touch. "Because you were very good, *chère*."

"No..." She tried to shrink away from him.

"You were unforgettably good, and unforgettably beautiful."

Eva closed her eyes a moment. He was deliberately, cruelly humiliating her.

"Underneath all that determination to be a perfect Martin, with a perfect life and a perfect man, there's a passionate, beautiful woman who wants to be free to find herself. Maybe that's why I can't let him kill you," he said softly. "I want to save that woman."

"Kill?"

His statement was so unexpected, so completely farfetched, that for a moment Eva could only gape at him. "Otto—kill me? That's crazy! You're the murderer."

Nicholas's grip tightened on her arms. That bleak dark look was in his eyes again.

"And you believed him, *chère?*"

"He showed me all the newspapers."

"Before or after he took you to bed?" His low tone was unspeakably cruel.

"You know so much. You figure it out."

"I already have."

"Fine. Just go. I was doing just fine before you showed up."

"It's easy to see why you think so. He told you you're going to be his princess. Your family probably approves. Do they know that you share his stateroom, his bed?" He lifted the ruby-and-diamond necklace from her throat. "He gave you this to wear around your neck like a dog collar. It's plain as day he owns you. Otto von Schönburg is a powerful, evil man. He can buy and sell newspapers, governments, human beings. He betrayed me, Eva. He had my men killed in Africa. He defamed my name with his lies. Now if I don't stop him, he's going to kill you, to get at me."

"I don't believe you."

"You never could believe in me."

She flinched. Maybe once she could have believed in him— if he had come back, if *he* had trusted *her*. But now he was a cruel stranger, whose dark cheek she wanted very much to slap. Instead she balled her fingers tightly into her palms and turned away. She did not know that their discussion—her rejection, her disdain, all these things—drove him past the point of madness.

He held her fast. "You were mine before you were Otto's. I can't stop myself from wondering whether the real thing is as good as the memory."

His long fingers curved painfully into the wet tangled mass of her hair, bringing her head back so that the creamy smooth length of her neck and shoulders was exposed to his insolent gaze.

"I should never have pulled you in," she whispered weakly. The comment seemed inane.

"So, you're just now figuring that out."

His dark head moved lower, and she could feel his breath against her cheek.

"No..."

"Yes," he murmured. Then his mouth came down on hers.

He had kissed her before, but never like this. Never with such greedy demand. Never with such angry passion and contempt. There were years of pain and need in his hot, savage kiss. And even as she fought him, she felt something darkly alive, some treacherous alien thing deep inside her, quicken in flaming, welcoming response. Her skin became warm satin beneath his callused fingertips, her body pliant beneath his. She let her mouth open.

He groaned. His tongue plunged inside the warm, sweet wetness of her lips. "Dear God..."

Their tongues mated; their mouths clung. She tasted pool water mixed with tobacco and rum, and that special flavor that was his alone. A bewildering tide of emotions made her ache for his physical embrace no matter how much she hated the man he had become.

"The real thing is damned good," he muttered hoarsely before he kissed her even harder than before.

"So you're alive," she whispered a long time later, after he'd torn his mouth from hers. She was running her hands through his damp shining hair, holding her cheek close to his, not letting him go, forgetting all the evil he had done, forgetting the lies he had just told her, not caring if only he would go on holding her in this dark time of fevered madness.

"Would you prefer me dead?" he demanded.

Weakly she shook her head. No matter what he'd done, she didn't want that. "All those years...you could have come back."

"Without making the real killer pay? With my name blackened? With everyone believing me a murderer? Could you have stood by me and borne that kind of scandal?"

Once she had thought... But what did it matter? The past was over. With good reason he had not believed in her then. There was nothing she could say to convince him now.

"There was nothing for me to come back to," he said grimly at last. "Besides, Otto would have killed me."

"But you did love me."

"It was a mistake. A dream. I woke up and found that I was a fool."

"So you can't forgive me the past, nor Otto," she whispered.

Nicholas was silent. His dark eyes grimly studied the sparkling necklace at her throat. "I was not blessed with a forgiving nature."

"I can't forgive you, either," she said wearily at last.

"I don't want your forgiveness, *chère*."

"Then?"

His fingers tightened at the back of her neck, and as he forced her face toward his again, the diamonds cut cruelly into her flesh.

"But I can't let him murder you the way he murdered my men."

Then his mouth grazed hers with hunger again. "And I still want this, too," he whispered, shoving the strap of her gown lower and then moving the material of her gown. He touched her breast. His hand felt slick and wet and warm against her. "Only this. Nothing more...ever again from you." His voice was as brittle as glass, and just as cold and loveless. But there was fire in him, too. Fire in the mouth that closed over her breast and suckled there until she was limp and breathless. "You were made for my kisses, but for mine alone."

At last she summoned the will to try to twist away, but he kissed her hard on the throat, on her mouth, possessively as if he were branding her with his kisses. A million liquid stars sparkled over the water like dancing diamonds. He pushed her against the side of the pool and pressed his hard body onto hers.

The water was icy, but he was hot, like fire. So hot he was melting her with his heat.

"Not here," he said at last, his voice harshly resonant with passion. "Not now."

With new horror she realized just how far she'd let things go.

"Never," she vowed, but she was shaking when he released her.

She felt his hands at the back of her neck roughly undoing the clasp of her necklace. He pocketed the necklace. Then he yanked off her clip earrings and her diamond ring.

"What are you doing?" she cried, furious again as he tossed the earrings and ring into his pocket, too.

He took her by the hand and pulled her out of the pool. "I came here to save you from Otto. Not to steal anything that is his. We've got to get out of here. Fast."

"No! Everyone will think I ran off with you."

"That's what always mattered—other people's opinions."

"No...but Connoisseurs— You don't know what Otto will do if I humiliate him like that."

"I have a hell of a lot better idea than you." With a single fingertip he made a swift slicing motion across the base of her slender white throat.

The mere gesture made her shake from the cold. She pulled her hand free of his and would have run back to the house. But he grabbed her and yanked her down the path that led to the docks beside the glimmering dark water of the harbor a thousand feet beneath.

"I don't have any clothes...and my contact lens stuff. And my cat! I can't leave Victor!"

"If I go after that cat, I *am* crazy!"

"Where are you taking me?" she whispered.

"Out there." He pointed at the lightning that burned the black sky with livid silver-white fire. "We're sailing straight out into the Med—into the teeth of that hell."

"That's suicide."

"That's why Otto won't follow us."

Eva tried to tear her hand away, but Nicholas gripped it tightly.

"You are crazy," she breathed.

His eyes were hard and dark and terrible. "I know."

"What about my cat?"

"Not that crazy, *chère!*"

But he was.

Chapter 5

Even the slight flutter of his swollen eyelids when he opened them caused waves of pain to pulse in Paolo's brain. His throat was raw. Through the blur of his own blood, he saw vivid red spatters all over the white-painted aluminum, and he knew that, too, was his own blood.

Dio.

His black suede pants were so damp with the stuff they stuck to his legs. The balcony looked like Girouard had mopped it with blood.

Paolo struggled heavily to his feet and shuddered convulsively. With a bloodied hand he pushed aside the pink curtains and stumbled back into the stateroom. Girouard had dragged him outside, nearly strangled him.

Except for the moonlight and the flashes of lightning, the room was dark. Still, he could see that Girouard had made a mess as he'd hastily packed. Signorina Martin's leather bag, most of her clothes, even her cat were gone.

Paolo had been waiting in the dark for him to come, and he would have gotten him if only he hadn't slipped on that damned cat.

Girouard had come from behind and struck him down.

A single piece of paper fluttered on the bed beside the dark glimmer of the woman's jewels.

Girouard was a fool for leaving the jewels and taking the woman. Paolo picked up the note and read the bold black scrawl.

There was a single word.

Revenge.

Girouard's taunt brought a fresh swell of bitterness into Paolo's heart, and he damned Girouard to the worst hell imaginable.

Paolo staggered to the balcony. What he saw made him utter a muted cry of rage. *Rouge Wave* was beating its way through the rough seas and high winds straight into the frothing violence of the Mediterranean.

No one deliberately left a safe harbor and sailed into a storm like that.

No one but a crazy desperate fool like Girouard.

Paolo crumpled the note into a bloody ball, struck a match and set the paper on fire, letting it burn down until he smelled the vile stench of his own flesh. Then he pitched the blackened fragments onto the priceless carpet.

Revenge would be his. Not Girouard's.

Girouard would pay dearly, and so would the woman.

Paolo imagined her slender white throat. He saw it covered with blood, and this vision made him swell with savage excitement and male power. He would make Girouard watch while he murdered her.

She would not be his first woman. But he would enjoy her more than most.

A cat's claw found its way through the soft leather bag and raked Nicholas's shoulder.

Damnation! Eva had been right. He was crazy. Crazy to go back to *La Dolce Vita.* Crazy to risk his neck for a cat.

Nicholas jammed his great bruised body into the doorway so he could brace himself against the yacht's bucking movements. He was holding the leather bag, struggling to unlock the door of the forepeak cabin where he had left Eva and dreading his reception all at the same time.

Outside the seas were streaked with foam; the gale-force winds were shearing the tops of the highest waves and pounding them onto *Rogue Wave*'s decks. Zak was at the helm, steering the boat so she would run with the storm. Nicholas had to get up there as soon as possible and shorten more sail. But first he had to deal with Eva. He had to find out if she had deliberately sent him to his probable death.

Nicholas threw the door open and saw her.

A single light glowed in the cabin. The room was tiny and plain after the magnificence of *La Dolce Vita*. The richly glowing teak walls smelled of teak oil—he had rubbed every layer into the wood himself. The brass fittings had been polished with equal tenderness and care.

Eva was exactly where he'd left her, still cowering on his bed in frozen terror, so wet and pitifully bedraggled, a different man in a different mood would have felt sympathy.

He remembered how close she'd once come to drowning, how terrified she'd been of boats and water afterward. She looked so fragile, so lost, that despite his foul mood, her appearance began to bother him. Her eyes didn't darken at the sight of him. Instead she looked relieved. Hers was not the face of a woman who'd sent a man to his death. But he couldn't weaken; he wouldn't weaken.

He tossed the black leather bag onto the bed. "Your cat, madam."

The boat heeled precariously, and the door slammed shut behind him.

"My—" She looked up, startled by Nicholas's cruel tone, by his stern expression.

A feline howl of outrage erupted from the bag.

"Why you beast!"

She wasn't referring to the cat.

"How could you? What kind of man are you that you would take pleasure in frightening a small, helpless animal?"

"That monster is about as helpless as a rabid sewer rat!"

She unzipped the bag carefully, and Victor clawed his way to freedom. He scrambled to the safety of the darkest corner and stared at them both with ferocious yellow eyes.

"What did he do to you, sweetie?" she whispered. Victor yowled plaintively back at her.

Nicholas felt an inane jealousy that she felt sympathy for the cat instead of for him. "A better question is what did he do to me? His claws are like ice picks. He sank every one of them into my hands when I put him in that bag. Then he scratched me again while I was carrying him here. I damned near died because of that cat."

If it hadn't been for the cat, Nicholas would have died for sure, but that was a bit of information he would keep to himself.

For the first time since Nicholas had come in, Eva seemed to forget her fear of the incessant pitching of the boat and the tremendous noise the yacht made slamming into the waves. Instead she concentrated on him. She looked at his hands that were crisscrossed with a dozen bloody scratches. At the purple bruise along his cheek.

"What happened to you?"

He had to fight his reaction to the concern in her eyes and to the slight quiver in her voice. She could be acting. He forced himself to move in for the kill. "You probably knew Paolo would be there waiting for me. Did you hope he would finish me off?"

With a gasp, she jerked back from him, letting go of the bunk railing. "No..."

The boat hovered on the top of an immense wave and then raced down it like a roller coaster car. She lost her balance and fell, tumbling across the bed, her head banging into the headboard. As she pulled herself up, he saw the faint trace of blood upon her lower lip. She touched her mouth, but said nothing. She merely looked at him with the hurt look of an abused child.

It was his fault she had fallen. His fault her lip was cut and bleeding.

He sank down beside her. Suddenly he felt terrible "Eva, I didn't mean it."

"Yes, you did. You are determined to be as mean and hateful as possible. Surely you must know I'm not such a horrible person that I would do a thing like that. No matter how furious I was at you, no matter how terrified."

"I know," he said quietly.

She took his battered hands in hers and gently touched the scratches one by one.

Her damp hair smelled of honeysuckle. Of home. Of all the beautiful things he had left behind, of the life he had once longed for, of all that was forever lost to him.

"You need to wash your hands. Cat scratches get infected easily."

"That figures. Everything about that cat is a nuisance."

Victor heard him and gave a faint yowl, almost as if he were defending himself.

Eva touched Nicholas's bruised cheek, and her fingertips were lightly caressing and deeply soothing. No other woman had hands like hers—long-fingered and slim that could either soothe or arouse. They smoothed the blood-soaked, wet tatters of his shirt. Gently she wiped the water that was streaming from his hair away from his brow, and though he willed himself to move away from her and the treacherous, warm pleasure of her satin touch, he couldn't. Her hand trembled just slightly above the blackest part of his bruise. "Oh, Raoul...Nicholas, I mean," she breathed. "It must have been a terrible fight."

"It was."

"Paolo—is he..."

Nicholas saw the look of horror in her beautiful eyes, and he grew angry all over again.

"No. Unfortunately there'll be no new...murder to further blacken my name," he jeered bitterly.

"You shouldn't joke about such things. Do you have a medicine chest?" Her voice grew softer still. "So I can clean these cuts."

His dark gaze met the gentle glow of her eyes. The hope for
some happiness with him seemed to tremble in her tentative
expression, and he felt drawn to her.

What was he doing? After all his resolutions to feel nothing
for her?

Too well he knew the dangers of her gentleness and kindness.
Ever since his mother had died when he was a baby, some secret
part of him had longed for a woman's kindness, making him
especially susceptible to it. Kindness was the one thing that
could rob his soul of anger. For eight years he had lived on
anger, on hatred, on revenge. Anger had driven him to make his
own fortune and destroy his enemy's. He had forgotten how to
live any other way, and he didn't want to learn.

"I'll do it myself," he said cuttingly, pulling his hand away
from her.

She glanced down quickly to hide from him the fresh sparkle
of tears in her golden-dark eyes. But he felt them. It was as if
her pain was his.

God, why was there this bond between them? How could she
still seem almost a part of himself? Why did she have to be so
beautiful? What made him so vulnerable to her shimmering eyes,
to her red hair and to her pale, translucent skin? To the velvet
sound of her voice? It alone could arouse in him feelings of
confused mutiny against every rule that he lived by.

Other women were as beautiful. She was a woman, like any
other woman.

But she wasn't.

He clenched his hands to keep from reaching out and drawing
her into his arms. He could understand the desire he felt for her,
but he could not understand why she alone could arouse all these
other complex feelings.

Because of him her graceful figure was coiled into a frightened, vulnerable ball. Because of him her eyes were downcast
and her pale fingers were tensed. He had always been able to
hurt her too easily.

He remembered the first day he had pulled her lifeless body

from the river. With his own breath, he had given her life. She had been a child gently raised, he a man with years of hard living behind him. He had been a Girouard, she a Martin, and their families had disliked each other for a hundred years. But from that first moment when he'd held her in his arms and prayed with all his heart for her to live, it had seemed she belonged to him.

He drew a shaky breath and got up. His cabin seemed suddenly too small for the two of them and much too intimate a thing to share.

In those brief two years when he'd loved her, when he'd waited for her to graduate from college, she'd shown him a softer side of life and made him see beauty in things and people and in nature. She'd loved as easily as he'd hated. But that golden time had been obliterated by Africa and Otto's betrayal, by the knowledge that such a woman could never really love him when his name was blackened with the foul stench of murder, and his heart blackened with the lust for revenge. He wanted no more softness, no more beauty—they only made the hard realities of his life more unbearable.

"Where will I stay?" she asked.

"In here. With me."

"There's no way I can share a room with you," she whispered.

"Do you think I want you to?" The hoarseness in his low tone betrayed him. "It was me or Zak." Not even to himself would he have admitted he would have killed any man who tried to sleep with her in his presence. "I drew the short straw."

She said nothing, but he saw a single tear slip down her flushed cheek. She looked young, lovely and infinitely sad.

Sheer strength of will was the only thing that enabled Nicholas to stand up, to move away from her instead of to her.

Rogue Wave fell sideways off a wave. The cabin light dimmed into total darkness. Pillows, charts and a flashlight tumbled from the shelves, and she screamed. The light flickered back on, and he saw the stark white terror in her face. Nicholas had to take the wheel and fast.

The only comfort he offered was to ignore the incident as if it were nothing to cause alarm. He moved to a locker.

"Paolo will tell Otto I took you. They will come after us."

"Then everyone will think I ran off with you?"

"I suppose they will," he said indifferently, rustling through the messy locker, his main concern *Rogue Wave*'s lousy performance. Zak was a great navigator, but as a helmsman he lacked something. The yacht was being beaten to pieces.

"Connoisseurs...my independence...are all gone because of you. You ruined my life once before. Now you're doing it again."

"Would you rather die?" He pulled out a shirt. "If your shop gets into trouble, get your rich father to bail you out. He's done it before. And more times than either of us can count."

"How can you, who prize your independence so much, say that to me?"

"I'm a man," he replied curtly.

It was going to be a long night, and Nicholas was wet to the skin. He stripped out of his wet shirt, and that was a mistake, too.

Not only terrified, but now furious, too, she was up on her haunches, watching him. When she saw the scars on his back, her expression changed again, and the deep concern he saw in her eyes made his hands unsteady as he pulled on his dry shirt.

"What happened to your back?" Her words were muttered shudderingly.

He turned away from her and yanked his foul-weather jacket on, pulled the hood over his head and snapped a dozen snaps.

"It was a long time ago."

"In Africa?"

"Yes, damn it."

"You were beaten." A spasm of pain passed across her beautiful face. "Brutally beaten."

"Like I said, it was a long time ago." His voice was angry and gruff. "I lived through it."

"Did you? Or did the scars go so deep they twisted the inside of you as badly as those outside lumps of flesh?"

"Damn it! If you don't like the way I look, don't look at me then."

Her gaze moved over his broad shoulders, his muscled back, his lean hips. "I didn't say I didn't like it."

Something in her soft tone made him forget the boat, made him forget the storm—made him forget everything else but her. He could feel the beat of his heart pulsing in his fingertips, in his throat.

His gaze slid over her. He could see the shape of her breasts beneath damp, clinging silk.

He made his voice as hard and cold as granite. "You need to get dressed yourself before you catch your death in those wet clothes." The leather bag lay between them on the bed. To vent his frustration he grabbed the bag, turned it upside down and started ripping clothes out.

A black bra got caught on his scratched hand. He shook it loose, but not before he felt the hot blood creeping up over his cheeks.

He was blushing! Like a high school teenager! Thank God for the dim light.

But she saw. "Are you going to watch me?" she whispered.

Nicholas grimaced and wondered if she suspected he'd done so before. "If you're smart, you won't play with fire."

"If you were smart, you wouldn't have brought me on board."

"Well, it looks like we're stuck with each other," he muttered. "For better or worse."

"That sounds too much like a marriage vow."

Suddenly a huge wave picked the boat up and rolled it on its side. Nicholas's great body was flung across the bed, on top of her.

For one long hideous moment, the boat stayed there. His arms and legs were intimately splayed across hers as they slid together down the width of the bed. He felt her breasts, her tiny waist, her long legs tangling around his. Under different circumstances he might have been tempted, but he heard water gushing inside the hull somewhere. If they took another knockdown before they could pump out the bilge, they could sink.

"I've got to get up on deck," he muttered brusquely, scrambling to free himself of her.

She clung to him and buried her face in the hollow of his neck, terrified. "Don't go out there."

He held her close as the boat slowly righted itself. Then he loosened her cold, clinging hands. "Stay below." When he saw that her eyes were still wide with fear, his voice gentled. "Hey, there. I'm not going to let anything happen to you."

"It's not me I'm worried about." There was a hush. "It's you."

He tore his gaze from her ravaged face. That was something he couldn't, he wouldn't accept.

Carefully he eased her back onto the bed. "Try to get some rest."

It seemed as if he'd been gone for hours. The reality was less than ten minutes. At first Eva had been cold and shivering in her wet silk gown, with her soaked hair. Now she lay in a pool of grit and sweat. The air in the cabin was dank, the salt from the sea air permeating everything. The cotton sheet was as rough as sandpaper against her hot skin.

Rest! Was he insane? To sleep down below as the boat pounded through the waves? As a little girl, she'd always thrown up after carnival rides. This was worse, infinitely worse, because the ride went on and on. The constant motion of the boat flung about everything that was loose. She was bruised all over from sliding and falling. As she struggled to hold on, she envied Victor his claws that were sunk deeply into the upholstery of the cushions.

Soon she was so nauseated she couldn't even feel anger toward Nicholas for inflicting this torture on her. She was too ill even to care about Otto or Connoisseurs. Those concerns seemed to belong to another world. All she cared about now was the boat and Nicholas, and despite his abysmal behavior, she was very worried about him on deck, risking his life, struggling to sail the boat and keep her safe.

Eva lay as still as was possible, and finally she felt slightly stronger. With Nicholas at the helm, the boat did seem to move more smoothly. She decided to change out of her wet clothes and brush her hair, but when she tried to stand up, she felt sick all over again. The boat was rocking so forcefully it was difficult to do even the simplest thing.

Somehow she managed to undress and pull on jeans and a shirt. Never before had she realized what a land creature she was. Fervently she longed to be back on dry land, to stand upright, to lie in a bed that did not move.

Every time the boat rode a wave to its crest, it hovered at the top before careening over it and slamming down into the trough with tornadic speed. Eva had heard of boats breaking up at sea, of sailors being washed overboard. What was happening to Nicholas, who was out there exposed?

Lightning crackled outside, and she stared out a porthole and saw a brilliantly lighted, rain and wind-scoured sky. *Rogue Wave* had tall aluminum masts. Where did lightning go when it hit a sail boat? What would happen to Nicholas if the boat took a direct hit?

She hadn't wanted to share this cabin with him, but not sharing it was worse. He exuded self-confidence. Even his deliberate insults distracted her so that she didn't worry quite so much about everything else.

The static blast of a radio in the main cabin made her jump. She heard the deep timbre of a man's voice. Hoping it might be Nicholas, she cracked the door. Instead she saw a tall black man with dark eyes and golden skin. He wore a T-shirt and white jeans, and he was huddled tensely over the radio. He looked up briefly and nodded toward her when she came in, but kept talking into the mike.

So this was Zak. He looked every bit as tough and hard as Nicholas.

"*Highlander Beauty,* we make our position to be..."

He spoke in a beautiful British accent.

Holding on to the walls, Eva made her way into the main cabin. She listened to every word Zak said, and watched everything he did. If only she could figure out how to operate the radio, she might be able to get a message out. The boat lurched wildly. Charts, gear, antennae, books and plastic containers flew off the shelves.

Zak seemed to take it all in stride as he answered another distress call on the radio.

"There's a lot of traffic in the Mediterranean. It's dangerous in any kind of weather at night, but in a storm it's even more so," he said after he finished the call.

Ships! They might be hit by a ship! Why hadn't she thought of that? She began imagining ships creeping up from all directions. A ship could crush *Rogue Wave* like a matchbox.

Again and again Zak used the radio, sometimes to answer a call, sometimes to make one. Every time he did, she watched him and listened intently.

During a lull, after making them cups of hot tea, Zak confided to her that he liked rough passages. As she set her cup in the sink where it couldn't roll, she sank queasily down beside him with the knowledge she was definitely in the wrong crowd.

The wind screamed outside, louder than before.

"Here we go. We're in for another squall," Zak warned her.

No sooner had he said it than a gigantic wave smashed into the boat, knocking her down, this blow a worse one than when Nicholas had fallen on top of her. Zak grabbed her and held her tightly. *Rogue Wave* lay on her side, sliding down the wave as still another crashed over her. Everything that wasn't a part of the boat came loose—tools, teacups, the coffeepot. Water was spilling into the cabin through dozens of tiny cracks, near the windows, the hatches.

Mon dieu. Were they going to die?

"If she goes over, we lose our rigging, and our skipper," Zak whispered, his voice like death.

Nicholas... As the boat hung there with the waves pounding over her hull, Eva's heart filled with a wild, mindless terror.

What was happening to Nicholas?

Slowly *Rogue Wave* righted herself.

The latch on the galley locker had come undone, and the door was banging. Cushions, pieces of the stove, life preservers, as well as other debris were floating on the floor. But Eva didn't care. She crawled over the mess toward the aft hatch. She had to know if Nicholas had been swept overboard. Before Zak could stop her, she flung the hatch open.

Rain poured inside, drenching everything, flooding into the bilges.

"Eva!"

Both men shouted at her to go back inside.

Her only thought was for Nicholas. He was alive! Her only desire was to be in his arms. She started to climb out.

"You don't have a safety harness or foul-weather gear!" Nicholas shouted. "Go back inside!"

Zak grabbed her, but she shook him loose and climbed out into the howling fury of the storm. She was immediately in another world, a world of black mountainous waves, a world that was brutal and overpoweringly destructive. The wet wind tore her hair back from her face as she crawled on bleeding knees toward Nicholas, clinging to the lifelines, clinging to the sheets, the winches, the railings, dragging herself when she could no longer crawl.

Nicholas watched her, his dark face white with terror.

"Go back! Dear God, go back!"

Suddenly she looked past him and saw what he saw—a wall of black water so immense that she knew *Rogue Wave* could never survive it. Eva would never reach Nicholas before the wave crashed over them. Without a safety harness, she would be swept overboard.

All of a sudden he was shouting at her, encouraging her. "Come to me, *chère*. You can make it."

But she was too paralyzed with fear to move.

The towering wave seemed to hang there. In reality it was rushing toward her with the power of a freight train screaming down a track at top speed. Within seconds it would smash her to pieces.

In that last desperate moment Nicholas lunged for her. His hard arms and hands were like steel holding her safely aboard while the great wave broke over them, flooding torrents and torrents of salt water over them until the decks and the cockpit were awash and the water swirled to their waists.

He was holding the wheel, holding her, too. She clung to him, wondering if they would live or die.

Against the hurricane roar of the wind and the waves, her scream seemed no louder than a whisper. "Are we going to die?"

"No."

She felt his incredible strength, the incredible force of his will. He was life—*her* life. With all her heart she believed his power was more than a match for the fury of the storm. She was slim and weak, but it didn't matter as long as she was in his arms.

The boat heeled dangerously. Water was pouring through the open hatch into the cabin. Zak was yelling and cursing and pumping madly down below.

In that endless black moment when *Rogue Wave* hung to the outer limits of a watery death and disaster, Nicholas stared into her eyes with a fierce intensity. All hatred, all desire for revenge were gone. They were no longer two separate people with two separate hearts and souls, no longer at odds, but together; they were one. He was inside her, and he *was* her. The terror of knowing they would either live together or die together was both exquisite pain and exquisite pleasure. She clung to him, consumed by the heat of his will to love her and to save her.

Even as she watched him in wonder, *Rogue Wave* slowly began to right herself and glide down the remnants of the shattered wave.

They were safe, and still Eva could not hold Nicholas close enough. The coiled sheets had come undone and were in tangles. A spar was broken, but they were safe.

She wanted to weep with joy, to cling to him forever, but he had regained control of whatever emotion he felt in the aftermath.

They were alive! But there was no joy in his face. Only a new and terrible hardness.

"Don't ever do that again!"

It took Eva's shocked brain a second to interpret the harsh bite in his voice and to realize that he was furiously angry.

"I—I came up to see if you were all right."

"You little fool, do you think that's any excuse? What could you have done if I wasn't? That wave would have swept you overboard."

"I'm surprised you even care."

A muscle jumped convulsively at the corner of his mouth. His lips were clamped together in a thin white line. "You could have jeopardized the boat." His tone was grim. "Get below and help Zak pump. Now!" The last word was like the blast from a cannon.

She stumbled through the companionway into water that was ankle deep. The life preservers and cushions were floating; the charts that had fallen to the floor were sodden pieces of garbage. There was the faint, almost undetectable, smell of chlorine gas.

His ebony face tight with tension, Zak jammed the hatch closed behind her. "It's like trying to bail a lake."

He resumed pumping with quick, deft strokes.

She stared at the ankle-deep water, the ruin and mess. The enormity of what she had done hit her full force. Numbly she put her hand beside his and lent her strength to his. A long time later, when every muscle in her back and arms ached with exhaustion, she whispered, "Nicholas is furious."

"With good reason."

This truthful remark, uttered without a trace of animosity, only made her feel worse.

Ten minutes later during another lull, Nicholas came down and Zak took the helm. Nicholas was sopping wet and haggard with cold and fatigue, but he gave her a quelling look. She wanted to apologize, yet she didn't dare do anything but keep pumping.

He went wearily to the stove and lit it. Soon the smell of fresh coffee mingled with the dank smell of the cabin. Her stomach quivered uneasily, and she clutched the side of the boat for support until she felt a little better.

He ignored her, sipping his coffee, savoring the hot warm liquid until, at last, his brooding silence drove her to despair.

"Well, aren't you going to say anything?"

His tired face turned in her direction. "All right, then, I'll say something. What you did was damned stupid. I didn't bring you on this joyride to get you and everyone else killed.

She forced herself to look at him.

"I—I'm sorry."

"From now on you'll do exactly as I say. If we're to get out of this alive, we have to work together, not against each other. You're going to have to help me."

"But what can I do?"

"You can cook, can't you?"

It didn't seem a very good time to tell him that she couldn't, so she nodded weakly.

"Hot drinks and hot food are very reviving in a storm when you're wet and cold. Come over here, and I'll show you how the stove works."

She stood beside him and watched as he lighted and extinguished the propane stove, which remained level because of gimbals.

She tried to concentrate as he explained Zak's and his "passage" routines, but the boat rocked continually. She began to feel seasick again.

"During storms I usually take six-hour watches and Zak

three-hour watches. He does the navigation, engine and systems maintenance and repair. Usually he cooks. But with you aboard, he can stand longer watches. You can keep us going.''

She was feeling sicker and sicker. His dark face swam in a queasy whirl. ''I—I think I'm going to be...'' Her voice was a curiously empty sound, trailing away.

The cabin reeked of teak oil, chlorine gas and stale salt water.

''Ooo.'' She put a frantic hand over her mouth to warn him.

That motion and her pale distraught face must have communicated her need, because he slid an arm around her to steady her, his face grave with concern. ''What's the matter.''

''I—I think I'm going to be sick.''

Very quickly he lifted her toward the sink and stood behind her, supporting her while she shuddered into the aluminum basin. Afterward, deeply ashamed, she wanted to cringe away from him.

''You were very...kind to help me,'' she whispered, hating the hot tears threatening to fill her eyes.

''Nonsense,'' he said gruffly as he reached past her and pumped cool fresh water from the reserve tanks into the sink and cleaned it. Then he poured her a glass of fresh water.

Even though the water tasted faintly of plastic, she drank deeply until he advised: ''Just a little.''

Then he led her to his cabin and helped her down onto the bed. When she was settled, he left her, and she thought he was done with her.

He returned almost immediately. ''Close your eyes, Eva, and I'll wash your face.''

She was too weak to resist. He had brought a rag, and he stroked her hot skin gently with cool, wet, soothing cotton, dampening her brow, her dry lips, her throat. Then he dried her face off with a fresh towel.

He was about to leave. ''Oh, I almost forgot—'' He pulled out a tiny, pink, circular adhesive.

''What's that?''

"A patch to put behind your ear. Zak uses them to prevent seasickness."

"You're a little late."

"Better late than never."

Her eyes met the tender, luminous darkness of his.

"Yes..."

He was talking about patches for seasickness. She was gazing at him, at the way his heavy dark hair fell across his forehead, at the way his harsh-featured face was soft now as he tended her, and she was thinking along very different lines. He had held her so fiercely outside when the wave had crashed over them. Then she'd been almost sure that he felt something beyond passion, something that was deep and eternal, something he could share only with her.

She lay breathlessly still while he fastened the patch behind her ear.

Her eyes closed, she enjoyed the feel of his callused fingertips against her neck, behind her ear. Gently he smoothed the tangled red curls back from her forehead. He readjusted the bandage at her wrist.

In spite of everything, there was something almost pleasant about being sick. He was being so kind.

With her eyes shut, she could almost imagine that he was always so tender in his regard for her. In that moment she wanted nothing more than for him to stay with her through this wild violent night. Then she wouldn't mind being sick. She wouldn't even mind that he had stormed back into her life and ruined everything. She wouldn't even mind being on a boat so much.

But when she opened her eyes to beg him to stay, she discovered that he had already gone.

Chapter 6

The dark gray dawn was massing with purple clouds when Nicholas dragged himself wearily to his cabin. He was icy and wet, and his bad leg burned where the bullet had ripped into his flesh all those years ago. Despite his pain, his overwhelming sense of fatigue and his knowledge that they were still in grave danger, when he opened the door, nothing existed but the beguiling curl of slender woman beneath the rough cotton sheets in his bed.

The joy he felt at the sight of her came as a shock. She'd almost gotten them all killed, and yet, ironically, it was that very action that had diminished his anger toward her. On deck in the midst of that howling fury, with her in his arms, he had seen something, felt something, in her and in himself, something incredibly powerful, and he was at a loss to explain it.

His disturbing thoughts dissolved, not due to exhaustion, but the sight of her.

It should have been a warning.

The sheet was thrown off. Her bare arms hugged his pillow tightly against her abdomen. Her red hair was spread in a pool of flame over her own pillow. Her thin T-shirt and tight jeans, unclasped at the waist for comfort, revealed the lush curves of her body. No longer did she look ill. Instead she seemed to be resting peacefully.

The picture was perfect until his gaze fastened upon a very contented black fur ball nestled against her hip. Pointed black ears cocked toward him. Yellow eyes slitted, observed him.

Nicholas felt a swift surge of jealous dislike, but since it erased the annoyance of those softer, maudlin emotions threatening to swamp him, allergic or not, he was almost glad the devil was there.

That cat kept coming in handy in the damnedest ways.

Not that Nicholas felt an ounce of gratitude nor the slightest intention of allowing that fleabag to remain where he was—in his bed.

Silently Nicholas began to strip in the darkness. He pulled on a dry shirt and briefs. Then he leaned down, caught Victor under the belly and scooped him onto the floor. The thud of four cat paws on teak made the most satisfying sound. There. He had shown the devil who the boss was.

The mattress dipped as he slid his icy body in beside Eva. He turned out the light, and the cabin melted into darkness. He stretched out his lean frame beside her, every muscle aching with cold and exhaustion, his old wound hurting more than the rest of him put together.

He had thought he could more easily ignore her in the darkness, but he was wrong. He caught the sweet delicate scent of honeysuckle. Another faint aroma drifted indistinctly to his nostrils. Her scent. The earthy, delectable scent of his woman. It was an elusive essence, but it made him remember long, hot, Louisiana nights when the air had smelled of damp earth, crepe myrtle and magnolia blossoms, of honeysuckle and wisteria. He'd lain with her, and they'd made love in the slanting, silver-white moonlight.

He remembered too clearly the way her mouth was soft and sweetly giving against his, the way her body had fit his perfectly, and the familiar memories stimulated masculine reflexes despite his aching exhaustion. She tempted him as no other woman could. She was French. A part of everything that he had been bred to. Dear God...

The warmth from her body seeped toward him beneath the sheets, and it took all his strength of will to cling to the hard wooden edge of the bunk and remain as far from her as possible. Adrenaline and other hormones—male ones, all of them, he was sure—pumped through his nervous system. His fingers knotted in an iron grip around the teak railing.

She exhaled softly, her breathing gentle. She was as undisturbed by his presence as he was violently disturbed by hers. He lay there, shivering and wretched, but with fiery desire torturing every cell in his body. *Rogue Wave* fought her way through the heavy seas, but he thought only of the woman beside him who seemed to breathe more gently, to sleep more easily now that he was near.

Surely this wild night was the design of the devil himself—first the storm, the long hours at the helm with blasts of black wind, waves and rain, and now to have to lie beside the one woman he wanted more than any other. He knew, though, that to take her would only make him all the more vulnerable to her.

He heard his own breath coming quick and harsh, and the sound of it shook him. He wanted her with an intensity that truly frightened him.

He did not know that she was awake, too; that she was as aware of his presence as he was of hers.

At last sleep came to them both. He dozed fitfully at first, as if all his muscles and nerves were wound tightly with tension. Then slowly a warmth stole through him, relaxing him, easing his exhaustion as well as the throbbing pain in his leg until he slept as carelessly as a child.

He awakened and was startled to discover the reason for the soundness of his sleep. She was beside him, her warm, satin-soft body cuddling against him trustingly, the perfumed waves of her honeysuckle-scented hair spreading over his chest and arms, her long jean-clad legs tangled deliciously in his.

She stirred in his arms, and without thinking he brushed his lips into her hair, against her throat. He felt her pulse race in response beneath his mouth. He stroked her breast, wanting more of her. All of her. Even as his hand drifted from her breasts to her belly where her jeans were unfastened, even as it slid inside to caress the bare flesh of her stomach, he told himself to stop. He had no right to touch her, nothing to offer her but more pain. Besides, to do so was to inflict the most exquisite form of torture on himself. With a groan, he rolled away from her to a spot where he lay shaking all over.

For a long moment he felt that he had to take her, that he had pushed himself too far this time, that he would die if he didn't have her. Then, with a supreme effort of will, he forced himself to remember Otto and Paolo, who would try to hunt them down and kill them as soon as the storm lessened. He remembered Paolo's stench of sweat and leather, his fist slamming against his jaw and pounding into his stomach in the stateroom. If it hadn't been for that cat and that blind, lucky blow into Paolo's thorax, Nicholas might be dead already because of her. Eva was dangerous, in too many ways to count.

Nicholas got out of bed and sank to the floor. The boat was pounding into the waves, but the teak felt cool against his feverish skin. He remembered Africa, the coldly savage murders of his men, and his own fierce need to gain revenge. Gradually he began to calm down sexually.

A velvet paw touched his hand. Then Victor curled up beside him. The cat did nothing else, and Nicholas pretended to ignore him. Since there was no one to see, he let him stay. They sat together, male to male, in silent camaraderie. After a long time Nicholas remembered he was allergic to cats, and he sneezed. But the beast seemed so settled, he let him stay anyway.

It was close to noon on that dark gray morning. One minute she was cosily nestled in warm sheets dreaming that she lay in Nicholas's hard arms. The next minute she was yanked brutally awake by hard arms that ripped the sheet from her body.

Nicholas looked bright and alert, as if he'd been awake for hours.

"Galley slave," he said provokingly, "get up. It's time you earned your keep! You damned sure weren't much use last night after you got sick!"

Her eyes snapped open. There he was, gypsy dark, his wolfish black eyes agleam as he loomed over her, rousing her in the worst possible way a woman could be awakened.

Forgotten was the tender lover of her dreams. Forgotten, too, was her fierce protector in the storm and the nurse who'd gently tended her.

"Get up! Your clothes are all over the floor. Your contact lens stuff and cosmetics all over the bathroom!"

"You!" She threw up her chin and glared at him.

"Who did you expect, *chère,* Prince Charming?"

"Certainly not with you aboard!"

"So you're feeling better?"

She nodded weakly, grumpily. "Not that much better." She dragged her fingers through her mussed hair. She still felt weak, and the patch made her sleepy.

"You'd better get up. You're in my bed, hogging my pillows, the covers. If you stay there much longer, I might decide to join you."

He made a move toward her.

"I—I'm getting up." That was wrong. She was fairly springing out of the bed. When his eyes raked her body, she snatched the sheet from him and pulled it around her.

He laughed in a superior, male way at that show of modesty. "Good. As I said, it's time you started earning your keep. I imagine you would prefer to earn it in the galley…rather than in the bedroom."

"As if those are the only places a woman belongs!"

"On this boat they are."

His expression altered subtly. His gaze ran from the curve of her slender neck down to the swell of her breasts. Her skin felt hot—almost as if he'd actually touched her. How did he do that with just his eyes?

"You belong in the dark ages."

"Most women who have sailed with me have not objected."

How dare he mention other women! It infuriated her that she cared. She glared at him fiercely. He grinned smugly at her obvious jealousy.

She remembered the way he'd clung to his edge of bed for hours and ended up on the floor. Then it came to her—he was deliberately baiting her. Why...he was bluffing. He was as afraid of seducing her as she was of being seduced. She turned this pleasant thought over in her mind. Her abductor was afraid of her, and he was covering it up with a bluster of sexist insults, hoping to rile her. What would happen if just this once she turned the tables on him?

She ran a hand through the fiery tangles of her hair, fluffed them, and let the radiant tendrils fall against her ivory cheeks. Remembering that he had always liked her shape, she tossed the sheet she'd been cowering behind to the bed so that the slim curves of her body were revealed.

"What are you doing?" he demanded in a hoarse low tone.

"I'm not much of a cook. Maybe...like those other women...I prefer the bedroom. You said I was...good. You were good, too."

At his dark frown, she smiled sweetly, lowered her fiery head and seductively peered at him through the thick, lush curls of her lashes. Then she got on the bed and crawled across it toward him, slowly like some hot wanton tigress on the prowl. She'd seen a movie star do it in an R-rated movie.

"Dear God. What are you doing?"

When she saw that his hand was trembling, she felt a fierce gleeful satisfaction. "You can have me," she whispered, moving her face very close to his. "If you want me." She made her voice huskily musical.

She remembered how he liked her voice. She remembered all the things that he liked.... He was so close, she could feel his warm breath brush her sensitive skin.

She saw his fear of her. Then she saw something stronger

than fear. His black eyes ate her, devouring her with a dangerous consuming passion.

Just for a second, her heart fluttered against the inside of her chest like a bird's frightened wings against its cage. She paled, terrified she'd gone too far.

With superhuman effort he tore his eyes away. "I'd rather have breakfast," he growled. Then he threw open the door and stormed out.

She collapsed onto the bed, weak with relief.

Eva opened the door to the main cabin and, clinging to the wall, tried to ooze out of it, but this attempt at a seductive slither was wasted because Nicholas didn't see it. She saw him, though. The bathroom door was ajar, and he was inside, stripped to the waist, with nothing on but a pair of sexy, snugly fitting, faded jeans. His lower face was a lather of white foam, and he was cutting away dark morning stubble with quick, deft strokes of his razor. His ink-dark hair was damp and slicked back—he must have run a wet comb through it.

The motion of the boat was not nearly so terrible as it had been the night before, but it was constant. He had to brace himself to stand. It obviously took great skill to shave under such conditions.

He had always been good with his hands. That single thought induced vivid, sensual memories that made her shiver.

He didn't know she was there. Mesmerized, she watched him for a second. He was such a virile specimen of manhood with his trim hips and broad shoulders that he would be dangerous for any woman to be around for very long. But he was especially dangerous to her.

Her gaze was drawn to the tangle of scars that ran the length of his back. What kind of inhuman monster had beaten him so mercilessly? Her eyes misted at the thought of the pain he must have endured. She doubted if he had ever cried out, if he had ever let on how he suffered. No, she was sure he had stood it with the same grim fortitude he had stood all the other hard things in his life—his mother's death, his father's rejection, Africa, even... Yes, even her foolish, long-ago determination to try to remake him into a weak shadow of the vital man he was. Why hadn't she seen she had loved him as he was?

He had a fierce primitive strength. Maybe that was what drew her to him. She didn't know. But there was a bond. A bond so strong that eight years hadn't destroyed it. Nor had the most terrible scandal, nor her conservative family's fierce disapproval, nor the foolish mistakes they had both made in their relationship.

The network of scars was terrible, but to her they only made him more ruggedly beautiful. She longed to reach out and touch them, to offer him comfort for the pain she knew he had suffered. But he didn't want comfort from her. So she had to content herself with watching the play of his muscles as he moved the razor back and forth and then washed his face with water. Just watching him sent tremors of excitement through her.

When Nicholas, caught unawares, turned and found her there, he shifted uncomfortably. Flushing darkly, he reached for his shirt.

"It damned sure took you long enough," he muttered. "Did you make the bed?"

Not the most encouraging of overtures.

She smiled at him anyway because he had always been susceptible to her smile. "No, I was such a mess myself, I forgot."

His eyes swept over her with a hot, dark look that told her she was a mess no more.

"You and everything you have anything to do with," he grumbled.

His insult didn't bother her. He was neat to a fault, and she knew she looked nice with her hair tied back by a saucy lavender ribbon. She was wearing her silky lavender bathing suit that molded her body like a second skin. Her angelic face was scrubbed clean of salt grit, her lips moistened with lipstick that matched her suit.

Lavender had been his favorite color on her.

"Couldn't you have picked something else to wear?"

"What's wrong with what I'm wearing?"

"As if you don't know. It's tight and sexy, and you're alone on this boat with two men."

"Whose fault is that?"

"I'm warning you, *chère,* don't play with me. You may find out you're playing a game that you'll lose."

"Yes, I know." She just smiled. But her stomach danced with excitement. It was such sweet revenge to taunt him for a change. Indeed, it was the only pleasure available under these trying circumstances.

"I'm starved," he said curtly.

"For breakfast?" she asked charmingly in her most musical tone. "Or for..." She batted her lashes.

"For breakfast, damn it."

But neither of them was entirely sure.

"Well, I can't cook. I thought we'd decided I'm a bedroom girl."

He ignored her last sentence and responded to her first.

"It figures that you can't cook."

"What do you mean by that?"

"I mean you're messy as hell, disorganized, too. Spoiled rotten by too many servants and a doting family. But it's time you changed. You're an adult. It's time you stood on your own two feet."

"I have Connoisseurs."

"No, your father's money bought that, and his money's bailed you out again and again. Every time you've gotten in trouble with a man or your shop, the Martins come to the rescue. You're so sweetly rotten, I wonder if you can do anything for yourself. You're marrying Otto so he'll take care of you and finance Connoisseurs."

Stung to the core, she shouted back. "I wasn't going to marry him!"

"Then why were you wearing his ring? I heard him announce the engagement with my own ears."

"He wasn't supposed to do that."

"Sure." Nicholas's face was white and still, his eyes red-rimmed from fatigue. "If you weren't going to marry him, then you damn sure were leading him and the rest of the world on."

"You once said I didn't believe in you. Well, you never believed in me, either! I'm telling you the truth."

For a moment something flared in his eyes, then vanished, and she saw that he wanted to believe her, but couldn't. "It doesn't matter," he said grimly.

But it did to her, more than anything. Suddenly tears welled in her eyes, silly ridiculous tears. She wiped her eyes, not wanting to cry. Not now!

"Look," he said, more on her side than he would ever readily admit. "I'm sorry. Your life is really none of my business. Believe me, I would have left you to it if I'd had a choice. I don't like this any better than you do. When it's safe, you and I will be done with each other for good. Can we just drop it? Zak and I are hungry. I wouldn't ask you to cook if we didn't really need your help."

Put like that, she was slightly mollified. But only slightly. Still, if she didn't cook for them, she would be acting spoiled and pampered.

He leaned down in front of her and lighted the stove for her.

"What do you want me to cook?"

He pulled out a box of dried eggs and put it on the counter. Beside the stove he set a loaf of bread, a pound of unopened coffee and a jar of marmalade.

"That ought to be easy enough for starters," he said dryly.

Easy? She stared at the two bare burners in desperation. How was she going to make toast—in a sauce pot?

Through the centuries other galley slaves had managed, most of them men, and everyone knew they weren't nearly so instinctually endowed with culinary talents as women. All she said was "Don't stay and watch me."

"I couldn't bear to." But he said it with just the flicker of a grin.

When she was done, she smiled proudly at the sight of her burned eggs until she saw that the galley looked like a dozen

guerrilla soldiers had made war with eggs and marmalade.
Spilled coffee was everywhere. Despite the gimbals, the eggs
had slopped onto everything.

But if Nicholas minded the mess in the galley or the fact that
the eggs were burned, he didn't say so. Below deck, at the table,
he and Zak both ate the hot food with a gusto that pleased some
secret female part of her nature that all feminists would deny
even existed. The men seemed to savor every bite, while the
electronic autopilot sailed the boat. The radar was turned on, and
the men assured her that an alarm would go off if there was the
slightest danger that they were on a collision course with a ship.

During the meal, Zak talked on the radio several times, and
as always she watched and listened to him intently, carefully
memorizing what he said about their latest position.

"Breakfast turned out rather well," Nicholas said when he
was done.

She beamed.

"But then—I picked the menu."

As always he was impossibly conceited.

Victor, who looked like a drunken caricature of himself as he
walked toward them at a decided slant, started to yowl at the
sight of plates and food.

"Does he like sardines?" Nicholas asked her.

Sardines... She had managed to eat little breakfast, but at the
mere mention of the word, her throat went dry and her stomach
flipped queasily.

"I think I need...another patch for seasickness."

"Here." Nicholas pulled one from his pocket. "I'll open the
can for the beast, to shut him up—even though it seems a terrible
waste of good sardines."

She was too weak to defend Victor. Besides she wasn't al-
together sure it was really necessary. Nicholas was going to feed
him, wasn't he? So, instead, she went to the forepeak cabin and
lay down so that she wouldn't have to smell the sardines.

Later Nicholas opened the hatches and aired out the boat for
her. When she was feeling better he showed her how to work

the saltwater pump so she could wash the dishes with seawater and thereby conserve their fresh water.

As he stood beside her in the galley, showing her how everything worked and where to stow things, she began to have the strangest feelings, dangerous feelings—like she belonged with him on this horrible boat, racing along in a stormy sea, with everything that mattered to her only yesterday not mattering to her at all today.

She hated the way he had taken control of her life, the way he had abducted her and carried her off on his boat. He was no better than a pirate, and yet for so many years she had longed for him. Every time she felt the dark force of his piercing gaze, or the accidental brushing of their bodies when the boat threw them together in the galley, she felt a quiver of spiraling excitement deep in the pit of her stomach that had nothing to do with seasickness.

Damn the man anyway! Intellectually she knew he was bad. But just standing beside him at the sink made her body react with a mind of its own. She felt tingly and soft and very feminine because he was so big and masculine. Beside hers, his hands were huge and darkly tanned. It was pleasant just to watch him dry a dish and put it neatly away. It was pleasant to breathe in the musky scent of his after-shave.

He was the bad guy.

What right did he have to be so virile and so awfully attractive?

But he said he'd come back to save her.

Paolo had beaten him.

Nicholas had risked his yacht, his own life, to take her away. He'd even gone back for her cat. More than anything she wanted to believe in him. It was difficult to imagine him sailing out into a storm just to recklessly amuse himself. But she'd never been any good at judging men, so she knew not to trust her instinct.

As he stood beside her, drying dishes, he was silent, seemingly unaware of her conflicting thoughts and emotions. When they were done with the dishes, he went up on deck to join Zak, closing the hatch because of the large swells.

Alone in the main cabin, she was still puzzling in confusion about Nicholas when the radio made a garbled sound.

The radio!

She was alone with it! This might be her only chance.

She scrambled across the bunks and table and grabbed the mike, hesitating only a fearful, breathless second. Then she flicked buttons and switches the way Zak had. Carefully she whispered into the microphone and made her distress call, giving the last position and heading she'd heard Zak give.

She waited as expectantly as an apprehensive child with a new toy.

Nothing. Frantic, she repeated the same call, terrified that Nicholas would open the hatch and discover her.

Metal slid against metal, and the hatch was flung open. A great whoosh of damp air sent charts flying everywhere. In the confusion, she hid the mike behind her back and glanced up innocently.

Zak's dark face was framed in the square of steel-gray light. She was so startled she nearly dropped the mike. Guilt over what she'd just done made her turn as white as paper.

"Oh, hi..." Her greeting was a croaky gasp.

Zak's dark gaze flicked to the radio and then back to her chalky face. "You don't look too good. You seasick again?"

She lied with a savage nod of her head.

"Why don't you lie down? I'll finish up in the galley."

Then he would come down. "N-no. I'm fine."

She wasn't though. She felt like a traitor—to Nicholas.

Nicholas's expression froze when he saw her step out of the cabin. The night was dark and moonless, but golden light from the open hatch backlighted Eva's hair and turned it to blowing flame. His fingers gripped the cold chrome wheel more tightly. She was beautiful, too beautiful.

All night, hour after hour, he had been clinging to the wheel, his deliberate intention to stay at the helm and avoid her by not going below.

She snapped the hatch shut, and they were alone together in the vast emptiness of the black night. Mist swirled around them.

"You must be dead," she said softly. "I brought you coffee. I made it the way you like it."

"Thank you." His tone was grim, but his fingers closed around the cup when she offered it to him. He felt the fleeting brush of her hand against his. Dear God, just her touch…just her being near…

Closing his eyes, he sipped the delicious hot liquid, but the warmth that spread through him was not from the coffee. It came from her presence. He wasn't used to anyone caring about his comfort. She paid too much attention to him. She noticed everything and did everything to try to please him. He was fastidious on board; she was messy by nature. But she had neatened the cabins, cooked and cleaned up after lunch and dinner. And everything she did made him more aware of her.

Not only was she turning into a most satisfactory crew member, but she was a pleasure to look at. Too much of a pleasure—in that tight lavender swimsuit that came so high on her thigh she seemed to be all curved golden leg. After the way she'd so wantonly teased him this morning—he knew now—just to bedevil him, he didn't trust himself to do the simplest thing with her without becoming aroused. Even teaching her to wash dishes had been a torment with her enticing body squeezed in the galley beside his, with the boat's movements causing too much accidental contact with each other. He had known then there was no way that he could spend another night in the same bed with her, without touching her—not unless he utterly exhausted himself first, which was what he had been doing for the past eight hours.

He'd liked having her on board, too much, which was dangerous. A single day had taught him what he'd been living without. He remembered the long months in prison, the trek across the desert, the years without her. Never had his life seemed so empty and lonely as it did now.

He had to remember he had taken her with him by force. She would never want him, never accept him, never believe in him. Nor could he allow himself to trust her. At any moment she might find a way to betray them to Otto.

He remained silent, determined to hold her at bay.

Naturally she couldn't leave it at that.

She inched carefully closer to him again, holding the lifelines, and he watched her lavender silk blouse ripple against her breasts. Always lavender…because she knew he thought she was beautiful in it.

Just watching her made his pulse begin to pound.

"How long before you let me go?" she queried softly.

Nicholas's gaze narrowed. "That depends."

"Surely you must see how impossible this whole situation is."

Oh, he saw.

"I can't stay. I have a life—"

"Which is why you *will* stay, so you will have that life. I don't like it any better than you do."

"What kind of man grabs a woman at a cocktail party and runs off with her?"

The muscles in his throat tightened. "I thought Otto told you what kind of man I was."

"Maybe I want to hear your side."

Her voice was like velvet. It made him want to pour out his soul.

His own low mutter was grimly rejecting. "That's a change."

"I do."

He stared past her. "You wouldn't listen."

"I listened before."

"To everyone but me."

"Tell me why you assumed a new name. I want to know about the scars on your back. About Africa. About everything. Please…" She put her hand very gently over his.

She was not forcing him to do anything, she was asking,

sweetly asking. Maybe he owed her his side. Slowly he moved his fingers so that two of them were warmly entwined with hers.

"All right..."

After a long time he began, and in telling her, he became caught up in his tale. His voice grew low and furious as he drew vivid pictures of Africa, of the desert, of the hot, choking dust, of death, of blood and the flies. Hatred made him paint the horror of no medicine, the betrayal and the stench of the dying with hideous detail. He told her about the real Nicholas Jones, about Paolo, about the dreadful march from the battlefield to the prison, about the privations of thirst and drought he and Zak had had to endure to escape. He told her about his own fierce vow to obtain revenge when he learned Otto had killed his men and fed the press all the lies that had ruined his name.

When Nicholas finished, she was weeping. At the sight of her crying for him, some of his anger melted. His breathing slowed and his fists unclenched.

"Oh, Nicholas," she moaned softly.

He put his arms around her. "It was a long time ago." But he made an inaudible and very blasphemous curse.

"No, it's now."

He held her hard against his body until finally her sobs subsided and she stood quietly against him. With a sympathetic, healing touch she eased her hands over his back, her fingers tracing his bones and the coiled ridges of flesh that ran the length of his spine.

She drew in a deep breath and stifled a sob. "It must have been terrible."

His arm about her waist contracted. He told her more, everything, while she clutched him silently, willingly sharing the grim horror of it all. He described his bed of rock and sand in the prison, and how he'd lain on it every night torturing himself with dreams of home, of Louisiana, of food too—of mouthwatering delicacies like fried chicken, steak and baked potatoes. He didn't tell her that most of all he'd dreamed of her. He told

her how terrible he'd felt when he'd found out Otto had bought
Sweet Seclusion, and she'd remodeled it.

"Because I didn't know...I didn't know. In my heart I was
restoring your home. Everything I bought, every board I had
painted—I did it all for you. When I was finished, I went to
London."

For a long time afterward they were silent as *Rogue Wave*
soared over the black waves and left a wake of glistening phos-
phorescence. Eva's hair flew against Nicholas's cheek, and he
breathed in the scent of honeysuckle and salt air. He did not
know if she believed him, but her mere presence soothed the
bitterness of his despair. No night at sea had ever been more
beautiful than this one with its misty darkness, with her in his
arms.

It was crazy to draw such pleasure in holding her, in talking
to her. Wrong in a dozen ways. But confiding in her had brought
a strange peace to him. Caution told him he should send her
below, that any emotional closeness with her was dangerous, but
the compulsion to go on holding her was too strong.

Despite the warmth of his arms about her, he forced a new
hardness to come into his voice. "I lost everything—maybe because I was too soft, too trusting. My men, my good name, my
soul, even you. All that is left of me is a savage desire for
revenge against Otto."

"So you took me."

The gentle accusation was like a blow.

*The little fool! Had she heard nothing then? Did she have no
concept of what murder was?* He could have shaken her.

Deliberately he dropped his arms from her shoulders, but she
didn't move away. She was so close he could feel the heat of
her body. He gripped the wheel. "Not exactly. I started a war.
You got in the line of fire. I had no choice but to take you."

A desperate tension filled him. "Believe me, having you on
this boat is the last thing I wanted."

That stung her. She backed away. "If you don't take me
home, you'll ruin my life all over again."

"There are always casualties of war," he replied with careful indifference.

"The hundred men who followed you—is that all they were?"

Everything in him went as still as death. His dark eyes glittered.

"Are you going to let Africa ruin everything you were?"

"Shut up," he snarled, indifferent no longer.

"I loved you. I thought you loved me. I made mistakes, and I've regretted them. But you've made them, too. You weren't a quitter then. It's as if you've given up on life, on what's beautiful about it. Is there nothing left...of Raoul? Of that wonderful man I loved even though I never knew quite how to handle him?"

Why did she have to be so damnably beautiful? Why did her delectable mouth have to look so inviting? Why did she ask questions that tormented his very soul?

"Nothing."

"I think you lie." She came very close again, standing only inches from him. "You remember me." Then she touched him. As no other woman could, with fingertips of flame that beguilingly traced sinew and corded muscle.

Yes, there was the memory of her and this feverish longing that refused to die even though he knew the world was a dark place and that such feelings were pointless.

She let her hand fall away, but he was mesmerized by the aftermath of its spell. His body raged to give up the helm, to know the velvet, encasing warmth of her, to hold her tightly. He'd gone through hell to get back to her, only to find she was lost to him forever, but he'd never forgotten the splendor of her love and passion.

When she spoke again, her voice was so soft he could barely hear her. "The women you've had, did you ever fall in love with any of them?"

He laughed harshly. He thought of Anya, whom he'd planned to use in his plot of revenge, but Eva had given him his chance.

"Love. You taught me the dangers of that trap. Never again. Women are to be used for the pleasure of satisfying an appetite."

He saw the desperate hurt in her eyes before she turned away.

"Let me go," she pleaded softly. "I promise that if you do, I'll run away—somewhere Otto will never find me."

"I can't take that risk."

"You don't care about me."

She turned away to leave him.

A sane man would have let her go.

Instead he uttered a low angry oath, secured the wheel and jerked her to him. His fingers embedded themselves in the thick waves of her hair. "No, I don't care," he muttered fiercely in a gravelly undertone that was unfamiliar to them both. "I don't care... At least not in the way a woman like you wants a man to care. You're like a fever in my blood, a disease that's devouring me from the inside out."

As he talked his hands were moving on her skin, sliding beneath her fluttering blouse, handling her with a rough expertise that left her gasping. "I want to hate you or to forget you, but ever since I saw you in Otto's stateroom, I haven't thought of anything else but taking you."

"Please...just let me go. Let me off this boat and we'll both come to our senses."

"It's too late." His fingers found her breasts, closing over the soft mounds of flesh. "I've lost mine completely. You're like a dangerous drug, and my craving for it is too strong." His jaw was set in a ruthless line. "I can't let you go. He will kill you."

Nicholas forced her back against the cabin, steadying himself and her. Then his mouth crushed down upon hers, silencing her murmurs of protest. Her hands splayed helplessly against his broad chest, Eva was trapped between the solid muscled wall of his powerful body and the wall of the cabin.

"Raoul." There was an unspoken plea in the way she said his name, her last futile attempt to stop him.

His hands roamed her body, noting that her breasts and hips were fuller, her waist slimmer. She was not so untried or girlish as she had been. She was a woman, fully formed. He was a man fully roused. She had teased him and beguiled him. What did she expect him to do?

She squirmed to resist him. She wouldn't have done it if she'd known that every move sent a jolt of electricity down the hard columns of his thighs.

"Be still," he growled, "Or we'll never make it to the bed."

From the cabin came two loud, frantic squawks.

Damn it to hell! The radar's alarm!

Directly ahead he saw the horror of red and green and white running lights. They were dangerously close! A giant black freighter loomed out of the misting darkness.

Nicholas jerked free of Eva, raced to the wheel and spun it fast and hard to starboard.

"Tacking!" he screamed.

The jib was cleated and backing. He rushed forward and released it. The big sail crackled wildly across the foredeck. He wrapped the sheet around the winch and trimmed.

Then he saw her white face. Her gold-brown eyes glittered opaquely as the freighter bore down on them. *Rogue Wave* seemed dead in the water.

Eva screamed and flung herself toward him, ready to die in his arms.

The freighter's bow wave crashed toward them, a deadly surge of white froth.

Chapter 7

Eva was safe from the ship.

But not from Nicholas.

Still quaking from the near miss, she lay in the dark listening to the waves slosh against the hull, knowing he would come to bed soon, and dreading it.

The aft hatch opened. She heard Nicholas inside issuing curt orders to Zak; then she heard Nicholas's heavy footsteps treading across the teak floor toward the forepeak cabin.

Nicholas hesitated at the threshold. Every nerve in her body went off like an alarm bell when his hand twisted the brass latch.

Her blood ran cold.

Or rather, hot.

She was suffocating in this airless room with a hot, tense excitement.

The door banged open, and he was inside, filling the tiny room with his presence, stumbling on his bad leg as he groped in the blackness for the light. A shiver of apprehension raced over her flesh. Tonight he did not creep inside and pretend to ignore her. She wished there was someplace she could run to or hide, but the yacht was like a prison, and the deep water that surrounded it was more confining than the highest walls.

He hit his hand against the tiny fan bolted to the wall and

cursed loudly and most descriptively before he finally managed to yank the lamp switch. The teak cell was instantly bathed with golden light.

She pretended to be asleep, but through her lashes she could watch him. His dark hair was windblown; his face was gray with exhaustion. Despite her fury and her despair, she ached because of the hard determined loneliness she sensed in him.

"That was close," he muttered grimly, ignoring her pretense of being asleep and loudly unsnapping his foul-weather jacket. "We missed her by no more than two hundred yards. Too close."

Yes. Silently she agreed with him.

He was speaking of the ship. She was thinking of his kiss, of the collision course their relationship was on.

"But close doesn't count."

It did to her. Especially now that they were alone together and would share the same bed for the rest of the night; especially now that she knew how completely changed he was from the man she had once loved. All day she had tried to please him. She had cooked. She had cleaned. She had listened to him when he'd talked about Africa and tried to understand all that he had been through. But this man was not the man she had loved.

Nicholas Jones was a stranger, determined to shut her out. It was as if he preferred to live in his world of darkness and deny that there was any other way to live. She was not a human being to him. All she could ever be was a pawn in the game he was playing with Otto or a temporary object of lust. She was on board Nicholas's boat. He was a man, she a woman who could serve a purpose for him any other woman could serve.

Through her lashes she kept a wary eye on his every move. She watched him hang his foul-weather jacket neatly on a hanger, strip off his boat shoes one by one, then his socks. Tidily he laid his socks and shoes on the shelf to dry.

Was this all that remained of him—a man who went through the mechanical motions of being a man? A man who was fastidious about his person, his boat—his *things*. A man who made vast sums of money in a complex, high-stake, international business while he played a deadly game of revenge. He could have written the owner's manual on any technical piece of equipment aboard *Rogue Wave*. He could sail her as though she were a part of himself. But when it came to being a real person...

He peeled off his shirt and jeans, and she gasped. Her pulse began to throb unevenly at the primitive, earthy, masculine vision. The less he wore, the more stunning he looked. When he sank down on the bed, she began to tremble with an emotion she understood all too well. Just his nearness cast a powerful pagan spell.

She stiffened, wary. She could not let his physical appeal blind her to the kind of man he had become. He had said that he used women solely for the pleasure of satisfying an appetite, and she now believed him.

If she had had any illusions, his violent kiss had dispelled them. Raoul was lost to her. The man Raoul had become, Nicholas, was so hardened he could never love again. He could only take and use, and destroy her all over again.

She remembered his harsh words and laughter with a sharp pang of guilt. "Love. You taught me the dangers of that trap."

Had she? Was she the cause of all that had gone wrong?

Years ago, Raoul had loved her desperately, and she had used her power to try to change him. He'd been a reckless entrepreneur, a brilliant maverick. But she hadn't appreciated his rare brand of talent, nor his courage to stand apart from the mainstream and excel. She had been so young, so incredibly foolish, too young to understand that loving someone did not give her the right to remake him. But hadn't she constantly tried to remake herself into the kind of person her family wanted her to be? Why would such an insecure person apply any different tactics to her love? She had believed she was helping him.

When her family had objected to his career, Eva had foolishly asked him to consider a more gentlemanly occupation, one like banking or medicine or law. He had laughed in her face at first and said a scoundrel would be a scoundrel whatever his trade and that an honorable man would behave honorably in any career, that he was good at his job, and happy in it.

If only she could have left it at that. Eva buried her head in her pillow but she couldn't escape the haunting memories.

After she'd succeeded in hounding Raoul into applying to law school just to please her, Eva's sister Noelle had suddenly ruined everything by becoming pregnant. At the time, it had seemed expedient that Noelle marry Garret Cagan and quickly. Since the Martins had disapproved of Garret as well as Raoul, the two sisters had decided that Eva should postpone her engagement to Raoul in order to spare their frail grandmother two misalliances at once. Eva had been so sure Raoul would be understanding. How could she have misunderstood him so completely?

She had hurt him and enraged him. Raoul had been so furious he'd hotheadedly leapt at the chance to rush off to Africa to check on Otto's oil fields. Eva remembered too well his last bitter taunt. "You know, *chère,* what really scares me is how close you came to remaking me into some whey-faced, namby-pamby hypocrite. I'd rather take a bullet in Rana."

Everything else had gone wrong after that. Noelle's baby had died. *Grand-mère* had had a stroke. Noelle hadn't married Garret, at least not then. Instead she'd run away to Australia. The Martins had covered up the scandal. Then war had broken out in Rana. A single letter had come from Raoul—he'd promised to be home for her birthday—to talk things out. Instead news of his death and treachery had come.

Her family had tried to be sympathetic. Otto had come around frequently to console her. When she'd remained depressed, they'd encouraged her to move to London and put the whole unfortunate affair behind her.

For so many years Eva had tried to forget Raoul. Now she couldn't help but realize that if she had believed in him and accepted him, he might never have gone to Africa. In a way, everything that had gone wrong in his life was her fault. If he was hard and bitter—if he was a killer, even—who had sent him to that fate?

Nicholas Jones snapped the chain on the lamp.

At the metallic sound, fresh pain splintered through her nerves.

The bed was shrouded in darkness.

The silent man and woman were as mute as two strangers, unable to sleep, unable to speak.

Eva's nerves tensed at his every sound, too conscious of the strength and animal fascination of him. His breathing seemed unusually harsh, and he twisted and thrashed like a great imprisoned beast, yanking the covers away from her, time and again. Rolling restlessly back again to his original position, he would throw them off.

She remembered his strong body crushing her against the cabin wall, her hair blowing against his face in the darkness, his hot lips against hers, devouring her mouth. He had admitted his fierce physical need of her. He was a hard, inhuman man. She kept dreading the time when he would reach out and take her—against her will.

An hour passed, and when his great body remained tensely coiled, as far from her as possible, gradually her fear of him lessened, and she began to weep silently for all that they had lost.

He lay beside her, still as stone, alert as a panther.

A strangled sob broke this silence. *Mon dieu.* To cry now… Why did the tears always come at the worst possible moment? She buried her hot wet face in a wadded pillow so it wouldn't happen again.

''Eva…'' His tortured, raspy voice flowed across the darkness, infinitely soft.

She didn't dare answer him for fear he would hear the sound of more tears in her voice, but she cried so hard her whole body was wracked with sobs.

Tentatively he edged nearer. Too upset to reply, she could only sense the nearness of his body, the warmth and power of him.

''*Chère*…''

He touched her hair, stroked the long silky waves.

"I—I didn't want to bother you." Her voice was a small choked sound. She tried to keep her face buried so he couldn't feel her cheeks, but he loosened her fingers, prying the pillow free and tossing it to his side of the bed.

"Pillow pig," he whispered gently. "You had both of them, you know. No wonder I couldn't sleep."

His hand curved along her slender throat, turning her face slowly toward him. His lips brushed her cheeks, kissing away the salty tears, one by one. She held her breath, not needing air, if only his mouth would continue its sensual exploration of delicate skin and bone.

She licked her lips, wanting him to kiss her there, but although his mouth hovered close, he didn't. Instead he pulled her into his arms, sliding her smaller body so that it fit beneath his, and cradled her until she quieted.

"I'm sorry for what I did, for what I said," he murmured in a low husky tone.

"Don't..." She put two fingers against his lips.

Involuntarily her two fingers trailed downward, tracing the hard firm curve of his chin, the line of his jaw. When a fingertip touched his earlobe, she heard his deep, indrawn breath.

She withdrew her hand.

A long hushed silence fell. They just lay there, her body nestled beneath his, the rhythmic rolling of the boat seductively moving them together. The hard feel of his naked flesh against her smaller shape rocked her senses. She felt the heat of his breath against her throat, the musky scent of him enveloping her.

Not that he was any more immune to her than she to him. She felt his pulse begin to pound. His arms fell away, and she knew that he clenched his hands into fists to resist the temptation of deepening their embrace.

She had always been bold, but only with him. So she touched him as only she knew how. With wanton fingertips of flame.

On a groan he rolled over, pulling her on top of him so that

her hair spilled over his perspiring face and shoulders, long satiny strands of it sticking to his skin.

"Are you sure?" His raspy voice was unsteady.

She felt him shaking with desire while she pretended to consider.

The emotion-charged seconds ticked by like hours while she
held him in thrall. His dilated pupils filled his eyes and made
them midnight black.

Then she leaned down and flicked his earlobe with her tongue,
her fingers curled into the wavy thickness of his hair.

"I think so," she sighed at last.

"You think so, huh?" But he laughed throatily, and the deep
vibrant rumble was as beautiful as music.

Because it was Raoul's laughter.

When he drew her face down gently to his, it was with
Raoul's lips that he kissed her. The hands that undressed her
and played over her body with reverent expertise were Raoul's
hands as well.

She released a quivering pent-up sigh of complete surrender.

A wild hunger swept them both.

Sex had always been good between them, but this was different. Fiercer, hotter. When he'd lain in prison with his leg so
infected he thought he'd surely lose it, he'd held on to his sanity
only by dreaming of her in his arms. For her he was the passionate lover she had lost and found again.

There was a ferocity in them both that neither had ever known
before. His tongue licked its way down her slim body, tickling
her nipples, delving into her navel, until she lay beneath him,
all hot and quivering, her eyes blazing, her shaky voice begging
him to take her.

He moved on top of her, only to draw back stunned at her
whimper when he found difficulty in entering her. She held him
close, her fingertips pressed into his spine, and whispered
fiercely, "it's only because...there has never been anyone but
you. Only you."

She'd been a virgin the first time. But this was better, infinitely better. He touched her cheek tenderly and murmured something in French that was low and inaudible. Then he was inside her and there was pleasure, immense shattering bursts of pleasure that saturated their minds and hearts. They were twisting and writhing, and everything that had gone wrong between them was forgotten in that one final melting explosion of ecstasy.

He gathered her to him closely, and she fell asleep cradled in his arms with the joyous knowledge that at last everything was going to be all right.

Early the next morning, Nicholas stood at the helm, coldly oblivious to the perfection of the sparkling morning. All trace of the storm had vanished from the skies and seas. Directly ahead he saw his island floating like a dazzling white jewel in a turquoise sea. The salty air blowing off the fringe of cliffs brought the scents of basil, bougainvillea, pine, and all the unidentified herbs Marcos planted every spring. At any other time the scene would have seemed paradisiacal, but this morning the bleached dome with its plunging cliffs loomed before Nicholas like the worst hell on earth. How many days—how many nights—would he be trapped there with Eva?

Nicholas was furious with himself. By sleeping with her he had complicated the hell out of an already complicated situation. He had planned to spend a week with her at most and be done with her forever.

She was still asleep. Thank God for that. He lighted a cigarette and carefully shook out the match. If only there was some way he could do as she'd asked and let her go in some safe harbor— but she didn't really understand the full extent of the danger. If she returned to London, one of Otto's men would be there to kill her. Nicholas had no choice but to stay with her and wait it out until he was sure she would be safe. Once Otto failed to make his interest payments later in the week, he would be receiving so much notoriety that he'd be afraid to make a false move.

Last night Eva had felt so good. Nicholas got aroused just thinking about it. He took a long pull on his cigarette, not wanting to torture himself by remembering. But it was no use. The memory of her arms and legs wrapped around him, of her muted cry of passion at the end, had driven him wild.

Grimly he pitched his cigarette into the water and turned the wheel hard alee so he could sail around the island once to make sure there were no other unwanted visitors moored offshore. When the main sail swung across, he tightened the sheet.

As he got closer to shore, he forced himself to concentrate on the island, noting how the rare sheltered folds of ground where Marcos cultivated the vines were unusually lush and green. But instead of the island, Nicholas kept remembering the erotic vision of Eva in his bed with her hair fanning across his pillows like a wreath of flame, with the sheet molding her shapely body.

His throat went dry.

The ruin of the Roman village at the foot of the cliffs came into view. He scarcely gave it a thought. Nor was he in any mood to admire his stunning house, which had been designed by one of the most famous architects in the world. The top floor of the mansion capped the island; the lower floors were carved into the side of the cliff.

Nicholas had chosen the island as the perfect hiding place because no one knew that he owned it. The house was equipped with sophisticated electronics—telexes, computers, fax machines, a network of telephone lines—everything he needed to conduct his business and stay abreast of what was happening.

The house was easily accessible to the water; paths led down from the terraces of the house to the beaches and natural swimming pools. More importantly there was a magnificent cave beneath his home that covered the deepest of these natural pools. There was a hidden elevator cut through solid rock cliff inside the cave. The cave's ceiling was high enough to moor and conceal *Rogue Wave* even with her tall masts. There was also a narrow cliff path within the cave that led to the house so that a man could go up and come down without being seen from the water or air.

Nicholas always came here alone. The island was a very romantic setting, the worst kind of environment to spend time with a woman a man wanted to avoid.

Not that Nicholas hadn't known this would be a problem. From the moment he'd seen Eva bathing in Otto's stateroom, the sight of her in that tub had stirred every repressed erotic male fantasy he had ever had of her.

Last night when he'd gone to bed it had taken a superhuman effort to leave her alone. Then she'd cried, the sound of her heartbroken tears luring him into her arms. Once there, he'd been lost.

Now he realized it was as clear as day that she'd known exactly what she was doing. She had known he had wanted her and yet all of yesterday she'd deliberately teased him.

She probably thought she had the upper hand now. But she was wrong.

Once, years ago, he had longed for Eva's love and a normal life with her, longed for it so cravenly that he had almost been willing to allow her to remold him in the image she had of the ideal man, until she'd shown him that no matter how he changed, he would never be acceptable. If he hadn't been good enough for her then, he damned sure wasn't now. He was too old to change, too old to risk his heart again—if he still had one.

The entrance of the cave was very close. Nicholas started the auxiliary engine and switched on the depth finder. When he put the engine in gear, the clutch slipped. Damn. He'd have to get Zak to check that.

Nicholas pointed the boat into the wind and hollered down below for Zak, who leapt up at once, racing to the foredeck to take down the jib while Nicholas lowered the main. Then they pulled out anchors and line and made them ready. Zak grabbed the boat hook to fend off from the walls of the cave as Nicholas slowed the yacht and headed it toward the tunnel of limestone walls.

The channel into the cave was narrow and cut through rock reef, its depth so uncertain in places that Zak had to call out constant readings from the depth finder.

"Twenty feet."

Rock walls on either side of the cave's entrance jutted dangerously close on both sides.

"Fifteen."

Nicholas cut the power.

"Seven!"

The *Rogue* drew five. Nicholas had to steer very carefully to keep her in the center of the channel so her keel wouldn't scrape bottom.

"Six!"

His breathing stopped. At just that moment, the worst of all possible moments, Eva emerged from the cabin to distract him.

"Five and a half!"

"Good morning," she whispered dreamily, looking lovely and sleep-mussed, her eyes softly aglow as she smiled at him, her red tangled hair glistening in the sunshine as the breeze blew it about her shoulders. She was wearing that bathing suit again that fit—what damned little of her body it covered!—like a silky lavender glove. Nicholas could see jutting nipples, everything— except where to steer. Standing amidship, her exquisite body completely blocked his vision of that. He felt a warm jolt of pleasure at the sight of her and then fury and panic.

"Five and a quarter," Zak yelled.

Terror gripped Nicholas.

"Damn it! I can't see through you! Get below," he yelled at her, cold anger in his voice, "before I wreck her."

The beautiful happiness in Eva's face died instantly. She went white, his harsh words like a blow. The bright tousled head disappeared below.

Zak shot him a peculiar look. Nicholas told himself there was no way he could know what had happened between himself and Eva. No way.

"Five and a half. Seven."

They were over the reef. They were safe—inside the shady

concealing coolness of thick limestone walls, the ship's white hull seeming to hang suspended over the crystal-clear waters.

"Twenty-five."

Nicholas saw Eva hovering uncertainly halfway down the stairs, her beautiful face ashen, her lovely eyes blurred by tears. Deliberately Nicholas made his voice even rougher. "Well, don't just stand there. Come up and help Zak with the dinghy while I set the anchors."

Without a word, she came up, turned her back on him and helped Zak lower the dinghy at the stern and tie and secure the painter. Zak was unusually nice to her.

And that grated, too. Especially when Zak called her to the foredeck to help stow the jib. Not that Nicholas thought she could be of much real help. But Zak was so patient and instructive that soon she was hanking the halyard to the mast, bagging the sail, and coiling lines like an expert, with Zak complimenting everything she did so excessively he had Eva beaming and Nicholas scowling.

Zak went below and helped her prepare breakfast. At the easy camaraderie between them, Nicholas ground his teeth. If Zak was going to cook, he'd have to see to the clutch himself.

Nicholas's bad leg throbbed from the awkwardness of squeezing himself into a tiny corner of the aft cabin so he could get to the engine. In the galley Zak and Eva laughed and talked.

Nicholas tried not to watch them or listen, but every time Zak smiled at her, every time she laughed at something he said, the knot inside Nicholas's gut wound a little tighter.

By the time the three of them sat down to breakfast together, Nicholas was green with jealousy. He had wanted her to ignore him. Well, she was ignoring the hell out of him. And seemingly enjoying the hell out of herself while she did so. She passed Zak the marmalade, not noticing that he hadn't had any himself.

Nicholas sat silently eating the unburned eggs and noted that her cooking was better. She was a quick learner, and for some reason that made him even madder, her virtues annoying him even more than her faults. Throughout the meal, Nicholas endured the friendly chatter of his woman and his best friend, his grim tension building like a storm cloud.

As the morning wore on, things got worse.

Nicholas wanted to ignore her, but whatever she did, she had his undivided attention. She sang a French love song as she washed the dishes, and her beautiful voice was such a distraction he couldn't do a thing with the transmission. Finally he threw his wrench down in frustration, and it hit his toe. Not that she so much as looked at him when he cursed about it. She never missed a note. In utter frustration he gave up on the engine and called Zak over to help him.

"Hey, don't act so riled. It's just the fluid, man. Here's the leak," Zak purred, his tone superior.

She heard.

"Then if it's so easy to fix, you do it," Nicholas growled, furious at them both.

Wisely Eva disappeared into the forepeak cabin, but Nicholas could hear her bustling about and couldn't forget she was there.

"So what are you going to do about her?"

Nicholas flashed his friend a dark look.

"I asked you a question."

Nicholas grimaced. "Which was none of your business."

"Hey, I have to live with the two of you. She cries. You sulk."

"That's your problem."

"That's why I'm asking you to do something about it."

Nicholas threw his oil rag to the floor, strode up the stairs and went outside, but Eva, who had opened the forward hatch and climbed out, was already up on the foredeck stretched out on a towel reading a paperback novel.

She never even looked up. Well, he damn sure wouldn't go back below just because she was there. That would only prove to her he'd noticed her.

Nicholas lowered a bucket and began to wash the cockpit with salt water and a brush. He was scrubbing so furiously he didn't hear her soft approach.

"Maybe it would help if I went ashore."

His black head jerked up. "What?"

The sunlight came from behind her, so he couldn't see how much her boldness was costing her—the quick flame of color in her cheeks, the overbright flare of hope in her eyes. All he saw was the dark outline of her body, the perfect female shape of her. All he felt was the unforgivable urge to drag her into his arms and make love to her violently. But that was a weakness he was determined not to give in to again.

"You heard me." Her voice was whispery, nervous. "My presence is obviously driving you crazy."

"The hell it is." A savage pulse had begun in his throat. "I don't give a damn about you one way or the other."

The sun blinded him. He couldn't see her whiten. "Well, then," she said with a calmness that infuriated him, "since it isn't, maybe we can start the morning over and try to have a normal conversation."

"I thought you were reading a book."

"I can't seem to get into it." Her voice was slow, husky, and somehow more unnerving than ever.

"Maybe you haven't tried hard enough."

"Maybe." She tossed it down and sank on her knees beside him, mindless of the book's pages fluttering in the wind. "Is this your private island? Or are we trespassing?"

Never had she shown him more naked golden skin...except last night. Damn it! He wasn't going to think about that. But her beautiful body was a soft coil of thighs, breasts arms, and he couldn't ignore her. What was she trying to do to him?

"Yes. It's mine."

"It's wonderful. Do you come here often?"

"Only in the summers."

"With friends?"

"Alone."

"Always alone?" she persisted.

"Damn it. I said it once, didn't I? I like being alone." His last sentence was a careful insult.

"Oh, you do?"

Her voice was naive, innocent. It compelled him to look at her. When he did, he felt the golden-brown dazzle of her eyes seeking his. His blood began to beat again, violently. "Look…"

"You could be alone if I went ashore," she said composedly, looking at him through her lashes.

"No!"

"Why do you care, if you want to be alone so much?"

"I don't, damn it!" What was he saying? "You're to stay because I said so." Even to himself, his sharp answer sounded unreasonable, like that of a child.

She wouldn't drop it. "I thought I saw a house on top of the island."

"The house is mine, too," he snarled.

"Can't we stay there?"

"No! A family lives there. Caretakers. A man, a woman, and a child. Stay away from them."

"I've been on this boat for two nights and two days. I want to go ashore. I want to stand up straight without having to hold on to something. I want to walk on solid ground."

It was a reasonable request, but he wasn't feeling the least bit reasonable toward her.

"Look. This isn't some pleasure cruise. Otto will be scouring the Mediterranean looking for us. If he sees you, or any of us, everyone on the island could die—including those people at the house. I want you near me, where I can watch you."

"I thought I saw a path through the cave."

"It's too steep and slippery. If you don't know it well, you could fall. One of us would have to go with you." He didn't mention that the cave had a hidden elevator that only he had a key to.

"Then I'll ask Zak."

"You leave Zak alone!"

"Why are you doing this?"

"Because of the danger."

"No. I—I don't mean that. I mean why are you being so

deliberately hateful? You've been awful, deliberately awful, all morning. Is all this…because of what happened last night?''

He couldn't see her tear-laden eyes, but he heard the sadness in her voice. And it stopped him dead. Then he told himself that she was doing it again, what she'd done last night, acting vulnerable, bringing out some insane masculine urge in him to protect her.

He wanted to take her in his arms again, to kiss away the tears, to ease the terrible pain he was inflicting, to tell her how much he wanted her. But when he spoke his voice was low and harsh. ''I told you my feelings on the subject. Don't make last night something it wasn't.''

''Then you just used me—to satisfy an appetite?''

He knew her softness could destroy him. He heard the break in her voice, but he made no denial.

''Oh, how could you?'' He heard her sudden intake of breath. ''And I thought…'' Her voice trailed away, bleak, pain-filled.

''Why are you surprised, when you've always considered me a scoundrel?''

''No, I never did. And I don't think I ever really believed Otto. Last night, when you were kind to me, I almost believed that I'd been right about you all along, that I do have the instincts to judge good from evil in men. That there is some remnant of a decent human being left inside you. Oh, how wrong I was.''

The heartbreak and anguish in her voice cut through him like a knife.

''You want to be alone!'' she cried. ''Well, fine—be alone!''

He heard her misery through the mists of his own pain. He reached toward her, but he was too late. She leapt up, and before he could stop her, she climbed over the lifelines and sprang, her slim form arched in a perfect swan dive into the water.

''Eva!''

There was a splash and she disappeared into the deep blue depths. Then her bright head broke the surface, and she swam with swift deliberate strokes away from *Rogue Wave* toward the island—in deliberate defiance of him. She could have gotten out at a nearby rocky ledge in the cave, but she was too upset to notice. She was swimming through the channel for the beach outside the cave, the only other place a swimmer could emerge safely. It was a long swim, much of it through deep water. There were currents around the island and dangerous undertows. He remembered her terror of deep water, how close she had once come to drowning. She would never have jumped in if she hadn't felt desperate to escape him.

If anything happened to her...

He pulled off his shoes and tossed them into the boat. Then he dived in after her. He swam through the channel into open water, but she was nowhere in sight. When he reached the beach there was still no sign of her. He fought against the first flicker of panic. Where was she? She had to be somewhere near.

He yelled for her. Not a sound from her. Only the echo of his own voice. Nothing but empty beach, a great wall of bleached rock towering above him on one side and an endless expanse of blue sea stretching away from him on the other.

"Eva!" he called her name, and when she didn't answer, his mindless fear mushroomed. He hadn't seen her emerge from the water. Dear God. He squinted hard, staring out at the turquoise water sparkling beneath a brilliant sun. Finally he sank to his knees in despair. Had she already drowned? He would never forgive himself.

"I'm up here," she called down to him after a long time.

She was standing above him on a narrow ledge next to another opening to the cave.

She had been deliberately hiding from him!

He was furious all over again. "Come down, damn you!"

She glared down at him mutinously. When he started to come up, she slipped back inside the cave.

Wild with anger, he climbed recklessly up the rocks, cutting his feet, his hands, his legs, but not caring. When he reached the path, he followed her into the cave. Inside it was dark and cool. Blinded from the brilliance outside, he couldn't see a thing.

"I'm right here," she said softly.

He whirled.

To his surprise she was standing a few mere inches from him. She had been waiting for him just inside. He saw that the ledge behind her narrowed dangerously. She was trapped.

He caught her to him, gripping her arms so hard she cried out.

Flesh to flesh. Wetly hot woman skin turned his every male cell to fire.

"What the hell kind of game are you playing?" His voice cracked like a whip in the hushed silence of the cave.

Rage, relief that she was alive, passion—all these things were burning in him as he held her nearly naked body against his own.

She said nothing. A tremor went through her. It was as if she knew that she had pushed him as far as he could be pushed. She moistened her lower lip with the pink tip of her tongue. He watched the movement, fascinated.

He felt a swift hot stab of arousal. His eyes met hers only to lose himself in those whiskey-dark eyes that blazed with a need as fierce as his own.

With fingertips of flame she touched him.

And then he knew her game.

But it was already too late.

He pushed her against the wall, his body pressing into hers, and he kissed her until they were both breathless. Then he picked her up in his arms and carried her down the narrow ledge. She clung to him trustingly even when he stooped and took her into a low-ceilinged, hidden grotto.

There in that sheltered darkness, on a bed of cool wet sand they made love. Gently, completely. It didn't matter that he came from a brutal world that she couldn't understand. It didn't matter that she could never truly be his. Nothing mattered but the glorious explosion of ecstasy they found in each other's arms.

Chapter 8

Enclosed within Nicholas's strong arms, Eva lay quietly beneath him, her beautiful face aglow with satisfaction.

He had fought the passion that bound him to her and lost, but he had no more rage for her, only wonderment that he had endured the long years without her. There could be no hope for a future. They had only today—at most perhaps the next day and the one after that.

A week—maybe.

The rest of his life to be lived in less than seven days.

Then she would be gone.

Nicholas put one hand on either side of her hot cheeks and with careful deliberation kissed her eyelids, the feathered black tips of her densely curled lashes; then her nose, her mouth.

She was sweet. Oh, so dangerously sweet.

She opened her languorous eyes, and for a few seconds they remained deliciously remote. Then she focused on him. "Nicholas," she whispered.

"Yes, *chère.*"

She touched his brow, smoothed back the black lock with the strands of silver from his brow. "I've made so many mistakes with you."

"So have I."

"If I'd only taken the trouble to really understand you." She paused. "Maybe—"

"Don't," he whispered. "No regrets..."

"I want to know everything about you," she persisted.

He smiled. "All the secrets of my scandalous life?"

She laughed. "Something like that."

"There are too many to tell."

"Just one then. When you were a teenager—why did your father really kick you out?"

His face tightened. She was digging deep. Too deep. He had to swallow hard to maintain control. "Why do you want to know about that?"

Eva softly kissed his cheek. "Because that's when everybody said you went bad. You never told me anything, and I was just a baby when it happened. All I've ever heard were the rumors. I can't believe they were true."

He tensed and pulled away from her, staring into the cave, his thoughts whirling away from the present, back down the dark corridor of time.

Dimly he heard her say, "You don't have to tell me, if you don't want to."

He didn't want to talk about it, but the gentle tenderness in her face and voice breached his defenses. She had a way of pulling the pain out of his soul and healing him with her kindness. His hand closed around a rock so hard it cut into his callused palm. "Which of the rumors did you hear?" His voice was rough with the effort it took to restrain all the old emotions and bitter resentments.

"That your father caught you in bed with your stepmother. You were only seventeen, she was twenty. Was it true?"

All the old hate and pain and fear boiled up in him. He remembered how lost he'd been when his father had thrown him out.

There was scorn in Nicholas's voice when he spoke. "In a way, I guess it was true. You've got the ages right. I had never lived around a woman. I resented it when my father married

Louise. He changed after he married her. He had been bitter with me, spending his nights with the bottle on a downstairs couch. After Louise came, he was always laughing.'' Nicholas paused.

''They hadn't been married very long when it happened. One night she called me into her bedroom to look for her earring that she said had fallen between the wall and the bed. She had the sheets pulled over her, and I didn't know she was naked beneath them. My father came up the stairs, and she threw off the sheet and started screaming. He caught us there and assumed the worst. She told him that I tried to force her to make love to me. He believed her. He grabbed a belt and would have beaten the life out of me if I hadn't run away. Later, when he changed his will in favor of her baby son, I figured out why she did it. Sweet Seclusion came from my mother. I never saw him again.''

''How awful.''

''I learned early how it feels to be wrongly accused.''

Tears of empathy sprang into Eva's eyes, and Nicholas clutched her to him. He told her of the wretched years that followed, how he'd drifted from one menial job to another, how he'd been picked up for vagrancy, how he'd been too wild, how he'd attempted and failed at college more times than he could count.

''Hell, it took me seven colleges, but I finally had the sense to stick it out and get a business degree. When I graduated at the top of my class, I decided that if I could do that, I could do anything. You know the rest.''

Her arms were about him, holding him tightly. She caressed his shoulders, his neck. She combed her fingers through the curling darkness of his hair.

''There was never anyone for me,'' he said.

''Never until now,'' she whispered.

She held his hand so that her slim white palm fit into his larger, darker one. Even this gentle touching of their hands coming together sent a charge of electricity through them both.

Her palm was fragile and soft, his roughly callused. His fingers overlapped hers by inches. He could have closed his hand and easily crushed her delicate bones. Instead he slid his hand against hers and massaged the velvet softness. The warmth of her skin seeped into his.

The black-and-gold onyx ring gleamed on her finger, his long-ago gift of love to her when she'd been an innocent girl. He stared hard at the ring she'd pressed into his hand to keep him safe when he'd left her to go to Africa. "I will wear it forever," she had said, "when you bring it back to me."

Nicholas met Eva's gaze and saw love and an innocent trust shining there. He saw as well the pure beautiful strength in her heart and soul, her belief in the possibility of happiness, in the future, her faith in everything that was utterly lacking in him. She was that innocent girl again, but a woman, too. A woman who had loved and lost and yet still believed in the redeeming power of love.

He laced his fingers through hers more tightly and dragged her beneath him again.

"You feel good, Eva," he whispered. "So good, you almost make me whole." His mouth found her lips, and he kissed them briefly, with an ache that filled his entire being. "Don't make this into something it can never be. For us there will be no tomorrow."

Eva lay on the deck, her book closed beside her, her fingers restlessly tapping the cover. Beside her were a bottle of teak oil and a rag. She could hear Nicholas and Zak down below dismantling the transmission again, the leak having proved difficult to repair.

No tomorrow...

That meant he would say goodbye again.

How Nicholas's words had haunted Eva in the three days that had followed them. Three days of golden sun, three days of passionate lovemaking in their secret grotto and in his bed at night. Every time Nicholas touched her, every time he looked at her, she was aware that precious time was running out.

Nicholas was gentler with her now. Although he never spoke

words of love or made any promises about what the future might hold, sometimes she caught him unawares, watching her with a sad tenderness in his eyes. The moment he saw she was watching, the poignant warmth would fade, and his old bleak mask would slip back into place.

Only when they made love was he different. Only when he was deep inside her would the mask slip away. He would hold her tightly, as if he'd never let her go, his face rapt with pleasure. Then in the wild tumult of their passion he was completely hers.

Otto had not come. Nicholas was frustrated because there was very little about him in the news. The lazy drifting days that were filled with fishing and swimming and reading made it impossible for her to believe they were in any real danger, yet there was constant tension in Nicholas and Zak. She was never allowed out of their sight for long.

Every afternoon Nicholas went up to the house alone and spent long hours on the phone, at his computers. He left her with Zak, and she had grown so restless and bored on the boat in his absence that Zak had set her to polishing chrome and teak. Every time Nicholas left, she begged him to take her along. She wanted to be with him, to see his house, to meet the couple and the child that lived there. He always, gently but firmly, stepped into the dinghy without her. The one surprise was that he allowed Victor to go along. "I'd do anything to get him off the boat awhile," Nicholas had explained. Sometimes Victor would stay ashore only to make a nuisance of himself by returning to the cave's lower ledge around midnight and yowling. Nicholas would have to go get him then.

Eva decided the reason Nicholas didn't want her to go was because he must be afraid that she would try to use the sophisticated equipment at the house to contact the outside world. Which was the last thing she wanted to do—now. Guiltily she remembered those two unanswered calls for help she had secretly made.

From the beach every evening, Eva had watched the couple walking with their small son at the top of the cliff. The man and woman had golden hair and skin, their son was slim and bronzed and black-headed. One evening the young woman had looked down and seen her. She had waved. Perhaps because the family was forbidden to her, Eva was filled with curiosity about them. She longed for female companionship, for someone different to talk to. Eva imagined that such a woman must be fascinating. Eva wanted to ask her what it was like to live on an island, cut off from the world with only her husband and child for company. Eva longed to meet the little boy as well.

Every day Eva's curiosity and boredom and restlessness grew. Thoughts of the house and the family took her mind off of Nicholas and their impossible relationship.

Eva's daydreaming was interrupted when high above the boat where she lay on the topmost ledge in the cave there was a sound. Then a rock splashed into the water near *Rogue Wave*'s hull.

Eva's fingers froze on her book. She looked up and saw the little boy and Victor together. The child, another rock in his hand, seemed to be staring down at her with a curiosity equal to her own. Victor was beside him. She called up to them. The child tossed the rock, and it landed closer, near the dinghy like an invitation, personally delivered.

She heard Nicholas curse down below. He was completely absorbed with his engine.

Was he her lord and master?

Not even considering such a silly question, she tiptoed across the deck, loosened the knot in the painter, and got into the dinghy as it slipped away. She glanced up and saw that the boy and cat had vanished.

Rowing all the way to the beach, she dragged the dinghy and its oars ashore and climbed the cliff. From time to time she had to stop to catch her breath. The sun beamed down; the northwesterly, as Nicholas called the perpetual breeze, blew her hair. The world seemed an eternity of warm hazy sky and undulating turquoise. It was impossible to imagine that there could be any danger.

She was breathless when she reached the magnificent house. Its terraces commanded beautiful views of the sea and the rest of the island. There were fig trees and prickly pears, fleshily fanned. She saw the satellite dish, antennae of all sorts, all partially concealed behind a tumble of boulders.

The blond woman and her dark-haired boy were walking with Victor beneath a grove of olive trees.

Victor meowed loudly when he saw her.

The beautiful young woman, her face radiant with welcome, came over at once. She was flushed and smiling. "You are Nicholas's friend," she said in a softly accented voice.

"I'm Evangeline Martin."

"And I'm Teresa. This is Nickie…"

Nickie came forward. His white smile and black eyes were brilliant as he tentatively offered his hand. Evangeline knelt down and took it, but hardly had she touched his tiny fingers than they had flown from her grasp. He moved like lightning. He was a small child, no more than six, Evangeline imagined. He was incredibly lively.

"He must be a handful, with all the high cliffs and the cave," Eva said.

Teresa smiled, the kindly tolerant smile of a mother. "He loves the island. We come every summer with my brother. Marcos helps me watch him when he isn't fishing."

"Oh, I thought you lived with your husband."

A fleeting shadow passed over Teresa's beautiful face as she fingered the plain gold band on her left hand.

"I'm sorry if I said something wrong," Eva said.

Teresa's gentle, accepting smile was meant to reassure. "It's all right. Would you like some refreshment after your long walk up the cliff?"

"Water would be fine."

"I have homemade wine."

"That would be lovely."

Nickie was playing on the ground with Victor beneath the olive trees. They seemed to be old friends. While Teresa was inside, Eva watched them. Nickie got up. He had a white cane, which he tapped on the ground. Victor chased after him, leaping for the tapping cane and pawing it.

A white cane?

Was Teresa's beautiful boy blind?

Eva was suddenly horrified the child would trip. "Victor!"

"It's all right," Teresa murmured soothingly, setting her tray with a bowl of ripe figs, a decanter of wine and wineglasses on a low table. "It's one of their favorite games. They like to play in the cave, too. There's an opening just beyond the grove. If you know the way, you can climb all the way down to the water through the cave."

"Nicholas told me." Eva sipped her wine, which was sweet and dark, and she complimented it.

"My brother, Marcos, cultivates the grapes on the island," Teresa said.

Eva's attention was on the child and the cat. "Is Nickie blind? Wouldn't it be dangerous for him to go into the cave?"

"He's only partially blind. His doctor says in another year he can have an operation that will help him. He's spent all his summers here. Look, there go the two of them. Nickie knows the cliffs in there as well as he knows his own room. He loves it here." There was no trace of concern in Teresa's voice.

"Do you mind if I follow them—just to make sure Victor doesn't trip him?"

Teresa shook her head. "I'll come, too." Teresa talked amiably. She said, "I get so lonely to talk to another woman. I have been begging Nicholas to bring you up or pleading with him to let me come down."

"So have I."

"Nicholas can be very stubborn."

They laughed together.

Inside the cave, the cliffs were steep and treacherous, but Eva could see the path leading all the way to the sea. Nickie and Victor were snugly ensconced on a narrow ledge. She could see *Rogue Wave*'s anchor line. Inch by inch her gaze followed it from the water to the yacht. Nicholas was standing at the pulpit, and even in the shadowy cave, she saw that every line of his body seemed grim and hard with anger the moment he caught sight of her.

Quickly she looked away. Too quickly. Her foot slipped.

A rock tumbled down the cliff and hit the water. She watched its spiraling descent to the bottom of the pool. The cliff was so steep, the path so narrow, she was suddenly dizzy. The walls of the cave seemed to sway in lazy circles. Shakily she pressed her back against the cool limestone and clung. Beneath she saw the dark water. Then it blurred. Her balance was gone. Panic stabbed through her, and she screamed in terror, afraid she would fall.

She heard Nicholas shout far below.

The world seemed to fade into darkness, and she imagined herself sinking down, down into that pool. She was drowning— as before. Burning water was filling her throat. Her body was pulled through currents, drifting deeper and deeper. She was choking.

Then she heard Teresa, right beside her saying, "Hey, every-thing's okay." Teresa's hand gently took hers. "I think we'd better go back outside. I'll lead the way."

Eva opened her eyes. Teresa was so kind, so gentle, so un-derstanding. Back at the house Eva told her that once she had nearly drowned, that for years she'd had a phobia about water, that she'd thought she was over it.

"Does Nicholas know?" Teresa asked.

"He was there when it happened."

"Then it seems odd that he would invite you on a cruise. He's usually so kind and thoughtful."

Eva could only stare at her. "Kind and thoughtful." Was that how Teresa saw him?

Teresa began to talk of her life on the island as well as her life away from it.

Innocently Eva asked, "Does Nickie go to school yet?"

"Oh, yes. Nicholas sends him to a special school every fall in London."

''Nicholas sends—'' Eva's voice broke. She could only stare at Teresa in dumb shock. Nicholas was paying for her son's education. Why?

Nicholas. Nickie. The similarity of the two names hadn't clicked. Perhaps because to Eva Nicholas was Raoul. Teresa had said she lived with her brother, not her husband. The golden band on Teresa's hand glittered in the sunlight.

Teresa was married to someone.

And she was living in Nicholas's house.

Eva's imagination speculated wildly. Was that someone a man who would send his son to school but refused to live with his mother? A man so callous he would bring another woman to the same island where his wife lived? Was he making love to both of them? Eva could not quite fathom that horror.

Why was she so surprised, Eva wondered?

But she was.

He had admitted to other women, to casual relationships, but never to this. Nickie was small. He must be around six years old.

It was all too easy to imagine what must have happened. Nicholas had returned from Africa and found solace in this lovely woman's arms. There had been a child, even marriage, although not a real one because Nicholas had been too brutalized for anything else. He had merely lived up to his responsibilities. Eva could almost have forgiven him, if only he had told her. Almost.

Teresa was so beautiful and golden, so saintly. The child could only have inherited his daredevil vitality and his darkness from his father. No wonder Nicholas hadn't wanted Eva up here. How could Teresa be so kind and accepting of her? How many others had Nicholas brought to the island?

Eva remembered the wanton ecstasy of Nicholas's recent lovemaking all too clearly, his fevered mouth against her skin, the torrid flow of excitement racing through her veins as hot as a forest fire. He'd made her wait and wait.

Their passion seemed a travesty now. Bitter shame washed through her.

Teresa stood before her looking lovely and troubled. It was impossible to imagine Nicholas touching this other woman, but even so the blonde's presence was like a knife that slashed Eva from heart to gut.

Eva stood there, just looking at her, with no words to say.

Before Teresa could speak, Eva was rushing away.

The sky was vivid violet and gold. The Mediterranean had been painted with the same brush.

Nicholas found Eva hiding among the bleached piles of boulders on the remote windward side of the island. She had been huddled beneath the shade of a lone carob tree for hours, wanting nothing but to be alone. When he called her name, she didn't answer.

When he knelt and reached for her, she jerked away. "Don't touch me. Ever again. I couldn't bear it."

Then her fierce bitter tears began.

"So he's got to be mine, right?" Nicholas's jaw clenched and unclenched. "And you were the one woman who would stand by me."

"Just tell me one thing. What is Teresa's last name? And Nickie's?"

"Why ask, when you have it all figured out?" Nicholas said in a voice that was deadly calm. "It's Jones, of course."

Eva shrank against the white rock, trying to hide from him. "You're married. You have a child," she whispered. "No wonder you kept telling me we had no future."

"Eva! Damn it! Are you going to listen to me or not?" He took her hands, and held her against the rock. But when he saw himself tried and condemned in her eyes, he let her go.

"Teresa—what kind of woman is she that she can endure this kind of treatment? A saint?" Eva asked bitterly.

"Probably." Wearily he lighted a cigarette and shook out the match. He stared past her, scanning purple sky and sea for a long moment.

"You don't deserve a wife like her."

"No, I don't." He spoke in a flat unemotional tone.

"How could you mistreat a child...Nickie..."

He stamped out the cigarette in fury and disgust. He had inhaled only once. "Damn it. I couldn't. As always, when it comes to me, you see but you don't see. Teresa was the real Nicholas Jones's wife. Not mine, you little imaginative fool. When he died, there was very little insurance. I took care of her. I would have died but for him. When I built this house, I hired her brother to see after it. It seemed the least I could do."

"Then she's not your wife?"

"I told you she wasn't."

"How old is Nickie?"

"Eight."

"But he's so small. I thought he was five or six."

"You've been wrong—about a lot of things."

She stared bleakly into his eyes and saw nothing of him there for her. He was closed off, remote. Again.

"Don't stay up here too long," he said. "It's too dangerous. Too exposed."

The sun was sinking into a darkening sea as he turned to walk away.

She felt without life or breath as she watched him go. Weary from the tears and the emotion, she pressed her fingers to her eyes.

She wanted to call after him, but couldn't.

She knew she had lost him all over again.

Chapter 9

After the cold way he'd been treating her, the last thing Eva expected was for Nicholas to smile and wave at her as he rowed the dinghy across the dark glimmering water toward *Rogue Wave*. She jumped up with barely concealed excitement and started to dash to the stern as eagerly as a puppy awaiting his master's return. Then she caught herself and salvaged a remnant of pride by walking with just a bit more reluctance.

But he had seen. Oh, yes he'd seen how her book had gone flying across the deck and nearly tumbled into the water.

Polishing chrome, pretending to read, she'd been waiting on deck practically the whole afternoon—waiting for him to return from the house. Hours ago he'd taken Victor and a briefcase full of papers up the cliff. To work, he'd said grimly, and to see if he could learn anything of von Schönburg.

At Nicholas's smile she'd felt the first flicker of hope in two days. Then she met his eyes and saw that they were as deep and as dark and as cold as ever.

For two long days she'd lived without his kisses, his smiles, his touches. Maybe that was why just the sight of him twisted her up in knots inside, that and the fact that he looked so heart-stoppingly handsome in a simple white T-shirt and tight jeans that molded his lean brown body to perfection.

He cut the engine and let the dinghy glide silently toward her. The slanting sun came from behind him and cast an iridescent gleam upon his black hair. The nearer he came, the more aware she was of a deep fluttering inside her breast, of her pulse racing out of control.

When she leaned down to help him secure the painter, he snapped the line out of her hand and looped it around the cleat by himself.

Her face froze. She turned away slightly, but not before he glanced up at her again and went momentarily still, his gaze roaming over her from head to toe, taking in the bright head with her feathery curls blowing in the faint breeze, her too brilliant eyes, her trim body in the tight lavender suit. Most of all he saw her tenderness and love for him flash fleetingly across her face, and suddenly he was vastly uncomfortable. He yanked his eyes away from her as brutally as he pulled and knotted the line he was tying.

"Where's Victor?" she dared to ask.

"He wouldn't come when I called him." Nicholas's reply was cool as he bent to stow the oars. "I have more important things on my mind than a cat."

"He won't just come. You have to go get him. You can't treat him like a dog."

"He'll climb down the path in the cave and yowl at us from the ledge when he's ready."

"That probably won't be till the middle of the night."

"He'd better come before then," Nicholas said abruptly. "Where's Zak?"

"Down below."

Nicholas and she were speaking to each other like strangers, trading necessary information with their carefully cool voices and polite sentences.

"He damned sure better have that transmission fixed."

Nicholas climbed up the ladder, managing to hold on to his thick briefcase at the same time. She expected him to walk past her.

But he didn't.

He stopped beside her, his great body coiled and tense. He was even smiling that terrible smile when his eyes stayed cold.

"Good news, *chère*."

She went very still. Somehow she was sure it wouldn't be.

"The war between Otto and me is over."

"What?"

"The deadline for Otto's interest payments is past. He couldn't pay his creditors. More ships have been seized. His empire is collapsing like a house of cards. It looks like there will be immense international legal repercussions. He's cheated some pretty important people who are high up in governments. He's sold arms to the wrong people, too. Otto will be too busy talking to lawyers and trying to stay out of jail to take an interest in you. Since the story about Otto broke, your running away with me has made headlines in all the European papers.

"My men have informed the proper authorities of my real name, of the fact that I once worked for Otto, of the fact that it was I who was betrayed in Africa, of the fact that I own Z.A.K. World and am Otto's arch-rival. I think Otto is in such a tight spot he won't risk his own neck by allowing anything suspicious to happen to you. You can go home. Back to your shop, your world. Back to your safe, respectable life. Only it won't be quite so respectable after all the headlines. I'm afraid you may get a taste of what it's like to live with an unfairly deserved reputation."

In an agony she listened to him. Didn't he understand that her world had become one man? Didn't he understand that never again would she care about headlines?

"So, just like that it's over?" she whispered. "It's goodbye."

He would have walked past her, but she touched his arm. The onyx and gold ring on her right hand flashed. He jerked away from her.

"Do I mean nothing to you?" she pleaded.

He did not answer, but his eyes had fastened on her white face.

"How do I know I wasn't part of your revenge plan? How do I know you didn't just take me because you thought I was his? Maybe that was the only reason you made love to me—to get revenge!"

His face darkened, but when he spoke his voice was still calm, controlled. "You would think that," he said quietly.

As always her eyes were too easily filling with tears. "I don't think it. I just said it. I love you. I believe in you. This past week has been like a miracle. I never want to go back. All my life I have wanted the one thing you alone can give me—to be loved, truly loved."

"No." He cut off her soft protestations of love. "It's not in me to give anything more to you, and even if it were, you'd never believe in me, *chère*. Maybe I have Otto where I want him, but the damage he did me in Africa will always be there between us. I can't ever be the man I was before. No matter how all this comes out there's no way I can ever completely clear my name. We can't live on an island for the rest of our lives, cut off from the world. There'll always be those who believe the worst of me. If I married you, everything I was accused of would taint you, too. You have always wanted approval."

"I want your love."

"Maybe, but not enough to live without all the other things you want as well. I'm not strong enough to give you only part of what you need to have. I couldn't stand for you to be my wife and doubt me. I can't be some lawyer with some safe career. I'm not a Martin, I'm a Girouard. And I have always lived differently than you."

Wife. Just the word made her want to weep. Before her ghastly mistake about Teresa, had he actually been thinking of marriage?

Eva had come so close, and that made everything so much worse.

He saw the sparkle of tears still trembling on her lashes. "Don't," he whispered. "You've always cried too easily. Don't waste tears now when it was all over a long time ago."

Not for her. For years and years she'd grieved, she'd put her life on hold.

"No...you're a part of me. If you leave me, that part will die."

"I *will* leave you, for your sake as well as mine."

It was no use. No use. He was too terribly disillusioned, and she had played a horrible part in his disillusionment. But she wouldn't beg. Not anymore. "When...when are we going?"

"Zak?" he shouted past her, relief in his voice that their conversation was over. "When will the transmission be fixed?"

"I think I've got it."

"It's about time." Nicholas turned back to her. "We leave in an hour."

Lonely black despair closed around her. "I have to go up and get Victor."

"Nickie went into the cave, and Victor followed him."

"That place gives me the creeps. The cliffs are so steep. Sometimes the footpaths are wet. The water—" she broke off, unwilling to even think about the water.

"I'll go then."

"No. You see to the boat. Sometimes it takes some doing to talk Victor into coming."

"Take a can of sardines," he suggested.

For a man who didn't understand cats, he was making progress.

"I want to say goodbye to Teresa and Nickie, too."

"Say it fast."

She saw all too clearly how anxious he was to be rid of her.

Then he was untying the dinghy for her, helping her cast off. She didn't know that he watched her row all the way to the beach, that he watched her until she disappeared high up in the rocks as she climbed the cliff.

But what he should have seen, he couldn't.

Eva was almost halfway up the cliff when she saw a boat hidden in the cove, but she couldn't see the owner of the boat.

Tourists, perhaps. Oh, well, they had to be down there somewhere.

When she came over the top of the cliff, a sullen man with lush Mediterranean good looks dressed totally in black suede was there waiting for her with a loaded automatic pointed right at her face.

Paolo laughed at her when he saw the wild fear in her eyes. She shrank away from him. "I've been looking for you, *Signorina*. Everywhere."

Then he reached for her.

At his touch, she began to shake. When she tried to run, scrabbling desperately across the hard dry earth, she stumbled and fell. He grabbed her and slammed her back against a rock wall. Terror made her oblivious to the gun barrel against her cheek. She was like an animal, her nails clawing and tearing at his face, ripping into his black shirt.

"We've got the boy." He laughed softly. She could feel his hatred of her that contaminated every male pore in him. His laughter came again and again, rolling over her in waves that were viciously evil and hideously sensual.

They had Nickie!

Her hands fell away weakly from his dark face. Her nails curled into her own palms like talons, slashing deep, vivid half-moons into her soft skin. She allowed Paolo to lead her up to the house.

Paolo shoved Eva through the door beneath the white vaulted ceilings arching over the cool blue tiles. The inside of the house looked as though it had been hit by a hurricane. A couch was overturned. A lamp had been shattered. The Aubusson carpet was stained with blood. There had been a violent struggle, but it was over now. Otto was leaning back in a white chair, with the arrogance of a victorious warrior-king lounging on his throne. Behind him the view of the Mediterranean was magnificent.

Paolo pitched Eva down on those cold tiles at Otto's feet as though she were a thing to be sacrificed.

Their eyes wide with terror, Teresa and Nickie were huddled together near the door with Victor crouched nearby. Eva saw a dark bruise across Teresa's blond brow, and blood was on her cheek and her dress. The monsters had struck her. Then Eva saw Marcos—lying beneath the overturned couch, his great golden body as still as a corpse.

Otto stared down at Eva indifferently. "Let her go."

"What?" There was barely contained fury in Paolo's deep voice, but his brutal hand fell away.

"We took the wrong woman, you fool. We should have taken Mrs. Jones and the boy. Eva, go down and tell Raoul that we are here and that we have his woman and child," Otto commanded.

Like Eva, Otto had jumped to the wrong conclusion.

Paolo regarded Eva with blood lust and hatred burning in his eyes. He would never let her live. They would use her to lure Nicholas to his death, and then they would kill her and everyone else.

"Tell him to come alone and unarmed," Otto ordered, "or the boy and the woman will die."

Eva stumbled outside and was blinded by the brilliance after the darkness inside the house. She blinked as if to wish the nightmare away. When she opened her eyes, she saw Nicholas emerging from the cave. He had taken the elevator, but even the short climb necessary to come from the cave to the house made his limp more pronounced. He looked tired. He was unarmed.

"Go back!" she screamed.

"Stay right where you are!" Otto's voice was soft with menace.

Behind her Eva heard Paolo's evil laughter. He was dragging Nickie and Teresa out of the house.

"Well, well, *Liebchen*, it looks like you can stay and enjoy the party." Otto's feral gaze held her spellbound. His automatic was aimed at Raoul's heart.

Eva knew they were all going to die.

"You thought to ruin me, Girouard. You are not the only one

with the desire for revenge. You made me. You destroyed me.
But I'm not going down alone. I am taking you with me. But
first, your woman and your child will die. Then you—and I
promise, my friend, you will die very slowly.''

''This is between you and me, von Schönburg. Leave them
out of it,'' Nicholas said gravely.

Otto laughed.

''It was clever of you to find the island.'' Nicholas was deliberately stalling, deliberately trying to keep Otto talking.

''Eva radioed for help. She gave your position, your heading.
Everything we needed. It was an easy matter then, after talking
to Anya. She had seen a chart once on board *Rogue Wave* with
this island marked on it. She wasn't quite sure of its location.
But she was humiliated after you ran away with Eva. A woman
scorned... Anya was quite anxious to help me find you. But we
had to search a dozen islands before we spotted this one.''

Nicholas looked at Eva, and she saw vivid anguish flare
briefly in his eyes. Then it was extinguished by a flood of dark
anger at this new betrayal.

''Nicholas, I didn't mean... It was days ago that I made that
call! I promise you....''

He wouldn't look at her. His hard face remained frozen with
dark rage, and she knew she had truly lost him. In this life. In
the next, too.

Nickie's tiny hand fluttered into hers. His fingers clung. Victor
curled his tail around her leg and began to yowl at her feet. She
felt Nickie's pulse beneath her fingertips—the delicate throb of
his young life.

Eva had made the radio call that had brought them to this. If
she didn't do something, they would all die because of her. They
would all be shot like Nicholas's men in Africa.

She had already lost everything. There was nothing more for
her to lose. But the child... The black cave was less than thirty
feet away.

Thirty feet. Logic told her it might as well have been a million, but something snapped in her tired desperate mind. She

hardly knew what was happening when her body catapulted forward. She scooped up Nickie and, protecting the child with her body, she fled to the caves. Victor raced ahead of them like a black bolt.

Everyone else went crazy, too.

There were heated shouts.

And a spray of bullets.

Behind her. Everywhere.

The distance to the cave seemed endless. Her legs were leaden. Their speeding steps seemed to be long, gliding, weightless leaps in slow motion.

Bullets shattered the rocks ahead of her and at her feet. All around her. Something stung her arm, but she felt nothing. She saw blood spatter against white rock and didn't know it was her own. She just kept running. Slower, now.

She was a child again running beneath the cypresses with Noelle along the bayou. *Grand-mère* was there in her black dress, scolding them for playing in their white lace Sunday clothes. They were laughing now at their stern grandmother as she wiped their muddy feet so they could come inside Martin House. The picture changed and Eva wore a gown of gold. Raoul was bending over her in the candlelight in a New Orleans restaurant, his dark eyes filled with love as his hand slipped an onyx ring onto her finger.

The black entrance to the cave loomed one step away.

Another bullet splintered off stone. Bits of rock cut into her face. She heard Raoul's ravaged shout, his voice, above the others, calling her name.

Was he dying? She couldn't look back.

Her memories faded into a blur. They were as meaningless as her life.

Then she and the child were in the cool, all-enveloping darkness of the cave. Eva couldn't see anything, and it was Nickie who pulled her along the narrow path.

It was cold inside, so cold. If only she had Nicholas's key to the elevator.

But there was no way down except the path.

Her eyes adjusted to the darkness. She looked down and saw the sheer rock wall tumbling away into black nothingness. The rocks became slippery with her blood. She was feeling faint. The pain in her arm was searing now, and everything seemed to be slipping away. Too weak to go any farther, she collapsed against cold wet rock, nearly unconscious.

Then she heard Paolo's muttered curse and knew that Nickie and she were no longer alone in the cave.

Was Paolo there because he'd already killed Nicholas?

Paolo would kill the boy, too, if she didn't stop him.

She didn't know if Nicholas was dead or alive. If he was dead she wanted to die, too. But first she had to save Nickie. First she wanted to destroy this monster who had killed her love. Her emotions were so fierce and terrible they brought her back to consciousness. For the first time she could almost understand the darkness in Nicholas, the savage desire for revenge.

She rose to her feet and let Nickie lead her down. Paolo grunted and stumbled along behind them. He was getting closer. The path got narrower and narrower. The rocks were wet with condensation. Or was it her blood? She looked down and again faintness threatened to overcome her. If she fell, she would hit the jutting ledge beneath. The terrible water was a dark glimmer, a long way beneath her.

She caught the thick smell of her pursuer. Paolo was so close he could almost reach out and touch her.

Suddenly Victor squalled.

Behind her Paolo screamed a shrill scream that was filled with utter terror. He had stepped on Victor and missed his footing.

Paolo was falling, but as he did he lunged forward and hooked his arm around Eva's throat. If he was going to die, he was determined to take her with him. Then her screams were mingling with his as she slipped and fell with him.

His body struck the ledge beneath, miraculously shielding her from the blow. But the strength of murderous life was in him even after that. His hard hand held on to her neck crushingly.

They hit the water together, and his heavy body was pulling her down, down.

The fingers around her throat kept squeezing, until she saw red stars streaming before her eyes. Together they slid through the water, their bodies falling and twisting weightlessly together in a macabre dance of death. It seemed to her that they fell forever down that dark, wet tunnel that was without end.

The meaningless memories were coming again, only this time they were all of Nicholas. She was in his arms as he shielded her from the fury of the storm at sea. He was making love to her in their hidden grotto on a bed of wet sand. Then she saw his face as she'd last seen it—hard with the bitter knowledge of her fresh betrayal.

The images were fading like the flickering shadows on a movie screen when the light comes on. Only there was no light. There was only endless darkness.

Nicholas was on the ground, his own blood filling his eyes, attacking Otto like a demon.

Then Nicholas heard Eva's screams, and the terror in them pierced all the way to his heart. Nickie came running out into his mother's arms. Eva was in the cave, dying, and Nicholas could do nothing to save her.

The two men rolled over and over until they were grappling on the edge of the cliff. Beneath them the rock wall dropped away to the hard stone beach a thousand feet below.

The death struggle seemed to go on and on. Then Nicholas twisted violently and Otto was beneath him, his silver head dangling over the face of the cliff. Nicholas was straddling him, pounding him to death. Nicholas's large hands closed ruthlessly around Otto's neck and he squeezed windpipe into bone so Otto couldn't breathe.

Nicholas knew a savage thrill as his fingers dug deeper into that dark thick throat, as he watched the feral eyes bulge and go blank.

Then Teresa was there with Nickie calling softly behind Nicholas, her hand tugging at his shoulders.

"Don't. Please, don't kill him."

"For Eva," Nicholas growled, his mind crazed, beyond reason so fierce was his desire for revenge.

"Let him live—for Eva," Teresa pleaded.

Nicholas's hands loosened ever so slightly around the thick neck. Nicholas saw his men in Africa, their red blood staining the sand. The stench of death was all around him. One of those men had been Teresa's husband. Nicholas remembered his own nauseating terror that he would be next when he'd lain in the dirt, unable to move, and Paolo had swaggered toward him with his bayonet drawn.

Otto had to die.

"Killing is his way, not yours." It was Marcos's voice this time.

Nicholas hesitated. He stared at the man beneath him, his heart raging with the savage need to do violence.

"He had Eva killed!" Nicholas muttered hoarsely.

"Maybe she's still alive," Teresa said. "It is no good to live for revenge."

"How can you say that? Your husband died because of this man."

"That's how I know."

Finally what she was saying penetrated his brain. For a long moment he remained frozen on top of Otto. Then in a daze he pulled his hands from Otto's throat, leaving Otto gasping for air. Marcos leaned down with a coil of rope and bound Otto's wrists together. Then his feet.

As if in a trance, Nicholas watched him. For years he'd lived with one purpose—to destroy von Schönburg. And now he was face-to-face with the terrible realization that the woman he loved might be dead because of his fierce desire for revenge.

The woman he loved...

He saw her as she'd looked down at him when she'd rushed to greet him this afternoon—with her face glowing in the shadows and sunlight. The rays coming through the entrance of the cave had turned her hair to flame. She had never looked more beautiful. And what had he done? With cruel words he had crushed that look. Destroyed her love. He thought of her courage, how she'd taken Nickie and run. The bastards had shot her. He remembered her last terrorized scream.

Killing Otto didn't matter. His death could change nothing.

Only Eva. Only Eva. With her tenderness and kindness and passion she had shown him that there was still some part of him that believed in the beauty of life. She had made mistakes in their relationship, but so had he. If only she was alive, he would forgive her everything. She had tried to teach him what it meant to love completely, without qualification.

He had treated her so brutally.

If she was dead, it was his fault. Not Otto's.

Nicholas knew he would never forgive himself.

If she was alive he would have to spend a lifetime making it up to her.

"Call the police," Nicholas said roughly.

Then he was racing, despite his bad leg, toward the cave.

Eva was cold, so cold. Her right arm burned with excruciating pain. But she felt the warmth of the sun on her skin. She heard the roar of the helicopter. Most of all she was aware of the raspy beauty of Nicholas's low-timbred voice.

Nicholas and Zak were hovering over her.

Through her lashes she could see Nicholas, his handsome face bloodstained and grim. She was afraid to open her eyes, afraid of the coldness and the darkness in his heart.

But she opened them anyway because she wanted to look at him just one more time before she released him forever.

She lifted her head. Oh, it hurt. Terribly. So much so that she couldn't quite suppress a moan.

Nicholas was staring at her when her lashes fluttered.

She saw the blazing warmth of his love. She felt his anguish, too. And his forgiveness.

She moved her lips to comfort him, but no sound came out.

"Don't try to talk," he whispered.

He was smiling, and it was Raoul's smile. "I thought I had

lost you and that I would never be able to tell you how much I loved you." He touched her hair that was all wet and tangled with grit from the beach. "Forgive me," he whispered. "Forgive me."

To her surprise she saw that there were tears in his eyes. For once there were none in hers.

"There is nothing to forgive, my darling."

The helicopter was landing on the beach. Nicholas knelt over her to protect her from the flying dust and pebbles. He was cradling her head in his hands and gently kissing her brow.

She closed her eyes, but she knew he was there.

At last he was hers. The future was theirs. No more ghosts to haunt them from the past. No more goodbyes.

Nothing mattered except that she and Raoul would be together. Always. She felt his strong arms lifting her to carry her to the helicopter.

All she wanted was for him to hold her close, against his heart, forever.

And she knew that at last he would.

Epilogue

Raoul stared down into the crib that was fringed with blue lace. As always when he came into the nursery filled with musical toys and teddy bears, he felt a soft glorious wonder and a love that was unconditional and all-encompassing.

Nestled against soft blue sheets and blankets was his son, whose hair was fiery like his mother's. Whose eyes were as black and sparkling with devilment as his father's.

Andrew Wade Girouard. It seemed a long name for such a little boy.

Gently Raoul reached down to touch his son, and when he did, the baby's tiny hand curled trustingly around his big brown finger.

Spread out upon an antique rocker were a starched white christening gown and cap. Next to pristine lace was a lazy ball of black fur. Victor had come up to hide from the fuss.

When the nurse saw the cat she would probably shriek about black cat hairs, but Raoul wasn't about to disturb Victor. He had learned a long time ago that that cat had a way of coming in handy.

"Today's the big day," Raoul whispered to his son.

Downstairs there was the sound of children playing—shrieks

of merry laughter. Noelle's two daughters raced through the house on a rampage.

"You're never going to knock over your mother's antiques and break her china, now are you?" Raoul said proudly.

Raoul didn't hear the door behind him open and close, nor the whisper of light feet across the blue carpet. But he caught the scent of honeysuckle.

He turned, and Eva was there, his wife, looking beautiful in green silk and pearls with her red hair flowing about her shoulders. Just knowing she was there made his happiness complete. She was the one person he loved above all else, even his son.

"You can pick him up," she prodded gently with laughter in her voice.

He still couldn't quite believe that.

"He's so small."

"He won't break."

"You keep telling me that."

Eva came to the crib and bundled the blue blanket around the child and handed him to his father, who cradled him a bit awkwardly but ever so gently in the crook of his arm. Together they all walked out onto the shady veranda.

The white columns of Sweet Seclusion gleamed through the hazy sunlight sifting through the dark green trees. Around the mansion was a freshly painted white picket fence upon which ivy and Carolina jasmine had already started to climb.

The family was gathered today for Andy's christening. The Martins had come even though they still couldn't quite accept a Girouard, especially Raoul, as one of their own, as their son-in-law. Zak and Zola had come. They were sitting in the summerhouse with Zola's little girl toddling at their feet.

Eva was an inveterate matchmaker. Raoul remembered how she had insisted that Zak come to London for the wedding. Naturally Zola had been there, too, to catch Eva's bouquet.

Raoul still couldn't believe that his lovely wife and his handsome son weren't all part of a dream. He had his home, and a family to share it with, everything he'd ever longed for since he'd been a child. He had assumed his real name, and they lived most of the time in London, but their vacations and summers were spent at Sweet Seclusion. Eva had her shop. She was as disorganized as ever. Running the shop was a constant challenge for her, but business was brisk.

There were still those who believed even the worst rumors about him. What hurt the most was the occasional accusing article that was written, the letter sent to him by the relative of one of his men who had died in Africa. Eva's family would probably never quite accept him. But none of these things mattered as much as he'd thought they would to either Eva or himself, because they had each other.

There had been great darkness in his life, and long years of emptiness when he'd lived only for revenge.

But Eva with her love had led him back into a world of light that filled every single one of his days with profound joy.

Above all things he trusted in her and she in him.

Who knew, perhaps in time even the illustrious Martins would come to accept him. Eva still wanted their approval, but more than that she treasured his love.

Carrying his son, Raoul led his wife from the deep shade of the veranda into the sunshine so that he could watch the light turn their hair to fire. They stood there basking in the brilliant warm light and in the glorious joy of their love for a long time. Beneath they heard children's laughter and all the rich warm sounds of familial happiness.

He felt Eva's fingertips that were like flame move against his skin. His hand tightened on hers, and he pulled her closer. She was a part of him. She was everything, the center of his world that was now as golden as the sunshine. Sometimes he was so happy he felt he would awaken and find that it was all a dream.

He heard her voice washing over him, caressing him with its husky sound. "I love you. I want to fill our house with children. Our children."

He remembered the long years of anguish and could not speak, but his eyes gentled with love as he held her.

With her at his side, he knew he could face anything.

* * * * *

THE BEST BRIDE
Susan Mallery

To my editor, Karen Taylor Richman,
for believing in me and encouraging me,
for seeing the vision in my stories and helping me
achieve that vision, for being kind and generous,
and wonderful to work with. You have my respect,
my friendship and my thanks. You're the best.

Travis's Bachelor Chili
(As created by Louise)

1 15-oz can kidney beans
2 15-oz can pinto beans
1 15-oz can corn
1 large onion, diced
1 large green pepper, diced
1 lb lean ground beef or turkey, cooked and drained
2 14 1/2-oz cans stewed tomatoes
1 cup water
1 cup spicy tomato salsa
1 tsp cumin
4 cups cooked white or brown rice

Drain canned beans and corn. Combine all ingredients—except for rice—in a large pot. Bring to a boil over high heat, then simmer for 15 minutes. Serve over rice.

Great for football Sundays, and even better the second day for lunch!

Chapter 1

The white T-bird fishtailed around the corner. It sprayed dirt and gravel up onto the left front of the patrol car parked on the side of the road.

Sheriff Travis Haynes turned the key to start the engine, then flipped on the blue lights. As he pulled out onto the highway, he debated whether or not to use the siren, then decided against it. He was about to mess up someone's long weekend by giving him a ticket; no point in adding insult to injury by using the siren. The good citizens of Glenwood had contributed enough money to buy a car equipped with a siren that could wake the dead. But that didn't necessarily mean they wanted him to use it on *them*.

He stepped on the gas until he was behind the white car, then checked his speed. He gave a low whistle and looked at the car ahead. He could see a mass of brown hair through the rear window, but little else. The lady was going somewhere in a hurry. He followed behind and waited.

It took her another two minutes to notice him. She glanced in her mirror, saw the flashing lights, did a double take, then immediately put on her blinker and pulled to the side of the road. Travis slowed and parked behind her. He shut off the engine, reached for his Stetson and ticket book, then got out and walked leisurely toward the car. His cowboy boots crunched on the gravel. He noticed the California license plate tags were current.

"Afternoon," he said, when he walked up to the open window. He glanced down at the woman and got a brief impression of big brown eyes in a heart-shaped face. She looked a little pale under her tan. A lot of people were nervous when they were stopped by an officer. He gave her a friendly smile. "You were going pretty fast there."

"I—I know," she said, softly, averting her gaze and staring out the front window. "I'm sorry."

She gripped the steering wheel tightly. He looked past her to the young girl in the passenger seat. The child looked more frightened than her mother. She clutched a worn brown teddy bear to her chest and stared at him with wide blue eyes. Her mouth trembled as if she were fighting tears. About five or six, he thought, giving her a quick wink.

Travis returned his attention to the woman. She wore her hair pulled up in a ponytail on top of her head. The ends fell back almost to her shoulders. It was a warm September afternoon. She was dressed in a red tank top and white shorts. He tried not to notice her legs. "I'm going to need to see your driver's license and registration, ma'am," he said politely.

"What? Oh, of course."

She bent over to grab her purse from the floor on the passenger's side. He thought he heard a gasp, as if she were in pain, but before he could be sure, she fumbled with her wallet and pulled out the small identification. As she handed it to him, it slipped out of her fingers and fluttered toward the ground. He caught it before it touched the dirt.

"I'm sorry," she murmured. Her mouth pulled into a straight line and dark emotion flickered in her eyes.

Immediately his instincts went on alert. Something wasn't right. She was too scared or too upset for someone getting a ticket. He glanced down at the license. Elizabeth Abbott. Age twenty-eight. Five-six. The address listed her as living in Los Angeles.

"You're a long way from home," he said, looking from her to the license and back.

"We just moved here," she said.

He took the registration next and saw the car was in her name.

"So what's the story?" he asked, flipping open his ticket book.

"Excuse me?"

"Why were you speeding?"

Her eyebrows drew together. "I don't understand."

"You're in Glenwood, ma'am, and we have a tradition here. If you can tell me a story I haven't heard before, I have to let you go."

Her mouth curved up slightly. It made her look pretty. He had a feeling she would be hell on wheels if she let go enough to really smile. "You're kidding?"

"No, ma'am." He adjusted his Stetson.

"Have you *ever* let anyone go?"

He thought for a minute, then grinned. "I stopped Miss Murietta several years ago. She was hurrying home to watch the last episode of *Dallas* on TV."

"And you let her off the hook?"

He shrugged. "I hadn't heard that excuse before. So what's yours? I've been in the sheriff's department almost twelve years, so it'll have to be good."

Elizabeth Abbott stared up at him and started to laugh. She stopped suddenly, drew in a deep breath and seemed to fall toward the steering wheel. She caught herself and clutched her midsection.

"Mommy?" The little girl beside her sounded frantic. "Mommy?"

"I'm fine," Elizabeth said, glancing at her.

But Travis could see she wasn't fine. He realized the look in her eyes wasn't fear, it was pain. He saw it in the lines around her mouth and the way she paled even more under her tan.

"What's wrong?" he asked, stuffing his ticket book into his back pocket.

"Nothing," she said. "Just a stomachache. It won't go away. I was going to a walk-in clinic to see if they could—" She gasped and nearly doubled over. The seat belt held her in place.

Travis opened the car door and crouched beside her. "You pregnant?" he asked. He reached for her wrist and found her pulse. It was rapid. Her skin felt cold and clammy to the touch.

"No, why?"

"Miscarriage."

"I'm not pregnant." She leaned her head back against the seat rest. "Give me a minute. I'll be fine."

Her daughter stared up at her. He could see the worry and the fear in her blue eyes and his heart went out to the little girl.

"Mommy, don't be sick."

"I'm fine." She touched her child's cheek.

Travis leaned in and unlatched the seat belt.

"What are you doing?" Elizabeth asked.

"Taking you to the hospital."

"That's not necessary. Really, I'll just drive to the clinic and—" She drew in a deep breath and held it. Her eyes closed and her jaw tightened.

"That's it," he said, reaching one arm under her legs, the other behind her back. Before she could protest, he slid her out and carried her toward his car.

She clung to him and shivered. "I don't mean to be any trouble."

"No trouble. Part of the job."

"You carry a lot of women in your line of work?"

Her muscles felt tight and perspiration clung to her forehead and upper lip. She must be in a lot of pain, but she was trying to keep it all together. He winked. "It's been a good week for me."

When they reached his car, Travis lowered her feet to the ground and opened the door to the back seat. He started to pick her up again, but she shook her head and bent over to slide in. He returned to the lady's car and slipped into the driver's seat.

The little girl was hunched against the door, staring at him. Tears rolled down her face.

"What's your name, honey?" he asked softly.

"Mandy."

"How old are you?"

She hiccuped and clutched the bear to her chest. "Six."

"I'm going to take your mom to the hospital, and they're going to make her feel better. I'd like you come with me. Okay?"

She nodded slowly.

He gave her his best smile, then collected Elizabeth's purse. After shoving her keys, license and registration into his pocket, he unhooked Mandy's seat belt and helped her out of the car. He rolled up the windows and locked the doors, then led her to the sheriff's vehicle.

Her tears stopped momentarily as she stared at the array of switches and listened to the crackling of the radio. "You ever been inside a patrol car before?" he asked.

She shook her head.

"You'll like it. I promise." That earned him a sniff. He settled her quickly beside him, then glanced back at Elizabeth. She lay across the seat, her knees pulled up to her chest, breathing rapidly.

"How you doing?" he asked.

"Hanging in there," she said, her voice tight with strain.

"I'm going to use the siren," he said, starting the engine and switching it on. Instantly a piercing wail filled the car. Travis checked his mirror, then pulled out onto the road.

Traffic was light and they were at the hospital in less than fifteen minutes. Two minutes after that, Elizabeth had been wheeled away on a gurney and he was filling out paperwork at the circular counter near the emergency entrance. Mandy stood beside him, crying.

She didn't make a sound, but he could swear he heard every one of those tears rolling down her cheeks. Her pain made it tough to concentrate. Poor kid. She was scared to death.

He bent over and picked her up, setting her on the counter next to him. They were almost at eye level. A headband adorned with cartoon characters held her blond hair off her round face. The same collection of animals, in a rainbow of colors, covered her T-shirt. She wore denim shorts and scuffed sandals. Except for the tears, she looked like just any other six-year-old.

"When did you and your mom move here?" he asked.

She clutched the tattered teddy bear closer. "Yesterday," she said, gulping for air.

"Yesterday?" There went his hope they might have made friends in town. "Do you have any family here?"

She shook her head and sniffed again.

He reached over the counter to a box of tissues beside the phone. The receptionist was also a nurse, and she had disappeared into the room with Elizabeth. Mandy wiped her face and tried to blow her nose. It didn't work. He took a couple of tissues and held them over her face.

"Blow," he ordered, wondering how many times he'd done this during summer T-ball practice. There were always a lot of tears as the kids skinned knees and elbows...and lost games.

"Where's your daddy?"

Her blue eyes filled again. "He's gone."

Gone meaning dead? Or divorced? "Where does he live now?" Travis asked.

"I don't know. He doesn't see us anymore. Mommy said he had to go away because he's big. She said he's never coming b-back." Her voice trembled.

He gave her a reassuring smile. Big? That didn't make any sense. Elizabeth Abbott must be divorced. He glanced down at the hospital forms. She had an insurance card in her wallet, so he copied that information. "Where do you live?" he asked, then realized that if they'd just moved here, Mandy wouldn't know her address yet.

"By the ducks."

"The duck pond?"

She nodded vigorously, her tears momentarily forgotten. "It's pretty. I have a big bed all to myself. Just like Mommy. And there's little soaps in the bath.'' She smiled. She had a dimple in each cheek and he could see she was going to grow up to be a heartbreaker.

He pictured the buildings around the duck pond in the center of town and remembered there was a small motel on the corner. So much for having an address here.

"What about your grandmother and grandfather? Do you know where they are?''

"They live far away.''

Before he could think of any more questions, the receptionist came bustling back into the room. "Appendix,'' she said, pulling her stethoscope from around her neck and placing it in the right hip pocket of her nurse's uniform. "Caught it in time.'' She looked at Mandy. "Your mommy is going to have an operation. Do you know what that means?''

Mandy looked scared again. "No.''

"The doctor is going to make her sleep for a little bit while he makes her feel better. There's an infection inside and he's going to take it out. But she'll be fine.''

Mandy didn't looked reassured. She bit her lower lip hard and tears filled her eyes. Travis felt like he'd taken a sucker punch to the gut. Apparently the kid didn't know a soul in town, and if the grandparents weren't local, finding them could take days. He didn't even know if Abbott was Elizabeth's maiden or married name.

He held out his arm, offering Mandy a hug, but letting her decide. She threw herself against him with the desperation of a drowning man clutching a raft. Her slight body shook with the tremors of her sobs. She smelled of sun and grass and little girl. So damn small to be facing this alone.

"Hush,'' he murmured, stroking her hair. "I'm right here and everything's going to be fine.''

It was nearly seven in the evening before Travis was able to take Mandy in to see her mother. The nurse had informed him children weren't allowed on the ward, but he'd ignored her and marched past, carrying Mandy in his arms. He was the sheriff. What were they going to do? Arrest him?

He should have gone off-duty at four-thirty, but he couldn't leave the kid on her own, and he didn't want to take her to the local child services office before she'd seen her mother. It didn't much matter, he thought as he walked down the hospital hallway. He hadn't made any plans for the weekend.

Although Glenwood was far enough off the beaten track not to get much tourist trade even over Labor Day weekend, the last celebration of summer usually kept him and his deputies busy. There were fights at the park as too much beer was consumed, and the teenagers would get involved in illegal drag races down by the lake. Come Monday afternoon, the small jail would be filled with red-faced citizens who would work off their sentences doing community service.

The last door at the end of the hallway stood partially open. Travis knocked once and entered. He'd already warned Mandy that her mother would be hooked up to tubes, but it wasn't as frightening as he'd feared. Elizabeth had an IV in each arm, but her color was good. Medium brown hair fanned out over the white pillow. The pale hospital gown set off her tan. For someone who had just had emergency surgery, she didn't look halfbad. Hospital smells filled the room: antiseptic and pine-scented cleanser.

"We can only stay a minute," he reminded Mandy in a quiet voice.

"I know. Is she sleeping?"

"Not anymore," came the groggy response. Elizabeth opened her eyes and looked at him. She blinked. "Do I know you?"

"We haven't been officially introduced," he said, walking closer and setting Mandy on the ground. Before the little girl could jump onto the bed, he laid a hand on her shoulder. "Stand next to your mommy, but don't bump against anything. I'm Travis Haynes. I stopped you for speeding."

"That's right." Elizabeth looked away from him and smiled at her daughter. He remembered when he'd stopped her he'd thought if she ever really smiled it would be a killer, and he'd been right. Even fresh from surgery, the lady was a looker.

"Hi, sweets," she said. "It's good to see you."

"Oh, Mommy." Mandy stood as close to the bed as she could without actually touching it. She clutched her bear to her with one hand and with the other stroked her mother's arm. "The nurse said you had something bad inside, but it's gone now."

"I feel much better." Elizabeth touched Mandy's hair and her face, then raised herself up on one elbow. She grimaced. Travis moved closer. She looked up at him. "I'm trying to get a hug here."

He picked up Mandy and held her close to her mother. They clung to each other for a second. He could see the fierceness of Elizabeth Abbott's love for her child in the way she squeezed her eyes tight and he heard it in her murmured words of encouragement.

"I'm fine," she promised. "Everything is going to work out."

He set Mandy on the ground and pulled a chair close to the bed. He sat down and pulled Mandy onto his lap. If Elizabeth was surprised by his daughter's acceptance of him, she didn't show it. But in the past couple of hours, he and the little girl had become friends.

Elizabeth settled back on the bed. She pushed a button and raised the head up until she was half reclining. "So you're the sheriff."

"That's me. I've just been voted in for another term."

Her brown eyes met and held his. The dark pain was gone and the lines around her mouth had relaxed. "Did I pass?" she asked.

"Pass what?"

She smiled. "Did I have a story you hadn't heard before? I mean how many people speed because they have appendicitis?"

"It's a first," he said, stretching his legs out in front of him. "I'm a man of my word. You won't be getting a ticket from me."

Mandy shifted against his chest and yawned. It had been a

long afternoon and evening for her. They'd gone to the cafeteria about six o'clock, but the kid hadn't been able to eat much. She'd fretted about her mother and beat him at checkers while they waited. Her slight weight reminded him of his oldest nephew. Drew would play video games in Travis's arms until he fell asleep and then have to be carried to bed.

"Thank you for looking after her," Elizabeth said. "You didn't have to stay and baby-sit."

"It was easy." He glanced down and watched Mandy's eyes close. "I filled out most of the forms for the hospital, but they're going to have a few questions. Do you want me to call your ex?"

She paled visibly. "What? Why?"

"To take care of Mandy until you're better."

"No!" She sounded upset. She raised her arm and stared at the IV taped in place on the back of her hand. "No." Her voice was calmer now, as if she had herself under control. "I'm not, that is, I wasn't ever married. There's no ex-husband."

"All right," he said, even though her claim made no sense. Mandy had talked about her father. Travis reminded himself this was the nineties and women didn't have to get married to have babies. He looked closely at Elizabeth. Somehow she didn't strike him as the type to have a child on her own. Still, she must have; Mandy was proof. Why would anyone lie about something like that? "Any next of kin nearby?"

She shook her head. "My parents live in Florida. Right now, however, they're cruising somewhere in the Orient. I can't..." She trailed off. "I can't call them. What am I going to do?" She shifted and winced. "I have to—"

"Shh." He pointed at the sleeping child. "You don't have to do anything tonight," he said softly. "You've just had emergency surgery and I'm not even supposed to be visiting. I thought this might be a problem, so I've already called and spoken with a friend of mine. Her name is Rebecca Chambers and she runs the local child services office. It's a county facility, but a great place."

"Rebecca?"

"Rebecca Chambers. She's the director. There are only about twenty kids there. It's on the other side of town, near the school. I've spent some time there volunteering. Mandy will be fine."

Elizabeth stared up at him. Her good humor had faded, and she looked tired and drawn. "You want to put my daughter in a home?" She blinked frantically, but tears spilled over onto her cheeks.

"Hey," he said, standing up and depositing a sleeping Mandy in the chair. He hovered awkwardly by the bed. "Don't cry. It's just for a couple of days. If you want me to call someone, I will. Just give me a name."

"I'm sorry," she whispered. "Everything is falling apart. It was going so well and now I don't know what to do or where to turn. I— There's no one to call." She looked up at him. "Can't she stay here, with me?"

"In the hospital? No. They didn't even want her to visit you, let alone spend the night. You're in no position to take care of her, Elizabeth. I know the home sounds bad, but it's not."

"You're right. I don't have another choice." She covered her face with her hands. "It just makes me feel like I'm an awful mother. It's not the place I'm worried about, I've been there. I'm going to work there." She wiped her cheeks with her fingers. "I'm Rebecca's new assistant. I moved us here to take the job. I'm supposed to start Tuesday. What's she going to think about me? I'm dumping my kid on her doorstep, and I'm going to miss my first day of work."

The sobs began in earnest. He hesitated about five seconds, then perched on the edge of the bed. Careful not to tangle the IV lines, he patted her shoulder. She clutched at his arm, all the while muttering how stupid she must look to him. The sheet slipped to her waist. He tried not to stare, but couldn't help noticing the shape of her breasts under her hospital gown.

Travis told himself he was at best behaving unethically, and at the worst acting like a pervert. He had no business noticing

Elizabeth's body. She'd just had surgery for God's sake. But he did notice, and admire, all the while calling himself names.

"I'm sure Rebecca will understand," he said. "It's not as if you planned this."

"I know, but Mandy will be there all alone. I wish—"

"Do all the women in your family leak this much?"

"What?" She blinked and looked up at him. Her dark lashes stood up in spikes, her nose was red and her cheeks blotchy. She was a mess. It brought out his knight-in-shining-armor side and he resisted getting involved. He knew what would happen then. Better for both of them if he just backed off.

"Between you and Mandy, I think we could have floated a ship today."

She smiled wanly. "Don't make me laugh. It hurts."

"Okay, then I won't tell you the one about the parrot with no legs."

"How did he stay on his perch?"

Travis stood up and winked. "You'll just have to wait until you get better to find out." He glanced at his watch. "I'm going to take Mandy over to stay with Rebecca. I'll call you in the morning and make sure you're doing all right, then I'll bring Mandy back here in the afternoon."

"Why are you being so nice to me?"

"Just doing my duty, ma'am." He gave a mock salute and picked up the sleeping child. "I'll leave my number with the nurse."

"Thank you for everything," she said, pulling the sheet up and smiling at him. "If Mandy wakes up, tell her I love her."

"You can tell her yourself when you see her tomorrow."

Chapter 2

"What do you mean chicken pox?" Travis asked. He stared down at Rebecca, seated behind her desk in her office at the local child services facility.

"I mean I have eight children in various stages of chicken pox, and the other twelve have been exposed. Sorry, Travis. If you'd explained why you were coming by, I would have told you what was going on and saved you the trip. I thought you were just going to mooch dinner. I know that when you're between women you hang out with me. I thought this was one of those rare weekends." Her brown eyes looked more amused than apologetic.

"But Mandy—"

"But Mandy doesn't know if she's had chicken pox, do you, honey?" Rebecca smiled at the little girl.

Mandy shook her head and tugged on Travis's pants. "Travis?"

"Hmm?" He didn't look down at her. Now what was he supposed to do? He couldn't just leave her in the street. "Rebecca, you're not helping."

"Travis?" Mandy tugged again.

"What?"

"Do I have to stay here?"

She looked up, her head bent way back, her wide blue eyes gazing at him with absolute trust. He felt as if he were torturing Bambi.

"Why don't I make a few calls," Rebecca said, coming to his rescue. She flicked her dark hair over her shoulder and reached for the phone. "There's a shelter about twenty miles from here. I'll see if they have room." She picked up the receiver.

"Travis?" Mandy tugged again.

"Yes?"

"I want my mommy."

Travis crouched down in front of her. "She's in the hospital. She needs to sleep tonight and get better."

Mandy held her teddy so tightly, he worried she might squish the stuffing out the side. She leaned close and whispered. "I don't know that lady. I don't want to stay here. I want my mommy."

He'd spent enough time with kids her age to recognize the quiver in her voice. Tears would come next and after that, he would feel like a heel and— He stood up and jammed his hands in his pockets.

"You think I should take her home with me?" he asked, already knowing the answer.

"It would be best for her. Elizabeth isn't going to need a sick kid on her hands, just as she's getting out of the hospital herself." Rebecca rose and walked around the desk. She wore a floral print jumper over a white T-shirt. With her long curly hair and conservative style of dressing, she looked like a Sunday school teacher. Travis suspected it was a facade and that deep inside, she had the wild streak of the best kind of a sinner.

When she'd moved to Glenwood six months ago to take over as director of the county facility, he'd asked her out. His big seduction scene had ended up failing badly. They were, he'd realized within the first ten minutes, destined to be good friends. Rebecca had promised to leave his reputation as a heartbreaker intact and not tell the world his kisses had left her cold. Travis stared at her big brown eyes and sighed. He felt mild affection for Rebecca and nothing else. He must be getting old and slowing down.

"You're the only friend Mandy has," Rebecca said. "If I could take her home with me, I would. But my staff is exhausted, and I'm staying here tonight. Anyway, you have Louise."

He thought of his housekeeper. Today was her day off but he knew if he called she would come over to help and show off her latest craft project. At least she wasn't knitting anymore. He already had two drawers filled with ugly, ill-fitting sweaters and socks she'd made for him.

"I suppose that might work. But I don't know anything about children," Travis muttered, trying to ignore Mandy tugging on him again.

"Your nephews stay with you."

"Travis," Mandy said.

"That's different."

"How?" Rebecca asked.

"Travis?"

"They're family. And boys." He looked down. Those blue eyes were killing him. "What?"

"I want to stay with you."

"You're the only person she knows in town. Come on, be a hero. It's what you're best at."

He glared at Rebecca. "Thanks."

Undaunted, she smiled. "Let me get you some supplies." She disappeared down the hall.

"Why me?" he asked no one in particular.

"Travis? Are you mad at me?"

"Mandy, no." He swept Mandy up in his arms and gave her a hug. She wrapped her spindly legs around his waist. "I'm not mad. We'll have fun. I'll read you a story tonight, okay?"

She nodded. "And Mr. Bear," she said, holding out the tattered animal.

"And Mr. Bear."

Rebecca returned with a small cloth bag. "I've packed a

nightgown, some underwear and a shorts set for tomorrow." She handed Travis the bag, then smiled at Mandy. "Do you want a pink toothbrush or a purple one?" She had both in her hand.

The little girl stared for a second, then pointed shyly. "Pink."

"You got it." Rebecca dropped that one in the bag and walked over to the door. "I'll be here, so call me if there's any trouble. It's only one night."

"Like you care," he grumbled.

"Stop it. You'll have a great time. Think of it as father training. For when you have your own kids."

"Not my style. Haynes men don't make good parents." It was a familiar argument between the two of them. The problem was Rebecca hadn't figured out he wasn't kidding.

She shook her head. "Let me know what happens. And tell Elizabeth not to worry about coming into work until she's completely healed. I won't be giving her job to anyone else."

"Yeah, I will." He shifted Mandy so that she was supported by one arm, then handed her the bag and dug in his pocket for his keys. "Say goodbye, Mandy."

"By." Now that she was getting her way, she smiled broadly. "Can we have the siren on?" she asked as they stepped out of the building and walked toward the sheriff's car in the parking lot.

"No."

She pouted and rested her head on his shoulder.

"Don't give me that look," he said. "I can't use the siren when it's not an emergency."

She thought for a minute. "I gotta go."

His heart sank. "Now?"

She nodded. "It's a 'mergency."

Elizabeth raised the hospital bed and stared out the window. From where she was lying, she could see the corner of the small parking lot and a plot of grass with a Chinese maple in the center. It was early Saturday morning and she'd seen only a handful of cars enter the hospital grounds.

Everything was going to be fine. She'd recited the phrase over and over, hoping by saying it enough she would start to believe it was true. But panic threatened, just below the surface of her carefully constructed facade.

She was scared. There was no getting around the lump in her throat and the cold hard knot in her stomach, just next to the tender incision the doctors had made yesterday. She wasn't frightened for herself. The surgery had gone well, and she was healing nicely, according to the doctor who had visited early that morning. She had medical insurance, so the unexpected stay in the hospital wasn't going to deplete her savings.

The lump in her throat got bigger and her eyes burned from unshed tears. She blinked them away and prayed that her daughter hadn't been too scared last night, alone in a strange place. Had they let her sleep with her bear? Had she had any bad dreams? There were, on average, twenty children at the county facility. Had Mandy gotten lost among all the other kids? Who would have been there to hold her if she cried?

Logically, Elizabeth knew she hadn't had another choice as far as her daughter was concerned. Having her spend the night in the county home had made sense. She would be fed and warm and have a bed to sleep in. But knowing her only child had been put there, like a stray puppy rounded up by the pound, made her feel like the worst kind of parent. Mothers were supposed to do better for their children. Of course, mothers were also supposed to know what they were doing when they picked out fathers—and look at how that had turned out.

She reached over to the black phone on the small metal nightstand and dialed the number she'd gotten from directory assistance. For the second time in fifteen minutes, she heard a busy signal. From what she remembered from her tour during her interview a month ago, the county facility only had one line. She hung up the receiver. She would keep trying until she got through. She wanted to check on Mandy and reassure her daughter that everything was going to be fine—even though she didn't know how.

Elizabeth forced herself to hold on to her control. She couldn't afford to give into the fear. Not now. If she started questioning herself, she might never stop. Six months ago her world had come crashing in on her. She'd managed to collect the pieces and assemble them into a life, but the structure was fragile, and this emergency was enough to send the whole thing crumbling again. The logistics of her condition whirled around in her head. How was she going to take care of Mandy when she was supposed to stay off her feet for a week and not drive for three weeks? What about feeding her, and registering her for school, buying her new shoes, and a hundred other things she'd planned to do over the long holiday weekend? What about taking her out to watch the ducks and playing tag and—

The sound of footsteps in the hallway caught her attention. She glanced over at her partially closed door and watched as it was pushed open. Sheriff Travis Haynes entered the room and smiled at her. She stared at him, surprise and a tiny spurt of pleasure temporarily hiding her worries. He'd told her he would come by today and visit, but she hadn't expected him to. He'd done too much already. Still, except for Rebecca and Mandy, he was the only other person she knew in Glenwood, and she couldn't help being pleased to see him.

Gratitude, she told herself firmly, trying to find the reason for the sudden surge of good spirits. Gratitude and nothing else.

"Hi," she said, managing a shaky smile. She pulled the sheet up to her shoulders and self-consciously touched the straggly ends of her hair. They hadn't let her have a shower yet, and she felt grungy. She'd planned to insist on getting cleaned up later that morning. She hadn't expected visitors so early.

"Hi, yourself." Travis crossed the room in three long strides and pulled a plastic chair close to the bed. "May I?"

"Please."

His khaki, short-sleeved uniform looked freshly pressed. A badge and a name tag had been pinned above the left breast pocket. He stood about six feet tall, with dark curly hair and a trimmed mustache that outlined his upper lip. He was the kind of man who, as her aunt Amanda used to say, made a woman get a crick in her neck just watching him stroll by.

As he settled himself in the chair, he tossed his beige Stetson across the bed. It sailed through the air and landed dead center on the table in front of the window.

"Neat trick," she said, trying to ignore the way his brown eyes twinkled when he looked at her. "You have to practice much?"

"Every day. I sit in my office, tossing my hat across the room. It impresses the ladies." He had a smooth, low voice, like liquid chocolate.

"Really?"

"Aren't you impressed, darlin'?"

Some, but she wasn't about to admit it. Once she'd let a man charm her and impress her and seduce her. Never again, she reminded herself. She'd learned a hard lesson from Sam Proctor. "I didn't expect you to visit," she said. "I'm sure you have other things you should be doing."

"You're the most important item on my agenda," he said, leaning back in the chair and resting one ankle on the opposite knee. The movement emphasized the muscles in his thighs.

She looked away. "Oh?"

"How are you feeling?"

"A little sore, but better than I was. The doctor says I'm healing nicely." She shifted in the hospital bed. "They gave me something to make me sleep, and that helped. I never got to thank you yesterday."

"Just doing my job."

She waved at the IV still attached to her hand. "They said that if I'd waited another couple of hours, the appendix might have burst. If I'd gone to the walk-in medical clinic like I'd planned, I might have gotten to the hospital too late."

"So it all worked out. You'll be released tomorrow."

"That's what they told me." She glanced at him sitting in the white plastic chair. He looked tanned and handsome and disgustingly healthy, while her insides felt as if a herd of buffalo had trampled through them.

"Where are you going to go when they release you?" he asked.

"Back to the motel." It wasn't a great solution, but it was the best one she'd been able to think of. Where else *could* she go?

"And then?"

"And then I'll get better and go to work. That is, if I still have a job. I need to call Rebecca and tell her what happened." She forced herself to meet his gaze, and prayed her expression looked as calm and confident as she'd made herself sound. She didn't want to foist her troubles on anyone, especially not this handsome stranger. One rescue per weekend was quite enough.

He folded his arms over his chest. His shirt stretched tightly across his broad shoulders. He had a solid look about him. He was the kind of man who could physically work for hours without tiring. He looked dependable. She shook her head. Looks could be deceiving.

Then he smiled. She told herself not to notice, that he was obviously an accomplished ladies' man, but that didn't stop her rather battered insides from responding favorably to the flash of white teeth.

"I have good news, bad news and good news," he said. "Which do you want first?"

She panicked. "Is Mandy—"

He cut her off. "She's fine. That's the first good news. The bad news is there's an outbreak of chicken pox at the children's home. I didn't know if Mandy'd had chicken pox, so I couldn't leave her there last night. Rebecca figured the last thing you'd need in your condition is a sick kid."

Elizabeth frowned. "If she's not at the home, where is she?"

"Downstairs, watching a clown make balloon animals." He shrugged. "They were having a party and she wanted to see what was going on. I thought you and I should talk first anyway."

"So where did Mandy spend the night?"

"With me. I called my housekeeper, and she took care of the basics of bathing and dressing. But I fed her breakfast." He looked sheepish and proud all at once.

"You?" Why on earth would he volunteer to take home her daughter? "Chicken pox? I can't believe this is all happening. Mandy hasn't had them yet. Thank God she wasn't exposed to them. I don't know what to say except thank you." She had a sudden thought. "I hope it wasn't too inconvenient for your wife."

"I'm not married."

She told herself she wasn't pleased by that fact. It was just a piece of information. It didn't *mean* anything. The last thing she needed in her life was a man. "I don't know how to repay you for all you've done."

"I'm responsible for the welfare of the people of this town," he said, and grinned again. "You *are* our newest citizen."

"You're very kind." She relaxed. Mandy was safe. Nothing else mattered.

The slow, sexy grin faded. "You're going to need help when they release you. Tell me who to call, Elizabeth."

She turned her head and stared out the window. "There's no one to call. I told you, my parents are on a cruise in the Orient. They're probably halfway between Australia and Hong Kong right now."

She didn't bother mentioning that she deliberately hadn't paid attention to her parents' travel plans. She didn't even know the name of the ship or the cruise line. In the past six months, she'd cut herself off from her family. She couldn't bear to tell them the ugly, disgusting truth about her life. She couldn't bear to see the shock and the shame in their eyes and to relive it all over again. She just wanted to forget everything. And she'd been on her way to doing just that. If only she hadn't had to have surgery.

"Then a friend from Los Angeles."

"No." All her friends knew what had happened. There'd been no way to keep it a secret. She hadn't been able to face them, and had quickly cut all personal ties. There was no one left to call. What about tonight? Where would Mandy sleep?

"Sheriff Haynes..."

"Travis."

"Travis," she said and paused. "I have no family, other than my parents. I know this is an imposition, but would you or your housekeeper be willing to keep Mandy tonight? I'd gladly pay you." Her hands curled into fists. She hated asking, but what choice did she have?

"I'll keep her and I don't want your money. But that only takes care of today. What happens tomorrow?"

Tomorrow she would handle whatever she had to. She turned toward him. "I really appreciate your concern, but it's not necessary. I'll be fine. In the morning, I'll get a cab. You do have cabs in Glenwood?"

"One or two."

"Good. Then I'll get a cab, collect my daughter from you and take her back to the motel. We'll be fine."

He stood up and walked over to the window. The view from the back—she caught her breath—well, it was just as good as the view from the front, she thought, staring at his tight, high rear end. The pants of his uniform fit snugly at his hips, then fell loosely over his muscled thighs. A black leather belt with snapped compartments hugged his narrow waist. His dark hair fell precisely to his collar, but didn't touch the starched material.

It was the anesthetic, she told herself. And the fact that she'd spent the last year living like a nun. It was the tension and the strain. It was the season, or the time of month, but it was certainly not the man. She wouldn't let it be.

"I have a couple of problems with your plan," he said, keeping his back to her.

"It's not your business." She allowed her temper to flare and the heat of anger to burn away the other kind of warmth threatening her composure.

"First," he said, ignoring her statement, "you're supposed to stay off your feet for a week. How do you propose to feed and take care of Mandy?''

''I'll—'' She hadn't solved that yet, but she would. She would get through it the same as she'd gotten through her other problems. One day, one step at a time. ''I'll think of something.''

''You're not supposed to drive for three weeks,'' he continued.

''How do you know?''

''I asked the nurse.''

''If the town has a cab service, I don't have to drive.''

''Then there's your job.'' He turned toward her and rested one hip on the windowsill. ''Which you still have.''

''What?'' She started to sit upright but the pain from the incision stopped her. She leaned back and stared at him. ''You talked to Rebecca about my job?''

''I explained the situation when I took Mandy over to her. She says to take all the time you need to heal. Your job will be waiting when you're ready.''

''Thank you,'' she murmured as relief filled her.

He was going to make her cry. After breaking down yesterday, she'd sworn not to cry again, but she could feel the tears forming. Maybe it was all going to work out. She'd been so afraid her life would never be normal again. Six months ago, when the police had shown up at her door, her world had collapsed. Slowly, so slowly, she was getting it back together. They were going to make it. They had to.

Before she could ask him what else Rebecca had said, the door pushed open and an attractive nurse came into the room with Mandy in tow. ''We do not allow children in this ward,'' she said sternly, then grinned. ''So I'm bringing her in here to get her out from underfoot.''

Mandy held her bear in one hand and clutched a balloon giraffe in the other. There was chocolate icing on her cheek and she was dressed in a cute pink-and-white shorts outfit that Elizabeth had never seen before.

''Mommy!'' When the nurse let her go, the little girl rushed toward her. Travis walked over and lifted her until she was sitting on the bed.

"Travis Haynes, I might have known I'd find you here with one of our prettiest patients," the nurse said as she paused by the door.

"You know me, Pam. I can't resist a female in distress."

Pam laughed, then looked at Elizabeth. "You watch out for this one. He's our resident heartbreaker."

"I'll be careful," Elizabeth said, knowing she wasn't ever going to get involved with any man, let alone one as charming and good-looking as Travis.

"You've got fifteen minutes," Pam said. "Then my supervisor gets back and Mandy will have to leave."

Elizabeth nodded and the woman shut the door.

"I missed you, Mommy," Mandy said, reclaiming her attention.

"I missed you, too." Elizabeth held out her arms.

Mandy dropped the bear and the balloon animal, and slipped next to her to snuggle close. Despite the tangle of IV's and the pressure on her incision as she leaned toward her daughter, Elizabeth wrapped her arms around her and held on, wishing she never had to let go. Mandy's warm body felt small and fragile cuddling against her, and so very familiar. Elizabeth stroked her head, then bent down and kissed her cheek.

"How are you doing, sweets?" she asked softly.

"There was a clown and he made me this." She picked up her giraffe. The rubber squeaked as she held it and she laughed. Bright blue eyes met her own. Sam's eyes, she thought with regret. Mandy had her smile and her nose, but her eyes and the rest of her coloring was all Sam's. It made it hard to forget her daughter's father. But forget him, she would. She'd promised herself.

Mandy laughed and tossed the balloon animal in the air, then wiggled to sit back and look up at her. "I had a cupcake."

"So I see." She wiped at the frosting. "Sheriff Haynes said you spent the night at his house."

Mandy nodded vigorously and grinned. "Louise made us another dinner. Then we had doughnuts for dessert." She sounded faintly scandalized, but quite delighted. "She gave me a bath but he read me a story. About nines and their end."

Elizabeth looked up at Travis who had returned to his perch on the windowsill. "Nines and their end?"

He cleared his throat. "You sort of had to be there. The San Francisco 49ers are looking for a decent tight end. I don't have any children's books in the house, so I read the sports page."

She grinned. "Whatever works."

"And we played with trains," Mandy said.

"I keep them for my nephews," Travis added helpfully.

"And I got a new nightgown with a bunny on the front from that nice lady, Becca."

"Rebecca?"

She nodded. "And a pink toothbrush."

Elizabeth brushed the blond hair out of her daughter's eyes. "Sounds like you had a full evening. Did you sleep all right?"

Mandy nodded. "I had one bad dream, but I hugged Mr. Bear and told him what had happened, and he said he'd take care of me until you were all better. Are you all better, Mommy?"

Elizabeth swallowed hard. She'd never loved anyone as much as she loved this little girl. She squeezed her. "Almost, honey. The doctor is going to let me go home tomorrow morning."

"Are we going to our house? The one with the bunnies?"

When she had accepted the job, Elizabeth had rented a house. While she'd stood in the kitchen and looked out at the backyard, she'd seen three rabbits scampering across the yard. She'd told Mandy about them and her daughter was very anxious to make their acquaintance. "No. We can't move in there until October first. That's about three more weeks."

"So where are we going tomorrow?"

Elizabeth could feel Travis's gaze on her. He'd asked the same question. She still didn't have a decent answer. "We'll be fine."

"Okay." Mandy picked up her bear and slid off the bed.

"Travis said we could go to the movies tonight, Mommy. He said we could have popcorn and hot dogs and candy." Her body quivered with excitement. "And if I'm really good, I can stay up past my bedtime."

Travis cleared his throat. "She wasn't supposed to tell you that last part."

"I appreciate you doing this for me," Elizabeth said, wondering how it had all gotten out of hand. "She's my responsibility and I—"

Travis pushed to his feet and held out one hand to stop her. "You're not in L.A. anymore. Glenwood is a small town, Elizabeth Abbott, and we take care of our own. As of Thursday night, you're one of us. I'm on duty today, so I'm going to take Mandy with me to the station. We're right across from the park. I'll see that she gets exercise and decent food and is in bed by nine. My housekeeper promised to come by and make sure I'm doing it all correctly."

"Why are you doing this?"

"Because I don't have any plans for the weekend and I've always been a sucker for a pair of beautiful blue eyes."

Elizabeth felt a rush of disappointment that her own eyes were brown. She wanted to believe him, believe that it was just about people helping each other. The way he said it, she was almost willing to buy into the myth of small towns. But she'd believed before, had trusted before, and that trust had been betrayed.

"I hate to impose," she said.

"You don't have a choice," he answered. "What else are you going to do with her?"

She glanced down at the IV needle taped to her hand. She didn't have an answer to that one, either. "Thank you. Again."

She looked up at him. Humor danced in his eyes, humor and a little bit of compassion. As long as it didn't change to pity, she could survive. And somehow, she would pay him back.

He retrieved his hat and settled it on his head; then he held out his hand to Mandy. The little girl collected her giraffe and tucked it next to her bear. She grinned at her mother and slipped her hand in his. "By, Mommy."

"By, honey."

Elizabeth watched her daughter act so trustingly with this stranger. Maybe Mandy hadn't been scarred by the experience as badly as she'd feared. Maybe Mandy was going to be fine.

Travis paused by the door and looked at her. The Stetson hid his eyes from view, but she saw the quick smile flash under his black mustache. Her heart fluttered foolishly. The man was handsome as sin.

"I'll call before the movie," he said. "So you can talk with Mandy."

"I'd like that."

"Rest," he commanded. "The nurse said you'll be released around ten in the morning. I'll be here around nine-thirty."

"You don't have to stay," she said quickly. "But I appreciate you dropping Mandy off."

"I'm not dropping her off," he said. "Unless you can come up with something better than that motel, Elizabeth, you're coming home with me."

Chapter 3

Travis left Mandy at the sheriff's office in the center of Glenwood and walked past his patrol car to Elizabeth's white car parked on the street. The T-bird started instantly. He shifted into gear and checked the mirrors before pulling out and heading for the motel.

Within ten minutes, he stood inside the small rented room, staring at the suitcases stacked in the corner and at the personal items scattered around. A pair of high heels poked out from under the bed. A yellow blouse rested over the back of a chair. The faint scent of perfume lingered in the air. He sniffed appreciatively. He missed having a woman living with him.

His wife had left both him and Glenwood three years ago, returning to town only long enough to sign the divorce papers and wish him well with his life. He didn't resent her or the split. He should have known better than to marry. Haynes men didn't make good husbands or fathers. He came from a long line of men who failed at marriage. But he'd wanted to prove his father, brothers and uncles wrong, so he'd married the pretty, dark-haired woman he'd met in college. She'd been shy but quick-witted—and hot as hell in bed. All the ingredients had been there. Still the marriage had fizzled and he'd learned his lesson firsthand. Haynes men made great cops, but lousy family men.

Travis placed an open suitcase on the bed. He folded Mandy's nightgown and picked up her toys. In the bathroom, an open cosmetic bag sat next to the sink. He collected the compacts, tubes and brushes on the counter and placed them into the bag, stopping long enough to pick up a bottle of perfume and sniff the cap. He would have thought Elizabeth Abbott to be the floral type, but the aroma was spicy. Not overpowering, just intriguing. He dropped the bottle in with the other cosmetics.

After checking the shower and behind the door for clothes, he returned to the bedroom and packed up the remaining items. A white cotton nightgown had been carelessly tossed over a dresser. He folded it carefully, noticing the row of tiny buttons up the front and the lace ruffle around the neck and arms.

He could see Elizabeth in something like this. It would fall about midcalf on her. Not the least bit sexy; the cotton wasn't see-through. And yet—

He brushed his thumb over the soft cloth. There were always plenty of women around him. Just because he wasn't good husband material didn't mean he wasn't a great date and an accomplished flirt. But he'd *liked* living with a woman. He missed the day-to-day familiarities, the verbal shorthand, the slow, sensual sex that could take hours. There'd been no need to hurry; he and Julie were supposed to have had a lifetime.

''Getting soft, Haynes,'' he muttered, then shoved the nightgown into the suitcase.

He opened drawers and pulled out clothes, ignoring the feel of the lacy panties and bras, quickly filling the luggage. When everything was packed, he loaded the trunk of the car and paid the motel bill. Then he headed for the hospital.

He didn't know what he was going to say when he saw her. If she'd made other plans, he would drive her to where she was going and be done with her. If she hadn't, she was coming home with him. There was no way in hell he was going to let her and Mandy tough it out in that tiny motel for the next three weeks. Tough it out, hell. They would *starve.*

As Travis walked down the hospital corridor he wondered

which it would be. He'd left her sputtering yesterday when he'd made his announcement that he intended to take her to his place. Last night, when he'd called to let Mandy talk to her mother, Elizabeth had been coolly insistent that she was not his problem. Louise had told him to use the famous Haynes charm, but he hadn't felt right about sweet-talking Elizabeth into anything.

He reached her door and pushed it open. She sat on the edge of the bed, dressed in the same shorts and tank top she'd been wearing Friday. Her hair was freshly washed and hanging loose about her shoulders in a mass of shining brown waves. A wisp of bangs reached almost to her eyebrows.

She was trying to pull on socks and didn't see him in the doorway. She bent down to slip on her socks, but she only got halfway there before grunting in pain and straightening. She raised her left foot toward her right knee, but that action caused her to clutch her side.

"Of course you'd rather rip out your stitches than ask for help," he said from his place in the doorway. He pushed back his Stetson and walked into the room.

She looked up and stared at him. Faint color stained her cheeks. "I'm not leaving with you," she said flatly.

"Fine. Where are you going?"

"Back to the motel." Fire flashed in her brown eyes. "I've already called for a cab."

He walked forward slowly, stopping when he was in front of her. Even sitting on the hospital bed, she had to tip her head back to meet his gaze.

"Not while I'm around," he said, folding his arms over his chest. "This isn't Los Angeles, Elizabeth. It's a small town, and it's Labor Day weekend. Most of the businesses are closed, including the restaurants. How are you going to feed Mandy? There's no kitchen in your motel room. Is she registered for school?"

Elizabeth slowly shook her head.

"Who's going to do that? Who's going to walk her to her class on the first day? Even if you find take-out places to deliver food, do you have the cash to pay for it, or are you going to have Mandy go to the bank to get more money?''

"Stop it," she said softly. "Just stop it."

Defeat darkened her eyes and made her shoulders slump forward. He felt like a heel, but there was more at stake here than her pride.

"You've got to think of Mandy," he said, perching next to her on the bed.

"She's all I have thought of. I've lain in this bed thinking about nothing else." She brushed her bangs off her forehead. "I just wanted to make a fresh start."

"You have. So things aren't going exactly as you planned them. It could be worse."

"Yeah?" She turned her head to look at him. "How?"

He grinned. "It could be raining."

A smile twitched at the corner of her mouth. "I happen to like rain."

"Sit back," he said, jerking his head toward the pillows.

"Why?"

He leaned forward until his face was inches from hers. He was close enough to see three faint freckles on her nose, close enough to inhale the scent of her body. It wasn't that spicy perfume, but it was still mighty appealing. Close enough to see the rise and fall of her breasts under her red tank top. Close enough to study the shape of her full mouth and feel the stirrings in his body. Women of all ages, shapes and sizes got his attention, but when the lady in question came in a package this tempting, it was hard to think about anything else.

It was part of his job, he told himself. He would have taken her in if she'd been a fifty-year-old man with grandkids. Yeah, he would have taken her in, but it wouldn't have been nearly as much fun.

"Do it," he growled.

She scrambled away from him and leaned against the pillows, drawing her legs up onto the bed. He grabbed one ankle and set her heel on his thigh. She started to pull away. He clamped down.

"You are the most stubborn woman I have ever met," he said, slipping the sock over her foot.

She had small feet, and her toenails were polished a bright pink, he noticed as he slid on her athletic shoe and tightened the laces. Trim ankles and a nice tan. He thought briefly about tan lines, where they would start and end and what color her pale breasts would be, then he told himself he was on duty and to can the sexual interest.

He put that foot down on the bed and grabbed the other one. When he pulled the sock over her instep, his thumb brushed against her skin. She jumped and giggled. He looked up. "Ticklish?"

"Very." Her smile faded. "Thank you for everything."

He studied her for a moment. "I live in a big old house on the edge of town. Six bedrooms. I'm restoring it. There's a yard and a playroom and a lock on the bedroom door. I'll charge you twenty bucks a night if it makes you feel better. When you can move around, you can cook me dinner on the nights my housekeeper doesn't work, because I'm damn tired of frozen dinners zapped in my microwave. If you still feel guilty, you can even do my laundry. Louise will be thrilled. In three weeks, when you can drive, you can move into your own place and we'll part friends. Deal?"

She searched his face as if trying to see what he got out of the offer. He wanted to tell her it was just his job, but he knew deep in his heart he would be lying. He would have made the offer if she'd been old and bald and male, but he wouldn't have wanted her to say yes so badly. It was, he realized with a touch of chagrin, his way of playing house. He would never have a family of his own, so for three weeks, he could pretend.

"It's not that I don't trust you," she said slowly, "it's just that—"

"You don't trust me."

She stared down at her hands. "I'm sorry. It's not personal."

"You don't have a choice, darlin'. I'm the best of a bad situation. Where else are you going to go?"

She bit her lower lip, then looked at him. The raw pain in her eyes made him straighten. It wasn't about physical discomfort, he thought, wanting to turn away, but unable to tear his gaze from hers. It was about some secret in her past. She'd said she'd come to Glenwood to make a fresh beginning. He understood that. Lots of people left places to start over. But she'd left something mean and ugly behind. Something big enough to make her not trust anyone. A man. He wondered what the bastard had done to her.

She nodded once. "If it wasn't for Mandy, I'd say no, but you're right. I don't have a choice. She's the most important part of my life. I accept your offer." She held out her hand, then drew it back. "But I won't do your laundry."

He laughed. "Deal." They shook hands. He finished putting on her other shoe, then stood up. "I'll tell the nurse you're ready to go."

Elizabeth watched him leave. In his cowboy boots and Stetson hat, he looked more like a cow town lawman than the sheriff in a sleepy California town. She wanted to trust him. Desperately. She sat up straight and shifted to the edge of the bed. It wasn't possible. She would never trust any man again. Worse, she would never trust herself.

Travis was right. He *was* her best choice. Right now her options were extremely limited. But when she could drive and move into her rented house, she would pay him what she owed him and disappear from his life.

She heard conversation in the hall. Travis came in, followed by a nurse pushing a wheelchair.

"All set?" he asked.

"Yes." She stood up and stepped toward the wheelchair. When she was settled, he put the small bag containing her personal belongings on her lap and pushed her out of the room.

She was surprised to see the T-bird parked in front of the hospital. "This is my car."

"I know. Did you want to go home in the patrol car? You're just like your daughter. She's always trying to trick me into using the siren."

She laughed. "I don't need a siren. I'm just surprised. I was afraid my car was still parked on the side of the road."

He set the brake on the wheelchair and opened the passenger door. "I had it moved to the sheriff's station. Not that we get much car theft up here."

She stood up slowly. He offered his hand and she took it. His fingers felt warm and strong as he guided her toward the car.

"Watch your head, darlin'," he said, wrapping his other arm around her waist and easing her down.

The incision pulled slightly and she winced. "I'm fine," she said, before he could ask. She looked up at his eyes and the thick, dark lashes framing them. For a heartbeat, his gaze dropped to her mouth. She had a fleeting thought that he was going to kiss her, and her body tensed in anticipation. Then he stepped back and the feeling disappeared, leaving her surprisingly disappointed.

What was wrong with her? she asked herself as Travis gave the nurse the wheelchair, then came around to the driver's side of the car. She wasn't interested in him or in any man. Dear God, hadn't she learned the biggest lesson of all?

Travis didn't glance at her as he slid inside. She wondered if he'd seen the expectation in her face. Embarrassment filled her. She slumped in the seat and closed her eyes.

Something warm brushed across her breasts. She jumped and her eyes flew open.

"Seat belt," Travis said, pulling the belt down and locking it into place.

She stared at him and her heart fluttered foolishly. He'd simply bumped her when he'd grabbed for the restraining device. *Why me?* she wondered and sighed.

"I thought we'd go straight to the house," he said, tossing his Stetson to the back seat. "I want to get you settled. Mandy is at the park with Kyle."

"Kyle?"

He started the engine and pulled out of the parking lot. "One of my deputies and my youngest brother. She's already twisted him around her little finger."

"How do you know?"

Travis shot her a grin. "When he left the office, he turned on his siren. Something tells me that was Mandy's doing."

"She can be stubborn."

"I guess she gets that from her mother."

She glanced at him out of the corner of her eye, but he was staring at the road. She relaxed in the seat and watched as he drove through the small town. As they neared the park, traffic became heavy. She saw families walking together. Her stomach clenched, not from the surgery, but from envy and regret. She and Mandy should have been part of a family like that. It had all been taken away from them. Stolen. She stared out the window and willed the tears away. No. Not stolen. They'd never had it in the first place. It had all been a lie.

As they passed the duck pond, she saw the motel. "Wait, I have to get my things."

"Already done," he said, not bothering to stop. "I went there this morning and checked you out. Your suitcases are in the trunk."

She didn't know whether to thank him or yell at him for invading her personal space.

"Before you get huffy and start hollering at me," he said, as if he could read her mind, "I knew you would want your things with you even if you'd made other plans. So I didn't *assume* you would take me up on my offer."

It took too much energy to get angry, so she simply leaned back in the seat and went along for the ride. He'd been right. She couldn't have made it work at the motel. They passed a sheriff's car parked on the side of the road by the park. Elizabeth looked around but she didn't see Mandy.

"When will Kyle bring her back?" she asked.

"I'll bring her home about four-thirty. There's a parade today, and a big barbecue. Games for the kids. I thought she might enjoy it and you need the rest. I'm going to have to drop you off then head back to the park myself. Have to make an appearance. Between Kyle and myself, we'll keep an eye on Mandy. Louise is off until Monday so you should have plenty of peace and quiet.''

He entered a tree-lined residential area. Elizabeth recognized it from her house hunting. He drove around the high school and along a narrow two-lane road she'd never been on before. The houses got larger and farther apart from each other on oversize lots.

''You mentioned Kyle was your youngest brother,'' she said. ''How many are there?''

''Four, counting me. Craig is the oldest, then me, then Jordan and then Kyle.''

''So Kyle is a deputy. Are you all cops?''

''It's a family tradition. My dad used to be the sheriff in Glenwood. All his brothers are in police work. Jordan is the only rebel. He's a fire fighter up in Sacramento.''

''A real black sheep.''

Travis grinned. ''We give him a hard time about it. Yup, the Haynes family grows boys and cops. Not a girl in the last four generations. What about you?''

''I'm an only child.''

''Too bad.''

''Why? It's all I know. My parents were older when I was born and they only wanted one child.''

''They got a pretty one.''

Elizabeth chuckled. This man could charm milk out of a snake. She would do well to remember talk was cheap. But she had to admit Travis Haynes had a certain amount of style to recommend him, and his heart was in the right place. She resisted glancing at his firm body so close to hers in the confines of the car. From what she had seen, everything else was in the right place, too. But the last thing she needed was to get involved with a heartbreaker. Her heart hadn't recovered from what Sam had done.

They pulled off the road and onto a long driveway. Maple trees and oaks grew on either side of the path. Up ahead she saw a peaked roof, and more trees. Then the path curved around and they drove up into a clearing and parked in front of a beautiful three-story house.

He'd told her he was restoring an old house, but he hadn't said it was a mansion. Big windows opened up onto a wide front lawn. A porch wrapped around the front. The columns holding up the porch covering had been painted white, as was all the trim. The rest of the building was dove gray, soft and light in the morning sunshine.

"You could get lost in there," she said, staring at the masterpiece.

"I did, the first couple of days. Stay in that seat and don't even think about moving."

He got out of the car and came around to her side. He opened the door, then helped her to her feet. Before she could take a step, he bent over and slid one arm behind her back and the other under her thighs.

"What are you doing?" she asked even as he lifted her against his chest. Elizabeth grabbed his shoulders to maintain her balance.

"And here I thought you were smarter than that." He started toward the house.

Her face bumped against his shoulder, and she could smell his masculine scent. He'd shaved only a couple of hours before, so his neck was smooth. She fought the urge to nestle against him. "Travis, put me down. I can walk."

He ignored her. There were four steps up to the porch. He climbed those easily and headed for the front door. She held on, ignoring the way her right breast flattened against his chest and the heated strength of his body. She was wearing shorts so the arm under her legs touched bare skin. Each of his fingers seemed to be leaving a warm imprint on her flesh. She thought about struggling, but her side hurt and she was tired of fighting. Instead, she gave herself up to the feeling of being safe and protected.

When he opened the front door and stepped inside, she stared at the beautiful interior and caught her breath. He had told the truth when he'd said he was restoring the house. Several of the walls had been stripped but not painted or papered. There wasn't a rug on the wooden floor, and she could see the pile of tools next to the front door.

But none of that mattered. He released his arm and she slid to the ground. Instead of moving away from him, she leaned against him and looked around. A crystal chandelier hung in the foyer. The cut glass caught the sunlight and diffused it into a hundred tiny rainbows. The long staircase swept up to the second story where it split and circled around both sides. Arched doorways led to high-beamed rooms. A giant fireplace filled one wall of the parlor to her left, while on the right, a study with floor-to-ceiling bookshelves held sheet-covered furniture.

"Wow." She looked at him. "You live here?"

He shrugged. "Yeah."

"All by yourself?"

"I do now. I was married when I bought the place. Some people have a baby to try and save their marriage. Julie and I bought this house." The humor left his brown eyes.

"I'm sorry."

He shrugged. "Don't be. There were no hard feelings. Sometimes it doesn't work out. Julie and I kept bumping into each other on the curves. Hell, it was no one's fault. Cops don't make good husbands and neither do Haynes men. I had no business trying."

She was about to ask why when he collected her in his arms again and started down the hallway next to the stairs.

"I'm going to put you in here," he said, using his shoulder to push open a door. "There's an attached bathroom. It's small, but I didn't think you'd want to hassle with the stairs."

Even though she hadn't moved much since leaving the hospital, her side was already aching. "You're right."

A double bed stood next to a window looking out on the side garden where roses had grown into a tangled disarray of blossoms. A single nightstand and a long dresser took up the rest of the space in the room. There was a half-open door and she could see through to a bathroom.

"This will be perfect," she said.

"Mandy's been sleeping upstairs." He set her on her feet. "She can stay there, or I can dig up a cot for her in here. It would be a little crowded, but—"

"Don't worry about it. I'm sure Mandy is happy where she is."

"I'll go get your luggage." He disappeared back the way they'd come.

Elizabeth settled on the bed and touched her healing incision. Just three days ago she'd arrived in Glenwood, hoping to make a fresh start. Many things hadn't worked out the way she'd planned, but they were getting better. She could feel it. She had to get on with her life. It was the only way to put the past behind her.

Travis looked at the empty plate on the table, then at Elizabeth. "Are you done?"

She laughed and patted her stomach. "Yes, thanks. It was wonderful. Here you had me believe you didn't know how to cook."

"I'm okay with omelets," he said, and carried the plates over to the counter. "And I know my way around a barbecue, but other than that, it's just me and the microwave."

"I can make French toast," Mandy announced proudly from her place opposite her mother.

"I know, darlin'. You made it for me this morning."

"How long did it take you to clean up the mess?" Elizabeth asked.

Travis rinsed the dishes and put them in the dishwasher. "About an hour."

She looked at him and smiled. "Amazing, isn't it?"

"I found eggshells everywhere."

"He ate four pieces," Mandy said.

"Good," Elizabeth said, but he could see she was more tired than enthused. There were dark circles under her eyes, and her smile wasn't as bright as it had been that morning when he'd brought her to the house.

He wiped his hands and turned toward the table. The kitchen had been the first room he'd remodeled. That had been before Julie had left. She'd picked out the cream tiles edged in blue flowers, and she'd been the one to insist on bleached oak cabinets. He'd wanted a more traditional kitchen but he had to admit her taste had been better than his. The rectangular room was bright and airy, despite an overabundance of storage and the large subzero refrigerator and six-burner range.

"Mandy, let's put your mama to bed. Then you can help me clean up."

"But it's early yet," Elizabeth said.

"You're dead on your feet."

"I can't be. After you left, I had a nap. I've only been up for—" she glanced at her watch "—three hours." She punctuated her observation with a yawn.

Mandy laughed. "You're tired, Mommy."

"I guess I am." Elizabeth braced her arms on the table and slowly pushed herself to her feet. Travis moved closer, but she waved him off. "I made it to the kitchen under my own power, I think I can make it back."

"Have it your way."

She took small steps. Mandy dogged her heels, and he brought up the rear, ready to jump to the rescue in case she slipped. Her nap wasn't the only thing she'd done while he was gone all afternoon. She'd also showered and changed clothes.

The shorts and tank top had been replaced by a loose-fitting summer dress. It dipped low in front and back and, as he had served his famous vegetable omelet, he got a flash of cleavage. He hadn't seen where the tan ended and her pale skin began, but the peek had more than stirred his interest. He'd spent most of dinner giving himself a stern talking-to.

Elizabeth was his guest. Despite his claim to want to be paid for the room, he would no more take her money than he would hurt Mandy. He was simply temporary shelter and the only friend she had in town. He couldn't take advantage of her, or the situation. It wasn't right. If he wanted a woman, there were plenty in town to oblige him. He'd never once had a problem finding company.

As she turned down the hallway, the last rays of sun caught the thick braid hanging down to her shoulder blades. Her hair gleamed with rich color, brown and gold with a hint of red, so different from Mandy's pale blond hair. Had Elizabeth's hair once been that color, turning darker with age, or had Mandy inherited her hair color from her father?

They reached the bedroom. Elizabeth sank onto the bed and smiled at her daughter. "I'm going to rest here for a few minutes before I get ready to sleep. Why don't you kiss me good-night now and then go help Travis in the kitchen."

Mandy reached up and kissed her cheek. "I love you, Mommy."

"I love you, too, honey."

"I'm glad you're not in that old hospital anymore. Tomorrow can you come upstairs and look at my room?"

"We'll see." Elizabeth stroked her daughter's head, then glanced at Travis. "Thanks for everything. I really appreciate it."

"Just being neighborly," he said from his place in the doorway.

"Hardly, but I do appreciate everything." She motioned to the room, and then smiled at her daughter. "I don't know what I would have done—"

He cut her off. "All you should worry about now is getting better. Leave the rest of it alone. Come on, Mandy. Your mother needs to sleep." He held out his hand.

Mandy looked from him to her mother. "But, Travis, aren't you going to kiss Mommy good-night, too?"

Chapter 4

Elizabeth looked up at him, obviously startled. Her big eyes got bigger and her lips parted slightly with surprise. But she hadn't flinched.

He pushed off the door frame and slowly approached the bed. Her gaze never left his. "I do my best work under pressure," he drawled.

"I'll bet," Elizabeth muttered, then looked away. "Look, you don't have to—"

"Mommy, you need to be kissed good-night," Mandy said, and bounced on the bed. "It'll make you feel better. Travis made me feel better when he gave me a kiss. I didn't have even one bad dream last night."

"Simply medicinal," he said.

"What's mecidinal?" Mandy asked, struggling with the strange word.

He didn't take his gaze off Elizabeth's face. Color steadily climbed her cheeks. She glanced at him, at Mandy, at her fingers twisting together in her lap. He approached the bed and bent over.

"It means doing something for medical purposes," he said. "Like taking medicine."

He rested his hands on her shoulders. Their eyes met. Mandy

asked another question, but he couldn't hear all the words. Elizabeth's irises were a pure brown, almost chestnut colored. Her sweet breath fanned his face. His stomach tightened in anticipation, which, he told himself, was stupid. She'd just had major surgery, her six-year-old daughter sat inches away. He was simply going to give her a quick peck on the cheek. So what was the big deal?

But he didn't kiss her cheek. He moved his head to the left side of her face, but at the last minute veered back and brushed his mouth against hers.

He'd expected some kind of attraction. He was a healthy single male, and she was damned good-looking. But he hadn't expected to get third-degree burns from the heat.

The contact, lasting no more than one or two seconds, seared his mouth and sent flames of need racing through his body. Instinctively, his hands tightened on her shoulders. Her arms reached up toward him. He felt them whisper by his sides then fall back. He wanted to haul her to her feet and pull her firmly against him. He wanted to feel her body pressing along his, thighs brushing, hips rotating, chest to breast in exquisite delight.

"Don't you feel better, Mommy?" Mandy asked.

He raised his head. Elizabeth's eyes were wide and unfocused as if she, too, had felt the conflagration. She swallowed and looked away. But not before he'd seen the answering desire in her gaze.

"Much," she answered, her voice low and husky. She cleared her throat. "I do feel better. Thank you."

Travis stared down at her. Who was this woman and what had brought her to Glenwood? Why was there no one, no man, for her to call in her time of trouble? He took a step back and fought a grin. Not that he minded the fact that she was single and in his house. If anything, their kiss had shown him the next three weeks could be very interesting. But why was she alone?

"Come on, Mandy," he said, holding out his hand. "Let's let your mom get some rest. I rented a movie for us to watch."

"Okay." Mandy jumped off the bed and gripped his fingers. "Night, Mommy."

"Night, sweetie," she said, and smiled at her little girl. Her gaze raised to the middle of his chest and stopped. "Good night, Travis. Thank you for...everything."

Yeah, he couldn't stop thinking about their kiss either, he thought. "Get some rest." He led Mandy from the room and closed the door behind them.

A large sofa with a matching chair in soft ivory leather sat in front of an oversize television. Mandy released him and ran over to the VCR. Expertly she pulled the rented tape from its protective cover and inserted it in the machine. Her chatter made him smile, but he had trouble concentrating on her words. He couldn't stop thinking about Elizabeth Abbott. He was sure there was a logical explanation for everything that was going on, but some sixth sense whispered there was a mystery.

As he sat on the sofa and Mandy climbed onto his lap, he mentally listed what he knew about Elizabeth and her daughter. It wasn't much. He was too good a lawman to let anything that intriguing go unsolved. If Elizabeth wouldn't cooperate and answer some questions, he was going to have to find out on his own.

Elizabeth got coffee going before her exhaustion and the pain in her side forced her to retreat to the kitchen table. She sank into one of the bleached oak chairs. She'd hoped the doctor had been kidding when he'd told her to stay off her feet for a week. Apparently not. He'd reminded her that despite all the improvements in medical technology, the fact was she'd had her tummy cut open, through all the muscles. There were multiple layers of tissues to heal. She hadn't realized how much she used those muscles until she tried to move around and they reminded her they weren't working well. She pressed her hand against her side and shifted on the chair. Maybe she would just sit here for a while.

She drew in a deep breath and inhaled the scent of the brewing coffee. At least she'd accomplished something. She smiled.

Maybe later, when she'd gathered her strength, she would get wild and attempt toast.

"What are you smiling about, darlin'?"

That voice. It made her think of something warm and rich and decadent slowly slipping through her fingers. It made her think of liquid satin on bare skin. It made her think of last night and their brief kiss. She turned to look at him.

Travis stood in the doorway with his arms folded over his chest. Her breath caught in her throat. She'd never seen him out of uniform before. Her gaze traveled from his scuffed black cowboy boots up the long, lean length of his legs. Worn jeans, faded with lines of white radiating out from the seams by his hips and crotch, clung with the familiarity of an old lover. A red polo shirt stretched across his chest and shoulders, emphasizing his muscles. He looked powerful, but more than that he made her think of a dependable man, a hard worker. His watch was black, some sports kind with a couple of buttons. He didn't wear any rings or other jewelry. Except for the glint in his dark brown eyes and his teasing smile, there wasn't anything flashy about him.

Solid, she thought. That's the word she'd been looking for. Travis Haynes was a solid man.

He took a step into the kitchen. His gaze moved over her face, pausing on her mouth long enough for the tingling to start in her toes and work its way up. Last night she'd lain awake in the dark reliving the brief touch of his lips on hers. It had been nothing significant. A teasing kiss instigated by her daughter. So why did she wonder what it would be like to be held in those powerful arms and pulled hard against that solid chest? Why was her heart beating faster and her breasts tightening in anticipation? Nothing had happened and nothing was going to happen. It couldn't. She knew better than to get involved.

"You didn't answer my question," he said, strolling over to check the coffee. The pot had stopped sputtering. He opened the cupboard above the machine and pulled out two mugs.

"I don't remember what I was smiling about." Her voice sounded completely normal, she thought with some relief.

"How do you take it?"

"With milk, please."

He stirred her coffee and handed her the mug, then took the seat opposite her. "How did you sleep?"

"Great. I feel better."

"You're supposed to be staying off your feet."

"I know. I just wanted some coffee, and I didn't know what time you got up."

She felt a little awkward talking about the intimate details of living together. She barely knew Travis. She tilted her head toward the table, then glanced up at him through her lashes. She liked the way his hair curled slightly around his ears, and the trimmed mustache outlining his upper lip. Last night she'd felt the faint tickle of his mustache against her skin. She wondered what that soft, groomed hair would feel like—

The back door opened, cutting off her dangerous train of thought.

"Yoo-hoo, Travis, are you up?" a loud female voice called.

He grinned. "If I wasn't, Louise, I would be now."

A woman entered the kitchen. She was in her mid to late forties with short blond hair and a figure that could only be described as an hourglass. Her pants were a bright lime green color, her short-sleeved blouse a blend of greens, yellows and oranges. A wide gold belt emphasized her small waist, while a trio of silver chains dipped toward her generous bosom. Dark eye shadow and lots of mascara highlighted her blue eyes. Her red lipstick clashed with everything, but somehow looked all right.

"You must be Elizabeth," Louise said, moving forward and holding out her hand. "Your daughter is the sweetest little girl." She smiled and her eyes got a faraway look. "Maybe I should have had children." She paused. "No, I think Alfred is more than enough trouble, don't you?"

"Alfred?" Elizabeth asked as they shook hands. "Your husband?"

Louise laughed. "No, my dog. Hi, I'm Louise."

Elizabeth didn't know whether to be embarrassed or laugh back. She settled on smiling weakly. Louise bent over and gave Travis a kiss on the cheek, then moved to the refrigerator and started pulling out food.

"Louise is my housekeeper," Travis said.

"I figured that."

"She works here three days a week—"

"But I'm willing to come in more while you're getting better, Elizabeth," Louise said, cutting Travis off. "When I heard what happened, well, I just had to rush over and do whatever I could to help." She set a pitcher of orange juice on the counter. "Maybe you would like to work on some crafts while you're recovering. I'm thinking of doing something with clay."

"Absolutely not," Travis said. "There will be no clay in this house."

Louise mumbled something under her breath about men being pinheads.

Travis leaned forward and lowered his voice. "Louise is going through a stage right now."

The chesty blonde glared at him. "I can hear every word you're staying and this is not a stage. I'm exploring my art."

"She's driving me crazy. She makes things and gives them to me."

"It's a sign of affection, but if you'd rather I didn't, then fine." She slammed the refrigerator door shut and turned her back on them.

"I have this drawer full of sweaters and socks."

Elizabeth stared at him. "Why is that a problem?"

"They're not—" he glanced from her to Louise and back "—normal. Most of the socks have no heel. The sweaters aren't anatomically correct."

Louise walked over to the table and grinned. "I'll admit I didn't quite get the hang of knitting. I never could figure out

parts of the patterns, but some of the wool was real lovely.''
She held two eggs in her right hand. ''How would you like them
cooked?''

Elizabeth blinked several times. ''Scrambled?''

''Fine.'' She glanced at Travis. ''I know what you want, but
the way you've talked about me this morning, I'm of a mind to
let you go hungry.''

''Your threats don't scare me.'' As Louise passed him, he
reached out and patted her rear end affectionately.

''Don't you try your wild ways on me, Travis Haynes,'' she
said, giving him a mock glare. ''I'm old enough to be your very
young and attractive aunt.''

Elizabeth couldn't help it. She started laughing. Even the
sharp pains in her side couldn't stop her from chuckling.

''Mommy.''

Mandy entered the room. She was washed and dressed in a
pretty blue dress with tiny white flowers. She came over to her
and held out her arms for a hug. Elizabeth pulled her close.

''Are you ready for your first day of school?'' she asked.
Travis was going to walk Mandy to the elementary school and
register her.

Mandy nodded. ''Travis helped me pick out this dress to wear.
Did we choose the right one?''

''Of course, Mandy. You look perfect.''

''I have ribbons.'' She held them out. ''Will you put them in
my hair?''

''Sure.''

Elizabeth turned and Mandy slipped between her legs. When
the girl saw Louise, she squealed with excitement. ''Louise, you
found us.''

Louise looked at her. ''Morning, baby girl. What do you mean
I found you?''

''Travis said you were lost.''

Elizabeth glanced at him. He'd taken a sip of coffee just as
Mandy spoke and now he started to choke. Louise came over
and pounded him on the back several times while he coughed.

Louise gave her a quick wink. "He probably said I was trying to find myself."

The next thud on his back sounded a little harder. He turned to her and held up his hand. "That's enough," he said, his voice raspy and faint. "I'm fine."

Elizabeth wasn't sure, but she thought she saw a flush of color on Travis's cheeks. She bit back her laughter and concentrated on Mandy's hair. When the braid was secured with the length of blue ribbon, Mandy pulled out a chair and climbed onto the seat. As Louise fixed breakfast, Many chatted with Travis and Louise about what Mr. Bear had told her in the night. Louise slid a plate in front of the girl, containing a waffle shaped like a popular cartoon mouse. Cut strawberries formed a bright collar at the bottom of the waffle. A glass of milk completed the meal.

Elizabeth looked up at the older woman. "Thank you for making that."

Louise shrugged. "It's nothing. The first day of school should be special for a little girl. And Alfred was never impressed with my waffles."

Elizabeth wanted to ask if Louise really did feed her dog waffles, but she didn't dare. As the smells of eggs, bacon and coffee mingled in the kitchen, she leaned back in her chair and savored her feeling of relief. She and Mandy were going to make it. In three weeks she would start her new job and move into her own place. In the meantime, they were safe here.

She glanced at Travis and found him staring at her. His gaze dropped briefly to her mouth. The sensation of being touched was so real, she wanted to touch him back. The attraction flickering just below the surface fanned to life.

He was her salvation and her greatest problem. This, this mindless reaction to him, had to stop. She knew better than to get involved with a man, any man. But he was even worse than most. She knew what his easy ways and quick, tempting smile meant. She'd already been seduced by one charmer and those results had been more awful than she could ever have imagined.

The only decent thing to come out of her relationship with Sam Proctor had been Mandy—and that had been an accident.

Louise served them breakfast, then poured more coffee. Elizabeth hesitated before picking up her fork.

"Dig in," Travis said. "Louise is a great cook."

"I don't doubt that, it's just..."

He leaned across the bleached oak table and laid his hand on top of hers. Heat flooded her fingers, warming her blood and making its way up her arm. She told herself to ignore it, and him, but she couldn't seem to look away from his dark gaze.

"It's just nothing," he said. "Everything is going to be all right. I'll make it all right. I'm the sheriff. I can do anything."

"I believe you," she said and was rewarded with a smile. She *did* believe him. That was the problem.

She picked up her fork. It was only for a few weeks, she reminded herself. She just had to stay strong and resist the powerful charm of Travis Haynes. She could do it, she had to. Her life depended on it.

Elizabeth sat in the family room and stared at the television. The screen was blank. She picked up the remote control, then tossed it down. She didn't want to watch television; she wanted to be with her daughter on her first day of school.

She swallowed against the lump in her throat, but the pressure didn't go away. Her eyes burned and she wanted to scream at the unfairness of it all. Little Mandy had gone off with Travis an hour ago. She'd waved and smiled, and promised to make her mom something pretty in class.

"I should have been with her," Elizabeth said softly, fighting the frustration. She touched her side, feeling the bandage under her shorts and panties. There was no way she could have made it from here to the school and back. It took all her strength to walk from the kitchen to the family room. But she'd so wanted to see Mandy's classroom and meet her teacher. Her daughter would only enter the first grade once and she'd missed it. What kind of mother did that make her? It wasn't enough she'd taken Mandy away from everything she knew in the world, but now the girl was going to a strange school, escorted by a strange man. It wasn't fair.

"Television is generally more interesting when you turn it on," Louise said.

Elizabeth looked up at her. The other woman stood in the doorway to the family room. She had a mug of coffee in each hand. "I wasn't really planning on watching," she said.

"Would you like some company?"

Elizabeth nodded. "That would be nice, if you have the time."

Louise handed her one of the mugs and plopped down at the opposite end of the butter-soft leather sofa. "I've got plenty of time. That boy hasn't even furnished most of the rooms in this monstrosity. There's not that much cleaning to do. I suspect he hires me so that he can have a taste of someone else's cooking and a friendly face to come home to a couple of days a week."

"Are you saying Travis is lonely?"

"Could be."

Louise fluffed up her bangs with her fingers. Elizabeth noticed she painted her long nails a bright red and had thin stripes of gold dotted on the tips.

"So what do you think of him?" Louise asked.

That was certainly subtle, Elizabeth thought, fighting a grin. "He seems very nice."

Louise's eyes narrowed. "Now I don't think any of the Haynes boys would appreciate being called 'nice.' Ladies' men, maybe. Irresistible, certainly. But nice?" She shook her head and smiled. "You'd better keep that opinion to yourself."

"I guess I'll have to." She took a sip from her mug. "Travis mentioned he has three brothers."

"That's right, and his daddy is one of five." She leaned her head back against the leather sofa. Her expression got soft and dreamy. "That means there are nine Haynes men walking around on this earth tempting women with their wicked ways. When I was in high school, Earl—that's Travis's father—came to speak to my class about drinking and driving. I don't remember a word he said, but I do remember how handsome he looked in his uniform. When he smiled, I about melted in my seat.'' She straightened and shrugged. ''I was barely seventeen, and my boyfriend and I had just broken up. Earl Haynes looked mighty good. Of course he was a much older man.''

''Of course,'' Elizabeth murmured. Louise was certainly a little left of center, but Elizabeth found herself liking the other woman.

''And his uncles. Hell-raisers all of them. I don't think they were ever faithful longer than a minute. Heaven help the women who tried to tame 'em. Of course the Haynes men did give this town something to talk about. Then when Earl went ahead and had four more boys of his own, there was even more talk. Do you know there hasn't been a girl born to the Haynes family in four generations?''

''Travis mentioned that.''

Louise laughed. ''Travis is the most easygoing of the four boys. Not like Jordan. That one's always been a mystery. But Travis knows what he wants and gets it.'' She winked. ''Maybe he'll decide he wants you.''

Elizabeth shook her head. ''I'm not interested in a relationship. Certainly not with a man like him. The last thing I need is some Don Juan upsetting my life.''

''Oh, you can't believe everything you hear about him. He's not exactly the heartbreaker everyone says. Despite what he thinks, he's nothing like his daddy.'' Louise grew serious. ''You can trust me on that one, honey. I know for a fact.''

It didn't matter how much of Travis's reputation was real and how much hype. Enough of what Louise had said was true for Travis Haynes to be trouble.

Sam had been a charmer, too. His easy smile and quick wit had seduced her in a matter of hours. Of course she'd been a willing participant. And young. Far too young for a man like him. She'd never had a clue as to what was going on. She'd known the relationship was in trouble, but even that hadn't prepared her for the police showing up at her doorstep in the predawn hours of morning. If she lived to be a hundred, she would never forget the feeling of horror when the Los Angeles Police Department officers had taken Sam away. Thank God Mandy had slept through it all.

Louise leaned forward and patted her leg. "You feeling better?"

"What?"

"I thought you might be a little down, what with missing Mandy's first day at school. You feel better now?"

Elizabeth looked at Louise, with her bright makeup and dangling earrings. The left one was a teapot, the right, a cup and saucer. "You probably don't want to hear this any more than Travis, but I think you're nice, too."

Louise gave her hand a squeeze and rose to her feet. "Just don't let word get out. I have my own reputation to keep up. Now I'm going to get to work on lunch. I heard Travis's truck in the driveway. He can tell you all about Mandy's classroom. Don't worry, honey. You'll get to see it soon enough."

She left the room and passed Travis in the doorway. Elizabeth half turned to face him. "How did it go?" she asked.

He studied her for several seconds. There was an odd look in his eyes, as if he'd never seen her before.

"Travis, is something wrong?"

"No. Everything went fine. Mandy loved her teacher and when I left, it looked like she'd already started making friends."

Elizabeth sagged back in the sofa. Some of the tension left her body. Maybe, just maybe, she hadn't destroyed her daughter's life.

"These might help," he said as he walked toward her. He held out several instant photos.

"You took pictures?"

"I thought they might make you feel like you'd been there."

She smiled up at him. "That was so thoughtful."

She took the photos and looked through them. The first showed Mandy smiling in front of the school. There were three shots of the classroom and one of Mandy with her teacher. The little girl was laughing at something the woman had said. Elizabeth felt tears forming in her eyes. She blinked them away.

"This is wonderful. I don't know how to thank you."

Travis shifted his weight from one foot to the other. "It's nothing special. I didn't even think of the idea. Craig does it for his kids. He says it's fun to look back later. You're not going to cry, are you?"

She sniffed. "No." She touched one finger to the smooth flat surface, as if she could touch Mandy's warm cheek. Her daughter's smile made her own lips curve up in response. "She *does* look happy, doesn't she? And the teacher looks nice. Did you talk to her?"

"I know her."

There was something about the way he said the words. "Oh?"

"I sort of, you know." He shoved his hands into his jeans pockets. "We dated for a while."

"Ah. Is she—" Elizabeth paused, then found the correct word. "Is she nice?" She had to bite her lip to keep from smiling.

Travis was obviously uncomfortable with the conversation. "Yeah, she's really great. With kids, I mean."

"I'm sure Mandy will like her."

"Most of the kids do."

He pulled his hands out of his pockets and walked over to the window. The bright light outside lighted his tall, muscular body. He was very handsome, with his dark hair and eyes. Elizabeth could see why he'd acquired his reputation. If his brothers were half as good-looking, then it's no wonder the town found the family a great source of gossip.

"Tell me about your ex-husband," he said.

She felt as if he'd thrown a bucket of cold water in her face. Every muscle in her body tensed. She had to put the photos down when she realized she was mangling them. She folded her hands in her lap and forced herself to relax.

"I don't have an ex-husband. I told you, I was never married." She could feel the heat of her flush climbing from the scoop neck of her T-shirt, up to her face. It had been six months, yet she was still embarrassed to remember what had happened. Would this ever get easier?

"You're sure?"

"I would hardly forget being married."

He walked to the sofa and braced his hands against the tall back. "The reason I ask is because when I registered Mandy for school, she got confused about her last name. When I first asked, she said it was Proctor. I reminded her that your last name is Abbott. She said that was her last name, too. So which is it, Elizabeth?"

He was still handsome as sin, but the friendly, teasing man who had shared breakfast with her had disappeared. In his place was a probing stranger. For the first time she saw the dark side of him. No doubt he made an excellent sheriff.

But she couldn't tell him the truth. It was too awful, too embarrassing, too unbelievable. She had trouble believing it had happened, and she'd lived through it. Besides, she didn't want to see that pitying look in his eyes. She didn't want to know he thought of her as less, or stupid. No, the truth was her own secret, one she would never share. She could, however, tell him part of the truth.

She raised her hand to flick her hair back over her shoulder. "Proctor is Mandy's father's last name. She used it for a while, but now she's using my name."

"I see." He drew his eyebrows together. "You mentioned you had rented a house here in town."

What did that have to do with anything? She nodded slowly. "I can take possession on October first."

"Is your furniture in storage?"

"Why are you asking me this?"

He moved around the sofa until he was standing in front of her. She had to tilt her head back to meet his eyes. She wished he was wearing his Stetson so she didn't have to see the cold black swirling through his irises.

"Is it?"

"No. I don't have any furniture. I left it all behind in L.A. I didn't want to move it. Travis, why are you acting like this? Why are you asking all these questions?"

"So you have no furniture, Mandy has very few toys. In fact, all your possessions can fit in the trunk of your car." He wasn't asking a question.

Her heart pounded in her chest. She wanted to stand up and stare him in the eye, but the tension was making her side ache too much. She could only sit on the edge of the sofa and fight the fear.

"Travis—"

He cut her off with a wave of his hand. "I want the truth, Elizabeth. Did you kidnap Mandy?"

Chapter 5

She couldn't have looked more stunned if he'd slapped her. All the color left her face and her lips parted, but she couldn't—or didn't—speak.

Travis noted her reactions, the cynical lawman side of him wondering if she was the genuine article or a very good actress. The male part of him, that part of his being that had reacted to her presence in his life, wanted to believe. He wanted her to be just a single mom looking for something better for herself and her kid.

It shouldn't matter, he told himself. He wasn't going to get involved. It would be better for his hormonal state if she was some kind of criminal. After his marriage had collapsed he'd acknowledged the futility of ignoring the truth. As long as he had Haynes blood flowing through his veins he didn't have a prayer of having a decent long-lasting relationship. So he shouldn't mind if everything about Elizabeth Abbott-Proctor, or whatever her name was, turned out to be a lie.

Except he knew it was too late. He couldn't get involved with her, but that didn't stop him from liking her. And Mandy. The kid had him wrapped around her finger. This morning—

Can it, he ordered himself. He couldn't afford to think about how great it had been to take Mandy to her first day of school.

So what if her trusting smile had given him a lump in his throat? Marriage, a wife and kids weren't for him. He didn't have whatever mysterious something it took to be a decent husband and father. He had to focus on Elizabeth and the mystery in her life. He might not be good domestic material, but he was a damn fine sheriff.

Elizabeth glanced up at him, then turned away. "It's a very effective technique," she said, her voice low and strained. "Glaring at people like that. I'm sure most of your prisoners crack under the pressure."

Only then did he realize how long he'd been staring at her. But he didn't look away. "Just tell me the truth. I'd have to be blind not to see there's some kind of mystery in your life."

She stood up slowly. Her mouth twisted, but he sensed it was from the strain on her incision rather than fear. When she was standing, she squared her shoulders and looked up at him. Emotional and physical pain darkened her wide eyes. All the color had faded from her cheeks, leaving her pale and drawn. He could see the beginning of tiny lines around her eyes.

Her long hair fanned out over her shoulders. He wanted to touch that hair, touch her and pull her close. He wanted to ease her pain and promise it was going to be all right. But he couldn't. He didn't know how it was going to be.

"I don't know whether to be furious or grateful," she said, and stepped away from him.

He knew she was too weak from the surgery to run, but instinctively his body tensed as he prepared to grab her if she went too far. He needn't have worried. She circled behind the sofa and leaned against the back.

"There's no mystery, Travis," she said softly. She studied the leather couch and traced a line of stitching back and forth with her finger. "I'm not and never have been married. Sam Proctor is Mandy's father. Our relationship—" She hesitated, then drew in a deep breath and looked at him. "Our relationship doesn't exist anymore. Sam is out of our lives. I came up here to make a fresh start. I left behind everything Sam had given me, includ-

ing the clothes and toys and furniture. I only brought what is
mine and Mandy's. Sam signed custody of Mandy over to me.
I didn't have time to open a bank account and get a safety-
deposit box, so I have the papers with me. I would be happy to
show you her birth certificate and anything else you'd like to
see.''

"I don't need to see the papers.''

"But you don't believe me.''

"I didn't say that.''

He didn't have to. They both knew she'd been lying. Oh, not
about Mandy. He did believe that. It almost made sense, the
leaving everything behind part. It seemed like an expensive, impulsive gesture, but nothing about women surprised him.

She'd only lied once. When she'd told him there was no mystery in her life. There was a damn big one and he was no closer
to figuring it out. She'd said she'd never married. He almost
believed that. So what did that mean? That she'd shacked up
with some guy and had his baby?

He studied her. With her hair loose around her face, she
looked younger than twenty-eight. Had she gotten involved with
a married man? He didn't want to believe that of her. It reminded
him too much of his father and the older man's string of young
women. Earl Haynes had gotten a kick out of seducing the innocents, making them believe he was going to leave his wife
and family. He'd never left them, at least not permanently. His
way of justifying his life-style had been waking up in his own
bed every morning. Every time Travis had heard his mother and
father fighting about his father's infidelities, Earl had glossed
over his behavior by saying he always woke up in his bed. What
more could a woman want?

Travis had been there once, when it had happened. A woman
in her early twenties had been in town visiting family. They'd
met in the hardware store. Within fifteen minutes, Earl'd had the
woman eating out of his hand and leaving the hardware store to
get a drink. Travis had run away as fast as he could. He'd only
been fourteen at the time, but he'd known what was happening.

He hadn't made it home before he'd had to stop and throw up in the bushes. He'd cried then for all he'd never had, cried for the loss of a father who was like other dads. A father who cared more about his wife and his sons than other women. It had been the last time he'd shed tears.

"Stop staring at me," Elizabeth said, and spun away. The quick movement caused her to gasp and clutch her side.

He moved toward her, but didn't touch her.

"I'm not going to faint or anything," she said, straightening. "I just wish you'd stop looking at me like I... Jeez, I don't know. I haven't committed a crime, okay? Isn't that enough for you?"

Anger radiated out from her, and that more than anything caused him to trust the feeling in his gut that said she told him the truth.

"I guess it has to be."

"I didn't ask to come here with you and I'll be happy to leave." She started for the door. "If Louise can't give me a lift back to the motel, then I'll call a cab."

He caught her in one stride and gently took her arm. "I don't want you to leave."

"I don't believe you." She pulled her arm free and glared up at him. "You keep staring at me as if I've just made off with the family silver. I haven't done anything wrong. None of this is my fault."

It was the fact that she didn't cry that finally convinced him. He could see the strength it took to hold on to her control. Her mouth quivered from the effort and perspiration dotted her forehead.

Maybe the guy had beaten her, he thought suddenly. Maybe her ex-boyfriend had been one of those sick types who got off on hitting women and children. He glanced at her bare arms, but there were no telltale marks. Of course she could have been on her own for several weeks.

Dammit, what the hell was her story?

She took another step and seemed to stumble. He caught her

up in his arms and carried her to the sofa. She clung to him for a moment. He ignored the way her curvy body felt against his chest, the long length of her legs and the soft pressure of her breasts against his shirt. When he set her on the sofa, she immediately tried to slide away. The movement caused her to clutch at her side and glare at him.

The anger in her gaze made him smile. Her temper he could handle.

"You're overreacting," he said mildly.

Her mouth dropped open. "*I'm* overreacting? Wait a minute. You're the one accusing of me of who knows what. Maybe it would be better if I just—"

"No." He settled next to her on the couch and touched her cheek with the back of his hand. She jerked her head away, but there was no fear in her eyes. Relief flooded him. If she'd been beaten on a regular basis, she would have been terrified. Instead she reacted with completely understandable indignation.

"Don't touch me, or try to sweet-talk me," she said. "You accused me of kidnapping my daughter."

"Given the little that you've told me, would you have thought any differently?"

"I—" She drew in a deep breath and brushed her hair out of her face. "I suppose not. But you didn't have to be such a cop about it."

"Just doing my job."

She nodded slowly. "I understand."

"So you're not going to make a run for it?"

"To the best of my knowledge I haven't committed a felony."

He winked. "Sometimes the misdemeanors can be even more interesting."

She smiled. "Oh, please. Don't get me started. I don't even want to know what you're talking about." Her smile faded. "I really haven't done anything wrong, Travis."

He hesitated and then said, "I know."

She held out her hand. "Friends?"

She wanted to shake on it. As Travis took her warm fingers

in his, he glanced at her full mouth and wondered if it would taste even sweeter if he kissed her without a six-year-old audience to censor the moment. Better to shake hands, he told himself. Safer. For both of them.

"Friends," he said and released her. Only then did he remember he still hadn't solved the mystery.

Elizabeth hobbled over to the table and gratefully sank into the seat. She was breathing heavily and all she'd done was assemble the ingredients to make cupcakes.

"From a mix," she said, disgusted with her weakened condition. She grabbed the package and ripped it open. The effort necessary to raise the box to dump it in the bowl made her incision ache.

She leaned back in the chair and took a deep breath. Thank God she wasn't trying to make it on her own in that small motel room. She and Mandy would have starved.

The line of thinking was a mistake, she acknowledged, as thinking of not being in the motel made her remember how she'd been rescued by the very handsome, the very inquisitive Sheriff Travis Haynes. Which made her think of this morning and what had happened between them.

He was not a man she wanted to cross. Despite the wicked charm and sinful good looks, he was intimidating when he was angry. All his questions had made her nervous, but he'd never once stumbled close to the truth. Of course, why should he? It wasn't the first thing anyone thought of. Things like that only happened in the tabloids. That's where she belonged. Right between the cover story on the aliens abducting the residents of a local pig farm and the woman giving birth to the four-legged child.

She felt guilty, too, knowing that Travis had given her the benefit of the doubt, trusting her when she hadn't told him the whole truth. She picked up an egg and held it. Was it so wrong not to want him to know? She *hadn't* done anything wrong, had committed no crime, save the one of being too young and too trusting. Okay, she'd been a fool. But was that illegal?

"Just what is it you think you're doing?"

Elizabeth jumped guiltily at the sound of the voice. Louise stood in the doorway to the kitchen. She planted her hands on her curvy hips and stared.

"I'm, ah, making cupcakes for Mandy."

Louise shook her head. "And you look like such a bright girl, too." She walked over and grabbed the egg from Elizabeth's hand. "The doctor told you to stay in bed for a week."

"I know, it's just—"

"A week is seven days. This is day two. If I have to tie you up, I will, but won't that be hard to explain to the neighbors?"

Elizabeth grinned and held up her hands in defeat. "I give. Just don't make me laugh. It hurts too much. If I promise to be good, can I at least sit here for a little while?"

Louise looked stern. "For a few minutes. Then I want you to go lie down until Mandy gets home."

"Yes, ma'am."

Louise took the seat next to her and finished pouring in the mix. "I remember when I was little my mama used to make cupcakes for me."

"Mandy loves them."

"So do I." The older woman smiled. "I haven't baked anything in ages. I wonder if Alfred would like some cake with his dinner." She thought for a minute. "No, he's still trying to lose weight." She leaned forward. "Alfred is a beagle and they tend to get a little heavy when they age."

Elizabeth hoped Louise was only kidding about making a cake for her dog, but she wasn't completely sure and she didn't want to ask.

Louise stirred in the other ingredients, then started pouring the batter into the cupcake pan. "So, I heard you and Travis fighting. You want to talk about it?"

"You aren't one to beat around the bush, are you?"

Louise shrugged. "I'm pretty straightforward," she admitted. "It would probably be easier if I'd just learn to keep my mouth shut. Maybe I'll get it eventually. But you seem like a real nice lady. Mandy is the sweetest little girl and I've found you can usually judge a mother by her children. Travis Haynes is one of my favorite people on earth. Why, if I was five or six years younger, I might just risk my heart on him." She paused, then shook her head. "On second thought, I'll leave the Haynes boys to the rest of you. I've already had my heart broken once by that family."

It was too much information to absorb, Elizabeth thought, not knowing whether to laugh, cry, be insulted or flattered.

"He's a good man," Louise said, carrying the full cupcake pans over to the oven and sliding them inside.

"Who?"

"Travis."

"I know that."

"He was just doing his job, asking all those questions, I mean." Louise poured herself a cup of coffee. When she held up the pot, Elizabeth shook her head. "Of course any woman would know you're that girl's mother through and through. She's got your smile. Her daddy must be some kind of looker."

"He is," Elizabeth said. Sam certainly was good-looking. Not nearly as handsome as Travis, but attractive enough to make any woman look twice. She'd been so caught up by his face and body, the charm and easy smile, she'd never thought to question anything except her good fortune. Imagine little Elizabeth Abbott catching someone like Sam. Only, she hadn't exactly caught him.

"So, you still mad at Travis?"

"No. I understand that he had questions." But she wasn't willing to give him all his answers. Still she couldn't blame him for asking. She'd expected him to wonder what her story was, but she hadn't expected him to come up with kidnapping!

"I'm glad." Louise sipped her coffee, then glanced at the clock over the stove. "Looks like it's time for me to leave. Travis and Mandy should be back in an hour or so. You're not going to get out of control and start vacuuming, are you?"

"I promise I'll behave."

Louise set down her cup. She picked up her purse from the counter, then crossed to the table, bent over and gave Elizabeth a hug. "I'm here if you want to talk," she said. "I might not have any answers, but I'm a great listener."

Elizabeth hugged her back. The other woman's perfume was a clingy Oriental scent that somehow suited her perfectly. Louise stepped back and waved, then left the kitchen. The back door banged shut behind her and the kitchen was silent.

Elizabeth stared around the empty room, wishing the digital clock would tick so there would be some sound. She was completely and totally alone. She wasn't afraid to be on her own. It was the questions that came to her, making her wonder if she'd made the right decisions for herself, and more importantly, for Mandy. Had she had other options and not realized it? Would she ever know how many clues she'd missed? She'd been worse than a fool.

The timer on the oven clicked down another minute. She thought about Louise who had offered to be a friend. Elizabeth knew that she needed to make some friends. She desperately needed someone to talk to and have fun with. Louise was a little offbeat, but that didn't matter. The reason Elizabeth couldn't reach out to her was because of herself, not because of the other woman. She couldn't dare be friends with anyone. She would always have to hold some part of herself back, be it from Louise or Travis.

Thank God he hadn't guessed the truth. She leaned back in the chair and sighed. Every time she thought she'd put it all behind her, something happened to remind her again.

She tried to think about nothing more complicated than whether or not she had the strength to frost the cupcakes. In the end, she decided she didn't and pulled the muffin pans from the oven and left them to cool. She lay down on her bed and closed her eyes, but she couldn't escape her past even there. So she tried thinking about other things. About the kiss.

Her eyes flew open. Not that. But now that she'd remembered it, she found it hard to forget the soft brush of his lips on hers yesterday. Today, when he'd sat next to her on the sofa and they'd shaken hands, for a moment she'd thought he might kiss her. Softly, tenderly, holding her close in those strong arms.

He carried her so easily, but that was an impersonal gesture made to aid an invalid. She wanted to be held close by a man who needed to hold a woman. She wanted to know if Travis could make her feel safe and secure in his embrace, if he could loan her a little of his strength and confidence. Foolish dreams. She hadn't answered all his questions. They both knew that. He might believe that she hadn't broken any laws, but she'd seen the look in his eyes. He was reserving judgment on her until he knew the truth. Imagine what he would think of her then.

The back door opened and she heard Mandy's laughter as she came into the kitchen.

"Mommy, Mommy, where are you?"

"In here," she called, sitting up slowly and leaning against the headboard.

Mandy flew into the room. She had several papers in one hand and her bear in the other.

"How was your first day of school?" Elizabeth asked, holding out her arms.

Her daughter scrambled onto the bed and threw herself into her embrace. Elizabeth held her close. Even the pain in her side didn't matter, she thought, as she stroked her daughter's hair.

Mandy leaned back and knelt on the bed. "I had fun."

"Did you?"

Mandy nodded. "Miss Brickman says we're going to learn to read."

Elizabeth touched Mandy's paint-smudged cheek. Her dress was wrinkled, her ribbons loose and coming undone, but there was a bright glow of happiness in her child's eyes that made her heart lighten. Maybe she had made the right decision after all.

"You already know how to read."

"I know." Mandy grinned. "She said she'd help me learn better. And we're going to do counting, too. Here." She thrust out her papers. "I did these."

Elizabeth looked at the drawing of what she was pretty sure was supposed to be this large house, a sheet with Mandy's name painstakingly spelled out in a childish scrawl, and a note from Miss Brickman outlining the homework schedule for the first half of the year.

"You're supposed to sign this one," Mandy said, pointing at the note from the teacher. "We're going to have homework, just like the big kids." She sounded delighted. Elizabeth wondered how long that would last.

"Someone's been busy."

She looked up and saw Travis standing in the doorway. He held a tray containing a plate with several chocolate cupcakes and two glasses of milk.

Mandy's blue eyes got big. "Mommy, you made cupcakes for me."

"I thought you weren't supposed to get out of bed," Travis said.

"Louise did all the work."

"Why don't I believe that?"

"Don't ask me, because she did."

"Sure." He put the tray down on her nightstand, then pulled Mandy off the bed. "Maybe you should change into play clothes before you get crumbs all over that dress. What do you think?"

Mandy looked at her mother, who nodded, then sighed. "Okay, but don't eat all the cupcakes before I get back."

"We won't," Elizabeth said and watched her daughter scamper out of the room. She glanced at the cupcakes and saw they'd been iced. "Thank you," she said. "I meant to get back to that, but I must have dozed off."

"Hey, I opened a can. How hard could it be?" He perched on the edge of the bed. "You're not overdoing it, are you?"

Exhaustion overwhelmed her with all the subtlety of being hit by a large truck. She tried to smile, but suddenly she was too tired. "Maybe just a little."

He leaned forward. For a second she thought he was going to kiss her. She found out she had just enough energy left to get excited by the thought, then was disappointed when all he did was lay his hand against her forehead.

"No fever," he said, "but you should stay in bed for the rest of the day. The last thing you need is to land yourself back in the hospital."

"I know." She picked at the bed cover, then looked at him. He'd shaved that morning, but the shadowy darkness of his beard highlighted his strong jaw. He had dark eyes framed by thick lashes. A firm mouth that was threatening to curve into a smile. Nothing in his expression reminded her of the questions he'd asked that morning. Yet that conversation sat in the room like a rather large intrusive elephant.

"I'm sorry," she said.

His expression hardened, and his mouth pulled into a straight line. "You don't have to apologize."

"I *want* to. You've been very kind to me."

"This is a full-service community."

She chuckled, then clutched her side. "Travis, don't make me laugh. It still hurts."

"Okay, I'll be serious."

He leaned closer, bracing one hand on the far side of her body. She wanted to reach up and pull him close. She settled on inhaling the scent of his body. He smelled like a fall day, with a hint of musk thrown in for temptation.

"Tell me your secret," he said softly.

When she'd first met Sam she'd thought she'd loved him with her whole heart and soul. He only had to look at her to make her want to be with him, next to him, touched by him. She'd learned later that her feelings for Sam Proctor were more about the newness of a physical relationship than anything else. But it had already been too late. She'd committed the ultimate foolish act and fallen in love with him.

Nothing about Sam's practiced charm had prepared her for Travis's lethal combination of strength and concern. It would be so easy to lean on those shoulders she admired, to tell him everything. But to what end? Once he knew the truth— She couldn't even bear to think about it.

"I can't." She met his gaze and held it.

"You won't."

"Yes. I won't. Please don't ask me again. I don't want to have to lie to you. I haven't done anything illegal. It's a silly little secret, but it's mine to keep. If telling you everything about my past is the price for staying, then I have to leave."

He studied her a long time. His gaze swept over her face, stopping at her mouth before dipping to her throat and returning. He reached up and touched her cheek, much as she'd touched Mandy's. But his caress was anything but maternal. Her stomach tightened and her breasts tingled in response.

Before she could say anything, or think about touching him back, he reached down for the comforter folded up at the foot of the bed. He pulled it over her and smoothed it in place. Then he leaned down and brushed his lips against her forehead.

"Go to sleep, darlin'," he said, and stood up.

She watched him leave the room and close the door quietly behind him. Her eyes burned with unshed tears. It would be so easy to let Travis into her world, she thought sadly. So easy to try to believe again. If she had the strength and the words, she would explain that it wasn't so much about him. Sure, she couldn't risk trusting a man again, but worse, she couldn't trust herself.

Chapter 6

"You're nervous," Travis said, taking off his Stetson and sending it across the family room. It landed neatly in the center of a writing desk on the left side of the window.

Elizabeth sank into the leather sofa and rolled her eyes. "Number one, if you keep doing that hat toss trick to impress me, I'm immune."

"Liar," he said as he crossed the room.

His khaki uniform, slightly wrinkled from his day at work, made his shoulders look broader and his legs longer. His wide black belt emphasized his trim waist. And yes, she had been lying. The nightly toss of the Stetson got her heart racing as if she'd just climbed three flights of stairs.

He settled on the sofa and grinned. "What's number two?"

"Number two is I have nothing to be nervous about."

"Double liar." He leaned closer, resting his weight on his elbow. His perfectly trimmed mustache outlined the teasing curve of his mouth. "I've made tougher women than you swoon with my cowboy hat, and while there's no reason to be nervous about having dinner with Rebecca, you are. I can see it in your eyes."

She opened her mouth to deny his statement, then closed it. He was right; she *was* nervous. "Okay, just a little."

He sat up straight, then leaned over and patted her bare leg. "Don't be. Rebecca's a sweetheart." He kept his warm hand on her knee. She told herself she should move away, but she liked it when he touched her.

She raised her eyebrows. "Do you realize that every time a female citizen of Glenwood is mentioned, you've dated her?"

"Only if they're between twenty-five and forty."

She reached behind her for one of the throw pillows and batted his hand away. "What's wrong with you?"

"I'm one of the Haynes boys. What else am I supposed to do?"

She'd been in Travis's house for six days. Louise had filled her head with enough stories to tell her what being a "Haynes boy" meant. "Settle down with one woman. Try monogamy for a change. There is something to be said for quality rather than quantity."

His good humor faded quickly. "I tried that, remember?"

"Oh." She did recall him mentioning a divorce. "Sorry." She was silent for a moment. "So what happened?"

He turned his head until he was looking at her. The lines around his eyes crinkled when he smiled. "You've been hanging around with Louise a little too much, don't you think? You could have been a bit more subtle with that question."

"Probably," she admitted shamelessly. "So what happened? Or don't you want to talk about it?"

"There's nothing to say. It just didn't work. I'm sure some of it was her fault, but I have to take most of the blame." He held his hands out in front of him, palms up. "It's a little difficult to get past who I am."

"So that's why you know Rebecca is a sweetheart?"

"Want to know a secret?"

She wasn't sure she did, but Travis was difficult enough to resist most of the time, and now, when he was rumpled and just tired enough to let his guard down, he was impossible to refuse. "Sure."

He slid closer to her. Her body tensed. Her incision had healed quite a bit, although it still hurt if she moved around too much. She wanted to pull back, but there was nowhere to go except off the sofa. Six days with Travis had taught her two important things. The first was that being in his presence made her very aware of her body, his body and the potential those two bodies had together. She told herself it was just hormones, and being lonely and afraid that brought on that thinking. The second thing she learned was that even if she was ever foolish enough to get involved with a man again. Travis Haynes was absolutely the worst one she could pick. He and his brothers had reputations for being lady-killers and heartbreakers. Louise had told her story after story about the female conquests made and cast aside. Elizabeth had to admit that in most of the stories, Travis had been honest, caring and had at least tried to make the relationship work. But the reality was he made Sam Proctor look like an amateur when it came to seducing women.

He leaned over so he could whisper in her ear. His chin rested on her shoulder, pushing aside the thin strap of her tank top. Stubble grazed her suddenly sensitized skin, making her muscles jump and her toes curl against the thick carpet.

"Rebecca is my greatest failure."

"What?"

She made the mistake of turning to look at him. He hadn't pulled back and their faces were inches apart. Breath mingled with the heady scent of his warm body. She clutched her fingers tightly together to prevent herself from reaching out toward him and touching his arm, his chest, anything she could get her hands on.

"Shortly after we met, I took her out on a date. It was supposed to be this great seduction. I had everything planned."

The pain in her midsection wasn't from the surgery, she realized, chagrined. It was envy, pure and simple. She prayed he couldn't see it in her eyes.

"I picked her up at seven-thirty. By eight-ten I figured out I'd made a large error in judgment."

"Which was?"

"Chemistry. It was all wrong."

She stared at him, at his dark eyes that suddenly seemed to be flickering with the most intriguing fire.

"What was wrong with it?" she asked, barely able to disconnect from the flames enough to follow the conversation.

"There wasn't any between us. Rebecca and me. We were destined to be good friends. But it's a secret. What would people say if they knew the truth? After all, the Haynes charm is supposed to be all-powerful."

It was working just fine on her, she thought as she lowered her gaze to his mouth. So close. She licked her lips. Three, maybe four inches separated them. The longing inside of her grew. She wanted to know what it would be like to be kissed, really kissed, by him.

She closed her eyes and forced herself to turn away. Why was she doing this to herself? Hadn't Sam taught her anything?

"Everybody needs friends, Travis. Rebecca seems very nice."

"Oh, she is."

He stood up and stretched like a powerful cat taking a moment's rest from stalking the mouse. That was *her* destiny: Elizabeth Abbott-rodent. She giggled.

"What's so funny?" he asked.

"Nothing. I'm pleased that you and Rebecca are friends. Now I get the chance to spend some time with her before I start my job." She smiled brightly, trying to banish the lingering lethargy and leftover passion, not to mention the image of herself with whiskers and a tail. "She's going to bring some paperwork by for me, to help fill the days." She pointed at the television. "I can only read so much, and TV is quickly losing its appeal."

"Just so you don't overdo it."

She gave him a mock salute. "Yes, Sheriff. I'll be careful. And I'll keep your secret."

"It's just as well it didn't work out," he said, walking over and picking up his Stetson. "I have two women in my life already. Even I couldn't handle a third."

"Two women?"

Her heart seemed to falter slightly. He was dating *two* women? She told herself the sudden dullness she felt was exhaustion. She'd probably done too much when she'd gone to the grocery store with Louise that morning. She could feel her smile fading and did her best to keep it in place. She didn't want Travis to know she was even slightly attracted to him. In fact she wasn't at all. He had two women. Good for him. She wished him well.

He paused by the doorway and looked back. "Although I have to say, of the two of you, Mandy is definitely my weakness. I guess it's those blue eyes of hers."

Elizabeth's mouth dropped open. She stared at him. The teasing glint in his eyes told her she'd been had.

She picked up the pillow beside her and tossed it at him.

He easily ducked out of the way. "Gotcha," he said and stepped into the hallway. Before she could finish fuming, he poked his head back into the room. His mouth straightened and those flames were still flickering in his dark eyes.

"For what it's worth, Elizabeth," he said slowly, never taking his gaze from hers, "the feeling is mutual."

With that, he left. She heard his footsteps as he walked down the hall, then made his way up the stairs.

Trouble. This was all very big trouble. She was willing to admit there was some kind of chemical reaction between her and Travis. Sometimes she worried that the heat between them was going to set the house on fire. But it didn't have to mean anything. It *couldn't* mean anything. She wasn't ready to get involved. She might never be ready for a real relationship. Even if she was willing to take a chance, it wouldn't be on Travis Haynes. The man was a walking, breathing heartbreaker. And she'd had enough heartbreak to last a lifetime. What woman would willingly give herself to someone who was destined to leave her for the next conquest?

She stood up and walked toward her room. Although she was healing, her side still gave her a little trouble. Travis had offered to move her to an upstairs bedroom so that she could be closer to Mandy, but she preferred to stay where she was. Her daughter was safe and happy in this big house, and Elizabeth wanted as much distance between her and Travis as possible. Just because she knew she would never get involved with Travis didn't mean she'd figured out a way to tell her body to get over its physical attraction to him.

She undressed then stepped under the warm spray of the shower. There was still over an hour until Rebecca was due to arrive, but everything took Elizabeth longer since the surgery. She was getting her strength back, but not as quickly as she'd hoped. The doctor hadn't been kidding about the recovery time needed. Her trip to the market with Louise had wiped her out for the entire day. She'd had to take a three-hour nap. But it had been worth it to get outside for the first time since the surgery.

As Elizabeth washed her hair, she wondered about Louise. The older woman had mentioned she was divorced. Elizabeth wanted to ask what had happened. For the most part Louise was funny and outgoing, but at the mention of her marriage, she'd gone all quiet. What made it all the more curious was her suspicion that Travis knew exactly what had happened. A couple of things Louise had said hinted at that. But Elizabeth wouldn't be asking anyone for the story. As much as she'd tried to hold herself back, knowing there were secrets she could never share, she and Louise were becoming friends. If Louise wanted her to know the truth, she would tell Elizabeth herself. If not…well, she certainly understood the need to keep some things private.

After drying off, she applied a little mascara and blush, then started blow-drying her hair. It still hurt to hold the dryer up for very long, so the process was slow. As she rested, she thought about Rebecca and hoped her new boss remembered to bring over some work for her to do. She would like to get a head start on her job so that when she went back full-time, she would know what was going on.

Elizabeth clicked the dryer back on and held it in one hand while fanning out her hair with the other. What must Rebecca think about her living arrangement? What must the whole town think? She was a virtual stranger, living with a single man, in his house. Was there talk? She shook her head and continued drying. Of course there was talk. She was living with Travis Haynes. One of *the* Haynes. A man with a reputation for women and trouble.

Elizabeth chuckled. That made Travis sound like a guy in a black leather jacket from some sixties B-movie. He certainly wasn't a troublemaker, although she wouldn't mind seeing him in a black leather jacket.

She put down the dryer and picked up a brush. The small bathroom was still steamy from her shower so her damp hair curled up toward her shoulders. She smoothed it with the brush, then slipped on a rose-and-green fabric-covered headband.

Despite his rather wicked reputation, she had to admit he wasn't at all what she'd thought he would be. Sam had left her alone so much, she'd practically raised Mandy on her own. She was used to making all the decisions and handling the responsibilities. She hated to admit it, but it felt kind of nice to have someone else making some of the choices. She even liked living with Travis. He was fun and easygoing. He made her laugh. Better than that, he helped her forget her past.

Her rose sundress had a sweetheart neckline and elastic ribbing in the back to hold it up. The skinny straps were more show than to secure the bodice. She pulled the dress down over her strapless bra and closed the side zipper. After slipping on a pair of high-heeled sandals, she stepped out into the hall.

She could hear a cartoon video playing in the family room. Mandy was excited at the thought of company at dinner, but even more thrilled that she was being allowed to watch her favorite show twice tonight. Elizabeth smiled. Life was certainly simple for a six-year-old.

She turned toward the kitchen to check on the dinner that Louise had made and left warming. A sound on the stairs caught her attention. She looked up and saw Travis.

He'd showered, as well. His hair was still damp, his face freshly shaved. She liked the clean look of his cheeks and jaw, but missed the darkening shadow of his afternoon stubble. He wore a long-sleeved white shirt rolled up to the elbows, and gray trousers. It wasn't all that different from jeans or his sheriff's uniform, but that didn't stop her heart from beating a little faster or her breath from catching in her throat.

She waited until he reached the first floor, then she looked him up and down. "Very nice," she said, struggling to keep her voice sounding normal. "Are you sure Mandy and I won't be in the way?"

"I told you, Rebecca is just a good friend."

"But it's Friday night. Shouldn't you be out on a date? You don't have to stay in to keep us company."

His dark eyes drifted over her face before dipping down to the bodice of her dress. She hadn't thought it was all that low-cut before, but she had the sudden urge to check to see exactly how much cleavage showed. His gaze left her feeling shivery and her knees threatening to buckle. Maybe the dress was a mistake.

"I didn't cancel a date to stay in with you, Elizabeth, so quit worrying about it. I want to spend time with you and Mandy, and I haven't had Rebecca over for a while."

He headed toward the front parlor. She followed, feeling that he was just being polite.

"But I don't want you to think that—"

He turned so quickly, she almost ran into him. As it was she stopped a scant inch from his tall, broad body and had to crane her neck back to see his face.

"I don't think anything," he said. His eyes darkened to the color of black velvet before brightening with a fire she didn't dare identify. "Except that you look very beautiful."

She blushed. Elizabeth wanted to put her hand on her cheek to make sure, but she knew the sensation of heat on her face could only mean one thing. "I— You—" She swallowed. "Thanks, but you don't have to say that. I mean, I'm just a paying guest here."

"Hardly that." He moved away to a stereo set on the floor in the corner. Wires disappeared into the walls. Louise had mentioned that he'd put speakers in the whole house. While he flipped through his CD's, she walked around the large empty room.

"This is going to be a beautiful place when it's finished," she said.

"I hope so. It's taking longer than I'd thought." He slipped a couple of CD's into the machine, then rotated the table to insert three more. "So what about you, Elizabeth? Why don't you have some guy from L.A. pounding down my door?"

"Me?" She laughed. "I haven't had a date in years." Seven years to be exact, she remembered. Her last date had been with Sam. That's when she'd told him she was pregnant with Mandy and had foolishly assumed they would do the right thing and get married. It was hard to believe her life had ever been that simple.

She touched the bare walls of the cavernous room, then looked up at the high ceiling. The basic structure of the house was lovely. Nothing like the cramped place she and Sam had rented. She'd wanted to buy a house, but he hadn't. She remembered the fights they'd had about that, and about having another child—she'd wanted four. That had changed, as well. She'd realized that with Sam gone so much, more children would be difficult. She'd practically lived as a single mother. She'd had such high hopes for the relationship, but the truth was it had been in trouble for the past two years. She'd been on the verge of leaving Sam when the police had arrived to take him away. What irony, she thought, stopping by the window and staring out into the night. She'd been wrestling with her commitment to Mandy's father, wondering if leaving was the right thing, or just the easiest solution to her unhappiness. She hadn't known that in a matter of days the question would be decided for her.

The soft sounds of classical music filled the room. Elizabeth turned and looked but she couldn't see the speakers. Travis stood up and brushed off his hands.

"Pretty impressive, huh?"

She nodded. "A regular seduction factory."

He grimaced. "Hardly. You might want to keep in mind that Louise does have a tendency to exaggerate things."

"Oh? You haven't seduced every female in a fifty-mile radius?"

He moved closer. "Nah. Now if she'd said a thirty-mile radius, that would be different."

"Oh, Travis, we are a pair, aren't we? You can't decide how many women you want, and I never want to get involved again."

"Is that why you haven't had a date in years?"

He asked the question so casually, she almost answered it. Almost. She nearly blurted out, "No, it's because I was married." But she caught herself in time.

"I was involved with Mandy's father. Call me a prude, but I've always believed in one relationship at a time."

"Me, too."

She stared at him in disbelief.

He put his hands on his hips. "Okay, what has she been telling you?"

"Nothing."

He raised his dark eyebrows. "She had to have said something for you to assume that I've never been committed to one woman at a time."

"Are you?"

"Yes. I believe in monogamy."

"For everybody, or do you exclude yourself?"

"Elizabeth!"

She shrugged. "I'm just asking. You have to admit you have this reputation in town. I heard it from the nurse, Louise—even Mandy mentioned something about it. You've dated her teacher, my boss. What am I supposed to think? That you're in training to be a monk?"

He grinned. The curve of his mouth and the flash of white teeth had her smiling in response. Realistically, she should be angry at him in the name of femalehood or something. But the truth was she liked Travis. Despite his obvious flaws, he was a good and kind man. At least he kept his socks picked up.

"I am involved with one woman at a time, Elizabeth Abbott."
His voice got lower and more seductive. She felt herself falling
under his spell and she couldn't summon the energy to care.
"That woman gets my complete attention, the total sum of my
energy and focus for as long as the relationship lasts."

His gaze never left hers. His hands stayed on his hips. So why
did she feel as if he were physically touching her all over? Her
skin grew heated, her fingers curled into her palms. How could
he do that with just a look and his voice?

"Oh."

With that he left the parlor and stepped into the hall. Before
she realized she'd been abandoned, he was back with a bouquet
of flowers.

"These are for you, darlin'," he said.

That woman gets my complete attention. She stared from the
flowers to him and back. No. He couldn't mean anything by
them, could he?

"Why?" she asked, almost afraid to hear his answer. What
if he wanted her? What if he didn't?

"It's been a week since your surgery. I thought you might be
feeling a little lost." He thrust the flowers at her and she was
forced to take them. "You can lose that panicked expression.
I'm not out to seduce you."

"You're not?" She wasn't sure if she was relieved or disappointed.

He shook his head. "Not while you're under my protection."

Which might mean she would have to watch herself when she
wasn't under his protection, or it might be a polite way of saying
he wasn't interested in her at all. Stop thinking about it, she
ordered herself. *She* was the one not interested, remember? She
was the one sworn to never get involved.

She lowered her head and sniffed the bouquet of flowers. The
colorful blooms smelled rich and sinful, not like those long-
stemmed roses Sam had often brought her after he'd been gone
for several weeks. She'd never had the heart to tell him she

didn't like those roses. They were so straight and scentless, almost mutated versions of natural flowers.

She touched the cheerful pink petal of a carnation. "Thank you." She turned toward him and smiled. "They're beautiful." He was close enough to touch. She reached out and placed her hand on his forearm. "This is probably going to make you cringe, but I think you're very nice."

The second to the last thing she expected was him to say, "I'm glad." The last thing she expected him to do was step closer and wrap his arms around her waist. She almost dropped the flowers before gripping them in her right hand. Emotionally she was too stunned to pull back; physically, she was too intrigued. Sam had been tall—maybe an inch or so taller than Travis—but Travis was powerful and strong. She could feel the muscles in his arms where they pressed against her side. She could see the strength in his shoulders.

And his eyes. She would like to stare into his brown eyes forever, warmed by the fire flickering there. Her gaze dropped to his mouth. He wasn't smiling. She was glad. She would have hated him to find this moment funny. She didn't think it was at all amusing. If anything, she was fighting the burning at the back of her eyes. She didn't know why she wanted to cry. Maybe it was because in his arms she felt safe and secure. She hadn't felt that way since she was a young girl, not much older than Mandy.

He pulled her close, until her thigh brushed against his and her breasts flattened against his chest. She reached up and placed her free hand on his shoulder. He was going to kiss her. For the first time since he touched her, she remembered she was supposed to be fighting this. Travis wasn't for her. But she needed him to kiss her. She needed to forget, even for just a moment. She sensed that once his lips touched hers, she wouldn't be able to think about anything else.

He didn't disappoint her. He breathed her name, then lowered his mouth to hers. Soft and hard and prickly and hot. She absorbed the sensations of his lips brushing back and forth on hers, the fire that flared between them. Her eyes drifted shut. Questions of right and wrong, her place in his house, Sam, her future and Mandy all faded, silenced by the powerful force of pleasure. He didn't assault her or press for more. He simply held her close and moved his mouth slowly, so slowly until she knew every millimeter of his lips.

She wrapped both her arms around his neck, carefully holding on to the flowers. But that was her only conscious thought. Everything else she simply felt. The hard chest flattening her breasts, the stroking of his hands up and down on her back, the shivers as his fingers grazed the bare skin by her shoulder. Her position pulled her incision, but not enough to matter.

He moved his head slightly so he could brush his lips against her jaw, then her ear. She arched her head back, liking the gentle caresses, the absence of pressure. Her blood flowed faster, hotter, fueled by the slow assault. His warm breath tickled, sending goose bumps rippling down to her toes.

He nibbled on her earlobe. She caught her breath, then whispered his name. With her free hand, she touched his still-damp hair, liking the way the smooth strands felt against her fingers.

He read her perfectly. When she grew impatient with his gentle teasing on her jaw and throat, he returned to her mouth. He didn't ask or hint, he simply opened his mouth on hers. As if she had no will, her lips parted to admit him.

Like his previous caresses, he moved slowly, tenderly, tracing her lips, touching the damp, sensitive inside, touching the edge of her teeth before stroking her tongue with his.

One small flicker was like the first faint flash of lightning. He moved against her again, touching, retreating, touching, circling, touching, tasting. The storm moved closer and closer. She felt the vibration of the thunder, the echoing of his heartbeat, matching the rapid cadence of her own. She saw the flash of light behind her closed eyelids.

Her body sought his, pressing harder to absorb his strength. Against her belly, she felt the hardness of his desire. Between her thighs an answering need flowered, leaving her warm and waiting. Her breasts tightened in anticipation. His hands moved lower, down her back, over the curve of her hip to cup her derriere in his large hands. He didn't pull her up against him; instead he squeezed gently, lovingly.

She reveled in the feel of being next to him. Every move was slow, not calculated as she might have thought, but savored. As if he had nothing more important in his life than this moment. As if he'd spent the whole day thinking about kissing her.

He wasn't as tall as Sam, but he was broader and she liked the way his size made her feel protected. Foolish needs, she thought, knowing that she was on her own. But for these few minutes it was enough to hold and be held, tempt and be tempted.

He sucked on her lower lip, the delicious sensations forcing all thoughts from her mind. He kissed her harder now, hungrily, the passion building between them. It was all she could do to stay upright and not sag completely against him. Her fingers had trouble holding on to the bouquet of flowers. His scent and warmth filled her body until she wanted him to be a part of her. He seemed to sense her need, moving even closer, tightening his arms around her as if he were as hungry for love as she.

Love. The word echoed in her brain, the cold reality of its meaning doused her passion and she pulled back. She wasn't hungry for love. She couldn't afford to be. Passion, maybe. Sex—well, it had been a while, so probably. But not love. Never love.

She stared at the open V of his white shirt and watched his chest rise and fall in a rapid cadence that matched her own. Not love. Never love. Love makes you blind. You can't trust it. Ever. She'd learned that lesson the hard way. She'd loved Sam with all her heart, and he had betrayed everything she'd held sacred and special. There had been a hundred clues, but she'd missed them all.

Travis was just like Sam. He was a womanizer, a smooth-talking charmer who made a hobby of breaking hearts. So what if he claimed to practice monogamy? That was part of the trappings of his disguise. She knew what he really was.

She realized they'd been standing there, breathing heavily for several seconds. She half expected him to say something, apologize. But he didn't.

The worst part of it was that her body still tingled from the power of their kisses. Her breasts ached, her thighs felt trembly and weak, and her blood hummed with a powerful need that even the most rational of arguments couldn't quench.

She swallowed thickly, then forced herself to look up at him. The fire in his eyes burned hotter than she'd ever seen it. His mouth was still damp from her passionate kisses. She wanted to look down but didn't dare. She couldn't bear to see the proof of his need. She would think about how he would feel next to her, inside of her. It had been over a year since she'd made love, but some chilling little voice at the back of her head whispered this wasn't all about simply doing without. It was more about the man in front of her than the need within her body, and that thought scared her to death.

"I'm sorry," she said, her voice shaking. "We shouldn't have done that. It's better if it doesn't get out of hand."

He smiled then, a slow, lazy, satisfied and very male smile. The skin on the back of her neck tingled and her breasts swelled painfully.

"What do you mean—'it'?" he asked.

"You know. Our relationship."

The smile turned into a grin. "I didn't know we had a relationship."

His amusement fueled her temper. "You're right," she snapped. "We don't have a relationship, and I would prefer to keep it that way." She turned and started to walk away.

He caught up with her instantly and touched her arm. She wanted to pull back, really she did, but she couldn't. It felt too good to have him touch her. A bright danger sign flashed before her eyes, but she had a bad feeling it was already too late.

"Don't be upset," he said, his thumb stroking her forearm.

"I'm not."

He arched his eyebrows. Yeah, well she'd never been a very good liar. So what else was new?

"It was just a kiss, Elizabeth."

She pulled free of his hand and continued walking down the hall. When she had turned the corner and was out of sight of the parlor, she raised the bouquet to her face and smelled the sweet flowers. Then she touched her free hand to her still-trembling lips. It had felt like a whole lot more than just a kiss to her.

Chapter 7

"And then there was the time the blood bank brought one of those mobile trucks. You know the kind. They stay for a few days and take donations." Rebecca paused long enough to finish setting the silverware, then looked up and laughed. "He dated both nurses."

"You're kidding?" Elizabeth asked. "Both. So much for monogamy, Travis," she called, glancing back at him over her shoulder.

"I *was* monogamous. The first one didn't work out, and her friend wanted to comfort me," he said from his seat on the floor at the edge of the big dining room. It was one of the few rooms he'd actually bothered to furnish. The rosewood table and hutch had once belonged to his mother. She'd left it behind, along with everything else when she'd left him and his brothers. Their father hadn't wanted the set. Both Jordan and Kyle lived in apartments. Craig had told him to take it because his three boys would destroy the beautiful pieces in a matter of days.

"Travis, it's your turn to move," Mandy said impatiently. "Hurry, 'cuz I'm winning."

"I'm hurrying," he told the little girl. He rolled the dice and counted out the squares with his marker. Mandy crowed when he landed on a chute that carried him almost to the bottom of the board. "Guess you're going to win, huh?"

She nodded vigorously, her blond braids bouncing on her shoulders. She grinned. "Mommy, I'm winning. Come see."

Elizabeth turned in her chair and looked down at the game. "Very good, sweetie." She gave him a quick glance. A tiny spot of color stained each cheek, but she didn't turn away.

Travis was glad. He'd barely had time to recover from his obvious and somewhat painful reaction to their kiss when Rebecca had arrived for dinner. So far he hadn't had the chance to make sure Elizabeth was all right. He told himself he hadn't meant to kiss her, but he knew he was lying. He'd been thinking about it ever since her first night here, when he'd briefly touched her lips with his. He'd wanted to know if the heat between them was real or imagined. The still-burning scars reminded him the heat was plenty real. Their kiss had only made him want more.

Which was, he acknowledged, an obvious problem. He didn't want to get involved with Elizabeth for several reasons. Not only was she a guest in his house, but he knew better than to risk it all with someone like her. She was the kind of woman who believed in commitment and forever. He didn't know how to do that. If he was honest with himself, he didn't have what other men had to make something special last. Four generations of failed relationships couldn't be argued with.

But the kiss had been tempting. He only wished he'd had a chance to ask Elizabeth if everything was okay. But Rebecca and Mandy were in the room. If that wasn't bad enough, his friend was taking perverse delight in telling Elizabeth a string of stories about his supposed conquests with women.

"What about that trick roper you dated?" Rebecca asked.

Elizabeth's eyes widened. "A trick roper. I don't think I want to hear about that one."

Travis shook his head. "That happened about six years ago. Long before you'd even heard of Glenwood," he said, turning to Rebecca. "You're repeating gossip."

"I know. Isn't it terrific?" She walked over and patted his

shoulder. "I love this guy. He is the ultimate male weapon against women. One look and they go weak in the knees."

He rolled the dice and moved three places. Mandy rolled and won the game. She laughed with delight, then leaned forward and gave him a big hug. He held her close. Funny how both Abbott women got to him. Elizabeth made him want dangerous things, while Mandy made him feel a fierce need to protect her. And a longing to be more. He would give his soul to be a decent father to some kid. She planted a wet kiss on his cheek. Deep in his chest, he felt a sharp stab of pain piercing his heart.

"You're the best, Travis," Mandy said.

"I rest my case." Rebecca headed for the kitchen.

Mandy scrambled off his lap and followed "Becca," as she called the other woman. He glanced up at Elizabeth still sitting in her seat watching him.

"I took each of the nurses out once," he said, wondering why he was defending himself. She wouldn't believe him. No one ever did. "I don't think I even kissed the second one good-night."

"Sure." She smiled.

"The trick roper was an old friend. I'd known her in college. You know people make up a lot of stories about me and my brothers. They think we get a lot more—" He hesitated, searching for a polite word.

"Action?" she offered helpfully.

"It wouldn't have been my choice."

God, she was beautiful. The skinny straps of her rose sundress showed off her tanned shoulders. The long line of her neck made him remember how she'd tasted when he'd kissed her there. Her mouth was perfect, pulling into a wide smile. It was her eyes that always got to him, though. There was a wariness in her expression that seemed out of place. Was it that Sam guy who had made her cautious? What had happened in her life? What was the big secret? Hell, a man could go crazy thinking about it.

He rose to his feet and took the chair next to hers. "A lot of people assume my brothers and I get a lot more action than we do. Part reputation, part circumstances.''

She tucked a loose strand of hair behind her small ear. ''Are you trying to make me feel sorry for you?''

''No, I'm trying to make sure we're still friends.''

''I would think you have so many women in your life that one more wouldn't matter.''

He leaned close to her, stopping only when their arms brushed. He was pleased that she didn't move away. ''I'm not talking about women in general. I'm talking about you. Friends?''

She glanced at the tablecloth. He couldn't see her expression, so he sweated it out. He hated that it mattered what she thought.

''I'm not a jerk, Elizabeth. I'm not what everybody says.''

''I know.'' She bit her lower lip. ''You're a nice guy.''

He winced.

''You are!''

''Great.''

''You want to shake on it again?''

He'd rather kiss on it, but hey, he would take what he could. Her hand felt small and delicate in his, but it was her smile that just about knocked him from his chair. She grinned up at him then leaned forward.

''So tell me the real story about the trick roper.''

They had barely sat down to dinner when the doorbell rang. Travis threw his napkin on the table. ''I'll get it,'' he said, rising to his feet.

He walked to the front door and pulled it open. He grinned. ''Austin, come in.''

Austin Lucas strolled into the hallway and paused. He sniffed the air. ''I smell dinner.''

''You hungry? Louise left plenty.''

His friend shrugged. ''I wouldn't say—''

''Travis, who is it?'' Rebecca called.

Austin raised his dark eyebrows. ''Sorry. I didn't know you had company.''

"It's not what you think." Travis grabbed his friend's arm and steered him toward the dining room. Austin let himself be pulled along, but Travis knew his heart wasn't in it. Austin didn't go out of his way to be sociable.

"Look who I found on the doorstep," he said. Elizabeth and Mandy both looked up expectantly. Rebecca rose to her feet and smiled, even though she couldn't see who was behind Travis. He stepped to one side and let Austin precede him into the room.

He raised his arm to Austin's shoulder, as much to show affection as to keep the other man from bolting. Austin didn't do crowds.

"Austin Lucas, this is Elizabeth Abbott and her daughter, Mandy. They're staying here while Elizabeth recovers from a bout with appendicitis. Next to my brothers, Austin is my oldest friend in Glenwood."

Elizabeth stood up and held out her hand. Travis watched her sharply, waiting for the inevitable reaction. She said hello and smiled at him, but that was it. Interesting, he thought.

"And you've already met Rebecca," he said.

Rebecca nodded several times. "The committee meeting on town support for the home. You were there." She paused. Her brown eyes widened. "I mean, everyone was there, weren't they? All the people in the town." She paused. "Not all of them, of course, but a good many. Not just you." Color flared on her cheeks. She smiled tightly. "Good to see you. Again. Here, that is." She reached for her water glass. Her fingers slipped and she knocked it over on the table. "Oh, no. I'll just—" She motioned helplessly toward the rapidly spreading pool of water. "I'll get a cloth."

"I'll help," Elizabeth said and followed her into the kitchen.

"What's gotten into her?" Travis asked no one in particular; then he glanced at his friend.

"Don't look at me. This is only the second time I've met the lady. She was a lot like this at the meeting, too. She must have dropped her pen a hundred times." He shrugged.

Elizabeth came back alone with a couple of dishcloths. She

mopped up the spill. Travis waited, but Rebecca never reappeared.

"Have a seat," Travis said.

Austin shook his head. "I just came by to tell you that I'll be here for the football game."

"Great. But really, there's plenty of food."

"You're having dinner with two beautiful women. I don't want to get in the way."

"You wouldn't be." Travis meant it. In the past several minutes, Elizabeth hadn't even given Austin a second glance. Good news because his friend's reputation with women rivaled that of any of the Haynes brothers. Austin topped Travis by at least three inches. He'd been described as handsome as the devil himself. Between his self-made fortune, his solitary ways and the gold hoop earring Travis and his brothers never tired of teasing him about, he drew women like a shell game drew suckers. So Elizabeth was somehow immune to the infamous Lucas charm. Too bad he couldn't say the same about Rebecca.

"Mister?"

Travis glanced down and saw Mandy was tugging on the sleeve of Austin's shirt.

"What?" Austin asked.

"I'm beautiful, too. Mommy said so."

Austin drew back his head and laughed. "You're right, Mandy. You are very beautiful. I'm sorry I didn't include you."

The little girl dimpled, obviously charmed.

"Tell me, Mr. Lucas, how long have you lived in Glenwood?" Elizabeth asked.

Austin looked at her. "It's Austin, and I've lived here since junior high school."

She folded her arms over her chest. The action pushed her full breasts up slightly. Travis remembered the feel of them against his chest. His mouth grew dry.

She smiled slowly. With her long hair curling over her almost-bare shoulders and the rose-colored dress outlining her feminine curves, he knew he didn't have the power to resist what she offered. Fortunately for him, she wasn't doing any offering. The last thing he wanted to do was hurt Elizabeth.

"I was wondering. I've heard all these stories about Travis and his women. Are the stories true?"

Austin glanced at him. Devilment twinkled in his pale gray eyes. "Every word, ma'am. Gospel."

Travis jerked his thumb toward the door. "Get out of here, you traitor." He followed Austin down the hall toward the front door, all the while accompanied by the sound of Elizabeth's laughter.

"I'll get you for this," he said as Austin got into his car.

"I'm scared." Austin gave him a salute. "Enjoy the ladies." He pulled his car door shut and started the engine.

When Travis returned to the dining room, Rebecca had come out of the kitchen.

"Oh, is he gone?" she asked, twisting her hands together. "I hate it when that happens."

Elizabeth glanced at the other woman. "What exactly happened?"

Rebecca sank into her chair and buried her face in her hands. "I can't be around that man without turning into a klutz. I have a master's degree, I got good grades in school. I run the entire child services department for the county." She looked up at Travis. "I do a good job, don't I?"

"The best." He had to fight back a grin.

"Don't you dare laugh, Travis," she said. "I'm a pathetic creature. Every time I'm around that man, I fall apart. I drop things." She grimaced at the tablecloth. "Or spill them. I can't finish my sentences. I've only met him three times, but it's getting worse." She sighed. "Maybe I should move."

Elizabeth giggled. Rebecca turned toward her. "This is not funny."

"I'm sorry." Elizabeth bit her lower lip, then burst out laughing. "You have a crush on him."

"I know. It's awful."

Travis reached over and rested his hand on Rebecca's shoulder. "Be careful, kid. Austin has broken more hearts than my brothers and I put together. He's not into relationships except for the convenient kind."

She looked up at him and smiled. She was dressed in a floral print dress that floated around her body. The garment was loose enough not to even hint at curves below. With her long hair, minimal makeup and flat shoes, she looked like everyone's stereotypical idea of a librarian. Or a Sunday school teacher. The innocence lurking in her gaze had been one of the reasons nothing had happened between them. He didn't want that on his already-full conscience.

"I know that," Rebecca said. "There's just something about him."

"He's dangerous."

"Yeah, kinda like you."

He and Rebecca sat on the front porch swing while Elizabeth put Mandy to bed. He could hear the sounds of Mandy's laughter floating out of the upstairs window. He liked the domesticity of their arrangement. If he couldn't have the real thing, this was a damn close second best.

"Elizabeth seems very nice," Rebecca said, pushing off the porch with her foot and causing the swing to rock.

"Uh-huh."

"That's what I like best about our friendship," she said, poking him in the side. "Your articulate statements."

He didn't bother responding. Rebecca had something to say, but he wasn't going to make it any easier for her.

"You're a fool if you let her get away."

He didn't answer.

"I know you probably think it's too soon to know if she's the one or not, but you two look right together. She's bright, funny, great with her daughter and—"

"Shut up." He softened the words by resting his arm on the back of Rebecca's shoulders and pulled her next to him.

"But—"

"No, Rebecca. I can't do this. I'm not a fool if I let her go,

I'm a fool if I try again. You're right. Elizabeth is great. Mandy's irresistible, but so what? I come from a long line of failures in the relationship department. None of my uncles, or my brothers have been able to make it work. Neither could I.''

"Maybe Julie wasn't the right one for you.''

"Maybe I should quit trying to be something I'm not.''

She looked up at him. The porch light illuminated her pale skin and the concern in her eyes. She was as slender and fragile as a porcelain figurine, and just as beautiful. He'd held her close, even kissed her once. And felt nothing. Damn. Why did Elizabeth Abbott have to be the one to make him crazy? It would have been easier to try again with Rebecca. He told himself it was because they were friends, but he knew better. It would have been easier with Rebecca because with her he didn't have as much to lose.

"You don't have to be like them,'' she said, snuggling closer. There was a slight chill in the air. He welcomed the decrease in temperature. Maybe it would cool his desire. "You're your own person. Blaze a new path. Start a new tradition in the Haynes dynasty.''

"If it looks like a duck and walks like a duck and sounds like a duck, it's probably a duck. No point in trying to be something else.''

She grinned. "What are you saying?''

He chuckled. "That I'm a duck.''

"Well, go ahead and be one if it makes you happy.''

The trouble was it didn't make him one bit happy. He wanted more. That was the hell of it. He couldn't be like his father, going from woman to woman. None of his brothers were. They all wanted to make a relationship work and settle down with one woman. Like them, he wanted to get married, have a herd of children and wake up in the same bed for the next fifty years. What right did he have to try for something that was doomed to failure?

"But maybe Julie *wasn't* the one for you.''

"She was the perfect wife. A guy couldn't ask for more.''

''Maybe you didn't love her.''

Interesting thought. He was beginning to think he didn't know what love was.

''Travis!''

He stood up when he heard Elizabeth call his name. ''Be right back.''

Rebecca rose and stretched. ''I'll come with you. I want to say good-night to Elizabeth and then leave. I have a lot of work tomorrow.''

She stood on her tiptoes and kissed his cheek. He waited, hoping for some reaction. Some hint of desire. Nothing. Not even the tiniest spark. She could have been his sister.

''Hang in there,'' she said.

''I will.'' He opened the front door for her to go in first.

Elizabeth watched Rebecca and Travis enter the hallway. They looked good together. Both tall and attractive. Rebecca said something, and Travis laughed. How easily they spent time together. Elizabeth fought down a feeling of envy. After the first year it had never been easy with Sam. He'd been charming, of course, but he'd never let her inside and never shared his feelings. Now, of course, she knew why. But then she'd always wondered what was wrong with her. Why wasn't she enough to keep her man happy?

Travis looked up at her.

''Mandy wants to say good-night to you,'' she said.

''Sure.'' He climbed the stairs two at a time and went into Mandy's room. Rebecca followed more slowly.

Elizabeth wanted to ask what they'd been talking about outside. She'd heard the creak of the swing. It had been an intimate sound. Elizabeth told herself she wasn't jealous. Why should she be? She wasn't interested in Travis. At least not romantically. She resisted the impulse to touch her nose to see if it was growing.

Tonight she was going to have to have a long talk with herself. She couldn't afford to get involved with anyone, and certainly not him. He would sweep her up in passion, muddle her thinking, pleasure her body and then leave her for the next one on the list. Which almost made it easier. If Travis wasn't such a flirt, she would have a more difficult decision. She would have to face trusting her judgment about a man. She shook her head. Never again. She was done making those kinds of mistakes.

Rebecca reached the landing. "I'm glad we got to spend some time together."

"Thanks for bringing me the work. I'll get started on it in the morning."

"Oh, please take your time." Rebecca frowned. "I don't want to be responsible for you not getting better. You don't have to do any of it if you don't feel up to it." Her frown turned into a smile. "Heaven knows the paperwork has waited for months now. A couple more weeks isn't going to matter."

"I'm desperate for something to do during the day. Between Louise and Travis, I barely have to move around at all. I'm looking forward to getting back to work."

"Your desk is waiting for you." Rebecca nodded toward Mandy's room. "Now you take care of yourself and that hunk in there. He needs some looking after."

Elizabeth rolled her eyes. "After all the stories I've heard, looking after is the one thing he doesn't need more of."

Rebecca sobered. "Maybe I shouldn't have passed on all those stories about Travis. He really is a nice man. Don't judge him too harshly."

"I don't judge him at all. He's been great to me and Mandy, but he's not my type."

"Too bad. He's not mine, either." Rebecca stared off in the distance for a moment. "There must be someone brave enough to take on this particular Haynes boy. I haven't known Travis for all that long, but I know him well enough to know it would be worth the trouble." She touched Elizabeth's forearm briefly. "Get better, but don't push yourself. The piles of paper aren't going anywhere. Good night."

She started down the stairs. Elizabeth moved to follow her but Rebecca stopped her with a raised hand.

"I'll find my own way out. You'd just have to climb the stairs again to tuck in your daughter. I'll talk to you soon."

"By."

Elizabeth watched as her boss left. When the front door closed, she stared at it for several minutes. Rebecca was great. She was looking forward to working for her. It would be nice to have some new friends in her life. Except—

She shook her head and turned toward Mandy's room. Except for the secrets she had to keep. They made it hard to open up. There was always a barrier between herself and anyone she wanted in her life. She knew she should put it behind her, but she couldn't. What would Louise and Rebecca think if they knew the truth? Worse, what would Travis think? She didn't want to even imagine that moment. He would know what a fool she'd been. He would blame her, as she blamed herself, for not figuring it out, for not getting the clues. There must have been hundreds.

Stop thinking about it, she told herself. But it was hard to forget what was keeping her from the life she really wanted. Tonight's dinner had reminded her how much she liked having people in her life. Being with everyone had taunted her with the vision of what she'd once imagined her life with Sam to be like. She'd thought they would be a family together; she'd been wrong.

Brushing aside the unpleasant thoughts, she moved toward Mandy's room. As she entered the room she saw Travis sitting on the edge of the bed holding Mandy in his arms. They both had their backs to her.

"Sometimes I miss my daddy," Mandy said.

"I know, honey," Travis answered.

Elizabeth felt as if someone had stabbed her in the heart. Mandy had adjusted so well to all the changes that sometimes she allowed herself to forget how this must be upsetting her daughter. Of course she missed her father.

She wanted to go to Mandy and comfort her, but Travis seemed to be doing a fine job. Besides, it was her fault the girl didn't have a father anymore. She'd been the one to demand Sam sign custody of their child over to her. She clutched the door frame. Sam hadn't given her any trouble. He'd signed the papers, then passed them to her. His blue eyes had spoken his silent apology as the prison guards had led him away. That quiet apology hadn't been enough.

Elizabeth knew this was hard on Mandy, but it was better this way. Sam had never really loved either of them. She'd finally figured out it had all been a game to him.

"How come your hugs make me feel better?" Mandy asked, settling back on her bed.

"They're magic hugs." Travis bent over and kissed her cheek. When he straightened, he saw Elizabeth standing just inside the room. "Hi. We were discussing her father."

"I heard," she said. Elizabeth addressed Mandy. "Were you feeling sad?"

"A little." Her little girl looked up at her with Sam's eyes. "Travis gave me a magic hug and I'm better now."

"Aren't you lucky." Elizabeth picked up her stuffed teddy and placed him next to her. "Are you ready to go to sleep?"

Mandy nodded.

"I love you, sweetie."

"I love you, too, Mommy."

Elizabeth fussed with the covers for as long as she could, knowing she didn't want to turn around and face Travis. What must he be thinking about her? Every time they came to some kind of agreement, something was there to remind him about the mysteries in her life. She knew he was curious. She just prayed he would stop asking her questions she couldn't answer.

Travis was waiting for her in the hallway. Without saying a word, he placed his hand on the small of her back and led her down the stairs. When they reached the foyer she was about to say good-night, but he opened the front door.

"Come outside," he said. "It's a beautiful night."

She hesitated. It would be better for both of them if she went to her room—alone. The two of them sitting in the dark could get into a lot of trouble. Their kiss this afternoon had proved that, and it had still been daylight. But the cool night beckoned. She was tired from her long day, but not in pain.

"I won't bite," he promised.

How could she resist him? "If you're sure," she said, and stepped out onto the porch.

The light beside the front door cast a soft glow down the steps. The swing was to her left, but she felt that would be tempting fate too much, so she sat on the top step and pulled her full skirt over her knees to her ankles. Travis settled next to her. The night air was full of sounds: crickets, the soft buzz of invisible flying wings, the hoot-hoot of an owl. She inhaled the smells. Damp earth from a brief afternoon shower, the last lingering sweetness of the roses by the porch rail and the hint of woodsmoke from some faraway fireplace.

A quarter moon hung just above the horizon. This was a different sky than she was used to. The lights of Los Angeles washed out most of the stars, but up here she could see the twinkling lights of the constellations.

Travis sat close enough for them to touch. Shoulder to thigh. She should probably pull away, but he was warm and familiar, her only anchor in her new world.

"You want to talk about Mandy's father?" he asked. He'd lowered his voice, but it still sounded loud in the quiet evening. "I assume you heard what she said."

"Most of it." She folded her arms on top of her knees and rested her chin on them. "I can't."

"How about your father?"

"What?"

She glanced sideways at him. He smiled at her. In the soft light, he looked like a chiseled statue. His hair and mustache were the color of midnight, his skin a polished bronze. If it wasn't for the warmth of his arm brushing her and the heat seeping through her dress from hip and thigh, she would have wondered if he was real. She'd escaped her past and had somehow stumbled upon this man. Was fate being kind or playing the most horrible joke on her?

"I'm changing the subject. Tell me about your family. Did you grow up in L.A.?"

"In the area. Near San Bernardino. A small town, a lot like this one. Then I went to the big bad city to go to college."

"And you're the only child."

"Yes. Mom was in her late thirties when I was born, and that was a lot less popular then. I was lonely growing up. I'd always planned on having three or four kids of my own to make up for it, but it didn't turn out that way."

"You could have them now."

"I'm not sure. Being a single mom is hard. I'm not getting married." *Again.* She almost said it, but at the last minute held back the word. Still it hung in the night like a winged creature before taking flight and disappearing into the silence. She cleared her throat. "What about you?"

Either he didn't notice that now she was the one changing the subject, or he was too kind to comment. She had a feeling it was the latter.

"Four boys, an assortment of uncles dropping by to visit. It was noisy." He shrugged. She felt the rise and fall of his shirt as it brushed against her skin. It was nice. "My dad was sheriff of Glenwood for about twenty-five years."

"Did you work for him?"

"Yeah." He chuckled. "For about a minute. He took an early retirement, but there was a month there when I was his newest deputy." He paused. When he spoke again, his voice was different. "He rode me hard."

"Did it make you angry?"

He turned to look at her. "Why do you ask?"

"You sounded…" She trailed off. "Bitter, I guess."

"Maybe I am. Not about the work, that was fine. Dad and his brothers were the original good ol' boys. They lived hard, drank hard, played hard. By the time I was ten, three of my four uncles were divorced. The fourth one, Bob, never bothered getting married. I knew my dad had a bunch of girlfriends, not to mention a mistress he kept in the next town.'' He drew in a deep breath. ''This is the seedy side of the Haynes family legend. Sorry. You don't want to hear this.''

She felt bad that he'd gone through that, but part of her was grateful to have something to focus on other than her own problems. She shifted until she was facing him. Her knees bumped his thighs. He leaned forward, resting his elbows on his knees and letting his hands hang loose.

''People in town think it was all good times and parties at our house,'' he said at last. ''It wasn't. My folks fought a lot. You can imagine what my mom thought of my dad's activities.'' His mouth twisted into a grim smile. ''He was so damn proud of himself. He had four sons and, no matter what else he did, he woke up every morning in his own bed. What a saint.'' He drew in a breath. ''She split when Kyle was fifteen. Packed her bags and left. Not a word, or a note. We thought about looking for her, but we figured if she wanted to stay in touch, she knew where to find us.''

''How old were you?''

''Twenty-one. It didn't really bother me. I'd just finished college and was about to find my own place anyway, but it hit Kyle hard. Jordan, too, but he wouldn't show it.''

Elizabeth's heart squeezed painfully. Jordan wasn't the only one who didn't want to show his pain. Travis might have been older, but she had a feeling his mother's abandonment had hurt him just as much. She was torn. Part of her couldn't blame the woman for walking out on Travis's father, but she didn't understand how a mother could abandon her sons.

''So you decided to punish all women for what she'd done?'' she asked.

''No. It's not like that. None of us are angry at women. Nobody has figured out how to make it work.'' He turned his head and looked at her. She saw the sadness in his eyes. Instinctively she reached out and rested her hand on his forearm. He didn't acknowledge the comfort, but she didn't mind. He felt warm and strong, even with all his pain. She liked to think she was giving a little back.

"Craig got married right out of college. Had three boys. But he couldn't make it work. I tried with Julie. You know what happened there. I come from a long line of ducks."

"What?"

"If it looks like a duck and walks like a— Never mind. We talked about it, my brothers and I. Watching our dad and the uncles fool around convinced us that we were all going to be faithful to the women in our lives. Wishing isn't enough, is it? Monogamy doesn't guarantee success. There's something else we all just don't get."

He stared into the night. Their backgrounds were so different, she thought. Yet here they sat together, facing their personal demons. She was glad that she and Travis could be friends. They needed each other.

"So you stay single forever?" she asked.

"There doesn't seem to be a choice."

"What about children?"

He turned on the step, shifting so his back pressed against the railing. He parted his thighs and rested his right foot on the porch, bending his knee. His other foot balanced on the bottom step. Her calves brushed against his inner thigh. It was a very intimate position. Her gaze seemed drawn to his chest, drifting lower to his trousers. She looked away before she reached dangerous territory, but their new positions made her hyperaware of his heat and scent. She clutched her arms to her chest.

"I'd like a family," he said, seemingly unaware of what he was doing to her. "But it's not in the cards for me."

"Too bad. You're wonderful with Mandy."

He brushed off her compliment with a flick of his wrist. "Speaking of Mandy, I've been thinking. There's a soccer league for the younger kids. It gives them something to do during football season. The teams are coed, but they match them up by size and skill. Sign-ups are tomorrow. I thought I could take her to the park. What do you think?"

"I think you're a sheep in wolf's clothing, Travis Haynes. All this tough talk, but underneath, you're a sweetie."

His slow, sexy grin chased the last of the shadows from his eyes. "Tell anyone, and you're dead meat."

"Tough guy, you don't scare me. Soccer will be great for Mandy. Thanks for offering to take her."

"No problem. I know the coaches. She'll have fun and make lots of friends."

She leaned forward. "Travis, you're wonderful with kids. This is a perfect example. You shouldn't dismiss that."

"The truth is, I'm a sprinter. It's easy to play daddy for a couple of hours, but it makes a big difference when the kids are yours. I know. I've seen Craig struggling."

"You keep saying that you don't have what it takes, but from everything I've seen, all the parts are in working order."

He raised his dark eyebrows. Instantly her gaze dropped to his crotch and she remembered the feel of his hardness pressing against her. She blushed and looked away. "You know what I meant."

"I prefer *my* interpretation of what you said."

She sank back against the railing. "I think it's time for me to say good-night."

"Not so fast."

He stood on the bottom step and loomed over her. His head moved lower, blocking out the night stars. His hands touched her almost-bare shoulders, making her instantly tremble. But at the last minute, she turned her face away. His mouth grazed her cheek.

"Elizabeth?"

"I can't," she whispered. She risked looking up at him. Confusion filled his brown eyes, fighting the fire there and slowly putting it out. She couldn't. For a thousand sensible reasons that all boiled down to being afraid of making the same mistake again.

If only she'd met Travis seven years ago. If only he'd been the one to steal her heart and seduce her body. But it hadn't been Travis, it had been Sam. Maybe if Sam had beat her or cheated on her, it would have been easier to get over what happened. But how was she supposed to recover from being a fool? How was she supposed to forget the lies?

Travis stepped back and held out his hand to help her up. She ignored him and rose. A pain jabbed her side as her movements pulled the incision.

"I'm sorry," she said, looking over his left shoulder. "I can't do this. I'm not what you think I am." She smiled sadly, knowing she either had to smile or cry. Already her eyes were burning. She prayed she made it to her room before she gave way.

"So it all comes back to that damn mystery," he growled. "What is so terrible?"

"Don't ask me, please. I really appreciate everything you've done. I'm very grateful."

"I don't want your gratitude."

She blinked several times, but it didn't help. One tear rolled free. She brushed it off her cheek. "It's all I have to give you, Travis. There's nothing else. Please believe me. I'm not who you think I am."

Chapter 8

The coach blew his whistle, but none of the kids on the field paid any attention. They continued to chase the white soccer ball, screaming with excitement in the frenzy of being the first one to actually kick the ball. When the ball made a sudden left turn, Mandy was right there. She stared down at it, her expression a mixture of confusion and delight; then she kicked for all she was worth. The ball sailed into the air and landed out of bounds. Travis stood up and cheered. The coach wearily shook his head and continued to blow the whistle. Finally the dozen or so six- and seven-year-olds quieted down to listen.

For the fifth time, the coach explained the rules of the game. Each of the children nodded earnestly, then scattered in an effort to find and kick the ball. Travis chuckled. Mandy was right in the middle of the pack. With her bright red shorts and T-shirt she was easy to spot. Her blond ponytail swung with each step.

"The kid's a natural athlete," he said.

"You sound like a proud papa."

He shifted on the bleachers set up on the side of the field and turned around. A sultry brunette with legs that stretched from here to forever smiled down at him. Her cropped T-shirt and microscopic shorts left little to the imagination.

"Unless you've been hiding something, Travis, she couldn't possibly be yours."

"No, Amber. She's the daughter of a friend of mine. I brought her to the practice. I'm surprised to see you here."

"Jimmy's playing." She motioned to the field. A short dark-haired boy ran tenaciously after the ball. "You know how Karl is about sports."

He did know. Karl was one of his deputies. A former college football hero, Karl had hoped for a career in the pros. He had the heart but lacked speed. Amber had married him before the 49ers released him from his contract. Rumor had it she wasn't happy about being cheated out of her role as the professional football player's wife. Travis couldn't confirm the rumors, but the last two times he'd stopped Amber for speeding, she'd offered to pay her ticket with something other than cash. He'd refused. Even if Karl hadn't been his subordinate and a friend, Travis didn't dally with married women.

"My husband's working today," she said, moving down closer to where he was sitting. "But then you know that, don't you? Are you going to be at all the practices? They take a couple of hours, don't they?" She moved closer and smiled. "Maybe we could get a cup of coffee, or something."

It was the "something" that had him worried. "Thanks, but I don't think so, Amber. I'd rather stay with the kids."

Her perfect features twisted into a snarl. "I always knew your reputation was a lot of hype, Travis. Figures there'd be nothing hot in this crappy little town." She jumped off the bleachers and stalked away.

It was starting to make sense, he thought, remembering how distracted Karl had been lately. Amber must be making his life hell. He grimaced. Looks like the Haynes boys weren't the only ones who couldn't keep their marriages together.

He returned his attention to the field. The coach was trying to set up drills for the kids. It wasn't working. Travis thought about volunteering his services, but he was already committed to a pint-size football team. In a couple of weeks the practices would overlap.

Mandy continued to run back and forth, laughing as she tried to kick the ball. Her smile made him think of her mother.

Life wasn't fair. Amber was ready to get involved in an affair. She would understand it for what it was and not expect more of him. He hadn't had a woman in months, so he should have been tempted. But Amber didn't do a thing for him. Not to mention the fact that she was married. He shrugged. He had a bad feeling that even if Amber had been single, he wouldn't have been interested.

Elizabeth, on the other hand, could turn him on in a heartbeat. She was single but not available, and certainly not the type a man played around with. If it wasn't for that damned feeling he got when he was around her—the sense of belonging—he could put her out of his mind.

But instead of trying to not think about her, he recalled their kiss. Hot and perfect. She'd gone all soft in his arms, holding on, kissing him back. His chest still burned where her breasts had pressed against him. She'd tasted sweet and ready. God knows he'd been ready. Even thinking about it made his jeans uncomfortable. He shifted on the bench and glanced at the kids still playing. Think about something else, Haynes, he told himself.

I'm not who you think I am. Her words haunted him. What could they mean? She said she wasn't married, and he didn't think she was a liar. So what was it? Damn. He should have made her tell him. Barring that, he should have kissed her again, kissed her until neither of them cared about her mystery, or anything but the feelings they generated when they were together.

A white sheriff's car pulled up, distracting him. He stood and stretched, then walked over to the vehicle. Kyle stepped out and walked around the car.

''What's up?'' Travis asked.

Kyle shook his head. ''Nothing's up. I called the house and

Elizabeth said you were here." Kyle grinned. "Is she as pretty
as she sounds?"

"What happened to Lisa?"

Kyle leaned against the car and folded his arms over his chest.
"We broke up."

"You dumped her."

"Yeah. I guess."

Travis studied his twenty-eight-year-old brother. He'd been
the one hardest hit by their mother's leaving. He was six-two,
lean, with the Haynes dark hair, eyes and good looks. Girls,
women and old ladies loved him. He dumped them all before
they could dump him.

"What happened this time?" Travis asked.

"You know, same old thing. She wasn't right. So tell me
about Elizabeth. I heard from Louise that she's really pretty. And
about my age."

"Don't even think about it," Travis growled.

Kyle grinned. "Jealous, old man? That's a first."

"I'm not jealous. Elizabeth is going through some things right
now and she doesn't need to get involved with a Romeo like
you."

Kyle leaned forward and mockingly punched him in the stomach. Travis feinted right and shot back a jab of his own.

"You've got it bad, big brother. The lady has you hog-tied
with *luvvvv*."

"It's been less than two weeks. We're just...friends."

Kyle dropped his arms to his side. "Sell it somewhere else. I
recognize the signs. You'll be parking your slippers under her
bed by the end of the month."

Travis shoved his hands into his jeans front pockets. "It's not
what you think, Kyle. I like her." How long had it been since
he'd admitted that to himself or anyone else?

Kyle's good humor faded. His mouth pulled straight and his
eyes darkened with sadness. "I guess that means you're going
to stay away from her, huh?"

"I don't have much choice."

"The Haynes curse." Kyle turned and braced his forearms on the top of the marked sedan. "We're all pretty bright. You'd think we'd have figured out a way to break the thing."

"You keep trying."

"Not anymore. I'm giving up on women."

"That'll last about a minute." He looked out at the field and watched Mandy play. She saw him and waved then went back to her game. "We make a sorry group, Kyle."

"That we do. And we're contagious. Austin was probably normal before we got ahold of him."

Travis shook his head. "I don't think so. Austin had trouble before he ever got to Glenwood. Maybe the five of us should start a twelve-step program. Hi, my name is Travis, and I don't know how to make a relationship work."

Kyle pushed off the car and stepped into the street. "Let me know if it helps. Are we on for the game this Sunday?"

Kyle, Austin and whichever of his other two brothers were around usually came over to watch football in the fall. He'd canceled last week because of Elizabeth.

"Sure. She's feeling better."

"So I will get to meet her." Kyle's smile didn't reach his eyes.

"Yeah, but watch yourself."

"I will."

Travis watched his brother open his car door. Before he stepped inside, Travis called, "Wait a minute." He walked around the hood of the vehicle and hesitated. "Can you run a name for me?"

"Sure. Who?"

He shouldn't do this. If Elizabeth found out, she would be furious. Worse, she would be hurt. She'd *said* she hadn't done anything illegal, but what if she'd been lying? He didn't want to think that of her, but there was obviously something she wasn't telling him.

He pulled a pad of paper out of his back pocket and borrowed

Kyle's pen. He vacillated another second, then wrote the name
"Sam Proctor" down and handed Kyle the sheet.

"Call me if you find anything. And keep it under your hat."

Kyle studied the name. "No problem. See you Sunday."

Travis watched the car pull away from the curb. What would
Elizabeth think when she'd found out what he'd done? What
would *he* think if he learned her secret?

Mandy licked her ice-cream cone frantically, but the drips
were faster. "Travis, help," she called, holding out her hand.

He grabbed two napkins and wiped her clean. By the time he
was done with that hand, the other one was a mess.

"You've got to learn to eat them quicker, honey."

Mandy giggled. She had several grass stains on her shirt and
shorts from the soccer practice. There was a smudge of dirt on
her cheek and chocolate ice cream on her chin. She was adorable.

"I'm done." She gave him the half-finished cone, which pro-
ceeded to drip all over *his* hand.

"Great. Thanks." He licked it a couple of times, then tossed
it in the plastic-lined trash container in the ice-cream shop. He
wiped both their hands, then collected their packages. Mandy
slid off her stool and followed him out onto the street.

"Hold this," he said, handing her one of the bags. He reached
in his back pocket and pulled out the list Elizabeth had made.
"Okay, we bought T-shirts."

"Three of them," Mandy said helpfully.

"Yes, three. And shoes. We got underwear."

"With pink bunnies."

"The bunnies are nice." It had been tough deciding between
bunnies, a popular female cartoon figure and flowers. He'd
picked out female lingerie before, but not cotton panties for a
six-year-old. He hoped Elizabeth approved of the bunnies. He
scanned the list. "That's it, kid. We just have to go by the post
office and collect your mom's mail. Then we'll head home."

"Okay." She started down the sidewalk.

"Mandy?" he called.

"What?"

"It's that way." He pointed in the other direction.

She smiled. "Okay." The bag was light, but almost as big as she was. He reached down and took it from her.

"I didn't mean for you to carry that, sweetie. I'll take it."

"But I want to help."

He sorted through the other packages. "Here. Take this one."

"Mommy's present?" She looked in the small gift store bag and smiled. "Mommy will like it."

"I hope so." It had been an impulsive purchase. A small yellow stuffed duck. She wouldn't get the joke, but seeing it would remind him not to try to be other than he was.

Mandy walked at his side chatting about school and soccer practice. He liked the sound of her voice and her stories. He liked how she looked up at him and simply assumed he would keep her safe. She accepted him with the tacit trust of a child raised in a house full of love and security. So where was the girl's father?

Thinking of Sam Proctor sent a shiver of guilt slipping down his spine. As they crossed the street and he saw a restaurant up ahead, he had the urge to step inside and use the phone to call Kyle at the station. It would be easy enough to tell his brother to back off. Why did it matter who Sam Proctor was? But he passed the restaurant without making the call.

They reached the post office. There was a short line. Mandy stood patiently, humming softly under her breath. He glanced down at her pretty face and beautiful blue eyes. Eyes she had to have inherited from her father. He smiled at her. She grinned in return and reached for his hand. The trusting gesture twisted his heart. A stab of loneliness caught him off balance. It was going to be hell when Elizabeth and Mandy moved into their own place.

When it was their turn, he approached the counter and collected Elizabeth's mail. She was having her forwarded correspondence held until she had her own place. He resisted the temptation to flip through the stack of envelopes. Checking on Sam Proctor was one thing, reading her mail quite another.

"Ready to go home?" he asked.

She nodded. "I had the best time, Travis. I like doing things with you. My old friends did stuff with their daddies but mine was always busy. I like soccer, too."

The slightly confused speech gave him the in he'd been hoping for. As they approached the car, he dug in his front jeans pocket for his keys.

"You haven't seen your daddy in a long time, have you?"

Mandy shook her head. "Mommy said he had to go away. My daddy left because he's big."

She'd said that once before. What the hell did it mean?

"Big?"

She nodded. "I heard her say that once. Mommy was on the phone. I was supposed to be in bed, but I got up for a drink of water. Mommy said Daddy was big. Then she started to cry." Mandy's mouth twisted into a frown. "I got scared and went back to my room. Mommy and Daddy fought sometimes. I could hear them." She handed him the bag then climbed into the front seat of his Bronco. As he bent over to fasten her seat belt, she glanced up at him. "It made Mommy sad when he went away. It made me sad, too."

He could see that sadness in her eyes and felt like the lowest kind of scum for questioning her. To distract her, he bent over and tickled her.

"Sad? No one is allowed to be sad in *my* car."

She twisted away and giggled. "Is it a magic car, like the magic hugs?"

"Absolutely." He handed her the mail and closed her door.

After tossing the packages on the back seat, he climbed in and started the truck. Mandy's good humor had been restored and she chatted happily. His mind reeled with curiosity.

My daddy left because he's big. Elizabeth Abbott, who are you? He signaled to turn out of the post office parking lot. Frustration welled up inside of him. He drew in a deep breath. He wasn't going to get answers anytime soon. Kyle might come up with something, or he might not. Until then, he would just have to let it go. He liked Elizabeth and found it hard to believe she was involved with anything shady. His gut trusted her, and he trusted his gut.

"Look at the pretty dog," Mandy said, pointing at a teenage boy walking a collie.

Travis stopped at a red light and turned to look. Mandy raised her hands to wave at the dog. The mail on her lap slipped off on the floor. He glanced at the light to make sure it was still red, then bent over and picked up the envelopes. He told himself not to, but he couldn't help glancing at the address. It was a suburb of Los Angeles. He looked up a line, to the addressee. His teeth clenched together. He flipped through the rest of the envelopes. Almost all of them were addressed to the same person: Elizabeth Proctor.

She'd lied.

Elizabeth wiped the kitchen counter. Again. It had been clean the last four times she'd wiped it. She was wasting time, trying to avoid the inevitable.

Travis had put up a good front through the late afternoon and even into dinner. But she knew there was something wrong. She could see it in his eyes, hear it in the way he hesitated before answering her questions. He'd held himself apart from her ever since he and Mandy had come home.

She looked around the clean kitchen, liking the way the cream-and-blue tiles complemented the bleached oak cabinets. It wasn't a traditional kitchen, but it suited her, and the house. She would miss it when she left.

She walked over to the coffeepot and poured out two cups. Sitting on the shelf above the sink was a stuffed yellow duck. The little creature seemed to smile at her, as much as a duck could smile. The gift had delighted her. Only Travis's seeming emotional distance distracted her from her pleasure. Something was wrong and she was going to find out what.

She carried the mugs carefully to the stairs and started to

climb. Travis was fitting cabinets in the big bathroom off the master bedroom. Mandy had been in bed for almost an hour. Her morning on the soccer field had worn her out. She had new clothes, thanks to Travis's patience at shopping, and several new friends. Life was good for the six-year-old.

Elizabeth walked down the hallway to the last door. Like most of the rooms in the house, the master bedroom was vacant, the walls stripped of wallpaper, the hardwood floor in need of repair. But even empty and abandoned, it was a beautiful room. Bay windows overlooked the back of the property, creating an intimate sitting area. There was a stone fireplace in the corner and a huge bathroom through the doorway at the far end.

She made her way over the stacks of supplies and tools. She could hear a file rubbing against wood.

"You ready to take a break?" she called. "Or should I come back later?"

"I can take a break."

"Good." She entered the bathroom. Molding for the ceiling lay stacked in the center. Travis had told her he planned to do the master bed and bath in a Victorian style. He'd even ordered a claw-footed bathtub. Several cabinets stood around the outside of the room. Pipes stuck out from the wall.

Travis sat in the middle of the floor, an open cabinet in front of him. He looked up as she entered. Something flickered in his eyes. Not passion, not even interest. It was almost a fleeting hint of sadness, followed by a healthy dose of mistrust. She stopped dead in her tracks.

"What's wrong?" she asked.

"Nothing." He blinked and the expression was gone, replaced by one she couldn't read.

Her stomach tightened as worry made her gnaw on her lower lip. She handed him a mug of coffee. He took it and nodded his thanks, then sipped the steaming liquid. Silence stretched between them. She didn't know what to say. Apparently he didn't, either, because the room stayed quiet.

She walked over to the rolls of wallpaper and studied the rose-

and-ivory pattern. She could feel Travis's gaze on her back. What had she done?

"You didn't have to stay home tonight to keep me company," she said at last, still staring at the wallpaper.

"I've been neglecting the house." He picked up his file and went to work on the cabinet.

She wanted to believe that was all it was, but she couldn't. The knot in her belly was too big to be ignored.

"Then tell me what's wrong. Are you angry with me?"

The file clinked when he dropped it to the floor. She heard him stand up and move close to her. She drew in a deep breath and turned around.

He'd set his coffee on the cabinet and stood with his arms folded over his chest. Worn black jeans hugged his strong thighs. His flannel shirt, rolled up to the elbows, had seen better days. The faded, soft fabric clung to him, highlighting his strength. When she gathered enough courage, she raised her head to look at his face. Dark eyes revealed nothing, nor did the straight set of his mouth.

"I didn't deliberately look through your mail," he said.

The knot in her stomach tightened. When he and Mandy had come back with her mail, she'd had a moment's unease. What if Travis had noticed who it was addressed to? But Mandy had proudly told her that she'd carried it all by herself. When Travis hadn't said anything, Elizabeth had assumed he hadn't looked.

"Mandy kept it on her lap. When it fell off, I picked it up. It's all addressed to Elizabeth Proctor. There's a postcard from your parents, Elizabeth. Your own parents use Sam's last name. Why did you lie?"

She expected the shame. When the hot emotion flooded her, she had to fight to keep from ducking her head. She could feel the blush creeping up her cheeks. Even in the soft light of the bathroom he would be able to see her embarrassment. But she hadn't expected to feel such sadness and regret. Travis had believed her. Despite the evidence against her, despite his questions, he'd trusted her to be who she said she was. He hadn't pressed to know her secrets. He'd been there for her, a good friend, and now that was gone.

"I'm sorry," she said slowly, gripping her mug tightly. "I didn't want anyone to know. I couldn't tell you because I knew what you would think."

"What's the problem?" he asked. His eyebrows drew together. He unfolded his arms and held out his hands, palms up. "It's no big deal. People get divorced all the time. Hell, I'm divorced. Why would you think anyone would care?"

"It's not that simple."

"What's not that simple? Did he beat you? Was he into men instead of women? Dammit, Elizabeth, tell me the truth."

She'd always known it would come to this. She should have known the secret would get out. What would Travis think of her when he knew? Would he despise her? Call her a fool? She shook her head. He couldn't say anything worse than what she'd already told herself.

"None of those things," she said at last. "Sam Proctor was already married when I met him. I didn't know, and he didn't tell me. Sam was a bigamist."

Chapter 9

If the situation hadn't been so sad and serious, Elizabeth might have laughed. Travis couldn't have looked more shocked if she'd stripped off all her clothes and started dancing around naked. The giggle in the back of her throat cracked and threatened to become a sob. She covered her mouth with her hand and turned away.

"You're the second wife?" he asked.

"Y-yes." She cleared her throat. It didn't help. Her legs started to tremble. She clutched at a stack of boxes of tiles, but the support wasn't enough. Shame, bitter regret, pain and confusion flooded her. She didn't want to lose Travis. Not yet. She needed him to be her friend. Now everything was lost.

She stopped trying to hold on and sank to her knees. The floor was cold through her jeans, but she didn't care. She clutched her arms to her chest and fought to stay coherent.

"I didn't know," she said, not turning around to face him. She didn't want to see the disgust in his eyes. "I swear I didn't know. I should have, of course. I was stupid. Young, naive. It was my fault for not questioning more. But I was barely out of my teens. Things like that didn't happen to girls from like me." She spoke quickly, as if by telling the tale fast he would be more likely to believe her.

"I met Sam at a lecture, at college. My parents had wanted me to stay home and go to a local junior college, but I wanted to get away. They seemed so old and out of touch with everything. I was working and going to school part-time. There was this lecture. I saw his picture. He was blond and good-looking. When he spoke, it was wonderful. The lecture was on staying motivated to achieve goals. He was very big on staying motivated." She paused to catch her breath.

"You don't have to tell me this," Travis said quietly. He was still behind her. She didn't dare turn around; she couldn't. Maybe if she explained it all correctly, he would understand. Maybe he would know that she'd tried, really tried. She hadn't meant to make such a big mistake.

"I sat in the back because I was shy." She sniffed. "Silly. I didn't have the courage to ask my questions in front of the group. There were probably two hundred people in the room. But afterward I went up to talk to him. There was a crowd, mostly women. They were older and well dressed. I was just a kid. When he spoke to me, I was enchanted. He looked at me as if I were something special. Something different. That meant a lot. When he asked me to go for coffee...well, I couldn't refuse."

"Elizabeth, don't."

"I have to. I have to make you understand."

"I understand."

"No, you don't." She looked up at him. Shock still flared in his dark eyes. He sat on the edge of the cabinet staring down at her. His arms were folded over his chest. His body language told her he'd pulled back. The teasing man who opened his home to her was gone, replaced by a judging stranger.

"I was a late bloomer. I didn't know how to dress or act around kids my age. My parents didn't help. The clothes they bought me were inappropriate for school. Too dressed-up and conservative. I'd never had a boyfriend. Sam was ten years older than me, but very hip and sophisticated. I was overwhelmed." She looked up at him and forced herself to smile. It felt a little shaky. "You know how that is, Travis. You've knocked your share of women off their feet."

"One or two," he admitted. "But I'm not judging you."

"Yes, you are. Of course you are. Do you think I don't judge myself? I made it so easy for him." She closed her eyes remembering how eager she'd been for his kisses, his touch. She'd never been with a man before. Sam was tender, teaching her the ways between a man and a woman. She'd fallen in love in a matter of days.

"He lived in Seattle but commuted to L.A. on business a lot. I even visited him there, once, at his apartment." She opened her eyes and stared at her clenched fists. She tried to relax her fingers, but she couldn't. She was holding on to all of herself to keep from breaking down. It was overwhelming, knowing what Travis thought, what other people would think. Knowing she'd been irresponsible and foolish and gullible. Feeling horribly alone. There was no one to turn to.

"I know now that apartment must have belonged to a friend. He was already married. He has two children with his real wife. A boy and a girl. When I got pregnant, I just assumed we'd be married. He'd never said anything about a wife. I never thought to ask. He said of course we would. He loved playing the odds. It was all a game to him. His dual life was exactly the kind of challenge he thrived on. I should have known."

"Elizabeth, I don't know what to say."

"I don't blame you. I didn't know what to say, either. I lived with that man for six and a half years." She laughed, then stopped before the laugh turned into a sob. "I found out when the police knocked on my door in the middle of the night. They arrested him, right there in my living room. You know the funny part?"

He didn't answer.

"I was going to leave him and get a divorce. The marriage— the whatever we had together—had been in trouble for a while. It didn't work with his separations. Of course his already being married would have put a strain on things, too, if I'd known."

''Elizabeth—''

''No, I know what you're thinking. Any kind of moron could have figured it out. My God, in six years there should have been hundreds of clues. There were. I know there were.'' She couldn't look at him anymore. She stared at the loose tiles in front of her. One was plain cream with tiny flecks of rose. The other was the same cream background with rose-colored flowers in each of the corners. The bathroom was going to be beautiful when he was done. She wondered if he would let her come and look at it then, or if he wouldn't ever want to speak to her again. She couldn't blame him. Her friends had stared at her with disgust. Most had stopped calling. The ones who had continued to speak to her had made her feel worse. She hated their pity.

''I should have known. There I stood on my wedding day, so happy. I knew I would be the best bride, the best wife, the best mother. It was all a joke.''

The colors on the tiles blurred. She heard a movement behind her. Travis crouched next to her and grabbed her shoulders. ''Dammit, stop beating yourself up.''

She stared at him, at his wavering image and only then did she realize she was crying. She raised one hand to her cheek. It was wet with tears.

''I told you,'' she whispered, her voice low and husky. ''I warned you I wasn't who or what you thought.''

''Give me a break,'' he said impatiently. ''You made a mistake. So what? People make mistakes all the time.''

''Not like this.''

''Hey, this isn't half as terrible as some of things I've been imagining.''

''You don't mean that.''

''Elizabeth, you aren't the bad guy. You didn't do anything wrong.''

''Except be stupid.''

He smiled slightly. ''That's not against the law.''

She pulled free of his grip. ''You haven't thought this through, Travis. It's not just about being stupid. I was never married.

Every document I have is a lie. I won't even bother with the details of what the IRS had to say about this. We had joint property together. It's still not all straightened out. And my daughter—'' Her voice started to shake. ''My daughter doesn't have a father anymore. I wasn't married when she was born. Even her birth certificate is a lie. I love her more than anything, yet I might have destroyed her life. I only wanted the best for her and look what happened.''

''I'm sorry.''

He reached for her, but she pulled back. She leaned against the pile of tiles. ''Do you know what it's like having the police show up at your door at four in the morning? Do you know what my neighbors thought or said the next day? Sam was gone about two weeks every month. I used to wonder why he didn't want to buy a house. Now I know it's because his other life would show up on the credit report. He didn't want me to go back to work, but thank God I did. When this all hit, I walked away with my daughter, my personal savings account and only what I'd paid for. I left behind everything else. I wanted to start over.'' The tears began to flow again. She felt her voice getting thick, but she couldn't stop. She had to explain it all. ''I didn't know. I swear I didn't know.''

''Hush.'' He reached for her and this time she didn't have the strength to resist him. After months of carrying around her guilty secret she felt cleansed, having spoken the truth at last. She knew that Travis would never be able to understand what she'd been through or look at her without feeling disgusted, but right now she couldn't deal with that.

He drew her into his embrace. He was warm and comforting, all the things her life lacked.

''Don't touch me,'' she said, willing herself to fight, but not able to find the strength. ''I'm incompetent. I ruined my life and Mandy's, and—''

''Never,'' he whispered. He rested her head on his shoulder and stroked her back. ''Never.''

''It's true. I am. I'm—''

He silenced her with his kiss. His firm lips brushed against hers, his mustache tickled her skin. He tasted salty; then she realized it was her own tears. She clung to him, to his strength, letting herself believe that this was real. Even for just a second, it was enough. His powerful body acted as a shield from the horrors of her past. In his arms, she could forget her part in the debacle that had been her life. She could ignore how it had affected Mandy, and caused them both to be cut off from friends and family. Even her parents didn't know the truth. She couldn't face telling them.

She turned her face away, breaking the kiss. "I wish you didn't know," she said, inhaling the scent of his warm body, knowing he would soon remove his strength from her reach and she would be alone again. "I wish I didn't have to see the disgust and pity in your eyes."

He touched her chin, forcing her to look at him. "What do you see in my eyes?" he asked.

She saw the flames that had been there the last time they'd kissed. She saw compassion, and something she couldn't identify.

"You haven't had time to think it through," she said, not willing to believe it was that easy.

"Give me a little credit for knowing myself."

She didn't say anything because she knew he was wrong. In time he would get angry at her for being so young and blind. Her friends had. She'd certainly gotten angry at herself. She was used to the weight of disapproval.

He rose and pulled her to her feet. Then he bent over and picked her up in his arms. She thought about protesting, but she didn't have the energy. She wrapped her arms around his neck and savored the feeling of being safe.

He carried her down the hall into his bedroom. She'd never been in here before. There was a large sleigh bed pushed against one wall. It dwarfed this room, but would look perfect in the master suite. An antique rocker stood in one corner. He settled down on the seat. She started to struggle.

"I'm not Mandy," she said. "I don't need to be treated like a child."

"Maybe not," he said mildly, "but you need a good holding anyway and this is the best way I know to do it. Relax, Elizabeth. Everything is going to be all right. I promise."

"You can't make it all right."

"Sure I can. Even if I can't make it right forever, I can fix it now. Close your eyes. Don't think about it anymore."

He held her head against his shoulder. His other hand moved slowly up and down her back. The comforting embrace weakened her resistance. She felt the tears forming. She clutched at his shirt and gave in to the pain.

It filled her, surrounding her. All the days and nights she'd lived with her shameful secret, all the lies she'd told, willingly and unwillingly. She'd hoped for a fresh start in this small town. Nothing was the way it was supposed to have been. This shouldn't have happened to her.

Travis murmured quiet words of encouragement. Her sobs lessened. She drew in a ragged breath and turned her face toward his neck. His shirt was damp against her cheek, his legs hard beneath hers. Big strong hands held her gently, as if she were the most fragile of creatures. Something precious. She wanted to believe his embrace. She wanted to know that she was fragile and special, something of value.

"Better?" he asked when she'd been silent for several minutes.

Elizabeth nodded slowly. "Thanks for understanding. Sometimes I'm so overwhelmed by all of it. Not just what went wrong with Sam, but for everything we've lost. I wanted to give my daughter a perfect home with two loving parents."

"Mandy is fine. You have a new job, you're healing from the surgery. You're both going to make it. So what's the problem?"

She stared at his neck, studying the way his evening stubble roughened his skin. She wanted to touch him there, to see what he felt like against her fingers, but she couldn't. It wasn't right to repay his kindness with her own selfish needs.

"I can't marry again. I would never trust myself to pick the right man."

"That's a big decision to make, based on one mistake."

She sat up and glared at him. "It was a hell of a mistake. Who are you to be telling me what I should think about marriage? You've had one bad experience, and you're never getting married again."

One corner of his mouth turned up in a smile. "I'm glad you're feeling better." She tried to wiggle out of his lap, but he held her firm. "It wasn't just one experience," he said, resting his hands on her waist.

She stopped fighting and sagged against him. "Does it hurt you, too? Does it hurt to know you'll always be alone?"

"Yeah. It hurts like hell."

He reached down for her at the exact moment she raised her head toward him. Their lips met. Unlike their other kisses, there was nothing gentle this time, no soft exploration. It was hard and hot, hungry and desperate. She could feel her own pain and his pain. The hurt, the bleakness of their futures compounded one another, growing until they were both close to drowning in need.

She clung to him, to his arms and shoulders, shifting to move her body closer. His strength would be her salvation. Just for this night, just for this tiny slip of time, she would steal what she had to, give all she could so he would be saved, as well.

His mouth angled over hers, his lips parted. She welcomed him, welcomed the sensations he brought, the forgetfulness of pleasure. That is what she needed, she thought, feeling his tongue with her own, tasting him, being tasted. She needed to forget everything in her life.

He touched her face, her hair, her shoulders, her back. Whisper-light touches that barely grazed her skin. They set her on fire. She moved closer so that her side pressed against him. Her breasts ached. She wanted him to touch her there, touch her everywhere. The heat of the fire helped her forget. She could get lost in the smoke. Disappear into the flames. He made her come alive in ways she'd forgotten existed.

His hands rested on her waist, then began to move higher. Her breasts swelled, her nipples puckered inside her bra. Against her hip she felt the hard ridge of his erection. An answering wanting moistened her panties.

"Travis," she breathed in anticipation as his fingers stroked her rib cage.

He buried his face in her neck, kissing the sensitive skin under her jaw, nibbling on her earlobe, whispering her name like a prayer. His lips were warm and damp.

His hands moved higher still, at last cupping her full breasts, taking their weight into his palms. His thumbs swept across her nipples, sending sharp jolts of pleasure down to curl her bare toes. She arched against his caress, searching for more and more of his touch. But instead of assuaging her need, he moved his hands up to her shoulders, then slipped his fingers through her hair and held her head in place.

She opened her eyes and stared at him. The fire burning in his dark irises left no room for any emotion other than passion. She reveled in the need and desire that matched her own.

Never taking her eyes from him, she touched his face. Her fingers traced the straight line of his nose, the shape of his jaw. She heard the rasp of her fingertips against his stubble, and felt the smoothness of his mustache. She touched his damp mouth, tracing the shape, enjoying the heat. He parted his lips and licked the tip of her finger.

She laughed. He smiled at the sound; then his smile faded and she saw the questions forming in his eyes. Questions that quenched the fire and overpowered the need.

The loss was more than she could bear. "Don't," she whispered.

"Elizabeth, you're reacting. It's too soon."

The disappointment tasted bitter. "I thought men always wanted to get women into bed. I guess it's not true." She tried to slide off his lap, but he held her in place. She flushed. "Or it's not true with me."

He thrust his hips forward, pressing his erection hard against her. "Do you need more proof that I want you? I'm trying to keep you from having regrets in the morning."

"You're thinking about my past." It hurt to be rejected out of hand. The feeling was made worse by the fact that he was the first man she'd been attracted to, or had even kissed, since Sam. She hadn't made love for over a year. She'd never once been tempted to stray, and since she found out the truth about her marriage, she'd been too ashamed to try dating. Nothing had changed. She was still the shy little nobody. The girl who didn't understand boys or know how to attract them. The boys had grown into men, but she was just as lost as ever.

"I'm sorry I embarrassed you," she said stiffly, wishing she wasn't turning bright red.

"Damn it, Elizabeth, what do I have to do to prove to you that I'm trying to act like a gentleman?"

"Nothing at all— What are you doing?"

He placed one arm around her back and slipped the other underneath her legs. As he rose to his feet, he pulled her against his chest. He walked four steps to the bed.

"You are the most stubborn woman," he growled as he bent over and placed her on the comforter.

"Stop. You don't have to do anything. In fact, I'd rather you didn't." She started scrambling off the other side.

He grabbed both her hands in his. One he held down at the mattress, the other he drew to his crotch and placed against him. Even through his jeans he was hard and hot. He held on to her wrist and moved her palm up and down. A tremor shot through his body, and he gritted his teeth.

"Had enough?" he asked, his eyes once again burning with the fire.

"No," she said truthfully.

"Elizabeth, don't tempt me like this. You're still recovering from your surgery. You're upset about your past. I don't want you to wake up and hate my guts. I like you too much for that.''

If he'd promised to love her forever, she would have never believed him. If he'd said the truth didn't matter, she would have never forgiven him for the lie. But liking her she could believe. She liked him back. He was the closest thing in the world she had to a friend. He knew the truth about her and hadn't turned his back on her. He might tomorrow. He might pity her or get angry. But for tonight he was her friend.

She reached for the first button on his jeans. ''It doesn't have to mean anything. It could just be about tonight.''

''Hell.'' He brushed her fingers away and bent down and kissed her.

He didn't wait for an invitation, but thrust inside her mouth savagely, hungrily, as if he'd been given permission to devour that which he most desired. He sucked on her lower lip, nipped her chin, then moved lower to the neck of her T-shirt. He paused long enough to slip off the offending garment and continue his journey of exploration.

His hands led the way, unfastening her bra to bare her breasts. The evening air was cool, in contrast to the heat of his mouth trailing ever closer. Damp kisses ignited her skin. His scent surrounded her, filling her with images of the man who touched her. She reached out to embrace his body, feeling the muscles in his arms and back, touching his short dark hair.

He murmured her name over and over again as if it were an incantation. His fingers reached for and found her puckered nipples, toying with them, readying them for his mouth.

He moved until he was straddling her. Their jeans slid back and forth creating friction. The bulging male part of him mated with her softer, damper center. Through the layers of clothing, she felt the promise of their joining.

Her hands fluttered against his chest and touched the buttons of his shirt. Before she could unfasten even one, he touched her right nipple with his tongue.

All rational thought fled. Her body awakened painfully to the joy of moist heat, the suckling that pulled exquisitely from her breast through her belly down to her swelling center. Her arms fell to her sides and her hands clung to the comforter. Her hips arched against him seeking the release of his touch.

Her breathing increased. She'd tried not to think about making love with Travis. She hadn't been as successful as she would have liked. She'd known he would be tender and patient, qualities she'd seen in him every day. She thought she might enjoy the feel of his body close to her, on top of her, his powerful strength reminding her of her femaleness. His broad shoulders made her feel fragile—and safe. She'd known she would enjoy his attentions, but she hadn't expected to lose control.

His fingers toyed with her other breast, teasing the hardened tip with the flick of his thumb. His kiss on her deepened, then he drew back and moved his lips over her nipple. The individual hairs of his mustache swept over her sensitized skin, making her gasp and bringing her shoulders up off the bed. She reached up and grabbed his head, holding him in place. She'd never been aggressive in bed before. She'd never offered any comments on Sam's performance. He'd pleased her most of the time, and she'd been content with that. He'd occasionally asked her to be the aggressor, but she'd never had the courage to act without being acted upon.

But now, she had no choice in the matter. Those tiny prickling caresses made her breath catch and legs tremble. She couldn't bear for him to stop. He kept moving back and forth against her breasts, taunting her with the movement. Her hips flexed again and again, pressing harder against his arousal. She was more ready than she had ever been. So close it hurt to breathe hard, and yet he hadn't even touched her there.

When she thought she would explode or go mad, he slid down her body, trailing kisses to the waistband of her jeans. He sat up and unfastened the button and slipped the zipper down. She had enough awareness to raise her hips to assist him.

It was only when she felt his mouth on her thigh that she realized he'd taken off her panties along with her jeans. Before she could be embarrassed, he moved his hands between her legs and urged her to part them.

She willingly availed herself to him, anticipating the skillful touch of his fingers. Something warm fanned her most secret place. A breath of air. Her eyes opened. Before she could react, his fingers drew her open and he kissed her moist, quivering center.

A thrill of pleasure shot through her. Her protest died unspoken. She'd read about this, of course, had even taken Sam into her mouth once, but he'd pushed her away telling her it was dirty. She'd wondered what it would feel like to have a man touch her so intimately. A thousand questions filled her mind. What exactly was he doing with his tongue? Did he like the taste and scent of her? Could he feel her muscle contracting as he—

Her breath caught in her throat. It was as if he knew exactly how to touch, where to touch. She relaxed back on the bed and forgot her questions. Nothing mattered except the feel of him against her, loving her over and over. The rhythm increasing in cadence, matching the thunder of her heartbeat.

She whispered his name without thinking, then got embarrassed. He paused long enough to tell her to say it again. So she did. She spoke his name aloud, gasped her pleasure, rotated her hips mindlessly and surrendered to his masterful touch. The fire grew, burning hot and brighter. The flames didn't frighten her— nothing frightened her. Travis was strong enough to save her. This night was a magical escape from her real world, from everything except the passion.

He moved faster against her, then shifted, slipping one finger into her woman's place, moving it slowly. Once again she was shocked, but this time there was no room for questions, no room for anything but the sudden tension that locked her muscles and the explosion that shattered her into a million tiny pieces of perfect pleasure.

He held her tightly in his embrace, comforting her as the aftershocks rippled through her. The dull ache in her side told her that she'd used her stomach muscles too much. Who cares, she thought sleepily, and sighed.

"That sounded very contented," he said, his voice rumbling against her hair.

"It is." She snuggled closer, rubbing her cheek against the soft flannel of his shirt. His shirt? She opened her eyes. "You're not even naked!"

"I know." His slow, lazy smile belied the erection she could see pressing against the fly of his jeans.

"Travis?"

"Hush." He brushed her hair out of her face and gently stroked her head. "Rest, darlin'. You've had a long and difficult day."

It didn't make any sense. If she'd taken too long with Sam, he had simply pleasured himself and left her unsatisfied. She'd always understood that a man's needs were more uncontrollable than a woman's, that a man had to find release or face a painful night. It had never been just for her.

"But you didn't...do anything."

"You're too sore," he said and reached down to touch her healing incision. "I saw you wince when you settled down. You can't even drive yet. There's no way your insides are ready for anything vigorous."

She drew her eyebrows together. She couldn't fault his argument. Just the thought of anything thrust inside of her was enough to make her side ache more. But this didn't *feel* right. It wasn't the way she'd planned it.

He moved his hand from her side to her breast and gently caressed the sensitized flesh. Her eyes drifted shut. It had felt so good when he'd loved her with his mouth. She couldn't remember ever experiencing such exquisite sensations. In fact—

The idea came to her full-blown. She rose up on one shoulder, then collapsed back on the bed.

"What?" he asked.

She didn't answer. Sam hadn't wanted her to do that. But

Travis wasn't Sam, she reminded herself. Sam hadn't done what Travis had done to her, either.

"Elizabeth?"

She exhaled deeply. "I was just wishing I'd had more lovers."

"What?"

She laughed. "Just so I'd know how to handle this situation."

He shook his head. "You're handling it just fine. Trust me. Now lay down and relax."

She shimmied closer, so that she could rest her chin on his chest. "I don't think so."

"What does that mean?"

"Nothing," she said, innocently and sat up. She straddled his hips and leaned forward so she could start unbuttoning his shirt.

"What are you planning to do?" he asked.

"Just wait and see. If you don't like it, I promise to stop."

Chapter 10

Travis warned himself not to blow it. Just because he was naked and she was sitting on his bare belly kissing his chest didn't mean she was going to reciprocate what he'd done to her. But he couldn't stop thinking about it. Couldn't stop imagining what it would be like to have her taste him, touch him in that most intimate way. He told himself just having her in his bed, trusting him with her body, was enough. The hardness between his legs throbbed in time with his heartbeat and told him he was a liar.

Her hands were everywhere. His shoulders, chest, neck, arms. Soft skin brushing, stroking. Her small hot mouth pressed against his flat nipples, teasing him to frenzied awareness.

She slipped back and down, settling between his legs. He thought about telling her she didn't have to do that. He could simply lie here a few minutes and explode from the need. He tried to think about other things, to get control, but every time he closed his eyes, he was back on top of her, touching and tasting *her,* loving her cries of pleasure, feeling her release against his lips. She'd been made to be pleasured by a man—by him.

Her hands rubbed up and down on his thighs. He looked at her. She nibbled on her lower lip as she studied him, obviously trying to figure something out.

"You don't have to do this," he said, cursing his mother for raising him right.

"Do what?"

Hell. "Whatever it is that has you confused."

She tossed her hair over her shoulders. The movement caused her breasts to sway slightly. The sight of her hard peach-colored nipples bouncing in the air made his erection surge toward her.

"I want to, but I'm afraid you won't like it."

He tried to laugh. It came out a little strangled.

"I've never done this before. I can't hurt you, can I? I don't want to, you know, do anything awful."

The muscles in his legs and arms started twitching. If it wasn't for the small red incision, bright and angry against her pale flat belly, he'd roll her on her back and bury himself deep inside of her. That would end the debate and the growing pressure.

"I doubt you'd do anything awful," he said, trying not to grit his teeth. "But we can stop now."

She smiled. "Did you know the veins on your forehead are sticking out?"

"I'm not surprised," he muttered, knowing he was being punished for some previous offense. It must have been pretty bad, whatever it was.

He couldn't stand it any longer. He started to sit up, determined to suffer the indignity of a cold shower when she reached forward and touched his arousal.

His groan sounded loud in the silent room. She bent over him, her brown hair falling like an erotic curtain, caressing the tops of his thighs. He sank back on the mattress and held his breath.

Her touch was sweet, wet and tentative. A delicate pressure, careful yet adventurous. He could have exploded then, but thought better of it. Her fingers traced small circles at the base of his desire, moving through the hair, slipping lower to cup his softer parts. Weighing them in her hands tentatively, then moving more boldly when he exhaled his pleasure.

It wouldn't take long, he knew. A few slow strokes, a flick or two with her tongue and he was ready.

"Elizabeth," he said, tensing his muscles, ready to stop and have her complete him just with her hands. "You can stop now."

She looked up and tossed her head. At that second their eyes locked. It was the most erotic sight of his life. Her heart-shaped face poised over his engorged maleness, her breasts swinging freely. Pale on tanned, he saw the lines of her bathing suit. She licked his sensitive tip once, then smiled.

"I don't want to stop," she whispered.

And she didn't.

It was nearly two in the morning when he woke up. He smiled in the darkness when he felt Elizabeth's warm body pressing against his side. One of her soft, delicate arms lay across his chest. Her face was buried against his arm. He could smell the scent of her body and the lingering aroma of sex.

In seconds he was hard. He didn't have to fully form the memory of what she'd done before he was ready to have her do it again and again. He figured he'd get tired of looking at her and making love with her in about fifty years. That thought scared the hell of out of him.

Slowly he slipped out of bed, being careful not to disturb her. He picked up his jeans and stepped into the hallway. After closing the door softly behind him, he pulled on his jeans and buttoned the fly.

He checked to make sure Mandy was sleeping soundly, then picked up her bear off the floor and set it on her pillow. Finally he made his way downstairs. Louise took care of the grocery shopping and kept him stocked with all the essentials. He reached in the back of the refrigerator for a bottle of beer and twisted off the top.

The cold liquid went down easily. Not bothering to turn on any lights, he walked into the family room and settled on the sofa. The leather was cool against his bare back. He shifted to get comfortable, then relaxed and closed his eyes.

A bigamist. He would never have guessed that one. It was hard to believe something like that had happened to someone as sweet as Elizabeth. It wasn't right. His hand tightened around the beer bottle as if the slick glass were Sam Proctor's neck.

She'd mentioned that her ex-husband—former husband, or whatever the hell he was to her—was still serving time in prison. Travis was glad. He hoped the bastard never got out. The anger inside of him simmered down to a slow burn, tempered by the question of what he was supposed to do now. Elizabeth had obviously been embarrassed when she'd told him the truth. He'd hated doing that to her. He'd tried to get her to stop talking, but she'd continued on as if finally telling someone about her past was the ultimate act of absolution.

He'd hated knowing she was uncomfortable around him. Had their lovemaking made it better or worse? He shook his head and took another swallow. The knot in his gut told him it was all about to get worse. Damn. He should have handled it better. He shouldn't have kissed her in the first place, or he should have tried harder to get out of making love with her.

He grinned mockingly. Oh, yeah, Haynes. Get out of it. As if making love with Elizabeth had been some irritating charity work instead of the most incredibly intimate, erotic act of his sorry life.

He rubbed his hand over his face, then scratched his chin. None of this was helping him answer the most important question. Now what? What did he do with the truth, and what about what happened between them last night?

Okay, knowing the truth. That was easy. Elizabeth would want it kept quiet. That wasn't hard to figure out. He just wouldn't tell a soul. He sat up straight and swore.

"Kyle." He'd asked his brother to run a check on Sam Proctor. Damn. He knew exactly what his deputy was going to find out. He would have to have a talk with Kyle and tell him to keep the information to himself.

The knot in his stomach tightened. He'd felt like slime when he'd asked his brother to run the check. He should have listened to that feeling.

A bigamist. It boggled his mind. He smiled suddenly, his

mood lightening as he remembered what Mandy had said about her father. He'd had to leave because he was big. The kid almost had it right, he thought, draining the beer and setting the bottle on the coffee table in front of him.

His smile faded. Where did they go from here? Despite his stellar reputation, he wasn't the casual sex, one-night-stand kind of guy. He'd had enough of that at college. He generally held back physically until there was an emotional connection. He knew nothing was going to last forever, but he'd never played fast and loose with a woman before. Elizabeth didn't strike him as overly experienced. With his luck, she'd only ever been with one man—Sam. Which meant she was going to be hating life and him come morning. Would she expect something of him? A commitment of some kind?

It wasn't, he realized with bone-chilling shock, a horrible idea. He liked Elizabeth, he adored Mandy. They got along well and—

Slow down, boy, he told himself. Nothing was going to happen between him and Elizabeth. Last night was a…a… He hated to use the word *mistake*. It hadn't been a mistake for him. Last night had been an unusual circumstance. They'd both needed each other. But there wasn't going to be anything permanent between them. He didn't have what it took to make that kind of relationship work. Even if he did, Elizabeth had made it clear she wasn't interested in getting involved with him or any man. After what Sam had done, he almost couldn't blame her.

In a week her medical restrictions would lift. She would be driving, and leaving him for her own place. If they both tried, they could put last night in its proper place and stay friends. It's really all he wanted.

The sounds of the night crowded in around him. The cool air made him shiver. He told himself to go back to his bed, to snuggle against Elizabeth's warm naked body and savor the moments while he had them. But he couldn't. Not yet. Not when he'd finally realized how hard it was going to be to let her go.

"It's a fumble on the twenty-yard line. Dallas recovers and runs it in for a touchdown. San Francisco is now down by fourteen points.''

Travis groaned and reached for the remote. He hit the mute button and sank back against the couch. Mandy looked up from her place on the floor where she was working on a jigsaw puzzle.

"Is your team doing bad, Travis?" she asked.

"They're getting their fannies kicked."

"Really?" She glanced toward the TV screen. "I don't see anyone kicking fannies."

He chuckled. "Hopefully it won't happen again."

She abandoned her puzzle and climbed into his lap. "I'll make you feel better," she said and gave him a hug. "They're magic, just like yours."

He hugged her back. "I do feel better. Thanks." He pointed at the puzzle. "What is it going to be?"

"A dog." She pursed her lips together. "Mommy says there's bunnies at our house and I can see them when we get there, but I was thinking maybe I could have a puppy instead. Do you think Mommy would like a puppy?"

"I don't know. You'll have to ask her."

She wrinkled her nose. "Maybe later. She's cooking, and if you ask her stuff now, she usually says no."

He'd heard the pots rattling in the kitchen and had decided to stay clear himself. He was giving Elizabeth time to recover from what happened between them last night. "You're a very smart girl."

"I know."

Her smile took a direct line to his heart. She wore sweatpants and a matching sweatshirt in bright pink with a redheaded mermaid on the front. Her pale blond hair was pulled back in a ponytail and her bangs hung almost to her eyebrows. She was going to be a heartbreaker in a few years; when she left with her mother at the end of the week, she was going to break *his* heart.

Elizabeth walked into the room. She stared at a point above

and to the left of his head. "Mandy, there are still a few flowers left in the garden. Why don't you pick some for the table?"

"Okay." The little girl slid off his lap and grinned. "I get to pick flowers."

"I heard."

She practically quivered with excitement. "You can finish my puzzle if you want to," she told Travis.

"I'll pass and let you do it."

She nodded and ran out of the room, singing a song about flowers. Elizabeth turned to leave, then hesitated.

She wore her hair as she had the first time he'd seen her, in a ponytail on top of her head. The loose strands tumbled down to her shoulder. A light touch of makeup accentuated her chestnut-colored eyes. An oversize peach sweater hung midway down her thighs. Matching leggings outlined her curves, taunting him with what he'd seen and touched and tasted the previous night. Her flat loafers didn't give her any height, and she looked small and ill at ease.

"What's wrong?" he asked, rising to his feet.

"Nothing." Her voice was hoarse, as if she was having trouble speaking. "I was just wondering if you wanted to cancel the party."

"A couple of friends over for a late lunch and football is hardly a party."

"I know, but..." Her voice trailed off. She clasped her hands together in front of her waist and stared at the ground. "I thought you might prefer to keep me away from your friends because of last night."

That didn't make any sense. "Because we made love?"

She shook her head. "No, the other thing."

The spot of color on each cheek had nothing to do with cosmetics. She looked as if she were praying for the ground to open and swallow her whole. It was all his fault.

In an effort to be a gentleman, he had left their bed that morning to give her the privacy to wake up alone. If he was going to be completely honest with himself, he would have to admit there had been something other than altruism in the act. He hadn't wanted to wake up and see the regret in her eyes. Unfortunately, she thought *he* was the one having regrets. She might say she was worried about her confession, but her body language told him she was thinking about the sex.

He crossed the room and reached toward her. Before he could pull her close, she stepped back. "Don't," she murmured.

"I'm not sorry we made love," he said quietly, aware that Mandy could return at any moment. "I left you alone this morning to give you some privacy, not because I didn't want to be with you in bed. I wanted us to make love again, but I was worried about you being sore and Mandy waking up. It was wonderful, Elizabeth. At least it was for me. I guess I'll understand if you're having second thoughts."

"I'm not sorry, either."

She looked up at him and he saw the sadness in her eyes. It puzzled him. If she didn't have regrets, then why was she sad?

"It doesn't change anything, though," she said dropping her arms to her side.

Make that: it hadn't *meant* anything. He'd been so damned worried about what she would be thinking and feeling that he hadn't spared a thought for his own feelings. "So you're saying, 'Thanks for the good time, no regrets, but gee, let's never bother doing that again'?"

"Not exactly."

He would have laughed but there was this pain deep in his chest. He'd been a one-night stand. Women across the county would be crowing with delight if they ever learned a Haynes had finally had his comeuppance. He'd been looking for something more, and Elizabeth was the one backing off.

"Don't worry about me," he said. "As for the company. Hey, why would it matter that people came over? Don't worry, I won't talk about your secret or last night."

"Thank you," she said, looking at him oddly.

"So nothing's changed. We're exactly where we were yesterday. Friends. Great."

"Travis, are you okay?" Her brows drew together in confusion. "Have I said anything to—"

The sharp ringing of the phone cut her off. "Excuse me," he said, and reached for the phone on the end table. "Hello?"

"Hey, Travis, it's Kyle." His brother sounded wary. "I ran that guy you asked me to. Sam Proctor. You're not going to believe what I found."

"I already know."

"About the bigamy?"

"Yeah."

"Elizabeth Abbott is in the report. The second wife, or whatever you'd call her."

"I know that, too."

"You okay?"

Travis turned back toward Elizabeth, but she'd left the room. No, he wasn't okay; he was never going to be okay again. She'd touched him and loved him in his bed, and now she was going to shut him down. Part of him couldn't blame her. He was the last guy in the world she should get involved with. He would only screw up the whole thing. But his brief experience of paradise had left him hungry for more. He wanted to be different, he wanted to be the kind of man who could marry and have a family. He wanted—

"Travis, are you there?"

"Sorry. I'm fine. Look, Kyle, I want you to keep this information to yourself, okay?"

Kyle exhaled in disgust. "I might be the youngest, Travis, but I'm not a kid. I know this could hurt Elizabeth. I won't say anything."

"I know. I'm sorry. Look, could you just get your butt over here as quickly as possible?" He needed someone to run interference before he said or did something stupid. Worse, before he made a promise he knew he could never keep.

"I can't sit out there with those boys if I know you're in here doing all the work," Louise said walking into the kitchen. "What can I do to help?"

Elizabeth closed the oven door and smiled. For the first time that day, her sense of doom lifted a little. "Nothing. I've got everything under control."

"You make me feel guilty. I'm supposed to be looking after you."

Elizabeth laughed and moved to the kitchen table. "I'm feeling great. Doing more things every day." She bit down on her lower lip. She'd almost blurted out, "Last night Travis and I made love, and I felt wonderful afterward." That would have given Louise something to talk about. "My incision hardly gives me any trouble at all." Except for a slight tenderness after they'd— Stop thinking about it, she ordered herself. It only made everything more difficult.

"Do you want some coffee?" she asked, pointing to the full pot. "It's fresh."

"I'll get it," Louise said. "You sit down for a minute and rest yourself. There's no point in spending all this time getting better if you're just going to wear yourself out in one afternoon."

She poured herself a cup, then offered one to Elizabeth. She shook her head in refusal. Louise poured in milk and added a rounded teaspoon of sugar.

Today she was dressed all in purple. A frilly blouse that did nothing to hide her generous curves, a calf-length ruffled skirt and bright purple cowboy boots. Her short blond hair had been puffed and sprayed into little spikes. She wore saddle earrings and lots of black mascara. The kindness and concern in her blue eyes made her look beautiful.

"I'm doing great," Elizabeth said. It wasn't an actual lie. Physically she was doing well. Emotionally, she was hovering about a half inch off the ground. Last night had been perfect, but this morning, when she'd woken up alone in Travis's bed, all her doubts had crashed in around her. They'd made a terrible mistake. The lovemaking had been so right between them, but the memory was tainted by the reason he'd reached for her in the first place. Once Travis realized that, he wouldn't want to remember what had happened at all. He would put it and her out of his mind. She hated to think about that. She knew there was no hope for any kind of long-term relationship between them, but she'd counted on them staying friends.

"You want to talk about it?" Louise asked, then took a sip from her mug. She walked to the table and plopped into the seat next to Elizabeth.

"I—"

"Don't bother lying, honey. I can see the pain in your pretty eyes. Did something happen here, or is this about whatever made you come to town in the first place?"

Elizabeth stared at her. Had the other woman guessed or had Travis said something?

"Don't give me that look," Louise said. "It doesn't take a lot of brains to figure out something is wrong with you. When you first arrived you spent most of your time looking over your shoulder. Who are you afraid of?"

Elizabeth fought the urge to confide in Louise. She'd felt better after telling Travis the truth. Confession was good for the soul. But she was afraid. She hadn't even told her own parents. She couldn't face the disappointment and shame she would hear in their voices. Would Louise understand? She gathered her courage together.

"If it's about you and Travis being lovers, then you don't have anything to worry about."

Her courage fled and with it her composure. Her mouth dropped open. "He told you?"

Louise leaned forward and smiled. "No one had to tell me, honey. I could feel it the second I walked into this house." She patted her hand. "Don't worry. The boys are too dense to figure it out. Your secret is safe with me."

"It doesn't make any difference," Elizabeth said, staring at the water glass in front of her. She moved it back and forth over the bleached oak table. "Travis isn't the kind of man a woman settles down with, even if I was interested."

"You be careful about believing all of his press," Louise said.

"He and his brothers paid a high price for their father's and uncles' ways. The boys have worked hard to be decent to the women in their lives. They mostly lack any kind of skills in relationships. No role models—at least that's what they usually say on those daytime talk shows." She smiled. "Maybe you should think about giving him a chance."

"I can't." She drew in a deep breath. The courage returned. "I came to Glenwood to get away from my life in L.A. Mandy's father was a bigamist, and I was his second wife."

She told the story quickly, even the embarrassing details about how stupid she'd been. She finished, then braced herself for Louise's well-intentioned scolding.

"That bastard," Louise said, glaring at her. "Excuse my French, but that's exactly what he is."

Elizabeth blinked. She couldn't have heard the other woman correctly. "No, you don't understand. It's my fault. I should have known."

"How were you supposed to know?"

"He was my husband."

"All the more reason to trust him. Oh, I just hate men like that."

"But, Louise—"

"Don't you 'but, Louise' me. You were a virgin when you met him, weren't you?"

Elizabeth was too surprised by her friend's anger to be embarrassed by the question. "Yes, but—"

"And you were faithful to him during your relationship."

"Of course, but—"

Louise rose to her feet and started pacing the kitchen. "I'd like to find him and give him a piece of my mind. No. I'd like him castrated."

Elizabeth giggled. "That sounds a little harsh, even for Sam."

Louise paused and leaned against the counter. "Okay, maybe we'll just threaten him with dismemberment. Just enough to put the fear of God into him."

Elizabeth's smile faded as she felt tears forming in her eyes.

Louise wasn't judging her, she was defending her. It was a miracle.

"Does this means we can still be friends?" she asked tentatively.

"Why in the world wouldn't we be?" Louise hurried over to the table and bent down to give her a hug. Her spicy perfume comforted Elizabeth, reminding her of her own mother.

"Thank you," Elizabeth said. "Thanks for giving me a chance."

"I'm not giving you anything." Louise straightened and smiled. "But while we're on the subject, you might think about giving yourself a chance. Travis, too. I know that boy, and I think he's smitten."

It would never work, Elizabeth told herself. If she gave Travis a chance, he would break her already fragile heart. Leaving Sam had been hard enough. If she got much closer to Travis, leaving him would be the end of her world.

Chapter 11

They finished eating close to four. Despite Elizabeth's protests, everyone helped clear the table and set out dessert. Travis looked at the small group sitting around the dining room table. Jordan and Craig couldn't make it back for the game, so it was just him, Elizabeth, Louise, Austin and Kyle. Oh, and of course Mandy who had seated herself next to him. He was torn between wanting to ease her shyness with Kyle and Austin and being pleased that she sought him out for protection.

"Of course I specialize in stopping long-haired types like you," Kyle said to Austin.

The other man ignored the teasing and gave Mandy a wink. His charm even worked on six-year-olds. She dimpled delightfully, then buried her head in Travis's arm. Travis glanced over at Elizabeth and saw she had noticed the exchange. She gave him a little smile. Better, he thought, remembering how she'd avoided his gaze for the first part of the meal. Every time she looked at Austin, his gut clenched as he waited for her to figure out his friend was handsome as sin and richer than God. So far she seemed singularly unimpressed.

"Kyle is leading the pack this month," Travis said, stroking Mandy's hair. "Giving out the most tickets."

''That must make him popular with the locals,'' Elizabeth said.

Kyle shrugged. ''At least I'm not like you, big brother. Always parking in the same place. He's got the worst record in tickets.''

Elizabeth began cutting the cherry cheesecake in front of her and placing the slices on plates. ''If you're the sheriff, why do you give out tickets at all? I wouldn't have thought that was part of your job.''

He made the mistake of looking at Kyle, who was making cow eyes at him, mocking him before he'd even started to answer the questions.

He balled up his napkin and tossed it across the table. Kyle burst out laughing, Elizabeth remained calm, Louise muttered about boys being boys and Austin stayed out of it. As always, his friend was on the fringe of the group, watching but never actually belonging.

''I don't ask my men to do anything I wouldn't do.''

''That's fair,'' Elizabeth said, as Kyle clutched his hands over his heart and pretended to swoon. ''If you don't behave, Kyle,'' she said, her voice staying even and friendly, ''I'm going to make you stand in the corner and not give you any dessert.''

Travis burst out laughing. Kyle looked suitably chastised. Even Austin smiled.

''He also parks his car in one place,'' Austin said, taking the plate she offered. ''By the main highway. Whenever he's out looking for speeders, we all know where to find him.''

Elizabeth glanced at him. ''I'm glad you were there,'' she said. ''If you hadn't been, who knows what would have happened.''

''Travis took Mommy to the hospital,'' Mandy said, taking her serving of cake and picking up her fork. ''I was scared, but he used the siren and made sure Mommy was all better.''

''Just doing my job,'' he said, slightly embarrassed.

Elizabeth saved him by changing the subject. She cut the last piece of cake and started to hand it to Kyle. His baby brother was her age, but she treated him as if he were several years younger. Travis couldn't help being pleased by that.

"Are you going to behave?" she asked, holding out the plate.

"Yes, ma'am."

"Good. No more trouble from you, young man." Her voice was stern, but her eyes danced.

Travis watched her tease Kyle and felt a warmth burning deep in his chest. He glanced around the table, at the people he loved most in the world. It felt right to have Elizabeth share in this part of his life. Louise chatted with Austin. Mandy scraped her plate clean. For the first time in years, he felt content.

Elizabeth looked up at him and their eyes met. The sadness and wariness from that morning was gone. In their place something soft and lovely flared to life. He wanted to make love to her. Instantly heat boiled through him, burning in his blood and engorging his groin. An answering passion made her lean forward slightly and lick her lower lip.

He wanted to feel her and taste her, loving her until she writhed with need. The room faded and all he saw was her. The V neck of her sweater had slipped slightly, allowing him to see the valley between her breasts and the hint of a curve. He wanted her naked, next to him. Under him. As much as he'd loved the feel of her mouth on him, this time he wanted to be inside, claiming her. He figured that line of thinking meant he was pretty primitive, but that didn't make his erection go away.

Louise stood up and asked if anyone would like coffee. Her prosaic question broke the spell between them, and Elizabeth looked away. After a few minutes, Travis managed to quench his desires. The conversation moved from speeding tickets to the local high school football team and the chance they had at the local championship.

Mandy climbed onto his lap. He put his arm around her back to support her. She leaned against his chest.

"You've got gravy on your shirt," he said, pointing to the spot on her sweatshirt.

She glanced down and held the shirt out so she could see it. "I always spill, huh?"

"Yeah, but I like it."

"You like it?" She grinned. "That's silly. You're not supposed to like it."

"Well, I do."

He bent over and tickled her under her arms. She squirmed and laughed. When he stopped, she sagged against him and sighed. "You're nice, Travis."

"You're not too bad yourself."

"There's a boy in my class. He said he lost his parents, but then he found new ones. I guess his mommy and daddy were too lost to ever find their way home."

He didn't know whether or not he should explain what the boy had meant by "lost." Before he could decide, she continued.

"He loves his new mommy and daddy, but he misses the old ones. He says new parents are fun. I lost my daddy. Mommy says he's not ever coming back. Could you be my new daddy?"

He felt as if he'd been hit by a speeding train. All the air rushed out of him and his chest ached. He tried to speak, but couldn't. His throat was too dry.

Mandy stared up at him, her wide blue eyes trusting him with her heart. He glanced around the table. Everyone else was busy with their own conversation. No one had overheard Mandy's question.

"I'm flattered you would ask me," he said at last, touching her soft cheek, then tucking a loose strand of hair behind her ear. "But I don't know how to be a daddy. I don't have any children of my own. Why don't I just be your friend instead?"

She frowned. "Do you have to learn how to be a daddy?"

"I think so."

She raised her shoulders and let out an exaggerated sigh. "Okay. You can be my friend, and then when you learn how to be my daddy, you can be that, too, okay?"

He hadn't cried in about twenty years, but suddenly he felt a burning behind his eyes. He pulled Mandy close and hugged her tight. ''It's better than okay, Mandy. It'll be great.''

The house was still. Elizabeth stood by the door and listened to the *creak creak* of the swing on the front porch. She balled her hands into fists, then consciously relaxed them. The company had gone home, Mandy was asleep in her bed. Elizabeth couldn't avoid Travis forever, even if she wanted to. But what was she going to say?

She shook her head. The problem wasn't what to say, it was where to start the conversation. They had many things to discuss, not the least of which was what had happened between them last night.

She walked toward the front door, placed her hand on the handle and paused. All of this would be a lot easier if she knew what she wanted. She knew what she didn't want. She didn't want to make another mistake like the one she'd made with Sam. She didn't want to be a fool again for a man. The easiest and safest way to ensure that was to never get involved again. Especially with someone even worse than Sam. Travis was too good-looking by far. He was kind, tender, sweet with her daughter and hot in bed. By comparison, Sam was an amateur, his smooth-talking ways falling far short of Travis's charm. Logically, she had to steer clear of Travis Haynes. If not, she would be risking herself all over again, and she would have learned nothing from her false marriage.

False. Just the word was enough to send waves of shame surging over her. Her cheeks heated. She pressed her hands against her face and prayed that she would one day be able to look back on what had happened and not feel so disgusted with herself. Friends had told her she was overreacting. Even Travis had told her to stop beating herself up about it. They didn't understand, she told herself. They didn't know what it was like to have made that big a mistake in judging someone's character. *They* weren't going to have to explain it to Mandy when she was old enough to understand. They didn't have to spend the rest of their lives knowing they had been taken in by a con man.

Elizabeth knew she had been so starved for love and affection, too eager to believe that someone—a man—finally loved her, that she hadn't wanted to see that Sam was using her.

She drew in a deep breath. One day she would be able to look back on this without wanting to crawl away and die. It had to get better; time was all she had. She grabbed the door handle and turned it, then pulled open the door and stepped out onto the porch.

The night was dark, the moon a faint sliver in the inky sky. Stars hung low, as if they wanted to eavesdrop on what she had to say. She knew Travis had seen her come outside, but the creaking of the swing continued in the same rhythm—slow, steady, seductive.

She told herself to go lean against the railing where it was safe. Better to keep her distance. But she was too tired and tense to be sensible. She moved over to the swing and sat next to him.

One long arm stretched along the back of the wooden seat. She relaxed and rested her head against the slats. He shifted, wrapping his arm around her shoulder and pulling her close against him. She told herself to resist, to stiffen and move away, but she couldn't. Her cheek rested against his hard chest. She could feel the muffled thudding of his heartbeat. The slow, steady sound reminded her of last night. She awakened several times to find herself in his arms. The warmth of his body, the scent of their lovemaking, and the sound of his heart had soothed her back to a restful sleep. For the first time in months, she'd felt safe.

"The meal was terrific," he said. His voice rumbled through his chest, vibrating against her skin. "Thanks for going to all that trouble. You've spoiled everyone. They're used to me cooking hot dogs or something out of a can."

"I enjoy cooking," she said, fighting the urge to look up at him. She wanted to see what he was thinking, she wanted to read the expression in his eyes. She was equally terrified of what she would see there. What if he didn't want her? Worse, what if he did?

"Do you cook a lot?" he asked.

"Some." She smiled and snuggled closer. "I used to think if I was a better wife, Sam would stay home more. So I took a couple of courses given by a restaurant and started really doing some exotic things. It didn't seem to help. For the longest time I assumed it was my cooking."

"It wasn't."

"Of course not. It was his wife and kids. The fanciest beef dish in the world can't compete with that."

"Elizabeth, Sam cared for you."

She grimaced. "Maybe. Sometimes, when I'm feeling rational, I believe that he did. In a sort of sick, twisted way. If he'd really cared, he would have told me the truth about himself." She shook her head. "I don't want to talk about him anymore. Thanks for including me today. I enjoyed having your friends around. Sam never wanted— Damn. Now that I've spilled the beans about him, I can't seem to stop talking about what happened. Sorry."

"Don't be."

Travis slid his hand up her shoulder to her head. His long fingers slipped through her hair to the band that was holding her ponytail in place. He tugged gently, easing it down the strands until her hair was loose and falling over her shoulders. She should probably tell him not to touch her so intimately. She was giving him the wrong idea. But she couldn't help herself. She liked the feel of his hands on her. He made her feel safe and cherished. She hadn't felt any of those things in a very long time.

He bent down and kissed the top of her head. "You were saying Sam never wanted what?"

"Sam never wanted us to have friends over. He didn't want me to have friends at all. But the crowd today was nice."

He chuckled low in his chest. "If you think this was a crowd, you should wait until my other brothers join us. Between Craig's three boys and everybody's dates trying to figure out who belongs with whom, it's a madhouse. I'll give you plenty of warning before letting that group descend on you.''

It sounded lovely, she thought wistfully, thinking of her own solitary childhood. She shifted on the swing. Her right breast pressed against his chest. Her nipples hardened in response to his body, but she ignored the tingling sensation.

''I wouldn't mind,'' she said, then realized she would be gone by the time Travis's family invaded. She would be driving at the end of the week and moving out to her own place next weekend.

A sharp stab of regret and disappointment startled her. She didn't want to think about what it meant, so she recalled what Travis had just told her.

''You mentioned dates,'' she said. ''I thought the Haynes brothers didn't want to get involved with anybody.''

''We all want it to work out, so we seem to keep trying. I guess each of us is praying for a miracle.''

The bitterness in his voice surprised her. ''You sound upset.''

''It gets damned lonely,'' he admitted. ''It's probably a matter of wanting what we can't have. Craig got burned big-time. His wife walked off with one of his closest friends, leaving him with a pile of bills and three little kids. Damn fool keeps looking for the right woman. Kyle dumps his girlfriends before they have a chance to dump him. I'm sure it has something to do with our mother abandoning him when he was fifteen and the string of women Dad brought into the house right after. We went through three stepmothers in three years. And then there's Jordan.''

Travis paused. Elizabeth wished she could move closer to offer him comfort. She could feel his pain. It radiated out from him like the heat of a fever. In the past, he'd talked about his family and his resistance to believing relationships lasted, but this was the first time she'd really understood all that he and his brothers had been through. She was the last one to be giving him any kind of advice, though. Her own track record was pretty awful. So she didn't say anything. She reached up her hand to his face and stroked his cheek. His evening beard poked at her palm. He felt warm and alive. A quivering began low in her belly; she told herself this wasn't about sex.

"Jordan, hell, I don't know about him. He keeps everything inside. He was always the odd one out. The rebel." He grabbed her hand and brought it to his mouth. His kiss on her palm was sweet and damp, his tongue tracing an erotic line from the base of her thumb to her little finger. She shivered.

"After all," he continued, "look at what he does for a living. He's a fire fighter, the crazy fool."

He laughed and she joined him. It felt good to be with Travis like this. He turned toward her, angling one knee across the bench. His position moved them a little apart, but now she could see his face.

He looked good by porch light, she thought, studying the way stubble darkened the hollows of his cheeks and made his eyes more mysterious. She wanted to lean close and touch him all over, relearning the body she had caressed so intimately the night before. His pleasing scent made her remember other smells and tastes, his laughter made her think of other sounds. The way he'd called her name, his voice husky with disbelief and pleasure. Her breasts grew more sensitive inside her bra; her most secret place dampened in anticipation. Desire filled her, but she kept it firmly in check.

"I had an interesting conversation with Mandy at dinner," he said, resting his palm on her thigh.

"I thought I saw you two talking. What about?"

"Her father."

She started to fold her arms over her chest. He grabbed her hands, pulled them down on top of his knee and held her in place. "She was telling me that a boy at school lost his parents. She assumes that they're physically lost and won't be able to find their way back to him. She thinks Sam is lost to her, as well."

Elizabeth tried to ignore the soft denim of Travis's jeans, the heat of his leg below and the warmth of his hand above hers. She tried to ignore the feeling of panic boiling to life in her belly. She'd known it would come to this with Mandy, but not yet. She wasn't ready.

"I told her that Sam wouldn't be able to see her again," she said. "But I can't explain the rest of it to her. Not yet. She's too young."

She dropped her head so that she could stare at her lap. No doubt Travis would disagree with her decision. She didn't care. When she'd asked Sam to sign away the rights to see Mandy, he hadn't even bothered to protest. He'd never been much interested in the girl. Not having him visit every few months would make it less confusing for Mandy.

"I agree," he said, surprising her. "But I think you should be willing to let her talk about missing her father if she wants to."

"Thanks for the advice," she said, surprised she wasn't irritated with his interfering.

He turned her hand over and placed his on top, palm to palm. His skin was rough from his carpentry work—warm, yet dry. He had large hands, strong, capable fingers. She trusted his hands as much as she trusted the man. A big mistake, she warned herself, hoping it wasn't already too late.

"She asked if I could be her father instead of Sam."

Elizabeth's heart clenched. Fierce jealousy and possessiveness poured through her. She wanted to jerk her fingers free and use that hand to slap Travis away. How dare he try to worm his way into her daughter's affections?

She opened her mouth to speak, then closed it again. He hadn't done anything wrong, a small rational voice whispered. He had been nothing but sweet to her and her daughter. Of course Mandy would respond to that affection. She'd spent more time with Travis in the past few weeks than with Sam in the past year.

"What did you tell her?" she asked, daring to look at him.

His dark eyes met and held her own. He shrugged sheepishly. "I told her I didn't know how to be a dad, but that I was willing to be her friend. I hope that's okay."

He was obviously concerned about her feelings. She was grateful she hadn't given in to that moment of jealousy and destroyed the special friendship she and Travis had built. It made sense that she would be protective of Mandy. Look at all that had happened to them. But Travis wasn't the enemy. She would do well to remember that.

She smiled softly. "You shouldn't have lied to her, Travis."

He straightened, obviously startled. "I didn't lie to her."

"Of course you did." She leaned a little closer to him, allowing the night to shut out the rest of the world. "You know exactly how to be a father. It's something you do very well." She held up her hand when he started to protest. "Think about it. You took her to soccer so she could have fun and make friends. You eat raw French toast and tell her that her cooking is wonderful. You hold her tight and protect her from the world."

He dismissed her words with a shrug. "That's the easy part. Anyone could do that."

"Sam didn't. It's not what you do with her, it's taking the time to make the little things matter. I think you're a terrific father. Mandy does, too, or she wouldn't have asked."

"I— Thanks," he said, looking distinctly uncomfortable. His gaze darted around the porch, to the ground, the sky—anywhere but at her. "I hope I can still see her. You know, when you guys move."

"Sure. She'll love it."

"And I think you should talk to her about Sam."

"Travis, I know what's best for Mandy."

"You don't have to tell her about the bigamy, just let her talk about being without him. Glenwood is a small town. We don't have a lot of single parents around here. Mandy probably feels different from everyone else she knows."

"I hadn't thought of that," she admitted. "It makes sense. I'll talk to her." She drew in a deep breath. She should have seen that on her own. "See, you're not the only one who questions about parenting skills." Would she ever get it right? First she messed up completely by believing Sam. Now she was concerned about making a mistake with Mandy. When would the second-guessing end?

"You're going to make yourself crazy," he said, taking her in his arms and pulling her toward him. "Stop worrying. Everything is going to be fine."

"But—"

"No 'buts,'" he said, covering her mouth with his finger. "That's enough thinking for tonight. I don't want you to tax your brain with anything more complex than how wonderful this feels."

He lowered his mouth to hers. She told herself she should stop him. They couldn't do this again. But it felt too good. Too right. His lips were hot against hers. His arms felt strong and safe as he enfolded her against his broadness.

He shifted, pulling her onto his lap. Of their own accord, her arms reached around his neck. One of his hands slipped up from her thigh to her waist, then to her breast. He touched her curves, stroked the puckering nipple. Elizabeth gasped her pleasure and knew that she was seconds from losing control.

She pulled her mouth away from his drugging kisses, away from the pleasure and escape he promised.

"I can't," she whispered, fighting the tightness in her throat and the screams of protest from her aroused body. "Please don't make me do this again."

"Darlin', no one's going to *make* you do anything."

She risked looking up at him. He wasn't smiling, but he didn't look angry. "I didn't mean it like that. Oh, Travis, you are wonderful and there's nothing I'd like better than to make love with you tonight."

"But?"

"But I don't want to fall in love with you or care about you more than I do. If we make love again, I won't be able to be just friends." She pulled free of his gentle embrace and stepped onto the porch. It was tearing her up inside to leave him, but she knew she had to. For both their sakes.

"I'm doing you a favor," she said, looking down at him, hoping that wasn't hurt she was seeing in his eyes. "After all, aren't you the one claiming you don't want to make another mistake? Aren't you the one who doesn't want to get involved again?"

Chapter 12

The question hadn't left him alone in two days. Elizabeth was right—he *had* told her he didn't want to get involved again. It went against everything he believed. Trying for a long-term relationship was a sure guarantee of heartbreak. Not only for himself, but for the woman involved. It would be crazy to start something he didn't intend to finish. The easiest thing for both he and Elizabeth was to stop playing footsie under the table and get on with being friends. At the end of the week, when she was able to drive and her rental house was available to move into, she would go back to her life and he would get on with his. No big deal.

He moved closer to the edge of the soccer field and watched Mandy race across the grass as she chased the elusive ball. She and her new friends squealed with excitement when she connected with her toe. The ball landed far short of the goal, but no one cared, least of all Mandy. She raced over to him and grinned.

"Did you see me kick it?" she asked, panting.

"You bet." He ruffled her bangs, then gave her a little push. "Go back to the game, honey."

"Okay, Travis." She raced off.

He shoved his hands into his uniform trouser pockets. He was supposed to be taking care of paperwork back at the station. But this morning when Elizabeth had asked him if he could take Mandy to soccer practice, he hadn't been able to say no. Time was ticking by too quickly and he wanted be with the little girl as much as possible.

He wanted to spend time with her mother, as well, but that was dangerous. And confusing. What the hell was going on with him? He should be pleased that Elizabeth was well enough to spend the afternoon with Rebecca at the office learning about her new job. She was certainly excited enough to be out of the house. But he'd hated dropping her off at the child services center. It wasn't because he didn't want her to have a job or be independent, it was that he didn't like the reminder that she was leaving.

"You thinking about taking on a new coaching job?"

He turned and saw Austin walking toward him. As always, his friend was dressed in jeans and cowboy boots. A small gold hoop hung in one earlobe. He looked like a modern-day pirate.

"Just baby-sitting," Travis said, pointing to Mandy. "What about you?"

"One of the deputies told me you'd be out here," Austin said, stopping beside him. "I wanted to let you know I'm going to be out of town for a few days."

"Vacation?" Travis asked, then grinned. To the best of his knowledge Austin had never taken a vacation.

"Nope. I'm giving a paper at a conference in France. Technical stuff. I'll be gone about five days."

Travis nudged his friend with his elbow. "You know what they say about French women, buddy. Have a great time."

"Are you going to start living vicariously, now that you've got the hots for Elizabeth?"

Travis started to deny the statement, then figured, why bother? "You saw?"

"Sunday, at your place? Sure. The way you two were looking at each other, you about set the table on fire."

"It's more than sex."

''Then you've got a problem.''

Travis looked at the field where Mandy was in the middle of the young crowd of soccer players. She darted left, the ball went right and she landed on her rump. He could hear her laughter from across the field. Involuntarily, he smiled.

''You know anything about being a father?'' he asked.

''No.''

''Me, neither. Except I wouldn't want to be like my old man. I'd want to be more interested in my kids than in other women.''

''So *be* more interested in your kids.''

''As simple as that?''

''Why make it hard?''

It made sense, Travis thought, in a twisted, Austin sort of way. ''You have any kids?''

For the first time since they'd started talking Austin smiled. ''I'm very careful.''

''I just bet you are. You don't want any gold digger getting a part of your money.''

Austin glanced at the playing field, then looked back at Travis. For once his guard wasn't up and Travis was able to see past the usual blankness in his cold gray eyes. Something ugly and painful flared there. Something that made Travis want to apologize for ever bringing up relationships, women or kids.

''It's not the money.'' The shutters went back down and Austin was once again in control. ''It's about belonging.''

Austin had never belonged. Travis remembered the first day his friend had shown up at the local junior high school. He'd been a skinny misfit of thirteen. Within two days he'd been in the middle of four fights and had a rainbow-colored black eye. He'd started an argument with Travis, not realizing that messing with one Haynes boy had meant getting involved with all four.

Travis looked over at the good-looking man next to him and wondered when he'd begun to change. He liked to think it had been at the moment Travis had stood with him, against his brothers. He always wondered why he'd done it. Maybe it had been the hopelessness he'd seen in Austin's expression, or the fear behind the bravado. Craig, down from the local high school had been willing to let Austin off the hook, but Kyle was too excited about his first fight with his older brothers. Jordan, more like Austin than any of them, had stood on the outside watching and waiting.

In the end no one could remember what the fight had been about. When the boys' vice principal had come to investigate, the Haynes brothers had closed ranks, including Austin as one of their own. He'd never forgotten, Travis knew. Austin hadn't said anything; he hadn't had to. Even after he'd run away from his foster home and gotten into trouble and been sent away, even when he turned up years later, never once saying where he'd been, even now that he was wealthy enough to live anywhere, he stayed close. Travis trusted him as much as he trusted any of his brothers. Maybe more. Austin stayed because he wanted to, rather than simply because of the loyalty of blood.

"You chose not to belong," Travis said.

"You chose not to get involved." Austin jerked his head toward Mandy. "Face it, Travis, you've got it bad for the lady and her little girl. You can run but you can't hide."

"No. It's not like that. I'll admit Mandy's got me by the short hairs. I would do just about anything for that kid. Her dad won't be showing up in her life anytime soon. I want to be there for her. Warn her away from guys like you."

Austin grinned. "Don't worry. I stay away from the innocents. Unlike you."

It was true. Austin only spent time with women who understood the rules of his game: no involvement. "Elizabeth's not an innocent."

"So you *are* involved."

Travis glared at his friend, then smiled sheepishly. "Okay, I'll admit I'm tempted."

Austin glanced at his watch. "I've got to get going if I want to make my flight." He turned to leave, then paused and looked back. The afternoon sun caught him full in the face, highlighting his strong features and boring into his gray eyes. For just a second, some emotion flickered there. Travis wasn't sure, but he thought it might be envy.

"You shouldn't believe it all, buddy," Austin said. "What people say about you. Sure you had some tough breaks with your dad and all. But it doesn't have to be like that again. You have a choice. Don't screw it up just because you think that's all you know."

With that he walked over to his car and climbed in. Travis was still staring after him long after he had disappeared down the road. He shook his head and turned his attention back to the game. Austin made it sound so damn easy. As if he'd *wanted* to mess up before, just because it was easier. It wasn't like that. He'd tried with Julie. They'd both tried. It hadn't worked out. Despite Austin's feelings to the contrary, Travis knew there was too much of his father in him to ever risk anything again.

"We make a sorry group," he muttered to himself. "Maybe men are just born stupid about women and love."

He watched Mandy sprint across the field and kick the soccer ball. It bounced off the goalie's shin, over his head and hit the net. There was a moment of stunned silence on the field, then the kids erupted into screams of delight. Mandy caught his eye and grinned victoriously. Travis called out his approval.

The coached strolled past him. "Are you working with her between practices?" he asked.

"A little."

"It shows. Most parents don't take the time."

Travis started to remind the man that Mandy wasn't his child. He shrugged. It would take too long to explain. He worked with Mandy because they both enjoyed the time spent together. The fact that it improved her soccer game was just a by-product of the fun. Practicing football with his brothers had been one of the best parts of growing up in his family, he remembered. Not that their father had spent much time with them.

Travis frowned. Earl had been kept pretty busy. Between his job as sheriff of Glenwood, and his extracurricular activities, there hadn't been a lot of spare time leftover for four growing boys.

Without even trying, Travis found himself remembering the past. One day in particular, that day in the hardware store, came back to him. He'd seen his own father pick up a woman and take her with him. He'd heard most of their conversation, had winced at the practiced lines, had been shattered and embarrassed as his father had touched a woman who wasn't his wife. He'd seen the lust in Earl's eyes, watched as his father's big hands, hands too much like his own, had rested on that woman's back, then slid lower to her backside. He remembered the smiled promise, the way the woman had brushed her breasts against his father's arm. He'd seen her nipples hardening to tiny points through her thin tank top. At fourteen, what he'd seen had disgusted him, but the woman's body had also aroused him. The conflicting feelings had forced him to run away before he confronted his father.

Even now, Travis could feel the burning in his lungs as he'd run farther and faster than he ever had. Away from his father and that woman, away from what was happening to his family, away from his own adolescent desires. He remembered he'd cried that afternoon. Alone on the banks of the stream, hidden from everyone by a screen of bushes, he'd sobbed out his heart, crying for the pain of what he'd lost. Thinking then it had only been for the loss of his father, knowing now those tears had been for the end of his innocence. He'd never told anyone about that afternoon at the hardware store. His mother hadn't asked why he didn't return with the items she'd sent him for. He wondered now if she'd seen the truth in his eyes.

It had been nearly twenty years since that day, but he could still remember every moment. He'd clenched his fists, raising them high toward the heavens, and sworn he would never be like his father. He'd declared that he would never treat a woman like his father treated his mother. He'd sworn to be faithful, no matter what. He'd risked his soul in a pledge of honor to his yet unknown wife. At fourteen he'd assumed that all emotional problems could be solved if a man didn't cheat. With the hind-sight of adulthood, he knew it wasn't that simple.

The soccer ball bounced past him, calling him back to the present. He reached over and grabbed it, then threw it back into the fray. The kids were tiring from their practice. A few wandered past the lines marking the playing field. Mandy was on the other side of the grass, kneeling on a stretch of dirt tying one of her shoelaces. Someone kicked the ball toward her.

Travis saw the bounce of the ball and in that moment, he knew what was going to happen. He started to call out her name, but it was too late. Before she'd even risen to her feet, he was partway across the field. She turned toward the ball, grinned and stepped after it. She hadn't finished tying her laces, though. When she took a step, she caught the loose lace, and tripped. She put out her arms to brace herself for the fall, but her forward momentum was too strong. She hit the dirt, hands and knees first, and went skidding.

The coach was closer and got there first. By the time Travis reached her side, she was crying hard enough to break his heart. The coach bent over to help her.

"No!" she screamed, pushing him away. "Travis! Travis!"

He was down beside her in an instant. "I'm here, honey." He gathered her close in his arms.

Her small body shook with sobs. He could feel her tears soaking his shirt, but he didn't care. The other children started to gather around, but the coach shooed them away.

"It's okay, Mandy." He bent over and looked at her knees. Dirt caked both of them and the right one was already bleeding.

"I have a first-aid kit," the coach said. "Let me get it."

Mandy looked up at him. Her pretty round face was blotchy and damp. Her long lashes had spiked together and her blue eyes were filled with tears. Her breathing came in gasps, between the sobs.

"I—I h-hurt my h-hand," she said, as fresh tears rolled down her cheeks. He looked at her palms. They were scraped and bloody, with bits of dirt and small pebbles stuck to the skin.

"Oh, baby. I bet it stings, huh? I'm going to give you a magic hug to help, then we'll get you cleaned up."

"M-make it really b-big magic, okay?" she said, clinging to him.

As he hugged her for all he was worth, the pressure in his chest grew. Damn, he didn't want anything to hurt this little girl ever. Unfortunately, reality was going to get in the way of that desire. He couldn't control the future, but he could control keeping her a part of his life.

He picked her up in his arms and carried her over to the water fountain. There was a small hose attached to the middle of the pipe. He stood Mandy up and took off her shoes and socks; then he turned on the tap and grabbed the hose.

"This is going to be cold," he warned, hoping it was cold enough to numb some of the stinging.

She stood bravely as he hosed off her knees. The dirt came out easily. Her hands took a little more work, but he was able to get them clean without having to hurt her more. The coach handed him a towel to dry her off, some antiseptic and a few bandages. By the time Mandy had stopped crying, she was patched up and ready to go home.

He knelt before her on the muddy ground, not caring that he was ruining his uniform trousers. She sniffed, then wiped her eyes.

"I need another hug," she said, holding out her arms.

He pulled her close. The tears started up again, but he knew they were more from shock than from pain. "It'll be okay," he whispered. "I promise."

Her body was slight against his chest. Her little-girl scent— part dirt, part sunshine—made him want to smile. The trust implicit in her embrace twisted in his chest like a dagger. He was probably ten different kinds of fool, but he couldn't let her go.

He and his brothers had decided long ago that cops made lousy fathers. The hours were long, the interruptions unavoidable. For all his thirty-four years he'd believed that as much as he'd believed in the existence of gravity.

But as Mandy clung to him with her sobs breaking his heart, he knew he couldn't believe it any longer. Not when he remembered his own father. No one had forced his old man to pick up that woman in the hardware store. No crime, or criminal had been the reason he'd come home late every night smelling of sex and booze. Earl Haynes had decided early that his right in life was to have lots of women, his wife and family be damned. He had chosen.

Travis swallowed hard. It had been a decision on his father's part. Not genes, not an unavoidable family curse. Earl had *chosen* his destiny. And he'd used his position as sheriff to hide away from his real responsibilities to his family.

Travis didn't want to risk hope and then have it blow up in his face, but Mandy wasn't leaving him a lot of options. In the past few weeks she'd stolen her way into his heart. He couldn't cut her out now. If it *was* a matter of choice, he could choose a different path from the old man's. After all, Craig was a great father. Travis could be one, too.

Mandy released him and stepped back. She smiled and wiped her face. "That *was* a magic hug," she said. "I feel better. Can we get ice cream before we pick up Mommy?"

"Sure," he said. He rose and held out his hand. Mandy slipped her smaller one trustingly in his and started walking toward the car.

He would talk to Elizabeth, he decided. Mandy needed a father and he needed the little girl. He would be there for her as much as Elizabeth would let him be. He'd made his decision and nothing was going to steer him off course.

Elizabeth stepped out into the bright sunshine and smiled. She felt wonderful being out of the house and back at work. If she had to be cooped up, then Travis's place was a wonderful home in which to recover, but after almost three weeks, she'd grown tired of staring at the same collection of walls.

She sat on the bottom step to wait for her ride. Late-September sunshine warmed her skin through the light cotton dress she wore. Beside her was a briefcase full of paperwork. Rebecca had teased her about not having to get it all done in one night. Elizabeth didn't mind the extra work. She had a lot of time to make up for. Besides, she liked feeling that she was actually accomplishing something.

A familiar black Bronco turned at the corner and pulled to a stop in front of her. She walked across the sidewalk as Travis leaned over and opened the passenger's door.

"Hi, guys," she said, slipping into her seat.

"We had ice cream," Mandy announced.

"Good for you." Elizabeth snapped her seat belt into place, then half turned to look at Mandy. Her breath caught in her throat. Mandy's face was tear-streaked and there were bandages on her hands and knees. "What happened?"

"I fell down, but Travis gave me a magic hug and now I'm almost all better." Mandy rubbed her left palm with her fingers. "But it still hurts a little."

"I'll bet." Elizabeth glanced at Travis.

He grimaced. "She tripped on her shoelace at practice. Unfortunately, she was outside of the grass playing field and on some dirt. I cleaned her up and patched the worst ones. I think she'll be okay."

"She looks fine. Thanks for taking such good care of her."

"No trouble."

They drew to a stop at a traffic light. He glanced at her. His normally open expression seemed slightly shuttered and cautious.

He faced front again. She took the opportunity to study his strong profile, the straight line of his nose, his trimmed mustache, the firm yet sensual curves of his mouth. How was she supposed to resist this man when even the faint scent of his body was enough to make her weak with longing?

Only a few more days, she told herself. She would already be driving her own car if the clutch wasn't so stiff. She'd tried it that morning, but shifting gears had caused a sharp pain in her side. Her gaze slipped over Travis again. Being chauffeured by him wasn't the worse punishment in the world.

"Would you mind if we went by my rental?" she asked. "The landlord dropped off the key at work. I'd like to take a look at what furniture is there and what I need to buy."

"Sure."

There was nothing in his voice to indicate that he was pleased or sorry to take her there. Did he think about her leaving as much as she did? Did he want his house back to himself or would he miss her? It wasn't fair, she told herself. She wanted Travis to miss her terribly, yet at the same time she knew she had no business staying involved in his life. She couldn't do anything but hurt both of them. She wasn't getting involved again. Ever. It was too dangerous. She didn't have the common sense to know when a man was right for her. Even if she did, everything about Travis warned her that he was all wrong. They were both relationship impaired, neither of them knowing how to make love work. It would be foolish to try.

So why was she thinking about it? She stared out the window and bit back a sigh. She had no answer. She was probably just tired from her first day back at work. Think about something else, she ordered herself.

As they drove through Glenwood, Elizabeth gave him directions to her rental house. The neighborhood wasn't anything like Travis's, she noted, eyeing the homes that hadn't seemed so small the last time she'd been here.

Mandy sat as far forward as her seat belt would let her. She peered out the window searching for the promised bunnies. "There were really three of them, Mommy?" she asked, her voice laced with pleasure.

"Yes, honey. I saw them from the kitchen window. They're probably hiding in the backyard. Maybe you could look for them."

Mandy bounced with excitement. "Okay."

Travis stopped in front of a small, tan-colored, one-story house. There were two windows facing the front, and a garage. She opened her door and slipped out. Mandy was already racing in circles on the lawn.

Elizabeth pulled the key from her dress pocket and led the way up the walk. She opened the door, then stepped inside. The house opened directly onto the living room. To her left was a small dining alcove, in front of her, the dark hallway. She could see the entrance to the kitchen beyond the dining room.

The carpeting was only a couple of years old. A muddy brown that would wear well and not show the dirt. Two gold patterned couches filled the living room. There were a couple of end tables and a big square wood-and-glass coffee table. The entertainment stand was empty. She would have to get a TV. She walked down the hallway. A green-tiled bathroom was flanked by two bedrooms, one slightly larger than the other. The master bedroom, if it could be called that, had a king-size bed and a single dresser. The other room was empty.

The kitchen hadn't been remodeled since the house was first built in the fifties, so the large tiles on the counter and up the wall were light and dark green. The refrigerator was newer, but the gas stove was large, with massive burners and curved edges. Over the kitchen sink, a window looked out onto a fenced backyard.

"There's no furniture in the other bedroom," Mandy said, bouncing into the kitchen. "Am I going to sleep on the floor?" She sounded slightly intrigued by the idea.

"No." Elizabeth brushed her bangs out of her eyes. "I'm going to buy you a new bedroom set."

"Golly!" Mandy's eyes got round. "Can I have a desk, too? So I can do my homework in my room like a big girl?"

"Sure." Elizabeth opened the back door. "Why don't you go see if you can find the bunnies?"

"Okay." Mandy raced outside. The screen door slammed shut behind her.

So far, Travis hadn't said a word about the house. She turned toward him. "What do you think?"

He stood in the doorway to the kitchen. With his arms folded over his chest, and his khaki shirt pulling across his broad shoulders, he looked like some kind of conquering warrior.

"It's very nice. I'm sure you'll be happy here."

There was something in his voice, something dark and broken. She wanted to ask what, but she was afraid. Instead, she dug in her purse and pulled out a small notebook. "I need tons of things. Do you have the time to wait while I make a quick list?"

"Sure." He stepped back to allow her to pass him.

But he hadn't moved back far enough, or the floor was uneven, or her feet unsteady because she managed to brush her arm against his chest as she went into the hallway. The heat from the brief contact sent a tremor up her arm and into her breasts. It was dark in the small house. Dark enough to make her forget it was still daytime outside and that her daughter was just a few feet away. Dark enough to give her the courage to look up at his face and meet his gaze. Dark enough to wonder if the fire would return to his irises and flicker there, matching the flames she felt burning inside.

The house smelled musty and unused. The furniture wasn't to her taste. After being in Travis's beautiful home, this place was a rude awakening. It could all be fixed, she told herself. A few throw pillows, some lacy curtains, a good scrubbing and airing out—then everything would be fine. But it wasn't the house at all. It was the man.

He tempted her. Even though she knew it was foolish and wrong and this time more than her pride would be at stake, she couldn't resist him. He made her care about him, even when she didn't want to. Even when it made her a fool twice in the same lifetime. Even when she knew they were doomed to heartbreak. Which is why she had to leave him as quickly as possible.

He reached out to hold her at the exact moment she stepped away. His arms hung there a moment, giving her time to step back into his embrace. He would kiss her. She could see the promise in his eyes. He would hold her and tonight he would make love to her. She turned her back on him and started down the hall.

Within twenty minutes she'd completed her list. Travis had followed her from room to room, offering suggestions. It was as if that moment in the hall had never happened. But it had. Her fingers trembled as she wrote out the items she would need. Her heart raced in her chest and her eyes burned with more than regret.

"I think that's it," she said. "The miniblinds will make a big difference at letting in light. Thanks for the suggestion."

"You're welcome."

She pocketed the small notebook and led the way back to the kitchen. "Is there some kind of mall around here? I need to buy Mandy furniture, as well as some other supplies for the house."

"There's a furniture warehouse store about forty miles away," he said as he followed her. "I have tomorrow off. I could drive you there if you'd like."

The screen door slammed open and Mandy ran into the kitchen. She glared at her mother. "I looked everywhere and I couldn't find even *one* bunny."

"I'm sorry, honey. Maybe they're hiding."

"But I looked!" Mandy's lower lip thrust out. "I don't care about any stupid bunnies. I want to stay with Travis and get a puppy."

Elizabeth drew in a deep breath. Of course, she thought, wondering why it hadn't occurred to her sooner. She wasn't the only one who was going to miss their host and his wonderful house. Mandy would, as well. She shook her head. She should have thought of that already.

"You'll like it here," Travis said, squatting down to the child's level. "There are lots of kids for you to play with right here on this street. You'll forget all about me, but no matter what, I'll still be around."

He paused, as if waiting for Elizabeth to disagree. She wasn't going to; she was pleased he wanted to stay in touch with Mandy. The little girl needed some continuity in her life.

"This house is dumb."

"It's not dumb," Elizabeth said, touching her daughter's hair. "I'm going to buy you a beautiful bedroom set and a real big-girl desk." She tried to ignore the flash of guilt. She didn't usually try to buy Mandy's cooperation, but desperate times called for desperate measures.

Despite the bribe, Mandy didn't look convinced. It was only after Travis tickled her into a giggling pile on the floor that her good humor returned.

While Mandy raced ahead to the car, Travis locked the front door.

"You should be able to get everything you need at the furniture store," he said. "The entire first floor is filled with household items. Linens, miniblinds…that sort of thing."

"Do you know if they deliver?" she asked, taking one last look at her new home.

"I think so. Are you thinking for the bedroom furniture?"

"Yes." She squared her shoulders. "Mandy is becoming too attached to you. I need to get us into our own place as quickly as possible."

Travis didn't answer. She wasn't sure if she was sorry or glad. Maybe a little of both. If he'd responded at all, she would have been forced to admit that Mandy wasn't the only one becoming too attached.

Chapter 13

They took the elevator to the top of the giant furniture warehouse, then started the circular descent to the ground floor. Sample rooms had been set up, followed by rows of couches, entertainment centers and end tables.

"Oh, good. They *do* deliver," Elizabeth said, pulling her list out of her jeans pocket.

"Yeah, within forty-eight hours," Travis replied, pointing to a sign posted on the wall.

"Great. If we buy Mandy's bedroom set today, it can be delivered Saturday when we move in."

She'd been reading the sign, but she felt Travis stiffen at her side. She risked glancing at him. He stared down at her, his normally readable face expressionless.

"That's quick. When did you make that decision?"

Yesterday, when I figured out how much Mandy and I were going to miss you, she thought. "It makes sense, Travis. I'm completely back on my feet. I've arranged for Mandy's afternoon daycare, although I'll be getting off work at three-thirty, so she'll need it for less than an hour. My car's clutch is still a little too stiff for me, but Rebecca is going to give me a ride to and from work for a couple of days."

"I see." He turned toward a fabric-covered sofa next to them. "You've got everything figured out."

"I guess I do. I'm sure you'll be pleased to see the last of us."

"Sure." He looked back at her and smiled. "We both need our lives to get back to normal."

If his smile didn't reach his eyes, she wasn't going to comment on the fact. If he noticed that she couldn't stop looking at him or brushing against him as they walked through the store, he didn't say anything, either.

The tension between them stretched until she could physically feel it tugging on her insides. She didn't want it to be like this. She wanted Travis to be her friend. She needed him to be there, to be strong. Was that wrong?

Before she could figure out the answer to the question, he darted across the aisle to a selection of leather furniture. There were three different rooms displayed, all in the same soft, buttery leather. He dropped down onto a black sofa and leaned back his head.

"This is wonderful," he said, closing his eyes. "I may do my entire house in leather."

"Even the bathrooms?" She bit back a giggle.

He opened one eye. "Laugh all you want, but this is *man* furniture."

"Oh, I see. So you'll want a gun rack right next to the TV. And what about your famous knife collection? You know, the ones you used to hunt the woolly mammoth."

She'd made the mistake of moving too close to him. He growled out a warning, but before she could jump back, he reached forward and tackled her legs, pulling her toward him. She landed in a heap on his lap. Their faces were inches apart; his breath fanned her cheek. It could have been a dangerous moment, but they were both laughing too hard.

His thighs were hard beneath her legs. Their jeans—hers blue, his black—rubbed together, generating an erotic heat. Low in her belly, wanting grew. She acknowledged the feeling, acknowledged that Travis's hands became less teasing and more caressing on her arms. But he didn't try to kiss her. In that moment of laughter, their friendship had been restored. Apparently neither of them wanted that threatened again.

The sound of someone clearing his throat broke through her musing. She looked up, then blushed like a high-schooler caught necking in the back seat of her father's car.

"May I help you?" the small, gray-haired man asked, his bushy white eyebrows raised above his wire-rimmed glasses.

Elizabeth tried to slide off Travis's lap, but his large hands held her in place.

"No, thanks," Travis drawled. "We were just testing the sofa."

"I see. Does it work to your satisfaction?" the man asked, glaring down at them.

"We're not sure yet." Travis winked. "I think it needs a little more testing."

The man turned on his heel and marched away. Elizabeth struggled to break free. "He's probably gone to get the manager."

"So what?" Travis leaned forward and kissed the tip of her nose. "The store is practically empty and we weren't doing anything wrong."

She couldn't help herself. She sagged against him and giggled. "Maybe you should have worn your uniform. At least then you could have threatened to arrest him."

"You just miss seeing me in my cowboy hat. If I'd known you were so attached, I would have worn it today."

"Oh, stop." She gave one last, hard push on his chest and broke free. She scrambled to her feet and smoothed the front of her shirt. Her fingers caught on an open button right above her bra. "I was flashing him," she said, horrified.

Travis chuckled. "He was getting a bit of an eyeful, but I doubt it's anything he hasn't seen before." He stood up and stretched. "Need some help?" he asked, approaching her.

"Don't even think about it." She slapped his hands away.

"No more pit stops. We have a list." She waved the piece of paper in front of him. "I want you to behave for the rest of the day. Do you promise?"

He put his arm around her shoulders and pulled her close. She knew she should resist, but it was just for one day, she told herself. They were in a public store. What's the worst that could happen?

"I'll behave," he said, whispering in her ear. "But I just might want to test-drive a mattress or two."

She managed to steer him clear of the adult bedroom section, but they spent almost an hour picking out Mandy's furniture. She stood between a bedroom done in white, with a canopy bed and delicate furniture, and one done in light pine. That bed was a four-poster design with a raised mattress.

"She'd practically need a step stool to get on it," Elizabeth said, gauging the distance.

"But it comes in a double. The canopy doesn't. If you get the bigger bed, she can have a friend over to sleep with her. Even if they use sleeping bags on top of the covers it'll be more fun than one of them on the floor."

She eyed him warily. "How do you know what little girls want?"

"Mandy tells me things."

"What kind of things?"

"Things like how she'd enjoy having a friend spend the night occasionally, and how much she wants a puppy."

"A puppy?" Elizabeth looked at the bed. "It would be a lot less messy to get the larger mattress. What do you think of the desk?"

It matched the pine dresser. There were two small and one large drawer on either side. A bookcase sat next to it.

Travis knelt down and ran his hands over all the edges of the desk. He checked the workmanship, then tested the drawers and the sturdiness of the shelves.

"I like it," he said. He glanced up at her. "If it's about money—"

"It's not," she said, cutting him off. She perched on the edge of the four-poster bed. "You might not understand my logic, but running off and leaving everything Sam had bought us wasn't something I did lightly. I know it wasn't the most sensible thing I've ever done, but it was a symbolic act for me. One that really proved to me I wasn't kidding about completely cutting him out of our lives. I think doing that is what has allowed me to heal as much as I have." She held up her hand. "I know what you're going to say. I haven't healed completely. I know there are a few things I'm working through, but I'll get there." She paused and drew in a breath. "Why are you grinning at me?"

He stood up and pulled out the desk chair. After turning it around, he sat down, straddling it, resting his arms along the slatted back. "You seem to know everything, so you figure out why I'm grinning."

"Travis!"

"I was just thinking about how strong you are. I believe that you will put this behind you and get on with your life. I admire that."

She ducked her head. "Thanks," she said softly. "Your support means a lot to me."

A different sales clerk approached. This one was a young woman in a navy suit. "May I write up an order for you?" she asked, her gaze locking on Travis's.

Elizabeth was too contented to care. "Yes, for me."

The young woman forced her eyes away from Travis. "What can I do for you?"

Elizabeth hesitated, then pointed at the pine set. "I'd like this bedroom set. All the pieces, please. Can you have it delivered on Saturday?"

They made the rest of her purchases quickly. They had one argument in the linen section, picking out sheets for Mandy. Elizabeth wanted something floral while Travis voted for the redheaded cartoon mermaid. In the end she bought them both.

"You're worse than Mandy," Elizabeth grumbled as she tossed the sheets into her cart.

"You love it," he said, coming up behind her and planting a quick kiss just below her left ear. Instantly a shiver raced through her body. She did love it. That was the problem.

They went through the kitchen accessories. She picked out some dinnerware and glasses. She started to hold up the box for his approval, then stared at him.

"What?" he asked, standing at the end of her cart. "Have I grown horns?"

"I don't care if you like these," she said.

"Thanks so much."

"No." She smiled. "I didn't mean it in a bad way. I meant, I don't have to get your approval on anything. I don't have to get anyone's approval ever again."

Travis frowned and planted his hands on his hips. "I have a lot of flaws, Elizabeth, but I'm *not* an ogre."

"Oh, I know." She put the dinnerware in her cart. "I suddenly realized that I don't have to get Sam's approval. Even though he was gone so much, I thought he should be a part of the decision making. I waited to get his opinion on drapes, dishes, what time Mandy should go to bed. I don't have to anymore. I can do what I want."

"It sounds like you're over him."

She glanced up at him. He held himself stiffly, as if regretting making the observation. Around them, shoppers chattered about their purchases. She could hear the faint electronic beeping of the cash registers. They stood alone in the middle of housewares discussing the state of her heart. Why did she feel her answer was so important? It couldn't be. Not now, not after she was just getting over what had happened.

"I am. The relationship had been in trouble for a long time. I was ready to ask for a divorce, and then it turned out I didn't need one. I know what he did to me has made me wary of trusting anyone again. But that's about pride, not about my heart. I've been over Sam Proctor for years."

"Soon you'll be over me, too," he said, his voice teasing.

But she didn't smile back. "Travis, I'll never get over what you did for me and Mandy. You came to my rescue when I was in dire straits, and I'll never forget that. You gave me more than a roof over my head. You were good to Mandy and a great friend to me.''

You showed me how it's supposed to be between a man and a woman.

But she didn't say her last thought aloud. Better for both of them if they simply put it out of their minds. If only it were that easy. If it had just been sex, she would have been able to forget. Being with him had been more than that. It had been warm and tender, loving and caring. He'd made love to her slowly and easily as if he'd been waiting for her all his life, as if he'd had all the time in the world.

He'd made her feel cherished.

''I'll never forget what you did,'' she repeated. ''I'm going to miss you when I move out.''

She waited, but he didn't answer in kind. And suddenly the warmth in her belly turned very, very cold.

Travis checked the rearview mirror for traffic, but the main highway was empty on a weekday afternoon. He looked in the mirror again, this time glancing at the boxes and bags stuffed in the back of his Bronco. They'd managed to fit everything in except for Mandy's bedroom set. That would be delivered to Elizabeth's new house in time for her to move in on Saturday. She was really leaving.

He didn't want to think about that, or how it made him feel. He tried to come up with some topic of conversation. The cab had been quiet for too long. Elizabeth sat in her seat, with her hands folded on her lap. She never once glanced at him.

He knew why. He hadn't said he would miss her, as well. He cursed under his breath. Those words were inadequate to describe what he was feeling. Hell, he didn't even know what he was feeling. Everything was confused. It had happened so fast. One minute he was living his life, with no concerns and no questions. A few short weeks later he was deeply involved with a woman and her daughter. He didn't know what he was supposed to do. Should he ask her not to leave, or just forget about her? Could he risk another relationship? Would she be willing to take that chance? Was it genetics or bad luck that kept the four Haynes brothers single? Was he or was he not a duck?

The last question made him smile. He saw Elizabeth glance at him out of the corner of her eye. He drew in a deep breath to plunge into an emotional discussion, but at the last second chose something more safe.

"Mandy's going to love everything you bought her," he said.

"I hope so." She brushed her hair off her shoulders. "Everything cost enough. If she doesn't like it, I think I'll make her get a job to pay me back for everything."

He grinned. "We can always use another deputy."

For the first time in almost an hour, Elizabeth grinned back. She looked at him, some of the concern leaving her eyes. "She'd love that. I suspect she'd spend her day running the siren."

"That would be a problem." His smile faded. "Look, I've been thinking about this whole money thing. I don't want you to pay me for the rooms. You're going to need it to get on your feet, financially."

She turned until she was facing him. He gave her a quick glance. Her mouth pulled into a straight line and her jaw was clenched.

"I insist," she said forcefully. "We made a deal, Travis. The money was the only thing that allowed me to accept your hospitality. It was too little to begin with, it probably didn't even cover food. If I can't pay you, it's too much like lying about everything."

He should have known she would make this more difficult than it had to be. He grabbed the steering wheel tightly, then moved into the right lane for the turnoff to Glenwood. "I don't need the money and you do. As for covering the food bill, give me a break. You two hardly eat anything. I want to do this for you. I want to help."

She rested her hand on his forearm. He liked the feel of her fingers brushing against his skin. It was hard not to get distracted.

"I don't need your help anymore," she said. "Even if I did, I can't accept it. This isn't about you, it's about Sam. He paid for everything. He didn't want me to work. When I did, after Mandy started school, he was very unhappy. He insisted that I keep my money for myself. I have almost a year's salary saved up. It might sound silly to you. You've always been responsible for yourself. But for six years a man controlled my life. I don't want that to happen again. Please don't start changing the rules on me now."

He drove past the sheriff's station and the small park with the duck pond. At the corner he turned left and entered the residential section where Elizabeth was going to live. He made a right on her street, then pulled into the driveway and turned off the engine.

He understood what she was saying, but he didn't have to like it. So much of her life was still tied up with Sam Proctor. He rubbed the bridge of his nose. Who was he to talk? So much of his life was tied up with his past and reputation.

"I don't care about the money," he said at last. "If you insist on paying me, at least let me use the money to buy Mandy something. A bike, maybe. Is that against the rules?"

Elizabeth shook her head. "No. That would be wonderful. I appreciate all you've done with her. She really cares about you."

"I care about her. I know you don't want the rules changed, but I don't have a lot of choice about this one. I can't let go of Mandy. I don't want to lose her. I'm not saying I'm a great father figure, but I'm not as bad as I thought. I want to stay involved with her." He shifted in his seat, turning to face her. "Can we make that work?"

He hadn't expected tears. Her big brown eyes glistened as she blinked frantically. One tear slipped onto her cheek. She brushed it away impatiently. "You're a damn fine man, Travis Haynes. Don't you dare let anyone tell you otherwise."

He could feel something uncomfortably like a blush heating

his cheeks. He cleared his throat. "Yeah, well, don't let it get around, okay? I have this reputation."

She leaned forward and touched her hand to his cheek. "I'm beginning to think your reputation is all talk. You're far too decent to be any kind of a heartbreaker. I would like it very much if you would continue to see Mandy. I'll work around your schedule or whatever it takes. She adores you."

In the close confines of the Bronco, the scent of her body—the sweetness of her woman's fragrance and the spicy temptation of her perfume—mingled together in a seductive aroma designed to drive him crazy. Her face was so near his, he could see the individual lashes framing her dark brown eyes. A few curling hairs drifted onto her cheek. The red lipstick she'd put on that morning had long since worn away, leaving her mouth soft and rose-colored.

This conversation was supposed to be about Mandy, but all he could think about was Elizabeth. Even as his mind screamed at him to just let her go, his heart protested the parting. He was torn between what he believed and what he wanted. Could he fight the legacy of his father? He and his brothers were so terrified of falling in love, of failing. Was it circumstance or destiny? He'd chosen to become involved with Mandy. Could he choose to become involved with Elizabeth? Could he choose to love her? Could he make it work?

He'd tried once, and failed. Julie had been his wife. But he'd never felt these powerful emotions before. He'd never needed her the way he needed Elizabeth. Was it enough?

"Travis?"

He had to let her go. It was the only sensible decision to make. Everything in his past warned him that he would fail if he tried again. Yet his heart begged for one more chance. What if everyone was wrong? What if he *could* do it? Making it work with Elizabeth would be worth anything. What did he have without her?

He took her hands in his. Her fingers were small and delicate, yet capable. She stared at him, her eyes concerned yet trusting.

They hadn't been together long enough.

She was moving out; he didn't have any more time.

"Don't go," he said.

Chapter 14

"What did you say?" Elizabeth asked, sure she must have heard him incorrectly.

"Don't go. I want you and Mandy to stay with me."

"Are you crazy?"

"Maybe. But stay anyway."

"No," she said loudly. "No, I can't. I won't. Don't ask me. Dammit, Travis. What are you doing?"

She didn't wait to hear the answer. After undoing her seat belt, she opened the truck door and jumped down to the ground. She moved to the back of the Bronco and started grabbing her packages. He stood and watched her.

"I care about you. I don't want to lose you."

Each word was a blow to her heart. Her chest tightened and her breathing became labored. "I asked you not to change the rules. Why are you doing this?"

"Why are you angry?" His voice was low and quiet. She could hear the pain in each word.

The anger would keep her strong, but she couldn't tell him that. When she'd collected as much as she could carry, she walked past him to the front door. After fumbling with the key, she stepped inside and dropped her bags on the ugly gold sofa.

The house still smelled musty. The small dark rooms would

never be more than what they already were: a temporary escape from her life, from her past and the shame that haunted her.

She stood in the center of the living room and fought the tears. Pain clawed at her stomach. She folded her arms over her belly and tried to hold it all inside. Not now, she prayed. Not like this. Not Travis. Didn't he know how much she'd grown to need and trust him? He couldn't change now. It wasn't right. It wasn't fair.

She heard him behind her. He set several boxes on the floor. "Elizabeth."

"Don't say anything." She turned to face him. "I don't want to hear it. We had everything planned. We were going to be friends. Travis, I desperately need you in my life, but only as my friend. I can't do more. It's too dangerous. I've made that mistake before and I'm never going to do it again."

He was tall and powerful standing there in the darkened room. His white, long-sleeved shirt emphasized his strength and good looks. She studied the lines of his face, the sadness in his dark eyes. His arms hung loose at his side, but his hands were clenched into fists.

"You don't understand," he said.

He was right, she thought. She didn't understand and she didn't want to.

"I love you."

His words hit her with the force of a lightning bolt, and she nearly went down. Her legs trembled and her breathing stopped. She stared at him, then gasped in a breath. He loved her?

"You can't," she said.

He shrugged. "All my life I've been told I couldn't be a good husband or father. My dad made a mess of both. My uncles are all failures in that department, as well. Every time I tried to make it work, I couldn't. After a while I gave up trying. If it looks like a duck and walks like a duck and sounds like a duck, it's probably a duck."

She remembered the small stuffed yellow duck he'd brought her when he'd gone shopping with Mandy. Even then he'd been wrestling with his feelings for her. She should have known. But what difference would it have made? Would she have left him? She wanted to say yes, of course she would have, but she wasn't sure it was true. Her time with Travis had been magical. Would she have willingly cut it short?

"What I have figured out," he said, continuing, "is that everyone has choices. Earl and his brothers didn't try hard enough. They could have made it work if they wanted to. I could have made it work with Julie. I cared about her. The marriage failed because of a lack of chemistry or each of us being lazy, not because I'm incapable of making a relationship last."

"I don't want to hear this." She started toward the hallway.

He grabbed her arm as she passed him. "You have to listen. It's important. This thing between us isn't going to go away. I'm willing to take a chance, Elizabeth. I know you've been burned. I have, too. I know it's frightening. It's too soon, we don't know each other well enough. But I can't risk losing you and Mandy. I love you both. I never thought I'd ever say those words again, but I believe them to be true with all my being. Trust me. Trust *us*."

She tried to pull away, but he wouldn't let her go. She was forced to look up at him, at the fire flaring in his eyes. These flames frightened her more than the fire of desire. His gaze burned with the heat of conviction. He did believe what he told her, that he loved her. That they had a chance. She wanted to weep from the sadness of it all. Couldn't he see that this was all a cruel joke? It would never work out; she wouldn't let it.

Oh, but she wanted to believe. Her heart had leapt when he'd said he loved her. For a single heartbeat, joy had filled her. Reality was too powerful, though, and couldn't be ignored.

"I don't want to hear this," she said and looked away from him. "I don't believe you. Even if I did, it doesn't change anything."

He was stunned. She could tell by the way he stiffened. He released her instantly and stepped back. "Why?"

She closed her eyes against his suffering and against the temptation he offered. If only she had never met Sam, she might have been able to respond to the gift Travis offered. But she had met Sam and he had changed her.

"Love isn't enough. I loved Sam and look what happened. In his own twisted way, he might have even loved me."

"I don't appreciate the comparison. I'm not a bigamist. I don't have a secret past. I'm not going to destroy your life, I'm going to make it better."

"I like my life just the way it is. Mandy and I don't need anyone. Sam disappeared, never bothering to say why he'd done it. He barely apologized. He signed over custody of his daughter as if she meant less to him than a car. I'm never going to risk that again. Never." She knew she was practically shouting, but she couldn't help herself. He wanted too much. She wouldn't take a chance, she couldn't. "I know. The loving doesn't keep you safe."

Travis moved close and placed his hands on her shoulders. "I am not Sam," he said, speaking slowly as if she couldn't make out the words clearly. "I would never do that to you. What I do is a part of who I am. The ideals of my job are here—" He touched his chest, then brushed hers, just above her left breast. "And here. You know that, Elizabeth. You've always known you could trust me. That's why you came home with me. That's why you're afraid now. You don't want to believe, but I'm not going to give you another choice in the matter. I'm not Sam Proctor. I won't leave you or lie to you. I'll take care of you and Mandy. I'll be here every night to protect you."

His words were like quicksand. The more she struggled, the deeper she sank. Soon she would be swallowed whole into his world. She fought against his spell. "I don't need rescuing. I'm fine on my own. Why won't you believe that?"

Suddenly she was free. He jerked away from her and the quicksand disappeared into nothing. His emotional bonds had snapped. She was alone, as she had requested.

He walked to the window and stared out at her front yard.

The pain radiated out from him. Waves and waves crashed over her, making her want to weep for both of them.

"Why?" he asked, without looking at her.

She had no answer because she didn't understand the question. Did he ask why she couldn't love him back, or why he had loved her at all? She didn't want to know which. He had come to the end of his journey, had shed the false covering learned from his family and had finally seen the true man inside. To what end? She was the last woman in the world to be able to give him what he needed. She would carry that guilt with her forever.

"I'm sorry," she whispered. "So very sorry. I want to be what you need, what you want, but I can't be. If it was just me, I might take the chance again. But I have to think about Mandy. I won't risk either of our hearts."

"Why won't you listen?" he asked, still staring out the window. "I'm not Sam."

"I know. I just wish it was enough."

He turned then. Anguish filled his face, drawing his mouth straight and tightening his jaw. "Have you considered the fact that it might be too late?"

She fought the urge to step back. Too late? Too late because *she* had already fallen in love with him? "It's not." It couldn't be.

He smiled then, a cold smile without humor. "You'd better pray that you're right."

"Please don't be angry with me. I wish I could explain."

"No!" He crossed the room in two strides and grabbed her. This time his grip was hard and bruising. Before she could start to fight, he pulled her up against him. "I'm the one who has to explain. Why can't I find the words?"

"Because there's nothing you can say."

"You're wrong."

She expected a verbal assault. Instead he began another campaign, one much more deadly to her peace of mind.

He kissed her. Not the hot ravishing kiss she might have expected. Despite his firm hold on her shoulders, his mouth was tender against hers. Familiar warmth curled through her, starting at her toes and working its way up to her breasts. The fingers on her shoulders began to knead her tense muscles, soothing them, relaxing her to the point of weakness.

He used his body to speak for him. His chest pressed against hers, offering strength and a place to rest. Long, powerful legs brushed her own. His arousal spoke of passion and perhaps even love if she was foolish enough to believe.

She told herself to push him away, to be cruel to be kind. Better for both of them. She raised her hands to his arms to give herself the leverage necessary to walk away; then she felt the sweet brush of his tongue on her lips.

Instantly her body responded to the caress. Her breasts swelled. Already puckered nipples sought the relief of his touch. Between her thighs the ache deepened as moisture dampened her panties. One last time. One last moment of passion. One last embrace. One last chance to lean on him, to accept his strength and his comfort. While his love frightened her, she could understand and accept the solace of his body. When he knew what she had done—willingly come to him, knowing it was never going to be more than this moment—he wouldn't forgive her. She wouldn't have to bother with sending him away. He would go on his own, hating her.

He was her weakness and her greatest strength. She would be with him, fully knowing that each moment of pleasure would cause her to die a little.

She opened her mouth to him, accepting him inside. He swept over and around, touching, tasting. She stroked his shoulders and back, then moved up to slip her fingers through his curly hair. When he stepped away from her, she murmured a protest. He picked her up in his arms and carried her toward her bedroom. She clung to him, kissing his neck, tracing the line where his afternoon stubble met smooth skin, wrinkling her nose at the slightly bitter taste of his after-shave.

The king-size bed had no sheets or covers. He placed her in

the center, then bent over her. Before he could touch her, she began to unbutton his shirt. She worked quickly, while she was able, then pulled the loose ends free of his jeans. She crushed the still-warm fabric in her hands, savoring the feel of his body heat. He sat up and shrugged out of the shirt.

His chest was broad and tanned, with a faint sprinkling of dark hair between his flat nipples. Slipping free of his long legs, she, too, sat up, mimicking his position and pulled her own shirt over her head. Their eyes locked. A smile tugged at the corner of his mouth. She caught the spirit of their game and reached for her shoes and socks.

Her athletic shoes hit the floor the same time as his boots. She settled back on the bed, kneeling in front of him. He reached for the first button on his fly. She did the same. As he unbuttoned, she unzipped.

The air around them grew thick with tension and the heady smell of desire. Her heart pounded harder and her fingers trembled. His hands moved to the waistband of his now-open jeans. She shook her head.

He raised his eyebrows questioningly. She touched his bare chest, then fingered the strap of her bra. They weren't starting from the same place. He sat back on his heels and watched.

She wanted to unfasten her bra and pull it off quickly. Instead she drew her fingers up from her belly, along her ribs to her breasts. Travis swallowed. She locked her gaze on his face, watching him watch her. His breathing increased.

He rested his hands on his thighs, motionless, and she could see his hardness straining against his white briefs. He was already large and swollen with desire.

Slowly, very slowly, she reached for the front fastener. It released and slid open across her pale breasts. The lace cups caught on her nipples. His breathing increased. She tossed her head, sending her hair back over her shoulders and freeing the bra. It drifted down her shoulders and she tossed it to the floor.

Travis returned his hands to the waistband of his jeans. She matched the movement. They pulled them off together. Clad only in briefs and panties, they stared at each other. She was already weak with desire. Every inch of her body was ready for him. Her breasts ached, her thighs trembled. She drew down her panties. His briefs followed, freeing his engorged maleness to view.

The silence in the room was broken by the faint sound of cars passing on the street and the occasional call of a bird. Their breathing blocked out all other noises. She would have thought she would find this dance unnerving, but it aroused her. She liked knowing what she could do to him without saying a word or even touching him. She liked that his skin gleamed with perspiration and his hands shook as they hung at his sides.

Their eyes met.

She raised her hand to his neck. He matched the motion. She wanted to see more of him, she wanted to know what pleased him. She needed these memories to carry her through the long winter of her life.

He took her breasts in his hands. She covered his flat male chest. When he tweaked her nipples, she did the same. The rate of their breathing increased.

She moved her hands lower, across his belly. His hands followed. Her gaze dropped to his hardened length. How powerful and male he looked.

Her eyes burned as tears threatened. He moved closer, at last drawing her down on the bare mattress. He kissed her face and neck and chest, then suckled her nipples into taut points of need. She felt his hardness probing her thigh. When he would have pulled back, she reached for him drawing him closer to her waiting moisture.

He hesitated before entering. She knew he worried about her healing muscles. She didn't care about any of that. She needed him to be inside of her. She arched her hips toward him, enveloping him in her heated dampness. He groaned once and thrust forward.

The feelings were too perfect, too intense. She clutched at his back, then lower at his buttocks, urging him deeper. Her breath came in pants. He'd barely begun to move when her muscles began to convulse around him. He stared at her, obviously surprised by the suddenness of her release. Fighting against her instinct to hide, she kept her eyes open, letting him see her wonder, her pleasure, her sorrow as her body spent itself. He moved back and forth, giving her all the time she needed to quiver against him, reveling in her soft cries of ecstasy. When the tension in her body had become a satisfied hum, he moved again, quickly bringing himself to the same place.

The game played on as he met her gaze, leaving his own emotions bare as his body shook with release. She saw the muscles in his chest and neck tighten, then relax. His eyes flashed with pleasure and promise, then flared with love.

As he held her close and she listened to the pounding of his heart, she at last gave in to the tears. She believed he loved her. Knowing that truth, she would still leave him. The tears fell silently in mourning for all she had lost.

Travis turned left onto his street and did his best not to speed. He'd left the station early, even though Kyle had been giving him trouble most of the day. His brother knew him too well not to notice his sudden lack of concentration. Thank God nothing out of the ordinary had happened that day in Glenwood. Of course any kind of serious crime was pretty unusual in the small community. Even so, Kyle had been on him from early that morning, making comments about his big brother being at the mercy of a woman. Travis had taken the teasing good-naturedly for two reasons. First, because there had been a note of envy in his brother's voice, and secondly because it was true.

He hadn't been able to think about anything but his night of making love with Elizabeth. After they'd gathered themselves together yesterday afternoon, they'd left her place to pick up Mandy, then had spent the evening together. He grinned as he pulled into the driveway. Elizabeth's car was gone, but he wasn't concerned. She'd taken it to work that morning. As she'd lain in his bed with him that morning, watching the sunrise, she'd said she felt better than she had in days. He knew the feeling.

Being with her, holding her, telling her he loved her, had changed him, as well.

It had been a night without sleep, but he didn't care. The promises her body had whispered had been enough for him.

He stopped in front of the house and got out of the car. After reaching in the back seat, he pulled out the bottle of chilled champagne he'd picked up on his way home, and a bouquet of lilies and exotic orchids. He was bearing more than gifts. In his back pocket was a list of arguments to convince Elizabeth that they belonged together. He understood her concerns. Hell, he even shared some of them. They had both been burned in a big way. She with Sam, and him with his whole damn family. But that didn't mean they were destined to fail at love. It just meant they had to try a little harder to make it work. He took the porch stairs two at a time. The victory would be that much sweeter for their effort. She was right for him. She needed him, Mandy needed him. And more important, he needed *them.* But he only had tonight to convince her.

He opened the front door and stepped inside. The quiet of the house was unsettling. He frowned and tried to figure out why. His brow cleared. He was used to coming home to Elizabeth and Mandy, but neither of them was there. Even Louise was off today.

He walked into the kitchen and stuck the champagne in the refrigerator. They would be back shortly. He would start talking to Elizabeth then. He had to convince her. If he didn't, she would leave him in the morning. He didn't doubt that he could eventually show her that they belonged together, but he knew it would be a lot easier when they were still living in the same house. If he had to, he would resort to guerilla tactics and seduce her.

He knew she cared about him. Last night her body had spoken the words for her. He'd told her over and over that he loved her and would never hurt her. She'd heard him. He liked to think she'd believed him. He shut the refrigerator door and leaned against it. He was in love.

He shut his eyes and smiled. Who would have thought it would happen to him? He'd given up hoping. All his brothers had. If he'd known what being in love was really like, he wouldn't have made the mistake of marrying Julie. He knew now that had been about pride and a desire to prove everyone wrong. Not the greatest basis for a marriage. This time he was getting involved for all the right reasons.

He laughed out loud for the sheer joy of it, then pushed away from the refrigerator. A piece of paper caught his eye. He turned to look and saw that Mandy had left him a new picture. He picked it up, staring at the three figures shown standing in front of a large white house. There was a brown blob in front of the three figures.

"It's us," he said aloud, his throat suddenly thick with emotion. Mandy had drawn a family scene with him—he recognized his khaki uniform and Stetson—Elizabeth, and Mandy herself. The brown blob was probably the puppy she wanted so much.

He put the picture back on the door, anchoring it with magnets. He would thank her when she got home. He started to walk out of the room, then paused. Slowly, very slowly, he turned back and stared at the sketch. It hadn't been there that morning. He would have noticed it. Which meant she'd done it that day at school. So Elizabeth had picked her up, brought her home and then...

And then what? And then she'd left? For where?

A cold feeling swept over him. Without thinking, he raced toward Elizabeth's room. The door was partway closed. He flung it open and stared at the perfectly made double bed. The dresser was clean, the end table bare of anything save a white envelope addressed to him. He didn't have to look at the signature to know who had written the note. He recognized Elizabeth's handwriting. There were no personal effects in the room, no half-packed suitcase, no nightgown hanging by the bathroom door. No smell of perfume or makeup.

He grabbed the note without reading it, then climbed the stairs and entered Mandy's room. His chest ached as if someone had wrapped a band around his ribs and was slowly tightening it. Her room was the same as Elizabeth's: clean and impersonal, as if no one of importance had ever lived there.

He couldn't breathe, he couldn't see. He couldn't do anything except feel the pain. It surrounded him, filling every pore of his being until it darkened to black and he fought against drowning in the hopelessness. She was gone.

She'd left without giving him a chance to convince her to stay. She'd left after they'd made love throughout the night. She'd left after he'd told her how much he loved her. None of that had mattered to her. *He* hadn't mattered to her.

When the honed edges of the razor-sharp emotion had faded to a mind-numbing ache, he opened the envelope. Several fifty-dollar bills floated to the floor. He held the single sheet of paper and read it.

Thanks for your warm hospitality, Travis. I don't know what we would have done without you. I hope you understand that I think it's time for Mandy and me to make our own home. We were both becoming too attached to you.

It wouldn't work, you know. No matter how much we wanted it to. I wish it could have been different. I wish *I* could have been different. But it wasn't meant to be. I hope you find someone as wonderful as you deserve, and that we can still be friends. I need a friend like you in my life, but I'll understand if that's asking too much.

He stared at the words, studying the shape of her letters and the way her signature scrawled across the page. He thought about the champagne and the flowers, the list of arguments and how he'd assumed loving her would be enough. He crumpled the note and let it fall to the ground, then walked down the stairs and out into the coming night.

Chapter 15

"How drunk are you going to get?" Rebecca asked as she stretched across the leather couch in Travis's family room.

Travis stared at the half-empty glass in his hand, then glanced at the bottle sitting on the coffee table. There were about three more inches of Scotch waiting for him. Through his slightly drunken fog, he wondered how much longer it was going to take for the alcohol to allow him to forget. The liquor was dulling his senses enough for him to breathe without feeling that his chest was going to cave in, but he could still sense the broken edges of his exposed heart. He could still remember everything. Damn Elizabeth Abbott and damn his own sorry hide for ever being stupid enough to care.

He drained the glass in his hand, then rose from the leather wing chair sitting at right angles to the sofa. It was exactly three steps to the coffee table. He kept the bottle that far away deliberately. As soon as he wasn't able to navigate those three steps, he would know it was time to stop drinking.

"A lot more drunk," he said carefully, conscious of the effort it took to form words correctly.

Rebecca stared at him. Her dark hair was held away from her face by a headband. Even though it was Saturday afternoon and most people were dressed in jeans and casual shirts, she wore a floral print jumper over a white silk short-sleeved shirt. He knew it was silk because she'd explained it to him once. He'd actually figured out the difference between it and cotton. That's how he'd known Elizabeth's skin had felt like silk against his body.

He stared at her white shirt and wondered if it would feel like Elizabeth's skin. Or would it feel differently because Rebecca wore it? Or if he was still sober enough to grab the Scotch bottle. Maybe if he asked politely, Rebecca would pour for him. He frowned. Judging from the way she was glaring at him, he didn't think she would be willing to cooperate.

As if she'd read his mind, she grabbed the bottle. He held out his glass hopefully. She shook her head and set the bottle on the far side of the couch. He sighed and sagged back in his chair. He didn't have a prayer of getting that far. Not with the buzz filling his head or the weakness in his legs. His coordination was shot. He just wished a benefit of his condition included a lapse in memory.

"I want to talk to you while you're still reasonably sober," Rebecca said, settling down on the edge of the sofa closest to him.

"Terrific. Pour me another drink—then I'll listen."

"I'm your friend, so no, I'm not going to pour you anything else. You're drunk enough. In the morning, you're going to wish you were never born."

He set the glass on the floor next to him. "I already wish I hadn't been born. Nothing's going to change that."

"Elizabeth needs time."

"What the hell are you talking about?"

"This isn't about you, Travis. This leaving. She needs some time to find her way. You've got to give her that." She spoke slowly and patiently, as if dealing with a slow-witted child. He thought about protesting, but he didn't think he could get the words out. His tongue was getting thicker by the minute, and who had started spinning the room?

He leaned back in the chair and closed his eyes. That was

better. "Of course it's about me," he said carefully. "I'm the one she left."

"Fool." She said the word affectionately. He thought about taking offense, but he didn't have the energy. "You're her knight in shining armor. Unfortunately, your timing couldn't have been worse."

That comment was almost worth opening his eyes for—almost. "That's me. A knight. Show me the dragon. I'll slay it. Maybe it'll slay me instead. That would be better."

"Travis."

He held up his hand, then let it drop to his side. When had his arm gotten so heavy? "Sorry. Didn't mean to get maud... maud..." What was that word?

"Maudlin?" she offered.

"Yeah. That. So my timing stinks. Nah. It's not that. It's me. I tried. Not supposed to try. Forgot who I was." He rubbed his hand over his face, then grimaced as he felt two days' worth of stubble. He hadn't shaved that morning. Hadn't done anything except drink more Scotch and try to forget. He couldn't forget; he made a lousy drunk.

"You've got it all wrong," Rebecca said, sounding slightly impatient.

"I know." He risked opening his eyes. Rebecca was glaring at him. He closed his lids again to shut her out. "It was all pretty pointless from the beginning. Who was I trying to kid? She figured it out. That I couldn't do it. Not the right type. Who'd want me for her kid's father?"

"I would."

Travis looked at her. "You're just saying that because I'm your friend and you have to be nice to me." He got so caught up in being pleased that he'd completed such a long sentence that he almost forgot what they were talking about.

Rebecca stood up and moved over until she was standing in front of him, looking down. Fire flashed in her eyes. She planted her hands on her hips, her chest heaved. She wasn't built like Elizabeth. Rebecca's curves were subtle. He'd never cared one way or the other because he'd never really been attracted to her. It didn't mean anything. But he still admired her.

"You are so beautiful," he said wistfully, wishing that staring at her got him aroused. He only had to think about Elizabeth and he was ready to make love, but Rebecca left him with a warm fuzzy feeling and zero passion. The great cosmic joke.

Rebecca drew in a deep breath, then let out a laugh and sank to the floor. She knelt between his legs and rested her hands on his thighs. "You need your butt kicked."

"That's pretty harsh." He raised his eyebrows, or thought he did. His face was getting numb.

"You're thinking about yourself, Travis, and none of this is about you at all. It's about Elizabeth. She's got the problem, not you. Finally you've figured out that you can make a relationship work. I think that's terrific. You're right, you do love her, and she left you." Her big eyes grew sad as they met his own. "Find it in your heart to forgive her. She's running because she's afraid. That's good. That means she cares back."

He covered Rebecca's hands and squeezed tight. "If it's so good, why does it feel so bad?"

"Because she hurt you. But hang in there. Give her time to understand what she's given up. She'll come around. I promise."

His face was completely numb, his tongue thick, his legs heavy beyond movement. None of it helped. He could still feel the sharp stabs of pain in his chest and gut.

"I told her I loved her," he said, softly. He had to look away from his friend's compassionate gaze. "I promised her the world, and she left anyway."

"Give her time."

"Why? Nothing will change." He forced his thick lips into a smile. "I can't blame her for leaving me. Look at what Sam did to her. Look at who I am. There's no way she's going to get past my reputation. I'm the last man on earth she'd ever want. That's why I'm drinking, Rebecca. So I can forget the truth."

She touched her cool hand to his cheek. "Is it helping?"

"No. I played the game and I lost." He shrugged. "I gave

her everything I had and it wasn't enough. Let it go, honey. I'm going to try my damnedest to do just that.''

Seven days later it didn't hurt any less and he still hadn't learned to forget. He'd given up the alcohol by Sunday morning. Mostly because he had a job to do and responsibilities he couldn't hide from. Also, because he was a lousy drunk. Even Rebecca had told him that when he'd awakened with the mother of all hangovers. He knew he had to get on with his life. Elizabeth had chosen not to be a part of that. Fine. He didn't understand her reasoning, but he respected her right to make that choice. But there was still the matter of a six-year-old girl.

He stood in front of Elizabeth's front door for several minutes before gathering the courage to knock. He heard voices from inside, then the sound of little footsteps hurrying down the hall.

''I want to get it,'' Mandy said. She opened the door and stared at him. ''Travis!''

She flung herself at him. He caught her in his arms and pulled her hard against his chest. Her thin legs came up around his waist.

''Hi, Mandy,'' he said, and was surprised his voice sounded so gruff.

She buried her face in his neck and sniffed, then glared up at him. ''You've been gone, Travis. You said you'd come to my soccer game, but you didn't. Mommy said you were working.'' Her pale blond eyebrows drew together mutinously. ''You promised me you'd come. Why weren't you there?''

Because I couldn't face seeing your mother, he thought, then kissed her forehead and set her on the ground. His relationship with Mandy was important to both of them, regardless of what was going on between him and Elizabeth. He squatted down beside the little girl. ''I'm sorry,'' he said, holding her shoulders. ''You're right. I *did* promise. I'll be there for the next one, and all the ones after that. I might have to leave early if I'm working, but nothing else will keep me away. Okay?''

Mandy thought for a moment, then grinned. ''Okay. I'm going to get a goal next time. You watch!''

Something small and brown scurried out the front door. Mandy shrieked. Travis leaned down and grabbed the fur ball by the scruff of its neck and raised the animal up to eye level. It was a small dog of undetermined breed. Big brown eyes stared into his face; then the puppy barked excitedly and licked his nose.

Mandy laughed. "That's Buster. He's our new dog. We got him at the pound. He sleeps in my bed and everything."

Travis smiled and handed her the puppy. Mandy held him carefully. Buster wiggled in her embrace, quivering with excitement. Apparently the dog had already figured out where his loyalties lay.

Travis heard a soft sound and looked up. Elizabeth stood in the center of her small living room. The band around his chest tightened as he looked at her familiar heart-shaped face.

Her mouth was pulled straight, as if she were in pain, and her eyes were dark with emotion. Her pale color, the shadows and lines of exhaustion, told him that she'd been suffering as much as he. Because he was a fool where she was concerned, he was pleased with the obvious signs of her distress. He had meant something to her.

His happiness faded as quickly as it had arrived. The operative word about her feelings was *had*. Whatever affection she'd maintained for him hadn't been enough to keep her in his house or his bed. It hadn't been enough to allow her to believe in him.

"Hello, Travis," she said, her voice soft and husky.

He rose to his feet. God, he loved how she sounded. Even now, just looking at her and hearing her, his whole body went on alert. From the ten or so feet that separated them, he could smell the scent of her perfume. She wore a cream sweater over jeans. Her hair was pulled back in a braid. He supposed there were men who wouldn't think her beautiful, but to him she was perfection itself.

"Elizabeth."

He was afraid she would see how she affected him so he stuck his hands into his leather jacket pockets. The business-size envelope there crackled as he touched it. His ace in the hole. Later, he told himself. Patience was the key.

Elizabeth studied him, her gaze drifting over his face, to his chest and lower. He saw the slight blush that appeared on her cheeks. He got to her. Good. Please God, let it be enough.

"Mandy, why don't you take Buster into the backyard and play?"

Mandy nuzzled her pet and giggled. "Okay." She turned away, then spun back. "Travis, there's a play at my school. I'm going to be broccoli and an Indian. Please come."

He tore his gaze away from her mother. "I wouldn't miss it for anything. Give me a kiss before you go."

She raised her face. Her lips were pursed. He bent down and brushed them with his own. She gave him a sweet smile that warmed him to the bottom of his soul, then ran through the living room and into the hall.

"Would you like to come in?" Elizabeth asked, moving to the door and drawing it back.

"Sure. For a minute. I still have some things to take care of today." He stepped inside and glanced around the small living room. She'd hung the miniblinds at the front windows. A lace shawl was draped over one of the ugly gold couches. "This is nice."

She closed the door and wrinkled her nose. "No. It's still small and dark, but it's ours. We're making it a home." She cleared her throat. "How have you been?"

He could have made it easy for her, but he was hurting too much inside. She'd gone and left him, and then had made a home for herself and her daughter. He'd been abandoned, cast aside without a second thought. "How do you think?"

She folded her arms over her chest, then straightened them. "I'm sorry," she said.

His hands closed into fists, but his jacket hid his reaction from view. "Are you? Why don't I think so? If you were sorry, you wouldn't have walked out of my life."

"I meant to call." She stared at the carpet.

"So you're a liar as well as a coward."

Her head shot up. Anger burned in her eyes. "How dare you say that to me?"

"If the shoe fits, lady. You're the one who snuck out of my house like some damn thief. You didn't even have the courage to say goodbye in person. I thought that we meant something to each other. I guess I was wrong." He stopped talking because it was starting to hurt too much. The act of breathing caused his chest to ache. Deep inside, around his heart, the hole deepened as pieces of his soul slipped away.

"You have no right to judge me," she said, leaning forward toward him. "No right at all."

"The hell I don't. What about all your concerns about Mandy? I'm more than willing to have her in my life. *You're* the one keeping her away from me."

"I—" Her anger fled as quickly as it had flared. Her shoulders slumped. "You're right. About everything. I'm sorry, Travis."

He wanted to go to her and hold her tight. He wanted to fight her battles and conquer her demons. The only flaw with the plan was the fact that he was her biggest problem.

"I didn't want to make love to you that day, but I couldn't help myself. You make me feel…" She shook her head sadly. "I can't explain it. You make me want things that I know I can't have. I can't do what you need me to do. I can't be that woman. I can't trust again."

"You mean you won't."

Their eyes met. Her pure brown irises shone with tears. "I won't," she agreed. "I wish I was stronger. You are a wonderful man. Strong, sensitive, caring, funny. Far too good-looking for your own good, or my peace of mind."

She was ripping him apart inside. He didn't know how much longer he could stand this. "You forgot about being dynamite in bed," he said, hoping the joke would make them both feel better. It didn't help him, and judging by the tears on Elizabeth's cheeks, she didn't find it all that funny.

"That, too," she whispered. She reached up and brushed

away the tears. "That's why I ran. Because it was too wonderful. I couldn't bear to believe and then have it turn out to be another mistake."

He'd expected to be sad, even disappointed. He hadn't thought he would feel the cold ice of rage. He pulled his hands out of his jacket pockets and clenched them into tight fists. He'd lost it all—they'd both lost everything—because she was afraid.

"I thought you were stronger," he said, fighting the urge to roar with anger. "My mistake."

She flinched as if he'd slapped her.

Before she could say anything he spoke again. "I don't claim to understand what you're thinking. But there are more than two people involved here. I have a commitment to Mandy, and I intend to honor it. Are you going to give me trouble with that?"

She mutely shook her head.

"Good. Then I'll be at her school play and her soccer games and anything else she wants me at."

"Thank you."

"Don't thank me. I'm not doing it for you. I'm doing it for Mandy and for myself."

There was a loose strand of hair floating around her face. He wanted to touch that strand, to brush it back and tuck it behind her ear. His rage disappeared as quickly as it had come. He wanted to stroke the smooth skin of her face and neck. His fingers ached to touch her. His body rebelled at being left unsatisfied. If it wasn't for Mandy, he would gladly go the rest of his life and never see Elizabeth Abbott again. She was going to be the death of him.

He reached in his jacket pocket for his keys. His fingers touched the envelope again. He pulled it out and looked at it.

"I thought there might still be a chance," he said. "But I see Rebecca was right."

"What did she say?"

"That this wasn't about me at all. This is your problem and there's nothing I can do to help you get over it." He looked at her then, studying the shape of her face, the smooth skin, the tears. He'd finally fallen in love. Unfortunately it was with the one woman who would never trust him enough to love him back. A perfect ending to a Haynes family story.

He handed her the envelope. "It's not worth the paper it's printed on, but what the hell. It'll give you a laugh. Years from now you can use it to remember me by. That crazy Haynes brother who was stupid enough to fall in love."

"Travis!"

She raised her hand toward him. He gave her the envelope, being careful not to touch her. It would be too easy to get lost in her for the night. Just one last time. However he knew if he did it again, he would never find his way back. This time he would stay lost.

She opened the envelope. He told himself to leave, but he couldn't help standing there watching. Just in case it got ugly, he reached back and gripped the door handle.

She pulled out the three sheets of paper and studied them. A slight frown drew her delicate eyebrows together. "I don't understand."

He opened the door and stepped onto the porch. "It's a report from a private investigator," he said and shrugged. "I paid to have myself investigated. Just so you'd know I have nothing to hide. His number is in there, along with his license information. The guy's legitimate. Check it out if you don't believe me."

"But why would you do this?"

"I wanted you to know I wasn't like Sam. I didn't realize it was already too late to change your mind."

The harvest play was held in the school auditorium. The seats weren't all that comfortable, but Elizabeth knew her restlessness was due to more than the hard wooden chair. Travis had promised to come and see Mandy in her acting debut. She, along with the other first-graders, had small parts in the school production.

Elizabeth had draped a sweater over the seat next to her on the outside left aisle. Her heart thundered in her chest. She prayed Travis would show up and not disappoint her daughter. With equal fervency, she prayed he *did* forget the date, time or location of the play. She couldn't face him again. Nothing made sense anymore, but she was getting used to living in a state of confusion.

Leaving Travis had felt horrible, but she'd known it was the right thing to do. What choice did she have? It was either leave with some small portion of her heart intact, or risk making the same mistake again. She'd judged so badly with Sam, how could she risk doing it all over again? It wasn't just about her, either. What about Mandy's feelings? She'd already lost one father. She would really be hurt to lose Travis.

But he was still seeing her daughter, a little voice in her head whispered. She tried to ignore the sound, much as she ignored her sweating palms and trembling legs. Good thing she was sitting down, she thought, trying to find the humor in the situation and failing badly.

She shifted on the hard seat, and smoothed her narrow wool skirt. The autumn weather had taken a cool turn. She'd bought several sweaters and a few skirts and trousers in a nearby town. Rebecca had accompanied her on the shopping trip. Try as she might, Elizabeth hadn't been able to gather the courage to ask her friend about Travis. She supposed her reticence was part embarrassment, part shame. If Rebecca had given Travis advice, then she knew the entire story. Elizabeth had wanted to say that it wasn't her fault, but she knew it was. She was the one who didn't have the courage to try. She sighed. No one understood what it was like to wake up one morning and find out her entire life was a lie. Okay, she should get over it, but not just yet.

The crowd of excited parents continued to file into the rapidly filling auditorium. Elizabeth looked over her shoulder, scanning for a familiar face. She nibbled on her bottom lip. What if he showed up? What if he didn't?

At last she spotted Travis threading his way through the other adults. She stood up so that he could see where she was sitting, then quickly sat back down. What if he didn't want to sit next to her?

She hunched down and stared fixedly at the stage. He'd already told her it was a lost cause. She still remembered the words as clearly as if he'd just spoken them. He'd been standing in her living room, handing her the detective's report.

Why had he done it? Why had he paid to have himself investigated? She'd called the man, then the state licensing board. Everything had checked out. Travis had no secrets in his past. She appreciated the gesture, but it didn't change anything.

"Are you saving that seat for someone?" a man asked.

She recognized the voice before she looked up and met his gaze. He wore his khaki uniform, with the Stetson she loved so much. The brim hid his eyes from view, but she could see his trimmed mustache, and the straight line of his mouth. He wasn't smiling. Why was she surprised?

"For you," she said, and moved the sweater.

He settled next to her. His arm brushed hers on the armrest. She started to move, then left her arm in place. If he didn't like them touching then he could be the one to shift in his seat.

Brave words, she told herself. They were in the middle of a crowd. Nothing was going to happen.

"You look very nice today," he said.

She glanced down at her new skirt and sweater, then smiled and looked at him. "Thank you."

Her smile faded when he removed his hat and she saw his eyes. Nothing flared to life in his brown irises. No emotion darkened the volatile color, no quick grin curved his lips. She was looking into the face of a stranger.

And then she knew the truth. He hadn't been lying when he'd said it was all a lost cause. Whatever feelings he'd felt for her had been locked away in a place she could never reach.

The room darkened and the first students appeared on the stage. There was no time for conversation. Elizabeth blinked several times and knew that it didn't matter. She'd turned her back on his offer of love, she'd taken the detective's report and had never called to discuss it with Travis. He'd gotten her message loud and clear. He knew she wasn't interested, so he was shutting her out. She'd gotten exactly what she'd asked for. Everything was working out perfectly.

Chapter 16

"What on earth did you expect?" Rebecca asked that night after dinner at Elizabeth's house.

Elizabeth shrugged. She cocked her head toward the living room. Mandy was watching one of her favorite cartoon videos. "I didn't expect him to ignore me like that."

"You tell the guy to take a flying leap, and now you're surprised that he's not all over you?"

Elizabeth took the chair opposite her friend. She placed her coffee mug in front of her. "No one ever mentioned the words *flying leap.*"

Rebecca sighed. "I saw him the next day, Elizabeth. He was in bad shape. You walked out on him without a word. In my book, that qualified as pretty cruel behavior."

Elizabeth stared at the table. She could feel the heated blush on her cheeks. "It was awful. I'm so sorry I did that. Travis is a great guy and he deserves better."

"I'm not the one you should be telling this to."

"I know that, too." She risked glancing up. "What am I going to do?"

"What do you want from all this?"

That was easy. She wanted him to sweep her off her feet and make mad, passionate love to her. She wanted to spend the night lost in his arms. She wanted him to promise to love her forever, then hold her tight and never let her go.

Her eyes began to burn. He'd already done that and more. She'd rewarded him by throwing it all in his face. But she couldn't risk another mistake.

"I don't know." She saw Rebecca's wide mouth twist with impatience. "Go ahead and yell at me, but you don't know what it's like. You haven't made the same mistakes I have."

"I've made others." Rebecca leaned back in her chair and tucked her long curling black hair behind her ears. "I've made plenty of mistakes. One thing they've all taught me is that the way to learn from them is to get on with your life. Hiding out accomplishes nothing."

"Is that what you think I'm doing?" Elizabeth demanded.

Her friend looked at her steadily. "Yes, I do."

"You don't know what it was like."

"You're right. I don't. So what? It's over, Elizabeth. Travis isn't Sam. You're losing a good man because you're terrified of making the same mistake again. Here's a news flash. Everyone makes mistakes. And everyone gets to deal with making at least one huge one. Forgive yourself and get on with your life."

"You make it sound so easy."

"You make it sound so hard. It doesn't have to be."

Elizabeth sipped from her coffee. After the play Travis had stayed long enough to congratulate Mandy and to warn the girl he wouldn't be able to stay for the entire soccer game the following Saturday. Elizabeth had offered to bring her home instead. They'd made the arrangements, then had parted. It had been so civilized, she'd wanted to scream. She didn't want calm, rational conversation with Travis. She wanted the passion.

"It's difficult to give up hiding once you've learned how," she said quietly.

"I know. But you have to try." Rebecca leaned across the table and squeezed her hand. "If you don't forgive yourself and get on with what's important, you'll have paid the highest price of all."

Elizabeth sighed. "I'll have lost Travis."

"Worse. You'll have lost yourself."

Elizabeth stood in the silence of her small house. It was lunch-time and Mandy was still at school. Buster was asleep on his bed in the corner of her daughter's room.

Normally, being alone was a pleasure. She reveled in the quiet, knowing it would soon explode into childish laughter, the sounds of the television and Buster's high-pitched barking. To-day she found no peace.

The pain in her heart hadn't gone away. If anything, it had grown, along with her sense of failure. She gripped her purse tightly in her hands and stared at the living room. When she'd left Sam, she'd been so sure she'd made the right decision. She'd protected herself and her child and had sworn to never make that kind of mistake again. She'd promised herself never to be emotionally vulnerable to love.

Had that been the lesson Sam's deception should have taught her?

She walked into the kitchen and studied the calendar pinned to the wall. Mandy had marked all her soccer games. Tomorrow Travis would arrive early and take the girl to breakfast. They would leave, laughing with each other. Elizabeth knew she would stand at the window and watch Travis smile at her daugh-ter. She would feel the loss when he touched her easily, perhaps even carrying her piggyback-style to the car. She envied her daughter's relationship with Travis. Elizabeth shook her head and wondered when she'd become a fool.

Next to the calendar was a bulletin board. Several of Mandy's class projects had been pinned up, as had a postcard from Eliz-abeth's parents. They were back from their trip. They'd called a couple of weeks ago to tell her all about the Orient. Elizabeth had listened politely and had avoided questions about her per-sonal life. She'd never had the courage to tell them the truth about Sam. Her parents sensed something was wrong, but they wouldn't ask.

She couldn't tell them the truth. They wouldn't understand

how she could have been so stupid. Elizabeth tossed her purse on the small table and balled up her fists. Damn him. She was tired of living only half her life.

It wasn't an emotional connection that kept her tied to the past. She knew that much. Her feelings for Sam had faded over the years. Looking back with the perfect vision of hindsight, she could see that she'd never loved him. He'd charmed her, showing up in her life just as she was ready to spread her wings.

So why couldn't she let go? She glanced down at her hands and slowly straightened them. Her fingers were bare. For over six years she'd worn a wedding band. She'd thought she was married. Mrs. Sam Proctor. It had all been a lie. That's what she couldn't let go. Being married had been part of her identity. It's as if she'd lost part of herself when she'd learned the truth. Her world had exploded, nothing had been as it seemed. She'd been left empty and broken, feeling as if she'd spent her whole life being a fool.

And lonely, she thought suddenly. Very, very lonely. Sam had kept her isolated from the world. He hadn't wanted her to work or have friends. Now she knew it was his way of making sure he controlled the game. She'd finally defied him and started working. That had given her a measure of independence, but hadn't taken away the feelings of isolation. She'd spent her entire marriage being on her own.

She stepped closer to the bulletin board and touched one of Mandy's drawings. It was a duplicate of the one she'd done for Travis. Three stick figures stood in front of a white house. Her daughter had even drawn in a puppy. The sight of the brightly colored picture made her smile. Mandy was going to be all right. Even as her world had been falling apart, Elizabeth had made sure she'd been there for her daughter. Her smile turned wry. Of course she'd had six years practice of being a single parent. With Sam gone so much, most of the responsibility had fallen on her shoulders. She knew she was capable of making it all work out.

So what was she trying to prove?

The thought came out of nowhere and stunned her. What *was* she trying to prove? That she was strong enough to make it on her own? She knew that already. That she had to punish herself for making a mistake? Maybe. She should have known. She should have seen the clues. She should—

"Stop!" she said out loud. "Just stop."

She hadn't known. She hadn't thought to look for clues. Did that make her a bad person? Was Rebecca right? Did everyone get one free big mistake? Was it time to let the whole thing go?

Her gaze drifted from Mandy's picture to the postcard her parents had sent. The feeling of loneliness swept over her again. She realized how much she hated hiding from them, hiding from the world. She'd been so worried about what everyone would think that she'd allowed the fear to rule her life. She'd left herself with no support to get her through the rough times.

Without giving herself time to talk herself out of it, she walked to the phone and picked up the receiver. She dialed from memory.

"Hello?"

"Hi, Mom. It's me."

Her mother laughed with delight. "Your father and I have missed you, honey," the older woman said. "How have you been?"

Elizabeth felt the hot tears flood her eyes and flow down her cheeks. She leaned against the wall and twisted the cord in her fingers. "Not that great, Mom. I have some things to tell you. About Sam. I don't know how to say this. I'm so sorry. I never meant to disappoint you. It turns out—"

"Just a minute, dear. Before you say another word, you don't have to apologize for anything to either me or your father. We love you, no matter what. Do you want us to fly out and be with you? We could get a flight today."

Elizabeth sank into a kitchen chair and smiled through her tears. "No. You don't have to. Mandy and I are okay. But thanks for offering." She drew in a deep breath to tell the rest of her story and realized she'd spoken the truth. She was okay. Probably for the first time in years.

"You're not eating," Mandy said, waving her fork at Travis's full plate. "Don't you like the pancakes?"

"I'm just not hungry." He winked at the little girl. "You sure wanted your breakfast, though."

Mandy looked down at her half-eaten meal. A thin pancake wrapped around a sausage was all that was left of everything she'd ordered. "I was hungry. I went to bed early, so I could sleep a lot. Mommy says I need to be rested to do good at my game. I'm going to score a goal."

"I bet you are."

She chatted about school and all her friends. He studied her small face, loving the way her eyes lighted up with her stories. Her hair was pulled into two pigtails. A red ribbon, matching her red-and-white soccer uniform, had been tied on each end. Her fresh-scrubbed face looked innocent and trusting.

He sipped from his coffee cup and tried to control the emotions swelling up inside of him. He adored this little girl. He missed the sound of her laughter and her cartoons, the endless questions, the way she crawled into his lap and demanded a story. He missed being loved by her.

He knew she still cared about him. They had planned several activities together over the next few weeks, but it wasn't the same as living with her. Or her mother.

Damn, he didn't want to think about Elizabeth. But he couldn't help himself. Staring at Mandy, knowing most of her features came from her father, he still saw traces of the woman he loved in her face. Loving and losing Mandy had broken his heart. Loving and losing Elizabeth was killing him.

The hell of it was he didn't know what to do. He couldn't think of any more words to convince her. He knew Rebecca had been right in telling him this was Elizabeth's problem and not his. Knowing the truth didn't stop him from wanting to fix everything. He couldn't, though. No one would tell him exactly what to fix. Louise preached patience and cooked his favorite meals. Neither made him forget. He'd tried words, he'd tried making love, he'd even tried giving Elizabeth that damned detective's report. Nothing had worked, and he'd run out of ideas.

"Mommy called Grandma yesterday," Mandy said, then nibbled on her sausage. "She told me."

"That's nice," he said, then frowned. Hadn't Elizabeth mentioned she didn't talk to her parents much because she was ashamed? She hadn't even told them the truth about Sam. A flicker of hope sparked in his chest, but he doused it with cold, wet reality. Calling her parents didn't mean anything.

"They're coming to visit us at the end of the month. Grandma's going to take me out for Halloween."

"Are you sure?" he asked.

Mandy nodded vigorously, her blond pigtails bouncing against her shoulders. "I talked to her last night. I'm going to be a fairy princess."

A phone call was one thing, a visit quite another. If they were coming out, Elizabeth would have to tell them the truth. Maybe she already had.

Hope threatened again. Travis did his best to ignore it. So what? They were her parents. She still hadn't contacted him in any way. This morning, when he'd driven up to get Mandy, she'd sent the girl outside without giving him more than a brief, impersonal wave.

Mandy put her fork down and looked at him. Something in her big blue eyes made him give her his full attention. "What's wrong?" he asked.

"Are you and Mommy fighting?"

He didn't have an answer for that one. They weren't angry at each other, but they sure weren't getting along. "Why do you ask?"

Mandy shrugged. "Mommy was crying last night. I heard her after I went to bed."

His gut clenched into a hard knot. Rather than give in to the impulse to jump up and find Elizabeth, he gripped the table. It wasn't his fault she was crying. If she wanted his comfort, she knew where to find him. He'd already told her he loved her. What else was there to say?

"We're not fighting," he told the little girl. Although he wasn't sure he hadn't made her cry.

Mandy seemed relieved. He changed the subject. "I told you I can't stay for the whole game," he reminded her. "I have to work this afternoon."

"I know," she said, nodding. "I'll score my goal early, okay?"

He leaned across the table and ruffled her bangs. "You do that, kid."

They left the restaurant and he drove them to the park. Most of the parents and children were already there. Mandy ran off to join her team. Travis walked to the edge of the field and stared at the players. He didn't want to look around and see Elizabeth. If there was any lingering trace of her tears, he would feel obligated to ask what was wrong. Maybe it was weak of him, but he couldn't face her shutting him down again. He needed a little time to let the wounds heal.

Apparently she didn't share his feelings. He'd barely been there a minute when he inhaled the soft scent of a familiar perfume. His body reacted instantly. His groin flooded with heat and his chest tightened.

"Hi, Travis."

"Elizabeth." He forced himself to look at her. She wore an oversize blue sweater over jeans. Her hair was loose and shiny in the autumn morning. All traces of tears were long gone. Her brown eyes glowed with something, but it wasn't pain or unhappiness. He wanted to believe it had something to do with him, or at the very least, was the result of talking to her parents, but his luck wasn't that good. He glanced around the field. There were several single men here. Any one of them could have put that special light in her eyes.

He wanted to ask about her parents and what had prompted her to call. He wanted to tell her how much he loved her and beg her to come back to him. He wanted to hold her in his arms until he convinced her that they belonged together. He did none of those things. He couldn't move, couldn't breathe, couldn't do anything but endure the heartache of knowing what could have been.

"Mandy mentioned you'll be leaving early," she said.

"Yes. Can you take her home?"

"Of course." Her gaze met and held his own. He tried to read her emotions, but he couldn't. Just as well, he thought, turning away. What was there to see?

"I've got to go," he said abruptly and walked away.

"Travis?"

He kept on going. If he moved fast enough, maybe the pain wouldn't be able to catch up with him.

Elizabeth stared at Travis's retreating back. The hurt and hunger in his eyes had left her with tangible wounds. She could feel the ache pouring through her body. Every part of her screamed at her to take a chance. One small risk. He wasn't Sam. He wasn't lying about anything in his life. He'd told her the unvarnished truth about himself, his past and his family. She'd seen his shame when he'd talked about his father. Travis had even risked telling her he loved her. He had no secrets left.

She took a step after him, then paused. Could she risk it? What about the mistakes she'd made?

"Take a chance."

Elizabeth spun on her heel and found Rebecca standing behind her. "What are you doing here?" she asked.

"One of the kids from the children's home is playing. I thought I'd come watch and show support." Rebecca stared at her. "Elizabeth, this may be your last opportunity. Don't be a fool."

"I can't." Elizabeth closed her eyes. "I can't risk—" Her eyes flew open. She clasped her hand over her mouth, then dropped her arm to her side. "I can't risk losing him, can I? What have I been thinking? Travis Haynes is the best thing that ever happened to me."

Rebecca grinned. "Finally. He went that away." She raised one finger and pointed.

Elizabeth hurried off in that direction. She scanned the growing crowd but there was no tall man in a Stetson anywhere. She stopped and looked toward the parking lot. Her heart sank. The sheriff's car was gone. Travis had left.

Disappointment dragged at her. Now what? Should she wait until he came off his shift? She shook her head. No, she couldn't wait another minute. They'd both suffered for too long.

She ran to a phone on the edge of the park. Dialing quickly, she shifted her weight from foot to foot. Finally the phone rang.

"Sheriff's Office."

It wasn't Travis, but the voice was familiar. "Kyle?"

"Yes."

"Hi, it's Elizabeth Abbott. I'm looking for Travis. Is he around?"

There was a pause. She bit her lower lip. Maybe Travis had told his brother about her behavior. If so, Kyle might not want to help her. Oh, but he had to.

"He's subbing for one of the deputies. He's out on patrol, giving out tickets."

"Oh, then I'll never find him."

"I don't know about that. Is this good news?"

She clutched the metal cord. "Very good news, Kyle. The best news."

"He's been walking around here like a kicked dog."

"I know. I'm sorry about that."

"He deserves something wonderful, Elizabeth." Kyle's voice got husky. "He's a good man."

"I know. Believe me, I know. I need to find him before it's too late."

There was a pause; then Kyle said, "Do you remember where he stopped you that first day?"

"Yes."

"He always parks in the same place. The locals know to avoid him. If you go now you'll be able to find him."

She thought for a second. "I have to wait until the soccer game is over. I can't leave Mandy alone."

"I'll be by in five minutes to get her."

"You'd do that for me?"

"I'm doing it for Travis."

She had to fight against the tears burning in her eyes. To think she might have lost the man she loved because of her own fears. "Thank you, Kyle. I really appreciate this."

"Yeah, well, don't make me regret it."

"I won't. I just hope it's not too late. By."

"Elizabeth?"

"Yes?"

"It's not too late."

She hung up and prayed he was right. She started toward the parking lot. At the sight of her car, she paused. Travis knew her car. She didn't want to give him time to get away from her or start to think up reasons why it wouldn't work. Not now. She glanced around the playing field and saw one of the coach's wives standing close to her. She rushed over.

"Mary, can I borrow your car for a few minutes?"

The young woman looked startled. "Didn't you bring your car?"

"Yes, but—oh, it's difficult to explain. I need to find someone and I don't want him to know it's me until it's too late and please, I promise I'll be careful."

Mary looked at her for several seconds, then grinned. "Sounds like man trouble to me."

"It is."

The blonde reached into her jeans pocket and pulled out a set of keys. "It's the red station wagon right there."

Impulsively, Elizabeth gave the other woman a hug. "Thanks. I'll be right back."

"Take your time."

She ran to the car, slid inside, fastened her seat belt, then started the engine. After drawing in a deep breath for courage, she pulled out of the parking lot and turned onto the main road.

*   *   *

Travis stared morosely down the highway. Even for a Saturday morning, the traffic was light. He'd only seen half a dozen cars and all of them had been going the speed limit. Not that he was in the mood to stop anyone.

He leaned his head back and groaned. Mandy was going to be upset that he'd left before her game had started. There was no way he could explain to the little girl that he hadn't had a choice in the matter. It had been too hard to stand there staring at Elizabeth and knowing he could never be a part of her life. Just seeing her had been difficult. How was he supposed to get through the torture of being her friend?

Friends. He swore. She might as well just shoot him in the back and get it over with.

He heard a car engine and straightened. A red station wagon barreled around the curve behind him and zoomed past onto the straightaway. Travis checked his radar and raised his eyebrows. Someone was going somewhere in a hurry.

He pulled out onto the highway and hit the gas. His patrol car was gaining, but slowly. He flipped on his blue light and accelerated, then frowned when he realized the driver in the red car was going faster than he'd thought. He stared ahead, but all he could see was the person wore a baseball cap. At last the driver glanced in the rearview mirror, saw him and turned off onto the shoulder of the road.

Travis parked behind the car and collected his ticket book and Stetson. He stepped out and walked over to the car. The window was already rolled down.

"You were going pretty fast there." He flipped open his ticket book, then glanced up at the driver. And about dropped his pen. "Elizabeth?"

"Hi." She jerked off the baseball cap and her brown hair tumbled over her shoulders. "I wondered if you'd see me."

"You were hard to miss, especially when you hit the straightaway doing eighty." He glanced at the unfamiliar car and frowned. "Why are you driving this?"

"That's not important." She opened the car door and got out. "I was speeding. Are you going to give me a ticket?"

He frowned. What kind of game was she playing? There was an odd flickering in her eyes, some suppressed emotion. Her mouth quivered, but he couldn't tell if she was upset or trying not to smile. None of this made sense.

"You *were* over the speed limit," he said.

"I know. Ask me for my story."

"What?"

"Travis." She planted her hands on her hips. "Isn't it a tradition here in Glenwood? If I tell you a story you haven't heard before, don't you have to let me go?"

He shoved the ticket book and pen into his back pocket, then folded his arms over his chest. He could feel his heart thumping. That damn hope flared to life again. This time he let it burn hot and bright. This time he dared to believe. But he wasn't going to ask. She was going to have to tell him.

"What's the story?" he asked cautiously, wondering if she was about to say something he wanted to hear, or if she would deliver the death blow.

The odd flickering in her beautiful brown eyes turned into something he could have sworn was caring. Her mouth curved up in a smile. When she leaned forward and placed her hands on his chest, it was all he could do not to pull her close.

"I love you," she said, then touched her lips to his.

Fire exploded through him. His mind echoed with the wonder of her words. He grabbed her arms and held her away from him. "What did you say?"

"Oh, Travis, I've been a fool. I was wrong to judge you by Sam's actions, and wrong to let the past destroy my future." She shook her head. "Our future. I could have lost you forever."

"Elizabeth." He breathed her name. "You would never have lost me. I have nowhere else to go. No one else to love."

"I love you."

He wrapped his arms around her waist and pulled her hard against his chest. He kissed her once, softly, savoring the reality of knowing they were at last together. Then he angled his head and thrust his tongue into her mouth. They met in a conflagration of sensation. When they came up for air, they were both breathing heavily.

"Does this mean I don't get a ticket?" she asked, and smiled.

He grinned in return. "It's a story I haven't heard before, so I guess not."

"Good. I would have been a little cranky on our wedding day if you had given me a ticket."

He stared at her.

Her smile faltered. "You do want to marry me, don't you? I mean I assumed that was the next logical step." She bit her lower lip and blushed. "Oh, Travis, we don't have to if you don't—"

He grabbed her hands and pulled them to his mouth. After kissing each palm, he stared into her eyes. "I love you, Elizabeth Abbott. Will you marry me?"

A single tear slipped down her cheek. "Yes."

"We can get married when your parents are here if you'd like." When he saw her confused frown, he kissed the tip of her nose. "Mandy told me. You'll be a beautiful bride, darlin'."

He bent his head toward her mouth again. The kiss quickly heated them both. He was thinking about which of their houses was closer when a burst from a siren made them jump apart.

Travis turned and glared at the patrol car rolling toward them. Kyle was driving, with a young girl bouncing at his side. When the car came to a stop, Mandy opened the front door and jumped out. Her smile about split her face in two and her blue eyes were shining.

"Mommy, Mommy, Uncle Kyle says you and Travis are getting married, and we're going to live happily ever after. Is that true?"

Elizabeth laughed and pulled her daughter close. "Uncle Kyle has a big mouth, but yes, it's true."

Kyle got out more slowly. "Sorry, Trav. I just thought the kid might want to know."

Travis pulled Elizabeth and Mandy into his embrace. "No problem, little brother. We are going to live happily ever after."

Mandy looked up at her mother. "Are you going to have a baby now?"

Elizabeth glanced at him. He swallowed hard. "Maybe," he said, not wanting to hope for too much.

"Yes," Elizabeth said firmly.

The joy in his heart doubled.

Kyle came forward and slapped him on the back. "Another Haynes son. You can name this one after me."

"Why a son?" Elizabeth asked.

Travis touched her cheek. "There hasn't been a daughter born to the family in four generations."

"I'd forgotten about that." Elizabeth looped her arm around his waist. "I just might surprise you all."

He held her close and felt the loving warmth of her body. "You already did, Elizabeth. You already did." She had been, he knew then, the best surprise of all.

* * * * *

Coming in January 2002 from Silhouette
Books...

THE GREAT MONTANA COWBOY AUCTION

by

ANNE McALLISTER

With a neighbor's ranch at stake, Montana-cowboy-turned-Hollywood-heartthrob Sloan Gallagher agreed to take part in the Great Montana Cowboy Auction organized by Polly McMaster. Then, in order to avoid going home with an overly enthusiastic fan, he provided the money so that Polly could buy him and take him home for a weekend of playing house. But Polly had other ideas....

Also in the Code of the West

A Cowboy's Promise (SD #1405)
A Cowboy's Gift (SD #1329)
A Cowboy's Secret (SD #1279)
The Stardust Cowboy (SD #1219)
The Cowboy Crashes a Wedding (SD #1153)
The Cowboy Steals a Lady (SD #1117)
Cowboy Pride (SD #1034)
The Cowboy and the Kid (SD #1009)
Cowboys Don't Stay (SD #969)
Cowboys Don't Quit (SD #944)
Cowboys Don't Cry (SD #907)

Available at your favorite retail outlet.

Silhouette®

Where love comes alive™

These New York Times *bestselling authors
have created stories to capture the hearts and minds
of women everywhere.
Here are three classic tales about the power of love—
and the wonder of discovering the place
where you belong....*

FINDING HOME

DUNCAN'S BRIDE
by
LINDA HOWARD

CHAIN LIGHTNING
by
ELIZABETH LOWELL

POPCORN AND KISSES
by
KASEY MICHAELS

*Available only from Silhouette
at your favorite retail outlet.*

Silhouette®
Where love comes alive™

LINDSAY M^cKENNA

continues her popular series,

MORGAN'S MERCENARIES

with a brand-new, longer-length single title!

She had never needed anyone before. Never ached for a man before. Until her latest mission put Apache pilot Akiva Redtail in the hot seat next to army officer Joe Calhoun. And as they rode through the thunderous skies, dodging danger at every turn, Akiva discovered a strength in Joe's arms, a fiery passion she was powerless to battle against. For only with this rugged soldier by her side could this Native American beauty fulfill the destiny she was born to. Only with Joe did she dare open her heart to love....

"When it comes to action and romance, nobody does it better than Ms. McKenna."
—*Romantic Times Magazine*

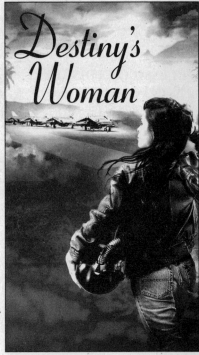

Available in March from Silhouette Books!

Where love comes alive™